'A book to make you smile and shiver, in every way a work of art and likely to establish Fay Weldon's reputation as a major writer'
London Evening News

'Wicked insight and amusement . . . the novel is unmistakeably Weldon'
Financial Times

'Weldon examines the conflicts of knowledge and ignorance, science and superstition, and the startling climax of the novel dramatises them in an effectively horrible way'
New Statesman

'Magical . . . she lays out the ingredients of her brew with a kind of manipulative glee, coolly moulding her characters and then neatly skewering them with mockery'
Daily Mail

'Gripping'
The Observer

About the author

Fay Weldon was born in England, reared in New Zealand, and educated in Scotland, where she took a degree in Economics and Psychology. After a decade of odd jobs and hard times she started writing, and is now well known at home and abroad as a novelist, playwright and critic. Her novel *The Life and Loves of a She-Devil* was screened on BBC TV last year and won the British Academy Television Award for Best Drama Series of 1986. Her other novels include *Praxis* and *The Shrapnel Academy*. She is married, has four sons, and is a Fellow of The Royal Society of Literature.

Puffball

Fay Weldon

CORONET BOOKS
Hodder and Stoughton

Printed and bound in Great Britain
for Hodder and Stoughton
Paperbacks, a division of Hodder and
Stoughton Ltd., Mill Road,
Dunton Green, Sevenoaks, Kent
TN13 2YA.
(Editorial Office: 47 Bedford Square,
London WC1B 3DP) by
Cox & Wyman Ltd., Reading.

British Library C.I.P.

Weldon, Fay
    Puffball.
    I. Title
823'.914[F]   PR6073.E374
ISBN 0 340 26662 7

In the Beginning

Many people dream of country cottages. Liffey dreamed for many years, and saw the dream come true one hot Sunday afternoon, in Somerset, in September. Bees droned, sky glazed, flowers glowed, and the name carved above the lintel, half-hidden by rich red roses, was Honeycomb Cottage and Liffey knew that she must have it. A trap closed round her.

The getting of the country cottage, not the wanting – that was the trap. It was a snare baited by Liffey's submerged desires and unrealised passions, triggered by nostalgia for lost happiness, and set off by fear of a changing future. But how was Liffey, who believed that she was perfectly happy and perfectly ordinary, to know a thing like that? Liffey saw smooth green lawns where others saw long tangled grass, and was not looking out for snares.

Besides, as Liffey's mother Madge once observed, 'Liffey wants what she wants and gets cross with those who stand in her way.'

Richard stood in Liffey's way that hot September afternoon, and Liffey was cross with him. Richard had been married to Liffey for seven years, and responded, as spouses will, to the message behind the words, and not the words themselves. 'I want to live in the country,' said Liffey, remarkably enough, for she did not often put her wants and wishes so straightforwardly into words.
'We can't,' said Richard, 'because I have to earn a living,' and it was unlike him to disappoint her so directly, and so brutally.

Liffey and Richard seldom had rows, and were nearly always

polite to each other, which made them believe they were ideally suited and happily married. She was small and bright and pretty; and he was large, handsome and responsible. She was twenty-eight, and he thirty-two. Madge was relieved that Liffey was, so far, childless; but Richard's mother, although an Anglican, had already lit a candle to the Virgin Mary and prayed for the grandchild she could reasonably have expected five years ago. They had been married for seven years, after all.

'But we could be so happy here,' said Liffey. The cottage stood on rising ground, at a point where smooth fields met wooded hillside. It looked across the plains to Glastonbury Tor, that hummocky hill which rises out of the flat Somerset levels, and is a nexus of spiritual power, attracting UFOs, and tourists, and pop festivals, and hippies, and the drug squad. The cottage was empty. Spiderwebs clouded the latticed windows.

'We are happy where we are,' said Richard. Adding, 'Aren't we?' in a half threatening, half pleading tone of voice, so she was obliged to forget his crossness and kiss him, and say yes. And indeed, their city apartment was small, but convenient and comfortable, and Liffey had never before complained about it, nor had any real reason to. If she gave voice to worries they were not so much personal as ecological, and were about the way the earth's natural resources were being eaten up, and what was happening to the blue whale, and baby seals, and butterflies, and what deforestation did to the ozone layer above Brazil. Richard, who knew that new developments in nuclear, chemical and silicon chip technology would soon solve all such problems, laughed gently and comfortingly at her worries and loved her for worrying. He liked to look after her, or thought he did.

After they kissed, he took Liffey round to the back of the cottage, through hollyhocks and wallflowers, and there, in the long grasses down by the stream, made love to her. It was a decorous event, characteristic of their particular mating

8

behaviour. Liffey lay still and quiet, and Richard was quick and dutiful.

'Isn't she skinny,' said Mabs, watching through field glasses from the bedroom of Cadbury Farm. Her husband Tucker took the glasses.

'They grow them like that in the city,' he said.
They both spoke in the gentle, caressing drawl of the West Country, mocking the universe, defying its harshness.
'You don't know they're from the city,' Mabs objected.
'They're not from round here,' said Tucker. 'No one round here does it in public.'

Cadbury Farm was made of stone, and so long and low and old it all but vanished into the fold of the hill above the cottage. Liffey and Richard, certainly, had not noticed it was there. Tucker's family had lived at Cadbury Farm, or on its site, for a thousand years or so. When Tucker moved about his fields, he seemed so much part of them he could hardly be seen. Mabs was more noticeable. She was reckoned a foreigner: she came from Crossley, five miles away. She was a large, slow, powerful woman and Tucker was a small, lithe man. So had her Norman ancestors been, ousting the small dark Celts, from which Tucker took his colouring and nature.

'Richard,' said Liffey, 'you don't think we can be seen?'
'Of course not,' said Richard. 'Why are you always so guilty? There's nothing wrong with sex. Everyone does it.'
'My mother didn't,' said Liffey, contradicting because the feeling of crossness had returned. Sexual activity can sweep away many resentments and anxieties, but not those which are bred of obsession and compulsion. 'Or only when she had me,' she amended.
'More fool her,' said Richard, who didn't want to talk about Liffey's mother. Richard's parents had described Liffey's mother, after the wedding, as wonderfully clever and eccentric, and Richard had watched Liffey carefully since, in case she seemed to be going the same way.

'If we lived in the country,' persisted Liffey, 'and had a bit of peace and quiet, I could really get down to writing my novel.' Liffey had secretarial training and did temporary work in offices from time to time, when it didn't interfere with her looking after Richard, but felt that such work could hardly, as she put it, fulfil her. So she wrote, in her spare time, poems and paragraphs, and ideas, and even short stories. She showed what she wrote to nobody, not even to Richard, but felt a certain sense of progress and achievement for having done it.

'You'd be bored to death,' said Richard, meaning that he feared that he would.

'You have your career and your fulfilment,' persisted Liffey, 'and what do I have? Why should your wishes be more important than mine?'

Why indeed? Richard could not even cite his money earning capacity in his defence, since Liffey had a small fortune of her own, left to her by a grandfather. And he had of late become very conscious of the communal guilt which the male sex appears to bear in relation to women. All the same, Liffey's words rang fashionable and hollow in the silence he allowed to follow them.

He made love to her again. Moral confusion excited him sexually – or at any rate presented itself as a way out of difficulty, giving him time to think, and a generally agreeable time at that.

'She's just a farmyard animal like any other,' said Tucker handing over the glasses to Mabs.

'Women aren't animals,' said Mabs.

'Yes, they are,' said Tucker, 'tamed for the convenience of men.'

Mabs put down her glasses and looked malevolently at her husband, frightening him into silence. Then she turned back to Liffey and Richard and watched some more.

'They're very quick about it,' she complained to Tucker. 'I

thought city folks got up to all kinds of tricks. Do you fancy her?'

'She's too skinny for my taste,' said Tucker.

'And you can do a lot better than him,' said Mabs, returning the compliment.

'I should hope so,' said Tucker, and did, pushing Mabs' old grey skirt up and reaching the oyster-coloured silk underwear beneath. She was fussy about what she wore next to her skin. She had surprisingly long and slender legs. Her bulk was contained in her middle parts. Tucker loved the way her sharp brown eyes, in the act of love, turned soft and docile, large irised, like those of his cows. The image of Liffey stayed in his mind, as Mabs had intended it should, and helped. Mabs made good use of everything that came her way, and Tucker did, too.

'If you would have a baby,' said Richard to Liffey, as they lay in the long grass, the late sun striking low across the land, 'there'd be some point in living in the country.' Liffey did not want a baby, or at any rate not now. She might be chronologically twenty-eight, but felt eighteen, and eighteen was too young to have a baby.

Liffey looked at Honeycomb Cottage. Generations of happy, healthy children, she thought, had skipped in and out of the door, along the path, under roses and between hollyhocks. There, loving couples had grown old in peace and tranquillity, at one with the rhythms of nature. Here she and Richard would be safe, out of the city which already had turned a few of his dark hairs grey, and was turning his interest away from her, and which threatened her daily with its pollutants and violence; the city: where there was a rapist round every corner, and rudeness at every turn, and an artificiality of life and manners which sickened her.

'All right,' said Liffey, 'let's have a baby.'

Panic rose in her throat, even as she spoke.

'All right,' said Richard, 'let's live in the country.'

He regretted it at once.

Mabs was in the yard of Cadbury Farm as Richard and Liffey drove back towards the main road along the bumpy track that passed both cottage and farm. Richard had to stop the car while Tucker drove his cows in. Mangy dogs strained and barked at the end of chains, and were yelled into silence by Mabs. She bent to give them bones and her rump was broad.

'So long as you don't ever let yourself go,' added Richard, and then Mabs stood straight and smiled full at Richard and Liffey. She was formless and shapeless in her old grey skirt and her husband's shirt. Her hair was ratty, she had unplucked whiskers on her double chin, and she weighed all of thirteen stone. But she was tall and strong and powerful, and her skin was creamy white.

'She looks like a horse,' said Liffey. 'Do you ever see me looking like a horse?'

'You'd better not,' said Richard, 'or we'll move straight back to town.'

Richard did not believe that Liffey, if offered the country, would actually want to live there. He believed he had called her bluff – which had begun to irritate him – and brought her a little nearer to having a baby, and that was all. He was realistic where Liffey was romantic, and trained, as business executives ought to be, in the arts of manipulation.

'Mind you,' said Liffey, 'horses are very friendly. There are worse things to be.'

Liffey, as horse, came from the Viennese stables. She tossed her head and neighed and pranced, precisely and correctly. She was trained in the arts of child-wifedom. Mabs, as horse, was a working dray – Tucker mounted her easily. She galloped and galloped and sweated and brayed, and what price breeding then? Who needed it? But how was Liffey to know a thing like that? Liffey never sweated, never brayed. Liffey made a sweet little mewling sound, as soon as she possibly could yet still carried conviction; a dear and familiar sound to Richard, for what their love-making might lack in quality was certainly made up for in frequency. Liffey felt that the act of copulation was a strange way to demonstrate the act of love, but did her best with it.

Tucker's cows moved on. Richard and Liffey left.

'They'll be back,' said Mabs to Tucker. He believed her. She seemed to have a hot line to the future, and he wished she did not. She had a reputation of being a witch, and Tucker feared it might be justified.

'We don't want city folk down Honeycomb,' protested Tucker.

'They might be useful,' said Mabs, vaguely. Glastonbury Tor was dark and rose sharply out of a reddish, fading sky. She smiled at the hill as if it were a friend, and made Tucker still more uneasy.

Inside Liffey (1)

There was an outer Liffey, arrived at twenty-eight with boyish body and tiny breasts, with a love of bright, striped football sweaters and tight jeans, and a determination to be positive and happy. Outer Liffey, with her fluttery smiley eyes, sweet curvy face, dark curly hair, and white smooth skin. And there was inner Liffey, cosmic Liffey, hormones buzzing; heart beating, blood surging, pawn in nature's game.

She put on scent, thrust out her chest, silhouetted her buttocks and drew male eyes to her. That way satisfaction lay: the easing of a blind and restless procreative spirit. How could she help herself? Why should she? It was her rôle in the mating dance, and Liffey danced on, as others do, long after the music stopped.

Liffey had lately been cross with Richard. Bad-tempered, so

he'd ask if her period was due, thus making her more irritable still. Who wants to believe that their vision of the world is conditioned by their hormonal state: that no one else is truly at fault, except that believing it makes them so?

'I've just had my period,' she'd say, 'as you surely ought to know,' and make him feel the unfairness of it all, that he should be spared the pain and inconvenience of a monthly menstrual flow, and she should not.
'Perhaps it's the pill,' he'd say.
'I expect it's just me,' she'd say, bitterly.

But how was one to be distinguished from the other? For Liffey's body was not functioning, as her doctor remarked, as nature intended. Not that 'nature' can reasonably be personified in this way – for what is nature, after all, for living creatures, but the sum of the chance genetic events which have led us down one evolutionary path or another. And although what seem to be its intentions may, in a bungled and muddled way, work well enough to keep this species or that propagating, they cannot be said always to be desirable for the individual.

But for good or bad – i.e. convenient for her, inconvenient for the race – Liffey had interfered with her genetic destiny and was on the pill. She took one tablet a day, of factory-made oestrogen and progesterone powders mixed. As a result, Liffey's ovarian follicles failed to ripen and develop their egg. She could not, for this reason, become pregnant. But her baffled body responded by retaining fluid in its cells, and this made her from time to time more lethargic, irritable and depressed than otherwise would have been the case. Her toes and fingers were puffy. Her wedding ring would not come off, and her shoes hurt. And although the extra secretions from her cervix, responding to the oestrogen, helped preserve her uterus and cervix from cancer, they also predisposed her to thrush infections and inconveniently damped her pants. Her liver functioned differently to cope with the extraneous hormones, but not inefficiently. Her carbohydrate metabolism was altered and her heart was slightly affected, but was strong and young enough to beat steadily and sturdily on.

The veins in her white, smooth legs swelled slightly, but they too were young and strong and did not become varicose. The clotting mechanism of her blood altered, predisposing her to thrombo-embolic disease. But Liffey, which was the main thing, would not become pregnant. Liffey valued her freedom and her figure, and when older friends warned her that marriage must grow out of its early love affair and into bricks and mortar and children, she dismissed their vision of the world as gloomy.

Was Liffey's resentment of Richard a matter of pressure in her brain caused by undue retention of fluid, or in fact the result of his behaviour? Liffey naturally assumed it was the latter. It is not pleasant for a young woman to believe that her behaviour is dictated by her chemistry, and that her wrongs lie in herself, and not in others' bad behaviour.

Holding Back

The next weekend Liffey and Richard took their friends Bella and Ray down to visit Honeycomb Cottage.

The trap closed tighter.

'When I say country,' said Richard, to everyone, 'I mean twenty miles outside London at the most. Somerset is impossible. But as a country cottage, it's a humdinger.' He had a slightly old-fashioned vocabulary.

Richard was, Bella always felt, a slightly old-fashioned young man. She wanted to loosen him up. She felt there was a wickedness beneath the veneer of well-bred niceness and that it was Liffey's fault it remained so firmly battened down.

'When I say have a baby,' said Liffey, 'I mean soon, very soon. Not quite now.'

Ray had a theory that wives always made themselves a degree less interesting than their husbands, and that Liffey, if married to, say, himself, would improve remarkably.

Bella and Ray were in their early forties and their friendship with Richard and Liffey was a matter of some speculation to Bella and Ray's other friends. Perhaps Bella was after Richard, or Ray after Liffey? Perhaps they aimed for foursomes? Or perhaps, the most common consensus, Bella and Ray were just so dreadful they had to find their friends where best they could, and choice did not enter into it.

Bella and Ray – who wrote cookery columns and cookery books – were a couple other couples loved to hate. Liffey and Richard, however, such was their youth and simplicity, accepted Ray and Bella as they were: liked, admired and trusted them, and were flattered by their attention.

Ray and Bella had two children. Bella had waited until her mid-thirties to have them, by which time her fame and fortune were secure.

When Bella and Ray saw the cottage they knew at once it was not for them to admire or linger by. Its sweetness embarrassed them. Their taste ran to starker places: they would feel ridiculous under a thatch, with roses round their door. They rather unceremoniously left Richard and Liffey at the gate and borrowed the car and went off to the ruins of Glastonbury to inspect the monks' kitchen with a view to a Special on medieval cookery.

'Richard,' said Liffey. 'The main-line station's only ten minutes by car, and there's a fast early train at seven in the morning which gets you in to London by half-past eight and a fast one back at night so you'd be home by half-past seven, and that's only half an hour later than you get home now.'

The Tor was distant today, swathed in mists, so that it rose as if from a white sea. And indeed, the surrounding plains, the levels, had once been marsh and sea until drained by monks to provide pasture.

'I want to live here, Richard,' said Liffey. 'If we live here I'll come off the pill.'
Richard nodded.

He opened Liffey's handbag and took out her little packet of contraceptive pills.
'I don't understand why someone who likes things to be natural,' he said, 'could ever rely on anything so unnatural as these.'

Richard took Liffey round to the field at the back and threw her pills, with some ceremony, into the stream, which recent rain had made to flow fast and free.

'I wonder what he's throwing away,' said Mabs watching through the glasses.
'So long as it's nothing as will harm the cows,' said Tucker. 'They drink that water.'
'Told you they'd be back,' said Mabs.

And Mabs and Tucker had a discussion as to whether it was in their best interests to have Richard and Liffey renting the cottage, and decided that it was, so long as they rented, and didn't buy. An outright purchaser would soon discover that the two-acre field, on the far side of the stream, belonged to the cottage, and not, as Tucker pretended, to Cadbury Farm. Tucker found it convenient to graze his cows there; but would not find it convenient to pay for grazing rights. 'You tell your sister to tell Dick Hubbard to keep his mouth shut about the stream field,' said Tucker.

Dick Hubbard was the estate agent responsible for Honeycomb Cottage, with whom Mabs' sister Carol was having an affair. Dick Hubbard was not married, but Carol was. Mabs disapproved of the relationship, and did not like Tucker mentioning it. Many things, these days, Mabs did not like. She did not like being forty any more than the next woman did; she was beginning to fear, for one reason and another, that she was infertile. She was, in general, suffering from a feeling she could only describe as upset – a wavering of purpose from day to day. And she did not like it.

'He'll keep it shut of his own accord,' said Mabs.

Something about Liffey upset her even more: the arrogant turn of her head as she sat in the car waiting for Tucker's cows to pass; the slight condescension in the smile; the way she leaned against Richard as if she owned him; the way she coupled with him, as she was doing now, in the open air, like an animal. Mabs felt that Liffey had everything too easy. Mabs felt that, rightly, Liffey had nothing to do in the world but enjoy herself, and that Liffey should be taken down a peg or two.

'Nice to have a new neighbour,' said Mabs, comfortingly, and Tucker looked at her suspiciously.

'I wouldn't fancy it down in the grass,' said Mabs. 'That stream's downright unhealthy, and nasty things grow there at this time of year.'

'You won't mind when I swell up like a balloon?' Liffey was saying to Richard.

'I'll love you all the more,' said Richard. 'I think pregnant women are beautiful. Soft and rounded and female.'

She lay on his chest, her bare breasts cool to his skin. He felt her limbs stiffen and grow tense before she cried out, her voice sharp with horror.

'Look! What are they? Richard!'

Giant puffballs had pushed up out of the ground a yard or so from where they lay. How could she not have noticed them before? Three white globes, giant mushroom balls, each the

size and shape of a human skull, thinned in yellowy white,
stood blindly sentinel. Liffey was on her feet, shuddering
and aghast.
'They're only puffballs,' said Richard. 'Nature's bounty.
They come up overnight. What's the matter with you?'

The matter was that the smooth round swelling of the fungus
made Liffey think of a belly swollen by pregnancy, and she
said so. Richard found another one, but its growth had been
stunted by tangled conch-grass, and its surface was con-
voluted, brownish and rubbery.
'This one looks like a brain in some laboratory jar,' said
Richard.

Him and me, thought Liffey, trembling as if aware that the
invisible bird of disaster, flying by, had glanced with its
wings. Him and me.

Bella and Ray came round from the back of the house.
'We knew we'd find you round here,' said Ray. 'Bella took a
bet on it. They'll be at it again, she said. I think she's jealous.
What have you found?'
'Puffballs,' said Richard.
'Puffballs!'
'Puffballs!'
Ray and Bella, animated, ran forward to see.
Liffey saw them all of a sudden with cold eyes, in clear
sunlight, and knew that they were grotesque. Bella's lank
hair was tightly pulled back, and her nose was bulbous and
her long neck was scrawny and her eyes popped as if the doll-
maker had failed to press them properly into the mould. Her
tired breasts pushed sadly into her white T-shirt: the skin on
her arms was coarse and slack. Ray was white in the bright
sunlight, pale and puffy and rheumy. He wore jeans and an
open shirt as if he were a young man, but he wasn't. A
pendant hung round his neck and nestled in grey, wiry,
unhuman hairs. In the city, running across busy streets,
jumping in and out of taxis, opening food from the Take
Away, they seemed ordinary enough. Put them against a

background of growing green, under a clear sky, and you could see how strange they were.

'You simply have to take the cottage,' said Bella, 'if only to bring us puffballs. Have you any idea how rare they are?'
'What do you *do* with them?' asked Liffey.
'Eat them,' said Ray. 'Slice them, grill them, stuff them: they have a wonderful creamy texture – like just ripe Camembert. We'll do some tonight under the roast beef.'
'I don't like Camembert,' was all Liffey could think of to say.

Ray bent and plucked one of the puffballs from its base, fingers gently cupping its globe from beneath, careful not to break the taut, stretched skin. He handed it to Bella and picked a second.

Tucker came along the other side of the stream. Cows followed him: black and white Friesians, full bumping bellies swaying from side to side. A dog brought up the rear. It was a quiet, orderly procession.
'Oh my God,' said Bella. 'Cows!'
'They won't hurt you,' said Liffey.
'Cows kill four people a year in this country,' said Bella, who always had a statistic to back up a fear.

'Afternoon,' said Tucker, amiably across the stream.
'We're not on your land?' enquired Ray.
'Not mine,' said Tucker. 'That's no one's you're on, that's waiting for an owner.'
He was splashing through the water towards them. 'You thinking of taking it? Good piece of land, your side of the stream, better than mine this side.'

He was across. He saw the remaining puffball. He drew back his leg and kicked it, and it burst, as if it had been under amazing tension, into myriad pieces which buzzed through the air like a maddened insect crowd, and then settled on the ground and were still.

'Him or me,' thought Liffey. But just at the moment Tucker kicked she felt a pain in her middle, so she knew it was her, and was glad, in her nice way, that Richard was saved. Her tummy: his brain. Well, better kicked to death by a farmer than sliced and cooked under roast beef by Bella and Ray.

'If you want to spread the spores,' said Ray to Tucker, 'that's the best way.'
'Disgusting things,' said Tucker. 'No use for anything except footballs.'

He told them the name of the estate agent who dealt with the property and left, well pleased with himself. His cows munched solemnly on, on the other side of the brook, bulky and soft-eyed.
'I hate cows,' said Bella.
'I rather like them,' said Ray. 'Plump and female.'
Bella, who was not so much slim as scrawny, took this as an attack, and rightly so.

They drove back to London with Bella's mouth set like a trap and Ray's arm muscles sinewy, so tight was his grasp on the steering wheel. Liffey admired the muscles. Richard, though broad and brave, was a soft man; not fat, but unmuscled. Richard's hands were white and smooth. Tucker's, she had noticed, were gnarled, rough and grimy, like the earth. A faint sweet smell of puffball filled the car.

Inside Liffey (2)

The pain Liffey felt was nothing to do with Tucker's kicking of the puffball. It was a mid-cycle pain – the kind of pain quite commonly, if inexplicably, felt by women who take the contraceptive pill. It is not an ovulation pain, for such women do not ovulate. But the pain is felt, neverless, and at that time.

Liffey, on this particular September day, was twelve days in to her one-hundred-and-seventy-first menstrual cycle. She had reached the menarche rather later than the average girl, at fifteen years and three months.

Liffey's mother Madge, worried, had taken her to the doctor when she was fourteen-and-a-half. 'She isn't menstruating,' said Madge, bleakly. Madge was often bleak. 'Why?'
'She's of slight build,' the doctor said. 'And by and large, the lighter the girl, the later the period.'

Liffey, at the time, had no desire whatsoever to start menstruating, and took her mother's desire that she should as punitive. Liffey, unlike her mother, but like most women, had never cared to think too much about what was going on inside her body. She regarded the inner, pounding, pulsating Liffey with distaste, seeing it as something formless and messy and uncontrollable, and being uncontrollable, better unacknowledged. She would rather think about, and identify wholly with, the outer Liffey. Pale and pretty and nice.

It was not even possible to accept, as it were, a bodily status quo, for her body kept changing. Processes quite unknown to her, and indeed for the most part unnoticeable, had gone on inside Liffey since the age of seven when her ovaries had begun to release the first secretions of oestrogen, and as the contours of her body had begun their change from child to woman, so had vulva, clitoris, vagina, uterus, fallopian tubes and ovaries, unseen and unconsidered, begun their own path to maturity. The onset of menstruation would occur when her body dictated, and not when the doctor, or Madge, or Liffey felt proper.

Her menstrual cycle, once established, was of a steady, almost relentless twenty-eight-day rhythm, which Liffey assumed to be only her right. Other girls were early, or late, or undecided: trickled and flooded and stopped and started. But as the sun went down every twenty-eight days, from the one-hundred-and-eighty-fourth calender month of her life,

Liffey started to bleed. Being able so certainly to predict this, gave her at least the illusion of being in control of her body.

Liffey never enquired of anyone as to why she bled, or what use the bleeding served. She knew vaguely it was to do with having babies, and thought of it, if she thought at all, as all her old internal rubbish being cleared away.

The mechanics of her menstrual cycle were indeed ingenious.

Lunar month by lunar month, since she reached the menarche, Liffey's pituitary gland had pursued its own cycle: secreting first, for a fourteen-day stretch, the hormones which would stimulate the growth of follicles in Liffey's ovaries. These follicles, some hundred or so cyst-like nodules, in their turn secreted oestrogen, and would all grow until, on the fourteenth day (at any rate in the years she was not taking the pill) the biggest and best would drop off into the outer-end of one of Liffey's fallopian tubes and there, unfertilised, would rupture, allowing its oestrogen to be absorbed. This was the signal for the remaindered follicles to atrophy: and for Liffey's pituitary to start secreting, for a further twelve days, a hormone which would promote the formation of a corpus luteum which would secrete progesterone and flourish until the twenty-sixth day, when the pituitary withdrew its supplies. Then the corpus luteum would start to degenerate and on the twenty-eighth day be disposed of in the form of menstrual flow – along, of course, with the lining of Liffey's uterus, hopefully and richly thickened over the previous twenty-eight days to receive a fertilised ovum, but so far, on one-hundred-and-seventy occasions, disappointed.

The disintegration and shedding of the uterus lining, signalled by the withdrawal of oestrogen, would take three days and thereafter the amount of blood lost would gradually diminish as the uterus healed.

On this, the twelfth day into Liffey's cycle, the seventy-seventh follicle in the left fallopian tube was outstripping its fellows, distending the surface of the ovary as a cystic swelling almost half an inch in diameter – but owing to the fact that Liffey had been taking the pill, her body had been hoodwinked so that the ovum would have no time to actually fall, but would merely atrophy along with its fellows.

Did a tremor of disappointment shake Liffey's body? Did the thwarting of so much organic organisation register on her consciousness? Certainly she had a pain, and certainly Mabs' eyes flickered as Liffey winced, but that too could be coincidence.

Mothers

Mabs and Tucker walked up to Honeycomb Cottage. They liked to go walking over their land, and that of their neighbours, just to see what was happening. As people in cities turn to plays or films for event, so did Mabs and Tucker turn to the tracks of badgers, or observe the feathers where the fox had been, or the owl; or fret at just how much the summer had dried the stream, or the rain swelled it. A field, which to a stranger is just a field, to those who know it is a battleground for combatant plant and animal life, and the traces of victory and defeat are everywhere.

Tucker came across another puffball and kicked it, taking a run, letting a booted foot fly, entering energetically into the conflict. 'Nasty unnatural things,' said Mabs. She remembered her mother before her sister Carol had been born, and the swollen white of her belly as she lifted her skirt and squatted to urinate, as was her custom, in the back garden. Mabs' mother Mrs Tree thought it was wasteful to let good powerful bodily products vanish down the water closet. This belief was a source of much bitterness and shame to her two daughters, and one of the reasons they married so early.

Mrs. Tree was a herbalist, in the old tradition. Her enemies, and she had many, said she was a witch, and even her friends recognised her as a wise woman. On moonlit nights, even now, she would switch off the television and go gathering herbs – mugwort and comfrey, cowslip and henbane, or any of the hundred or more plants she knew by sight and name. She would scrape roots and strip bark, would simmer concoctions of this or that on her gas-stove, at home with distillations and precipitations. The drugs she prepared – as her mother's before her – were the same as the local doctor had to offer; psychoactive agents, prophylactics, antiseptics, narcotics, hypnotics, anaesthetics and antibiotics. But Mrs. Tree's medicines served, in overdose, not just to restore a normal body chemistry, but to incite to love and hate, violence and passivity, to bring about increased sexual activity or impotence, pain, irritability, skin disease, wasting away, and even death. She made an uneasy mother.

'Does your mother use puffballs?' Tucker asked Mabs.
Mabs didn't reply and he knew he should not have asked. She liked to pretend that her mother was just like anyone else. But Tucker, as was only natural in the circumstances, would roll food around in his mouth before he swallowed, searching for strange tastes. Such knowledge passed from mother to daughter.

'Puffballs are too nasty even for my mum,' said Mabs, presently. 'They're the devil's eyeballs.'

'Isn't it dark and poky!' said Mabs, pushing open the front door of Honeycomb Cottage. 'I'd rather have a nice new bungalow any day. But the view's good, I'll say that.'

Mabs waved at Glastonbury Tor, in a familiar kind of way, as she went inside. The sun was setting behind the hill, in a blood red sky.

'I wonder if they'll live like pigs,' said Mabs, 'the way they act like pigs,' and she looked at Tucker slyly out of the corner

25

of her eye so that he started grunting and waddling like a pig
and pushed her with his belly into the corner and bore down
upon her, laughing: and they made love in the red light that
shone in diamonds through the latticed windows.

'So she's too skinny for you, is she,' said Mabs, presently.

'Yes,' said Tucker.

'You might have to learn to like it,' said Mabs. 'Just once or
twice.'

'Why's that?' asked Tucker, surprised.

'It's important to have a hold,' said Mabs. 'You can't be too
careful with neighbours.'

'You wouldn't like it,' said Tucker. 'Not one bit.'

'I'm not the jealous type,' said Mabs. 'You know that. Not if
there's something to be got out of it. I don't mind things
done on purpose. It's things done by accident I don't like.'

They walked back hand in hand to Cadbury Farm. She was
so large and slow, and he was so small and lively, they had to
keep their hands locked to stay in pace with one another.

The dogs in the courtyard barked and Tucker kicked them.

'They're hungry,' Mabs protested.

'A good watchdog is always hungry,' said Tucker. 'That's
what makes it good.'

The children were hungry as well, but Mabs reserved her
sympathy for the dogs. Mabs had five children. The eldest,
Audrey, was fourteen. The youngest, Kevin, was four. Mabs
slapped small hands as they crept over the tabletop to steal
crusts from the paste sandwiches she prepared for their tea.
All her children were thin. Presently Mabs picked up a
wooden spoon and used that as a cane, to save her own hand
smarting as she slapped. One of the children gave a cry of
pain.

'You shouldn't have done that,' said Tucker, taking notice.

'My children. I do as I please.' She did, too, according to
mood.

'You're too hard on them.'

She said nothing.

Her breasts were full and round beneath the old sweater. Tucker's eyelids drooped in memory of them.

'Get the bleeding sauce,' Mabs shouted at Eddie. Eddie was her third child, and irritated her most, and she slapped and shouted at him more than she did the others. He took after her, being large and slow. She preferred her children to take after Tucker. That cruel audacity which in Mabs was almost attractive, was in Eddie something nasty and sly: she had slapped and startled him too often: he lived in the expectation of sudden disaster, and now cringed in corners. Nobody liked him. He was eight now and it would be the same when he was eighty. Audrey, Mabs' eldest, looked after him. She was kind where her mother was cruel, and clever at her books. Mabs took her books away because she put on airs.

Mabs and Tucker ate fish fingers and tinned spaghetti. The children made do with the sandwiches.

That night Mabs sat at the window and watched a sudden storm blow up over the Tor. Black clouds streamed out from it, like steam from a kettle, and formed into solid masses at the corners of the sky. Lightning leapt between the clouds. Thunder rumbled and rolled, but the rain did not start.

'Come to bed,' said Tucker.

'There are people in Honeycomb Cottage,' said Mabs. But Tucker couldn't see them, although he came to stand beside her. Lightning lit up the interior of the rooms, and made strange shapes which could have been anything.

'What sort of people?' he asked, cautiously.

'Him and her,' said Mabs. 'It won't be long now.'

'At it again, are they?'

'No,' said Mabs. 'They were in opposite corners of the room. She was holding a baby.'

'I know what's the matter with you,' said Tucker. 'You want another baby.'

'No I don't,' she said, but he knew she did. Her youngest child was four years old. Mabs liked to be pregnant. Tucker wondered how long it would be before she began to think it was his fault, and what means she would find to punish him. 'Come to bed,' he said, 'and we'll see what we can do.'

It was a rare thing for him to ask. Usually she was there first, lying in wait, half inviting, half commanding, a channel for forces greater than herself. Come on, quick, again, again! Impregnate, fertilise; by your will, Tucker, which is only partly your will, set the forces of division and multiplication going. Now!

Inside Liffey (3)

Liffey was off the pill.

Liffey's pituitary gland was once more its own master and stimulated the production of oestrogen and progesterone as it saw fit: no longer, by its inactivity, hoodwinking her body into believing it was pregnant. Liffey became a little thinner: her breasts a little smaller: her temperament a little more volatile. She was conscious of an increase in sexual desire although she was still obliged to pretend, for Richard's sake, and in the interest of her own self-esteem, to have orgasms. Not that this affected her fertility, for orgasm and ovulation in the human female are not connected, as in other species they sometimes are. And although sexual desire itself can on occasion prompt ovulation, overriding the pituitary's clock-work timing, the element of surprise which brings this rare phenomenon about (and much distress to rape victims and deflowered virgins) was not present in Richard's love-making with Liffey.

Liffey's menstrual cycle was thus quickly restored to its normal rhythm. Liffey, all the same, did not become pregnant.

Two more lunar months went by. Two more ova dropped, decayed and were disposed of.

Liffey's chance of becoming pregnant, which was ninety-five per cent when she was a teenager, was by now down by some six per cent and would continue to diminish, slightly, year by year, as would Richard's, until by the time he was sixty, his fertility rate would be down by ninety per cent, and hers, of course, would be nil.

In their favour, both were still young: intercourse occurred at least four times a week, and Richard's sperms were almost always present in the outer part of Liffey's fallopian tubes, waiting for ovulation to occur. Against them, was the fact that Richard had flu in November, and his sperm count was perhaps temporarily rather low: and Liffey had only just come off the pill. There were the many other statistical probabilities of conception to take into account. Had Liffey known all this, she would perhaps not have lain awake at night, fearing – for although she did not want a baby she certainly did not want to be infertile – that she was barren and that some cosmic punishment had been visited upon her.

It was a matter of time, nothing else, before she conceived.

In-Laws and Secretaries

Liffey's mother Madge was a lean, hard-drinking, prematurely white-haired teacher of chemistry in a girls' school in East Anglia. She had never married, nor wished to, and Liffey was not so much a love child as a gesture of defiance to a straitlaced world. Madge had thought to bear a warrior son, but had given birth to Liffey instead, and Liffey had compounded the error by attempting, throughout her childhood, to chirrup and charm her way into Madge's affections.

Madge, hearing that Liffey was trying to have a baby, commented then to a friend, 'Silence for six months and then this. Not that she's pregnant, not that she's miscarried – just that she's *trying* to have a baby. How's that for a piece of non-news?' 'I expect she thought it would please you,' said the friend, who was only there for the whisky.

'It doesn't,' said Madge. 'Liffey is an only child and an only grandchild. Nature is clearly trying to breed the line out. Trust Liffey to interfere with the proper course of things.'

Madge did not want Liffey to be pregnant. She did not want to think of herself diluting down through the generations. She craved mortality.

Richard's father, on the other hand, living in early retirement in a fisherman's cottage in Cornwall, was glad to think that his line might well continue, now that Liffey was off the pill. Richard's mother was made nervous by the news – as if some trouble, pacing for years behind at a steady distance, had suddenly broken into a jog and overtaken her. She started knitting at once, but there was a tenseness in her hands, and the nylon wool cut into her fingers.

The Lee-Foxes looked a placid enough couple – well-heeled, grey-haired, conventional and companionable – but the effort to appear so cost them a good deal in nervous energy. He had ulcers; she, migraines.

'It's too early to start knitting,' said Mr. Lee-Fox. 'She's not even pregnant: they're just trying.'

'Richard always does what he sets out to do,' said Mrs. Lee-Fox, loyally.

'Your fingers are bleeding,' said Mr. Lee-Fox. 'Whatever is the matter?'

She wept, for answer.

'Little garments,' said Mr. Lee-Fox, in wonder, 'stained by blood and tears!'

Mr. Lee-Fox could not understand why, having worked

hard to achieve a reasonable home and a happy life and done so at last, troubles should still keep occurring. It was his wife's fault, he concluded. She was discontented by nature. He hoped, for his son Richards's sake, that Liffey was not the same.

'You mustn't worry,' he said. 'Liffey will come through with flying colours. Wait and see.'

Liffey was at the time extremely discontented, which made her more loving and lively than ever. Chirruping and charming. Sometimes, when she woke up in the apartment, opening her eyes to the concrete wall of the house next door, and the sound of traffic instead of the sound of birds, she thought she was a child again, and in her mother's house.

The trouble was that Richard, telephoning Dick Hubbard the estate agent about Honeycomb Cottage, had been told that the cottage was for sale, and not to rent, and Richard had said they could not afford it.

'We could spend some of my money,' said Liffey.
'No, we couldn't,' said Richard firmly. 'I'm not going to live off you. What kind of man would that make me?'

By mutual consent, throughout their marriage, Liffey's money had been used to buy small things, not large things. Confectionery as it were, but not the matrimonial home.

'Then let's sell this place and buy that.'
'No. It isn't ours to sell.'

The apartment had been a wedding gift from Mr. and Mrs. Lee-Fox. Disapproving of Liffey as a bride for Richard, they had sacrificed their own comfort and security and spent an inordinate amount on the present. Thus they hoped both to disguise their feelings and remain securely sealed in the ranks of the happy and blessed.

When Richard came home from his boarding school bruised

and stunned, victim of bullying, they would seem not to notice.

'Such a wonderful school,' they'd say to friends. 'He's so happy there.'

Liffey searched the newspapers for cottages to rent but found nothing. Another month passed: another egg dropped, and failed. Liffey bled; Richard frowned, perplexed.

Liffey took a temporary job in a solicitor's office. The quality of her cooking deteriorated. She served Richard burnt food and tossed and turned all night, keeping him awake. She did not know she did it, but do it she did. She had come off the pill, after all, and still they lived in London.

'If Liffey can't have children,' asked Annie, Richard's secretary, 'would you stick by her?'
'Of course,' said Richard immediately and stoutly. But the question increased his anxiety.

Annie read cookery books in her lunch hour, propping them in her electric typewriter. She took an easy and familiar approach to her job, and felt no deference towards anyone. She had spent a year working in the States and had lost, or so it seemed to Richard, her sense of the nuances of respect owing between man and woman, powerful and humble, employer and employed.

Her fair hair hung over the typewriter like a veil. She had a boyfriend who was a diamond merchant and one-time bodyguard to General Dayan. She had wide blue eyes, and a rounded figure. Liffey had never seen her. Once she asked Richard what Annie looked like – tentatively, because she did not want to sound possessive or jealous.
'Fat,' said Richard.
And because Annie had a flat, nasal telephone voice Liffey had assumed she was one of the plain, efficient girls whom large organisations are obliged to employ to make up for the pretty ones they like to keep up front.

Besides.

When Richard and Liffey married they had agreed to tell one another at once if some new emotional or physical involvement seemed likely, and Liffey believed the agreement still held.

Christmas approached, and Liffey stopped work in order to concentrate upon it, and decorate the Christmas tree properly. She had her gifts bought by the second week in December, and then spent another week wrapping and adorning. She was asked to Richard's office party but didn't go. She did not like his office parties. Everyone looked so ugly, except Richard, and everyone got drunk.

Liffey arranged to meet Richard at a restaurant after the party. She expected him at nine. By ten he had not arrived, so she went round to the office, in case he had had too much to drink or there had been an accident. In no sense, as she explained and explained afterwards, was she spying on him.

The office was a massive new concrete block, with a marble-lined lobby and decorative lifts. Richard's employers were an international company, recently diversified from oil into films and food products – the latter being Richard's division, and he a Junior Assistant Brand Manager. If it were not for Liffey's private income, she would have had to work and earn, or else live very poorly indeed. As it was, lack of financial anxiety made Richard bold in his decisions and confident in his approach to his superiors, which was duly noted and appreciated, and boded well for his future.

Liffey went up in the lift to Richard's office, walking through empty corridors, still rich with the after-party haze of cigarette smoke and the aroma from a hundred half-empty glasses. From behind the occasional closed door came a cry, or a giggle or a moan. Liffey found Richard behind his desk, on the floor with Annie, who was not one of the plain ones after all, just plump and luscious, and all but naked, except for veils of hair. So was Richard.

Liffey went home by taxi. Richard followed after. He was maudlin drunk, sick on the step, and passed out in the hall. Liffey dragged him to bed, undressed his stubborn body and left him alone. She sat at the window staring out at the street.

She felt that she was destroyed. Everything was finished – love, trust, marriage, happiness. All over.

But of course it was not. Richard's contrition was wonderful to behold. He begged forgiveness: he held Liffey's hand. He pleaded, with some justification, total amnesia of the event. Someone had poured vodka into the fruit cup. It was Annie's fault, if anyone's. Richard loved Liffey, only Liffey. Love flowed between them again, lubricating Liffey's passages, promoting spermatogenesis in Richard's testes, encouraging the easy flow of seminal fluid from seminal vesicles and prostate to the entrance of the urethra, and thence, by a series of rhythmic muscular contractions, into Liffey.

Love, and none the worse for all that: but earthly love. Spiritual love, the love of God for man, and man for God, cannot be debased, as can earthly love, by such description.

Still Liffey did not get pregnant.

Annie was transferred to another office. After the annual Christmas party there was a general shifting round of secretarial staff. A stolid and respectful girl, Miss Martin, took Annie's place. Her plumpness was not soft and natural, as was Annie's, but solid and unwelcoming, and encased by elasticated garments. Her face was impassive, and her manner was prim; Richard was not attracted to her at all, and was relieved to find he was not. He had lately been having trouble with sudden upsurges of sexual interest in the most inappropriate people. He confided as much in Bella.

'For heaven's sake,' said Bella, 'you can't be expected to stay faithful to one person all your life, just because you married them.' Richard quite disliked Bella for a time, for giving voice to what he saw as cheap and easy cynicism. He still believed in romantic love, and was ashamed of his lapse with Annie: his sudden succumbing to animal lust. He decided that Liffey and he would see less of Bella and Ray.

Christmas Pledges

Liffey's birthday was on Christmas Day, a fact which annoyed Madge, who was a proselytising atheist.

They were to spend Christmas with Richard's parents. They journeyed down to Cornwall on the night of Christmas Eve: there was a hard frost. The night landscape sparkled under the moon. Richard and Liffey were drunk with love and Richard's remorse. The back of the car was piled high with presents, beautifully wrapped and ribboned. They took with them a thermos of good real coffee, laced with brandy, and chicken sandwiches. They went by the A303, down past Windsor, on to the motorway, leaving at the Hungerford exit, and down through Berkshire and Wiltshire, crossing Salisbury Plain, where Stonehenge stood in the moonlight, ominous and amazing, dwarfing its wire palisade. Then on into Somerset, past Glastonbury Tor, into Devon and finally over the Tamar Bridge into Cornwall.

Liffey loved Richard too much to even mention Honeycomb Cottage, although they passed within five miles of it.

Christmas Day was bright, cold, and wild. Mr. and Mrs. Lee-Fox's cottage was set into the Cornish cliffs. A storm arose, and sea spray dashed against the double glazing but all was safe and warm and hospitable within. The roast turkey was magnificent, the Christmas tree charming, and Liffey's presents proved most acceptable – two hand-made patch-work quilts, one for each twin bed. Liffey loved giving. Her mother, Madge did not. They had once spent Christmas

35

with Madge, rather than with Richard's parents, and had a chilly bleak time of it. Madge liked to be working, not rejoicing.

Mr. and Mrs. Lee-Fox agreed, under their quilts on Christmas night, that at least Liffey kept Richard happy and lively, and at least this year had worn a T-shirt thick enough to hide her nipples.

On their way back to London they made a detour out of Glastonbury and into Crossley, and passed Dick Hubbard's estate agency. There was room to park outside, for the Christmas holiday, stretching further and further forward to grab in the New Year, kept most of the shops and offices closed. And Dick Hubbard's door was open. Richard stopped.

'Townspeople,' said Dick Hubbard, looking down from his private office on the first floor. 'Back from the Christmas holidays, and looking for a country cottage to rent, for twopence halfpenny a week. They're out of luck.'

He was a large, fleshy man in his late forties, at home in pubs, virile in bed; indolent. His wife had died in a riding accident shortly after his liaison with Carol had begun. Carol was smaller and slighter than her sister Mabs, but just as determined.

'There's Honeycomb Cottage,' said Carol.

'That's for sale, not for rent. I'm holding on until prices stop rising.'

'Then you'll hold on for ever,' said Carol. 'And in the meanwhile it will all fall down. Mabs says it's already an eyesore. She's quite put out about it.'

'Mabs had better not start interfering,' said Dick, 'or she'll lose her grazing.' But no one in Crossley, not even Dick Hubbard, liked to think of Mabs being put out, and when Richard and Liffey enquired about Honeycomb Cottage, they were told it was to rent on a full repairing lease for twenty pounds a week.

'Done,' said Richard.

36

'Done,' said Dick Hubbard.
They shook hands.

'In the country,' said Liffey, as they got back into the car, 'the word of a gentleman still means something. People trust one another. You're going to love it, Richard.'
'It's certainly easy to do business,' said Richard.

They decided to rent the London apartment to friends, and let the income from one pay for the outgoings on the other. 'We could get thirty a week for the flat,' said Liffey. And the extra can pay for your fares.'

It was a long time since she had been anywhere by train.

After Richard and Liffey had gone, Dick Hubbard returned to his interrupted love-making with Carol.
'Didn't they even ask for a lease?' asked Carol.
'No,' said Dick.
'You'll do all right there,' said Carol.
'I know,' said Dick.

Friends

On the morning of December 30th, Liffey rang up her friend, Helen, who was married to Mory, an architect. The friendship was not of long standing. Liffey had met Helen in the waiting room of an employment agency a year ago, and struck up an acquaintance.

After the manner of young married women, still under the obligation of total loyalty to a husband, Liffey had cut loose from her school and college friends, as if fearing that their very existence might merit a rash confidence, a betrayal of her love for Richard. She made do, now, with a kind of surface intimacy with this new acquaintance or that, and since she did not offer any indication of need or distress, or any real exchange of feeling, the friendships did not ripen.

Liffey did not like to display weakness: and weakness admitted is the very stuff of good friendship.

Mory and Richard had met over a dinner table or so, and discussed the black holes of space, and Richard, less acute in his social than his business relationships, thought he recognised a fellow spirit.

So now Liffey went to Helen and Mory for help.

'Helen? Sorry to ring so early but Helen we've rented a *most darling* cottage in the country and now all we have to do is find someone for this flat and we can move out of London in a fortnight, and I was wondering if you could help?'
There was a pause.
'How much?' enquired Helen.
'Richard says forty pounds a week but I think that's greedy. Twenty would be more like it.'
'I should think so,' said Helen. 'If you can't find anyone Mory and I could take it, I suppose, to help you out.'
'But that would be wonderful,' cried Liffey. 'I'd be so grateful! You'd look after everything and it would all be safe with you.'

Liffey sorted, washed, wrapped, packed and cleaned for two weeks. Friends rather mysteriously disappeared, instead of helping. She had no idea she and Richard had accumulated so many possessions. She gave away clothes and furniture to Oxfam. She found old photographs of herself and Richard and laughed and cried at the absurdity of life. She wrapped her hair in a spotted bandana to keep out clouds of dust. She wanted everything to be nice for Helen and Mory. Charming, talented, scatty Helen. Mory, the genius architect, temporarily unemployed. Lovely to be able to help!

'Friendship,' Liffey said, 'is all about helping.'
'Um,' said Richard. Five years ago the remark would have enchanted, not embarrassed him.
'Don't you think so, Bella,' persisted Liffey, not getting the expected response from Richard.

'I daresay,' said Bella, politely. Ray was out visiting friends who had a sixteen-year-old daughter he was helping through a Home Economics examination. Bella was in a bad, fidgety mood. Richard knew Ray was making her unhappy and from charity had lifted the embargo on the friendship. And Bella was being very kind; the kindest, in fact, of all their friends, offering packing cases, time, concern, and showing an interest in the details of the move. Now, on the eve of their departure for the country, she gave them spaghetti bolognese. The sauce came from a can. Richard followed Bella into the kitchen. Liffey had gone to the bathroom.

'Liffey's a lucky little girl,' said Bella, 'having a husband to indulge her so.'

Bella kissed Richard full on the lips, startling him.

'If you're not careful,' said Bella, 'Liffey will still be a little girl when she's got grey hairs and you're an old, old man.'

She dabbed his mouth with a tissue.

'You're going to hate the country,' said Bella. 'You're going to be so lonely.'

'We have each other,' said Richard.

Bella laughed.

Liffey came back from the bathroom with a long face.

'No baby?' asked Bella.

'No baby,' said Liffey. 'I'm sorry, Richard. Once we're in the country I'm sure it will happen.'

The removal van arrived on the morning of Wednesday, January 7th. Liffey's period was soon to finish. She was in a progesterone phase.

Richard took the day off from work. They followed the furniture van in the car, and left the key under the mat for Mory and Helen. There was no need of a lease, or a rentbook, between friends.

'Goodbye, you horrible town,' cried Liffey. 'Hello country! Nature, here we come!' Richard wished she wouldn't, Bella's words in his mind. And, he rather feared, Bella's lips. He had never thought of her as a sexual entity before.

Mory and Helen moved in a couple of hours after Richard and Liffey had left. With them came Helen's pregnant sister and her unemployed boyfriend, both of whom now had the required permanent address from which to claim Social Security benefits.

Honeycomb Cottage, in January, was perhaps colder and damper than Liffey had expected, and the rooms smaller: and the banisters had to come down before any furniture could get in, and Richard sawed the double bed in two to get it into the bedroom, but Liffey was happy, brave and positive, and by Wednesday evening had fires lit, decorative branches, however bare, in vases, and a cosy space cleared amongst chaos for a delicious celebration meal of bottled caviar, fillet steak (from Harrods), a whole pound of mushrooms between them, and champagne.

'All this,' marvelled Liffey, 'and five pounds a week profit!' She'd forgotten how much she'd asked Helen to pay, in the end. 'You're leaving out the fares,' murmured Richard, but not too loud, for it was always unkind to present Liffey with too much reality all at once. Fares would amount to some thirty pounds a week. Liffey had bought a whole crate of new books – from thrillers, new novels, to heavy works on sociology and philosophy, which she intended to dole out to Richard day by day, for the improvement of his mind on the morning journey, and his diversion on the evening train – and Richard was touched.

'It's very quiet,' said Richard, looking out into the blank, bleak wet night. 'I don't know what you're going to do with yourself all day.'
'I love the quietness,' said Liffey. 'And the solitude. Just you and me – oh, we are the most enviable of people! Everyone else just dreams, but we've actually done it.'

That night they slept on foam rubber in front of the fire, but did not make love, for they were exhausted. Richard wondered why someone so old and scraggy and cynical as

Bella should be so attractive. Perhaps true love and sexual excitement were mutually exclusive.

Realities

On Thursday morning Liffey's little alarm watch woke them at six. Liffey was up in a trice to make Richard's breakfast. The hot water system was not working and there was ice in the wash basin, but he laughed bravely. Liffey had the times of the trains written out and pinned up above the mantelpiece. She tried to light the kitchen stove but the chimney was cold, and filled the room with smoke. She could not get the kettle to boil: she plugged in the toaster and all the electricity in the house fused: she could not grind the coffee beans for coffee. The transistor radio produced only crackle – clearly here it would need an aerial. Richard stopped smiling. Liffey danced and kissed and pinched and hugged, and he managed a wan smile, as he found the old candles he'd noticed in the fuse box.

'I suppose,darling,they'ddieifyoutookanotherdayoffwork?'

'Yes, they would,' said Richard, longing for the warmth and shiny bright order of the office, and the solidarity of Miss Martin who never pranced or kissed, but offered him hot instant coffee in plastic mugs at orderly intervals.

Richard left the house at seven-thirty. Castle Tor station was twelve minutes' drive away, and the train left at seven fifty-two.

'Allow lots of time,' said Liffey, 'this first morning.'

Richard was delayed by the cow mire outside Cadbury Farm. The little Renault sank almost to its axles in the slime, for it had thawed overnight, and what the day before had been a hard surface now revealed its true nature. But revving and reversing freed the vehicle, though it woke the dogs, and he arrived, heart beating fast, at Castle Tor station at seven fifty. The station was closed. As he stood, open-mouthed, the fast train shot through.

Richard arrived back at Honeycomb Cottage at five minutes past eight. He stepped inside and slapped Liffey on the face, as she straightened up from lighting the fire, face blackened by soot.

Castle Tor station was closed all winter. Liffey had been reading the summer timetable. The nearest station was Taunton, on another line, twenty miles away. The journey from there to Paddington would take three hours. Six hours a day, thirty hours a week, spent sitting on a train, was clearly intolerable. And another eight hours a week spent driving to and from the station. To drive to London, on congested roads, would take even longer.

Richard hissed all this to Liffey, got back into his car, and drove off again.

Liffey cried.

'I wonder what all that was about,' said Tucker, putting down the field glasses.
'Go on up and find out,' said Mabs.
'No, you go,' he said.

So later in the morning Mabs put on her Wellington boots and her old brown coat with the missing buttons and paddled through the mire to Honeycomb Cottage and made herself known to Liffey as friend and neighbour.

'Do come in,' cried Liffey. 'How kind of you to call! Coffee?'

Mabs looked at Liffey and knew she was a bubble of city froth, floating on the scummy surface of the sea of humanity, breakable between finger and thumb. Liffey trusted the world and Mabs despised her for it.
'I'd rather have tea,' said Mabs.

Liffey bent to riddle the fire and her little buttocks were tight and rounded, defined beneath stretched denim. The back-side of a naughty child, not of a grown woman, who knows the power and murk that lies beneath, and shrouds herself in folds of cloth.

So thought Mabs.

Liffey was a candy on the shelf of a high-class confectioner's shop. Mabs would have her down and take her in and chew her up and suck her through, and when she had extracted every possible kind of nourishment, would spit her out, carelessly.

Liffey looked at Mabs and saw a smiling, friendly country-woman with a motherly air and no notion at all how to make the best of herself.

Liffey was red-eyed but had forgiven Richard for hitting her. She could understand that he was upset. And it had been careless of her to have misread the train timetable. But she was confident that he would be back that evening with roses and apologies and sensible plans as to how to solve the commuting problem. And if it were in fact insoluble, then they would just have to move back into the London apartment, apologising to Mory and Helen for having inconvenienced them, and keep Honeycomb as a weekend cottage. Liffey could afford it, even if Richard couldn't. His pride, his vision of himself as husband and provider, would perhaps have to be dented, just a little. That was all.

Nothing terrible had happened. If you were an ordinary, reasonably intelligent, reasonably well-intentioned person, nothing terrible could happen. Surely.

Liffey shivered.
'Anything the matter?' asked Mabs.
'No,' said Liffey, lying. Lying was second nature to Liffey, for Madge her mother always spoke the truth. Families tend to share out qualities amongst them, this one balancing that, and in families of two, as in the case of Madge and Liffey, the result can be absurd.

At that very moment Mory, who had brutal, concrete architectural tastes, looked round Liffey's pretty apartment and said, 'Christ, Liffey has awful taste!' and then, 'Shall we burn *that*?' and Helen nodded, and Mory took a little bamboo wall shelf and snapped it between cruel, smooth, city hands and fed it into the fire so that they all felt warmer.

'I hope Dick Hubbard's given you a proper lease,' said Mabs.
'You can't trust that man an inch.'
'Richard sees to all that,' said Liffey and Mabs thought, good, she's the fool she seems.

Mabs was all kindness. She gave Liffey the names of doctors, dentist, thatcher, plumber and electrician.
'You don't want to let this place run down,' she said. 'It could be a real little love nest.'

Liffey was happy. She had found a friend in Mabs. Mabs was real and warm and direct and without affectation. In the clear light of Mabs, her former friends, the coffee-drinking, trinket-buying, theatre-going young women of her London acquaintance, seemed like mouthing wraiths.

A flurry of cloud had swept over from the direction of the Tor and left a sprinkling of thin snow, and then the wind had died as suddenly as it had sprung up, and now the day was bright and sparkling, and flung itself in through the window, so that she caught her breath at the beauty of it all. Somehow she and Richard would stay here. She knew it.

Mabs stood in the middle of her kitchen as if she were a tree grown roots, and she, Liffey, was some slender plant swaying beneath her shelter, and they were all part of the same earth, same purpose.

'Anything the matter?' asked Mabs again, wondering if Liffey were half-daft as well.

'Just thinking,' said Liffey, but there were tears in her eyes. Some benign spirit had touched her as it flew. Mabs was uneasy: her own malignity increased. The moment passed.

Mabs helped Liffey unpack and put straight, and half-envied and half-despised her for the unnecessary prodigality of everything she owned – from thick-bottomed saucepans to cashmere blankets. Money to burn, thought Mabs. Tucker would provide her with logs in winter and manure in summer: she's the kind who never checks the price. A commission would come Mabs' way from every tradesman she recommended. Liffey would be a useful source of income.

'Roof needs re-doing,' said Mabs. 'The thatch is dried out: it becomes a real fire-risk, not to mention the insects! I've a cousin who's a thatcher. He's booked up for years but I'll have a word with him. He owes me a favour.'
'I'm not certain we'll be able to stay,' said Liffey sadly, and Mabs was alerted to danger. She saw Liffey as an ideal neighbour, controllable and malleable.
'Why not?' she asked.

Public tears stood in Liffey's eyes at last, as they had not done for years. She could not help herself. The strain of moving house, imposing her will, acknowledging difficulty, and conceiving deceit, was too much for her. Mabs put a solid arm round Liffey's small shoulders, and asked what the matter was. It was more than she ever did for her children. Liffey explained the difficulty over the train timetable.
'He'll just have to stay up in London all week and come back home weekends. Lots of them round here do that,' said Mabs.

Liffey had not spent a single night apart from Richard since the day she married him, and was proud of her record. She said as much, and Mabs felt a stab of annoyance, but it did not show on her face, and Liffey continued to feel trusting.

'Lots of wives would say that cramped their style,' said Mabs.

'Not me,' said Liffey. 'I'm not that sort of person at all. I'm a one-woman man. I mean to stay faithful to Richard all my life. Marriage is for better or worse, isn't it.'

'Oh yes,' said Mabs, politely. 'Let's hope your Richard feels the same.'

'Of course he does,' said Liffey stoutly. 'I know accidents can happen. People get drunk and don't know what they're doing. But he'd never be unfaithful; not properly unfaithful. And nor would I, ever, ever, ever.'

Mabs spent a busy morning. She went up to her mother and begged a small jar of oil of mistletoe and a few drops of the special potion, the ingredients of which her mother would never disclose, and went home and baked some scones, and took them up to Liffey as a neighbourly gesture and when Tucker came home to his mid-day meal told him to get up to Liffey as soon as possible.

'What for?' asked Tucker.

'You know what for,' said Mabs. She was grim and excited all at once. Liffey was to be proved a slut, like any other. Tucker was to do it, and at Mabs' behest, rather than on his own initiative, sometime later.

'You know you don't really want me to,' said Tucker, alarmed, but excited too.

'I don't want her going back to London and leaving that cottage empty for Dick Hubbard to sell,' said Mabs, searching for reasons. 'And I want her side of the field for grazing, and I want her taken down a peg or two, so you get up there, Tucker.'

'Supposing she makes trouble,' said Tucker. 'Supposing she's difficult.'

'She won't be,' said Mabs, 'but if she is bring her down for a cup of coffee so we all get to know each other better.'

'You won't put anything in her coffee,' said Tucker, suspiciously. 'I'm a good enough man without, aren't I?'

Mabs looked him up and down. He was small but he was

wiry; the muscles stood out on his wrists: his mouth was sensuous and his nostrils flared.

'You're good enough without,' she said. But in Mabs' world men were managed, not relied upon, and were seldom told more than partial truths. And women were to be controlled, especially young women who might cause trouble, living on the borders of the land, and a channel made through them, the better to do it. Tucker, her implement, would make the channel.

'I'll go this evening,' he said, delaying for no more reason than that he was busy hedging in the afternoon, and although he was annoyed, he stuck to it.

Liffey ate Mabs' scones for lunch. They were very heavy, and gave her indigestion.

A little black cat wandered into the kitchen, during the afternoon. Liffey knew she was female. She rubbed her back against Liffey's leg, and meowed, and looked subjugated, tender and grateful all at once. She rolled over on her back and yowled. She wanted a mate. Liffey had no doubt of it: she recognised something of herself in the cat, which was hardly more than a kitten and too young to safely have kittens of her own. Liffey gave her milk and tinned salmon. During the afternoon the cat sat in the garden and toms gathered in the bushes and set up their yearning yowls, and Liffey felt so involved and embarrassed that she went and lay down on her mattress on the floor, which was the only bed she had, and her own breath came in short, quick gasps, and she stretched her arms and knew she wanted something, someone, and assumed it was Richard, the only lover she had ever had, or ever – until that moment – hoped to have.

Gradually the excitement, if that was what it was, died. The little cat came in; she seemed in pain. She complained, she rolled about, she seemed talkative and pleased with herself.

Farmyards, thought Liffey. Surely human beings are more than farmyard animals? Don't we have poetry, and paintings, and great civilisations and history? Or is it only men who have these things? Not women. She felt, for the first time in her life, at the mercy of her body.

Richard, four hours late at the office, had to fit his morning's work into the afternoon, re-make appointments, and re-arrange meetings. It became obvious that he would have to work late. His anger with Liffey was extreme: he felt no remorse for having hit her. Wherever he looked, whatever he remembered, he found justification for himself in her bad behaviour. Old injuries, old traumas, made themselves disturbingly felt. At fifteen, he had struck his father for upsetting his mother: he felt again the same sense of rage, churned up with love, and the undercurrent of sadistic power, and the terrible knowledge of victory won. And once his mother had sent off the wrong forms at the wrong time and Richard had failed as a result to get a university place. Or so he chose to think, blaming his mother for not making his path through life smooth, recognising the hostility behind the deed, as now he blamed Liffey, recognising her antagonism towards his work. It was as if during the angry drive to the office, a trapdoor had opened up, which hitherto had divided his conscious, kindly, careful self from the tumult, anger and confusion below, and the silt and sludge now surged up to overwhelm him. He asked Miss Martin to send a telegram to Liffey saying he would not be home that night.

Miss Martin raised her eyes to his for the first time. They were calm, shrewd, gentle eyes. Miss Martin would never have misread a train timetable.

'Oh Mr. Lee-Fox,' said Miss Martin. 'You have got yourself into a pickle!'

Farmyards

Mabs' children came home on the school bus. Other children wore orange arm bands, provided by the school in the interests of road safety. But not Mabs' children.

'I'm not sewing those things on. If they're daft enough to get run over they're better dead. Isn't that so, Tucker?'

Today the children carried a telegram for Liffey. Mrs. Harris, who ran the sub post-office in Crossley had asked them to take it up to Honeycomb Cottage. They gave it instead to Mabs, who steamed the enevelope open, and read the contents, more for confirmation than information, for Mrs. Harris had told the children, who told Mabs, that Richard would not be coming home that night. He was staying with Bella, instead.

Bella? Who was Bella? Sister, mistress, friend?

Tucker consented to take the telegram up to Liffey. No sooner had he gone than Mabs began to wish he had stayed. She became irritable, and gave the children a hard time along with their tea. She chivvied Audrey into burning the bacon, slapped Eddie for picking up the burnt bits with his fingers, made Kevin eat the half-cooked fatty bits so that he was sick, and then made Debbie and Tracy wipe Kevin's sick up. But it was done: they were fed. All were already having trouble with their digestions, and would for the rest of their lives.

When Mabs was pregnant she was kinder and slower, but Kevin, the youngest, was four, and had never known her at her best. He was the most depressed, but least confused.

Liffey, wearing rubber gloves and dark glasses as well as four woollies, opened the door to Tucker. She knew from his demeanour that he had not come to deliver telegrams, or to mend fuses (although he did this for her, later) but to bed her if he could. The possibility that he might, the intention that he should, hung in the air between them. He did not touch her, yet the glands on either side of her vaginal entrance responded to sexual stimulation – as such glands do, without so much as a touch or a caress being needed – by a dramatic increase in their secretions.

Like the little black cat on heat, thought Liffey. Horrible!

She made no connection between her response and Mabs'
scones, with their dose of mistletoe and something else. How
could she?

I am not a nice girl at all, thought Liffey. No. All that is
required of me is the time, the place, and the opportunity: a
willing stranger at the door unlikely to reproach me; and
dreams of fidelity and notions of virtue and prospects of
permanence fly out the window as he steps in the door.

Love is the packet, thought Liffey, that lust is sent in, and
the ribbons are quickly untied.

If I step back, thought Liffey, this man will step in after me
and that will be that.

Come in, come in, Liffey's whole body sang, but a voice from
Madge answered back, 'Wanting is not doing, Liffey.
Almost nothing you can't do without.'
Liffey did not step back. She did not smile at Tucker. But
her breath came rapidly.

Tucker introduced himself. Farmer, Neighbour. Mabs'
husband. Owner of the field where the black and white cows
grazed. Kicker of puffballs. Liffey remembered him now, by
his steel-capped boots. She remained formal, and friendly.
But Tucker *knew*, and knew that she knew, what there could
be, was to be, between them.
Tucker handed over the telegram.
'My husband can't get back this evening,' said Liffey,
brightly and briskly, reading it. She knew better than
to betray emotion at such a time. But she minded very
much.

A fighter plane zoomed over the Tor, startling both, and was
gone. Tucker Pierce smiled at Liffey. Liffey's eyelids
drooped as other parts of her contracted, in automatic beat.
Oh, little black cat, squirming over the cool ground, the
better to put out the fire within! Tucker moved closer. Liffey

stood her ground, chanting an inner incantation, of nonsense and aspiration mixed. Richard, I love you, Richard, I am spirit, not animal: Tucker, in the name of love, in the name of God, in the name of Richard, flawed and imperfect as he is; Tucker, stay where you are.

Tucker stayed; Tucker talked, still on the step.
'Come the spring,' said Tucker, 'you'll be wanting our cows in your field. Keep the grass and the thistles down.'
'Not to mention the docks,' said Tucker. 'Docks can be a terrible nuisance.'
'Don't thank me,' said Tucker. 'We're neighbours, after all.'
'Any little bits and pieces you need doing,' said Tucker. 'Just ask.'
'Looks cosy in there,' said Tucker, peering over Liffey's shoulder into the colourful warmth within. 'I see you've a way with rooms: making them look nice, Feminine like.'

And indeed Liffey had: tacking up a piece of fabric here, a bunch of dried flowers there. She adorned rooms as she hesitated to adorn herself. She loved silks and velvets and rich embroideries and plump cushions and old, faded colours.

Tucker looked longingly within. Liffey stood her ground.
'Come on down to the farm,' said Tucker, remembering Mabs' instructions, 'and have a cup of coffee with Mabs.'
'Mabs is always glad of company,' lied Tucker. 'One thing to be on your own when you expect it,' observed Tucker, with truth. 'Quite another when you don't. You'll be feeling lonely, I dare say.'
'Not really,' said Liffey, with as much conviction as she could muster. 'But I'd be glad to use your telephone, if I could.'

They walked down together, along the rutted track. Tucker Pierce, farmer, married, father of five, muddy-booted, dirty-handed, coarse-featured, but smiling, confident and easy, secure in his rights and expectations. And little Liffey,

51

feeling vulnerable and flimsy, a pawn on someone else's chessboard, not the Queen. She saw herself through Tucker's eyes. She saw that her frayed jeans could represent poverty as well as universal brotherhood, and skinniness malnutrition, rather than the calculated reward of a high protein, low calorie diet.

Liffey had to run to keep up with Tucker. Her country shoes, so absurdly stout in London, appeared flimsy here, while his clumsy boots moved easily over the hollows and chasms of the rutted path.
'It's quiet up here,' said Tucker, turning to her.
Not here, she thought, not here in the open, like an animal: and then, not here, not anywhere, never!

Liffey rang Richard's office from the cold hall of Cadbury Farm. Miss Martin said Richard was not available, having gone to a meeting at an outside advertising agency, and she did not expect him back.
'Didn't he leave a message?'
'No.'

Liffey rang Bella and the au-pair girl Helga answered. Bella and Ray were dining out, with Mr. Lee-Fox. Perhaps if Liffey rang later? At midnight?
'No. It wouldn't be practical,' said Liffey.
'Any message?'
'No,' said Liffey.

'You do look cold,' said Mabs. 'Pull a chair to the fire.'
And she poured Liffey some coffee, in a cracked cup. The coffee was bitter.

Mabs chatted about the children, and schools, and cows and smoking chimneys. Tucker said nothing. The kitchen was large, stone flagged, handsome and cold. The same pieces of furniture – substantial rather than gracious – had stood here for generations – dresser, tables, sideboards, chairs – and were half-despised, half-admired by virtue of their very age.

Tucker and Mabs boasted of the price they would fetch in the auction room, while using the table, almost on purpose, to mend sharp or oily pieces of farm machinery, and the edge of the dresser for whittling knives, and covering every available surface with the bric-à-brac of everyday life – receipts, bills, brochures, lists, padlocks, beads, hair rollers, badges, lengths of string, plastic bags, scrawled addresses, children's socks and toys, plasters, schoolbooks, and tubes of this and pots of that. Neither Mabs nor Tucker, thought Liffey, marvelling, were the sort to throw anything away, and had the grace to feel ashamed of herself for being the sort of person who threw out a cup when it was chipped; or a dress when she was tired of it, or furniture when it bored her.

Cadbury Farm, she saw, served as the background to Tucker and Mabs' life, it was not, as she was already making out of Honeycomb Cottage, a part, almost the purpose, of life itself.

Liffey went home as soon as she politely could.
'It's getting dark,' said Mabs. 'Tucker had better go with you. I'm not saying there's a headless horseman out there, but you might meet a flying saucer. People do, round here. Mostly on their way home from the pub, of course. All the same, Tucker'll take you. Won't you, Tucker?'
'That's right,' said Tucker.

But Liffey insisted on going by herself, and then felt frightened and wished Tucker was indeed with her, whatever the cost, particularly at that bend of the road where the wet branches seemed unnaturally still, as if waiting for something sudden and dreadful to happen. But she hurried on, and pulled the pretty curtains closed when she got to the cottage, and switched on the radio, and soon was feeling better again, or at any rate not frightened; merely angry with Richard and upset by her own feelings towards Tucker, and fearful of some kind of change in herself, which she could hardly understand, but knew was happening, and had its roots in the realisation that she was not the nice, good, kind, pivotal person she had believed, around whom the rest of an

53

imperfect creation revolved, but someone much like anyone else, as nice and as good as circumstance would allow, but not a whit more: and certainly no better than anyone else at judging the rightness or wrongness of her own actions.

Desire for Richard overwhelmed her when she lay down to sleep on the mattress on the floor. It was, for Liffey, an unusual and physical desire for the actual cut and thrust of sexual activity, rather than the emotional need for tenderness and recognition and the celebration of good things which Liffey was accustomed to interpreting as desire, for lack of a better word. Presently images of Tucker replaced images of Richard, and Liffey rose and took a sleeping pill, thinking this might help her. All it did was to seem to paralyse her limbs whilst agitating her mind still more; and a sense of the blackness and loneliness outside began to oppress her, and an image of a headless horseman to haunt her, and she wondered whether choosing to live in the country had been an act of madness, not sanity, and presently rose and took another sleeping pill, and then fell into a fitful sleep, in which Tucker loomed large and erect.

But she had locked the door. So much morality, prudence, and the habit of virtue enabled her to do.

In Residence

At the time that Liffey was taking her second sleeping pill Bella offered one to Richard. Bella sat on the end of his bed, which Helga the au-pair had made up out of a sofa in Bella's study. Bella wore her glasses and looked intelligent and academic, and as if she knew what she was talking about. Her legs were hairy beneath fine nylon. Richard declined the pill. 'Liffey doesn't believe in pills,' he said.
'You aren't Liffey,' said Bella, firmly.
Richard considered this.
'I decide what we *do*,' said Richard, 'but I let Liffey decide

what's good for us. And taking sleeping pills isn't, except in extreme circumstances, and by mutual decision.'

'Liffey isn't here,' Bella pointed out. 'And it was she who decided you'd live in the country, not you.'

It was true. Liffey had edged over, suddenly and swiftly, if unconsciously, into Richard's side of the marriage, breaking unwritten laws.

'You don't think Liffey misread the timetable on purpose?' He was on the downward slopes of the mountain of despondency, enjoying the easy run down: resentments and realisations and justifications rattled along at his heels, and he welcomed them. He wanted Bella to say yes, Liffey was not only in the wrong, but wilfully in the wrong.

'On purpose might be too strong,' said Bella. 'Try by accident on purpose.'

'It's unfair of her,' said Richard. 'I've always tried to make her happy, I really have, Bella. I've taken being a husband very seriously.'

'Bully for you,' said Bella, settling in cosily at the end of the bed, digging bony buttocks in.

'But one expects a return. Is that unreasonable?'

'Never say one,' said Bella. 'Say "I". "One" is a class-based concept, used to justify any amount of bad behaviour.'

'Very well,' said Richard. '*I* expect a return. And the truth is, Liffey has shown that she doesn't care for my comfort and convenience, only for her own. And when I look into my heart, where there used to be a kind of warm round centre, which was love for Liffey, there's now a cold hard patch. No love for Liffey. It's very upsetting, Bella.'

He felt that Bella had him on a pin, was a curious investigator of his painful flutterings. But it was not altogether unpleasant. A world which had been black and white was now transfused with colour: rich butterfly wings, torn but powerful, rose and fell, and rose again. To be free from love was to be free indeed.

Bella laughed.

'Happiness! Love!' she marvelled. 'Years since I heard anyone talking like that. What do you mean? Neurotic need? Romantic fantasy?'

'Something's lost,' he persisted. 'Call it what you like. I'm a very simple person, Bella.'

Simple, he said. Physical, of course, was what he meant. Able to give and take pleasure, and in particular sexual pleasure. Difficult, now, not to take a marked sexual interest in Bella; she, clothed and cosy on his bed, and he, naked in it, and only the thickness of a quilt between them. Or if not a sexual interest, certainly a feeling that the natural, ordinary thing to do was to take her in his arms so that their conversation could continue on its real level, which was without words. The very intimacy of their present situation deserved this resolution.

These feelings, more to do with a proper sense of what present circumstances required than anything more permanent, Richard interpreted both as evidence of his loss of love for Liffey, and desire for Bella, and the one reinforced the other. That, and the shock of the morning, and the evidence of Liffey's selfishness, and the sudden fear that she was not what she seemed, and the shame of his striking her, and the exhaustion of the drive, and the stirring up of childhood griefs, had all combined to trigger off in Richard's mind such a wave of fears and resentments and irrational beliefs as would stay with him for some time. And in the manner of spouses everywhere, he blamed his partner for his misfortunes, and held Liffey responsible for the cold patch in his heart, and the uncomfortably angry and anxious, lively and lustful thoughts in his mind: and if he did not love her any more, why then, it was Liffey's fault that he did not.

'All I can say,' said Bella, 'is that love or the lack of it is made responsible for a lot of bad behaviour everywhere; and it's hard luck on wives if misreading a train timetable can herald the end of a marriage: but I will say on your behalf, Richard, that Liffey is very manipulative, and has an

emotional and sexual age of twelve, and a rather spoilt twelve
at that. You'll just have to put your foot down and move back
to London, and if Liffey wants to stay where she is, then you
can visit her at weekends.'

'She wouldn't like that,' said Richard.

'You might,' said Bella. 'What about you?'

Spoilt. It was a word heard frequently in Richard's
childhood.

You can't have this: you can't have that. You don't want to
be spoilt. Or, from his mother, I'd like you to have this but
your father doesn't want me to spoil you. So you can't have
it. It seemed to Richard, hearing Bella say 'spoilt' that Liffey
had been the recipient of all the good things he himself had
ever been denied, and he resented it, and the word, as words
will, added fuel to his paranoic fire, and it burned the more
splendidly.

As for Bella – who had thrown in the word half on purpose,
knowing what combustible material it was – Bella knew she
herself was not spoilt, and never had been. Bella had been
obliged to struggle and work for what she now had, as Liffey
had not, and no one had ever helped her, so why should it be
different for anyone else?

Richard sat up in bed. His chest was young, broad and
strong. The hairs upon it were soft and sleek, and not at all
like Ray's hairy tangle.

'I wish I could imagine Liffey and you in bed together,' said
Bella. 'But I can't. Does she know what to do? Nymphet
Liffey!'

Bella had gone too far: approached too quickly and too near,
scratched Liffey's image which was Richard's alone to
scratch. Whatever was in the air between herself and
Richard evaporated. Bella went back to her desk, typing, and
Richard lay back and closed his eyes.

The wind rose in the night: two sleeping pills could not wipe out the sound or ease the sense of danger. Liffey heard a tile fly off the roof: occasionally rain spattered against the window. She lay awake in a sleeping bag on a mattress on the floor. The double bed was still stacked in two pieces against the wall. Liffey ached, body and soul.

Liffey got up at three and went downstairs and doused the fire. Perhaps the chimneys had not been swept for years and so might catch light. Then she would surely burn to death. Smoke belched out into the room as the hot coals received the water. Liffey feared she might suffocate, but was too frightened to open the back door, for by letting out the smoke she would let the night in. When she went upstairs the night had become light and bright again; the moon was large: the Tor was framed against pale clouds, beautiful. Liffey slept, finally, and dreamt Tucker was making love to her on a beach, and waves crashed and roared and stormed and threatened her, so there was only desire, no fulfilment.

When she woke someone was hammering on the front door. It was morning. She crawled out of the sleeping bag, put on her coat, went downstairs and opened the door.

It was Tucker. Liffey stepped back.

Tucker stepped inside.

Tucker was wearing his boots, over-trousers tucked into them, a torn shirt, baggy army sweater, and army combat-jacket. His hands were muddy. She did not get as far as his face.

'Came up to see if you were all right,' said Tucker.

'I'm fine,' said Liffey. She felt faint: surely because she had got up so suddenly. She leaned against the wall, heavy-lidded. She remembered her dream.

'You don't look it,' said Tucker. He took her arm; she trembled.

'How about a cup of tea?' said Tucker. He sat squarely at the kitchen table, and waited. His house, his land, his servant. Liffey found the Earl Grey with some difficulty. Richard and she rarely drank tea.

'It's very weak,' said Tucker, staring into his cup. She had not been able to find a saucer and was embarrassed.

'It's that kind of tea,' said Liffey.

'Too bad Hubby didn't come home,' said Tucker. 'I wouldn't miss coming home to you. Do you like this tea?'

'Yes.'

'I don't,' said Tucker. He stood up and came over to stand behind her, pinioning her arms. 'You shouldn't make tea like that. No one should.'

His breath came warm and familiar against her face. She did not doubt but that the business of the dream would be finished. His arms, narrowing her shoulders, were so strong there was no point in resisting them. It was his decision, not hers. She was absolved from responsibility. There was a sense of bargain in the air: not of mutual pleasure, but of his taking, her consenting. In return for her consent he offered protection from darkness, storm and fire. This is country love, thought Liffey. Richard's is a city love: Richard's arms are soft and coaxing, not insistent: Richard strikes a different bargain: mind calls to mind, word evolves word, response evokes response, is nothing to do with the relationship between the strong and the weak, as she was weak now, and Tucker strong upon her, upon the stone floor, her coat fortunately between her bare skin and its cold rough surface, his clothing chafing and hurting her. Tucker was powerful, she was not: here was opposite calling to opposite, rough to smooth, hard to soft, cruel to kind – as if each quality craved the dilution of its opposite, and out of the struggle to achieve it crested something new. This is the way the human race multiplies, thought Liffey, satisfied. Tucker's way, not Richard's way.

But Liffey's mind, switched off as a pilot might switch off manual control in favour of automatic, cut back in again once the decision of abandonment had been made. Prudence returned, too late. This indeed, thought Liffey, is the way

59

the human race multiplies, and beat upon Tucker with helpless, hopeless fists.

It was the last day of her period. Surely she could not become pregnant at such a time? But since she had stopped taking the pill her cycle was erratic and random: what happened hardly deserved the name of 'period': she bled for six days at uneven intervals, that was all. Who was to say what was happening in her insides? No, surely, surely, it would be all right, must be all right; even if it wasn't all right, she would have a termination. Richard would never know: no one would ever know.

She was worrying about nothing: worrying even as she cried out again in pleasure, or was it pain: Tucker now behind her, she on her side, held fast in his arms. They were like animals: she had not cared: now she began to: she wanted Richard. Where was Richard? If he hadn't missed his train none of this would have happened. Richard's fault. It could not happen again: it must not happen again: she would have to make clear to Tucker it would not happen again: so long as he understood what she was saying, peasant that he was. Even as she began to be horrified of him he finished, and whether she was satisfied or not she could not be sure. She thought so. It was certainly a matter of indifference to Tucker. He returned to the table and his cold tea. He wanted the pot filled up with boiling water. She obliged in silence, and poured more.

'I suppose you could develop a taste for it,' he said. 'But I'd better be getting back to Mabs.'

He left. Liffey went back to bed, and to sleep, and the sleeping pills caught up with her and it was two in the afternoon before she woke again, and when she did, the dream of Tucker and the actuality of Tucker were confused. Had it not been for the state of her nightshirt and the grazing on her legs and the patches of abraded roughness round her mouth, she would have dismissed the experience altogether as the kind of dream a woman dreams when she sleeps alone for the first time in years. But she could not quite do that.

Liffey balanced the incident in her mind against Richard's scuffling with his secretary at the office party, and decided that the balance of fidelity had been restored. There was no need to feel guilty. At the same time there was every reason not to let it happen again. She had the feeling Tucker would not return, at any rate not in the same way. He had marked her, that was all, and put her in her proper place. She felt sure she could rely upon his discretion. She was even relieved. Now that Richard had been paid out, she could settle down to loving him again. She felt she had perhaps been angrier with him than she had thought.

'Well?' enquired Mabs, when Tucker returned. The children were off on the school bus. Eddie had a bruise on his back. She had given him a note to take to his teacher saying he had a sore foot and could he be excused physical training, which was done in singlet and pants.
'Skinny,' complained Tucker. 'Nothing to it.'
She pulled him down on top of her, to take the taste of Liffey out of him as soon as possible.
'Not like you,' said Tucker. 'Nothing's like you.'
'But we'll get the cows in her field,' Mabs comforted herself.
'We'll get whatever we want,' said Tucker. He felt the distress in her and kissed her dangerous eyes closed, in case the distress should turn to anger, and sear them all.
'She's just a little slut,' said Mabs. 'I knew she was from the way she talked. Don't you go near her again, Tucker, or I'll kill you.'

He thought he wouldn't, because she might.
If he'd been a cockerel, all the same, he'd have crowed.
Taking and leaving Liffey. He liked Liffey.

Mabs asked Carol, later, if she knew what it was her mother mixed in with the mistletoe, and Carol said no, she didn't. But whatever it was, it had got her Dick Hubbard.

'It's not that I believe in any of mother's foolery,' said Carol, 'any more than you do. It's just that it works. At least to get things started. It would never get a river flowing uphill – but if there's even so much as a gentle slope down, it sure as hell can start the flood.'

In Richard's Life

Richard, taking Bella's words to heart, if not her body to his, went round to the apartment before going to work, to explain to Mory and Helen that a mistake had been made, and that he and Liffey would have to return to London. Liffey, Richard had decided, would have to put up with using Honeycomb Cottage as a weekend retreat, and he would have to put up with her paying for its rent – not an unpleasant compromise for either of them – until his verbal contract with Dick Hubbard, to take the cottage for a year, could be said to have expired. 'Never go back on a deal just because you can,' Richard's father had instructed him, 'even if it's convenient. A man's word is his bond. It is the basis on which all civilisation is based.' And Richard believed him, following the precept in his private life, if not noticeably on his employers' behalf.

'Never let a woman pay for herself,' his mother had said, slipping him money when he was nine, so he could pay for her coffee, and confusion had edged the words deeply into his mind. 'Never spend beyond your income,' she would say, 'I never do,' when he knew it was not true.

Now he earnestly required Liffey to live within his income whilst turning a blind eye to the fact that they clearly did not: that avocados and strawberries and pigskin wallets belonged to the world of the senior executive, not the junior. The important thing, both realised, was to save face. She seriously took his housekeeping, and he seriously did not notice when it was all used upon one theatre outing.

It was difficult, Richard realised on the way up the stairs, to fulfil the obligation both to Dick Hubbard and to Mory, who had been promised a pleasant apartment and who now must be disappointed. It could not, in fact, be done; and for this dereliction Richard blamed Liffey. He resolved, however, out of loyalty to a wife whom he had gladly married, to say nothing of all this to Mory.

The familiar stairs reassured him; the familiar early morning smells of other people's lives: laundry, bacon, coffee. The murmur of known voices. This was home. Three days away from it and already he was homesick. He could never feel the same for Honeycomb Cottage, although for Liffey's sake he would have tried. Wet leaves, dank grass and a sullen sky he could persuade himself were seasonal things: but the running, erratic narrative of the apartment block would never be matched, for Richard, by the plodding, repetitive story of the seasons.

I am a creature of habit, said Richard to himself.

'I am a creature of habit!' Richard's mother had been accustomed to saying, snuggling into her fur coat, or her feather cushion, eyes bright and winsome, when anyone had suggested she do something new – such as providing a dish on Tuesday other than shepherd's pie, or getting up early enough in the morning to prepare a packed lunch for Richard, or going somewhere on holiday other than Alassio, Italy. 'I am a creature of habit!' Perhaps, Richard thought now, one day I will understand my mother, and the sense of confusion will leave me.

Richard knocked on his own front door. Helen's sister Lally, pregnant body wrapped in her boyfriend's donkey-jacket, opened the door. She wore no shoes. Richard, startled, asked to see Mory or Helen.
'They're asleep,' said Lally. 'Go away and come back later whoever you are,' and she shut the door in his face. She was very pretty and generally fêted, and saw no need to be

pleasant to strange men. She believed, moreover, that women were far too likely for their own good to defer to men, and was trying to stamp out any such tendency in herself, thus allying, most powerfully, principle to personality.

Richard hammered on the door.
'This is my home!' he cried. 'I live here.'
Eventually Mory opened the door. Richard had not seen Mory for three months. Then he had worn a suit and tie and his hair cleared his collar. Now, pulling on jeans, hopping from foot to foot, hairy chested, long haired, he revealed himself as what Richard's mother would describe as a hippie.
'Don't lose your cool, man,' said Mory. 'What's the hassle?'
'Is that really you?' asked Richard, confused more by the hostility in look and tone, than by the change in Mory's appearance, marked though it was.
'So far as I know,' said Mory, cunningly.

He did not ask Richard in. On the contrary, he now quite definitely blocked the door, and Richard, who had just now seen himself as a knight errant, was conscious of a number of shadowy, barefoot creatures within, and knew that his castle had been besieged, and taken and was full of alien people, and that only force of arms would win it back.
Richard explained. He was cautious and formal.
'That's certainly shitsville, man,' said Mory, 'but it was on your say so we split, and our pad's gone now, and what are we supposed to do, sleep on the streets to save you a train journey? Didn't you see Lally was pregnant?'
Richard said he would go to law.
Mory said Richard was welcome to go to law, and in three years time Richard might manage an eviction.
'We've got the law tied up, man,' said Mory. 'It's on the side of the people, now. You rich bastards are just going to have to squeal.'

Mory's language had changed, along with his temperament. Richard remarked on it to Miss Martin, when he reached the office. He was already on the phone to his solicitor.

'He may have been popping acid,' remarked Miss Martin. 'Or he may have been like that all the time. People's true natures reveal themselves when it comes to accommodation. It's the territorial imperative.'

The solicitor sighed and sounded serious, and said Richard should come round at once.

Richard drove up to Honeycomb Cottage at eight that evening. He parked the car carefully on hard ground, in spite of his apparent exhaustion. He covered the bonnet with newspaper before he came in to the house. He did not mean to risk the car not starting in the morning. Liffey waved happily from the window. Last night's nightmares and suspicions, and the morning's bizarre event, were equally washed away in expectation, excitement and a sense of achievement. She had worked hard all day, unpacking, putting up curtains, lining shelves, chopping wood: reviving last night's uneaten sweet-and-sour-pork in the coal-fired Aga which, now it had stopped smoking, she knew she was going to love. She had the hot water system working and the bed assembled. She had bathed and put on fresh dungarees, and washed her nightshirt.

Richard was not smiling as he came in the room. He sank in a chair. She poured him whisky, into a warmed glass. That way the full flavour emerged.
He was silent!
'Haven't I worked hard? Do say I've done well. You've no idea how I missed you. There was such a wind, I was quite frightened in the night.'
Still he did not speak. Hearing her own voice in the silence she knew it was the voice of a child, playing bravely alone in its lighted bedroom, dark corridors between it and parents: making up stories, speaking aloud, filling up space, taking first one rôle, and then the other. Mournful, frightened prattle.
'Did you really stay with Bella?' She heard her own voice growing up, growing sour. No, she begged, don't let me. But she did.

'Why didn't you drive back last night? You must have known I'd be miserable on my own.'

Still silence.

'And you hit me.'

'Do shut up, Liffey,' said Richard, in a conversational and uncondemning voice, thus enabling her to do so. 'What's for supper?'

She fetched out the sweet-and-sour-pork. She lit the candles. They ate. It was almost what she had dreamed, except that Richard hardly said a word.

'We are in a mess,' said Richard over the devilled sardines she had prepared in place of dessert. She could see that getting to the shops would be difficult. She would have to get a telephone installed as soon as possible, if only in order to call taxis.

'We're not,' said Liffey, 'we're here, aren't we, and it's lovely, and if you say we have to move back to London I won't make any trouble. But I would like to stay.'

Did Liffey have Tucker in mind as she spoke? Opening up whole new universes of power, and passion; laying instinct bare.

'We can't move back to London,' said Richard, and even as Liffey's eyes lit up, said, 'I'm going to have to stay up in London during the week, and come back at weekends.'

Liffey wept. Richard explained.

'At least until we can get something sorted out with the lawyers,' said Richard. 'Three months or so, I imagine. I can stay with Ray and Bella, on their sofa. It won't be very comfortable but I can manage.'

Did Richard have Bella in mind as he spoke, filling his black-and-white world with rich colours of cynicism and new knowledge.

How long since Liffey had really wept? Not, surely, during

all the time she had been married to Richard. Tears had fallen from her eyes for the plight of the helpless, or for abused children, or forsaken wives, or for the tens of thousands swept away by floods in far-off places, but she had not wept for herself.

'I don't want to be away from you,' said Richard. 'Do you think I enjoy sleeping apart from you? But what else can I do?'

'Helen and Mory are supposed to be our *friends*,' wept Liffey.
'How can friends behave like that?'

Richard tried to console Liffey. He told her about army wives whose husbands were away for months at a time, and light-housemen, and submariners on nuclear submarines who sometimes didn't come home for years. And the wives of convicts and political prisoners.

'But those are other people,' cried Liffey. 'This is *me*.'

Richard told Liffey how nice she'd made everything in the cottage, and how he would look forward to coming home at the weekends, and how absence made the heart grow fonder and she believed him, and he believed himself, and they went to bed, tearful but entwined; and he fell asleep, so tired was he, before he could do more than embrace her, and in the morning both slept through the alarm, which was set for five-thirty, so that Richard had to leap out of bed and be gone before she could possibly speak to him.

Liffey without Richard

When Richard had gone Liffey snuggled back into the warm bed and half wondered and half wished that Tucker would come knocking at the door, but he did not. Liffey did not lust after Richard. She never had. They were too well suited, too polite for that. He could produce in her, by kissing and loving, a delicate desire: but not the personal, angry focusing of lust.

Liffey, waking properly a second time, with the winter sun shining across white frosted fields and the Tor raising its crystalline arm into a pale brilliant sky, felt happy enough. But realising that despondency might soon set in, Liffey made lists.

> Get telephone.
> Learn to drive.
> Organise shopping.
> Invite friends.
> Read gardening books.

Presently she added:

> Writing paper and stamps.

And then, later:

> Bicycle, to get to postbox. Powered bicycle, perhaps?

Later, she added:

> Write book.

That one frightened her. If there was time and opportunity she might actually have to, and be judged. She would rather have it as a dream, than a reality. She crossed it out.

Afterwards she wrote:

> Make friends.

These things, surely, added up to contentment. Madge, in times of trouble, had written lists and posted them up. Earn more money, spend less, stop Liffey picking her nose (or had it been worse? Liffey had a feeling that it was something far more sinister she had to be saved from) find lover, buy brown bread not white. Messages from her good lively self to her depressed self. Stop drinking, she'd even written, in the days when she did: when Liffey would come home from school and find her mother asleep and snoring on her bed. Or had Liffey herself written that one? She thought perhaps that she had. And Madge, as a result, had picked herself up and stopped drinking, and in so doing had given Liffey the encouraging feeling that life was not a gradual descent from good to bad, from youth to age, from health to decay, but rather flowed in waves, good times turning to bad, bad turning to good again. Wait, be patient, shuffle the cards.

Wait, Liffey; use your time well. Shuffle the cards. Write lists. If you fear loneliness, turn it into solitude and rejoice. Cultivate inner resources, wrote Liffey.
'There is nothing to worrry about,' Liffey told herself. 'So long as you are healthy and have money in the bank, there are no problems which cannot be solved.' She believed it, too.

Liffey composed a reasonable letter in her head to Mory and Helen, and wrote it out on a brown paper bag, having no writing paper, and then used it, by mistake, to re-light the Aga stove.

In the afternoon Liffey walked a mile and a half across the fields to the village of Poldyke, where there was a shop, a garage, and a post office, and a doctor came over on Wednesday afternoons from the big village of Crossley. At Crossley there were schools, and pubs, a greengrocer and a chemist. To get to Crossley, five miles away, meant a walk up the lane, past Cadbury Farm, and then along a stretch of main arterial road, where it narrowed alarmingly, and the lorries passed, and did not like pedestrians.

Liffey arrived at Poldyke one minute after the surgery was closed, in time to see the doctor drive off in his big new car. He was a small, desperate-looking man, with strained eyes in a dark monkey face, not so much older than Liffey: he drove off past her, both gloved hands gripping the wheel, hunched into a great coat, sunk into rich upholstery.

In the village shop Liffey cried out with delight over a rack of farm overalls, and bought one.

'For your husband? He'll be working the land up there, then?'

'No. For me,' said Liffey, before she could stop herself, and had to watch the look of puzzlement appear on Mrs. Harris's narrow face. Mrs. Harris worked the land behind the shop. Once or twice a day the shop bell would sound and Mrs. Harris would dust off hands and boots and come in to serve. 'She acts as if everything's toys,' Mrs. Harris complained to Mabs' mother later, 'not real things at all.'

Liffey was now eight days into her new, somewhat irregular menstrual cycle – the fourth since she had stopped taking the contraceptive pill, and her body was still recovering from a surfeit of hormones, as might a car engine flooded by the use of too much choke, and obliged to rest. She had not been made pregnant by Tucker, though who was going to believe a thing like that? And had had no opportunity of becoming pregnant by Richard.

Richard without Liffey

'The thing about Liffey,' said Bella to Richard that evening, 'is that she's so gloriously positive. Of course it can be a drawback. Well, look at you! Swept away on the powerful tides of Liffey's whims!'

'She's so wonderfully young,' said Ray. 'What a pity we all have to grow up.'

Richard badly missed Liffey, sitting there without her at Ray and Bella's table. He thought of himself as a tree with its main branch wrenched off, leaving a nasty open wound down the trunk, vulnerable to all kinds of disagreeable infections.

There were beans on toast and fish fingers for supper, prepared by Helga. Bella and Ray dined excellently in public, but meagerly at home. The dishes for their dinner parties were brought in by a deserted wife and mother of four who lived down the road. She also tested the recipes in the many recipe books which Bella and Ray devised together. Their speciality was fish dishes, but they knew a thing or two about edible fungi. She looked after Tony and Tina, Bella's children, on Helga's day off, but was now suffering from nervous exhaustion, so that Helga seldom could have a day off. Helga came from Austria, and worked for her keep, and pocket-money.

Ray and Bella lived busy lives. They had Marxist leanings. They applied their intellectual energies, every now and then, to the practical details of domestic life, so that the home ran smoothly on machinery and the labour of others. Tony and Tina picked up their own toys, lay their own places at table, washed up their own plates and cutlery when they had finished with them, plus one saucepan and mixing bowl each, and put their dirty clothes in the laundry basket and collected them clean from the dryer. They were quiet children. Other parents became quite disagreeable about them.

Richard had sometimes wished in the past that Liffey was more like Bella, and had a capacity for money-making and public-speaking. But Liffey devoted all her energies to the actual business of living, not doing, and that, he supposed, was that. And Liffey was restful, and Bella wasn't. And though Liffey, as Bella had pointed out, might be an emotional challenge, she was certainly not an intellectual one, and that was restful.

Richard found himself vaguely mistrustful of Bella and Ray's kindness in offering him, so readily, the use of Bella's sofa. He would have felt reassured had they suggested he baby-sat, but they had not. He told himself, over tinned peaches and custard, that he must not become paranoic.

That Mory and Helen's perfidy must not blind him to the essential goodness of others, and justness of the Universe. Business, after all, proceeded by trust, and the world, so far as he could see, was given over to big business.

Mory's 'shitsville, man' had been a shock, no doubt of it. The aggressions and hostilities that Richard had met, in his thirty-two years, had been of the muted, civilised kind; confined to office memos or gentle, if confusing, parental words. Richard, like Liffey, had learned early to placate, and smile, and turn away anger, and mix with others of a like frame of mind. 'If you didn't read the papers,' Liffey once said to Richard, 'but only looked about you, you'd really believe the world was a nice place.' And not recognising hate, spite or anger in themselves, and so not understanding how these things show their greater face in the dealings of management with labour, governments with governed, and so forth, could only look to communism or socialism, or facism, or any other available ism, as the source of conflict. Trouble, seen as coming from the outside, and working its way in, and not the other way about.

During the rest of the week Richard developed a whole assortment of fears and suspicions. He suspected that money was missing from his wallet, that taxi-drivers were cheating him by going the long way round, that his fellow employees were talking behind his back, that Miss Martin was going to make amorous advances, and that Liffey had organised his absence from her in order to be unfaithful. Such a thought as this latter had never crossed his mind before. He murmured it to Bella who only laughed and said, 'Projection, Richard,' which he did his best not to understand.

Miss Martin made call after call to Richard's solicitors. He confided in her now, and she in him. She seemed, marginally, in this new world of treachery, less dangerous than Bella.

Miss Martin was saving through a building society. In three

years she would marry her fiancé, then they would own their own house from the beginning. No rented accommodation for them. Richard marvelled at how well people of no ambition could run their lives. Miss Martin's boyfriend Jeff was finishing an apprenticeship as an electrical engineer. He would call for her, at the office, on occasion, and was a surprisingly handsome, tall and lively young man. Miss Martin was a virgin. She told Richard so. She believed in saving herself for marriage. She thought perhaps she was under-sexed, and hoped it didn't matter. There were more important things in life. Miss Martin was very capable. She never forgot things. She plodded around the office, thick-ankled and knowledgeable. The danger that she might turn into a seductress evaporated.

Liffey was more educated more cultured and sophisticated than Miss Martin, but Miss Martin would never have misread a timetable.

And Miss Martin would never expect her Jeff to drive six hours a day, just so that she could live in the cottage of her dreams. On the contrary, Miss Martin let herself be guided by Jeff's will in everything other than in sexual matters, where her will prevailed.

Lonely nights without Liffey.

Brave Liffey.

Richard had quite a lot to drink one night. Richard rang through to Cadbury Farm.
'Take a message to Liffey,' he said. 'Tell her I love her.'

The Underside of Things

Mabs and Tucker thought Richard was daft, wasting good money on such a call. There was a wistful look in Mabs' eye, all the same.

'Don't you start sticking pins in her,' said Tucker.
'Now why should I want to do that?' asked Mabs, virtuously.
'I don't know why women do anything,' said Tucker.

Once Mabs had made a model out of candle-wax to represent a farmer who had wronged Tucker and stuck a pin through its leg, and shut it in a drawer, and the farmer had developed thrombosis in his leg and gone to hospital. Just as well the pin had not been driven through the chest: Mabs had desisted from that obvious course because the farmer's daughter had once done her a good turn.

But Liffey was a different and difficult matter. It was Mabs' experience, and her mother's before her, that spells worked only upon angry and disagreeable people, and Liffey was neither. Moreover, if the spellbinder herself or himself was angry, then the spell could turn back like a boomerang. That was why a third party was so useful, to curse or spite for payment – in the same way as a psychoanalyst is paid, to receive spite and curses on behalf of others: sopping up the wrath turned away from cruel mothers and neglectful fathers and unfeeling spouses. The witch or spellbinder did more; and passed the evil on.

Mabs' mother, along with everyone else, said that spells were a lot of rubbish and she'd rather watch television any day; if you wanted to do anyone a bad turn these days all you had to do was ring up the Income Tax Inspector, or now, even better, the VAT man.

All the same, when Mabs and Carol had been little, they'd once nailed their mother's footprint to the ground – one damp day when she'd been hanging out the washing – and sure enough she'd developed a limp. That was a sure test of a witch.

'It's not magic,' their mother would say, limping, as she mixed her powders and potions, "it's medicine. Natural, herbal medicine.' And Carol and Mabs would listen, not knowing what to believe. She'd cured old Uncle Bob Fletcher of cancer. Everyone knew that. He'd gone on to ninety-nine, fit as a fiddle, and left her five hundred pounds and three acres in his will.

Dirty old man: some said Carol was his daughter; Carol and Mabs couldn't have come out of the same bag. One so small, the other so large.

Mabs went up to Honeycomb Cottage with Richard's message – Liffey was out walking so Mabs left a little note, and a bag of home-made sweets which Liffey didn't eat. She thought they tasted bitter.

Liffey, on the Tuesday of that week, organised a taxi to take her in and out of Crossley two days a week. She bought a new motorised bicycle at Poldyke garage, and on Friday a brand new Rotovator at Crossley. On Saturday she returned the bicycle. The engine was faulty. The village counted the cost of it all and marvelled.

Liffey's grandfather, Madge's father, had left Liffey a large sum of money, by-passing his daughter. What is the use, he asked her, bitterly, of handing wealth on to those who despise it? To those who would rather eat cheese sandwiches than steak au poivre? Madge had made nonsense of her father's life. She was as like as not to give away an inheritance to something she believed in – nuclear disarmament one year, save the whale or women's liberation the next. No, Liffey would have to have it. Liffey at least enjoyed spending money, and acted as most people did, on whim rather than principle. Liffey did not open bank statements. She put them straight into a drawer. Thus Richard's face was saved, and the illusion that they were living off his money preserved. Liffey would, from time to time, offer money to Madge, but Madge always refused it. Madge lived in a tiny cottage in a Norfolk county town, taught at the local school and ate school dinners, and now she had given up drinking whisky, was able to save most of her salary. Madge wanted nothing that Liffey could give. Never had, thought Liffey sadly. Not smiles nor gaiety nor prettiness nor money, which was all Liffey had to offer. Nothing of solid worth. Just what she *was* – nothing she had achieved.

At seven o'clock that evening Tucker came up to see if he could help Liffey with the Rotovator. Liffey's breath came short and sharp as she opened the door – but the tension between them had evaporated, and she was alarmed to see how ordinary he looked, and unattractive, and not in the least worthy of her. He stood in the kitchen, knowing more about her business than she cared to acknowledge, but no cause at all for erotic excitement. Grimy nails were just grimy nails, and not black talons of lust and excitement.

'I can manage,' said Liffey. 'I have the manual and am quite good mechanically.'

That was his cue to say she was quite good at other things too, but he didn't, so she knew it was over for him too, and was, when it came to it, relieved.
'My husband's coming back soon,' she said boldly. 'Stay and meet him properly,' which Tucker did, settling down in front of the Aga, easing off his working boots.

'Rotovator's no good for virgin land,' said Tucker. 'You'd need a tractor, your side of the stream. Bad soil, too. You'd be lucky to grow an onion. All right for cows but that's about all.'

Liffey was making mayonnaise. She squeezed in garlic.

'Strong stuff for eggs,' commented Tucker. 'Eggs are delicate.'

It had not all been rough and powerful: no. His fingers had been hard and calloused, but his mouth had been soft, and his tongue gentle.

No, Liffey, no. Enough.

Oh, lonely nights without Richard.

Richard arrived at seven minutes past eight, looking forward to his weekend. He was loving, cheerful and eager, and loaded with good things. Ray and Bella lived around the corner from the Camden Town street market, and Richard had bought aubergines and peppers, celeriac and chicory; and olives from the Greek shop, green and black, both, and fetta cheese and pitta bread: and whisky and a new kind of aperitif and good claret; and a joint of the best available lamb in all London.

Richard had resolved not to tell Liffey about the film he had seen the previous night with Bella and Ray, and how they had all gone off to a new fish restaurant afterwards, on expenses, for Bella and Ray were writing the place up for the column, or about the fun they had choosing the most expensive dishes on the menu, finding fault, and sending them back to the kitchen. The management had not seen it as fun, and Richard had wanted Liffey to be there, so he could discuss the whole thing afterwards, but where was Liffey? At the end of a muddy lane, a hundred and more miles away, which she loved more than she loved him.

Richard unloaded the good things on to the table, kissed Liffey, and was glad to see Tucker sitting there, since the presence of a stranger made the lie in his heart less likely to show in his eye.

How quickly Liffey makes friends, thought Richard. At least

he would not have to worry in case she were lonely, stuck away here by herself.

'Tucker and Mabs have been so helpful,' said Liffey.
'Until we get her driving, and get a telephone put in,' said Richard to Tucker, 'we're going to be dependent on your good services, I'm afraid. Sorry about the call the other night. Too much to drink.'
'That's what neighbours are for,' said Tucker.

Liffey had the uncomfortable feeling that Richard was in some way shelving his responsibility towards her, and handing it over to Tucker and Mabs.

Tucker suggested they both go over to Mabs for a meal, and Richard accepted with what Liffey saw as unseemly alacrity.
'But I've got supper waiting—' she began, but didn't finish. She moved the meat from the fast to the slow oven. They could eat it tomorrow.

Mabs saw the lights in the kitchen go out, and knew they were on their way up, and determined that Liffey should have an uncomfortable weekend. She could in no way see that Liffey deserved Richard's love as well as Tucker's attentions. Those who must be up and doing, as was Mabs, have little time for those who are content just to *be*, as was Liffey. And the need to be pleasant to her, for the sake of a pound here and 50p there, and an acre of free grazing, no longer seemed of pressing importance.

Mabs served a lamb stew from an enormous pot on the cooker. Liffey was given the gristly bits.
'Wonderful flavour!' marvelled Richard.
'It's because they're home-grown,' said Liffey. 'Everything here tastes wonderful.'
'No time to grow vegetables,' said Tucker. 'We do manage a drop or two of cider; come November you'd best be bringing your apples over for the pressing. You get quite a nice little crop off of some of your trees. No good for eating, mind. Not

if you've got a sweet tooth.' And he grinned at Liffey, and Liffey wished he wouldn't.

Liffey was well into her menstrual cycle. Some twenty-five or so follicles ripened nicely in her ovaries, one ahead of the others. In a couple of days it would reach maturity, and drop, and put an end to the generative energies of the rest. Nature works by waste.

There was apple pie and real cream for pudding, and afterwards Mabs handed round home-made Turkish delight. She pressed the mint-flavoured piece on Liffey. Liffey didn't think it was very nice.

Liffey and Richard walked home down the lane. The night was crisp and clear. The moon had a chunk out of it.
'Wonderful people,' said Richard. 'Real people; country people.'
'Those are my lines,' said Liffey.
'With none of the false romanticism about the country you get from townfolk.'
'Those are Bella's lines,' said Liffey.
They were, too.

Liffey was getting grumbling pains in her stomach. Her hand clenched Richard's.
'What's the matter?'
'Pains.'
'Ovulation pains?' asked Richard, knowledgeable.
'No, not like that.'
'What like, then?' He used the childish vocabulary that was their habit, and heard himself, and despised himself.
'Indigestion. Perhaps it was the stew.'
'Delicious stew. Why don't you make stews, Liffey?'
'Perhaps I will, now I'm in the country.'
'We're still going to have our baby, aren't we?'
'Of course!'

Bella had said that having a baby might be the making of Liffey. Responsibility might mature her.

'The Turkish delight tasted peculiar,' said Liffey. 'Why would a woman like Mabs make Turkish delight?'

Richard discovered that he was critical of his wife, that he jeered inwardly at her absurdities, and felt the desire to mock what had once entranced him. He blamed Liffey for the loss of his love for her. Richard had been to bed with Bella.

Full Moon

Mabs stared at the moon. The moon stared at Mabs. Tucker couldn't sleep.

Other people looked at the moon.

In Liffey and Richard's former apartment Mory lay in bed in the moonlight while Helen tweezed hairs from her chin. He had a sharp, pale face and a straggly beard which jutted above the bedclothes.

'No need to get uptight about anything,' said Helen, comfortingly. She was plump, pretty, dark and hairy. She was a freelance TV set designer, usually out of work. 'Liffey has money to burn. They can afford to live anywhere. We certainly can't.'
'I'm really hung up about Richard,' said Mory. 'I can feel my ulcer again. What sort of friend is he, writing solicitors' letters when he could just as well phone?'
'And there's Lally to think about,' said Helen.

Lally, Helen's sister, out-of-work model, and eight months pregnant, lay on foam rubber in the room next door, in the arms of Roy, out-of-work builder. If they married, her Social Security payments would cease. She was cold. She tossed and turned in the moonlight and presently decided the warmth was not worth the discomfort and told him to get the hell out of her bed, and build a fire. 'What with?' he asked.

'With that,' she said, and pointed at a Japanese bamboo screen of Liffey's and a little wickerwork stool. 'People before things,' she said.

'He's got it all ways,' observed Mrs. Martin, Richard's secretary's mother. She was a plump, busy little body, with a husband two years dead. She was ashamed of her widowhood, as if in letting her husband die she had committed a criminal offence – a feeling which the neighbours up and down the suburban street reinforced, by ceasing to call where once they had called, or even going so far as to cross the road when she approached. That they might have acted thus from embarassment, or from a primitive fear that misfortune might be catching, and so could hardly be any more responsible for their reactions than she was for her husband's death, Mrs. Martin failed to appreciate. She kept herself to herself, and studiously read the more profound of the women's magazines, scanning the pages for truth and understanding about wifehood, mistresshood, motherhood, never quite knowing what she was looking for, but feeling sure that one day she would find it; in the meantime she passed on to her daughter what she found out about the ways of the world.

'He's got it all ways,' she said now. 'Bachelor life all week, and country cottage at the weekends. Trust a man.'

'Oh no,' said Miss Martin. 'It wasn't his idea, it was her idea.'

'He'll be after you next,' said Mrs. Martin, 'in that case. You be careful. Men always cheat on women who organise their lives.'

'I'm not the type,' said Miss Martin, wishing she were. She felt cheated by life, which had taken away her father, and turned her mother into someone whose advice was based on reading, not on experience. Mrs. Martin thought it unwise of her daughter not to sleep with her fiancé Jeff; but Miss

Martin knew well enough that the only reason so handsome and eligible a young man as Jeff wanted to marry her, was that all the other girls did, and she didn't. He was a Catholic and divided women, in the old fashioned way, into good and bad. The good ones, Virgin Marys all, who had a man's babies by as near to an immaculate conception as everyone could manage; and the bad ones whom you loved, humiliated and left. Miss Martin saw all this quite clearly, and still wanted to marry Jeff. Mrs. Martin also saw it clearly, and didn't want her daughter to marry Jeff: her advice was directed, if unconsciously, to this end.

Their little white cat yowled to be let out. Miss Martin opened the back door and it darted out between her solid legs.

'Why should Mr. Lee-Fox choose me?' she asked.

'Because you're there,' said her mother. 'All a man needs is for a woman to be there.'

Miss Martin's boyfriend Jeff was on the Embankment doling out soup to vagrants and alcoholics. Once a week he did voluntary social work. 'There but for the grace of God,' he'd say. He took girlie magazines in his briefcase, to read in the early hours, when the flow of mendicants and suppliants dried up. Tonight the moon was so bright that he did not need his torch, and a shimmering mystery was added to an otherwise brutal reality, and he was glad. He put his trust in Miss Martin's virginity to cure him, in some magic way, of his unseemly lusts.

Bella and Ray lay far apart in their big double bed. Bella thought of the love of her life, who had been married for five years to someone else, and Ray thought of his hopeless love for Karen, schoolgirl. Bella and Ray held hands across the gulf which separated them, and felt better.

'Helga fancies Richard,' said Bella, with satisfaction. Bella lived in fear of losing Helga, for if Helga went, so would her own freedom from domestic and maternal duties. Au-pairs were becoming hard to find, and harder still to control. They demanded nights out, and lovers in their beds, and exorbitant wages. Helga had been showing signs of restlessness. A romantic interest in the house, in the form of Richard, would do much to keep her quiet and docile.

'So long as you don't,' said Ray, more out of marital politeness than any real anxiety.

'Of course I don't,' said Bella. 'He's much too simple for me.'

The moon, shining through the Georgian window, making shadow bars across the bed, made her think she was in prison, which in turn made her feel she could yet be free.

Helga, indifferent to a foreign moon, slept soundly in her box-room. She worked hard, too hard: she was always tired. She was a warm, rounded, sleepy little thing with busy hands, for ever cleaning and wiping and tidying. Sometimes she thought she would look for a new job with less work but there was never time. And if she went home, who would look after the children? They needed her. Those who responded to others' needs live hard lives, and go unrewarded. She knew it, but could do nothing about it.

Mabs' sister Carol, allegedly spending the night at Cadbury Farm, was in the back of Dick Hubbard's car. Later they would go to his office in the market square, letting themselves in when the pubs had closed and there was, they wrongly believed, no one about to see. While they waited, they indulged the passion that obsessed them both. It was true, the whole village agreed, that he was a better partner for her than her husband Barry, but she made her choice, and the village said she should stick to it. Carol was lean and dark as Mabs was broad and pale. Her limbs were silvery in the moonlight, smooth and slippery as a fish seen under water.

Dick Hubbard was worried because he had let Honeycomb Cottage when he should have sold, and allowed short-time interest to stand in the way of long-term benefit. He had recognised, long ago, that to act in this way was to doom himself to financial mediocrity. But still he let it happen.

'She bought a Rotovator,' he complained now to Carol.

'She'll soon get tired of it,' said Carol, comfortingly, 'and the weeds will be back.'

'She was even asking round for a builder.'

'Then have a word with the builder. You can pay a builder a fortune and the chimney will still come through the roof. What's the matter with you, Dick? Where's your spirit?'

'I don't know,' he said. 'The energy seems to have left my brain and gone down between my legs. I suppose that's how you like it.'

'I'll supply enough brain for both of us,' said Carol. 'You just supply the other.'

Mr. and Mrs. Lee-Fox lay under the moon and worried about Richard. He was their only son.

'Perhaps I brought him up wrong,' said Mrs. Lee-Fox.

'You did the best you could. Every mother does.'

It was their normal way of speaking – she agitating, he comforting. Now, in the middle of the night, it came like automatic speech.

'He should never have married her.'

'She's a nice, bright girl. His choice.'

'We'll never have grandchildren.'

'Give them time.'

'Our lovely apartment. And they've let the squatters in!'

'The law will get them out.'

'All our savings went to get him started.'

'And he is started,' said Mr. Lee-Fox. 'That's the way life goes. As his starts, ours closes in. We're left with the pickings of his takings. Once it was the other way around. You did it to your parents, I did it to mine. Now it's our turn.'

'I don't want it to be,' she said, as if he, like Superman, could turn the world the other way, but he just grunted and fell asleep. The moonlight cratered her skin as if it were the moon's surface, so she looked fifty years older than the modest fifty-three she was.

As for Liffey, the gripes in her stomach became worse. She spent the night groaning on the sofa or moaning on the lavatory seat. Liffey was not good at pain. Stoicism was her mother's prerogative. Madge, even if stung by a wasp, would manage to clamp her teeth before the involuntary scream could be fully released. Liffey, similarly stung, would shriek and jump and fling her arms about, breaking dishes and spilling food, giving easy voice to pain, shock and indignation.

Liffey was afraid of pain, as people often are who have endured little of it. She had never had toothache, never broken a bone, and had spent a healthy youth, unplagued by unpleasant minor illness. She avoided emotional pain by pulling herself together when nasty or uncomfortable thoughts threatened, and diverting herself conscientiously if she felt depression setting in. It could not always be done, but she did her best. Liffey was afraid of childbirth because she knew it would hurt. How could it not, if so large an object as a baby was to leave so confined a space? And the cries and groans of women in childbirth was part of her filmic youth: yes, that was pain, PAIN. And supposing the baby were born deformed? The fear would accompany her pregnancy, she knew it would. She could not say these things to Richard: women, though allowed to flinch at spiders and shudder at the thought of dirtying their hands, were expected to face pregnancy and childbirth with equanimity. Nor could she expect sympathy from Madge, who would see it as further proof of her daughter's errant femininity. And as for her friends – ah, her friends. Only a few days away, and she could scarcely remember their names or their faces. Liffey kept her fears to herself, and let others believe her reluctance to have a baby was, in the terms of an older generation, 'selfish', and in those of her contemporaries 'political' – namely, that she feared to lose her freedom and her figure, and sink into the maternal swamp.

Richard gave up waiting for Liffey to feel better and fell asleep at two-fifteen. He had had a long day. Up at seven, the strain of breakfast with friends, not family: then the office, a business lunch, a conference: then the long drive back to Liffey, then supper with the Pierces: and now poor Liffey groaning and clutching her stomach. He doubted whether he could have managed to make love to Liffey, even had she been feeling well, even had her pains been due to ovulation and she at her most fertile.

Richard slept. Liffey groaned.

It was not until after three that a cloud covered the moon: or, as Tucker felt, that Mabs let the moon go, stopped staring, and slept.

The cloud passed: the moon shone bright and firm again. In the morning, when the sun rose, it could still be seen as a pale disc low in the sky. Mabs waved to the disc as if to a friend, when she rose early to help with the cows. Lights flashed behind the Tor; she could not be sure why. She had noticed the phenomenon before.
'Something's going to happen,' she said to the moon, feeling a small excitement grow within her.

Mabs cast an eye over to Honeycomb Cottage and noticed that no smoke rose from the chimney, and presumed, rightly, that the kitchen range had gone out and that Liffey had had a bad night after the Turkish delight, and laughed.

Good and Bad

All the next day too Liffey moaned and groaned and shivered. The tiny bathroom was unheated, and there was no hot water, since the kitchen stove had gone out overnight.
'Oh, Liffey,' Richard reproached his wife, gently enough,

for she was a poor, weak, pale, shivery thing, 'it's one thing to live like this from necessity, but I can see no virtue in doing it from choice.'

'It would be all right if everything was working smoothly,' said Liffey, but she hardly believed it herself any more. She could see Richard was being brave and trying hard not to complain, and to enjoy what she enjoyed: and also perceived that he never would, and never could, had had to accept that though they were one flesh, yet they were different people, and that one or the other would have to submit. And that she had.

Richard cleared the flue with a broomstick and went up on the roof and extracted the matted twigs of jackdaws' nests which blocked the chimney. In one of the nests he found silver foil, bottle tops and a piece of Woolworth's jewelry, which he would have presented, ceremoniously, to Liffey, had she been in a fit state to receive it, or he, indeed, to give it. She was ill and he was dirty. He had to boil kettle after kettle of water before he could clean away the soot from his face and neck and the grime beneath his nails.

'But I like you dirty,' said Liffey. 'It's natural.' She was wrapped up warm and cosy on the sofa, and feeling a little better. She had been purged of her sin, her liaison with Tucker. 'What has nature got to do with us?' he asked. 'We've left the cave. Too late to go back.'

Outside, the trees were gaunt and bare against the winter sky, and snow clouds massed grey and thick behind the Tor. That pulled one way: Richard the other.

'Do you want to sell soup all the days of your life?' asked Liffey, 'live in an artificial world entirely?'

'Yes, Liffey I do. I want you to have babies and me to be their father and that's enough nature for me. I want to have light and heat at the touch of a button, and never to have to clear a flue in all the rest of my life. I find the country sinister, Liffey.'

It was an odd admission from him, who liked to deny the

existence of anything that science could not properly understand. 'That's because you fight it,' said Liffey. Smoke puffed out of the chimney and made Richard cough, but swirled round Liffey, leaving her alone. Liffey deduced, wrongly, that nature was on her side. She was its pawn, perhaps, but scarcely an ally. Mabs could have told her that.

'In the meantime,' said Richard, 'we shall make the best of it, since we have to, and I will put up with being away from you during the week, and you will put up with being separated from me, and I promise not to look lustfully at anyone and you must do the same.'

Now that Richard was with Liffey again he regretted his sexual lapse with Bella. It had happened while both were under the influence of drink, so much so that neither could (or at any rate had the excuse not to) remember the details the next day. Both had quickly resolved that it should not happen again, or Richard had. In the clear light of Liffey's gaze, he was happy enough that it should not.

Both had agreed, on marriage, that sexual jealousy was a despicable emotion, and, while playing safe, and pledging mutual fidelity, had taken it as a matter for congratulation that neither was a prey to it. That it might more reasonably be a matter for commiseration – inasmuch as neither offered the other so profound a sexual satisfaction as to make them fear the losing of it – did not occur to them.

Nevertheless, Liffey had certainly suffered a whole range of unpleasant emotions – disappointment, pique, humiliation and so on – over what Richard now thought of as 'The Office Party Episode', and he did not wish her, or indeed himself, to go through that again.

And he regretted even more than the physical infidelity, the more subtle betrayal of Liffey of which he was guilty – the discussion of her failings with others. Prying himself loose from her, as if he was the host and she the parasite, he had let in so much light and air, that the close warm symbiosis between them could never quite be repaired. They had been one: he had, in self-defence, rendered them two.

He could see, moreover, the threat to their happiness which their weekly separation entailed. He would see her, each weekend, more and more clearly. She, because she waited, would see what she expected. He, the one waited for, and for that reason the more powerful, would see reality. He feared that marital happiness lay in being so close to the partner that the vision was in fact blurred.

But it was a situation she herself had brought about. He could not be responsible for it, nor suffer too much on account of it. It was comfortable and convenient at Bella's, and exciting, too, in a way he would rather not think about.

'I'll bring down paint and wallpaper next weekend,' said Richard. 'We'll make everything lovely.'
'And guests,' said Liffey. 'Friends! Perhaps Bella and Ray would come?'
'They're very busy,' said Richard. And they went through their friends, and discovered that most would be too busy, or too frightened by discomfort, or too in need of crowds, or too quarrelsome, and in general too restless, to make good guests.

They made themselves think of Mory and Helen, although the subject upset them, and decided, or at any rate Liffey did, that Helen had fallen under the influence of her sister Lally, and that Mory was suffering from some kind of brainstorm consequent upon unemployment, and that it could not be concluded that there was anything disagreeable at all about the nature of human beings or the foibles of friends. It was, as it were, a one-off experience and should not embitter them. So said Liffey. Richard merely concluded, in his heart, that the business world and the personal world were pretty much the same, after all. Everyone behaved as well as they could afford to, but not one whit more.

'All the same,' said Liffey, 'let's just have you and me at weekends.' She suspected that was what Richard wanted: that after a week at the office and in Bella and Ray's home, he would be glad of peace and solitude at weekends. And he thought that was what she really wanted, and was relieved. 'Money isn't important,' said Liffey, a little later. 'Money can't buy love.'

It was a favourite phrase, and one which came easily to the lips of someone who had never gone short of it.

Liffey's fortune, although she did not know it, was in fact down to seventeen pounds eighty-four pence. The cheque made out for the Rotovator, at present passing through the central banking computer, albeit at its slow Sunday pace, would overdraw her account by five hundred and thirty pounds and eight pence. Three years ago Liffey had instructed her bank to sell stock at will in order to keep her current account in balance, and this they had dutifully done. There was no more stock to sell. A letter to this effect had been delivered to her London home on the very day she left for the country. Mory and Helen had neither the will nor the inclination to forward letters, and this one now lay behind an empty beer can on the mantelpiece.

'If they want their mail,' said Lally, 'let them come and get it. I don't see why you should do them any favours!'

The apartment, which once had been warm with the smell of baking and the scent of the honeysuckle Liffey had managed to grow in a pot on the windowsill, and sweet and decorous with the music of Dylan and Johann Sebastian Bach, was now a cold, hard, musty place, stripped of decoration, echoing with righteous murmurings.

'Richard needn't think I'm going to pay him a penny rent,' said Mory. 'Because I'm not. I'm not the kind of person other people can send solicitor's letters to, with impunity. I give as good as I get.'

'It's not even as if we could pay the rent,' said Helen, 'as Richard knew perfectly well when he asked us in to caretake this dump of a place.'

'He's let this place run down,' said Lally's builder boyfriend, pointing out a damp patch in the ceiling, the blocked bathroom basin overflow, and the flaking plaster under the stairs. He pulled at a hot water pipe to demonstrate the rottenness of the wall behind it and the pipe broke in two and it was some time before anyone could find the stop cock of the water main. 'People who don't look after places don't deserve to have them,' he said, rolling another joint. He had given up building since meeting Lally. He referred to himself as Lally's piece of rough.

'I think Richard's got a nerve,' said Helen, the next day, pulling out the gas cooker to adjust a pipe so that the supply would bypass the meter, 'asking any rent at all for a place like this. Look at the wall behind the cooker. It's thick with grease! Liffey needn't think I'm going to clear up after her.'

'It's just a slum,' said Lally, feeding the fire with the remains of a bentwood rocker, 'everything in it's broken.' Liffey had left the chair, an original Tonne, under the stairs, while she found a responsible caner to re-do the broken canework.

'I say,' said Mory, uneasily, 'I think that might be rather a good chair you've been burning.'

'It was broken,' said Lally. 'Same as everything else in this dump.'

'Possession is theft,' said her boyfriend, going to sleep.

'All this antique junk,' said Helen, 'I really used to dig that scene, didn't I, Mory? Remember? Then I realised it was part of the nostalgia which keeps the human race dragging its feet. Chairs are things you sit in, not mementos to the past.'

Mory said a little prayer, however, as the flames licked in and out the little bevelled squares of golden cane. Sometimes he wondered where the womenfolk were leading him: whether living by principle couldn't go too far.

During that weekend Mory and Helen took in a pregnant cat who settled in the linen cupboard and had kittens in a nest of Victorian tablecloths. Helen loved the kittens. Lally had pains from time to time, and thought she might be having the baby, but Helen looked up the *Book of Symptoms* and all decided she was not. They had given up doctors, who were an essential part of the male conspiracy against women, and were seeing Lally through her pregnancy themselves. At the very last moment, the plan was, they would dial 999 for an ambulance for Lally, who would then be taken to the nearest hospital too late for enemas, shaving, epidurals, and all the other ritual humiliations women in childbirth were subjected to, and simply give birth to the baby.

'I suppose you must know what you're doing,' said Lally's builder boyfriend, whose name no one could remember but which in fact was Roy, whose father had been a hard-line Stalinist, and who was fighting – at least they hoped he was fighting – a severe indoctrination in authoritarianism.

'There's a positive correlation,' said Helen, 'between the hospitalisation of mothers and infant mortality rates. We know what we're doing all right.'

Lally's pains were quite severe.

'That means it's not labour,' said Helen, 'it can't be. You don't have pains when you're having a baby, you have contractions. All that stuff about pain is part of the myth. Having a baby is just a simple, natural thing.'

Helen was excited by her new view of the Universe. Acid-tripping for the first time, six months previously, at Lally's instigation, had caused her radically to rethink her life and attitudes. If Lally showed signs of reneging, falling back into the accepted framework of society, Helen was there to prevent it.

Lally's pains stopped, and later she had diarrhoea and other symptoms of food poisoning, so Helen was vindicated. She put Lally on a water-only diet for two days. They clustered round the bamboo fire, which burned yellowly and brightly, and had a consciousness-raising session.

Were they all to be made homeless by the whims of the likes of Richard and Liffey? No. Would they fight for the roof over their heads: fight individual landlords: fight the system which denied them their natural rights? Yes. Would they join the Claimants' Union, just around the corner?

Tomorrow! All went to bed invigorated, cheerful and fruitful.

During Saturday night Liffey's pains returned, and when Richard moved his hand on to her breast, speculatively, she pushed it gently away. Liffey was worried. She thought it might have something to do with Tucker. Perhaps the introjection of his body into hers, so foreign to it, had started up some sinister chain of reaction? She worried for Richard's sake, in case something disagreeable of Tucker passed itself on to him, through her. It was nothing so crude as the fear of a venereal disease, but of something more subtle – a general degeneration from what was higher to what was lower. Tucker was mire and swamp; Richard a clean, clear grassy bank of repose. The mire lapped higher and higher. It was her fault.

Richard let his hand lie: they drifted off to sleep. Richard, to his shame, dreamt of Bella, and in the morning did not pursue his amorous inclination towards Liffey, but cleared damp leaves from the paths around the cottage, and missed his Sunday paper and the droney communal somnolence of the city Sabbath, and said nothing. The countryside did not soothe him. He felt it was not so much dreaming, as waiting. Its silence, broken only by a few brave winter birds, made him conscious of the beating of his breast, the stream of his own blood, and his mortal vulnerability. He could not understand why Liffey loved it so.

Mabs came over in the afternoon with home-made mayflower wine for Richard – which she claimed was unlucky for women to imbibe – and a dark, rich, sweet elderberry wine to soothe Liffey's insides.
'I don't know how you knew about my tummy,' said Liffey, gratefully sipping, and Richard wondered, too, how Mabs could know. Then they both forgot about it, as people will, when the penalty of unravelling truth is extreme.

Mabs carried Richard's wine in a brown carrier bag, and the

bottle was wrapped for safety in old magazines, which, inspected when Mabs left, turned out to be crudely porno-graphic. Liffey's little nose crinkled in mirthful disgust.

'Aren't people funny!' she said, sipping the sweet elderberry wine, which indeed soothed her tummy, and contained a drop or two of a foxglove potion with which Mabs' mother had dosed her daughters in their early adolescence, to keep them out of trouble. 'The things they have to do to get turned on.'

The thought came to Richard, after several glasses of the mayflower wine, which was dry, clear and heady, and contained the same mistletoe distillation which Carol put in Dick Hubbard's brandy and soda, that Liffey had never in fact been properly turned on herself, that her love-making, was altogether too light and loving and childish – a reflection, in fact, of herself – and that though he loved and cherished her, in fact *because* he loved and cherished her, he could never through her discover what lay in himself. The thought was quite clear, quite dispassionate, and final.

Richard put his arms round Liffey, but she moved away from him. Mayflower and elderberry do not mix – they belong to different seasons. They do not understand each other: any more than do foxglove and mistletoe, the one of the earth, the other of the air.

Carol was the next to call.

'Well,' said Richard to Liffey, 'at least you'll never be lonely here.' He thought that Carol looked at him with direct invitation, as she warned them not to spend too much on the house, as it would never be anything but damp, not to bother to try and grow vegetables, as the soil was poor, and to leave the roof alone, as it was so old that interference by builders would only make it worse.

It seemed to Richard that what Carol was saying, in effect, was that time and money spent on things was wasted: energy should be preserved for sexual matters. That the highest good was the union of male and female, and had Liffey not been in the room, and some scraps of discretion left to him, he would most certainly have made a sexual advance towards her.

Carol's lips mouthed words about damp-courses, potatoes and thatch but her eyes said come into me, and he could feel the warmth of her body even across the room, and it seemed to him that all the ingenuities and activities of the human race, and all its institutions – state, church, army and bureaucracy – could be read as the merest posturing; diversion from the real preoccupation of mankind, the heady desire of the male to be into the female, and the female to be entered by the male. He had another glass of mayflower wine. Liffey looked at him anxiously. He was flushed.

When Carol had gone, he kissed Liffey chastely on the brow. 'What's the matter?' she asked, puzzled.
'I'm glad I married you,' he said.

For those very qualities in Liffey which earlier in the day had seemed his undoing, he could now see as God-given.

Richard wanted Liffey to be the mother of his children. He wanted her, for that reason, to be separated out from the rest of humanity. He wanted her to be above that sexual morass in which he, as male, could find his proper place but she, as wife and mother, could not. He wanted her to be pure, to submit to his sexual advances, rather than enjoy them: and thus, as a sacred vessel, sanctified by his love, adoration and respect, to deliver his children unsullied into the world. It was for this reason that he had offered her all his worldly goods, laying them down upon the altar of her purity, her sweet smile. And he wanted other women, low women, whom he could despise and enjoy, to define the limits of his depravity and his senses, and thus explain the nature of his being, and his place in the universe.

Richard wanted Bella. Richard wanted anyone, everyone. Except Liffey.

Richard sat rooted in his chair.

'What's the matter?' asked Liffey, but he would not, could not speak, and presently said he would have to go back to London that night, instead of the next morning, which upset her and made her cry, but could not be helped. These cataclysmic truths had in some way to be properly registered in his mind through his actions, lest they become vague and be forgotten, washed away by the slow, slight, sure tides of habit and previous custom.

'Now have a good week,' Richard said, kissing Liffey goodbye. 'And look after yourself, and prune the roses round the door, and by this time next year we'll have a baby, won't we!' His breath smelt of mayflower wine, and she, redolent of its opposing elderberry, could not help but be a little pleased that there had been no opportunity for love-making that weekend.

'You didn't put anything in that wine, I hope,' said Tucker to Mabs.

'Why should I do a thing like that?' asked Mabs. 'None of that stuff works, in any case. Or only on people who're stupid enough to believe in it.'

'You can't change people,' said Audrey, Mabs' oldest daughter, listening when she had no business to. 'But you can make them more themselves.'

'What do you know about it, Miss?' Mabs was angry, and surprised that one of her children should have a view of the world and contribute it to the household.

'Only what Gran tells me,' said Audrey, putting a table between herself and Mabs. She had her father's protection, but that only made her the more nervous of her mother.

Mabs looked at Audrey and saw that all of a sudden she was a young woman with rounded hips and a bosom, and Mabs' raised fist fell as she felt for the first time the power of the growing daughter, sapping the erotic strength of the mother. She was quiet for a time, and felt the more pleased, presently, that she had dosed Liffey to keep her off Tucker, and Tucker off her; and dosed Richard so that he should pay Liffey out properly while away during the week; and hoped again that she herself was pregnant, and still young.

Solitude

During the next week the wind turned to the north and rattled through the cottage windows, and the sky was grey and heavy, and the Tor hidden by cloud and mist.

Liffey cleaned and painted and patched and repaired by day, and shivered by night. She came to know the pattern of wind and rain around the house, as she lay in bed listening, hearing the wainscot rustle with mice, and the thatch with restless birds, and further away the hoot of an owl or the bark of a fox, and when all these noises for once were stilled, the tone shifts in the silence itself, as if the night were breathing. Once she heard music, faintly, on the wind, and was surprised to remember that the night world had people in it, too.

Liffey was lonely.

Liffey admitted defeat in her heart, and that she had been wrong, and not known what she had wanted, like a child, and not cared what Richard had wanted, like an unhappy child: and wanted Richard back the sooner to apologise. As soon as Mory and Helen were disposed of, she would join Richard in London.

Liffey walked to the Poldyke pub one evening, in search of companionship, and the host of friendly young couples whom she had come to believe inhabited every corner of the world, but found instead only old men drinking cider who stared at her in an unfriendly way. She walked back home in the dark, stumbling and groping, without a torch, having forgotten how black the night could be. Wet trees behind her whispered and gathered.

Liffey was frightened.

Mabs came up once or twice for coffee and a chat, and Liffey was grateful.

Liffey wrote a change-of-address letter to her mother. It did not mention loneliness or fear, merely hopes fulfilled and desires gratified. She had always found it difficult and dangerous to confide in her mother, and was accustomed to prattling on, instead, filling silence as now she filled the space on the page. Madge read the letter and recognised its insincerity and screwed it up and put it in the fire, and thereafter had no record of her daughter's new address.

Liffey walked to the telephone box at Poldyke to call friends, but once there lacked the courage to put in coins, and speak. It seemed as if she were having to pay for friendship, and she was humiliated. She walked home over the icy stubble of the fields and in the shadow of herself that the low sun cast in front of her, perceived a truth about herself.

She was someone shadowy, inhabiting a world of shadows. She had not allowed the world to be real. She had been accustomed to sitting beside a telephone, and summoning friends up out of nothingness, dialling them into existence, consigning them to oblivion again, putting the receiver down when they had served their purpose. She had no friends. How could she have friends, who had never really believed that other people were real? It was her punishment.

And if Mory and Helen were real, not cut-out figures set up by Liffey in the play of her life, to flail about for a time in front of paper sets, then perhaps they could not be man-oeuvred and manipulated: perhaps they could not be got rid of.

Liffey cried.

She wondered whether Richard was real, and whether she wanted him to be real. Her life since she had left her mother's house had been a dream. And still her mother would not write to her. Perhaps, thought Liffey, I am as unreal to my mother as everyone except her is unreal to me. A child might very well seem unreal to the mother. Something dreamed up, clothed in flesh and blood, which sucked and gnawed and depleted.

Liffey cried some more.

The north wind grew stronger and came through the missing roof tiles in sudden cold gusts.

Liffey walked to Poldyke again and made herself telephone friends and talk and invite them down, but they were all too busy to talk much, or thought the winter too cold to come and stay, and though all were polite and friendly, Liffey sensed the displeasure of those who remain, towards the one who had wilfully absented herself: and marvelled at how out of sight could so quickly become out of mind, not from carelessness or malice, but from a desire to preserve self-esteem.

Liffey ran out of butter and walked all the way into Poldyke again, and saw six tins of loganberries on Mrs. Harris' shelf, and loving tinned loganberries, bought all six, thus leaving none for Mrs. Harris' other customers, and nearly breaking her arm as she carried loganberries and butter back.

Liffey thought, I must get back to civilisation quickly.

Liffey rang Richard from Cadbury Farm to tell him all these things, but Miss Martin who answered said Richard was in a meeting, and would not fetch him out of it.

The grey sky groaned and heaved: dark, lonely days drifted

99

into darker, lonely nights. Liffey wanted Richard again. She dreamed he was making love to her and she cried when she woke.

There was no sign of Tucker.

Inside Liffey (4)

Although all was not well without, all was very well within. Liffey's uterus had settled down nicely after its recent state of confusion. It lay like an inverted pear, settling upon the upper end of her vagina, narrowing into the cervical canal, finished off (where in a pear the stalk would be) by the cervix itself. This, on a good day, could be detected by Richard's engorged penis as a hard knob, and by a doctor's hand as a firm, dome-shaped structure. The walls of Liffey's uterus were some half an inch thick, and composed of a whole network of muscles, some up and down, some oblique, some spiral, all extraordinarily flexible, and all involuntary – that is, uncontrollable by the conscious Liffey. The blood supply, simple, ample and good, came from the main blood vessels in Liffey's pelvis; and the nerve supply, anything but simple, enabling as it did the muscle to contract rhythmically during menstruation and more dramatically during labour, would only send messages of discomfort when uncomfortably stretched. These nerves could be cut or burned or ulcerated and Liffey would be none the wiser.

Now, as the fifty-first of Liffey's potential ova for the month ripened, the walls of the uterus lined themselves richly and healthily in preparation for its fall and fertilisation. Liffey's fallopian tubes (the pair of ducts attached to the outer corners of the uterus) waited too, secreting from their own mucous membrane the substances which nourished all visiting sperm, and, more rarely, any fertilised ovum. Of the four hundred million sperms which Tucker had released into Liffey the week before, on the sixth day of her cycle, some forty million had reached her cervical canal, but only a few dozen had survived the quick, forty-five minute journey up the uterus and along the fallopian tube. Here, in spite of the warm, sugary, gently alkaline environment which did its best to preserve and nurture them – and Tucker's were good strong sperm – all had inevitably perished, since no ovum arrived within the forty-eight hours of their life span. All died, but surely, surely, some molecular vestige of Tucker remained within Liffey?

One way or another, like it or not, we are part of more people than we imagine: one flesh.

Be that as it may, on the fourteenth day of Liffey's cycle, now nicely re-established at twenty-eight days, an ovum released by Liffey's left ovary, and swept up by the fimbriae, the little fingers of tissue where the fallopian tubes curl round to meet the ovary, swam into the healthy canal of the tube itself.

Ins and Outs

Liffey knew nothing of all this. She gave these matters even less attention than a car driver might give to his car. All she knew was that it was Friday night, and that she was looking forward to Richard's return: that dinner was cooked, candles lit, and everything in order. She wore a swirly skirt, a blouse instead of a T-shirt, and scent. Everything in fact was ready and prepared – an outer symbol of an inward state.

In the conscious and the unconscious world alike, this is the pattern. Things are made ready, offerings are prepared, fulfilment is hoped for, and sometimes occurs. The cosmic soup prepares for life, birds prepare nests, men prepare for war, wombs prepare linings, priests are prepared for ordination. Friday washing and ironing prepares for Saturday Sabbath. It was not surprising, then, that Liffey prepared for Richard, and found pleasure in it.

Things get ready, then burst into life. Nature, like its subsidiary processes of love, and friendship, and learning, proceeds by halts and starts.

Reverently, Richard made love to Liffey. She found him gentler and more considerate than ever, and although this should have gratified her, she found it oddly irritating.

Richard was not gentle with Bella, nor had been with the motorway whore he had picked up on the journey away from Liffey, back to London, the previous Sunday night. They were the users-up of surplus seed, not of intended seed; they were instruments of his anger, inasmuch as a man who has conscientiously decided to respect and adore his wife, to project rather than to incorporate his resentment of her – must find something to do with his anger, and the erect penis can be used to punish and destroy, as well as to love and create. So can soft words.

These were the five women Richard had made love to, since his adolescence. Mary Taylor, a forty-year-old barmaid, whose habit and pleasure it was to seduce sixth-form boys from the local boarding school.
Liffey, his wife.
His secretary, on the occasion of a drunken office party.
Bella Nash, his friend and landlady and best friend's wife.
Debbie, a fifteen-year-old delinquent, who travelled the motorways.

His encounter with Debbie of the unknown last name, precipitated by fate and the emotional tumult brought about by sudden self-knowledge – or else a physical irritation induced by Mabs' mistletoe and mayflower – and his on the whole unvoiced resentment of Liffey's recent behaviour, had gratified and satisfied him. To use, pay, and forget a more than willing girl hurt, so far as he could see, no one. It did not interfere with his uxorious love of Liffey, his more complex and imaginative lust for Bella, or his work.

If Richard was saddened by anything, it was by the new knowledge of years of sexual opportunity lost – a common enough sadness in those whom circumstance or conditioning have prevented from making full use of youthful sexuality. Richard resolved that while he could, he would: that Liffey's living in the country, though adventitious, would in the end help them both. It would help him, Richard, to know himself and by knowing him, to love her, Liffey, better, and in the end, surely, as they both grew older, to love and want Liffey alone. He could see fidelity as something to be travelled towards, achieved in the end; and the journey there could surely be made as varied and exciting as possible.

Mabs the while, lay in bed with Tucker and laughed out loud.
'Now what?' He was nervous.
'I don't know,' she said. 'I just feel things are going the way I want.'
'Up at Honeycomb Cottage?'
'That's right.'
'Leave them alone,' he begged. He should never have let himself be pushed by her, right into Liffey. She'd done it to him before once, with a former schoolfriend she'd come to envy.

'That Angie,' Mabs had deplored, with sudden savagery, 'what's she got to be so stuck up about, anyway?' And Tucker had been sent over before Angie's big wedding, and Angie had ended up with an arm mangled in a hopper, and a drunk for a husband, and one single stone-deaf child, big wedding or not. It was as if he, Tucker, had been sent in to prepare the way: make an entry through which Mabs could pour ill-wishes.

But these were night thoughts. In the morning, he knew,

Mabs would be just another farmer's wife, in Wellingtons and head scarf.

He rolled over her, as he could feel her needing, as he knew controlled her, if only for a while. Mabs was a sweep of forested hill, of underground rivers, and hidden caves, and dark graves and secret powers. Liffey was a willow-tree, all above ground. He liked Liffey. He would do what he could to protect her.

'Well,' thought Liffey, lying there, revered by Richard, 'at least he loves me. He won't get into trouble in London.' For she saw now that sexual opportunity is more powerful than sexual discrimination, and that by and large those who can, will, and there was Richard, by himself in London all week, and a young and handsome man: although of course Bella would keep an eye on him for her, and what's more it had all been her doing.

'I miss you and love you,' said Richard, as they lay together, wind and rain swirling around the chimneys outside, snug and warm beneath a hundred per cent eiderdown quilt from Heals, and it was true. He missed her and loved her. She was his wife.

She missed and loved him. He was her husband.

Inside Liffey (5)

Meanwhile some forty million of Richard's sperm were starting their migration from the vault of Liffey's vagina to the outer part of her fallopian tubes. Her orgasm or lack of it, made no difference to their chance of survival. The sperms had been formed in the testicles suspended in the scrotum beneath Richard's penis. Here, too, the male hormone testosterone was formed. Richard's testicles produced perhaps a little less than average of that particular hormone, rendering him in general kind and unaggressive, not given to using force to solve his problems, and needing to shave only once a day, not twice: but not so little that he did not berate Mory over the telephone and feel the better for it. It was some months since Richard's sperm had been so plentiful. The electric blanket he and Liffey loved, and which now Mory and Helen delighted in, had overheated his testicles, and moreover the tight underpants Liffey so admired had overconstricted the overheated testicles, thus causing a degree of infertility. But now, deprived of the electric blanket, wearing more comfortable pants, the sweat glands of his scrotum were once again able to maintain the testicles at their correct temperature and enable spermato-genesis to occur. The sperms, once produced, were stored in the slightly alkali, gelatinous fluid produced by his prostate gland, which lay at the base of the bladder at the root of the penis.

Richard ejaculated four millilitres of seminal fluid, each containing one hundred million sperm, well within the normal sperm count (which can vary between fifty and two hundred million sperms per millilitre and be ejaculated in quantities between three and five millilitres). Each sperm was about one-twenty-fourth of a millimetre long and consisted of head, neck and tail. The head of the sperm contained the chromosomes required to fertilise the ovum. The neck contained the mechanism which moved the tail. The tail propelled the sperm forward, at a rate of one millimetre every ten seconds; not bad going for an organism so very small. If it came up against a solid object it would change direction, like a child's mechanical toy. So doing, a sperm would even get by a cervical cap; or the vinegar-soaked sponge Liffey's grandmother used to trust, before she had Madge. Liffey's cervical canal was that day receptive and benign to Richard's sperm: the mucus there, mid-cycle, had become transparent and less viscous than normal. As the hours passed, so the sperm moved, readily and more plentifully than Tucker's before them, up into Liffey's fallopian tube.

Conception

Saturday morning came, and lunchtime, and then it was time for supper.

Mabs suddenly and unexpectedly leaned forward and slapped Eddie for slurping his tea. He cried. She slapped him again and snatched away his bacon and baked beans. All the children snivelled. They were having a late tea. Earlier, Tucker had taken Mabs to the pictures.
'What's the matter with you, then?' asked Tucker. 'Can't you just leave the children be?'
But she couldn't. Something had gone wrong. She knew it had.

Baked beans fell from Mabs' fork on to her tweed skirt. Audrey ran for a damp cloth.
'Little creepy crawler,' said Mabs to Audrey, but she took the offered cloth, and darted Tucker an evil, glinting look as she wiped, as if it was all his fault. He knew she was thinking about Liffey.
'You sent me up there,' said Tucker. 'It was what you wanted.'

Mabs strode about the kitchen, her face distorted. Tucker nodded sideways to the children, who slipped away quickly.

'Calm down,' said Tucker. He was frightened, not knowing which way Mabs' anger was to turn. Mabs stood at the window and looked at the Tor, and he could have sworn that as she did the clouds that hung above it swirled and churned in the moonlight.

'How funny the clouds look, above the Tor,' said Richard to Liffey. They stood side by side on the stairs, leaning into each other, dreamily.

'They often look funny,' said Liffey. 'It quite frightens me, sometimes. But it's just air-currents.'

Richard's sperm, now in Liffey's left fallopian tube, had there encountered a fully-fledged ovum, some five hours old and in good shape. By virtue of the enzymes that they carried, en masse, they liquefied the gelatinous material that encased the ovum, enabling one of their number to penetrate the ovum wall, running into it head first, leaving its tail outside.

And there, Liffey was pregnant.

'I do love you,' lied Richard.
'I love you,' said Liffey.

'Calm down,' said Tucker to Mabs, once again, and surprisingly, she calmed down. She moved away from the window.

'It's her I blame,' said Mabs, smiling at Tucker, 'not you. Did she wear a bra?'

'No,' said Tucker.

'Well, there you are,' said Mabs, as if that explained everything. And then, 'What's bad news for some is good news for another.' It was something she often said, and her mother too. Dick would say it to Carol, sometimes, referring to Carol's husband Barry, as a counter-point to their lovemaking, making Carol laugh.

'Tucker,' said Mabs. 'What size shoe does she wear?'

'Little. Three or four, I should say.'

Mabs looked down at her own large feet and sighed. She scraped all the children's teas into the pig-bin, yelled down the corridor for them to get to bed, and she and Tucker went to their bedroom together, like an ordinary couple, and she not at all hooked up to the hot lines of the Universe.

Inside Liffey (6)

Liffey slept. The female nuclei of the ovum and the male nuclei of the sperm, each containing the chromosomes which were to endow her child with its hereditary characteristics, both moved towards the centre of the ovum, where they fused to form a single nucleus. The nucleus divided into two parts, each containing an equal portion of Liffey and Richard's chromosomes. Liffey's brown eyes: Richard's square chin. Her gran's temper: his great grandfather's musical bent. And so on.

That was Friday night. By Sunday night, as they listened to Vivaldi on Richard's cassette player and toasted their toes by the wood fire, the two cells had divided to make four, eight, sixteen – by early Monday morning, when Richard left for London there were sixty-four, and could be termed a morula. The process was to continue for another 263 days; and 266 days from the time of conception, when the specialisation of different tissues was complete – some that could see, others that could hear; some to breathe, others to digest, stretch, retract, secrete; some to think, others to feel, and so on – and then when all were ready a baby would be delivered, weighing seven pounds or so. If Liffey's nature and physique were such that she would not abort the child, by accident or on purpose, or die from the many hazards of pregnancy: if Richard's were such that he could protect it until it was grown; if the combination of genes that formed the child allowed it health and wit enough to survive – a naked, feeble creature in a cold world, with only mews and smiles to help it – and then fulfil its designed purpose and itself procreate, successfully – the human race would be one infinitesimal step forward.

Nature works by waste. Those that survive are indeed

strong, but not necessarily happy. Auntie Evolution;
Mother Nature; bitches both!

Inside Richard's Office

Offices do, for some, instead of families: and for others, more
prudent, as a useful supplement to them. Bosses are as
parents, subordinates as offspring, and colleagues as siblings. For entertainment there is the continuing soap opera
lives which brush past each other, seldom colliding, seldom
hurting.

It does not do, of course, to mistake office life for real life.
For if a desk is emptied one day by reason of death, or
redundancy, or resignation, or transfer, it is filled the next,
and the waters close over the departed, as if they had never
been. In offices no one is indispensable; in real life people
are.

Mother dies, and is gone for good. The Personnel Officer
dies, to be reborn tomorrow.

It does not do, either, to mistake office sex for real sex, least
of all carry the fantasy into the outside world. Secretaries
marry bosses, it is true, but must remain secretary and boss
for the rest of their lives, hardly man and wife. He parental:
she childish. And colleague may marry colleague, but the
quality of comradeship inherent in the match, of fraternal
common sense and friendliness, keep them for ever like
brother and sister, hardly man and wife.

Miss Martin was in love with Richard. Why should she not
be? He was young, he was pleasant, he was good-looking, he
was forbidden; above all he was there. He had come to
confide in her. She was sorry for him too, regarding Liffey as
a bad wife, who could not even consult a railway timetable

accurately, and who rang the office at inconvenient times, distracting Richard when he most needed to concentrate, intruding and interfering in a world which was none of her business.

Miss Martin knew that hers was a hopeless love. She could place herself quite accurately in the world. She was sensible, but dull. She had a solid, pear-shaped figure which no amount of dieting would make lissom. She preferred to serve rather than be served. She was deserving, so would never get what she deserved. She did not understand her fiancé Jeff's regard for her, and rather despised him for it. If he loved her, who was not worth loving, how could she love him? He seemed lively and handsome enough now, but would soon settle down, and be as dull and plain as she was.

Miss Martin, in fact, following the death of her father, was in a sulk which might well last her whole life. She was consumed by spite against the Universe, which had spited her, and taken away the object of her love. She would find no joy in it. The determination glazed her eyes, dulled her hair and skin.

In the meantime, Richard would do to be in love with. The passion, being forbidden and unrequited, would serve as its own punishment. It made her heart beat faster when he came into the room, and her hand tremble when she handed him his coffee, and her typing perfect, and her loyalty fierce. It was a secret love. It had to be. It would embarrass Richard to know about it. The love of the socially and physically inferior is not welcome, especially if the object of the love is male. Miss Martin, in other words, knew her place.

She knew it, as it transpired, better than he did.

On Monday Richard arrived in the office, and hung his coat upon the hook provided. (Later, Miss Martin would re-arrange it, so that it hung in more graceful folds.) She had waiting for him upon his desk a list of the day's appointments. There was mud upon his shoes, and she tactfully remarked upon it, so he could attend to it before encountering his boss.

'That's country life,' said Richard. 'All mud and stress. But Liffey loves it. Have you ever lived in the country, Miss Martin?'

'I'm a suburban sort of person,' she replied. 'Neither one thing nor the other.'

'I need a nail file,' he remarked, and she provided it. She did not find these attentions to his physical needs in any way humiliating. They set him free to attend to matters which by common consent were important – the making of the decisions which kept them all employed. She could have made the decisions as well as he, of course, but nobody would then have believed they were important, let alone difficult.

Messengers came, telephones rang and files were circulated. Currently obsessing Richard's department was the maximising of the salt content of a particular brand of chicken soup, and the growing conviction that some kinds of salt acted saltier than others, a fact verifiable by common experience, but not scientific experiment. Pleasing the public palate is not easy.

'Of course Liffey would have everyone keeping their own chickens and boiling them down for soup,' said Richard. 'She's not a great one for packets.'

'I wouldn't have the heart,' said Miss Martin. 'Poor chicken!'

Before lunch Richard took out an unlabelled bottle of white wine.

'All this talk of salt has made me thirsty,' he said. 'Will you have some, Miss Martin? It's home-made. A neighbour of ours made it. Mayflower. It's supposed to be unlucky for women to drink it, and Liffey won't, but you're not superstitious, are you?'

'No,' said Miss Martin, drinking too. Richard noticed the

stolid fleshiness of her behind as she bent to a filing cabinet, and found himself rather admiring it. Liffey's buttocks proclaimed themselves to the world, moving in open invitation, cheek by cheek beneath tight jeans. Miss Martin had something to hide. But what? He took another glass.

'I love you,' said Miss Martin, two glasses later. The love induced by the mistletoe, parsley, and mystery ingredients in the wine was of an elemental, imperative kind, and overrode inhibitions induced by low self-esteem.

Richard flinched, as if physically assaulted, but quickly recovered. Miss Martin was an excellent secretary, he liked her, and for some reason pitied her, as he pitied certain kinds of dogs, who look at humans with yearning eyes, as if able to conceive of humanness, but know they can never aspire to it, and are doomed to creep on four legs for ever.

'That's just the wine talking,' said Richard more truly than he knew. 'You'd better not have any more.' But he poured her another glass, even as he spoke.
'I don't see why I shouldn't love you,' complained Miss Martin. 'No skin off your nose.'
'Well,' said Richard, 'since it's sex that makes the world go round—'
Miss Martin felt argumentative. She often did, but was accustomed to keeping her arguments to herself.
'I'm not talking about sex,' she said, 'I'm talking about love.'
'You're only not talking about sex,' said Richard, 'because I suspect you know nothing about it.'
'I'm a virgin,' she said.

Miss Martin rang up the colleague with whom Richard was supposed to be lunching, and said he had been delayed by a crisis, and they went off to lunch together, oblivious to those who saw them. He strode on long, cheerful legs, and she trotted alongside on her little dumpy ones. It wasn't right. He was a kestrel; she was a sparrow doomed to pick at leavings. In nature everyone knows their place.

Mabs would have been pleased at the un-rightness brought about by her mother's potion, and would certainly have thought it served Miss Martin right. Mayflower wine is unlucky for women to drink, and she had been warned.

'I think,' said Richard, blindly, 'I would be doing you a kindness in saving you from suburbia and a life of proper propriety.'

And in a room at the Strand Palace Hotel, after lunch, for her sake rather than his, or so it appeared to him, he did not so much as save her from these things, as make them intolerable to her for ever.

By five o'clock both were back in the office: Miss Martin was pale and stunned and at her typewriter, and he was trying to catch up with his work. Neither could quite believe that it had happened, and Richard certainly wished that it had not.

Miss Martin told no one. There was no one to tell. 'I was drunk,' she told herself. 'You know what home-made wine is.'

Justifications

Richard quite wanted to tell Bella about the astonishing episode of himself and Miss Martin, but prudence forbade it. She would have laughed at him, from her lordly position, sitting astride him on the study sofa, exacting response from him, payment, this pleasure for that, as if she was the queen and he the subject. Boadicea. Knives on the wheels of her lust, cutting into self-esteem.

'I took her virginity,' he could have said. 'It seemed my right, even my duty. She certainly expected me to.'

'Took her virginity,' Bella would have sneered. 'A poor Victorian dirty old man, that's all you are at heart.'

But he knew there was power in it. That he would never be forgotten: thus his life lasted as long as hers. He would keep that to himself.

'Don't you worry about all this?' he asked Bella. He had to ask her something. She demanded rational conversation until the very last minute of their love-making, and question and answer seemed the least troublesome means of providing it.

'Why should I worry?'

'In case Ray finds out. He might come home early.'

'Ray never comes home early.' She was bitter, but he could see her logic. Bella was doing what she was because Ray came home late: it was the grudge she bore against him. It circled and circled in her mind – words rather than meaning. Ray Comes Home Late. Ray could not, therefore, come home early, or she would not be doing this. He could see that the logic might well apply to Bella, making her husband inaudible and invisible if he returned early from his visit to the nubile Karen and her homework problems – perhaps taken ill, or overcome with emotion – but would hardly save him, Richard, from Ray's anger and upset.

He said as much.

'Ray wouldn't be angry or upset,' said Bella. 'Why should he?

He likes me to enjoy myself. And what else can he expect, the way he never comes home until late. And you're a friend after all.'

'You don't think this is an abuse of friendship?'

'It might be a *test* of friendship. Whenever I go away my friend Isabel sleeps with Ray. She and I are still the best of friends.'

'I expect you compare notes,' said Richard, gloomily.

'Of course,' said Bella.

'I don't want you to talk about me,' said Richard.

She sighed and raised her eyes to heaven, revealing an amazing amount of white.

'I don't think Ray treats you very well,' said Richard.

'In what way?' Bella was interested.

'The way he talks about other younger women in front of you. And complains about your tits.'

'That's just his insecurity.'

'He calls you "the old bag".'

'He projects his fear of ageing on to me,' said Bella, 'that's all.'

'Well,' said Richard, 'I do feel bad about doing this, in spite of what you say.'

'Of course you do. It's the only way you can get it up.'

He found her crudeness horrific and fascinating, and was unable to continue talking.

On evenings when Richard did not accompany Ray and Bella on some gastronomic jaunt, or was keeping Bella company on Ray's late nights out, he ate simply enough, with the family. The staple food of the household was fish fingers, baked potatoes, and frozen peas. Food, except on special occasions, was regarded as fuel. Tony and Tina, the children, watched television and read books while they ate. 'Today's children have no palate,' mourned Bella.

The Nash household was for the most part quiet, as if saving its strength for uproar, or recuperating its strength from the last outburst. Helga the au-pair washed and cleaned and fried fish fingers and ironed: the children did their homework, Ray wrote in the attic, Bella and Richard silently worked or studiously made their secret love.

Sometimes it reminded Richard of his parents' home: the semblance of ordinariness, of kindness and consideration and warmth, as passions gathered and dams of rage prepared to burst.

Married to Liffey, in the little sweetness of their love, he had forgotten all that. He had learned, as a child, to smile and please and be out of the way when storms broke. Liffey had learned the same lesson.

Richard would do things with Bella as he believed debased the pair of them.
'No such thing as a perversion,' Bella would say, 'so long as both enjoy it.'
But Richard knew that she was wrong: that in dragging the spirituality of love down into the mist of excitement through disgust, he did them both a wrong. He would never do such things to Liffey. She was his wife. But he had to do them with someone, or be half alive.

All Bella's doing, thought Richard. Bella's fault.

Or he could have lived with Liffey for ever, in the calm ordinariness of the missionary position, as had his mother and father before him, and known no better.

Miss Martin had trembled and moaned so much he'd simply got it all over as soon as possible.

Richard could see that Miss Martin too might come to enjoy it. Perhaps it was his duty to ensure that she did: to bring her to the enjoyment of sex, before casting her back into the stream of life from which he had so tenderly fished her? The more Richard contemplated the notion, the more attractive and the more virtuous such a course appeared.

There were, Richard thought, three kinds of women, and three kinds of associated sex. Liffey's kind, which went with marriage, which was respectful and everyday, and allowed both partners to discuss such things as mortgages and shopping on waking.
Bella's kind, which went with extra-marital sex, and self-disgust, and was anal and oral and infantile, and addictive, and so out of character that nobody said anything on waking if only because the daily self and the nightly self were so divorced.

Miss Martin's kind, which involved seduction: the pleasure of inflicting and receiving emotional pain: in which the sexual act was the culmination not to physical foreplay – for orgasm was in no way its object – but of long, long hours, days, weeks, of emotional manipulation.

It would not be possible, nor indeed desirable, Richard thought, to find these three different women in one body; he could never satisfy his needs monogamously. Could any man?

On Wednesday morning Richard said to Miss Martin, whose hand shook more than ever when she handed him his coffee, whom he had had to reprove more than once for carelessness in typing, and who was now wearing her hair curled behind her ears – 'I like your hair like that.'

It was the first personal remark he had made to her since their return from the Strand Palace Hotel.

Miss Martin blushed. Later he asked her out to lunch. He knew she would not refuse: that she would make no trouble for him: and make no demands. She was born to be a picker up of other people's crumbs. Well, he would scatter a few. She needed the nourishment: and the more wealth that flowed from him, the more there would be to flow. Richard knew that in sexual matters the more you give out, the more there is to give.

Nature

Inside Liffey, a cystic space appeared in the morula of her pregnancy, which now could be termed a blastocyst. It grew sprout-like projections, termed choriomic villi. It drifted down towards the cavity of the uterus. So each one of us began: Nature sets us in motion, Nature propels us. It is as well to acknowledge it.

And by Nature we mean not God, nor anything which has intent, but the chance summation of evolutionary events which, over aeons, have made us what we are: and starfish what they are, and turtles what they are: and pumpkins too, and will make our children, and our childrens' children what they will be, and an infinitesimal improvement – so long, that is, as natural selection can keep pace with a changing environment – on what we are. Looking back, we think we perceive a purpose. But the perspective is faulty.

We no longer see Nature as blind, although she is. Her very name is imbued with a sense of purpose, as the name of God used to be. God means us. God wills us. God wants for us. We cannot turn words back: they mean what we want them to mean; and we are weak; if we can not in all conscience speak of God we must speak of Nature. Wide-eyed, clear-eyed, purposeful Nature. Too late to abandon her. Let us seize the word, seize the day; lay the N on its side and call our blind mistress Σature.

On Thursday night the calm of the Nash household was disturbed. Ray and Bella had a row. Both thought they behaved as rational people do when provoked beyond endurance, and both were in error. Ray and Bella acted as people act when their metabolisms are disturbed, as Σature works its terrible, its integrating changes in the body, and the messages received from the outside world are both distorted and distorting.

Bella wept. Ray shouted. Ray said he was in love with Karen because she was sixteen, had a mass of red hair and a tiny mouth.
'It isn't love,' cried Bella. 'It's lust.'
'It's love, Bella, love,' he shouted, and the volume of his voice made African objects d'art, lean mahogany phallic things, tremble on the pine bookcase.

'But she's a fool. How can you love something that's less than you.'

'Perfectly well,' he shouted.

'What do you mean by love?' she yelled.

'What any teenager means.'

'You're not a teenager. You're a poor impotent old man.'

'And you're a jealous old cow.'

She snatched up a sharp fruit knife and advanced upon him and he was frightened and fled, and in the bedroom Helga reading Tina and Tony their bednight story, raised her voice and tried to protect her charges from the noise of adult life.

Bella, having taken up her knife and wielded it, felt better. She was indeed jealous. Σature had rendered her jealous, thus giving her children (or so Σature thought, living as she does so much in the past) a better chance of survival. Even as Bella was ashamed of the emotion, so did acting upon it fulfil and satisfy her – as to act upon all the major impulses which Σature dictates – whether they be aggressive, defensive or procreative – fulfils and satisfies.

If it feels right, it is right, according to Σature, but not, alas, to man. At the same time as feeling better, Bella felt ashamed, and upset, and confused.

The voice Bella gave to confusion, grief and resentment was the more violent inasmuch as her unused ova – laid down, waiting for delivery, when she herself was still in the womb – were beginning to atrophy with age, and her cyclic production of oestrogen and progesterone was at a critically low level. She was suffering, as the months went by, from an increase in premenstrual tension, and from mild indigestion. She was forty-four – an early age for such symptoms of menopause, the average being forty-eight point five – but such things happen. Though by and large, those whose periods begin early, continue late. In sexual matters, to those that hath, is given more.

The voice that Ray gave to anger and despair was the more

violent, inasmuch as his supply of testosterone was uncomfortably diminishing, leaving him prone to sulks, moods, depressions and outbursts of rage. Karen, being young, even tempered, clear of complexion and of spirit, seemed the more enchanting. He felt that youth was infectious, and it was true enough that by stimulating his sexual appetite, Karen might stimulate his supply of testesterone, and make him better tempered, for a while. In the meantime, his tongue was acid and his moods were black.

Presently their parents stopped shouting, crying and stamping, and Tina and Tony slept. Next morning Helga swept and cleaned with a set face.

'I only stay because of the children,' she said. It was her theme song. She ironed Richard's shirts, beautifully.
'How can I thank you?' he asked.
From her look, he could tell. He wondered why he had suddenly become so desirable to the opposite sex, and concluded it was because he had become available.

Richard, observing Helga, suspected that there was perhaps a fourth kind of woman, and a fourth kind of sex.

Helga, and sex-as-payment. Helga would iron his shirts, and then demand to be brought to orgasm. She would work as busily and concentratedly on that as she did his shirts. As the iron was to the shirt, so would his penis be to her satisfaction.

He did not wish to put his theory to the test. Later, perhaps. Bella was upset enough as it was.

'You know,' said Bella on Friday night, after he had sent Liffey a telegram to say he'd been delayed at a meeting, and would return on Saturday morning. 'You're terribly angry with Liffey.'
'Why should I be angry with Liffey?'
'Because she won't let you be a man. She wants you to be a little boy, so you can romp hand in hand with her through green fields, for ever.'

'I'm not angry with Liffey,' he repeated.

'Yes you are. That's why you're doing these terrible primitive things to me. I'm her stand-in.'

Richard wished Bella would leave the inside of his head alone. There were a thousand motives which could be attributed to every act, but none of them made the act any different.

He had been angry with Liffey. Now, he was not. Or so he believed.

Inside Liffey (7)

By Saturday morning the fine hairs of the blastocyst inside Liffey had digested and eroded enough of the uterus wall to enable it to burrow snugly into the endometrium and there open up another maternal blood vessel, the better to obtain the oxygen and nutrients it increasingly required.

This implantation, alas for Liffey and her doctors, occurred in an unusual part of her uterus – in the lower uterine segment. Too far down, in fact, for safety or comfort. Perhaps this was a mere matter of chance – perhaps, who's to say, it was a matter of Mabs' ill-wishing? If prayers can make plants flourish, and curses wilt them, and all living matter is the same substance and thought has a reality, and wishing can influence the fall of a dice, and kinetic energy is a provable thing, and poltergeists can make the plates on the dresser rattle, why then Mabs can curse Liffey's baby, and Liffey protect it, as bad and good fairies at the christening.

Liffey looked up at the sky and thought it was beautiful, and the blastocyst clung where it could, not quite right but not quite unright, and growth continued and the so-far undifferentiated cells began to take up their specialist parts, some forming amniotic fluid, some placental fluid, and some becoming the foetus itself. The degree of specialisation which these later cells would eventually achieve would be rivalled nowhere else in the Universe, enabling their owner to read, and write, and reason in a way entirely surplus to its survival.

Σature intends us to survive only long enough to procreate. We have other ideas. Ask any woman past the menopause, withering like a leaf on a tree, and fighting the decline with intelligence, and oestrogen. Ask any man, reading *Playboy*, whipping up desire. These extras, too, Σature gave us. Why? Are we to assume Divine Intent, and fall on our knees, set the Σ the right way up, go back to Nature, and retreat to God? Never!

Liffey's child was to be male. Liffey contributed her share of twenty-two chromosomes plus the X chromosome which was all she could, being female, hand over. Richard handed over twenty-two chromosomes, plus as it happened, a Y sex chromosome. Forty-four plus an XY makes a male. Had Richard handed over an X sex chromosome – and there was a roughly fifty per cent chance that he would do so -- the forty-four plus an XX would have made a female. The sex of the child was nothing to do with Liffey – who left to herself could only have achieved a girl – but was determined by Richard.

The ratio of male to female babies conceived is some 113 to 100 but by the time of delivery has dropped to 106 to 100, since the male embryo is marginally the more likely to perish. So Liffey's baby, being male, and placed too low in the womb for maximum safety, already had a few extra odds working against its survival. Nevertheless, it had survived a few million obstacles to get this far, and if there is such a thing as a life-force, a determination in the individual of a species, as distinct to the group, not to give up, not to perish, not to be wasted, why then Liffey's baby had that determination.

Marvels

On Sunday morning Tucker and two of his children, Audrey and Eddie, came round to visit.
'You didn't go to church, then?' enquired Tucker.
'We're not really believers,' said Liffey.
Tucker looked amazed.
'Somebody had to make it all,' said Tucker.

While their elders talked about the weather, crops, and cider apples, Audrey wandered and Eddie leaned, and fidgeted. They were not like Tony and Tina. They did not believe the adult world was anything to do with them.

Audrey wore platform heels, three years out of date, a short skirt, holed stockings, and a shiny green jumper stretched over breasts which would soon be as robust as her mother's. Her large eyes followed Liffey, making Liffey nervous, but sometimes she would look sideways at Richard, and smile. She sidled round the perimeter of the room, as if her natural habitat were out of doors.

Eddie leaned against the wall, and shuffled from foot to foot, and fidgeted. His face was pale and puffy, his little eyes were sad, he had cold sores round his mouth, and coarse stringy hair. If Audrey looked as if she were biding her time, Eddie, at the age of eight, looked as if his had run out. His nose dripped a thick yellow mucus, which from time to time he would sniff back up his nostrils.

Eddie, fidgeting and fumbling, pushed a glass ashtray from a shelf and broke it.

Slap, went his father's hand across his cheek, and slap again.

'Oh don't!' cried Liffey and Richard in horrified chorus. 'Oh don't! It doesn't matter.'

'He's got to learn,' said Tucker, surprised, slapping again. Eddie snivelled rather than cried: as if life, already despaired of, was now merely continuing on a slightly more disagreeable level.

Liffey, half horrified, half fascinated, by this exercise of power, of parent over child, strong over weak, raised her eyes and found Tucker looking straight at her.

Tucker hadn't forgotten. She knew he would be back.

Liffey retreated to the kitchen to make real lemonade for the children, from whole chopped lemons, blended and then strained, and sweetened with honey. Audrey followed her in.

Audrey spoke.

'I've had nothing to eat all day,' she said, 'and won't till the end of it, that's according to my Mum. I was cooking bacon and eggs for all our breakfast, the way she told me, but then she changed her mind and made me make the beds and when I came back breakfast was cold, and I said don't make me eat that I'll be sick, but she did make me, so I ate it, and then of course I threw up over everything and she made me wipe it up and then she made me go to my room but my Dad made her let me out.'

Liffey did not believe Audrey. Mabs loved children and wanted more. She often said so.

'Would you like a sandwich?' Liffey asked, all the same, but Audrey refused, having taken a look at the brown wholemeal bread. 'I only like white sliced,' she explained, and then, as if in apology, 'you be careful of my Mum. She's got it in for you. You only see the side of her she wants you to see. You don't know what she's like.'

It was a clear warning, and Liffey disregarded it. Nobody nice, ordinary, and well-meaning wishes to believe that they have enemies, let alone become the focal point of energies they do not understand. Liffey had assumed a discretion and secrecy in Tucker that did not exist: and that Mabs could have instigated the seduction did not even occur to her and that the same convulsions which animate a mindless cluster of single cells – of division and multiplication within, and incorporation and extrojection along the outside perimeter – applies to the whole of existence, from galaxies to groups of human beings, she did not know. She could not see the dance of the Universe, although she was part of it.

'You'll feel better about your mum tomorrow,' said Liffey, and offered Audrey some of her lemonade, but Audrey, preferring the bottled kind, only distantly related to the lemon, declined to drink.

Richard went back to London. Liffey waited for Tucker to call, and was relieved when he did not. She locked the door at night, and was placating towards Mabs, whose bulky figure she would see, at odd times of the day, trudging over the fields, making Liffey feel both secure and anxious. On Thursday Liffey expected her period to start, but it did not. Her pituitary gland, out of its accustomed season, was producing extra progesterone: too much for menstruation to begin. The inner surface of Liffey's uterus had, in general, become highly secretive and active, and thus would continue until the end of her pregnancy, whether this ran to term or otherwise.

A week passed. Two weeks. Richard came and went. They agreed that they loved each other and that a little absence made the heart grow fonder, and that there were things about the Universe which could be learned singly, and which could not be learned together. That these things included, for Richard, sexual knowledge, did not occur to Liffey. He gave an account of his days which included Bella and Miss Martin, and she knew that Bella was old and his best friend's wife, and that Miss Martin was stodgy and plain, and why should he anyway, since he had her, Liffey, and Friday,

Saturday and Sunday nights – on a good weekend – were three nights out of seven.

Liffey dug the garden. Dick Hubbard came over to inspect the roof and told Liffey not to bother with the garden since the soil was so poor it was a waste of time. There were prowlers about, and the local prison was where they sent sexual offenders and the security was shocking and there were always break-outs, hushed up of course, and Honeycomb Cottage was on the direct escape route, over the fields, from the prison to the main road.

But Liffey, who wished to harm no one, feared no harm.

Mabs came over with seeds for the garden and talked of the prison working parties too, describing the prisoners as without exception harmless and amiable.

Liffey started a compost heap, having read that artificial fertilisers were the ruin of the soil. Richard scoffed, and marvelled at his wife's capacity of handling what to him was better churned up as quickly as possible in a waste disposal unit. Mory and Helen failed to answer solicitor's letters, pay rent, or answer the door when Richard knocked upon it.

Illegal, his solicitors said, to knock down your own front door.
Wait, wait.

The other side of the door Lally's pains came and went. Her legs swelled. Spots swam before her eyes, and she had headaches.
'You don't think I should call a doctor?' she would sometimes say, plaintively. But Helen said no, doctors would only interfere with the course of nature.
'I think the baby's overdue,' Lally ventured one morning. The flat was almost bare of furniture now. Bedding could not be burned, conveniently, as it filled the rooms with a choking smoke.

'How can a baby be overdue?' asked Helen. 'When a baby's due it comes out,' and Lally was obliged to admit that that was so. Helen was her elder sister, and had known best from the beginning.

Neither Mory nor Roy liked to interfere. Helen had a determined and positive nature: once given over to the winning of Pony Club rosettes and hockey colours; since her conversion equally determined to bring about the New Society. She smoked less than the others, as they smoked more and more, which gave her, if only by default, definite qualities of leadership.

'I suppose the wicked weed doesn't do the baby any harm,' murmured Mory.

'It stops me feeling the pains,' said Lally, who had never at the best of times been prepared to sacrifice comfort and entertainment in the dubious interests of the baby ('all these dos and don'ts are just punitive – part of the male plot to make the pregnant woman miserable' – Helen) and at the moment felt happiest in a stupor.

The apartment became increasingly damp, dirty and un-comfortable. Helen declined to make Roy's coffee, Lally could not, and Mory did not. There was no cooked food, and Roy felt bad without at least one dish of meat, potatoes and vegetables a day. He started doing sums on pieces of paper, and concluded that he could not be the father of Lally's child and moved out, taking Helen's amber beads and all their supply of marihuana with him. Helen wept: Lally groaned and started to haemorrhage. Mory ran into the street and stopped a police car who called an ambulance. Lally was taken to hospital where the next day the baby was still-born, of placental insufficiency, the baby being six weeks beyond term.

'Liars, murderers,' sobbed Helen, 'you should never have called them in, Mory.'

But he had lost his faith in her, and threw about a great deal of Liffey's blue and white Victorian china.

Lally went back to stay with her mother, 'Just for a time,' she said.

'Traitor,' stormed Helen. 'Don't give her my love, whatever you do.'

The doctors said that Lally's fertility might be henceforth somewhat impaired, but Lally did not mind, at least for the moment.

The bank wrote another letter to Liffey, and Mory and Helen failed to pass it on. But Mory made telephone calls to Argentina, in the weeks before the Telephone Company acted on Richard's instructions to disconnect the telephone, where he had heard of a job, and where truly creative architects, artists in concrete, were appreciated. Helen said it was an impossibly reactionary and oppressive society, and they were not going to such a place, not even for a week, and Mory said he was, he didn't care about her.

Still Liffey's period did not begin. Three weeks late! She felt a little queasy and put it down to some vague virus infection: and was sick one morning, and her breasts were tender – but so they often were just before a period – and she had to get up in the night to pass water, but put this down to a chill on the bladder.

No, no, thought Liffey, I can't be pregnant. Not this month. Not while Tucker might be remotely connected with the event. Which surely he wasn't, because surely—

Liffey discovered she knew next to nothing about pregnancy, or what went on inside her, and really had no particular wish to know. It is hard to believe that the cool, smooth, finished perfection of young skin covers up such a bloody, pulpy, incoherent, surging mass of pulsing organs within: hard to link up spirit to body, mind to matter, ourselves to others, others to everything. But there it is, and here we are. Hearts beating, minds running; fuel in, energy out.

Liffey, trembling on the edge of a train of thought which

would both enhance and yet debase her, make her ordinary where she had thought herself special, special where she had believed herself ordinary, was pushed by guilt and trepidation to go into Poldyke and buy the one paperback book on pregnancy that they had in stock.

News quickly got back to Mabs.

Mabs stood and stared at the Tor. It was very cold that day, and deathly still. The cows stopped rustling in the fields and the birds waited in the trees. Tucker stayed out of the house and sent the children to Mabs' mother.

'No reason to think it's mine,' said Tucker, to the trees.

To Mabs, Tucker said, 'Just because she's bought a book, doesn't mean she is.'

But Mabs did not reply, and both knew, as surely as one knows a death before it's verified, that Liffey was indeed pregnant.

Liffey wondered: Mabs and Tucker knew.

Everything Mabs felt, but gave no voice to, partly because she scorned to, partly because she did not have a vocabulary to express the complexity of the things she felt: fear of ageing, fear of death, loss of father, fear of mother, hate of sister, resentment of her children (who, once born, were not what she had meant at all), jealousy of Tucker, sexual desire towards other women, pretty women, helpless women; resentment of women who spread their possessions, their homes, delicately around them and stood back in pride: envy of brainy women, stylish women, rich women, women who could explain their lives in words: all these things Mabs felt, surging up in a great wordless storm, on knowing that Liffey was pregnant.

She, Mabs, could stump about the fields, and put her

powerful hands before her, and spread her fingers wide, and the whole power of the Universe would dart through them – but what use was that to Mabs? It could not make her what she wanted to be.

Mabs, pregnant, felt the fury of her unconscious passions allayed, and could be almost happy. And, so, pregnant, became ordinary, like anyone else, and used her hands to cook, and clean, and sew, and soothe, and not as psychic conductors.

Mabs knew, too, that there are only so many babies to go round, and that if Liffey was pregnant, she would not be.

Mabs thought all these things, and since she could not voice them, then forget them; she knew only that she liked Liffey even less than before, and that the answer to her dislike was not to keep out of Liffey's way. No.

The air grew warmer: the cows rustled in the fields; the birds found the courage to leave the trees and look for food in the thawing ground: clouds passed easily over and around the Tor.

Tucker fetched the children back. Tucker liked the idea of Liffey being pregnant. It was as if Mabs had barred the light of the world, eclipsing it, and suddenly he could see round her, and all this time she had been hiding wonderful things.

Liffey was in her fifth week of pregnancy. The baby was two millimetres long, and lay within a newly formed amniotic sac. It's backbone was now beginning to form.

Liffey felt her tender breasts, and thought no, no, surely not. She was not ready to have a baby. She had not grown out of her own childhood: a baby was something which would grow at her expense: which would diminish her: which would bring her nearer death. It seemed bizarre, not natural at all.

She said nothing about it when Richard came home the next weekend. And he told her that he thought Bella was a repressed lesbian, and that Miss Martin had announced her engagement in the local papers, and they both laughed a little, but kindly, at the hypocrises of the one and the modest aspirations of the other.

'As for Helga,' said Richard, 'she's the original Hausfrau! The three Ks. *Kirche, Küche, Kinder*. I thought women like that went out with the dinosaur. Of course she's the size of one.'

But Richard's shirts were clean and ironed, and he brought no washing home for Liffey. She was glad of that. She was feeling a little tired.

She felt an increase in her sexual desire for Richard. She wished to try new positions, but Richard seemed embarrassed so she quickly desisted, marvelling at herself. It was as if her body, no longer needing to insist on procreation, had at last found time for its own amusement. Richard went back to London on Sunday night. She hoped her conduct in bed had not driven him away early.

On the Monday morning Liffey was sick, and on the Monday afternoon went into Crossley and bought, with some embarrassment, a pregnancy testing kit and by Tuesday mid-day, having dropped some early-morning urine into a phial, adding the provided chemicals, and putting it to set, soon knew that she was pregnant.

A certain elation began to mingle with her fear. The sick feeling, which might have been brought on by anxiety, and uncertainty, lessened a little.

Liffey went round to Mabs.

'I'm pregnant,' she said. 'Can I use the telephone to ring Richard?'

'But that's wonderful!' cried Mabs, and insisted that they open a bottle of blackberry wine to celebrate, and delayed Liffey getting to the telephone until well after one o'clock, by which time Richard had gone to lunch.

Or so Miss Martin said. In actual fact Richard had just kissed her gently on the eyes, to kiss away her tears, and she had had to break away from his embrace to answer the telephone. The tears had come after a full office week in which Richard had ignored her except for sending letters back for re-typing and reproving her in front of other people: she thought, she hoped, that the cause of his unkindness was her having announced her engagement to Jeff, but how could she be sure? She knew that tears irritated him, but by Tuesday lunchtime could no longer hold them back.

And instead of shouting, he kissed her.

'Who was that?' asked Richard.
'It was only your wife,' said Miss Martin, and he had to stop himself from striking her. *Only* Liffey! He knew that Jeff, poor Jeff, would end up beating her. She invited it, mingling tears with acts of hostility.
'But it was your lunch-hour,' Miss Martin put in her feeble excuse, 'you said you didn't want to be disturbed in your lunch-hour.'

He made her ring back Cadbury Farm, and get Liffey on the line. But Mabs answered. Her broad accent rang thick and strange in the quiet office.
'Your Liffey's here tippling with me,' said Mabs, 'and she's got something important to tell you. She's pregnant.'

There was silence. Mabs had the receiver away from her ear.
'I'll bet that shook him,' she said, aside to Liffey.

Liffey took the phone. There were tears in her eyes. She felt that a moment had gone, lost, never to be recaptured. It was one in which she might have lost her fear of having the baby, and in Richard's spontaneous pleasure learned how to accept it.

'Are you sure?' Richard was saying. 'Liffey, are you there? You're sure you haven't made a mistake?'

The telephone went dead, and although Miss Martin, sobbing, denied that it was her doing, and did her trembly best to re-establish the connection, Liffey at the same time was trying to get through to Richard, and by the time she did he had indeed gone off to a meeting.
'Is there any message?' asked Miss Martin, who had recovered her composure, and blamed Liffey because she had lost it in the first place. 'I'd ask him to ring back, but he is so busy this week, and we're expecting a call through on this line from Amsterdam.'

Liffey put down the phone.
'I don't like the sound of that secretary,' said Mabs. 'She sounds for all the world like a wife.'

Suppositions

Knowledge of pregnancy comes early to modern woman, perhaps too early, before body and mind have settled down into tranquillity.

Liffey, all alone, trembled and feared and cried. She thought her life was over. She thought that to be pregnant was to be ugly, and that afterwards her body would be spoiled; she would have pendulous breasts and a flabby belly.

Her mother Madge had strange creases over her stomach, flaps of ugly skin, for which she held Liffey responsible. 'Stretch marks!' she would observe, making no attempt to hide them. Madge viewed her body as something functional: if it worked that was all she cared about. But Liffey loved her body and cherished it: she feared maturity, she wanted to be looked after, for ever; to be placed, physically, at a point somewhere between girl-child and stripling lad: hips and bosom all promise, waiting for some other time, but not now, not now. Not yet.

Richard wanted a boy-wife, she knew it. She knew it from the way he groaned at biscuits and moaned at buns and worried in case she grew fat.

On the way home from Cadbury Farm Liffey slipped and fell, and lay for a moment, stunned and shaken, with the world slipping and sliding about her.

A face loomed over her. It was Tucker. Tucker helped her up and set her on her feet, calmly and kindly.
'You look after yourself,' he said. 'And don't go drinking too much of Mabs' wine. It isn't good for you.'

Liffey ran home, as quick as she could over slippery ground, for light snow had been falling, and locked the door. During the night more snow fell, fine and light and driven by strong winds, which in the morning left a blue, washed sky. And such a brilliant tranquillity of white stretched across the plain to the Tor, broken only by the sketched pencil-lines of the half-buried hedgerows, that tears of wonder came to her eyes, and she felt better.

Richard woke on Bella's sofa to the sight of Bella's books: the works of Man, not nature, and found it reassuring. The news of Liffey's pregnancy had come as a shock. He was glad, but not altogether glad.

If Richard was to be husband and father, how could Bella continue his education? How could he in all conscience continue to lie on his back with Bella on top of him, wresting from him any number of degrading pleasures?

How could he discover what it was in Miss Martin that made her cry when she lay beneath him, as if she had the key to all the sorrows of the Universe?

How could he discover the nature of Helga's being, which he now passionately desired to know?

But to be a father! There was pride in that, and pleasure in looking after Liffey, and wonder in the knowledge that a man was not just himself, but so stuffed overfull with life that there was enough to pass on – and here in Liffey was the proof of it.

Richard decided to give up Bella and Miss Martin and concentrate on Liffey.

It was a decision he was to make frequently in the following months, as a dedicated but guilty smoker decides to give up smoking.

Six weeks. The limb buds of the foetus began to show and the tail to disappear. The heart formed within the chest cavity and began the activity which was to last till the end of its days. Blood vessels formed in the cervical cord. Parts of the stomach and intestine formed.

Liffey wondered how to be rid of a baby she did not want, without telling anyone that she did not want it.

Richard wondered how to subdue in himself that part of his being which did not dovetail with his nature as husband and father.

Liffey thought she was growing a malformed baby, which would have a lolling head and tongue, and flippers for arms, finished off by Tucker's black fingernails. Liffey was guilty, in other words, and believed that no good could come out of her.

Mabs walked about the hills and fields, and the rain poured

out of the heavens so hard it stirred up the ground where she trod, and there was little to choose between heaven, or earth, or her. The Tor vanished altogether, obscured by water, fog and cloud, in which occasionally, sheets of lightning danced. Earth, water, fire and air no longer retained their separate parts.

Seven weeks. Budding arms and legs, and little clefts for fingers and toes. Blood vessels throughout, and the liver and kidneys forming. A spinal cord, and a well-shaped head with the beginnings of a face, and a brain inside. It was not, all the same, conscious. It was an automota, as the jellyfish are, and the whole kingdom of the plants, and much but not all of the insect world. It was not yet truly a mammal. Mammals have the gift of consciousness: decision can over-ride instinct, and often, but perhaps not as often as we assume, does.

'You are looking poorly,' said Mabs, and made Liffey a brew of ergot and tansy tea; a rich abortificant, which had, fortunately for Liffey but unfortunately for Mabs, no effect on Liffey or her baby beyond giving the mother slight diarrhoea. 'This will do you good.'

Liffey had become a little frightened of Mabs, and drank whatever she suggested, for fear of offending her.

Richard succumbed to loneliness, vague resentments of Liffey, various worries connected with the varying saline content of the water flow at the soup works, and fornicated as much as possible with Miss Martin and Bella.

'I shouldn't,' whispered Miss Martin. 'Not if your wife is pregnant.' But she did, and even left out her own contraceptive cap, once, and fortunately did not get pregnant, an episode which led her to believe she was infertile, and did nothing for her self-esteem. She knew nothing about ova, where they were, or how long they lasted. All she knew was that her very being cried out to have Richard's baby, if Liffey did: and her conscious mind, that glory of the mammal kingdom, did very little to protect her.

'Live as much as you can while you can,' said Bella. 'Before life and Liffey close in.' Bella was old, by nature's standards, and her conscious mind had less trouble over-riding her instinctive drives. All that remained of naturally rivalrous behaviour was her current irrational dislike for, and impulsive disparagement of, Richard's pregnant wife Liffey.

Mabs' period began, staining oyster silk underwear. Mabs scrubbed away, hating Liffey, and focused her ill-will. And in London Helen looked up and saw the letters to Liffey on the mantelpiece and said, 'I suppose I'd better post those,' and did, and Mabs at once felt better and actually baked a cake for tea.

Liffey opened the letters and understood that she was no longer rich, that she was to live as the rest of the world did, unprotected from financial disaster; that she was pregnant and dependent upon a husband, and that her survival, or so it seemed, was bound up with her pleasing of him. That she was not, as she had thought, a free spirit, and nor was he: that they were bound together by necessity. That he could come and go as he pleased; love her, leave her as he pleased: hand over as much or as little of his earnings as he pleased; and that domestic power is to do with economics. And that Richard, by virtue of being powerful, being also good, would no doubt look after her and her child, and not insist upon doing so solely upon his terms. But he could and he might: so Liffey had better behave, charm, lure, love and render herself necessary by means of the sexual and caring comforts she provided.
Wash socks, iron shirts. Love.
And that to have been unfaithful was a terrible thing. That financially dependent wives are more faithful than independent wives. That she must go carefully.

Liffey thought of all these things for the space of three days.

'You're looking worse,' said Mabs, and offered Liffey more ergot and tansy tea, which Liffey pretended to take, but emptied instead into a pot plant which was altogether dead two days later. Had Liffey known this she might indeed have drunk the tea.

On the fourth day Liffey ran up country lanes, and over rough ground, fleeing her past, and her present, and her mother, and trying to shake her baby free. But the baby barely noticed any change to its environment. How could it?

Annunciation

The wind sang in Liffey's ears, and told her she was wasting effort and energy: that all things were destined, that she was what she was born, and would never change: would for ever be the girl without a father who wished she had no mother; and that though she ran and ran she would never escape herself. As Liffey ran, so antelope run over the African plain, and kittens across the domestic lawn, frightened by themselves, seeking refuge in flight, running as likely into danger as to safety. Her muscles ached: her energy drained. Liffey stopped running.

Liffey looked about her. The rain, which had poured and poured for weeks, had stopped, and the sky was washed and palest blue. She could still see the Tor, but now from a different angle, so that its slope was less acute, and the tower on top was clearly man-made, not eternal. It was friendly: scarcely nuministic at all. It had been weeks, she felt, since she had looked about her and noticed the world in which she lived. She saw that the leaf buds were on the trees, and that new bright grass pushed up beneath her feet, and that there was a sense of expectation in the air. All things prepared, and waited.

Liffey sat on the ground and turned her face towards the mild sun. She felt a presence: the touch of a spirit, clear and benign. She opened her eyes, startled, but there was no one there, only a dazzle in the sky where the sun struck slantwise between the few puffy white clouds which hovered over the Tor.

'It's me,' said the spirit, said the baby, 'I'm here. I have arrived. You are perfectly all right, and so am I. Don't worry.' The words were spoken in her head: they were graceful, and certain. They charmed. Liffey smiled, and felt herself close and curl, as a sunflower does at night, to protect, and shelter. The words dispersed, and the outside sounds came in. Birdsong, traffic, distant voices.

'I have been blessed,' said Liffey, to herself, walking carefully and warily home, eyes inside and misting from time to time. She did not say it to anyone else, for who would believe her?

'Richard, I felt the baby's spirit arrive. It was the soul that came. I know it was.'

No.

'Madge, mother, did you know I was pregnant? No? Well, I am and what's more the Holy Ghost, or something, descended and now inhabits me.'

?

No.

'Mabs, friend, you know how I slept with your husband, Tucker, well you don't, but I did, except it isn't his baby; well, I just *know*, because the baby's said so—'

?

No.

'Mr. and Mrs. Lee-Fox, your daughter-in-law speaking, the flimsy one who trapped your only son into marriage: the never-quite-accepted, never-to-be-accepted one, who tried to charm her way into your hearts but failed, who now says just to have Richard's child isn't enough, but has to have an Annunciation instead, as if Richard was some Middle-Eastern carpenter and she was Mary—'

?

No.

'Bella and Ray, Liffey speaking. You know, Richard's wife, your lodger's wife, who chose to live in the country and apart from her husband and is now pregnant and poor but compensating with quasi-religious experiences—'

?

No.

Liffey made up the fire and polished the windows to let every scrap of light in, and settled down to cherish the baby.

Growth

Richard, told of the loss of Liffey's wealth, frittered away on pretty things and useless things and delicious things, was first irritated, then relieved, and then filled with a great sense of protectiveness and love for Liffey, as if by her very helplessness she solicited something from him which she hitherto had not. He moved through the world with an added weight and dignity, so that presently his colleagues remarked to one another that Richard had changed.

'He's older than one thinks,' somebody said, and at meetings his voice was listened to, and not just heard.

Richard resolved to give up Miss Martin and Bella, and kept the resolution for a full week.

Then Bella got him drunk, on free champagne at a restaurant opening, and if he did with Bella, then why not Miss Martin?

And Helga was sulking slightly, as if thanks were not sufficient recompense for her ironing of his shirts, and the folding of his socks in the neat Continental way, not the angry convoluting inside out way the English had.

Eight weeks. The baby's heart beat strongly now. The inner ears were growing fast, although they still showed no external part. The face had nostrils and a recognisable mouth, and black pigmentation where the eyes were to be. Elbows, shoulders, hips and knees were apparent. The spine moved of its own volition, for the first time, although fractionally. The length of the foetus was two point two centimetres. There was no apparent room within for the soul which gave grace to its being.

Mabs, or so she thought, knew everything there was to know about Liffey. She certainly knew about Liffey's new poverty. Liffey used Mabs' telephone, having none of her own; and if she wished to be private had to walk a mile to the public call-box at Poldyke – a manual exchange, where it so happened that the operator was a friend of Mabs. Letters to and from Liffey were left at Cadbury Farm, for the postman would not walk up the track, and Mabs was not above steaming open any she thought interesting. Shop assistant friends gave an account of what Liffey purchased, and the doctor's receptionist, also a friend, passed on details of her health.

'She's having to learn to live like anyone else,' said Mabs smugly, observing that Liffey now bought groceries much as anyone else did, and that her order at the butcher's was for mince and sausage, no longer fillet steak and stewing veal. 'Her Richard won't like that!'

And it was true that Richard did not like it very much. The euphoria of his compassion and tenderness faded; difficulties, so bravely anticipated and overcome in principle, remained in detail to plague and depress him. With the merest suspicion in the mind that Liffey's skinny, shabby clothes might be chosen because they were cheap, she stopped looking chic, and looked dowdy instead. Her cooking – when she was obliged to use inexpensive ingredients, and deprived of the cream and brandy she liked to add to everything, from soup to stewed apples – was not as seductive as before. And what Richard had construed in Liffey as sexual delicacy, now seemed rather more like sexual limitation – for without a doubt what had occurred to Liffey had occurred to Richard too – that once a wife is financially dependent, she is sexually dependent too. Richard felt by that token the more in a position to criticise.

He cherished Liffey, of course he did, but no longer quite as an equal. He was almost sorry for her; he came down at the weekends because he ought, not because he wanted to. Nothing was said: the movement in their relationship was slight: too slight to find voice, but both sensed it.

Now he was rich, and she was poor.

Mabs knew it, and she was glad.

Mabs knew everything about Liffey except what she could not know – that Liffey's baby had spoken to her; settled clear and bright inside her and promised that everything would be all right. That Liffey, now, had powers of her own: that Mabs could no longer have Nature all her own way: that forces worked for Liffey too, and not just Mabs. Winter winds were on Mabs' side, and frost, and lightning and storms. Liffey loved sun, and breeze, and warmth; and they loved her. And spring was coming.

Danger

Tucker put the cows on Liffey's side of the stream field. One of them was pregnant. It bellowed and groaned one misty evening. It lay down: it shuddered: it jerked its limbs and arched its neck. It rolled its eyes in a terrifying manner, showing an expanse of red-veined white. Could any eye on earth be so large? A single leg, Liffey was horrified to see, stuck out from under its tail. A single leg, a calf's leg, in a frozen wave to the world, as if a frame of a film had been frozen. Blackish mucus gushed out around it, even as Liffey looked, and with it came a stench strong and disagreeable. Liffey looked and gasped and ran, crying for Mabs and Tucker.

Tucker was out. But Mabs was in the kitchen, watching television. She took a long time deciding what to do: whether to wait for Tucker or call the vet, and then finally came herself, pulling on a long pair of rubber gloves. Together they set off back up the lane. Liffey wanted to go back inside the cottage but Mabs wouldn't let her.

'Why don't you watch? It's always nice to watch animals being born.'

But it wasn't. The calf was dead when Mabs pulled it out by its emergent leg, tugging and grunting, while the cow lowed and moaned. When the calf's head came out, it was putrid; pulpy and liqueous. Then the cow heaved and groaned and died.

'Three hundred pounds down the drain,' said Mabs, furious. 'At least she wasn't a good milker or it would have been nearer four.'

And she left cow and calf lying there, and walked back to the cottage with Liffey. Liffey composed herself as best she could: she felt sick and wanted to sleep, but Mabs wanted to talk, it seemed.

'So you're going through with your baby,' Mabs said.
'Of course,' said Liffey, surprised.
'I'd have thought you'd have waited until you and your Richard are more settled.'
'Why?'
Mabs just shrugged, and Liffey felt, for once, wary, and as if forces she was not quite in control of were abroad, and dangerous. Supposing what happened to the calf happened to her baby? She wished she had not seen it.

Liffey feared the contagion of ill-fortune, as pregnant women do. Oh, show me no bad sights: sing me no harsh songs: let good fairies only cluster around the baby's cradle.

'Nothing to a termination these days,' said Mabs. 'Girls I know have it done in order to get away on holiday in peace. They don't mind a bit, up at the hospital. Funny thing, that cow that just died. Her fourth calf, and still something can go wrong. We mostly lose them first time round. Just like people. First babies are always the trickiest. Longer labours, that's what does it.'

Liffey folded her mind around the baby, to guard it.
'I couldn't possibly have a termination,' said Liffey.

Mabs did not like the firmness of Liffey's response. Liffey's baby, she began to feel, might be harder to get rid of than she had imagined. She felt it more and more acutely as the supplanter of her own, product of some process set up by Tucker and so stolen from her: she despised Liffey for a fool; she despised the baby for choosing where it had to grow. She smiled warmly at Liffey, dispelling most of Liffey's doubts, but not all. Liffey, for once, had noticed Mabs' ill-will.

'You'd better get up to the doctor soon,' said Mabs. 'You look a little peaky.'

'I'll wait a bit,' said Liffey, and spoke gently, and smiled, as people do when they sense danger, and know better than to aggravate it, and went inside her cottage.

Mabs stood, still in bloodied rubber gloves and thick muddied Wellingtons, and stared after her for a little, and then moved off towards Cadbury Farm.

The lane was very, very old. The hedges were so high that in summer they would form a tunnel of green. Earthworks and barrows stood at the summit of the hill above the Cottage. Here the people of the Bronze Ages had lived, and died, worked their magic and honoured their dead, until the Iron Age invaders had arrived, and driven them out, and lived off a past which was none of their own. Once messengers had hurried up and down the lane, with good news and more often bad, and mothers, at their coming, had clutched their children to them, and fathers wondered how to turn ploughshares into swords, and stood there wondering too long.

Liffey stood in the kitchen and watched Mabs plod away, and wondered why she was afraid, and realised, of course, it was the dead calf and the dying cow which had upset her. Unreasonable to blame Mabs for what was Nature's fault.

At about the same time as Liffey witnessed the death of the cow, Richard was obliged to rescue the Nash's cat from the gutter, where a passing car had flung it to die. In the end he could not nerve himself to pick the animal up, fancying its dead eye was glaring at him, and while he was hesitating Helga, with alarming speed, came running out of the house, scooped the remains up into a plastic bag and dumped them into the dustbin, and got back to her cleaning as if nothing had happened. Richard was sick.

Liffey rang her mother and told her the news.

'I suppose you know what you're doing,' said Madge. 'Is it what you want?'

'Yes.'

'Why?' asked Madge, disconcertingly.

'I suppose because it's natural,' said Liffey, brightly.

'So are varicose veins,' said Madge.

'It's not as if I had a career,' said Liffey tentatively, over the crackling line to her mother far away. 'It's not as if I was good at anything else. I might as well use up my time having a baby. I might even be a born mother.'

'Not if you take after me,' said Madge, which might almost have counted as an apology. 'Aren't you too frightened? You know what you're like about pain.'

Liffey realised at that moment that she would never, ever, receive her mother's whole-hearted approval. Marks would be given, but marks would always be taken away. Six out of ten for overcoming cowardice: three out of ten for indulging her own nature and having a baby: and there she was, with an average four-and-a-half out of ten, when a pass-mark to mother's love was five.

So we live, as daughters; and, as mothers, are astonished that we elicit the same sad anxiety from our progeny. It was not how we meant it to be, when we dandled them on our knees.

'So you're having a baby in the country,' said Madge, 'while Richard works in London. Is that wise?'

'It's what has to be,' said Liffey. 'Not what I want. As soon as Richard gets Mory and Helen out of the apartment we'll be together again.'

'You could afford something else,' said Madge. 'What's the matter with you?'

Liffey did not want to hear the note of relish in the mother's voice when she explained about the money; she put it off. 'I like it down here,' said Liffey, and a ray of sun broke through the clouds, and she knew that it was true. Only that some danger lay across the land like a sword.

Madge hiccuped on the other end of the line, and Liffey wondered if she were drunk again, and along with the dreary everyday feeling that she had failed to live up to her mother's expectation of her, there now travelled another strand, sharply painful: of anxiety for her mother's welfare. The fear of the child, back from school, whose footstep hesitates at the gate of the house, wondering what's to be found within. Liffey remembered that, too. Her heart beat faster: her hand trembled: tears started in her eyes.

'It's all right,' said the baby, suddenly and unexpectedly. 'All that is past. Be calm, be still.'

And Liffey was, and Mabs, listening in on the extension, knowing only what was available to her to know, wondered why the tone of her voice changed.

'Why don't you come down and stay?' asked Liffey. 'It's going to be so lovely now spring is coming.'

'I was never one for nature,' said Madge, presently, cautiously, 'or for family either. But I suppose it is the kind of thing a mother is expected to do. Once you're given a label you never escape it. I'll come down presently if I can find the time.'

Liffey, to be hung for a sheep as well as a lamb, telephoned Richard's parents.

'A baby!' cried Mrs. Lee-Fox, 'how wonderful.' But in her voice Liffey could hear shock and despair. Now Richard and Liffey were married for good, for ever: they had joined not as children join, for fun and games, but as man and wife, together, as parents, to face trouble and hard times. Mrs. Lee-Fox was in danger of losing her son.

Liffey wondered if she had always heard the other voice, the tone that lies behind the words and betrays them: and if she had heard, why she had not listened? Perhaps she listened now with the baby's budding ears? And certainly this disagreeable acuity of hearing diminished within a week or two: perhaps because Liffey could not for long endure her new sensitivity to the ifs and buts in Richard's voice when he assured her he loved her: perhaps because the matter of hearing was, once properly established, less in the air so far as the baby was concerned.

Mrs. Lee-Fox handed Liffey over to Mr. Lee-Fox, who repeated his wife's enthusiasm, and the phone, following a misunderstanding as to who was actually to talk to whom, went down rather abruptly. Liffey did not telephone back.

Mabs put down the extension and called Liffey into the kitchen for a cup of tea.

Later in the week Mabs sent Tucker up with some new-laid eggs from her hens. Tucker smiled at Liffey in a friendly and ordinary manner, and did not outstay his cup of tea and biscuit.

Liffey used two of the eggs for breakfast the following day. On the mornings she did not feel sick, she felt extremely hungry: with a kind of devouring, none-selective hunger, as if already feeling the need to stock up now for hard times ahead. This was one of the hungry mornings, when she was glad Richard was not about to witness her greed.

The first egg plopped perfectly out of its shell into the pan: the ball of orange yolk held firmly in a strong white. The second fell out in a runny, smelly, thin flow, yolk and white already mingled, leaving the inside of the shell stained a yellowy green, and spread across the bottom of the pan with unbelievable speed, so that the first egg was contaminated.

Liffey's heart beat: her hand flew to her mouth. She knew beyond doubt that Mabs had sent a message of ill-will. Her earlier doubt of Mabs had been transitory: had been washed away by civility, smiles and cups of tea. And as Richard had pointed out, to ask a barely pregnant woman to witness the delivery of a dead calf may be tactless, but can hardly be called a conspiracy. And he had laughed, and Liffey had tried, and managed, to laugh too.

The reasonable part of Liffey told her that she was being absurd, that an addled egg sent by a neighbour is a mistake, not an attack; she assured herself that Mabs had no reason to dislike her, that what had passed between her and Tucker was over, secret, and of no consequence; and that Mabs was truly the friend she seemed. The other unreasonable part of Liffey cried out in wild alarm, and would not be pacified. Her sins would find her out.

Liffey was not accustomed to being unfaithful. She did not suffer, as did many of her married women friends, from sudden overwhelming sexual passions for this inappropriate person or that. She was not practiced, as they were, in the arts of forgetting, and self-justification and mendacity. Liffey tried to forget, and could not. She tried to justify and failed. She wanted to tell Richard, but the longer the time that passed between the event and the confession, the more difficult that became: and the more occasions on which she and Richard, Mabs and Tucker were in the same room, sharing the same conversation, the same meal, the more implicit deceit there must be in her silence, and the more difficult it was to break.

It came to Liffey that she and Mabs were linked, through Tucker, in the mind, in a more compelling and complex way than ever she and Tucker had been in the flesh. It flitted through her consciousness that this was perhaps what Mabs had intended, but so fleetingly the notion did not take root, did not settle, did not open itself up for contemplation. Liffey continued to feel uneasy, as people do, when clues are offered, and in the interests of peace of mind and self respect, ignored.

Liffey walked to Poldyke and rang Richard from the phone-box there; and Miss Martin graciously allowed them to speak.

'Richard,' said Liffey, 'do you think Mabs could be a witch?'

Now Richard was in a meeting with a marketing man who wanted money to set up a feasibility study on the subject of community salinity centres, which he, Richard, could not recommend. When Liffey asked her question he already felt much practised in patience, and answered politely and quietly.

'No, Liffey, I don't. What are your reasons for suggesting it?'

'She sent up some rotten eggs this morning, saying they were fresh.'

'Liffey,' said Richard, reasonably, 'it is hard, even for a farmer's wife, to know what is going on inside an egg.'

Liffey accepted Richard's version of events; she was a stay-at-home wife: she had already begun to believe he knew best. She looked at the weather from out of her window: he journeyed into strange places, and knew many things, and understood them all. 'If you don't mind, Liffey,' he said. 'I am rather busy,' so she put the telephone down, and he reproved Miss Martin mildly for putting through a telephone call while he was in a meeting. Miss Martin wept secretly because he had reproved her, but her heart leapt at this rebuff of Liffey. Perhaps, she thought, he was at last beginning to see Liffey for what she was. Foolish, empty and useless.

Carol, in the telephone exchange, dialled through to Mabs to report.

Later in the morning Mabs came up to Liffey and said she did hope the eggs had been all right; one of the hens had been laying outside the nesting box and Audrey had found the cache and not told her until after Tucker had come up with them.

Mabs smiled and chatted about husbands and elm trees and babies and said it was high time Liffey went to see the doctor, wasn't it, and Liffey agreed, and realised she was being silly about Mabs, who was a good friend, just sometimes tactless.

'What was all that about witches?' asked Richard at the weekend.

'Just a silly idea,' said Liffey. 'One gets silly ideas when pregnant.'

Mabs asked them over for supper.
'Let's not go,' said Liffey. 'We haven't really got all that much in common.'
But Richard wanted to go.
'You wanted to live in the country,' said Richard. 'I would have thought you could find plenty in common. It's not as if you were the greatest intellect in the world, Liffey.'

He had come home on Friday, resisting the temptation to stay over with Bella for a smoked salmon festival, because he had been a little worried by his brief and surprising exchange with Liffey on the telephone. Now, since she seemed perfectly well and cheerful, he resented having made the sacrifice. He found it difficult to wind down on Friday evenings; he found himself looking round for people to confide in, or chivvy, or engage in argument or sexual provocation, while Liffey wanted him to sit quietly and stroke her hair, as if they were some still-life of a young married couple: by Saturday he wanted to do nothing but sit, and recover, while Liffey wanted him to be out mowing or digging and painting, and on Sunday he waited for the evening, passing the time with the Sunday papers, so that he could return to London, and real life.

It would be better, he told himself when Mory and Helen were eased out of the apartment and Liffey and he were together again. He would not need Bella or Miss Martin then. He would not have to justify his infidelities by finding fault with Liffey. He could still see some kind of future for them both – even a rosy one – it was just the present he found difficult, and in particular Friday evenings.

'You're never at your nicest on Fridays,' observed Liffey.
'I'm tired,' he said.
'But not too tired to go up to Mabs and Tucker?'
'No,' said Richard.

There was something different about Richard these days, thought Liffey. A kind of snap of power; a glint of ice behind the boyish eyes: she saw that he might indeed become something significant in his organisation. She was not sure she wanted that. They were to have roamed together, hand in hand for ever, through the long tangled grasses of life.

She sat at Mabs' dinner table and felt frail, and rather ill, and tired, while Richard and Tucker talked about fertilisers, about which Richard was surprisingly knowledgeable, and milk yields, and Mabs urged Liffey to eat up the gristly, fatty lumps of pork in her plateful of meat stew. Richard thought how peaky Liffey looked, and had a sudden longing for Miss Martin's solid plumpness. He caught Liffey's eye, and she smiled at him, and there was a quality of sadness in her smile, as if she mourned a lost innocence.

Resolutions

'Bella,' said Richard, later in the week, 'all this is getting on top of me. It has to stop. It's not as if it were love.'
Bella just laughed. It was not easy to hurt Bella. She sat on top of him, breasts full and firm, swaying backwards and forwards calmly and slowly and smoking a cigarette, which he supposed was ridiculous but nevertheless appealed to him.
'If it were love,' said Bella, 'I wouldn't be doing it. Love hurts. This is just sex.'
Richard's feelings were wounded. He thought she ought to love him. He thought that her not loving him might be dangerous, making him more inclined to love her. He would wait until she loved him and then, having given her back a whole range of feelings she had forgotten that she had, would quietly and gently leave. That was what a man could, and did, do for an older woman.

He could wait until Miss Martin was out of love with him,

and then quietly and gently leave her. That was what a kindly man did, when the object of someone else's unrequited love. Richard wanted to do his best for everyone.

Mr. and Mrs. Lee-Fox rang Richard and said they'd pay for Liffey to have her baby as a private patient, so she didn't have to go through the ordeal of a public ward.

It was a light, friendly, easy telephone conversation: one parent on each of two telephone extensions. Richard knew it had taken them a good week of urgent, desperate, anxious conversation, planning and sleeplessness, to achieve this ease, and unanimity. So major decisions had always been dropped into his life. First closed doors, raised voices kept determinedly low: the feeling of agitation and argument in the house, then bombshells presented like grapenuts at breakfast. You're going to boarding school. We're going away: you're to stay with Aunt Betty. We've written to your school: you're having extra tutoring.
'Not in front of the child,' the Lee-Foxs had agreed on their honeymoon – both having been the victims of naked parental conflict. Never in front of the children. Our child, as it turned out to be. Had it been children, such resolutions might have been abandoned.

Richard, at his office, was a great protagonist of open decision making. His every thought, his every conclusion, his every action was recorded by Miss Martin, and circulated throughout the department. Never, thought Miss Martin, was there an office from which streamed so many memos and minutes.

'We'll hide nothing from our child,' Richard said to Liffey on one of the rare occasions he spoke about their coming baby. 'We won't let happen to it what happened to me.'

He passed on the news of his parents' offer to Liffey.
'Have it privately?' Liffey was unenthusiastic, thus surprising Richard. 'No. I'd rather have it like anyone else. I don't want to be thought special. I'm not.'

So then Richard had to ring his parents back, and in refusing their offer sound both ungracious and ungrateful.

'No,' said Bella, darkly, nibbling Richard's ear. 'I don't think this is the dawn of social conscience in Liffey. I think it is self-interest. In private wards you bleed to death by yourself. At least in the public wards there are other patients there to help you.'

'You're not at all nice about Liffey,' complained Richard. 'You should remember I'm married to her and be more tactful. Don't you feel in the least guilty about her? You are taking what is hers by rights.'

'No man is the rightful property of any woman, and vice versa.'

'But you're liberated. I thought Liffey was supposed to be your sister.'

'So she is. She is welcome to Ray any time she likes. Perhaps she would like to come and stay for the weekend?'

'I don't want Liffey anywhere near this house,' said Richard with some passion, but Bella curled her tongue around his, and although the texture of her flesh between his thighs did not have the resilience of Liffey's or the firm solidity of Miss Martin's, it had a kind of practiced feel, as if sexual impulses travelled a well-worn, easy path, coming and going with conviction, and marvelling at this, he stopped worrying about Liffey.

Miss Martin was not so outspoken when it came to her feelings towards Liffey. She confined her comments to ums and wells and I sees, but timed so that Richard would begin to see Liffey as Miss Martin saw her – as someone damaging to his professional, emotional, financial and physical well-being. I am one of the world's givers, said Miss Martin, by her very lack of sexual response, lying beneath Richard in hotel, or board room, or cloakroom; I am not one of the world's takers. Not like Liffey.

Liffey, whom she had never seen. Liffey, the boss's wife. Above her in status: the marriage partner, not the concubine. Concubines travel through the house by night, with long needles to plunge into the hearts of wives. They kill if they can, through love, spite and anger mixed.

Investigations

Eleven weeks. Liffey's baby had eyes beneath solid eyelids, a nose and rudimentary hands and feet. It weighed two grams. It lay safely in a sac of amniotic fluid. It rocked as Liffey walked.

Liffey felt that her baby was sufficiently rooted in the world to stand a little classification and investigation, of a scientific and medical nature, and made an appointment to see Dr. Southey on his weekly visit to Crossley.

Mabs kindly drove Liffey in, but mistook the time of the doctor's first appointment, and did not wait to check that the surgery was open, so that Liffey had to wait in the cold and rain for nearly an hour.

Dr. Southey, the same young man who had once nearly run Liffey over, in a car which appeared too big for him, was serious, kind and well trained in psychosomatic medicine.

When he reproached Liffey for not having attended earlier she made no reply, and he took her reluctance – how could she say that she had not wanted the baby frightened away – as a sign that she was unenthusiastic about her pregnancy. And the fact that she was cold to the touch reinforced his sense of unease. She was at first reluctant to be examined internally, and he suspected that she was neurotic.
'Why did you have to do that? What did you discover?' she demanded, afterwards.
'That your dates are about right, that there are no tumours,

or abnormalities of your pelvis, no major infections, no ulcers on your cervix, and that the size of the pelvic cavity, and its outlet, are reasonable.'

'You mean I have minor infections.'

He sighed.

'Giving information to pregnant women is impossible,' he said. 'All I mean is, if you have minor infections, I cannot detect them.'

She looked at him, strong chinned and mutinous, and he decided that he liked her. But that she was too thin.

'I want all the information you have,' she said. 'It's my body and my baby, and I'm not a fool.'

'I daresay not,' he said, 'but that won't stop you going into a grey depression because you misunderstood what I say. Better, in my experience, to say nothing. I took a cervical smear while I was about it.'

'What makes you think I have cancer?' she demanded, and he laughed, thinking his point well made. Presently she smiled, too, and after that they got on better.

He took blood from a vein.

'What's that for?'

'To see if you have syphilis.'

'Is it going to be like this all the time? One indignity after another?' she asked presently and he replied yes, that having babies was not the most dignified of processes. It was, he added, the ultimate triumph of the body over the mind.

'And of desire,' she said, 'over common sense.'

He thought she meant sexual desire, but she did not. She meant the overwhelming desire, of which she was now so conscious, to be part of the world about her: to be a woman like other women; to feel herself part of nature's process: to subdue the individual spirit to some greater whole. When, now, she knelt in the flower beds and crumbled the earth between her fingers to make a softer bed for a seedling, she felt she was the servant of Nature's kingdom, and not its mistress. And what sort of common sense was that?

He asked her what she did all day.

'I wait for my husband to come home at weekends,' she said. 'I wait for the baby to grow. I garden, I think, I listen to the radio. I walk up to see Mabs, my friend. Sometimes I'm sick, and then I wait to feel better. I do a lot of waiting.'

It occurred to him that she might have invented the husband, away in London; when she had gone he wrote a memo for the social worker to check.

Liffey Lee-Fox, whom everyone had envied, now the object of compassion and concern! Mabs, hearing about the social worker from Ellen, the doctor's receptionist, felt both gratified and annoyed. She asked Richard and Liffey over for Sunday lunch and added mistletoe-tansy to Richard's glass of nettle wine, and a distillation of pure ergot in Liffey's elderberry.

Audrey, the previous autumn, had searched the heads of rye stalks for the violet-black grains with their fishy, peculiar odour, where the ergot fungus had attacked the grain. She had done well, and her grandmother had been able to prepare quite a quantity of fluid ergot, and told Audrey to tell her mother to use sixty drops if she wished to abort a baby. Audrey wasn't listening properly and told Mabs to use six drops and the dose had in fact a beneficent effect on Liffey's system. She was twelve weeks pregnant; her period would in normal times have been due; she was suffering from a slight hormonal imbalance, and on the verge of losing some of the uterine lining – a process which, once started, can continue until all the contents of the uterine cavity, baby and all, have been lost. The few drops of ergot caused the uterus to contract, but mildly, and Liffey's condition being marginal, the bleeding stopped. Had her elderberry wine been fractionally more strongly dosed, the uterine contractions would have been powerful, and Liffey would have miscarried.

Richard, his entire system agitated by mistletoe poison, and mistaking his general restlessness for sexual ardour, wanted to make love to Liffey as soon as they arrived home, but she refused. Intercourse can be dangerous during pregnancy at the time of a threatened miscarriage; one contraction, as it were, leading to another, although at all other times in pregnancy is perfectly safe; an hour before the baby is born; an hour after.

Liffey, refusing Richard again! It made him angry. He went home on Sunday evening – he now thought of London as home – and went to Bella's bed, not she to the sofa in the study. Thus he defied the last of the proprieties. But where was Ray? At a discotheque with Karen – with one ear pierced by a silver earring. Bella had lost single ear-rings by the dozen over the decades – and could never bring herself to throw away the one remaining. Now Ray, following male teenage fashion, made good use of them.

Mabs waited, and waited in vain, for Liffey to come running with news of blood and disaster. She could not understand it. Mabs looked at another full moon, and at the Tor, riding the skies beneath it.

'I suppose it looks like a woman's breast,' she said to Tucker. 'And the tower on top is the nipple. Perhaps all those hippies are right, prancing about mother-naked up there. Do you think so, Tucker?'

Alterations

Tucker was not feeling so frightened of his wife. Mabs minded about his going with little Liffey, who was anyone's for the asking, and being able to make Mabs mind made Tucker powerful.

Mabs had noticed the change in Tucker and gone to her mother, who was already compounding a mixture of belladonna together with the bark and twigs of the Virginia Creeper which grew above Carol's door, to ensure Barry's fidelity and sobriety. But Tucker was not to know that.

Carol's husband Barry was as unaware as Tucker of the changes in his nature brought about by his wife. It was Carol's habit to mix foxglove pollen into the egg of his daily sandwiches, thus sparing herself from his sexual attentions. She herself took an infusion of lignum vitae – a hard and rare wood much imported from the West Indies in the nineteenth century and used for the axles of horse-drawn vehicles – dissolved in whisky, the better to respond to the advances of Dick Hubbard. The blacksmith at Poldyke had a few old lignum vitae timbers left, and in exchange for a kiss and a pinch and the promise of more was happy enough to let Carol scrape away at the black, hard, heavy wood. He could not see how it harmed him, let alone benefited her.

Carol and Mabs' mother was now teaching Audrey her skills and sometimes Mabs wondered if it was Audrey's doing that she did not get pregnant, in spite of the infusion of coca which she, Mabs, took daily, and which made her, sometimes, visionary; so that Glastonbury Tor swam towards her through the sky. Perhaps it was the coca, too, which gave her frequent rages a force which superseded the ordinary rules of cause and effect, and sent her perceptions a little beyond the ordinary, piercing extra deeply into the crust of reality.

Inside Mabs (1)

But coca or not, visions or not, Mabs did not become pregnant. Tucker's sperm swam obediently to meet her monthly ovum, and fertilised it well enough; the ovum dutifully developed the required choriomic villi with which to embed itself into the waiting uterine wall, but then proceeded with too laggardly a pace along the fallopian tube, arriving in the cavity of the uterus eight days after fertilisation instead of the required seven, and by that time had ignobly perished, for lack of a suitable foothold, or villihold.

It would require a very special drug to meet such a specific need, and the drug was not coca.

Inside Liffey (8)

Thirteen weeks. Liffey's waist thickened. She had to tug at her jeans to do them up. Her uterus was distending: the amniotic sac within measured four inches in diameter and the foetus was three inches long. The baby's face was properly formed: its body curled in an attitude of docility; resting, waiting, listening, growing. What it most needed now was time, which Liffey, by her love and caution, must supply.

Twenty-seven weeks to go. The most dangerous days were over, for the baby's organs had properly formed and no major congenital abnormality had become apparent – nor, now, were likely to – which might lead to miscarriage. Although the baby could still, of course, be expelled if the mother body for some reason or other rejected it – even though there was nothing in the baby's own ordination, as it were, to lead to this sorry conclusion. But any drugs or infections introduced into the mother's body would now have the barrier of the placental wall to cross and could harm only in extreme circumstances.

And there was, of course, the one great hazard to this baby's survival, still undiagnosed by the outside world, in the fact that the placenta, now fast forming, had lodged in the uterine wall beneath the foetus instead of to one side of it. For here the choriomic villi of the fertilised egg had clawed and stuck and now, where they had first attached, were developing with vast speed, into the complexity of the placenta, linking itself with arteries to the foetus, separating the mother's circulation from the baby's, selectively transfering to the baby oxygen, carbohydrates, fatty acids, proteins, amino acids, vitamins and essential elements, removing excreted products, carbon dioxide and urea for the mother to dispose of through her own system – but also, alas, by virtue of its unusual position, blocking the baby's eventual path to the outside world.

It was as if the fertilised egg, on its way out of Liffey's uterus, had grabbed its last chance: clung where it could and not where it ought. A lucky, hopeful, still surviving baby.

Upsets

Richard wrote to Liffey in the middle of the fifteenth week.

It's ridiculous, we really ought to get a telephone. I've been promoted and I can't even ring you to tell you! £60 extra a month! Of course tax will take £30, but never mind. When the baby comes at least we'll get an allowance for that. Only another six weeks, when the summer train services begin, and I'll come down mid-week as well as weekends.

Liffey cried. She had expected that Richard would commute every day once the summer came. So had he, once upon a time. But circumstances changed.

'I'm now Junior Product Manager on Beesnees Soup,' wrote Richard, in a letter which was delivered by Audrey, and bypassed Mabs:

It's a real challenge: the salinity factor has yet to be solved. It means a certain amount of travelling, to factories, sales conferences and so on, but at least all in this country. The jet-set life comes later! Darling, I'm afraid I have to be in Edinburgh this weekend, so do look after yourself. And please try and make some friends: you keep yourself much too much on your own. Shall I ask your mother to come down? I hope you're seeing something of Mabs and Tucker: they're real friends to you: you mustn't get all funny about them, the way you sometimes do. I'm enclosing £20 for food and so on. Now be careful and write down what you spend. You know what you're like. Love, in haste, Richard.

'Isn't Richard coming home this weekend?' asked Mabs that Saturday morning, bringing round a drop of cider for Richard to try. She and Tucker did not drink cider themselves, finding it a sour and disagreeable drink, but they knew that Richard delighted in it, detecting species of apples and vintages as he drank, with an interest and knowledge that country people seldom displayed.

'Richard's away on business. He's been promoted. Isn't that wonderful?'

'But what about the cider?' Mabs seemed quite disappointed.

'I'd like to try it,' offered Liffey.

'It wouldn't do you any good,' said Mabs, 'in your condition.'

But Liffey insisted, and tasted it, there and then, and presently, quite liking it, drank a glass or two more, and later that night had an uprush of sexual desire which disconcerted her. Had Tucker put in an appearance, she would have unlocked the door to him, but Tucker did not: Mabs entwined her long legs around Tucker's middle and held him fast.

While Richard, in and out of Miss Martin, passed through the wilds of Cumberland on the way to Edinburgh, Bella and

Ray went together to a newly opened fish restaurant in Fulham.

'There's nothing wrong with what I feel for Karen,' said Ray. 'I don't want you to think that, Bella. I don't want to upset you.'

'The only thing that upsets me,' said Bella, 'is your taste. Why don't you fuck her and get it over?'

Bella rose and left the restaurant, but not before slipping twelve oysters into a plastic bag.

'Where are you taking those?'

'Home to the children.'

Bella forgot to put the oysters in the refrigerator when she got home and left them on the kitchen table. The cat, an instant replacement of the one run over, ate them and was found ill to the point of death the next morning, and had to be taken by Helga to the vet. It was a journey of two miles but Bella would not let Helga take a taxi. She had to walk.

'The vet's bill's going to be bad enough, let alone a taxi!'

'Don't think I'm going to pay the bloody vet's bill,' said Ray to Bella, but absently, without acrimony. Really, he could think of little else than Karen: her long, somehow unformed legs, her plump, smooth face, still unmarked by woe and indecision: her little hands: the way she moved about the world, choosing between one happy option and the next: living by choice and not necessity.

The cat died in the carrier bag on the way to the vet. Helga did not cry, but Tony and Tina did, when they heard the news.

'Supposing it had been us?' asked Tony. 'The oysters were meant for us.'

Everything seemed upset that weekend. Routines were altered and not for the better.

That Saturday night Carol told her husband that she was going over to Mabs, and made him a nice cup of tea before she went. He did not drink the tea, since the shepherd's pie she'd made had given him indigestion – the onion was still raw, the mince lumpy and the flour thickening barely cooked – and as a result did not fall asleep over Match of the Day. He heard mice nibbling and rustling and rang Mabs to ask to speak to Carol, and Tucker answered and said no, Carol hadn't been round. Funny, thought Barry, but quite soon Carol came back and said she hadn't gone up to Mabs after all but had stopped by her Mum's, who was having trouble with a bee swarm. The fright, or suspicion, or unease, or whatever it was which had churned round in his heavy, kindly, trusting mind, stirred him strangely, and he paused in the middle of his swift, embarrassed, usually silent love-making and asked his wife if she loved him.

'Of course I do,' she said.

'Idiot,' said Mabs to Tucker, when she finally got back to bed. 'I had to run all the way down to the estate office. Haven't I got enough to do?'

'I'm not going to tell lies for anyone,' said Tucker. 'Especially not for your sister, who is a married woman but having it off with Dick Hubbard.'

'She fancies him,' said Mabs. 'She can't help herself. And Dick Hubbard's more use to us than Barry ever will be. Thank your lucky stars it's you I fancy, Tucker.'

'It'd better be,' said Tucker, 'or I'd knock his bloody head off, whoever he was. Yours, too.'

He would have, as well.

In other rooms at Cadbury Farm Mabs' children slept, uneasily. They were left-over children; out-grown their usefulness as Mabs' babies, left to get on with their lives as best they could. Eddie, of all of them, wouldn't accept his fate. He would sidle up to his mother and muzzle into her crutch, as if trying to get back in. All it did was disgust her. She disliked him for his soppy ways, his running nose, his watery eyes and the dull reproach therein. The others were tougher, or more sensible, and kept their distance and grabbed the baked beans, and shut their eyes and minds to night-time visions of strange people who belonged to long ago. There had been a farm on the site when the Romans came, and uncooperative people there who had to be killed to be quieted, but still weren't quiet.

To Tucker, the children were part of the landscape, like the cows and the farm, and the dogs. He hoped that when the boys grew bigger they would help on the farm. He did not see how the girls could be much use to him. Cattle were fed a carefully calculated amount in terms of cost and nourishment, in order to return a profit in milk and meat yield. Sometimes it cost too much to keep the animals alive, and then it was best to slaughter. You knew where you were with animals. But the girls just ate and ate and grew and grew and what return was there in that? Some other man would presently have the benefit of them. To nurture girls seemed to Tucker an absurd philanthropy.

Mabs slept. Tucker couldn't.

Better, thought Tucker, Mabs dreaming beside him, to satisfy the pleasure of begetting via some other man's purse – Liffey's body; Richard's income. Richard was a good enough man on a fine day in a rich season, but not much use when the cold wind blew. In the meantime there was something to be learned from Richard – the fresh wind of new ideas. He could feel them ruffling the surface of his mind. And such was Tucker's sense of mastery, via Liffey's body, Liffey's baby, (which he had come to assume, if only from Mabs' attitude, was his) that he could condescend to Richard, secretly; while Richard condescended to him, openly. Tucker thought he would visit Liffey again, before long, so she did not forget.

Tucker grew sleepy. He saw the world was composed of virgin ground: of furrows waiting to be ploughed. Seed to be dropped, watered, nourished: then to grow. That was the wonder of it. Perhaps if Mabs was to have her baby, visiting Liffey again was not a good idea. Perhaps a man used his fertility up: burying himself too often in already fertilised ground might weaken his capacity. Tucker would resist the temptation, which was, after all, not the temptation of the flesh, but the temptation of laughing at Richard. Who spoke well, wrote well, thought well, earned well, dressed well, but could not look after a wife.

Tucker laughed and slept.

The sun, rising in the east, sent streams of early light westward and caught the Tor in brilliance, beneath lowering dawn clouds.

Sixteen Weeks

The baby weighed five ounces and was six inches long. It had limbs with working joints, and finger and toes, each with its completing nail. It was clearly male. It lay curled in its amniotic sac, legs crossed, knees up towards its lowered head, which it sheltered with little arms. Its lifeline, the umbilical cord, curled round from its stomach and into the nourishing placenta. The baby stirred, and moved, and exercised, according to its own will and not its mother's: a little being within a greater being, grown out of it, and from it, but now itself, no longer part of the greater whole. It moved, but Liffey could not detect the movements: she would have to wait another month or so for that.

It was time to see the doctor again. Liffey remarked on it to Mabs.

'You look healthy enough to me,' said Mabs.

'They like you to have a check-up every month,' said Liffey.

'They like to claim their various allowances,' said Mabs, 'and keep their clinics open and their files full of forms, and if they're men they like peeking up your insides. Is it Dr. Southey you have? Tucker won't let me see him. They got him for indecent assault up in London. That's why he's working down here.'

The baby laughed, amused. Liffey heard.

'And when you think of that thalidomide business,' said
Mabs, 'I think it's best to keep out of their way. Those poor
little babies with flippers. Baby kicking yet?'
'Not yet.'

All the same Liffey used the telephone to make the appointment and Mabs was annoyed. Liffey was proving more
difficult to control than she had thought possible. The way to
bring her back to heel, of course, would be to send Tucker
down again, but that was now out of the question. Mabs felt
hollow and cold in her insides. She missed the movement of
the kicks and shruggings of an unborn child. Tucker filled
her up a little, from time to time, but it was not enough. And
if Tucker went to Liffey, ploughed about in those already
warm and packed places, she might find herself trying to kill
the baby by killing the mother. And that she recognised
would be wicked. The baby, being Tucker's was hers to kill.
Liffey was not.

Mabs offered to drive Liffey into the surgery.
Liffey declined.
'The walk will do me good.'
'Suit yourself,' said Mabs, and Liffey felt she had behaved
ungraciously. Liffey felt it was important to stay on the right
side of Mabs. She now looked to her, as a pregnant girl will to
an older and more experienced woman, for advice, company
and reassurance. She recognised that the advice was often
bad, and the reassurance marred by a blunt tactlessness, but
she did not doubt Mabs' good will.

All the same, if she could help it, she did not travel in Mabs'
car. Mabs' driving frightened her, and the way she was jolted
over the rutted tracks made her worry for the baby, and there
was something about the car itself which worried her. She
thought it was haunted.

Cadbury Farm, too, was haunted, but in a more positive

way. It was suffused with a sense of activity, both past and present. It had sprung out of the ground two thousand or so years ago, had fallen down, been raised again, been added to, a new beam put here, a rotten one replaced there, the generations passing the while; children born, others dying, genes shifting and sorting all the time within, languidly, but to a steady, beating, almost cheerful purpose. But the Pierce's car had none of this richness. It sopped up the energies of its occupants – Tucker's fixed and narrow will, Mabs' flourishing discontent, the children's sly and secretive passions – and all to no purpose, except the eventual disintegration of plastic upholstery and the rusting of metal parts.

Dr. Southey thought Liffey looked puffier and heavier than she ought. She seemed tired and anxious.
'Wouldn't you be better off back in London, with your husband?'
'There are problems about that.'
'What sort?'
'Oh, just practical. Not matrimonial.' She believed it, too.
'Anyway I love the country.'
'In what way?'
'It makes me feel more important.' She had the capacity to surprise him. He looked forward to her visits.

She lay on the couch, her stomach bare. Her uterus, normally hidden away in the pelvis, had now risen to a point halfway between her pubic mound and her umbilicus. His hand felt it out. He thought her dates were correct: the uterus was at the expected height for sixteen weeks.
'I have pains in my side,' she said, 'low down.'
'They'll go away.'
'What are they?'

The pains were caused by the shrinking of the corpus luteum of her ovaries – no longer required to produce the progesterone which had inhibited the shedding of the uterus wall during the first months of her pregnancy. The placenta had taken over the task. It was a sign that all was well, not bad. He said as much.

'You're sure it's nothing wrong?' she insisted.
'Of course it's not.'
'I do worry about it. I'm not used to worrying. I used to leave it to Richard to do the worrying. He always worried about his parents, if there was nothing else. Now he seems to have stopped and I've started.'
She laughed, rather nervous and embarrassed, reminding him of a hen gone broody, changing its nature from something greedy and silly, into something prepared to die rather than expose its eggs to harm, looking out at the world with a stubborn, desperate wisdom. And for what? To lead ten fluffy chicks back into the hen coop – and forget them a week or so later.
'Is there any treatment?' Liffey asked.
'The passage of time,' he said. 'Come and see me next week if you're still worried.'

Liffey went home.

The pains went. Others came. Liffey's ovaries were enlarged and developed a series of small cysts, which may have accounted for some of the fleeting pains. Her vaginal secretions increased; she passed water frequently.
'Yes, but why?' she made a special journey to ask him.
'I don't know,' he said, impatiently, 'these things just happen to pregnant ladies.'
He was busy: he had two patients with terminal cancer. He wished he could keep his respect for pregnant women. They seemed to him to belong so completely to the animal kingdom that it was almost strange to hear them talk.

The weather turned cold. A wet west wind blew day after day and took the blossom from the trees.

Liffey's body, which normally contained ten pints of blood, now had some twelve pints coursing through it, the better to supply her uterus and markedly swelling breasts, but diluting the concentration of red cells therein. Liffey became anaemic.

Mabs knew Liffey was anaemic because Carol's friend worked in the laboratory at Glastonbury and did the blood counts. The doctor prescribed Liffey iron tablets, and she took them, although they gave her indigestion.

Mabs felt that time was working for her. Mabs comforted herself with the thought that perhaps all she need do was wait, and the baby would leave of its own free will, and natural justice would be served.

'Why are you hiccuping?' Richard asked.
Sometimes he worried for Liffey's health, in case the punishment of the Gods was diverted from him to her. He was having altogether too good a time.
'It's the iron pills. I don't think I'll take them any more.'
'Don't be irresponsible, Liffey. You ought to be thinking of the baby, not yourself.'

Richard had a few bad weekends after that. His skies clouded over, for no apparent reason. Nothing had changed, of course, except his attitude to them. He was concerned for Liffey and her baby, and now his concern afflicted him. There were enough things in the world to worry about, surely, without the gratuitous addition of another? Parents, job, income, the car, accommodation; worries heaped in upon him one upon another: wives, surely, were meant to decrease the load of anxiety, not increase it with anaemia, with hiccuping, and puffy eyes, and the threat of the thing within? Miss Martin implied as much, all week. Hard to throw it off, at weekends.

The curse of the irrational, moreover, descended upon him. He dug the garden, he planted peas and beans; he hammered and painted when he meant to do nothing but rest and relax and compare cider and home-made wines with Tucker. He saw that the chains of fatherhood were already around him: he was preparing for the baby. As well be a humble cock-sparrow lurching to and fro, to and fro, straw in the beak for the nest: exhausted, bored and foolish, helpless in the face of his nature. Richard pulled a muscle in his back, and blamed Liffey.

Bella sent him to an osteopath, who made it better, and the next Friday Richard returned to Honeycomb Cottage with a car loaded with food and drink, and was loving and kind and considerate.

'We can't go on living like this,' he said. 'We don't see nearly enough of each other. But, oh, Liffey, London is such a terrible place.' And he reeled off tales of vandalism and violence: a colleague's wife mugged on her way home; someone's daughter's friend raped: someone else's apartment burgled: lead pollution in the air: the pale faces of children: the grey look of the elderly.

Liffey's words, once upon a time. Now Richard's.

Mabs and Tucker came over for a drink. Richard sat with his arm round Liffey, and Liffey, blooming in his new-found protection, wore a smock and looked really pregnant.

'You are looking well,' said Mabs. 'How's the anaemia?'
'Much better,' said Liffey.
'Wonderful,' said Mabs. 'It's the elderberry wine's done that.'
Mabs gave Richard a bottle of nettle wine to take back to London.
'Give some to your secretary,' said Mabs. 'Perhaps it will sweeten her.'
'Take more than drink to sweeten Miss Martin,' said Richard automatically.

Richard kept his second appointment with the osteopath, and the back pain returned. He decided to spend the next weekend in London. Ray had gone off to Brussels on a free fish-tasting excursion for two, but taking Karen with him instead of Bella, who had a dentist's appointment she couldn't miss. Bella was left at home, angry, which meant sexually extremely active: and Miss Martin's Jeff was also away for the weekend at an Encounter Therapy course, which meant that Miss Martin was free all Friday night, and her mother staying with relatives, so there was an empty house available for their love-making. Richard told Bella that he was with Liffey on Friday night, Miss Martin that he was with Liffey on Saturday night, and Liffey that he was at a weekend conference on permitted saline additives. Unfortunately, as often happened when he stayed away from home, his potency was unaccountably diminished and both Miss Martin and Bella were disappointed. Moreover Miss Martin had looked forward to making him a proper English breakfast, with bacon, eggs and sausages, and not the bread and jam and coffee with which Bella and Liffey apparently fobbed him off – but Richard only toyed with the plateful, and left the sausage altogether, and she felt he found her home rather ordinary and suburban. But of course he had hurt his back, and that clearly affected his enthusiasms – sexual, culinary and aesthetic.

Richard blamed the osteopath.

Trouble

Mabs thought she might be pregnant. Her period was late. She felt heavy. She brought the children home iced lollies, and took Eddie to the dentist and let him sit on her knee in the waiting room.

Then her period started.

Storms clashed and banged around the Tor. Tucker laughed and Mabs' eyes flashed. Mabs went out with her mother before dawn and gathered wild arum, cherry laurel and henbane, in the grey light. Or rather Mabs pointed and her mother picked; Mabs was bleeding and wasn't supposed to touch. In any case old women make better herbalists than young. Mabs' mother chanted Hail Marys as she picked.

'Do shut up, Mum,' complained Mabs. 'That's the wrong sort of mumbo-jumbo.'

'It'll do,' said Mabs' mother. She didn't look like a witch, any more than did her daughter. She had a round, lined face and open features and wore spectacles which swept up at the sides in the fashion of thirty years ago. She was proud of her straight stature and good figure, wore tweed skirts and ironed blouses and went to Keep-Fit classes.

'And what are you up to, anyway,' she asked of her daughter, 'that the Blessed Virgin wouldn't like?'

Mabs smiled.

'Just putting a few things right, Mum,' she said.

'Because if you want to get pregnant,' said Mabs' mum, 'this is the best way I can think of, of making sure you're not. And what do you want more children for? You don't look after the ones you've got, and you're too old anyway. Now stop snivelling, or I'm going straight home back to bed.'

And indeed, Mabs stood up to her large knees in the long grass of the graveyard and snivelled, because her mother was being unkind. She might have been anyone's daughter.

Mabs persuaded Audrey to do the distillation, and added a whole half-glassful to a bottle of the previous year's elder-berry wine, and gave it to Tucker to take over to Honeycomb Cottage. Liffey would not be the only one to drink it, but she was beyond caring.

The six or seven drops of the distillation which Liffey swallowed did indeed lower her blood pressure, but without harming the baby. Her blood pressure, as the pregnancy advanced, and the level of progesterone in her body dimin-ished, was returning to normal. She no longer felt so faint, nor so disinclined to stand for long in one position, as the

173

circulation of blood through her various tissues proceeded more normally, although the blood vessels were not quite so relaxed as before. She was, in fact, beginning to feel well. Her complexion was smooth, her eyes glowed, her hair shone; she moved more lightly: she flung her arms around Richard; she bubbled and burbled and overflowed; she drank the glass of elderberry and felt obliging and friendly.

'How was she?' Mabs asked Tucker on his return.
'Looking better everyday,' said Tucker.
'Country air, country food, and country wine,' said Mabs. But he did not trust her.
'Mind you be nice to her,' Tucker said. 'She's done you no harm.'

Mabs was heating up hen food on the stove, and a musty smell filled the kitchen. The hens were off-lay again, and warm food for a day or two often started them off again. He came up behind her and ran his hands up her sides.
'She's pregnant and I'm not,' said Mabs, not looking at him. It was a confidence, and a question, and contained no threat.
'It might be,' said Tucker cautiously, 'that you're your own worst enemy when it comes to that. Takes a soft and gentle woman to have a baby, not one full of hate.'

She thought he might be right, and resolved to try leaving Liffey's baby alone for a while. Liffey was mid-pregnancy in any case, and the baby harder to shift now than at any time, and she could always return to the kill later on, if it did not work.

Time passed. Liffey had to use a safety pin to do up her skirt. She had gained twelve pounds: she had lost weight, as many women do, in the first three months of pregnancy, but the change in her diet from expensive protein foods to cheap carbohydrate bulk, had more than compensated. The extra twelve pounds, of course, included the weight of the foetus, the placenta and the amniotic fluid, and the increase in the circulating blood. Liffey could expect, through the course of

174

the pregnancy, to add about twenty-eight pounds to her normal weight. Now, at four-and-a-half months, she had added eight pounds more than Dr. Southey thought proper, but on the other hand her colour was better, her face less strained and the quiet life she led for five days of the week did her more good than the two weekend days with Richard could do her ill.

Richard's solicitor, in the meanwhile, wrote three more letters to Mory, which Mory did not even see, as Helen now destroyed all letters as they came through the letterbox. The kittens loved playing with paper shreds. Richard's solicitor, moreover, was having domestic troubles, his files were in confusion, and migraine headaches sometimes kept him away from his office for weeks at a time. He was a friend of Richard's father, had once known Richard's mother well and felt headaches coming on whenever he stretched out his hand to Richard's file, thus considerably delaying Richard's cause.

'Everything's under control,' he would say, whenever Richard rang, or Miss Martin, asking for news, 'these things can't be hurried. Tenancy disputes always take time.'
'Is that what we're in?' Richard asked, troubled. 'A tenancy dispute? I thought they were in illegal possession?'
'I know what I'm doing, young man,' said Richard's solicitor, merrily enough, but with a hint of asperity behind the merriment, putting Richard properly in his place. And when Liffey asked Richard if he trusted his solicitor, Richard replied, 'I know what I'm doing, Liffey. Tenancy disputes always take time. And he's an excellent solicitor. My father swears by him.' So that Liffey, in her turn, was put in her place.

Mory's application for a job in Argentina went unanswered.

Miss Martin's mother read an article aloud to her daughter, over tea. Its title was 'The Sticky Snare of the Married Man', and Miss Martin was worried enough to say to Richard, 'This can't go on.'

'What can't go on?' he asked, blankly, and she felt at once that she had been presumptuous, and fell into silence, and was the more easily manipulated afterwards.

She did suggest to Jeff, however, in desperation, that if he really wanted it, she would sleep with him before their marriage. But he said he wanted their married life to begin properly, and that he valued her purity very much, and explained what she had not known before, that his mother had been a 'wild' woman and disgraced the family very much, and he was determined to have as a wife someone who would not repeat that sordid pattern. So she apologised, and felt even more guilty than before, and interpreted that emotion as a new flux of love for Richard.

Mabs sat at the kitchen table, and glowered. The room was cold, although outside the sun shone. The cows went off milk, the hens stopped laying again, one of the mangy dogs lay down at the end of his chain and died. Mabs dragged the body inside the house, and wept with pity and frustration mixed. She laid it upon the kitchen table, considered it, rang up her mother to ask if she had any use for a dead dog, and her mother said no, but Carol might; and Carol sent Barry over in the van to fetch it back. Before he came Audrey stole a few of the coarse hairs from beneath its tail and taped them across Eddie's ear, which had started discharging as a result of Mabs' frequent cuffs.

Mabs contemplated the nature of a world which could kill a dog she loved, but keep Liffey's baby, whom she hated, safe.

Mabs decided that being good was no way to become happy, let alone pregnant.

Visitors

Madge came to visit Liffey. She thought it was expected of her. She came by taxi from the station, and fretted at the extravagance. She thought the thatch was unhygienic and the rooms damp, but grudgingly admired the view. She said that Liffey should not be pregnant, in as much as she had no job, no training, and now no likelihood of getting one.

'Richard will look after me,' said Liffey.

'I'm sure I don't know where you get it from,' said Madge, sourly.

'Get what?'

'Naïvety.'

'It isn't naïvety. It's trust and love.'

'There's always Social Security,' said Madge, 'when the money runs out, which I suppose it will soon. Do you keep check?'

'Of course,' lied Liffey.

Madge conceded that Liffey looked well; she advised her not to eat fish, which contained a great deal of cadmium and other poisons, and asked her if she were not worried about fall-out from Hinkley Point, a nuclear power station some twenty miles distant.

'I used to worry about that kind of thing,' said Liffey. 'Not any more.'

Mabs came round with damson wine, which Madge at first refused. Then she accepted, and sipped the deep red, sticky mixture.

'It hasn't fermented out yet,' said Madge, firmly. 'It has a bitter edge which will soften in time.'

And she poured her glassful back into the bottle and did the same for Liffey's.

'I see you're not drinking any yourself,' she said to Mabs.
'Doctor's orders,' said Mabs, vaguely.

'I think you're very foolish to drink that stuff, Liffey,' said
Madge, when Mabs had gone. 'Goodness knows what it does
to the baby.'
'I'm afraid you offended her,' said Liffey, reproachfully.
'She's my only neighbour and I'm dependent on her, and
she's very proud of her home-made wine.'
'I didn't like her and I didn't trust her,' said Madge. 'I get
girls like her at school sometimes. Wherever they are, there's
trouble. Heavy girls with good legs. They cheat at exams and
steal from cloakrooms and if they offer you chocolates, you
can be sure they're stale.'

But Liffey took Madge's advice in the wrong way, and felt
that her mother, far from trying to protect her, was
attempting to upset and worry her. She did not wish to be
told bad news, only to hear good news. It was a tendency
apparent enough in normal times, but emphasised now that
she was pregnant. Disaffection made her bold.

'Mother,' said Liffey, startling Madge. 'Will you tell me who
my father is?' It had been laid down between them long ago
that Liffey did not enquire into the circumstance of her
birth. Enough, Madge's look had always said, that I had you;
that I introduced you into the world, with considerable
difficulty, and without any great pleasure to myself.
'It's only natural to want to know,' said Liffey, into Madge's
silence.
'It might be better for you not to,' said Madge, filling Liffey
with instant fear, that her father had been monstrous or
deformed, or that she was the result of rape and that her child
would inherit criminal tendencies. She had told Richard, for
lack of any other way of accounting for herself, that her
father had been a student friend of her mother's, who had
died in an accident shortly after her, Liffey's, conception:
and Richard had amended that part of it to 'shortly after the
wedding' for his parent's ears.

Lying, which had once seemed an essential part of Liffey's life; the very base, indeed, on which it was founded – though a changing, shifting base, the consistency of an underfilled bean bag – now seemed inappropriate. The baby gave her courage: compounded the reality of her existence. She could not be wished away, or willed away.

'I want to know,' persisted Liffey, and heard the baby murmur its approval, and leap in delight. She put her hand on her stomach. 'The baby moved,' she said to her mother. 'Moved for the first time.'

'I expect it's indigestion,' said Madge, but Liffey knew it wasn't. The flutter came again.

'He was an actor,' said Madge. 'He assured me he was infertile. He'd had mumps when he was sixteen. When he made me pregnant he refused to believe it, thought I was trying to pull a fast one, and wouldn't have anything to do with you or me. Mumps in men makes only a very small minority infertile, of course, but you know what men are. They believe what they want to believe, and expect you to do the same.'

'What sort of actor was he?'

'Shakespearean.'

'Was he a good actor?'

'He certainly thought so. I didn't. He was the sweet-faced, curly-haired kind. Heterosexual, but who'd have thought it. He was very charming, and very boring. You know what actors are.'

'How old was he?'

'Twenty-five.'

It seemed strange to Liffey to have found a father who was younger than she was.

'You didn't want to get rid of me?'

'I did,' said Madge brusquely, 'but it was illegal and expensive and dangerous, so I didn't.'

'Could I get in touch with him? If he didn't want a child, he might want a grandchild.'

'I doubt it very much,' said Madge. 'He went to Canada to avoid a paternity suit.'

Madge left on the Friday afternoon – missing Richard by a few hours.

'Much as I'd love to see him,' she lied, 'I have a pile of examination papers waiting. I must get back. And they may have forgotten to feed the cat.'

Liffey knew that the minute she was out of sight she would be out of her mother's mind: she realised that children do not forget mothers, but that mothers forget children. That Madge had done her duty by her: had manfully taken the consequences of misfortune, had seen them through, and then put the whole thing from her mind – in the same way as, year after year, she would put a whole Upper Sixth out of mind, as it passed from the school into adult life, and out of hers.

Liffey waved her mother goodbye and knew that the parting was for ever. They would see each other again, no doubt, but that small part of Madge which had been mother, had been firmly swallowed up by the rest, and ceased to be mother.

Movement

Eighteen weeks. The doctor laid a stethoscope to Liffey's swelling abdomen, and she heard the beat of her baby's heart. 160 a minute.

Liffey, listening, wore on her face an expression of satisfaction, gratification and calm.

'What are you so pleased about?' asked the doctor. 'Anyone would think it was your doing. All you have to do is just exist. The baby uses you to grow. You don't grow it.'

Liffey knew better. She hugged her baby in her heart. Ah, *we*: we have done it. We are doing it. It is all going to be all right. Listen to the heart; there it is, the pulsing of the Universe. It never stops. It is available to those who listen.

'I felt the baby move,' she said.
'Indigestion,' he said. 'It's too early.'

Richard brought his washing home every weekend. Bella had told Helga not to do it any more.
'Liffey has nothing better to do,' said Bella, 'and you have, Helga.'
Bella's jealousy was spreading: ripples from the central pool of her feelings towards Karen. She did not mind Helga's eyes so often upon Richard, but objected to Richard's upon Helga.
'Women are so wonderful, so extraordinary,' Richard would keep saying. 'All so different.'

'We are half the human race,' snapped Bella, but he failed to get her point, and she ruthlessly sorted through the washing baskets and hauled out all Richard's underpants and sweaters and vests and shirts and socks and jeans and shoved them in a pillowcase and sent them back to Liffey.

Liffey washed them lovingly, treated them with softener, and dried them in the wind and sun, and ironed them and folded them; and presently Miss Martin, Bella and Helga were all to admire her handiwork. Miss Martin the whiteness of his shirt as he divested it, Bella the softness of a sock, and Helga the smoothness of vest.

Liffey looked in the mirror and was surprised. She was darker than she remembered. The increased pigmentation which accompanies pregnancy was more noticeable in her than it would have been in a fairer person. Freckles, moles, nipples, all became darker; and the hair on her legs, usually so light as not to need removing, had become darker and more plentiful. Liffey noticed them with alarm, as she took off Richard's safety-pinned jeans and lay on the doctor's couch, knees up, legs apart, at the twentieth week.

He put on a fine rubber glove to perform the examination, and did it, as before, with a cool professionalism which belied any notion that it might count as a sexual assault. 'Do you have to do this again?' Liffey asked the doctor and he replied, 'Yes, mid-term.' But offered no further information and she did not ask. She had accepted his part in her pregnancy: the father's part.

Ellen, the doctor's receptionist let slip to Mabs how well Liffey was doing. The next day Mabs brought Liffey round a tonic, made, she said, with honey and rosemary, but containing also dried mushroom powder, which she did not mention. Liffey took a tablespoon every morning.

Twenty weeks. The baby moved, there could be no doubt of it. A pattering, pittering feeling, like the movement of butterfly wings. Extraordinary. She walked all the way to Poldyke to tell Dr. Southey.

But listen, doctor, we have the whole world here inside!

Liffey told him, too, that her mouth felt oddly dry. That he could not explain, nor did he understand it. Her haemoglobin count was high, yet she complained of listlessness, she was pale, and her eyes were dull. The doctor sent the health visitor up to visit Liffey. Mrs. Wild, a competent lady in her middle years, reported a quiet, clean, orderly household. No, there wasn't much food in the cupboards but then it was a long way from the shops. The husband worked away, but then so do many in rural districts. He came home at the weekends. Most weekends. The garden was beautifully tended. No phone, but neighbours were close at hand. Nothing to worry about.

The doctor worried about her, all the same. He would have asked her over to supper at home, but Liffey had no transport, and he could not find time to collect and deliver her himself, and his wife could not drive. Besides, where would it end? The world was full of listless young women.

He did not have the strength to give them all the kiss of life. Nevertheless, he did what he could for her. He persisted: he asked Mrs. Wild who the neighbours were.

'Tucker and Mabs Pierce,' said Mrs. Wild.

'Eddie's mother?'

'Eddie's just accident prone,' said Mrs. Wild, defensively. He did not comment. He studied Liffey's card.

'I know what it is,' he said, laughing. 'She's overlooked. Mabs Pierce is one of the Tree sisters.'

Tales of old Mrs. Tree filtered through to the surgery. She was reputed to have dosed her husband to death with a cure for rheumatism; to have made horses limp and hens go off-lay. A woman whose son had jilted Carol had lost her hand in a food press the day after news got out – crushed to a pulp, and injuries by crushing were, as everyone knew, witch's doing.

'Because the mother's a witch doesn't make the daughter one too,' said Mrs. Wild, who had been born in Poldyke, although trained elsewhere.

'I hope you don't believe in witches,' said the doctor, surprised.

'Of course not,' she said, saving herself.

'Just as well,' he said, 'or they might have power over you. Those who don't believe in them can't be harmed by them, and Liffey Lee-Fox is not the kind to believe in witches. So let's rule out overlooking, and find another reason why someone with a high haemoglobin count – up in the mid-eighties – should be pallid and listless.'

'Marital troubles,' said Mrs. Wild.

'Quite so,' said Dr. Southey.

He asked Liffey to come to the surgery every week, instead of every two weeks: the two-week arrangement was a measure of vague unease about her: the one week of something nearing anxiety. A visit a month is the normal arrangement in mid-pregnancy.

'He must be worried!' said Mabs, when Liffey told her. 'And

you're not looking very well. I hope you're taking your tonic?'

'Oh yes,' said Liffey.

'Well, make sure you do. It's honey and rosemary. Best thing in the world if you're poorly.'

'It certainly tastes delicious,' said Liffey, and it did.

Tucker noticed the change in Liffey. He was angry with Mabs. He defied her.

'You stop doing whatever you're doing to her,' he said. 'Just stop doing it. What's bad for one is bad for all.'

'She's taken what's mine,' said Mabs.

'That's where you're wrong,' he said. 'There's always more than enough to go round.'

'But there isn't,' said Mabs. 'How can there be? If one has it, another one hasn't.'

It was a deep doctrinal point: a profound rift. Tucker had a vision of continual creation, streaming outward: Mabs of a fixed state Universe, of strictly limited riches. Her children felt it, dividing up the fixed and miserly amount of her love, and starving.

'Anyway,' said Mabs, 'what makes you think it's me who's harming her? More like the doctor's poisoning her with his iron pills. I know of a child who died, taking them out of his mother's bag and thinking they were sweets. If they'll kill a child, they can't be good for the mother. Someone should tell her.'

Tucker took Mabs, all dressed up, to the Farmers' Ball. She wore real sapphires and a green silk dress and they went in the new Rover they kept in the barn for special occasions. They had bought it with the help of a government grant for the purchase of farm machinery. He wore a suit and a tie. Dressed up, they looked quite ordinary: almost negligible. But they were pleased with themselves and took the Rover down the track to show themselves off to Liffey.

Liffey looked pathetic and wan, standing on the path outside Honeycomb Cottage, waving. The garden, beyond Liffey's energy now to control, was overgrown and tangled, and the evening light sombre. Liffey herself was too fat in parts, and too thin in others. Mabs, secure in green silk, thought she could afford to be kind.

Tucker put it to her another way.

'If you want to get pregnant,' he said, 'you'll have to do as I say. A man has to be boss in his own house. Look around you.'

And looking round, Mabs saw the force of his argument, saw, as he did, a natural order in the world about her, of male dominance and female receptivity: saw the behaviour of hens around the cockerel, the cow submissive before the bull: the bitch accepting the dog, the little female cats yowling for the tom.

Mabs even contemplated leaving the mushroom powder out of Liffey's tonic, but she talked the matter over with Carol who snorted and said, 'What are you talking about, Mabs? People aren't animals. Tucker talks like that because it suits him, not because it's true.'

Richard said to Bella, 'Liffey's looking awfully ill.'

Bella said, 'I don't want to hear about your wife, Richard.'

Richard rang up Mr. Collins, his solicitor, in the hope that there would be news of the apartment, and the routing of Mory and Helen, but only an answering machine replied, taking a message and promising a return call. No return call was made.

'You don't really want your wife to come back to London,' said Miss Martin, sadly. 'You're having the best of both worlds, the way things are.' That was, according to her mother's magazines, the way men were, and she believed them.

And even while Richard worried for Liffey, Richard knew that what Miss Martin said was true. His duty lay towards Liffey, but no longer his inclination. And what was a man to do about that?

Liffey, on her next visit to the surgery, accepted a lift in Mabs' car. She did not think she had the strength to walk. The rutted path was baked in the sun, and the car jolted and jerked fiercely.

Dr. Southey looked quite shocked when she came into his surgery.

'You're taking your vitamin supplement?'

'Yes. And Mabs next door makes me up a tonic.'

'What's in it?'

'Only honey and rosemary. I take it every morning.'

'Then don't,' he said, and added, on impulse. 'You're not still being sick?'

'Yes, quite a lot. Isn't that normal? You said not to worry about it, just to put up with it.'

'For God's sake, woman,' he shouted, 'where's your common sense?'

Where indeed? Out the window, along with independent judgment. The pregnant woman leans upon her advisor; no longer thinks for herself. He had heard it often enough at the ante-natal clinic. 'I feel like a cabbage: I look like a cow.' Large-bellied women, sitting in their stolid rows, legs apart, for comfort's sake.

Liffey looked quite startled.

'I meant not to worry for the first three months,' he said, more gently, relieved to have discovered the cause of her trouble. He prescribed some tablets, and Liffey fetched them from the chemist – as Mabs discovered from her friend the girl in the dispensary, but too late to do any switching – but in fact did not take them, memories of thalidomide in her mind. But she did stop taking Mabs' tonic and instantly felt better, and stopped vomiting. But she did not make a connection between the two events.

Dr. Southey assumed that the cessation of vomiting was due to the anti-histamine drug he had prescribed.

Mabs watched Liffey grow plump and bloom again. She

burned the bottoms of saucepans out, and slammed doors and hit Eddie and shook her fist at the sky, which provided a flash of lightning and a crack of thunder but little more.

Glastonbury Tor looked black from a distance, like a coconut cake covered by flies. It swarmed with tourists and hippies, and little knots of people trying to focus cosmic energies down from the skies with one device or another. It was a shoddy place this time of year, Mabs felt, its powers divided amongst too many purposeless people: covered with litter. She felt displaced. Liffey, on the other hand, felt merry and bright and companionable and more like other people. Ramblers came past the door, and mushroom hunters, and Mrs. Wild called again, and Audrey would come up and talk, and sometimes Eddie would just come and stand and stare.

'I hope you're taking your tonic,' Mabs said to Liffey. 'Oh yes,' lied Liffey, to save embarrassment and trouble. So she had lied to her mother, when asked if she had brushed her teeth, or done her homework. She had not quite given up lying, for it is a hard habit to break; it was to her advantage, now as then: she lied convincingly, and Mabs believed her, as had Madge before her.

Inside Liffey (9)

The baby was unharmed by the general depletion of Liffey's energies. The placenta took priority over the normal demands of Liffey's system. Liffey, as she vomited, suffered from lack of calcium, vitamins, proteins, fats and carbohydrates – but the baby did not. Liffey's fat deposits were broken down, as necessary, to provide what was needed.

Liffey was now seven months pregnant. Her heart was

enlarged. Its workload had increased by some forty per cent, it beat at a rate of seventy a minute – nine more than was its custom before she was pregnant. Her heart was, little by little, pushed further up her chest by her enlarging uterus. All this was normal, if extraordinary and uncomfortable. Liffey's lungs too, were working at considerable disadvantage, being pushed into a smaller and smaller area within her chest: her ribs were having to spread sidewise to accommodate them. She took large breaths from time to time: she was comfortable only on high chairs, sitting straight. If she slumped, she felt she could hardly breathe at all. She started piling up the pillows behind her at night. Just as well, perhaps, that Richard was only with her, now, on Saturday nights. He pleaded pressure of work on Friday evenings, and on Saturday took the early morning train to the country, and the one back to London on Sunday night. The local station was open again now, and had been for some months, but the notion of Richard being a daily commuter had long been abandoned.

He made love to Liffey reverentially, and she wished he would not. She had developed, through her pregnancy, a marked interest in sexual matters, and a desire for sexual experiment, and an almost seedy interest in pornography, as if her body was anxious to keep her in practice and her genitals lubricated. She did not understand it, and did not like it, finding herself searching through drawers for the sex magazines Mabs used to wrap her offerings of this and that, and which she had meant to burn but never got round to. She told no one, feeling ashamed: and as Richard seemed shocked if she wanted to change her position from that gentle one of nesting spoons, which was the most sedate her pregnant shape would allow, Richard felt uneasy and embarrassed. Sex with Liffey, for Richard, was an expression of affection and a mark of dedication, not of need fulfilled, or passion gratified, or desires sated.

Liffey suffered now from vague aches and pains. Her ligaments, in particular those in her pelvis, became softer and liable to overstretch. A group of moles on her forearm enlarged. The hair on her legs were so dark and so obvious she took to shaving her legs with Richard's razor. Her skin became rather dry and she itched and scratched a good deal. The veins in her legs, now slightly varicose, irritated. Her vulva did too, for the same reason. She developed thrush and painful little ulcers as a result, but they responded at once to fungicidal pessaries prescribed by the doctor.

'Thrush!' she cried in horror. 'But I'm so careful to be clean.'

He explained that the thrush fungus flies through the air, and that there is nothing it likes more than a warm, moist, pregnant vagina. Liffey, he said, was lucky not to have developed piles, or they would be irritating too.

In the City, in the Summer

In the city the streets baked, drivers and pedestrians alike were bad tempered, dog turds withered where they lay, sight-seeing buses held up the traffic, exhaust fumes hung about the unhurried air, and were breathed in by the foreign visitors, who sat outside cafés on makeshift tables, holding up the city's flow of business.

Mory and Helen kept the windows wide open: the electricity supply had been cut off so there was no refrigerator, and the butter melted before it could reach the bread: they had no money for the launderette – or rather none they were prepared to waste on it – and dirty clothes lay in heaps upon the floors. Helen would not wash by hand, and Mory could not. They seldom left the apartment together, fearing that if they did someone would nip in when they were away and bar the door against their re-entry. For these misfortunes they blamed Liffey.

On one of these hot days Helen recognised the writing on an

envelope, and saw that it was addressed to her, and refrained from destroying it and opened it. It was from her younger sister Lally, accusing her of murdering Lally's baby.

> You always hated me, [wrote Lally] because I was so much prettier and brighter than you, and could walk and talk before you, although I was ten months younger. And then you married Mory and thought you were one up because you were married before me, but then I got pregnant without even bothering to marry, so you had to have your revenge. I know all this because I am in treatment with a wonderful man who has explained it all to me.

Helen screamed and cried and grew purple and Mory thought she would choke.

'We can't live like this,' he moaned. 'What's gone wrong with our lives?'

Helen took a whole lot of sleepers and when she woke, said, 'It's this place. Everything's gone wrong since we came here. We've got to get out.'

'How?' asked Mory.

'Write to Richard,' said Helen, 'and say we'll get out if he gives us a thousand pounds to find somewhere else. Then we can have a holiday, get to the sun and out of this dump.'

Richard received the demand, and telephoned his solicitor, who was not there.

'You can't respond to threat and blackmail,' said Miss Martin, righteously.

'You haven't got a thousand pounds,' Bella pointed out.

'Your wife would suffer if you moved her now,' Helga pointed out. On those rare evenings when both Bella and Ray were out together Richard now joined Helga in her little attic room. He had been right about the exacting nature of her sexuality: he interpreted her neglect of his washing as a reproof, concluding that he failed her in some way. Indeed, he was so nervous of discovery by Bella, as to be unduly hasty in his performance with Helga.

Richard thought that Miss Martin, Bella and Helga judged the situation rightly, and said nothing to Liffey about Mory's offer. Pregnant women, he knew, should be spared undue worry. He had looked through the letterbox, in any case, on one or two occasions and seen the filth within, and wished Liffey to be spared the sight.

Richard felt inadequate in his dealings with Mory and Helen. He had been emasculated by the law; his instinct was to break down the door and snap Mory's neck, and throw Helen down the stairs, and regain both his territory and his pride, but these things were illegal and uncivilised. Nor could he find the courage to hurt his family's feelings by changing his solicitor. Frustrated in his masculinity in these respects, he felt obliged to reassert it by taking Miss Martin, Bella and Helga to bed: and inasmuch as it was Liffey's doing that Mory and Helen featured in his life at all, accounted her responsible for its general current unquietness.

He found his weekends at home increasingly unsatisfactory. Liffey was not so active about the house as she had been. There were dead spiders in his toothmug, and she put food on the table in saucepans, instead of dishing up properly. And there were no napkins. He had become accustomed to napkins, in the restaurants he frequented. But in his heart he knew that the trouble lay not in Liffey, but in his own guilt. He would find fault with her in order to justify his conduct: and the worse his conduct was the more he would diminish her. Liffey fails me in this respect, and that: therefore it is only reasonable for me to find consolation elsewhere.

He could not look her in the eye. He would rather be in London, compounding his offences, than face her trust.

Ray made matters worse by confiding in him.
'What am I going to do about Bella,' asked Ray, 'now that I have Karen? It isn't just the infatuation of a middle-aged man for a young girl – it is more like an appointment made by

destiny. Of course I'll wait. She's only sixteen. I shan't sleep with her until she's nineteen. It wouldn't be right. And then of course we'll be married. But that's three years pretending to feel husbandly towards Bella when I'm waiting to marry someone else.'

'So long,' said Richard cautiously, 'as Karen feels the same in three years time.'

'Karen's one of nature's innocents,' said Ray, with confidence. 'I wouldn't dream of presenting her with my feelings: she would be shocked and alarmed. But I just catch her looking at me sometimes – those pure green almond eyes beneath the long blonde hair – and I *know*, and she *knows*, and she'll wait for me—'

'Of course Bella might find someone else.'

Ray looked startled.

'I hardly think so,' he said. 'She's far too old in the tooth for that. Besides I trust her implicitly. It's just one of nature's cruel tricks – to keep a man attractive long after a woman is past it.' 'Quite so,' said Richard.

Complications

In the thirtieth week of Liffey's pregnancy Mabs went out into the night with a dead candle, and melted it down, and moulded the soft wax into an image of Liffey, stomach bulging, and drove a pin through its middle. An owl flew out of a hedge just as she struck, hooting and flapping, and quite scared her.

And then when she went back into the house to put the image into a drawer she found Audrey at the kitchen table, complaining of stomach pains. It quite took Mabs aback. She took the pin out, and in the morning Audrey's pains were gone. Mabs asked her mother to stick the pin for her. 'I'm not sticking no pins in any poor girl's stomach,' said

Mrs. Tree, crossly, 'just because you want to breed a football team. Why don't you look after the ones you've got? Something terrible will happen if you go on like this, and it won't happen to her, it will happen to one of yours, and serve you right.'

So the image lay in Mabs' drawer, without a pin, but with a hole through its middle all the same.

Next time Liffey went to see Dr. Southey and lay on her back on his couch while he felt, with firm chilly fingers, the outline of the baby, she noticed a flicker of surprise on his face. She always watched his expression carefully as she lay, thinking she might find out more from that than from his words.

'What's the matter?' she asked, sharply.

'Nothing,' he said, 'but I think we might send you up for a scan.'

'What's a scan?'

'A sonic picture.'

'Is it bad for the baby?'

'No.'

'Does it hurt?'

'No.'

'Why do you want me to have one?' she snapped the question out, first things first.

'The baby seems rather high, that's all.'

'Too high for what?'

'It might be nothing. It might be placenta praevia.'

'What's that?'

'The placenta is attached below the baby, not beside it or above it.'

'Is that dangerous?'

'If there weren't doctors and hospitals in the world, it might be. But as there are, it isn't. You can go in for the scan, by ambulance, tomorrow.'

'Ambulance? Am I delicate?'

'No. It's simpler and more comfortable and I'll be sure you've gone. Your husband might like to come too. It's nice to see a picture of the baby, after all.'

Liffey rang Richard from the surgery. Miss Martin answered the telephone.

'I'm afraid he's at a meeting, Mrs. Lee-Fox. Is it important?'

'No.'

'I can take a message if you like.'

'No thanks.'

Sad, thought Liffey, putting down the phone, that nasty things are thought important, but nice things aren't. News of death travels faster than news of triumph. Miss Martin did not tell Richard that Liffey had rung. He was not in fact at a meeting, but chatting with a colleague down the corridor. She did not think Richard would go home that weekend, and if any question of the phone-call arose, the passage of time would have clouded the issue, by the time he saw Liffey again.

Liffey went by ambulance to the hospital, and marvelled at how smooth the ride was, compared to what it was like when she drove with Mabs. She sat between two white-coated ambulance men, who were friendly, and wondered at her courage, living all alone miles from civilisation, nearing her time, and without a telephone. Liffey, hearing it put like that, felt, for the first time, almost sorry for herself.

'I have friends and neighbours,' she said. 'The Pierces.'

'Mabs Pierce? Old Mrs. Tree's daughter?' said one. 'Well, as long as she's a friend and not an enemy.'

'Why do you say that?' Liffey asked, but neither man would answer directly.

Liffey lay on a slab with her stomach oiled, and a technician moved a scanner back and forth, back and forth, over the mound of the baby, building up a picture on a screen, as a child makes the pattern of a coin on tissue paper, shading the circle with pencil. There was the curve of the baby's backbone, the little hunched head. Liffey felt both reassured and shocked, at what seemed an untimely manifestation of spirit into flesh. The technicians pointed and murmured. Beneath the baby's head, banning its exit to the world, was the shadowy boat-shape of the placenta.

Mabs felt her spirits rise. She dressed up and went into town and had coffee with Carol, and had her hair done, and looked at her face in the hairdresser's mirror, and saw again the face of a young girl, Tucker's bride, happy to have left her mother's cottage and become mistress of Cadbury Farm, pregnant and fruitful, in the days before she knew the depths of her own malice, and anger and greed. That's what I was, thought Mabs; that's what I still could be: happy and simple and good. What happens to all of us, with time? But when she got home, all the same, she stuck a pin into Liffey. Tucker's baby was not to live in Liffey: she had every right to stop it. Debbie complained of a pain, but Mabs took no notice. Liffey came to Mabs in tears.

'They think I'll have to have a Caesarian,' she said.

'That's bad,' said Mabs. 'Why?'

'Otherwise when labour starts I'll just bleed to death, and the baby will suffocate.'

'They always exaggerate,' said Mabs. 'Dr Southey loves to frighten women. He's famous for it. Have some tea? Or a glass of wine to cheer you up? I've got some of last year's plum.'

'I'll have some tea.'

Mabs made some rosemary tea and sweetened it with honey and put in a pinch of dried mushroom powder.

'Placenta praevia,' marvelled Mabs. 'Dr. Southey said I had one of those with Eddie. But it moved over by itself: they always do. I had a perfectly normal labour.'

'And I'm so far from the hospital; supposing I don't get there in time.'

'We'll look after you,' said Mabs. 'Come to that we could always deliver you ourselves. Think of all the cows Tucker and I have done.'

It was meant to be a joke and Liffey tried to smile.

Mabs rang Richard on Liffey's behalf since she seemed the only one able to get past Miss Martin, and told him that Liffey was upset and why, that the doctor was just being an alarmist, and that Liffey looked all right to her, and a

Caesarian, in any case, was perfectly routine. Liffey listened.
'I expect she's got it all wrong anyway,' said Richard. 'You
know what Liffey's like.'

Liffey went off to be sick and attributed it to nerves, not
Mabs' tea. After all, Mabs had drunk it too. But it was the
sort of thing she noticed, these days. When she got back
Mabs had put down the phone.

'He had to take a transatlantic call,' said Mabs. 'But he sent
you his love. He said Tina and Tony had got German
measles. I don't think he ought to come down until he's out
of quarantine, do you? If you get it the baby can be born
blind and dumb.'

'I thought that was only in the first three months.'

'That's what they say, but I had a friend had it at six months
and her baby was a mongol.'

Richard did not come back at the weekend, at Liffey's
request. Tina and Tony coughed and groaned and sweated,
out of sight and out of their parents' mind.

Richard had become suddenly afraid that the baby would be
born deformed, that out of the once beloved, wholesome
Liffey, a monster would emerge.

'That's guilt speaking,' said Bella. 'You believe you're so bad
you can't produce anything good.'

'I expect it's true,' he said, and wept.

'Christ,' said Bella, 'don't I have enough with Ray, without
you starting as well?'

Bella curled her legs around the small of his back and they
rocked and rocked, and Richard's tears passed.

'You'll feel better when the baby's born,' Bella assured him.
'When I was pregnant with Tony, Ray went on a gastro-
nomic tour of New Zealand; and with Tina, it was Tierra del
Fuego. At least you've kept within telephonic distance.'

'I don't like the thought of Liffey being cut open,' said
Richard.

'Saves you having to do your paternal duty and watch,' said
Bella. 'I'm sure it's unnecessary, anyway. Doctors just make

more money out of the National Health doing operations, than leaving things to nature.'

Liffey was frightened. The baby was silent. She felt that the scan had been in some way an insult to him: she'd been checking up on him. Giving him physical shape before he was ready.

The weather grew colder. It rained and rained, and slugs got the poor, sodden strawberries. Four cows broke through from Tucker's side of the stream, breaking down the fence, splashing through the water, trampling and munching her patch of vegetables. She asked Tucker to move them and he didn't, and she had been afraid to persist, for his kind and friendly eyes, as she asked, had taken on a speculative look and he had lain his hand on her stomach in the half-pleased, half-envious way people did sometimes, but which was somehow something different in Tucker, reminding her of what she would rather not remember. So there the cows stayed, staring and munching and splattering round her back door, and Richard not coming back for seventeen days, which was the incubation period for German measles, and a pain in her stomach every now and then, as if someone had pierced her through the middle with a laser beam, but which Dr. Southey told her was nothing.

As if a placenta praevia was not enough.

In-Laws

Richard's parents came down to stay as soon as Richard was out of quarantine. Liffey made the house as pleasant and pretty as a shortage of money and energy would allow. She dusted out cobwebs, and turned sheets side to middle, and noticed how quick the processes of dilapidation and depression were – when cracked cups were kept because there was no money to replace them, and burned saucepans scraped, not thrown away: and stained carpets merely scrubbed, and damp wallpaper patched. The houses of the poor take longer to clean than the houses of the rich: rooms must be tidied and polished before guests appear; a wealthy disorder is tolerable; the jumble of desolation is not.

Mr. and Mrs. Lee-Fox were shocked by the change in Liffey's appearance, but felt she was wholly to blame. She was letting herself go: she would depress Richard – she was young and healthy and had nothing else to do all day but look after herself – why was she not doing it properly? Mrs. Lee-Fox told Liffey how well she was looking, and remarked on how pregnancy evidently suited her, and looked forward to at least another six grandchildren.

Mr. Lee-Fox went further into the matter of Mory and Helen's occupancy of the London apartment.
'Of course it was a gift to you and Richard freely given,' he said, 'but we hardly expected it to be given away so soon!' He appeared to be joking; he smiled and smiled as he spoke. 'All the same,' he added, 'Collins is a fine solicitor; he'll get them out of there in no time. Of course the law of the land, these days, is on the side of thieves and vagrants.'

Mr. and Mrs. Lee-Fox liked their cups to rest on saucers, and their saucers on tablecloths and their tablecloths on polished tables, and Liffey did what she could to oblige. Her own daintiness seemed a thing of the past, her swelling belly on too large a scale to allow for a retreat into little, pretty, feminine ways.

When Richard arrived, having been delayed, or so he said, by queues of traffic leaving London, his car was laden with the exotic foods which once had been their staple diet. His parents marvelled.
'How well he looks after you, Liffey!'
'Worth waiting for, after all, Liffey.'
'All the goodies of the world on your doorstep, Liffey!'

'Why live near to the shops with a delivery service like this!'
'Isn't Richard a wonder! Where does he find the energy. Not to speak of the time. Makes the money, does the shopping, drives a hundred miles for a kiss, and comes up smiling!'
'Whose friends were they, Liffey, this Helen and Mory? Yours or Richard's?'

'Mine,' said Liffey.

Richard was kind, charming and hard-working all week-end. He was up early to make the breakfast, bring tea in bed for Liffey; then he fetched the papers, weeded the garden, mended the banister, peeled the potatoes, and washed up.

'Good heavens, Liffey, it isn't a husband you've got here, it's a servant.'

That night Liffey placed Richard's hand on her stomach, but he withdrew it as soon as he tactfully could. Being in his parents presence had focused the matter for him, forcibly. He did not want to be a father. He did not want to join the grown-ups. He wanted to be a boy-husband and have a girl-bride. Liffey was making him old beyond his years.

On Sunday afternoon, while Richard was out walking with his father, Mrs. Lee-Fox enquired further into Liffey's side of the family.
'Of course I met your mother at the wedding. What a brave and independent lady! I only wish I could have been like her, and flouted convention. But I never had the courage. What was your father like, Liffey?'
'Slippery, from the sound of him,' said Liffey. 'Apart from that I don't know.'
'But your mother *is* a widow.'
'No,' said Liffey. 'Unmarried and deserted.'

Mrs. Lee-Fox's hand trembled as she sipped Mabs' home-made plum wine. The wine contained a distillation of the seed of a flower known locally as 'Tell-the-Truth' and had been given to Liffey and Richard by Mabs on the grounds that, one way or another, it was bound to cause trouble.

'I'm glad you told me the truth, Liffey,' said Mrs. Lee-Fox. She wore many rings on her once pretty fingers and a thick gold charm bracelet on a still slender wrist. Her hair was grey and curled, and sad eyes battled for predominance over a mouth composed into an enduring smile.

'Thank you for telling me your secret, Liffey,' said Mrs. Lee-Fox, sipping plum wine.

'I shall now tell you my secret,' added Mrs. Lee-Fox. 'It's bigger than yours and I've kept it longer.'

'I've never really loved Richard,' said Mrs. Lee-Fox, her head spinning from Tell-the-Truth, 'because you see Richard isn't his father's child.'

'He has his father's nose and his father's neck,' confided Mrs. Lee-Fox, 'and his father is Mr. Collins the solicitor who treated me very badly. Talk about being seduced and abandoned!'

'No use looking shocked, Liffey,' reproved Mrs. Lee-Fox, 'because all women are sisters under the skin, and if this child of yours is Richard's I'll eat my hat. If it was his, he'd be here all the time. He's acting completely out of character, all this sweet talk and washing up; you're both of you putting on an act and I know what it is. You've cheated on him, Liffey, and he's agreed to stand by you.'

'No,' cried Liffey, on her feet. 'No!'

'Another secret,' said Mrs. Lee-Fox, calmly, 'is that Mr. Collins is an extremely bad solicitor, but I can hardly tell my husband that, in the circumstances, let alone my son.'

'I did my best to raise Richard properly,' wept Mrs. Lee-Fox into her glass, 'but he always reminded me of what I'd rather forget. And Liffey, Mr. Collins had a grandmother who was an Asiatic. I remember him telling me so. If the baby has slanting eyes, Liffey, for my sake, say it comes from your father's side. I have lived in fear of this for so long. It has clouded my whole life.'

Liffey put her mother-in-law to bed with a hot-water bottle.

When the older woman woke she seemed perfectly normal and the smile was back, and she and her husband departed with little conventional cries of pleasure and admiration and apparent ordinariness.

Inside and Outside

Thirty-four weeks.

'Still a placenta praevia,' said the doctor to Liffey. 'But never mind. We'll take care of you. And the baby will be saved the struggle of getting out, won't he?'

Ah, but what about me, doctor? What about my tight and stretching tummy? Where are you going to take your knife and slit it? From top to bottom or side to side?

'You'll have to ask the specialist,' said the doctor. 'I'll send you to see him this week.'

The hospital was large and new, hot and carpeted. Pregnant ladies walked bright corridors up and down, up and down, dressing gowns stretched to cover swollen tummies. Young men waited at telephones: faces elated or anxious or bored.

'We'll give you a bikini scar,' said the specialist. 'Just below the line of your pubic hair. Almost unnoticeable. That's if all goes well, of course. If we're in a hurry we do the best we can, for you and baby, and without a doubt the old-fashioned navel to pubis cut is quicker and safer; but there you are: you girls think of your figure more than your baby.'

Liffey didn't like the specialist. Nor did he particularly like women.

'We'll keep the baby inside you as long as we possibly can. If

you start to bleed, which you probably will, soon, because
the placenta's likely to tear when it's down there, you'll go on
bleeding until the baby's out. So when I say come in quickly
if you see so much as a spot of blood, that's what I mean. A
placenta praevia is rare in a first pregnancy. You're sure you
haven't been pregnant before?'
'Quite sure.'
'You're not hidinng anything?'

She began to think perhaps she was, such was the force of his
suspicion, his determination that all women were fools, and
knaves, and the enemies of their babies. She tried to think,
but could not: to give her past a reality acceptable to him.
Yes, I have had measles, and mumps – but a baby? Did I?
Her silence irritated him.
'Well, let's say you're just unlucky.'

Liffey thought, all of a sudden, Mabs did this to me. If she
was unlucky it was because Mabs had done it to her. She had
never been unlucky before. The baby danced and laughed,
to confirm her conclusion. Mabs was not a friend, she was an
enemy.

'Active little beggar,' said the specialist. His hands, she
acknowledged, however much she disliked them were experienced and competent. 'You're lucky to have kept him
inside this long. You're sure there's been no bleeding?'
'No.'
'No, you're not sure, or no, there's been no bleeding?'
Ah, he was a bully.

Never mind, sang the baby, never mind. I'll be all right. So
will you. Liffey felt she had to protect such charming
naïvety.

'No bleeding.' There will be no bleeding, either, until my
baby is forty weeks old, give or take a day or two. My baby's
no fool. Nor am I. I'll keep him in and he'll cooperate.

'He isn't the most tactful of men,' said the doctor, tentatively, of the specialist. 'But on the other hand, he won't let you die.'

Liffey was elated. She felt that things were better now between herself and Richard. She felt sure the baby would nudge the placenta praevia over when it felt like it. She did not believe her mother-in-law's account of her husband's birth. She would keep out of Mabs' way, and things would go better.

Thirty-four weeks. Oh, she was heavy, breathless, and languid, but she was still happy. Richard, had, for some reason, turned vegetarian so she worried in case she was not eating enough meat for the baby's welfare. Richard assured her that animal flesh did more harm to the human body than good. He wore a lovely pair of thonged sandals. They had a good weekend. He took her to the pub, which she liked but knew he hated. He had enough of people during the week. So he said.

Richard had lately met up with a girl called Vanessa. She had auditioned for a part in a television commercial, for oxtail soup, and failed to get it, but had given Richard her telephone number. She was an actress, had a degree from Oxford, a flat and slender crutch across which jeans strained, a mother who was a Countess and her own apartment. Richard thought she was just about right for him. She was a vegetarian and thought that sex was yucky and pushed off roving hands but Richard thought she would soon be cured of that. She was twenty-one.

He was particularly animated and cheerful that weekend. He told Liffey about Ray's love for Karen, and how it upset Bella.
'So long as she doesn't expect you to comfort her,' said Liffey.
Richard shuddered at the thought.

'Bella,' he said, 'is a withered hag who talks too much. I'm sorry for her, and she's good to me, but I could no more – oh, really, Liffey!'

'What about Helga?' Sometimes Liffey wondered about Helga.

'Helga is a Hausfrau and I don't go for Hausfraus. You'll be laying the finger on poor Miss Martin next.'

'You did go off with your secretary last Christmas.'

'Go off with? You mean she fell on top of me at a drunken party and if you hadn't been spying you'd never even have known.'

'I wasn't spying.'

But he was angry, and made her drink up and took her home. He relented as they passed Cadbury Farm and kissed her proffered cheek. Her skin, these days, was hot to the touch, as if fires burned inside her.

'I think Mabs *is* a witch,' said Liffey, as they passed the farm.

'That's a very unkind thing to say about a neighbour,' said Richard.

'If you nailed her footprint to the ground,' said Liffey, 'I bet she'd limp. That's how you can tell a witch.'

The next day, giggling and absurd, as in the old days, they crept down the lane when Mabs and Tucker were out, and found a footprint made by Mabs in the marshy ground where she went to feed her ducks, and hammer, hammer, Richard drove a nail right into it.

Then they watched and waited for Mabs to come back, and sure enough, when she did she was limping. They laughed and laughed, and went up later to the farm and asked what was the matter with Mabs' foot, and Mabs replied she'd stubbed her big toe and all but broken it, hadn't she, Tucker, and Tucker said yes, she'd walked straight into a tree stump, what's the matter with you two, for they were stifling giggles, but of course they couldn't say – ah, like the old times back again. Happy days. That night they lay curled like spoons together, and Richard stayed until Monday morning and kissed Liffey goodbye as if he meant it and didn't want to go. And he didn't.

Honeycomb Cottage, as he looked back at it from the car, nestled amidst hollyhocks and roses like a childhood dream of the future. This was surely what he wanted and enough for any man.

And Liffey, waving goodbye, sensed it, and hoped yet to achieve what her mother had not – an ordinary marriage, an ordinary family, and ordinary happiness.

But the next day she had a nasty pain in her sacroiliac joint, at the top of her buttocks, three inches to the right of mid-point, and could hardly walk.

Mabs came over by chance with some honey, and sent Tucker over to drive her at once to the doctor's surgery. Liffey was in such pain she almost forgot her dislike of the Pierce's car.

'Was that Tucker Pierce?' asked the doctor, manipulating the joint.
'Yes.'
'He's changed,' said the doctor. 'It's not in his nature to do good turns. Not in anyone's round here, come to that.'
He'd just sent the ambulance for the body of a recluse, found badly decayed in the caravan he'd inhabited for fifteen years.
'His wife makes him,' said Liffey. She'd forgotten all the nonsense about Mabs being a witch; all, all had been washed away again in loving laughter, annd trust of Richard.

Liffey's back creaked and cracked as the doctor pressed and dug, and the pain went, although the joint remained a little tender.

'Well,' said Tucker, 'here we are, just you and me. Time we had a little talk.'
'What about, Tucker.'

'Don't get all la-di-dah with me. That's my baby you've got in there and don't you forget it.'

'Tucker!' she was horrified. 'You can't think that. It couldn't possibly be yours.'

'Mabs thinks it is. According to her sister's friend who works up at the doctor's, it's as like as not my baby.'

'You mean Mabs *knows*?'

'Of course she knows. She's my wife. We have no secrets.'

'You *told* her?'

'Of course.'

Liffey was quite cold with shock. Gentlemen did not kiss and tell, but Tucker, after all, was no gentleman. And secrecy rose out of guilt, but Tucker felt no guilt: and if Mabs knew what was there to stop her telling Richard?

Tucker's hand was unbuttoning her Mothercare blouse.

'No please, Tucker.'

'Why not?'

'I'm pregnant.'

'Anyone can see that. It's not comfortable in here. Come out on the grass.'

'No.'

'Why not? What you do once you can do twice.'

'Tucker I can't, I mustn't. Please. My back still hurts.'

'I expect it does, at that,' he said, kindly. 'I'll be over in a day or two. No hurry.'

He started the engine and they bumped back to the cottage. I can deny it, thought Liffey, wildly. I can deny everything. That's all I have to do. Tell Richard that Tucker tried to rape me – tell Richard I'm coming up to London, I can't stay here, he has to think of something, some way we can live together.

Liffey packed a hessian bag with some meagre belongings, hitch-hiked with a startled salesman to the station, and used the last of the week's housekeeping for a ticket to London. She had to change trains at Westbury, wait two hours for a connection. The journey took five hours. She wondered how she had ever thought Richard could do it daily. She arrived at Ray and Bella's at half-past nine in the evening.

Events

Helga was cleaning up the kitchen. Liffey had met Helga once, in the old days, and not bothered to speak to her, since she was an au-pair, and au-pairs, like servants, were uninteresting. Helga did not much like Liffey, but was shocked by her appearance. What had seemed gamine now seemed undernourished, ill and almost ugly. Helga told Liffey that Bella, Ray and Richard were at the pictures. In fact Ray was at a discotheque with Karen but she thought that fact could perhaps emerge more kindly in the course of time.

'I only stay for the children,' said Helga. 'Every night I get to bed at midnight. It is a very messy family.'

'Doesn't Richard do a lot of baby-sitting?' asked Liffey. For that was how Richard described his evening occupation: sitting in the kitchen, working on papers from his briefcase, while the rest of the household had a good time.

'Oh yes,' said Helga. 'Of course.'

At midnight Richard and Bella came home. Ray wasn't expected until after two. Helga intercepted them in the hall.

'Liffey's here,' she hissed.

'Oh, Christ,' said Richard, furious. He had pushed Bella into her house with his buttocks and was looking forward to thus edging her up the stairs.

'Ask her up,' said Bella. 'She might as well know. Everyone might as well know.'

She had been drinking. So had Richard.

'I couldn't be so cruel,' said Richard. 'She only has me in the world.'

But he stood undecided until Helga pushed him into the kitchen, and Liffey ran into his arms.

Liffey did not mention Tucker. She merely said she missed him so much she'd decided to come to London, on the spur of the moment.

'But where are you going to stay?'
'I can share your bed, Richard.'
'My bed is the sofa. But you can have that tonight and I'll sleep on the floor. I've got meetings all tomorrow, too. I was hoping, just for once, to get some sleep.'

The temptations of power are indeed terrible. Richard succumbed to them. To hurt, subtly, yet appear not to hurt, made up for a little of his sense of loss in regard to Bella.

Liffey slept badly on the sofa. The noise of the London traffic kept her awake. Yet it appeared friendly, and companionable. She wondered how she had ever found it oppressive. To look out of the window and see not grass and cows, but people and buildings, and the safety of civilisation - was this not good fortune? Not for nothing had men yearned, over the generations, to escape the solitude of the countryside and make for the pleasure of the town.
Too late.

Breakfast with Ray and Bella was humiliating.
'Well,' said Ray, 'pregnancy has certainly made you look more like a woman and less like a boy. Everything going all right?'
'Well,' said Liffey, 'it's not really. They say I have to have a Caesarian.'
'They give everyone Caesarians these days,' said Bella, 'at the drop of a hat. The hospitals have to justify their monstrous expenditure on capital equipment. So the knife's back in fashion.'
'But I have a placenta praevia,' replied Liffey. 'It's nothing to do with fashion.' But Richard was reading *The Times*, and

Ray and Bella fell into an argument as to who was to talk to the Selfridges' Fish Buyer.

'I suppose you'll be meeting Karen out of school,' said Bella. 'That's why you can't do it.'

'She has her A-level Art today. I said I would, Bella. She's only a kid. She depends on me. Her own father neglects her terribly: she has to have someone.'

'Oh yes. Incest's so fashionable.'

'You are disgusting,' said Ray. 'You see sex in everything.'

'Please,' said Helga, 'not in front of the children.'

Liffey, out of the city for six months, started to cry. Mabs and Tucker back home; plotting: Richard reading his newspaper here; indifferent. Liffey fainted.

Helga took Liffey round to Bella's doctor, since Richard had an important meeting at half-past nine. The doctor said her blood pressure was up, what was she doing gadding about London, she should be safely at home in the country, and with a placenta praevia anyway she should try not to be too far from the hospital where they had her records.

'I'm not trying to frighten you,' said her doctor. 'I just don't want you to be silly. You have to think of the baby.'

Liffey rang Richard's office and got Miss Martin and left a message. Miss Martin gave Richard the first part, that Liffey was on her way home, but left out the part about the blood pressure and staying near a hospital, as he had another important meeting and she didn't want to worry him.

Liffey remembered, on the way back in the train, that she had no means of getting from the station to Honeycomb Cottage, and cried.

But Tucker was waiting for her at the station. It seemed inevitable. She did not even ask him how he came to be there. In fact, Richard had rung through and asked him to meet Liffey. Miss Martin had dialled the call, with reluctant fingers.

'I can't stand helpless women,' said Miss Martin. 'It isn't fair. If you're silly and helpless like your wife, you get looked after. No one ever looks after me.' And she cried into her typewriter – the big, ugly sobs of despised womanhood.

Later that morning Miss Martin said that she wanted to confess to Jeff, and Richard knew that once she did, once her guilt had been evaporated, puffed away in a careless word or so, she would begin to see herself as a proper person with feelings to be considered. She would stop being a humble typist, grateful for her boss' caress, and see herself as a mistress, with claims and aspirations to all kinds of impossible things.

Richard regarded his situation as dangerous. 'You'd be unwise to tell Jeff,' he said, as casually as he could manage, knowing that those who want too badly never get, and that to care too much is to lose power. 'He'd only get upset. It's not as if you and he ever slept together. You're doing him no harm: I'm only warming his bed for him a little.'

It was a phrase Bella used. Bella's phrases swam through all their lives. Even Karen had to put up with it. Bella was feeling thwarted and unsatisfied. She too seemed to be becoming a danger.
She said there ought to be more, somewhere, somehow, the other side of sexual acrobatics. She bought Richard a flat Victorian carpet-beater and asked him to thwack her bottom with it, but either her flesh was not young and smooth enough to be excited by chastisement, or he did it wrong, for all that happened was Helga threatened to give in her notice, since the noise they made upset the children.

'You must not,' said Helga. 'I will have to speak out. Mr. Ray will find out and we will all be murdered.'

Bella laughed at the idea of Ray as murderer. Part of her wanted to be murdered, another part of her wanted Ray to know, another part wanted the nights with Richard simply to continue.

So did Richard.

'Helga loves the drama,' said Bella, to Richard. 'She hasn't the guts to do it herself, so she lives through us.'
'Perhaps you ought to be quieter,' suggested Richard. 'It might upset the children.'
'Christ,' said Bella. 'It's how they were born, weren't they?'

Bella could justify anything in the world she wished to justify, thought Richard. Perhaps everyone could.

Ray bought Karen a pound of the first cherries of the season. She bit into them with her little white teeth. Red cherry juice ran down her chin. In the car he held her hand and bit into it with his own rather yellowed teeth.
'Your chin's all stubbly,' she said. Peter's hair grew fine and soft on his chin. Peter was young. Ray was old. She had not told Ray about her boyfriend Peter, a gardener drop-out, with whom she was sleeping. She thought he might be hurt.

Richard rang Vanessa but she was off to a summer school for the New Atlanteans, where communication was through the spirit not the body.

Richard thought about giving up Vanessa. Vanessa didn't think about it at all.

As for Liffey, little Liffey: Liffey lay naked on the bed, on her side, while Tucker entered her from behind. To submit gracefully, calmly, had seemed the best way of protecting herself and her baby and her blood pressure. Tucker had met her on the station: she owed him something for that.
'You shouldn't go rushing up to London like that,' he said. 'Bad for the baby. Bad for you. I wasn't going to harm you. Do anything you didn't want.' He spoke kindly, and what he said was true. He was concerned for her. She was grateful. Liffey grateful to Tucker!

He took her home, made her put her feet up, and made her

tea. 'I don't know what you're so frightened of,' he said. 'All you've got to do is what you want.'

'I know what pregnant women are like,' he said. 'I've had Mabs pregnant more times than I can remember. I like the feel of my child inside.'

'It's not yours,' she whispered. But she did not persist. She had to stay calm and bring her blood pressure down. Liffey felt the baby warning her. Careful now. Lie down. Do as he wants. It doesn't matter.

Tucker put his hand on her bare tummy: he lay down his head to listen to the baby's heart beat. That answered some kind of craving in her, too.

It was almost pleasurable; then it actually was: she forgot herself, she cried out. Liffey had an orgasm. Afterwards she cried: floods; all kinds of things, it seemed, got washed away with her tears.

Liffey, rightly or wrongly, felt she had changed. She would never easily look like a little boy, feel like a little girl, ever again. It was a loss: she knew it: she was at her best when very young. All charm, no sense. The days of charm were gone. Now she was real, and alive.

Liffey looked to no kind of future beyond the day of delivery. Everything worked towards that end.

Tucker seemed to like her tears. He made no comment on them. 'Don't tell Mabs,' he said, as he went, and Liffey was safe again, knowing he was cheating too. Their interests once again coincided.

She sang as she worked in the garden. She had to sit on the ground to weed; she found it hard to bend.

Waiting

The weather was hot. Liffey spoke to the birds, and the butterflies. Tucker came up from time to time to see how she was. She quite looked forward to his visits: she ran to make him tea – ordinary tea bags now, not Earl Grey – discussed the cows, Dick Hubbard's perfidy, the knack of making silage. Tucker made no more sexual assaults upon her. He seemed satisfied, having made his mark, having made her remember.

The baby kicked and heaved, and made her laugh and pant: it seemed to have a foot wedged under her ribs. She hoped he was all right: that a leg wouldn't grow crooked for being so long in one place.

The doctor said that was highly unlikely.
'No bleeding?' he asked.
'No bleeding,' said Liffey. Liffey still believed she would have her baby naturally. She felt that fate had dealt her quite enough blows. It could not be so cruel as to make her submit to the surgeon's knife.
Slice into the smoothness, the roundness, the taut health of her tummy? Ah, no. That was a bad dream. Liffey loved her tummy now. She lay on her back and sang to it. The earth was warm and so was she.

Liffey looked better. She was almost pretty again. The doctor said she would be delivered on October 10th. It was now the beginning of September.

Thirty-six weeks.

The first puffball of the season appeared. A blind white head pushed its way out of damp warm ground, down in the dip by the stream where once, a year ago, Richard and Liffey had made their ordinary everyday love and thought themselves much like other people. Then, when the world was innocent, and Liffey was not pregnant, nor Mabs so desperate to be so; and Richard was faithful and Bella nothing worse than bored; and Karen was a virgin and Ray was not a laughing stock: when Miss Martin still looked up to her fiancé, and Tucker contented himself with looking, through field glasses, at Liffey in the act of love – then indeed, the world was young.

Mabs was the first to see the puffball. She was out early, bringing the cows in. This was normally Tucker's job, but the night before she and he had drunk a bottle of whisky between them, almost inadvertently, one on either side of the fire, while the children, barred the kitchen, snivelled and snored upstairs.

Mabs was having trouble with Debbie. Debbie was dirty. Debbie wet the bed. In the mornings she'd stand at the sink crying and washing out her sheets, cheeks red from a slapping, and doing her best – even Mabs had to admit it – but she was a cack-handed child, and never seemed to get through before it was time for the school bus, so she'd have to leave it, and then Mabs would have to load the dripping mass into the washing machine and finish it off. And now it was school holiday time, it was even worse, for Debbie would spend the entire morning washing and getting in Mabs' way.

Debbie was eleven. She was a delicate-looking child: the prettiest of the girls and a throw back to some obscure ancestry. Mabs had the heavy jowly features and prominent eyes of the Norman invaders of these parts: Tucker the smaller, darker, cautious looks of the Celts. Once, in any case, the general belief was, in the very old days, there had been two races about, the giants and the little people, but time and civilisation had diluted the strain, and now everyone was much of a muchness – only Mabs would look out, as it were, from the surface of her head, and Tucker from within it. But Debbie seemed a new, neater breed, incompetent with her hands, full of whims and fancies, uncertain of necessities, a decoration placed on the face of the earth instead of something part of it – and reminding Mabs for all the world of Liffey.

Slap, slap. You dirty little thing!

Mabs sent the whole lot of them to bed early and then drank more whisky than she meant, to calm her nerves. Soon she was talking about Richard and Liffey.

'Of course he won't put up with her for long,' said Mabs. 'Dumping her down here is just the first stage. He's on his way up in the world and she's a millstone round his neck.'
'You can't tell what goes on between man and wife,' said Tucker.
'I can,' said Mabs. There was still a light left in the sky. The Tor seemed very near tonight, as it did when rain was about. 'Judging by the things he lets slip,' added Mabs.
'I think he's interested in a whole lot of things,' said Tucker, 'not just his office.'
'It's going to rain,' said Mabs, as if willing it, and the Tor stepped nearer, listening. Tucker told himself it was only a sudden shift in the pattern of clouds above Glastonbury.
'I wonder who it will take after when it's born?'
'Not me,' said Tucker, rather too quickly.
'It had better not,' said Mabs.
'Well,' said Tucker, 'I don't know what you're complaining about. We got the cows in Honeycomb field, didn't we?'
'Not for long,' said Mabs, and the rain started and drove against the window pane in sudden gusts. 'She's a slut and a thief and she came out of nowhere and stole my baby.'
'That's nonsense,' said Tucker.
'Then why haven't I got one?'

Mabs went to the cupboard under the sink, where the candles were kept in case of powercuts, and lit one, and waited until the wax began to melt, and then took the drips and began to mould them. First came the head, white and blind, with a pinch for the neck, and then a half-pinch, not at the waist, but where the trunk joined the legs, so that the belly curved out round and full.

'Don't do that,' said Tucker, 'it gives me the creeps. Who is it?'

'Who do you think?' said Mabs. 'Liffey. I've done one for the baby; that one's in a drawer keeping its strength, but this one's the mother. I'll get them both. Why not?'

She took a hairpin from her head and was about to pierce the belly, but Tucker thrust her hand aside and slapped her, and then bore her down on the floor, pushing up her old skirt and down her pretty, slippery knickers, and had her, while she laughed and panted and struggled.

'Why do you do it?' Tucker asked, later. 'It's a wicked thing to do.'

'She stole my baby,' Mabs persisted.

'If she did, it's not her fault,' said Tucker, doubtfully. Perhaps such things did happen: who was to say? Certainly Liffey was pregnant, and Mabs was not. And Liffey had never been pregnant before, and Mabs usually was.

'That's neither here nor there,' said Mabs. She slept peacefully afterwards but Tucker did not, and he groaned and moaned, so in the morning Mabs kindly rose and brought in the cows on his behalf from Honeycomb field. And there, down in the long grass, as a kind of omen and reward, was the puffball.

Mabs stared long and hard at it and after breakfast went up and knocked on Liffey's door. Liffey was hemming cot-sheets. Liffey quite enjoyed the task: to sit patiently, sewing, each stitch an act of faith in the future of both her child and herself, stemmed up anxiety and sorrow and made her feel at peace. But Mabs wouldn't have it.

'It's unlucky to sew for babies before they're born,' said Mabs, peering over Liffey's shoulders.

'I hadn't heard that,' said Liffey.

'Well, now you have. It's tempting providence.'

'I suppose it is, in a way.'

'Come over and use my machine. And stay for lunch,' said Mabs.

So Liffey took the pile of old flannelette sheets which Mrs. Lee-Fox senior had sent her by parcel post, and walked over to Cadbury Farm and sat in the kitchen where Mabs' children yammered and cowered and snivelled and were slapped and shouted at, and used the sewing machine and wondered if she really wanted a child.

The baby kicked Liffey. It had changed its position. Its head lay somewhere over her left groin: its legs tucked under her right ribs. Sometimes it waved its elbows and made her gasp. It's not what *you* want, it seemed to say, it's what *I* want.

Tucker was out with the cows. A cat sat by the fire. Eddie crouched beside it, poking at its eyes with a stick. Jab, jab. 'You leave the cat alone,' shrieked Mabs, 'or I'll have you put away.'

Jab, jab, jab, went Eddie, until his mother seized him and flung him half across the room.

Mabs served cabbage and bacon for lunch. She would let the cabbage cook for a couple of hours, then squeeze and press some of the water out of it, and cut it into wedges.

Mabs walked with Liffey back to the cottage, after lunch. She said she wanted the exercise. Liffey wished she didn't. Moreover, she ran her large hands over Liffey's tummy before they set out, and Liffey wished she wouldn't do that either.

'It's a girl,' said Mabs, 'you can tell. What do you want? A boy?'

'I don't mind,' said Liffey. 'So long as it's human.'

It was a little joke she made, but Mabs seemed to think she was serious.

Mabs saw the puffball.
'Look,' she said. 'Isn't it horrible!' And she pulled back the long grasses, and ran her hands over its surface rather as she had run them over Liffey's tummy.
Then she straightened up and kicked the puffball, and it spattered into pieces.
'I can't abide those things,' Mabs said. 'Coming up from nowhere like that.'

Liffey felt quite sick, and trembled, but Mabs smiled pleasantly and they walked on.
'They're only big mushrooms,' said Liffey presently. 'They don't do any harm.'
'Can't abide them,' said Mabs. 'Nor does Tucker. No one round here does.'

Liffey sat for a while after Mabs had gone. It was a lovely, warm afternoon. Bees droned, sun glazed, flowers glowed.

Preparations

Changes had recently been occurring in the lower part of Liffey's uterus. It was gradually softening and shortening, in preparation for labour, and it was to this lower part, of course, that the baby's placenta was attached. Now the placenta separated itself fractionally from the uterus, and Liffey lost a few drops of blood, but failed to notice. For there was a thunderstorm over the Tor that evening and lightning struck a cable, so that there was a powercut. Mabs had to take out her candles again, but Liffey had none and had to undress in the dark and did not notice the staining.

218

'Make the lights come on again,' said Tucker to Mabs, half-joking, and no sooner had he spoken than they came on. 'You're a witch,' said Tucker, 'that's your trouble,' and then had to spend half the night pacifying her. She did not like to be called a witch by anyone, let alone her husband.

The doctor sent Sister Davis the midwife up to see Liffey. Sister Davis was a slender, doe-eyed girl, who had no intention of ever having a baby herself.

'No bleeding?' she asked.

'No,' said Liffey.

'The minute there is,' said Sister Davis, 'you'll come along in to hospital, won't you.'

'Of course,' said Liffey.

'I don't know why they haven't taken you in already,' said Sister Davis. 'Of course, they're short of staff up there, and it's a question of priorities.'

'I feel fine,' said Liffey. 'I really do.'

'Up here, on your own,' said Sister Davis, running expert hands over Liffey's tummy. 'No telephone, no husband. It isn't right.'

'It's very peaceful,' said Liffey.

'And you have good neighbours,' said Sister Davis, 'that's the main thing. Mabs Pierce is an old hand at motherhood. I wonder when her next will be? She's leaving it longer than usual.'

'I don't think she wants any more,' said Liffey, surprised.

'No? What a pity. She's such a lovely mother. The babies slip out like loaves from a greased tin!'

Sister Davis reported to the doctor that Mrs. Lee-Fox seemed in good health and spirits, and she was sure that Mabs Pierce would keep an eye on her. The doctor replied that somebody ought to be keeping an eye on Mabs Pierce and sent the health visitor up.

The health visitor called in to see Mabs.

'You'll keep an eye on Mrs. Lee-Fox, won't you,' said the health visitor, an eye on Eddie's facial bruises.

'Of course,' said Mabs.

'What's the matter with Eddie's face?' asked the health visitor.

'Fell into the grate,' said Mabs, 'didn't you, Eddie?'

'That's right,' said Eddie. Mabs clasped Eddie to her, with a spurt of genuine affection. She was feeling better. She felt that in some way or other she'd off-loaded a bit of bad.

Eddie looked up at his mother with such evident pleasure and gratitude that the health visitor decided she'd better let well alone. Even if you feared a child was being battered, the problem of alternatives remained. Mrs. Wild was of the opinion that short of death, a natural home was better than an unnatural one, with changing foster parents or in institutions. The child's spirit died, in any case, if the mother failed to love it, no matter who intervened; just the same way as its body would die if she failed to nurture it. And once the spirit died you could do what you liked with the body, and make yourself feel better, but scarcely ever the child.

Eddie's spirit hovered on the brink of life and death.

Liffey's baby floated free and wild. In normal first pregnancies the baby's head descends into the cavity of the pelvis at the thirty--eighth week: a process known as lightening, inasmuch as the pressure on lungs and heart and digestive organs lessens and the mother thereafter feels more comfortable. Liffey's baby's head did no such thing: it could not. The placenta barred its way. Liffey's baby did not care. Liffey's baby, headstrong, trusted to a providence which had already acted against it, whether twisted by Mabs' malevolent will, or merely by the laws of chance. One pregnancy in a hundred is a placenta praevia: does every one of those foetuses have a Mabs in the background? Surely not; such foetuses are merely accident prone, or event prone, as some individuals are; at one time or other in their life. Ladders fall on them or pigs out of windows, or bombs go off as they approach; or, in country terms, their crops fail and their cattle sicken and a witch has overlooked them.

Liffey's baby, overlooked or accident prone, take it how you will, leapt in Liffey's womb, and its umbilical cord – now twenty inches long – exerted gentle pressure on the upper side of the placenta, so that it slid further over to cover Liffey's cervix fully. And then it leapt again and contrived an actual knot in the cord, but fortunately – or whatever we mean by that word – the knot did not tighten, and the cord continued to supply the foetus with blood, through its two ingoing arteries, and remove it, through its single outgoing vein. But there the knot was, annd should it tighten, that would be the end of that.

The baby sang to Liffey: Liffey drowsed: the knot did not tighten. Nor did Liffey's blood pressure rise: it stayed at around 20/77 of mercury – the upper figure being the pressure reached within the blood vessel at the height of a heart beat, and the lower figure being the minimum level to which the pressure falls between heart beats. The upper figure could vary, safely enough, with exercise, fatigue, excitement and emotion – and indeed had risen dramatically when Mabs kicked the puffball to pieces – but the lower figure could only vary as a result of some fundamental change in the circulation, which might tend to reduce the blood supply to the uterus, placenta and baby, and result in, what must at all costs be avoided, premature delivery.

Catharsis

In London the sun shone day after day. It was hot. Karen's boyfriend Pete was found asleep in the potting shed and lost his job. He turned up at Karen's house and introduced himself to Karen's mother. Karen's mother was a psychotherapist, and asked him in.

'How dare you have him in the house without asking me first,' shouted Karen, all red hair and spoilt pout, already on her way to Ray's.

Helga let her in. Ray and Bella and Richard were all out. Karen watched Helga wash dishes and peel potatoes and despised her.

Ray came home and was both disconcerted and delighted to find Karen in his kitchen.

'I've left home,' said Karen.

'You can stay here,' said Ray. 'Bella won't mind. You can help Helga with the children.'

They went upstairs. Helga clattered and crashed. Karen revealed to Ray that Bella was having an affair with Richard, an item of news she knew from an unkept confidence in her mother. Ray hit Karen, so shocked was he; Karen fell into Bella's arms, as she returned home with Richard. Ray knocked Richard down the stairs and Karen ran shrieking from the house.

Ray's nose bled heartily from Bella's blow, and she had to mop him up in the bathroom, her own eyes blurred with tears of remorse and indignation mixed. Richard rose, dazed and alone, from the floor, and gathered his belongings and prepared to leave, out into the night, wondering where he would go.

But Bella and Ray barred his way.

'Don't go,' said Ray. 'We must talk everything out,' and they led him by the hand to the kitchen, and there they sat all night, eating French bread and Brie, and drinking coffee, and more coffee, and whisky and more whisky, while tears ran and voices grew husky, and childhoods were remembered and rankling incidents recalled, and marital failures and erotic disappointments mulled over.

Richard realised that he was a bit-part player in Ray and Bella's drama: and he feared he had much the same rôle in Miss Martin's life. He was her route to self-esteem, not the gratification of her desires; and in all fairness, she was his.

He understood at last that Liffey, his marriage partner, was his true love, his true security, his true faithful companion and his happiness. Richard said as much. He wept. They all wept.

Ah, what a night it was, the Night of the Confessional, of remorse and whisky and embraces and the signing of pacts and the announcement of good intentions, and as the day broke and the noise of traffic grew, and the grass of the park emerged out of dawn grey into brilliant morning green, all felt purged and re-born.

It was only when *The Times* was stuffed through the letterbox, and Tony and Tina were still asleep, and the replacement kitten yowling with hunger, that it was realised that Helga had gone.

Packed her bags and gone.

Richard left for the office. Tina and Tony emerged startled from their bedrooms and organised their own breakfast and departure for school, and wrote their own notes apologising for their lateness, which they presented to Bella for signing. Ray took offence at this. Both children were weeping over Helga's leaving, but neither parent showed much concern. 'For God's sake,' snapped Bella. 'Stop whining. She was only the maid. It's not as if she was your mother.'

Richard knew he must break off his relationship with Miss Martin. She made it easy for him.
'You're never going to marry me, are you, Richard?' she blurted, out of her typewriter.

Richard was startled. He could not remember her ever using his first name. She had so far avoided it, as he avoided hers. He was not even sure, come to think of it, what her first name was.
'No,' he said.

'I'll tell your wife about us,' said Miss Martin: her eyes were hollow and her cheeks sunk. Her figure, no longer solid and shapeless, seemed scraggy and shapeless. Her eyes were malevolent.

Richard rang through to the Personnel Department and arranged to take its head out to lunch.

Miss Martin was sent for by Personnel during the course of the afternoon and transferred to the Computer Room.
Her replacement was a young woman with downcast eyes, a demure look and practised ways, lately transferred from the Manchester branch. Richard read invitation in the eyes, eventually raised to his over lunch – it was customary for bosses to take secretaries out to lunch on the first day of their appointment, so they could get to know each other – but steadfastly refused the invitation.

Now he was free of Bella, Helga and Miss Martin, he would concentrate on loving Liffey. It was clear to him that the world and the people in it were not perfectable; that one person's happiness could only be gained by the unhappiness of another; that if Liffey were to be happy, Miss Martin must be unhappy, and Bella, and Ray, and even himself. For deprived so suddenly of the sexual activity of which he had been accustomed, Richard was restless and wretched and irritable, and dissatisfied, and jealous, and very very hungry. But he bore all for the love of Liffey and in a mood of self-congratulation and sorrow mixed, and with a feeling of achievement and some kind of personal storm weathered, did he return, on that the thirty-eighth week of Liffey's pregnancy.

Bella, Ray, Tina and Tony went too. Bella thought Tina and Tony would benefit from a weekend in the country. Ray wondered if Liffey would be up to it, but Bella said of course she would: anyway, she, Bella would look after Liffey: she felt she had behaved badly towards her and wanted to make amends.

It was the children's half-term the following week and Bella thought perhaps she should leave them behind, to look after Liffey. They were really very good. Tony could help carry shopping and Tina could make beds and bread or whatever.

Didn't Richard think so?

Inside Liffey (10)

Thirty-eight weeks.

Liffey's baby was eighteen inches long: its weight was six pounds one ounce; it was layered nicely with subcutaneous fat. The vernix creased richly in the folds of its body. It lay head down, knees meeting wrists, ankles turning little feet towards each other, buttocks jutting out at a point just above Liffey's umbilical cord. The baby was now almost fully mature, and had it been born into the world that day would have had a ninety per cent chance of survival. Only the lungs were not quite ready, and would have had some trouble in performing their required task, the converting of oxygen.

Liffey herself was languorous and uncomfortable, and the normal relief expected at such a time, when the baby's head drops into the pelvis, and the maternal organs are relieved of this untoward pressure and that, did not occur. It could not. The placenta, positioned as it was, prevented it. The baby swayed and moved, and stayed free. What yet might prove its undoing remained for the time being a blessing.

Liffey moved slowly about the house. From time to time she breathed heavily and deeply. Every now and then her uterus contracted, painlessly, but growing taut and hard. It was a reassuring sensation, as if the body at least knew what it was doing. The contraction would last some twenty seconds and then fade away.

Liffey dreamt. How she dreamt! Were they the baby's dreams, or hers? She dreamed of strange landscapes, and of the dark, warm, busy world that was inside her. She dreamed that the baby was born: that it jumped out of her side and ran off laughing. Its hair was curly and it was aged about two. She dreamed she gave birth to a grown man and when he turned his face to look at her, it was Richard. She dreamed she gave birth to herself: that she split into cloned multitudes. She dreamed that Madge tied her feet together and forbade her to give birth at all. She dreamed that Mrs. Lee-Fox shut her in the seaside cottage and the waves rose and broke against the window; and rockets flew overhead: and she escaped in a junk. But there was a kind of blank panel in the mural of all her dreams, where the face of Mabs should have appeared but never did.

In the mornings she woke slowly, and dressed slowly, and the evenings came before the day had scarcely passed. She had very little sense of the passage of time; she functioned, yet her senses closed down around her: she saw and heard and touched the world through a dark film, as if preferring to see and hear and touch as the baby must – rocked and lulled in the dark.

Guests

And here they were, on Friday evening, pouring out of Richard's car, and yes, they were real: Richard and Ray and Bella and Tony and Tina: and yes, they were chattering and laughing and looking for sleeping bags and oh, they were hungry and tired, and no, Liffey mustn't move, not an inch, they were going to do everything, everything, only where was the tea and were there any more towels and no, Liffey, don't move the beds, get Ray to do it – where's Ray? Looking for flying saucers: everyone is, these days, and this is UFO country, isn't it – and Liffey, is there any brown paper we can use for the loo; newspaper is so crude, isn't it? And Liffey, no Liffey, sit down – just tell us where the onions are so we can make a sauce for the spaghetti – oh, in the garden – where in the garden? – ah, there – where are the plates, Liffey? Liffey is there any hot water, and Liffey, Tina's fallen and hurt her knee on the torn mat; yes, thank you for the plasters, and I do think the mat ought to be moved – where's Richard? Ah, taken Ray to try Tucker Pierce's cider, how like a man, to leave everything to the womanfolk. How long, Liffey? Two weeks! Now if we can just get the table laid and the candles – where are the candles? – lit, everything will be ready by the time the men get home. Can Tony just have some cocoa and go to bed?

That's one dinner saved! And Tina had better have some too. They simply love the country. You're so lucky, Liffey, right out of the rat-race, and I'm sure one gets on better with a husband for not seeing him all the time and of course Richard, as everyone knows, adores you, Liffey, and is fundamentally absolutely, totally faithful to a vision of you, Liffey. Liffey, is there any ice? I can't seem to get it out of the tray. Most people have plastic, Liffey, not tin. Now you're not to overtire yourself.

Liffey, exhausted, faded back into a kind of gentle stupor. Richard came back from Cadbury Farm in a luxurious and loving mood. His arms were full of puffballs. He laid them in rows of ascending size upon the kitchen table.

Who needs shops, when the fields are so abundant?

Liffey waited until the guests were in bed, and Richard had made gentle, affectionate remorseful love to her and fallen asleep, and got up and cleaned the kitchen and laid breakfast, feeling that this was the way she could best allocate her strength, and then went back to bed and propped pillows beneath her back, and slept as upright as she could manage. A light, uneasy sleep. She thought the baby did not want the visitors. But they kept Mabs away.

In the morning Richard sliced a sharp knife into the biggest puffball, and where the cut was the flesh gaped wide, as human flesh gapes under the surgeon's knife, and Liffey stared, aghast.

'What's the matter?'

'Nothing.'

He dipped the slices of puffball into first flour, then egg, then breadcrumbs and fried them in butter. Bella and Ray and Richard ate with enthusiasm; Tina and Tony politely declined and made do with Weetabix, and Liffey fainted dead away.

'Perhaps we'd better call the doctor,' said Ray, when Liffey had been patted and coaxed awake, which took only half a minute or so.

'Honestly, I'm all right,' said Liffey.

'I'd better leave Tony and Tina,' said Bella. 'She shouldn't be on her own, should she.'

'I don't know why puffballs should have such an effect,' said Richard.

'It's because of the operation,' said Tina, softly. No one, usually, listened to Tina.

Liffey wondered about whether or not to go to the doctor about her fainting fit, but the assembled company, now sitting in the garden in the early sun, drinking coffee, clearly did not want to get into cars and drive her anywhere so boring. Liffey, the general feeling was, was showing her hypochondria again. Pregnant women fainted; everyone knew that.

Liffey went inside and swept floors and made beds. Tina helped, and told her about Helga, and how Helga was now working for her girlfriend's boyfriend, making Indian sweetmeats. She had no work permit for anything other than domestic work so was earning only fifteen pounds a week but don't tell Mummy because her visa has expired and if Mummy tells the Home Office Helga will be deported and we'll never see her again.

'Why should Bella do a thing like that?' asked Liffey, surprised.

Tina shrugged. She was a sad, sallow little girl with a round face and button eyes. She kept her eyes fixed on Liffey's tummy.
'I don't think I want a baby,' she said.

Her brother Tony wandered around the garden, kicking at tufts of grass and slashing the heads off what he claimed to be weeds but were usually budding flowers. He stared at Liffey's stomach too, but in a more prurient, less sympathetic way.

'It's because Helga's left, I'm afraid,' said Bella. 'She really was an irresponsible little bitch.'

Tony watched Liffey and Richard together, and giggled, and sniggered, as if imagining them in the act of love.

'I don't know why it is,' complained Bella. 'I thought if you brought children up to be open about sex, they didn't get like that. I expect it was Helga. What a little prude she always was.'

Ray lay in the sun and Bella rubbed his back with oil.

'Do we really have to stay here two whole days?' asked Bella. 'I'm missing a perfectly good publishers' party on Sunday.'
'We can't just dump the children and go,' said Ray.
'It's not dumping,' said Bella.
'Anyway, I like it here,' said Ray.
'I don't,' said Bella. 'It's tiny, and scruffy and fancy having to eat pork and beans at our time of life, and the beds are uncomfortable and Liffey lumbers round making everyone feel bad – she used to be such fun, do you remember? – and Richard can only talk about freeze-dried peas.'
'You don't like seeing Richard and Liffey together. You're jealous.'

'I could have Richard any time I wanted him but I don't want him any more.'

She didn't either. She felt quite happy with Ray. She had forgiven him for not being her rightful husband. Anger and guilt had been purged by the confessional. She could even accept the episode of Karen as her rightful punishment for past sins. Like candyfloss in the mouth – so much abundant glory gone, melted, nothing. All she was now was bored.

'Can't we go tomorrow morning?'

But no, Richard had accepted an invitation to Sunday lunch at Cadbury Farm.
'Oh Christ,' said Bella to Ray. 'Now we'll all get food poisoning. What does Richard see in those boring peasants anyway.'
'They're *real* people,' said Ray, turning his mottled chest to the sun. 'Bred out of the soil.'

He still yearned for Karen. Karen told her friends how she had seduced Ray, and about the sorry state of his legs, and the funny mottled colour of his member, and was believed; and wherever they saw his picture at the head of his column in the *Evening Gazette* she and her friends laughed, and felt less powerless in the world.

Miss Martin's mother had a bad night with her daughter, who presently demanded to be admitted to a mental hospital. They spent a long morning waiting in the out patients department of a psychiatric hospital, only to be told that the case did not require in-patient treatment, and that pills would do. Jeff was most supportive, but believed on balance that Miss Martin was fantasising, and feared his own liking for pornographic magazines was somehow to blame.

While Bella oiled Ray and complained, and Liffey toiled, and Tony and Tina mourned, Richard talked to Tucker about the benefits of planting in phase with the moon.

'Never heard of anything like that,' said Tucker.

'It's part of the old knowledge,' said Richard. 'It's died out here where it originated. Now the city folk have to bring it back to the countryside. Root crops are planted at the waxing of the moon: leaf crops at the wane.'

'His brain's weakened,' Tucker complained to Mabs. 'I hope you haven't been giving him anything.'

'I've no quarrel with him,' said Mabs. 'Only with her, and that's your fault.'

'I don't really want to go to the farm tomorrow,' said Liffey to Richard, at tea. He was cutting open another puffball. Its rich, sweet, sickly scent stood between her and the fresh clean air her lungs demanded. She opened the window. 'You are full of whims and fancies,' he complained. 'Why not now?'

'Mabs frightens me,' said Liffey.

'Mabs!' he laughed.

'She kicked one of those puffballs to pieces,' Liffey said.

'Country people are superstitious about them. I don't know why.'

'She wants to harm me, Richard.'

'Why, Liffey?' Richard sounded quite cross.

'I don't know.'

'Perhaps you've been messing with Tucker?' He was joking.

He sliced into the next puffball and Liffey thought of her own pale, stretched flesh.

'Supposing the baby starts early?' she asked. 'Supposing I start to bleed.'

'Liffey, you are making ever such heavy weather over this pregnancy.'

'Sorry. I suppose London's full of girls just dropping their babies in a corner of the office, and going straight back to the typewriter?'

'Well, yes. More or less. That sounds like the old Liffey.'

The old Liffey. Little lithe silly Liffey. Liffey remembered her old self with nostalgia, but knew it was gone for good.

Tucker had driven it out of her. Mabs flew shrieking through her mind, perched on a broomstick; heavy, smooth, nyloned legs ready to push and shove and get her in the stomach. All Richard did was slice puffballs, and smile, and pretend that nothing had changed. But it had. Richard had changed, too. He had grown from a boy into a man and she was not sure that she liked the man.

But she had to. He paid the rent. He bought the food. She and the baby had to have a home. And he was the baby's father. Richard, I like you. I love you.

Please, dear God, let me like you, love you, trust you.

'Don't you love the smell of puffballs?' Richard asked. 'Wonderful!' said Liffey. 'Of the earth, earthy.'

Tucker, with earth beneath his nails. That was not love, nor lust, nor folly, nor spite: that was nothing to do with the will, with the desire for good or bad, that was simply what had happened. An open door, and someone coming through it, further and further until he was not just inside the room but inside her as well.

'I don't know what you had to go and ask them over for,' grumbled Mabs. She was preparing a distillation of mother-wort for herself, and syrup of buckthorn for Debbie, who complained of stomach pains, presumably due to con-stipation. Debbie was locked in her room for not having properly cleaned the kitchen and was using the pains as an excuse.

Mabs was in good spirits. Tucker had taken her to a dance at Taunton. She'd had her hair done at the hairdresser and bought a new flowered skirt.

The milk yield accepted and paid for by the Milk Marketing Board was higher than it had ever been; the cattle sheds could be retiled: it had been a good spring for silage, and a fine summer for hay. Apart from Liffey's baby, and her own inability to conceive, it might almost be called a lucky year.

The bad times were nearly over. Mabs felt that once Liffey's baby was delivered she would start her own. That was the way things went. And she confidently expected Liffey to die under the surgeon's knife.

Mabs gave Tucker a twist of thornapple in his elderberry wine, which made him mellow and complaisant, and took the edge out of his complaints, and she felt it was rather an improvement. His lovemaking lasted longer, too.

Early on Sunday morning Ray took Tony out for a walk. They went up the hill and stopped at the point where there was an excellent view of the Tor. As they paused, and puffed, for neither were in good condition, they saw a round red spinning disc of considerable size but unclear distance from them, move towards them, move away again, vanish, reappear, shift colour from red to orange, and depart again, not to reappear.

Ray and Tony were silent.
'That was a flying saucer,' said Ray, eventually.
'Don't be stupid, Dad,' said Tony, embarrassed. 'Anyway don't call them flying saucers. They're UFOs.'
'But you do agree we saw one?'
'No, I don't,' said Tony, wretchedly.

Ray ran back to report his sighting, and had to wake a sleeping house to do so. Bella was angry.
'Your brain's gone to jelly,' she shouted. 'You're so afraid of your own mortality you've taken to seeing things.'
'It was real, Bella.'
'Tony, did you see the same thing as your father?'
'There was something, Mum, but it could have been a fireball or a shooting star or something.'

Ray took hold of Tony and shook him.

'If you ask me,' said Bella, 'that's the first physical contact you've had with your son since the day he was born.'
Ray stopped shaking.

'Everything wonderful in my life,' he said to Bella, sadly, 'you destroy. I can't even see a flying saucer but you entirely spoil and diminish the event.'
'UFO,' said Tony.

The quarrel continued until it was impossible for Bella and Ray to stay under the same roof. Tony and Tina wandered in the garden. Bella demanded that Richard take her to the station at once, and Ray got in the car at the last moment and Liffey did what she could to comfort Tony and Tina. Their parents did not have the spiritual energy left to say goodbye.

Bella got to her publisher's party.

Richard was laughing when he got home.
'Oh Liffey, darling,' he said, 'how lucky we are. We've had our hard times but things are going to be better from now on.'

He touched no wood as he spoke.

The Unexpected

Sun glazed, flowers glowed, bees droned. Richard and Liffey walked down the lane from Honeycomb Cottage to Cadbury Farm, on the way to Sunday lunch. They held hands. Tony and Tina, taken aback by their parents' sudden departure, walked behind, subdued.

Now, in late summer, after a season of Liffey's tending, the cottage might have graced the top of a chocolate box. Hollyhocks, roses and wallflowers tumbled together against the whitewashed walls; swallows dived and soared above the thatch; Tucker's black and white cows grazed serenely in the field behind; down on the stream moorhens paddled against the current, in the dappled shadow of weeping willows. Peas and beans and carrots flourished in the small vegetable patch: and there would have been potatoes in the field had it not been for the cows.

'You do make the best of everything, Liffey,' said Richard, contentedly, as they walked.

He carried a puffball with him. It was tucked under his arm. It seemed to stare ahead, as he walked; there were, by chance blemishes spaced like eyes and mouth on its smooth surface. He was taking it as a gift for Mabs.

'I'm not sure she'll appreciate it,' Liffey said.
'But they're so nourishing,' Richard replied, 'and so delicious. I'll convert her.'

They came to the end of the wood. The long grey building of Cadbury Farm lay before them, with its crumbling dry stone walls, and the neglected outhouses, with their collapsing red tiled roofs. Away to the right of them, the ground swept down and across the levels of the valley, past small villages and hedgerowed meadows, threaded by ribbons of road, where toy cars and lorries trundled, to where the Tor rose, suddenly and dramatically, at odds with the gentle landscape which surrounded it.

'They say there's a magnetic force line straight from the Tor to Jerusalem,' said Richard.
'Who says?'
'Can't remember,' said Richard. It had been Vanessa. She had told him to find a pine tree on a ley line and lean against it, when ever his system needed revitalising. She had told him about twisted apple trees and yews which marked the radiating force lines from the Tor; about the old roads between Stonehenge and Glastonbury; about how it was no coincidence that he lived in London in the shadow of

Primrose Hill – also a seat of power – and in the country, in the shadow of the Tor. Deciding, by virtue of his dwelling place, that Richard must be a rather special person after all, she had allowed him to sleep with her, and declared herself revitalised by the encounter and not – as she had feared – enervated. But she would not repeat the experience, no matter how his by now practised hand strayed over her long, young, cool body. Once was enough – she said. They knew all there was about one another now – she'd as soon recharge herself against a pine tree or a ley line. But could he get her another modelling job?

Richard thought he probably couldn't, but since then had regarded the Tor with more respect, as something with spiritual meaning, which could bring good things about, rather than a tourist trap for ruined abbey and UFO freaks. Things had gone wrong, since then. He'd talked to Vanessa about Liffey.

'I didn't know you were married,' she'd said, surprised. 'I don't want to get into all that scene. You should have told me.'

'I didn't think marriage mattered to you lot, one way or another.'

But it had seemed to; she had said she'd ring him when she'd worked things out, but hadn't rung: and Richard was vaguely sorry, since Vanessa was restful, and her expectations from sex so few that he was bound to please, and his attempts at seduction for that reason unclouded but relieved as well. All that was behind him now.

'You're not tired?' he asked, now, solicitously.

'No,' said Liffey. But she was. From time to time she had a dragging pain in her abdomen.

Labour

Thirty-eight weeks. The average duration of pregnancy is forty weeks, but can vary from woman to woman, and from one pregnancy to another, and from one marriage to another. Each pregnancy differs: each woman differs. Liffey's baby was ready. All through life the muscles of a woman's uterus, like the muscles in the rest of her body, contract and relax from time to time, lest they waste away. All through pregnancy uterine contractions occur, every half hour or less, for about half a minute at a time. In late pregnancy, they become noticeable, though not painful: they are known as Branston Hicks contractions. When labour begins, these contractions become regular, stronger, and more forceful. They last for forty seconds or more: they mount to a crescendo more slowly, fade away more gradually. As labour progresses, uterine contractions come at shorter and shorter intervals; they are designed to eliminate the canal of the cervix without damaging its muscle, incorporating it into the lower uterine segment, so that the baby can be expelled. The upper uterine segment, where the contraction begins, and which consists almost entirely of muscle, behaves during labour in a unique way, known as retraction. It shortens itself slightly after every contraction, thus increasing its pulling power on the lower segment, which is already much stretched and weakened by the baby it contains. The pressures produced inside are considerable. The cervix, as the canal above it is, little by little, inexorably, drawn up, widens, or dilates, eventually making an opening some nine-and-a-half centimetres in diameter, enough for the baby's head to pass through – all going well with the baby, that is. This first stage of labour, as it is called, takes a different length of time in different women, varying from two hours to twenty-four but with some exceptions either side. It is not possible to anticipate the duration of a labour, nor whether the contractions will be experienced as discomfort or pain: but as a rough working estimate it requires some one hundred and fifty contractions to produce a first child, about seventy-five for a second or third child, and about fifty for a fourth.

Liffey, walking down the lane with Richard, had a mild backache, and a slight dragging pain in her tummy: but so she'd had from time to time over the past few weeks. Earlier in the morning she'd had an uprush of energy: had swept and cleaned and even scrubbed, under and around her warring guests, but this had now passed, leaving her soft and languid.

'What a pity,' said Mabs, when they got to the Farm, 'I was expecting your smart London friends. So was Tucker. Weren't you, Tucker!'
'They had to get back in a hurry,' said Richard.
'London folk are always in a hurry,' said Mabs, shooing Tina and Tony out into the yard. 'I suppose my invitation wasn't good enough for the likes of them.'

She was annoyed. Richard offered her the puffball by way of pacification. It made her laugh.
'God-awful things,' she said. 'You're quite mad, Richard.'
But she consented to slice it, a little later, and place it under the roast to catch the drippings, and serve it like Yorkshire pudding.
'Just because I never have,' said Mabs, nobly, 'is no reason why I never should.' Her annoyance seemed to have evaporated. She smiled at Liffey, and pulled back a chair for her, saying, 'Don't go into the parlour, since it's only you. Stay and talk while I work.'

Tucker served elderberry wine, clearing a space on the crowded table for bottle and glasses.
'How are you keeping, Liffey?' he asked. 'No pains?'
'No more than usual,' said Liffey.
'She's not allowed to produce for another two weeks,' said Richard. 'I can't take time off until then.'
'You're not going to be *there*,' said Mabs, in horror.
'Fathers are supposed to be,' said Richard, helplessly.
'Liffey, you wouldn't want him to see you in that state?' demanded Mabs.

Both Mabs and Tucker wore their Sunday best. Tucker was wearing a collar and tie, which somehow diminished him. It made him seem uneasy and ordinary, and grimy rather than

238

weathered, as if the ingraining accomplished by sun and wind was the mark of poverty. Mabs wore an oyster coloured silk blouse, already splashed by juices from the rib of beef she was roasting and the sprouts she was stewing, but her hair was pulled firmly and neatly back, showing her broad face to advantage. She has lost weight recently, Liffey decided, and that made her high cheek bones more prominent and her dark eyes larger and more glittery than usual. Moreover, Mabs, who seldom so much as looked in a mirror, but saw herself, as it were, defined by sky and hills, had today outlined them with black.

A witch, thought Liffey. A witch preparing for witchery. The ceremonial has begun.

Nonsense, thought Liffey. My neighbour, about whom I sometimes get strange fancies, connected, no doubt with my pregnancy. My neighbour, the salt of the earth.

'I don't think it's going to apply,' said Liffey. 'I'm going to have a Caesarian, anyway. Or so they say.'
'They only say you might, Liffey,' said Richard. 'Don't exaggerate.'
'It's natural for her to get nervous,' said Tucker, 'at this stage.'
'The way I look at it,' said Mabs, 'a man's place during childbirth is down at the pub.'

Everyone laughed, Even Liffey.

Tony and Tina had been given a bag of crisps each and sent out to play with the others. The others were nowhere to be seen, so they sat on a wall and swung their legs and waited, with some alarm, for further events to transpire. They were hungry, but relieved not to have to sit down with the grownups for dinner. They were accustomed to the stripped pine furniture, uncluttered lines and primary colours of home, and found the rich dark mahogany and oak, the dust, and litter and the crumbling walls of the Pierce's kitchen oppressive. They were accustomed, moreover, to adults who talked to them, and who did not offer them crisps in lieu of conversation. They were accustomed to Richard, but did not trust him; liked Liffey but judged that she was hardly in a condition to look after them; were angry with their parents for abandoning them; and missed Helga. They munched and crunched their crisps, and were silent, faces impassive.

Mabs had got their names wrong: had taken Tina for a boy, Tony for a girl.

'You can't tell which is which,' she complained, in their hearing. 'I'd be ashamed to let my children out, looking like that.'

Debbie was locked in her room again. Today the reason given was that she failed to clean her father's Sunday shoes. She lay with her legs drawn up to her chest, occasionally vomiting and groaning. She had had another dose of buckthorn to cure her constipation.

Buckthorn was a tall shrub which grew in the woods around. It had little creamy white flowers in spring and inviting black berries in autumn; and grew, in these parts, without thorns. The thorny kind, or Spinachristi, provided Christ's crown of thorns; Mabs' kind, though without thorns, provided a powerful cascara-like purgative, which she prepared, with sugar and ginger, from the dried berries, and with which, as her mother, grandmother and great-grandmother before her, she dosed her children, doing them one damage or another. It was a local custom so to do. Dr. Southey would suggest to mothers that they keep it for cows, but they politely agreed and kept on dosing. Sometimes he thought he would emigrate, and take a post in Central Africa, where superstition and witchcraft would be something clear and definite to be grappled with, not a running, secret thread through the fabric of life.

Eddie played silently in the corridor outside Debbie's room.

He crouched on the floor, listening to her groans, zooming his hand over the rug like a dive-bombing plane. There were blue bruises on his upper arms. Eddie was waiting for Audrey to come back from church. Audrey had a nice voice and a natural ear and had joined the church choir, partly because she could make 35p a wedding and more for funerals and partly because she fancied the curate, Mr. Simon Eaves. She looked at him with large, glittery, inviting eyes and he struggled to believe there was no invitation in them; she was a child.

Today Audrey asked if she could stay behind after church and speak to him, and Mr. Eaves felt he could not very well refuse, and also that it would be prudent not to see her alone.

'Well,' said Mabs, preparing the puffball for the oven, 'I don't know about you lot, but I'm certainly looking forward to the baby. You've really made me feel quite broody, Liffey.'

She sliced into the puffball with too blunt a knife, so that the edge crumbled as if it were a ripe Stilton she was parting, and not an edible fungi.

As she cut through the flesh, not cleanly, but bruising and chipping on the way, she stared at Liffey's stomach.

'I'm imagining it,' thought Liffey. If she were doing it on purpose, surely Richard would have noticed? But Richard smiled amiably on, his mind on good red meat juices and the creamy texture of roasted puffball. And Tucker stared into space and drank.

'But why does Mabs hate me,' wondered Liffey. 'I am not a hateful person. I am a nice person. Everyone likes me. They may forget me, but if I'm around, they like me.'

'I have slept with Mabs' husband but Mabs doesn't know that. Mabs can't know. Tucker was lying.'

When the knife had pierced to the very centre of the puffball Mabs gave it another twist.

'She hates my baby, too. She wants to kill it.'

Liffey looked at Richard for help. Richard was speaking. 'Puffballs are truly amazing. Nature's richest bounty. And you can hang them up and dry them, and then they make wonderful firelighters. Did you know that, Tucker?'
'Can't say I did,' said Tucker. 'We use a gas poker to light our fires, in any case.'

He smiled at Richard as he spoke, as a grown-up might smile at a rather slow child; and then he looked at Liffey with a sympathetic expression on his face, which would have been pleasant enough except that Mabs was watching Tucker watching her, and Mabs' eyes seemed not just brown, dark brown, but deepest black.

Things fell into place.

'Mabs knows Tucker comes up to see me. Tucker wasn't lying. Mabs knows. Knows he came up again, and I let him.'

Make it a dream.

Dinner is served, in the cold dining room, on the French polished table. It is a room that is hardly ever used.

'So, Liffey,' said Mabs brightly. Tucker carved. Mabs served. A face appeared briefly and hungrily at the window, and disappeared again. Tina's. 'Only two weeks more to go. I expect you'll be glad when it's over.'
'I like being pregnant,' said Liffey, brightly. Liffey knew that she must now assert her will against Mabs: must oppose bad with good: must send out against her such spiritual forces as she could muster. Mabs had a strong, evil battalion already assembled: as she doled out mixed thawed peas and carrots, and roast and mashed potatoes both, she doled out

242

spite, anger, enmity and mystery. They were hers to distribute.

Wonderful dinner! Liffey said so.

Liffey must be cheerful, honest, ordinary, positive and kind. Then all might still be well. She must set up a bulwark of good will. Her defence must be an armoury of opposites. She had no attacking weapons. She could not love Mabs, who had stuck a knife through Liffey, into Liffey's baby, and twisted.

Mabs, who limped when you drove a nail through her footprint.

Ha-ha.

Yes, Richard. Mabs, witch. Do you know? Are you part of it, too?

O madness! Paranoia! Pregnancy!

Liffey looked down at her plate. On Richard's plate, and Tucker's, were good thick lean and shapely slices of roast rib of beef. On her, Liffey's plate, was a little mound of fat and gristle.

Mabs watched Liffey watching her plate. Liffey raised her eyes and stared at Mabs.

Mabs smiled. Mabs knew. Mabs knew that Liffey knew that Mabs knew.

Richard noticed nothing, or pretended to notice nothing. He was fishing for more puffball slices with Tucker's carving fork.

'Give Liffey a decent piece of meat,' said Tucker, mildly. 'She doesn't want too much at this stage,' said Mabs, 'do you Liffey?'
'I'm fine,' said Liffey, 'really fine with what I've got.'

Well done, Liffey.

Of course what it's all about, thought Liffey, with the calmness born of certainty, is that Mabs thinks it's Tucker's baby.

'Have some puffball, Liffey,' said Mabs, 'now Richard's found it. I was hoping he'd forget but no such luck.'
'No, thank you,' said Liffey. Ah, that was wrong. She should have accepted, devoured her own flesh and blood. Or at any rate her own white, bloodless flesh. The life blood drained away. Too late.

'Liffey,' said Richard, 'you must at least taste. I insist. After all the trouble everyone's been to.'

Eat, said the baby. You must choose now not between good and bad, but between the lesser of evils. Eat, smile, hope.

'Really, Liffey,' chided Richard, 'you're supposed to be eating for two.'
'Don't upset her,' said Tucker. 'Not in her condition.'
'It's an entirely natural process,' said Richard. 'Nothing to worry about. African mothers go into the bush, have their babies, pick them up and go straight back to work in the fields.'
They all looked at Liffey, to see how she would take this.
'And then they die,' said Liffey, before she could stop herself.
Open a chink to let doubt out, and a tide of ill will would surge back in.
Bright, brave, bold! That's the way, Liffey. If ever you fought, fight now.

Liffey laughed, to show she didn't mean it.

'Exactly when is the baby due?' asked Mabs.
'October 10th,' said Richard for Liffey.

Mabs got up and rummaged in a drawer amongst old batteries, dried-out pens, bills, string, ancient powder puffs and tubes of this and that with stubborn tops, and rusted skewers, and brought out a leaflet the cat had walked upon with muddy paws. 'The doctor gave me this,' she said. 'After the fifth baby, in just about as many years. He said I might work it out for myself.'

'Work what out?' Tucker was nervous.

'When it was, you know, conceived. It's wonderful the way they can tell, these days. They know everything there is to know in hospitals.'

'It was back in December or January, some time,' said Liffey, swiftly, vaguely.

'According to this,' said Mabs, 'it was over Christmas.'

'We moved in on January 7th,' said Liffey, thankfully.

'So you did,' said Mabs. 'Do you remember, Richard? What a terrible time you both had? You had to rush straight off back to London, Richard, didn't you, and then that weekend poor Liffey had an upset stomach. I remember clearly thinking, you poor things; if you expected a second honeymoon, you certainly weren't getting one then. Such lovebirds you seemed. Of course if Liffey was pregnant that explains her upset stomach.'

'Yes I expect it did,' said Liffey.

'Nothing to do with my cooking after all,' laughed Mabs. Then she seemed to look at the leaflet more carefully. 'No, wait a minute. Christmas was your last period. The baby must have been conceived just around the time you moved in. I must say, Richard, you don't lose much time! In between all that running around and train catching. Remember?'

Richard remembered very well. The days were seared into his memory.

'Of course Tucker was over a lot, helping Liffey out,' said Mabs, into the silence. 'That's so, isn't it Tucker?'

Mabs laughed. Tucker grunted.

'Of course you London people are different,' said Mabs, 'but I don't see anyone round here so easy about rearing another man's child.'

Nobody laughed or grunted or spoke.

Richard blinked, as if by shutting his eyes he would then wake up into a more real and more believable world.

Upstairs Debbie screamed, but the sound went unnoticed.

'Do shut up, Mabs,' said Tucker, 'or I'll break your bloody jaw.'

'I think you'd better take me home, Richard,' said Liffey. 'I don't feel very well.'

The dull pain was gone but the piercing pain now seemed established as a permanent reality and was increasing in intensity. A sizeable segment of placenta had torn away from the uterine wall. Liffey, although ignorant of this fact – indeed, having known remarkably little of what had been going on inside her for the last nine months – nevertheless felt something was going wrong somewhere. Mabs' allegations and revelations seemed to Liffey, now, of no particular relevance.

But for Richard, of course, they were.

'Home,' he said. 'What do you mean by home, Liffey? I don't think what we have is a home.'

Mabs, Liffey realised, was on her feet, arm outstretched, pointing at Liffey: black eyes staring.
'Thief,' she cried. 'You stole what was mine. I hope you die.'

'Richard,' observed Liffey, 'I do have a pain. I think we ought to go.'
'You can't pull the wool over my eyes,' said Richard. 'What do you think I am? A fool? I could see the way things were

going.' But of course he hadn't. All the same, the claim to knowledge lessened the humiliation, just a little.

Tucker spoke.

'No reason to think it's my baby,' said Tucker to Richard, man to man. 'Might be yours: might be mine.'

Richard turned his blue eyes, no longer merry, but still crinkling, of executive habit, to Liffey's, and found them abstracted. He slapped her. Her head shook, and her body, but her look of indifference remained.

'Don't you see what you've done!' shouted Richard. He had trusted Liffey with the better part of his nature, and she had betrayed his trust. There was, he felt, nothing good left in the world. And she had stolen so much of his past as well. She had invalidated so much – the love and concern she had elicited from him; his worry about the growing child; the guilt and inconvenience he had endured; the conscience, and indeed the money, he had expended – all had been for nothing, had meant nothing: had been as little to Liffey as it had been, once, to his mother. And Liffey seemed not even to notice his distress.

The placenta tore a little further. Liffey's uterus began to bleed. No doubt Mabs' curse – for curse it was, a malevolent force directed along a quivering outstretched hand, and not a mere overlooking or ill-wishing – had something to do with it, if only by virtue of the sudden alteration in Liffey's hormonal levels, as shock and anxiety assailed her, and the rise in her blood pressure occasioned by sudden emotion.

Liffey was not aware, so far, that she was bleeding. But the pain intensified.
'Take me home, Richard,' said Liffey.

Richard was staring at Tucker. Little grimy Tucker in his collar and tie. Richard did not really believe that Tucker, by virtue of his way of life, was his superior. Richard had been playing games, as the rich and confident will do with the humble and struggling. Richard despised Tucker.

A wife may be unfaithful with a prince, and not be considered defiled. Glory can be transmitted via the genitals. But Tucker!

'Richard,' Liffey was saying, 'I have to be looked after.'

'Let him look after you,' said Richard, and left Mabs and Tucker's house, head hunched into his shoulders, walking briskly, stonily through the yard, mangy dogs yapping at his crisp blue denim, Tony and Tina falling in behind, up the lane, looking neither to left nor right, to where his car was parked outside Honeycomb Cottage, and piled Tony and Tina in the back, while they protested about hunger and clothes and homework left behind, and drove to London. Quickly, for fear of further pollution, as if evil followed him from the Somerset sky, as if Glastonbury was beaming out some kind of searchlight of dismay, meant especially for him.

Richard, too, got to Bella's publishing party in time, but he was feeling sick with misery, resentment and disillusion, and possibly also from Mabs' dinner, and did not enjoy the party at all. Afterwards he went to see Vanessa, who was pleased to see him, in the way a rather busy person is pleased to see a stray cat, and told him she'd been stoned out of her mind for the last few weeks but had now reformed, and encouraged him to cry gently into the night for his lost Liffey, while she, Vanessa, rang girlfriend after girlfriend to discuss the ethics of whether or not she should own a car, positing the good of comfort against the evil of lead pollution of the sky. He heard himself referred to as a strung-out executive hung-up on a wife who was having it off with a cow-hand, and fell asleep, reassured by the ease with which words could modify experience.

Tucker left shortly after Richard did. He just took the car and went.

'You'd better walk on back up to Honeycomb, girl,' he said

as he left. 'There'll be no sense out of Mabs for an hour or two.'

Mabs strode the room, up and down, up and down. She seemed to have forgotten Liffey, who drooped over her belly, willing the pain away. The floor seemed to shake beneath Mabs' footfall, although surely it was made of solid stone. Mabs seemed larger then life, like a giantess.

Liffey's baby was quiet. Liffey knew it was apprehensive: she had not known it like that before. All right, said Liffey to her baby, reassuring where no reassurance was, all right. She made a conscious effort to modify her own mood: to lessen shock and fright, to accept pain and not to fight it, as Madge had once tried to teach her, while Liffey had refused to learn. Little Liffey, long ago, refusing Madge's knowledge, that the world is hard and you'd better learn to manage it.

All right, mother, you win.

Liffey stood up. Blood streamed down her legs. It was bright, almost cheerful.

'Mabs,' said Liffey, 'can I use the phone?'
Thus the habit of politeness spoke, foolishly. Madge would just have grabbed, before worse befell.

Worse befell – Mabs, barely pausing in her pacing, answered by ripping the telephone wire out of the hall and throwing the receiver across the room and breaking it.
'Mabs,' said Liffey, 'I'm bleeding.'
'Good,' said Mabs.

Liffey went to the door.
'Tucker,' she yelled. 'Tucker!' There was no reply. There were tyremarks in the dust of the yard. Tony and Tina were gone. A swallow swooped down, and up again, and was gone. It was quiet. The dogs did not yap and prance, as they usually did. They sniffed around, the rich red smell of Liffey's blood, perhaps too strong and strange for them.

Liffey had another pain now, of a different kind: a more patient, slow, insistent pain, travelling round from back to front, as the uterus, damaged as it was, began the business of taking up the cervical canal.

'Mabs,' said Liffey, 'get me to hospital.'
'Can't,' said Mabs. 'The car's gone.'

There was a trail of blood wherever Liffey moved.
'Mabs,' said Liffey, 'I'll die.'
'Good,' said Mabs.

Missions of Mercy

Audrey put her hand trustingly into that of the curate. Hers was warm and small. His was cold and bony. They were alone in the vestry, and he wished they were not.
'What's bothering you, Audrey?'

Audrey sang loud and lustily in the choir, but gave the impression, in church, of being some kind of emissary from a foreign power, and not a particularly friendly one at that. It might, he thought, have had something to do with the way her eyes roamed, with prurient speculation, over the males in the congregation. Most of them were elderly.
'It's my sister Debbie. She's ill. She needs the doctor.'
'Then surely your mother will fetch one?'
'My mum's not like that.'
'But why come to me? Why not go straight to the doctor?'

He knew the answer even as he asked. Audrey did not even bother to reply. Audrey fancied him. She did not fancy the doctor. He wished he were back in theological college. He did not know why he felt so helpless. Audrey's hand, which he had thought to be so childish, moved like an adult's in his, suggestively.

'My mum says Debbie's just constipated, but I know she's not, because she keeps messing her pants, and I'm the one who washes them so I should know. And my mum keeps on giving her buckthorn.'
'What's that.'
'It's all right for the cows, I suppose. It's just berries she boils up. Makes your mouth green.'

The curate took back his hand. Audrey looked disappointed and concluded the interview.
'Anyway,' she said, going, 'I really am worried about Debbie.'

Liffey stood bleeding in the yard of Cadbury Farm.
Mabs had slammed the door behind her. The piercing pain was worse: her brow was clammy, her clogs were full of blood. She took them off.

Well, thought Liffey, no good standing here. No good screaming, or crying, or fainting. No use lying down, either. If I do nothing, I will simply bleed to death. If it was only me, I wouldn't mind. I really wouldn't. I am not sure, on my own account, that I wish to stay in the world, considering its nature. What about you, baby? She felt the touch of its spirit, almost for the last time, still clear, still light and bright, almost elegant. The baby didn't have to want to live: it *was* life. She felt the touch on her hand, and there was little Eddie, standing in front of her, looking up at her, mumbling something incoherent, talking about Debbie. He pulled her forward, down the lane towards the road.

Liffey started walking.
'Only blood,' said Liffey aloud. 'Not even the baby's blood. My blood. Lots more where that came from, Eddie.'

But she wasn't so sure. She walked as fast as she could, but she was also aware that that was very slow, because Eddie kept standing in front of her, facing her, waiting for her to catch up. And as soon as she did, he was off again. Pain counted now as sensation. It had to. She had no idea what the time was, or how long she walked, and bled. The sun glazed in the sky behind the Tor; it was surprisingly high. She walked into it. She did not suffer, particularly. She travelled because she had to, as a bird might travel to a warmer climate, or a salmon cross the sea to the river it had to find.

The curate, though delayed by Audrey, presently arrived at a drinks-before-Sunday-dinner party at the new solicitor's house, and here he encountered the doctor, who was telling the solicitor's wife, not without pride, of the extent to which the old herbalism was still practised in the neighbourhood, and the fact that the village even boasted a wise woman, old Mrs. Tree, who claimed to have cured one of his terminal cancer patients with stewed root of Condor Vine – and admittedly the patient was still in remission. The curate, casually enough, mentioned buckthorn berries and his conversation with Audrey, at which the doctor groaned, said all Sundays were much the same, left his drink unfinished and his wife without transport, and took off for Cadbury Farm. 'His partner once had a child die from buckthorn,' said the doctor's wife, sadly. She finished her husband's sherry. The new solicitor was not going to be lavish with the drink.

The doctor found Liffey just where the lane joined the main road. He took Eddie into the car as well, since he could not leave a small, half-daft child standing by himself on a main road. He drove to the hospital, stopping briefly to talk to a policeman on the way.
'Aren't you going rather fast?' Liffey asked.
'Not particularly,' he said. 'Why didn't you use the phone?' He went through a red light as if it wasn't there at all.
'It was out of order,' said Liffey.
'Where's your husband? Isn't he home? It's Sunday, isn't it?'
'He had to get back to London,' said Liffey, easily. She rather enjoyed the ride; the piercing pain had dulled and she could now allow the other ones to come and go at will. She was sitting on a pile of curtains the doctor happened to have

in the car, on the way to the cleaners for his wife. He had prudently put them under Liffey to save his car upholstery. What funny bright red damp curtains, thought Liffey. I'm sure I have better taste than his wife.

Three nurses and a doctor and a wheeled stretcher, with two drips already set up, one clear, one red, waited at the top of the hospital steps.

'I say!' said Liffey.
'She might be drunk, or something,' said the doctor. 'She's euphoric. Tell the anaesthetist,' and hoped they heard him as they ran down the corridor away from him.

There had been valerian and coltsfoot in the elderflower wine; Mabs thought now that perhaps she had overdone the coltsfoot, and made everyone quarrelsome, including herself. Well, it was too late now. What was done was done. She wiped up the blood on the doorstep and worked out a story to tell when Liffey's body, with any luck, was found, and went upstairs to tell Debbie to stop that racket.

The doctor had forgotten all about Eddie but of course there he was, still sitting in the back of the car, crying.
'Christ,' said the doctor. 'This is supposed to be my day of rest.'

He sped and jerked Eddie all the way back to the village, and then bumped and banged him all the way down the lane, and parked amongst the yowling dogs because there was nowhere else, just as Mabs came out of the front door with Debbie's unconscious, or dead, body in her arms. The doctor got out of the car and ran, kicking at the dogs. He'd forgotten about the buckthorn berries.

'The phone's out of order,' offered Mabs by way of explanation, 'Eddie broke it, and Tucker's gone off God knows where, and I came back in from the cows and found blood all over the step and Debbie fell out of bed and must have banged her head because I went up and found her like this.'

'The blood is Mrs. Lee-Fox's,' said the doctor, laying Debbie flat, running his hands over her stomach. She groaned. Good. 'Fine neighbour you make: never in when you're wanted. She's in hospital now.'

'My, that was quick,' said Mabs. 'She was right as rain at lunch. Had a bit of a row with her husband, though. Well, she imagines things.'

'Why was the child in bed?'

'She's dirty. Wets the bed. She's got to learn. Is it bad?'

'Ruptured appendix,' said the doctor. 'Stands to reason. Help me get her in the car, quick.'

'I'll come to the hospital too,' said Mabs. 'Might as well. Will Mrs. Lee-Fox be all right?'

'I'd worry about the child, if I were you,' said the doctor, but he'd known mothers like this many a time, the object of their concern shifted to something more tolerable than danger to their own child. At least he hoped it was that.

'Mrs. Lee-Fox is in good hands.'

'It's a punishment on me,' said Mabs, and began to cry, though what was the punishment she did not make clear. Eddie had stopped crying. He stayed in the car while the doctor drove back to the hospital. This time they did not pass a policeman and when they reached the hospital the doctor had to stamp and roar to get attention, by which time he feared all hope for Debbie was probably lost.

'Two emergencies in one afternoon,' grumbled the theatre sister. 'You can tell it's Sunday.'

Birth

Bells rang, red lights glowed, people ran.

Liffey had been in the operating theatre for twenty minutes.

254

She had gone in fully conscious, been given one injection to reduce the secretions from her throat and mouth, another one which part-paralysed her and prevented her struggling, and an anaesthetic which was of necessity light, in case the baby was anaesthetised too. Liffey sensed the passage of time, and of terrible, painful, momentous events. Of struggle, and endeavour, and of the twists and turns of fate, and of life taking form out of rock.

'Was there breakthrough?' enquired the anaesthetist later. 'Sorry. Sometimes it's hard to judge, not too much, not too little and there wasn't much time.'

The foetal heart had showed no signs of distress. The baby's supply of oxygen remained adequate, in spite of the knot in the umbilical cord, in spite of the haemorrhage behind the placenta, in spite of the frequency of the uterine contractions – each one obstructing the blood and oxygen supply to the placenta for, at their height, one minute in every three: in spite, in fact, of anything, everything Mabs could do. The umbilical knot remained loose; the area of haemorrhage was limited; the placenta remained able to provide enough oxygen in two minutes to carry the baby through the next. The heart remained at a steady 140 beats, falling to 120 at the height of a contraction.
'Lots of time for baby,' said someone, surprised. 'What a lucky baby. Not much for mother, though.'

The uterus had to be emptied before it could fully contract. Until it was fully contracted, it would continue to bleed. Difficult to drip as much into Liffey as she dripped out. The surgeon made an inverse incision from side to side across the abdomen, just above Liffey's pubic mound. He then separated the muscles of the lower abdominal wall and opened the abdominal cavity. The bladder was then dissected free from the lower part of the anterior of the uterus. A transverse incision was then made in the lower uterine segment, exposing the membranes within. The baby's head slipped out of the surgeon's hand: membranes closed.

Mabs seated herself, coincidentally, in the waiting room of the theatre block, and took up a magazine and flicked through it.

Poor woman, thought the voluntary worker who organised the tea bar there.

The baby, conscious of distress, moved violently, tumbled and turned and pulled the umbilical knot tighter and the surgeon re-exposed the membranes and found the baby's buttocks, and Liffey, conscious of struggle within, tried to cry out and could not.

The surgeon found the head: used forceps. He sweated. 'Little beggar,' he said. 'You seem to like it in there. If only you knew how unsafe it was.'

The surgeon lifted out the baby.

'A boy,' someone said. Someone always names the sex. Everyone wants to know. It defines the event. Liffey heard.

'I'm really sorry,' said the anaesthetist later. 'Still, we do our best.'
'At least,' said Liffey, 'I am left with a sense of occasion, not just in one minute and out the next.'

The baby was held upside down. The baby did nothing. Then the baby breathed, spluttered, coughed and cried, and tried to turn itself the right way up, slithering in restraining hands. His colour was pinkish blue, changing rapidly to pink, first the lips, then the skin around the mouth, then the face. He was covered, beneath the slippery vernix, with fine hair. His muscles were tense.
'Doesn't seem premature. Got her dates wrong, I expect.'
The umbilical cord was clamped in two places, and divided between the clamps.
'A knot, too. See that? Only eight lives left.'
'About five, I'd say. How far did she walk?'
'A mile, someone said.'

'Christ!'

More anaesthesia. The placenta was removed. Ergometrine,
to contract the uterus.

'How much has she lost?'
'Two, three pints since she's been in. Can't say, before.'

The bleeding stopped. A morsel of puffball, undigested – for
during labour the digestive processes stop – rose up in
Liffey's gullet, propelled by retching muscles as the anaesthetic deepened, and such was its light yet bulky texture,
might well have been inhaled had the nurse stopped
bothering to exert pressure on Liffey's neck. But she was
young and frightened and doing as she was told. So much so
that Liffey's neck retained the bruises for some weeks. But
she lived.

Mabs, sitting outside in the waiting room, was conscious of
defeat, annd sighed and was brought a cup of tea by the
voluntary worker.

Repair

The incision in Liffey's now firmly contracted uterus was
repaired with catgut. The bruised bladder was stitched back
over the lower uterine segment. Liffey's fallopian tubes and
ovaries were inspected. They looked young, healthy, and
capable of function in the future. The anterior abdominal
wall was sutured. The incision in the skin was then closed
with individual stitches.

'I wouldn't want to do that again,' said the surgeon. 'Next?'

The baby lay in an incubator in the special care unit. His

temperature was ninety-eight degrees. His heartbeat, 120 at the moment of delivery, had fallen to 115, and would slow gradually over the next three days to between eighty and a hundred, where it would stay for the rest of his life. He breathed at forty-five breaths a minute, with an occasional deep, sighing breath. The breathing came mostly from the abdomen – the chest itself moved very little. He grunted a little but that would soon stop. He was immune, for the time being, to measles, mumps, and chicken pox, thanks to antibodies present in Liffey's system which had crossed the placenta.

With his first breath he had inhaled some 50cc of air, opening up the respiratory passages in his lungs, forcing blood through the pulmonary arteries, establishing an adult type of circulation. He weighed six pounds and six ounces, he was nineteen-and-a-half inches long. Grasp, sucking, swallowing, rooting and walking reflexes were present. That is, his palm would clench when pressure was applied to it, any pressure on his palate would start him sucking, a handclap would make him throw out his legs and arms, he would swallow what was in his mouth, he would root for food, following touch on his jaw: when he was held under the arms and his feet touched a firm surface, he would seem to walk.

His nails reached the end of his fingers; his eyes were blue, but already, unusually, changing to brown. He could not see, in adult terms, but could differentiate light from dark. His tear ducts worked so well he could not cry. He sneezed from time to time. He could hear. He had already passed a quantity of meconium, the sticky dark green substance present in his intestine at birth. Liver and spleen were slightly enlarged at birth, which was normal. His testicles had descended, and his urinary passage was normal.

Everything was well with the baby. Very well.

In the operating theatre next door Debbie hovered between life and death, and finally came down on the living side. The nurse who went to tell the mother so, found her eventually in a phone booth, where she was having a long, wrangling conversation with her sister Carol. as to whose fault it was.

Mabs seemed annoyed at having to bring the call to an end, rather than gratified with the message brought. 'What a fuss!' she said, 'about nothing.'
Mabs did not enquire too closely into the nature of Debbie's illness, its cause, or its prognosis.
'I expect you'll want to stay with your little girl, till she's out of the anaesthetic,' said the nurse.
'Well, I can't get back till Tucker comes with the car,' said Mabs. 'How's Mrs. Lee-Fox doing?'
Liffey had been wheeled past her on the trolley, ashen white, head lolling.
'She'll be all right,' said the nurse. 'We only lose one mother a year and we've already lost her!' It was their little joke.

Murder

Mabs heard Liffey's baby cry. A pain struck through to Mabs' heart, not just at this final, overwhelming evidence of her impotence to prevent this birth, but at the injustice it presented. Tucker's baby emerging from the wrong body, so that she, Mabs, was left ignored in a waiting room while the gentle, powerful concern of authority, and the dramatic indications of its existence – masks and lights and drugs and ministering hands – focused down on the wrong person. Mabs sat beside Debbie's bed and waited for her to wake up, and scarcely saw her.

Liffey woke up to ask how the baby was and was told it was fine, which she didn't believe, and sank back into sedated sleep. When she woke next she cried with pain, exhaustion and lack of a baby to put in her arms.

259

'Baby's perfectly all right,' said the nurse. 'Don't fuss. All Caesar babies go into special care for a couple of days, that's all.'

The staff treated Liffey with automatic kindness; moving her up in the bed when she slipped down, changing pillows, sponging her face. The desire to empty her bruised bladder was enormous; the ability to do so lacking: the pain and humiliation of being lifted to use a bedpan overwhelming. She had more drugs.

She remembered the baby.

'Don't let Mabs get the baby,' she said. Of course this was hospital and Mabs was at the farm, but Liffey kept saying the same thing. 'Bring the baby here. Please bring the baby here,' and they promised her they would, to keep her quiet, knowing her sense of time was confused.

The Almoner's Department tried to trace her husband but he could not be found at his office, and had a new secretary who was not helpful. They did rather better with the Personnel Department, who proferred the information that Mr. Lee-Fox might well be having a minor breakdown: that this sometimes happened to executives under stress at the time of a major life event; of which having a first baby was certainly one. They were concerned but not anxious, and thanked the hospital for their help.

Liffey lapsed back into slumber and pain and woke to find Mabs in the room. Liffey tried to sit up but could not. She had no strength in her abdomen, thighs, arms or shoulders.

'Well, well.' said Mabs. 'Feeling better, are we? Congratulations!'
Liffey said nothing.
'I never had to have a Caesar,' said Mabs. 'Perhaps you have narrow hips? You should have taken some of my rosemary tea. I always drink it when I'm pregnant and never have any trouble. Is Richard pleased?'

Liffey said nothing.

'I do think a girl's easier for a man to accept,' said Mabs, 'but there's not much we can do about that. Do you mind me just chatting on? Don't talk if it tires you. I know what it's like by now. The doctor told me you lost a lot of blood, too. Why didn't you come down to me instead of setting off like that, all by yourself. Mind you, the phone was out of order. Eddie broke it, the naughty boy; I didn't half wallop him. Debbie was taken ill with appendix, and of course the one time I really needed the phone, it wasn't working.'

'Is it visiting hours?' asked Liffey. Perhaps she was dreaming Mabs?

'No,' said Mabs, 'it isn't. I'm living in, with Debbie. She's been quite poorly. Isn't it a coincidence, the two of us here together? So I can pop in any time I please. Where's baby?'

Dreamed or not, Liffey wasn't replying to that.

'In the special care unit, I suppose?' went on Mabs. 'I'll just nip down and see him. Poor little mite, all wired up. No baby of mine ever went into special care.'

Mabs saw the bruises on Liffey's neck.

'Who ever tried to strangle you?' she asked, as she left. 'Now who would want to do a thing like that?'

And Mabs was gone.

I dreamed it, thought Liffey. There was a great hollow under her ribs where the baby used to live, and a hole in that part of her mind which the baby had used. She had endured some kind of fearful loss. Liffey sat up and cried for help.

No one came.

No. She had not dreamed Mabs. Mabs had been real.

Liffey remembered Richard's going, the pain, the broken telephone, the slammed door, the blood, Eddie, the walk. Mabs. Witch, Murderess.

Liffey got out of bed. She took her legs with her hands and dropped them over the side of the bed, and let the rest of her fall after them. Once she was out of bed and on the floor, progress was possible. Surprisingly, movement begat movement. Liffey began to crawl. She still wore a white surgical gown, tied with tapes across her back.

Mabs was already at the special care unit, at the far end of a wedge of post-natal wards. The walls of a corridor turned to glass, and there, behind the glass, under the bright yet muted lights, were ranks of plastic incubators, and in them babies, wired up to monitors by nostril and umbilicus, or linked to drips or life support machinery: tiny mewling scraggy things.

Baby Lee-Fox, there only for observation, unwired, unlinked, lay in a far corner, breathing, sighing, snuffling, doing well. Masked nurses sat and watched, or moved about the rows on quiet urgent missions. An orderly at the door handed out masks and gowns for parents and close relatives. 'Baby Lee--Fox?' asked Mabs. She looked like many women in these parts, large and strong, yet soft.

The name Lee-Fox with its pallid hyphenated ring, its overtones of refined home counties, sat strangely on her tongue, but not strangely enough for the orderly to doubt Mabs' right to be where she was so clearly at home; amongst these small babies, hovering between dark and light, at that moment of existence where the ability, the desire, to go forward peaks again towards reluctance.

At Honeycomb Cottage doors and windows stood wide. Rain had fallen in the night and splashed unheeded on to papers and books. A column of ants now filed through the sunny front door and into the sugar bowl on the kitchen table. The rain had washed out most, but not all, of the marks where Richard, in his anxiety to be away, had scored the lane with his tyres.

Up at Cadbury Farm Tucker was in charge. He liked being

alone with the children. They sat round the kitchen table eating large plates of cornflakes, liberally sprinkled with sugar and swimming in milk. Audrey made a cake. Eddie sat on his father's knee and poked his fingers up Tucker's nostrils. They missed Debbie. The radio was on. All remembered a time when Mabs had been kind, and Tucker felt at fault for not having earned them, of late, a remission. Each remission, of course, meant another mouth to feed for the next fifteen years. Now, it seemed, he had earned one by proxy.

Mabs leaned over Baby Lee-Fox. Mabs laughed. The tone of the laugh disturbed a nurse, who came over and looked as well.

Baby Lee-Fox clenched and unclenched fists; struggled to open eyes.
'Lovely little baby,' said the nurse. 'Of course Caesar babies usually are. They don't get so squashed.'

Mabs laughed again: it was a strange deflating sound, as if all the air and spirit was draining swiftly out of a balloon, so that it tore and raced annd hurled itself about a room, before lying damp and still.
'Is it that funny?' asked the nurse, puzzled.
'He's the image of his father,' said Mabs.

'Just like Richard,' said Mabs to Liffey, laughing again. Liffey had been picked up from the floor outside the special care unit and put back to bed, and the drips set up again, and Baby Lee--Fox brought into her room, since she was apparently earnest in her desire to see her baby.
'Why shouldn't he be?' asked Liffey, wearily.

Mabs smiled, a really happy, generous smile.
'All's well that ends well,' said Mabs, 'and Debbie's fever has broken. If they'd let me give her feverfew in the first place we'd have had none of this trouble. What a fuss they make in here about every little thing.'

Mabs leant over and picked Liffey's baby out of its crib. She did it tenderly, and reverently. Liffey was not afraid. Mabs had dwindled to her proper scale. The world no longer shook at her footfall. Mabs handed Liffey the baby.

'But where's Richard?' asked Mabs, all innocence. 'Where's the father?'

Liffey's memory of the Sunday lunch was vague, over-shadowed by the events that had followed it. She remembered as one remembers on waking from sleep, the feeling tone of the preceeding day rather than its actual events – that Richard had left angry and that this had been a practical inconvenience rather than an emotional blow. As to the details of the rest, it seemed irrelevant.

The baby lay in Liffey's arms, snuffling and rooting for food. She sensed its triumph. None of that was important, the baby reproved her: they were peripheral events, leading towards the main end of your life, which was to produce me. You were always the bit-part player: that you played the lead was your delusion, your folly. Only by giving away your life, do you save it.

'The little darling,' said Mabs. 'How could anyone hurt a baby?'
The baby smiled.
'Only wind,' said Mabs, startled.
'It was a smile,' said Liffey.
'Babies don't smile for six weeks,' said Mabs, uneasily.
The baby smiled again.

Resignation

Liffey slept. The baby slept. Mabs went home.
'It wasn't your baby after all,' she said to Tucker, and they went upstairs to try for another one. This time sufficient of Tucker's sperm survived the hazardous journey up to Mabs' fallopian tubes to rupture the walls of a recently dropped ovum – fallen rather ahead of time, by virtue of the emotions

264

of tenderness and remorse, mixed, which had flooded Mabs when she marvelled over Baby Lee-Fox, and laughed at his looks. Richard's bemused air of competence combined with innocence, Liffey's gentle generosity: as if the baby, wonderfully, had captured both their good qualities as they flew, and let the others pass.

Mabs, being pregnant, became quiet and kind as if, in her, body alone dictated mood. She had no rational knowledge that she had conceived: only her body, setting off on its forty-week journey, conveyed a general impression of contentment, which the mind accepted.

Mabs came downstairs, smiled at the children, and brought them all fish and chips, and even lemonade to go with it.

The doctor came up to Cadbury Farm presently to say that Debbie was to be sent off to a convalescent home, and to take a general look around.
'Rather them than me,' said Mabs. 'She's a dirty girl. She wets the bed. Still,' she added, magnanimously, 'the others miss her.'
'You nearly lost her altogether,' said the doctor.
'No,' said Mabs, 'I knew I wouldn't.'

There had been no signs, after all – no owls hooting out of nowhere, no lightning out of a clear sky, no yew brought into the house – no signs or portents. Only Mabs twisting a pin in a wax image when she should have left it to others: enough to damage and frighten, but surely not to kill. Debbie had always been safe enough; but how could she tell the doctor a thing like that?

'I'd like to hear a little less about home remedies,' said the doctor, 'and a little more about visiting the surgery when anyone's ill.'
'All right,' Mabs acquiesced. It was a genuine capitulation. She yawned. She was tired. It occurred to her that Tucker and she were not as young as once they had been.

265

She allowed the doctor to put Eddie on a course of antidepressants, and Audrey on the pill, and she herself on valium to cure the rages she now admitted to, and Tucker on Vitamin B because he drank so much home-made wine. With every act of consent, every acknowledgment of his power, her own waned. She felt it. She didn't much mind.

Mabs told the doctor that she and Tucker would fetch Liffey and the baby home from hospital. They'd look after Liffey. Well, the husband had finally gone off.

Liffey's drips were removed. Her stitches came out. Snip, snip – eight times. The skin that had stretched and smarted around the catgut resumed its natural place. She could sit up now, of her own accord. She could lie on her back and lift her legs. She could do without the physiotherapist, who thumped her hard from time to time to make her cough and clear her lungs. She could take a bath, albeit on her hands and knees. She rang her mother, hardly knowing what to say. Madge was cool but friendly, and busy with a Royal visitor to the school.

Mrs. Harris from the shop came to visit; and Audrey brought the curate, who saw God's hand in the deliverance of both Liffey and Debbie. The incident had even reached the local paper. Audrey wished to be confirmed; he was undertaking it. Mabs and Tucker came, with flowers. Tucker wore collar and tie, and sat on the edge of his chair and seemed embarrassed by his surroundings, but he was robust and solid, and dignified: powerful, dark and male in a pale female world.

And certainly as Mabs lost power, Tucker gained it. He knew it: he was rough with Mabs now; he told her what to do: he shouted at her if she behaved badly to the children. He recognised that she was deflated, that although she still stared at the Tor, the clouds around its summit neither reflected her will nor shadowed her intent. Her sly looks requested rather than commanded, and he performed at his own pleasure, and not hers. He thought she was a better mother, and high time too. As one set of energies drained out of her, others took their place.

Richard did not visit Liffey.

Ripples

Richard, after a whole week's absence, unaccounted for and so far unexplained, went back to the office.

'Welcome back!' said Personnel. 'We'll ask no questions and be told no lies. You have a fine son and mother's doing well. Can we be of any help?'
'No, thank you,' said Richard.

He knew he had a son. His attention had been drawn to an advertisement in *The Times* which said, 'Lee-Fox. To Liffey and Tucker, a son'. Miss Martin, Richard rightly guessed, had inserted it. Miss Martin, as did everyone in the company, via Vanessa's connection with the director of the Canadian ox-tail soup television commercial, knew all about the fathering of Liffey's baby. Malice does not evaporate: it bounces round like a rubber ball, striking here and there, sometimes in the most unexpected places, gradually losing energy. It almost stops. Then up it starts again – the cosmic ball of ill will.

Richard wangled Vanessa another modelling job, so that she could buy a car for herself, but after that left her alone. She had heard him weep: she would never respect him. The battle, he could see, was to find a woman who would.

He had spent the whole week with Vanessa: she had made him, for a while, believe that his work was unimportant, that he was only money-grubbing in a rat race: fortunately, common sense reasserted itself. He wished to behave well towards Liffey: to shame her with kindness; to continue to support her. For that he would have to earn more. He owed it to his parents to get promotion, do well, carry on along the road on which they had first set his stumbling footsteps. He could not fail Liffey, or disappoint them.

When he hated Liffey, it was because of the distress her behaviour would have given his parents. He put off telling them. How was he to put it? Yes, mother, Liffey has her baby but it is another man's child. Not your grandchild. Not, after all that, after all those years, your flesh and blood.

Ah yes, I am sure. So sure. It explains so much. Why I betrayed her. It was all her doing. Once the sacred tie is loosed, chaos ensues; the forces of love, of trust, and faith are in disarray: lust sweeps in. Liffey loosed them, quite deliberately. Untied the snowy white robe of her purity and let Tucker in.

Mrs. Lee-Fox senior telephoned.

'Darling, what *is* happening? How's lovely Liffey?'

Lovely Liffey had Tucker's child, mother.

Mrs. Lee-Fox senior wept. See, Liffey, what you have done? My mother weeps. All my life I have dreaded this minute, this moment. I knew it lurked somewhere, waiting.

Liffey, I hate you. I would kill you if I could.

Richard went to stay with Bella and Ray. Bella still couldn't get over the way Liffey had behaved towards Tony and Tina.
'Not even bothering to pack their homework!' said Bella. 'Not even making them a sandwich. They were dreadfully upset. I can't help thinking you're well out of it, Richard.'

'Next time choose someone who can cook,' said Ray. 'Does that sound crude? But it's no good being romantic. You're past the age of falling in love.' Ray had felt infatuation for

268

Karen, not love. Bella had explained it all. Ray was glad it was over.

No one has a baby alone. Every pregnant woman carries with her the aspirations, the ambitions and the fears of others – friends, relatives, and passers-by – and good and ill wishes of such intensity as might put the sun right out.

Good Fortune

As Mabs' ill-wish evaporated so Liffey's good fortune returned. Or perhaps it was merely that now she carried the baby in her arms, the ordinary up-and-downness of life returned.

Tucker and Mabs brought Liffey home from hospital. Their car no longer reeked of menace. It was an ordinary, shabby, littered family car. The baby seemed to enjoy the motion. Home was cosy and familiar. Mabs had put flowers in vases: Tucker had dug over the garden.

The telephone had been installed.

There was a pile of letters. One was from the bank to say that a final payment from the trust fund had been paid in on her last birthday but had inadvertently not been entered to her credit. Twelve thousand pounds. Another was from Mory and Helen. 'Wonderful about the baby!' they wrote. 'Just to say the flat's yours if you want it, even without the £1000 Richard couldn't raise. Mory's been offered a wonderful job in Trinidad, and Helen can't stand the British climate any more. She's pregnant.'

Cruel Richard, thought Liffey. Cruel, cruel Richard. But she did not want the flat back. She wanted very few now of the things she had wanted before.

It was a wonderful month for late sun and over-ripe roses. Liffey could take off the baby's clothes, and let the sun get to his little chicken limbs.

The telephone rang. Friends, who had seen the announcement in *The Times*, and wanted to know what was going on. Liffey told them. Liffey, they thought, was quite fun again.

Fortunately no one who knew Tucker and Mabs read *The Times*, so news of the announcement did not reach them. Personnel fired Miss Martin, however. Enough was enough.

On Friday nights Liffey would find herself nervous, wondering if Richard would come back: half wanting him to, half not. She needed the full width of the double bed for herself and the baby, rolling over in the night as he woke, to pick him from his crib and feed him. Richard would have been in the way.

'What's his name?' people asked.
'Baby Lee-Fox,' she said. She was waiting.

Madge wrote out of the blue saying that the name of Liffey's father had been Martin, and in retrospect had behaved well according to his lights. They just weren't Madge's lights. Why didn't Liffey call the baby Martin?

She called the baby Martin.

'After his grandfather,' she told milkman, dustman, postman, proudly. They all came up the drive now.

The baby's legs looked more human: he lay in his cot working rather than resting, making sense of the world, recognising kindness, censorious of carelessness.

There was a brief rain-sodden autumn. The last of the rose petals fell. A few last blackberries stayed on the brambles. The days became cold and short.

Eddie would come up with firewood; he liked to hang close by Liffey's side. Audrey came to talk about sex, and religion, and whether she preferred the vicar to the curate, the former being older, wiser and richer, but married. Debbie, though still pale and fragile, would trudge over the fields unasked, to get Liffey's shopping. Liffey thought perhaps she was quite content with the company of children.

Local events became important in her life. Carol's husband broke Dick Hubbard's jaw in a brawl and was sent to the local prison for two weeks to teach him what the magistrates called a lesson. Carol did not visit him on visiting day, but was seen in the car park in Dick Hubbard's car. Public opinion finally turned against Dick Hubbard.

Mabs laughed. She and Tucker drank a bottle of sherry between them. They let Audrey have a sip. Mabs was pregnant; the price of beef was high, of foodstuffs not so high as usual; one of the dogs had a puppy, unexpectedly: they were happy. Liffey lived in Honeycomb, properly subdued. It had taken them a year to achieve it. Christmas was coming.

Conclusion

Liffey's baby lay in its cot by the fire and smiled. It seemed, to the outside eye, a perfectly ordinary baby. It spoke to Liffey, silently, but less and less, as its body grew into better proportion to its being. It gave up all apppearance of being in charge, of knowing best. It left all that to Liffey, now.

Liffey looked at herself in the mirror and laughed. She thought she seemed a very average person: no longer pretty, or elfin, or silly, or anything particularly definite, any more. She was much like anyone else. She thought that she too had become what Richard wanted. He had triumphed in his absence.

She put on another jersey. The baby wore two pairs of leggings. The wind turned to the north. Black clouds heaved around the Tor: sometimes it was obscured altogether by mist and rain. In the very cold weather the fire smoked to such an extent it would put itself out, like a scorpion which stings itself with its own tail. On Christmas Eve Liffey ran out of kindling wood to relight the fire. It was raining, and the branches and twigs outside were wet and useless. She went into the outhouse and there found the withered remnants of Richard's puffballs. They were tough, withered and leathery, and she remembered what Richard had said about their use as firelighters, laid them in the grate, and lit them. They burned slowly, patiently and brightly, and she thought there was some good in them after all.

She wanted the baby to speak, to mark so momentous a thought, but his spirit was finally cut off from hers. He smiled at her and that was all.

The fire lit by the puffballs stayed in over the Christmas holiday, to Liffey's satisfaction. The baby smiled at the flames. On Boxing Day a car drew up outside. It was Richard, and his arms were full of soft fluffy toys – white bears and pink fish and orange lions. Liffey thought that vitamin drops and disposable nappies would have been more sensible.
'Christ, Liffey,' he said. 'I am sorry. I don't care whose baby it is.'

Liffey opened the door, not without reluctance. But she knew the baby liked to see people. He enjoyed company more than she did. He would smile at everyone, Liffey told herself, at Mabs and Tucker and the postman and the milkman. But now he smiled at Richard too, claiming him for a father, shuffler of the genes, and she knew that that was that. He claimed them all, everyone, as bit-part players in his drama, dancers in his dance, singers to his tune.

Come in Richard. Here is Liffey.

Clare Morrall was born in E̶̶. She works as a music teacher, ̶̶̶̶̶ ̶̶̶̶̶ two daughters. Her first novel, *Astonishing Splashes of Colour*, was published in 2003 by Tindal Street Press and was shortlisted for the Man Booker Prize. Her second, *Natural Flights of the Human Mind*, was published in 2006 and her third, *The Language of Others*, in 2008.

'Compelling . . . In clear, concise prose, Morrall movingly depicts Kate's strength in the face of adversity, and Felix's excoriating regret at the damage done.'

Marie Claire

'Morrall controls her material brilliantly, taking us back into Felix's past, scattering clues to his psychology, switching back and forth to the present, to Kate somehow coping, into the heads and hearts of the children, their inner voices pinned to the page . . . There are evasions, confrontations, and an outcome that's raw but faithful to every shred of what's gone before.'

Scotsman

'An imaginatively written novel with well-drawn and believable characters, it's a compelling read'

Choice

'The greater complexity she gives Felix works out as the novel progresses and the estranged husband and wife are irretrievably changed by their experiences . . . Morrall is in firm control of her material, contrasting stagnant stability with fluid, dynamic relationships and showing that, in a world that won't stand still, the future belongs to those who understand that and can adapt to it.'

Sunday Herald

'An absorbing novel about deception and self-discovery'

Grazia

CLARE MORRALL

The Man Who Disappeared

SCEPTRE

First published in Great Britain in 2010 by Sceptre
An imprint of Hodder & Stoughton
An Hachette UK company

First published in paperback in 2010

1

A CIP catalogue record for this title is available from the British Library.

ISBN 978 0 340 99429 0

Typeset in Sabon by Hewer Text UK Ltd, Edinburgh
Printed and bound by CPI Mackays, Chatham

Hodder & Stoughton policy is to use papers that are natural, renewable
and recyclable products and made from wood grown in sustainable
forests. The logging and manufacturing processes are expected to
conform to the environmental regulations of the country of origin.

Hodder & Stoughton Ltd
338 Euston Road
London NW1 3BH

www.hodder.co.uk

To the Blue Coat children who think I should dedicate a book to them and all the others who are too polite to ask.

Part One

Chapter 1

Felix Kendall stands in the darkness, outside the friendly circle of light from the streetlamp. Cold seeps into him, numbing his fingertips. A breeze rustles the larches in the front garden of a house behind him on the opposite side of the road.

He watches.

Through a bright window, close to the pavement, he can see a family sitting in their dining room. The mother is spooning out the steaming contents of a casserole dish that she has just brought to the table, putting a piece of meat – chicken, lamb, pork? – on a plate and then pouring the sauce over it. She hands the meal to one of the children, a boy, who starts to help himself from the vegetable dishes placed in the middle of the table. He must be about six. Felix can see the round softness of his cheeks, his wayward dark hair, a little too long, the fringe soft and floppy over his forehead, his earnest concentration as he balances a potato on a spoon.

Rory – oh, Rory . . .

Two other children are waiting, talking to each other, arguing perhaps. There's some animosity between them, and they appeal to their father, who's sitting at the other end of the table.

It's a portrait of a family, a Dickensian scene of harmony, lit by a central light that hangs over the table. Everything is too perfect, too good to be true. Felix tries to convince himself that they hate each other, the husband and wife. They're probably about to divorce: the father is having an affair with

3

someone at work; the mother's running a successful business, living her life apart from the rest of the family; the meal is ready-made from Waitrose.

But he can't accept it, can't absorb the cynical chill of reality. He wants to believe in this cosiness, this world of families, this labyrinth of deeply entwined love.

That's the key, of course: love. He has been told this for as long as he can remember. 'We love you, Felix,' one of his aunts used to say, 'and that's all that matters.'

What have I done, Kate?

Frost glints on the road, nearby car windscreens are clouded with ice. Felix blows on his hands and shuffles his feet around, trying to bring some feeling back to his toes.

The father gets up suddenly and goes to the window. Felix forces himself into stillness and holds his breath, wondering if his movements have attracted attention. The man pulls down a blind, shutting him out into the night.

It's very dark out here. Felix thrusts his trembling hands into his pockets. The darkness is inside him, a black, black pit with no bottom.

He walks away, studying the houses he passes in the hope of another tableau, another family. He sees empty rooms, half lit from a hall beyond. There are bookshelves, tables, armchairs, Swiss cheese plants, photographs on mantelpieces. Occasional isolated people watching television, sitting at a computer. But no more families.

Lawrence, Millie . . .

Alfred's Mart is warm and brightly lit, an open-handed invitation to join the generous club of everyday life. Felix selects a few items for his supper, aware that he has only a limited supply of cash, and queues behind a woman with a trolley containing twenty loaves and sixteen cartons of milk. Is she a mother with dozens of children? She's far too well

4

kept for that – chic spiky haircut, long shimmery silk scarf with a bold green and purple geometric design.

'Sorry,' she says to him, seeing him watching her. 'Do you want to go in front?' Her voice is soft and breathy, as if she has asthma.

'No problem,' he says. He's got all evening, all night, for ever. 'I'm in no hurry.'

Compassion looms ominously out of her eyes. 'Oh dear. No one to go home to?'

What gives her the right to ask personal questions? She's not going to tell him why she has all those cartons of milk. At least, he hopes she isn't. 'My house got hit by lightning,' he says, 'and my wife went off with the fire brigade.'

She clearly hasn't heard him properly, because a tap of sympathy opens up and starts to flow. 'You poor thing—'

'And my six children got run over by the fire engine as they cycled home to see what was going on.'

Ladybird, ladybird, fly away home—

Millie at two, fresh from the bath, her eyes drooping, then snapping alert, warm and cosy in his arms. White, plump pillows, the smell of fresh air and washing-powder.

Your house is on fire and your children are gone—

I can't go home. It's no longer possible. I would if I could – but I can't.

There's a shift in the woman's manner, a pause while she decides how to interpret Felix's reply. She doesn't have enough information to know how to react. She manages a distant half-smile and turns her attention to packing her shopping.

Felix is ashamed of himself. He's slipping out of the character he has spent years perfecting. Be friendly, be nice. The roadmap to success. He wonders if he should help her. It would redeem him, perhaps, and it would speed up her departure. But he stands and watches, his arms heavy with the paralysis of indecision.

She pays, and snatches a last glance at him out of the corner of her eye before wheeling her over-laden trolley away. Her tights are navy with seams at the back. A prostitute who offers her clients tea and toast afterwards?

He shouldn't have spoken to her. He mustn't draw attention to himself.

He packs his meagre purchases into a carrier-bag, wondering why he has bothered to buy anything. How could he possibly put his mind to food?

'Have you signed the petition for a pelican crossing outside the store?' asks the girl on the till, as he hands her a twenty-pound note.

Without thinking, Felix picks up the pen she's offering him – and stops. He can't use his own name. He searches for inspiration and sees the chocolate selection next to the till. *Martin Cadbury*, he writes with a flourish. 'What other action have you taken?' he asks.

She looks at him blankly. She's only about sixteen, not at all pretty, with her hair scraped back into a severe ponytail, accentuating her plump cheeks. 'What do you mean?' she says.

Felix is assailed by a familiar organisational streak, full of righteousness. Don't they know anything? All his years with the parent-teacher association at the children's schools qualify him to offer advice. Fêtes, concerts, trips to the theatre, summer balls. His work for the local volunteer group cleaning up the area, protests against planning applications, the fight against the proposed mobile-phone mast. He's done it all. He's good at it. It's like the smell of baking bread, fresh and mouth-watering, rushing through him with an unexpected pain of pleasure.

'A petition won't do it,' he says. 'These people only glance at the signatures, check there's nobody like Paul McCartney or the Queen on it, and then put the piles of paper into a convenient corner where they'll get taken away for recycling. You have to do something much more significant if you want a chance of success.'

She stares. 'Like what?'

'A demonstration, a feature on local television, a trip to Westminster to involve your MP, embarrass him in front of his colleagues, that kind of thing.'

She seems to be having difficulty taking it all in. 'Oh,' she says. 'You need to talk to my boss.'

'Another time,' says Felix. He puts his shopping into a carrier-bag.

'Haven't I seen you somewhere before?' says the girl.

Panic jolts through him. How could she possibly know? With some difficulty, he turns away from the till. His legs are stiff and his knees won't bend properly.

'Hey!' calls the girl. 'You forgot your change.'

It doesn't matter. I don't need it.

She leans over and grabs his arm. 'Here,' she says, putting the coins into his hand. 'You can't leave your change. I'd get into awful trouble.'

He produces his charming smile, the one that always gets him where he wants to be. He can feel his mouth opening, the lips parting. 'Thank you,' he says, and turns away.

The hotel lobby is filled with dozens of French schoolchildren when Felix returns with his shopping. They are congregated in groups, heaps of luggage arrayed around them, chattering with high-pitched excited voices. Their teachers are working hard, issuing instructions and trying to calm them down, but without much success. Felix is forced to take a diversion through the bar to reach the lifts.

On a low table, stationed between two white leather sofas, a well-thumbed copy of *The Times* catches his attention.

He stops.

He and George are staring out from the front page, their photographs side by side, with a smaller one of Kristin underneath.

It's as if he's been punched in the stomach. This must be a mistake. Someone must have picked up the wrong photograph.

With trembling hands, he leans over the table and grabs the newspaper. He reads his name below and the headline above.

He glances around to see if he's being watched, suddenly convinced that someone will recognise him, but everyone is caught up in the drama of the French schoolchildren. He hurries round the corner and decides to take the stairs. He can't wait for the lift – he can't stand still.

He drives himself up to the twenty-first floor, his breath uncontrolled and painful. He's not pacing himself now, not in training for a marathon, not having to prove himself. He's running with fear, terrified of what the newspaper is going to tell him.

Panting, he fumbles with his card in the lock, putting it in upside down at first, all the time checking over his shoulder that no one else has arrived on the floor. Once he's in, he slams on the light and drops his shopping. Standing there, he reads through the article. Then he reads it again.

Someone's got it horribly wrong. Of course there would inevitably be some media interest, but it should be a short paragraph on page seven, not headline news, not photographs on this scale. They seem to think he and George have masterminded a worldwide operation.

But I didn't know any of this. George didn't tell me the whole truth.

Why would you expect a dishonest man to be truthful?

I could have stopped it and I didn't.

He drops to the floor and hunches up on the carpet, wrapping his arms round his legs, staring into space. His mind races through a tangle of replayed conversations and missed connections, and a torrent of guilt and shame floods through him.

Two hours later, he arranges himself on the hotel-room floor, stretching his legs out in front of him. His purchases are laid on the carpet by his side. A bottle of Scotch; a wedge of strong Cheddar; a packet of water biscuits; a sharp cheese knife.

He's tried examining himself in a mirror, next to the newspaper, and concluded that it must be obvious he is the man in the photograph. His face is buried under an emerging beard and there are new hollows under his eyes, but it's so clearly him that he can't understand why the police aren't already knocking on his door. If he goes out again, he'll be spotted immediately. One of the hotel staff must have recognised him. His time is limited.

Everything has led to this hotel room in a small corner of a city far away from his home. His whole life, his record of achievement, has turned out to be inconsequential. A speck of dirt flicked by a duster, brushed aside, tossed out for the bin-men without a thought.

One minute he was cruising along, in control of his life, enjoying the breeze, and the next, everything had crumpled into a major pile-up that wasn't his fault.

Not true. It was his fault. He'd been driving with full headlights, miles over the speed limit, without looking far enough ahead.

How to lose your identity in five days. On Tuesday he didn't go to Hamburg. On Thursday, in a lucid moment, he sent an email to Kate from an Internet café, wanting to reassure her, even though she wouldn't know yet that he had gone. It was a mistake. He shouldn't have sent it. He'd tried to sound normal but it was difficult – impossible—

Everything he's done has been for Kate, for the family. As a child, he dreamt of having a family, imagining his own place within it, the complicated interactions between parents and children. The dream was a twenty-carat diamond, nurtured over the years, cut and polished, and he was willing to plough

9

through mud, dig through rock to get it. He'd constructed a family with as much skill as he could manage, pulling it all together with an expertise that he acquired from books, newspapers, advice from colleagues. He'd collected all the essential ingredients, mixed them up, created a work of art, an edifice of love.

He keeps telling himself it was real.

How could everything crumble so spectacularly? Was it really his fault? Was it the result of his actions, or had it been inevitable? Had he just built up a story, an ideal, that was ready to collapse the moment a small breeze blew from the north? Iceland, to be precise.

He sees a child sitting on a bed, alone, listening to clocks ticking in the empty silence. Rory? Or himself as a child?

The room is lit by a bedside lamp that is absurdly inadequate. Nobody could read in this light. You need brightness for reading. Perhaps people don't read any more. Perhaps he's unreasonable in his expectations.

No, his expectations haven't been unreasonable. He's believed in himself. He's always known he could do it, right from the beginning. How could he have predicted this?

But was his family just a painting hanging in a gallery, a figment of an artist's imagination? An English interior, a semi-sentimental portrait of life in the early twenty-first century?

He was expecting to go to Hamburg. For work. He'd delivered Rory to his friend's house and Millie to her school, where she was going to board for a week. Kate was in Canada. The world was organised, everyone was in the right place, there was no reason why anything should go wrong.

Except – something had happened on Monday that made him nervous. Ken, his driver, had been taking him home from a meeting in Bristol and they'd stopped for a break at a motorway service station. When Felix went to pay for their coffees, the girl at the till dropped his change on the floor and there was some confusion, so when he finally picked up his tray, several people were watching him. One of them was a small man sitting at a table on his own, reading a newspaper. He was peering over the top of the pages, an ordinary man, middle-aged, dark hair, glasses, in a suit, nothing to distinguish him from anyone else.

But this was the fourth time Felix had seen him in the last week. He'd first stood next to him in the queue for taxis at Exmouth station, then he'd noticed him at a newsagent's in Budleigh Salterton and only yesterday, he'd caught a glimpse of his back as he left the foyer of his office block.

He studied the man in the motorway service station. Surely this was one encounter too far. For a brief second, their eyes made contact. Then the man's gaze slipped away as he folded his newspaper, stood up and left the room.

Was it coincidence? Or was he being watched?

On Tuesday, at six o'clock in the morning, Felix's driver dropped him by the entrance to Exeter St Davids station. 'Thanks, Ken,' he said, getting out.

'Have a good trip,' said Ken.

Felix stood and watched the Mercedes glide out of the station car park, go round the mini roundabout and head up the hill towards the city centre.

It was still dark. Orange lights lit the car park, and the station glowed with the welcoming yellow of electric warmth. The ticket office wasn't open yet, but there was a young woman drinking a cup of coffee behind the newspaper kiosk. She was wearing a hat and scarf and her hands, encased in woolly gloves, wrapped themselves round the plastic cup for warmth. Her breath escaped into the air in puffs of white steam.

Felix was earlier than he needed to be. He always allowed plenty of time to buy a newspaper, find the right platform, establish which end of the train would be First Class.

His mobile rang. Kate, he assumed. She'd miscalculated the time difference in Canada.

But it wasn't Kate. 'Felix—'

'George?'

'Felix, my man.' George's voice was distant, uneven, as if he was running.

'What's going on?' asked Felix.

'It's the Big Man,' said George.

'What are you talking about?'

A sharp memory of the Big Man, their headmaster from more than thirty years ago, thundering along the corridor towards them, his grey wispy hair awry, his eyes fixed on them from behind thick-lensed glasses, his voice booming: 'Kendall! Rangarajan!'

'Get out now, Felix, while you can—' There was a lot of crackling and the phone went dead. Felix took it away from his ear and stared at it. Did George mean what he thought he meant? He dialled back, but the line wouldn't connect.

A train was waiting on Platform One, hissing and wheezing as passengers climbed in and settled into their seats. Felix made for the exit, thinking his mobile would work better outside, then changed his mind and turned back abruptly. The height of the bridge crossing the platforms would give better reception.

As he doubled back, someone caught his attention, a flicker in the edge of his vision. A man, a small, inconsequential figure, was heading straight for him, but changed direction as soon as he realised they were going to collide and hurried towards the café. It was the man he had seen yesterday at the motorway service station. What was he doing at Exeter St Davids so early in the morning? Why was he so anxious to avoid Felix?

The icy bite of the morning frost seized Felix's arms and legs so that he couldn't move. The oxygen seemed to have been sucked out of the air.

His mobile rang again. Forcing himself to react, he put his finger to the button, ready to answer, then stopped. *It's the Big Man.* What if it wasn't George this time? What if there were other people on the station, watching him?

The train on Platform One was preparing to leave. Two men were working their way along, slamming the doors shut. Without conscious thought, Felix ran, tossing his mobile phone under the wheels of the train. He could hear shouting behind him, pounding footsteps, a whistle. He sprinted to the last open door and leapt on just before it was closed behind him. After a few seconds, the train started to move, gliding gently along the platform before accelerating.

The shadows in the room are creeping closer. Felix picks up the whisky, unscrews the top and raises the bottle to his lips. He gulps a couple of mouthfuls. He puts the bottle down and picks up the knife. His childhood had ended with a knife. It seems right that his adult life should end in the same way. He feels the blade. It slices into the soft part of his index finger and a wafer-thin trickle of blood squeezes out. Dark, dark red, almost black.

'Ouch!' His voice is oddly loud in the thick space around him. He's five years old again, paralysed by the sight of blood.

A deep sigh shudders through him.

Chapter 2

Kate Kendall stretches out her legs in the generous space of the luxury car and gazes through the window at early-morning Toronto. Snowploughs have been out already and great mounds of snow line the edges of the streets. The pavements have been cleared and pedestrians are on the move, bent forward to preserve their heat, huddled into thick coats, wrapped up in hats and scarves. They're queuing for trams, heading for subway stations, striding along the side of the wide, traffic-clogged roads.

'You want to sit in the front?' the taxi driver had suggested, in a heavy accent, when he picked her up. 'Make you more comfortable for long journey.'

Why not? she thought. He's not likely to be dangerous, and if he is, he's hardly going to be interested in a middle-aged woman in a quilted anorak, flat-heeled boots and a woolly hat.

'Where are you from?' she asks the driver. He looks like the Tamil refugees who run the corner shop near her home. Short. Very black.

'Italy,' he says. 'You like Toronto?'

'Very much.' She likes the people, who are friendly but not overwhelming, the easy way in which ethnic groups seem to integrate, and the twenty-four-hour weather programme on television. It pleases her that Canadians analyse the weather so much. She'd expected them to accept the snow, since there's so much of it, but instead they discuss it, complain about it and take as much interest in the extreme conditions as the English would.

It's the first time she's been away without the family and she's been enjoying herself. Once or twice she has caught herself turning round to discuss something with Felix, only to find he wasn't there, but the empty space she finds inside herself without the constant presence of chatter and laughter and arguments isn't as wide as she had expected because she knows it's only temporary. She's phoned Rory and Millie a couple of times, but they seem distracted, involved in their worlds, so she has stopped worrying about them.

She feels refreshed by the interruption to her normal routine. It's like changing the oil in an engine or putting the homemade bread aside to rise overnight. She's going home tomorrow and has a sense of being pulled back to them all with some urgency, but the elastic that binds them has stretched much further than she had anticipated.

They cross the lanes of the Gardiner Expressway and speed up. In a sudden break between the buildings, Lake Ontario appears, stretching into the distance, merging with the low clouds on the horizon. Small waves ripple the surface, grey and bleak in the winter gloom.

'The lake hasn't frozen,' she says, surprised.

'Doesn't happen often,' he says. 'Toronto is warmer than rest of Canada.'

She's here for the art. For the last three years she's been doing a part-time MA in art history and her final thesis is due in by October. She was browsing on the Internet, trying to decide on a suitable subject, when she discovered Canadian art and the Group of Seven. Vibrant images of wilderness jumped out at her, mountains, lakes, storms, snow, all alive with movement and colour.

She was so excited she sent them through to Felix's computer. 'Look at these!' she said.

'Very nice,' he replied.

He's no good at art. He likes numbers, calculations, lists.

'You're so boring,' she wrote.

'Thank you,' he wrote back. 'What is your view on the impact of the housing market on the long-term UK economy?'

She went to find him in his study. He was working on the computer, his face intense with concentration, his abundant hair glowing copper in the pool of light from his desk-lamp. No sign of grey.

'You'd probably like the pictures of villages,' she said. 'The way the houses grow out of the land, the textures of the snow . . .'

He clicked the cursor back on her email and studied the images again. 'OK,' he said. 'I can see a certain something. But they seem a bit flat, not quite real somehow.'

'You're too literal,' she said. 'It gives them strength.'

'Why haven't I heard of the Group of Seven?'

'Hardly anyone has, except the Chinese.'

He raised an eyebrow. 'You'll have to explain that.'

She was pleased to know something that he didn't. 'The Group of Seven gave the first foreign art exhibition allowed into Communist China. Chairman Mao knew a Canadian doctor who died helping the Chinese Communists and wrote an essay about him, which is still studied by Chinese schoolchildren. So Mao had a soft spot for Canadians and let them exhibit at a time when nobody else was allowed in.'

'What was the doctor's name?'

'Nathan Bethune. They've got statues of him all over China.'

'I've never heard of him.'

'That's because you're not Chinese.'

'Write about the Group of Seven for your thesis,' he said. 'If you're excited, it's bound to be good.'

'I don't think I could study them properly without examining the originals. They're just not accurate enough on the computer.'

'Go and see them.'

'I can't. There are hardly any in Britain.'

'Then go to Canada.'

'But we're going to France at Easter, and if I wait until the summer holidays, it'll be too late.'

The suggestion of a smile tugged at the corner of his mouth. 'I didn't mean all of us. I meant you.'

'On my own?'

'Why not? You could go in the week when I'm in Hamburg. I'm sure we could sort the children out.'

And it just happened. They booked a hotel and a flight. Millie was thrilled to be offered the chance to board and Rory, who was always amenable, seemed happy to stay with a friend.

She's spent most of the week in Toronto, in the Art Gallery of Ontario, but on this last day she's heading for the McMichael gallery at Kleinburg, outside Toronto. According to her tourist guide, you can look past the pictures, through the windows to the landscapes that inspired the painters. The fact that it's not possible to get there by public transport adds to the sense that she's penetrating the original wilderness they captured in their pictures.

The sky starts to descend, the clouds dark and heavy, and white flakes drift down, gradually increasing until the cars are engulfed by wild, swirling snow. They're travelling in their own private compartment, separated from the other vehicles by a curtain of ethereal whiteness. The taxi driver keeps going, but reduces his speed.

'Will we be able to get there?' asks Kate.

'No problem,' he says. 'Roads always stay open. Not like England, eh, where everything stops for a few bits of snow?'

'I wouldn't call this a few flurries.'

'This is Canada,' he says, and laughs. 'We're used to it.'

They continue for a while. 'I need to put radio on,' he says. 'Find out which routes are clear.'

'Of course,' says Kate.

The driver fiddles with the radio, steering with his left hand. Snatches of words drift out, moments of clarity in the middle of an aural snowstorm. '. . . big freeze . . . Iraq . . . burger-eating competition . . . Felix Kendall—'

'Stop!' says Kate.

The driver puts his foot on the brake and they jolt forward in their seats.

'No,' she says. 'I'm sorry – I meant the radio. I could have sworn I heard my husband's name. Can you go back and search for the channel?'

He takes a deep breath and accelerates more gently. 'Phew!' he says. 'You had me scared there, lady.' He puts both hands on the steering-wheel for a few seconds, watching his rear-view mirror until the speed picks up. Then he reaches out for the radio again and presses the button. More words, fragments of sentences jump out, but no further references to Felix. 'Why your husband go on radio? Is he famous?'

'Not really,' she says. 'He's written a book about accountancy, but not many people would have read it.'

'A book, eh?' He seems pleased. 'What's it called?'

'*Counting the Beans*.'

He thinks for a while. 'No,' he says sadly. 'I haven't heard of it.'

Kate sits back and tries to make sense of it. Did she mishear? Or could it have been another Felix Kendall? It wasn't beyond the bounds of possibility that there was someone with the same name in the huge expanse of Canada. She wishes the driver could find the right channel again. It would have been comforting to hear the name again, even if it wasn't her Felix. She has a sharp sense of loneliness, as if the intimacy of the mention of his name makes him further away.

She'll try phoning him again tonight. She's only heard from him a couple of times since he's been in Hamburg

– she'd known he would have a very busy schedule – but she's left messages. He might be home this evening, or early tomorrow.

She gazes out of the window. The snow has eased a little, but continues to twist through and over the traffic, softening the factories that line the edge of the motorway, transforming everything into the charming, benevolent landscape of a postcard.

The energy of the paintings in the McMichael gallery, their vitality, is exhilarating. The starkness of the snow against a background of forests and mountains, whose shapes have been simplified into large, bold symbols. Remote islands pushing up out of lakes like mini volcanoes, their asymmetry mirrored in the icy water. Water viewed through trees, serenely lit by the gold and orange of autumn or whipped to a fury by dark, chilling storms.

Kate stands in front of the paintings for hours, absorbing their colours and composition. Carmichael, Varley, Jackson, Harris, Johnston, Lismer, MacDonald. And Tom Thomson, the forerunner, who died alone in Canoe Lake at the age of thirty-nine before the Group of Seven was formed. It's difficult for her to grasp that these names are over-familiar in Canada, part of the background, when hardly anyone in Europe has ever heard them. Discovering these paintings was like seeing van Gogh's work for the first time, not knowing that his sunflowers had appeared on bags, jigsaws, posters, book covers and umbrellas for more than a century.

Kate had thought she knew about art, the historical movements, the landmark works of genius, and here was a new concept, a wild, fresh culture, whose existence she had never suspected. Her lack of knowledge was an added stimulant. There was a delicious excitement in discovering that she didn't know as much as she'd thought. It was like peering into a vast library of information and experience that was there all the time but outside her limited perspective.

Windswept trees bent jagged on the horizon. The dramatic silhouette of a lone jack pine, the edges of its leaves tinged silver by the light from the setting sun. Small settlements huddled together in a sculpted landscape of shadows and snow.

She has lunch in the café, enjoying the leisure of her last day in Canada. She goes back to examine the paintings again. She buys books and prints. The woman on Reception phones for her taxi driver to come back and pick her up. 'It's stopped snowing,' she says to Kate.

A party of schoolchildren come out of the activity room, clutching their own attempts to re-create Thomson's *Autumn, Algonquin Park*.

The taxi ploughs through the slush, hooting at any car that shows signs of indecision. Ridges of snow have accumulated along the edge of each lane of the expressway, brown and polluted.

'So, what do you think of our Canadian artists?' asks the taxi driver.

'I love their energy,' says Kate. 'I can't believe I've never seen them before.'

He settles back in his seat and snorts. 'You English are too interested in unmade beds and pickled sharks.'

'To be fair,' says Kate, 'that was a long time ago. We've moved on since then. Are you interested in art?'

'In Italy we all grow up surrounded by art, we have no choice.'

'Do you like Canadian art?' says Kate.

He slaps one hand on his chest in an unexpected dramatic gesture. 'The Group of Seven, the soul of Canada,' he says. 'I am an artist. I know these things.'

'Really?' Kate is unsure how to take this. 'What sort of artist?' She sounds patronising, she thinks, but doesn't know how to avoid it. Does he mean artist as in 'art' or is he referring to something else – music or even his driving skills?

'I was art student in Italy. We were taught to draw, to see. When you are artist, you see the world different. Like through spectacles of your own . . .' he searches for a word '. . . sensibilities.'

Goodness, thinks Kate. It's difficult to imagine him sitting in a class of art students, charcoal in hand, studying a life model. He looks like a taxi driver. He's small, his head barely rising above the level of the steering-wheel, but his movements are fast and sudden, as if he has too much energy and can't slow himself down. He brakes too heavily, accelerates too unpredictably, swerves to avoid other cars at the very last minute. How would he manage the delicate work of an artist? How would he trace the fine lines round the eyes or the stray strand of hair? 'But you drive taxis,' she says.

He shrugs. 'It's a job. It earns money. I love driving.'

They come off the expressway and join the slow-moving cars along the outskirts of Toronto.

'Have you been out to the Beaches?' he says.

'Should I have done?'

'It is beautiful. Every day I take my dogs out for a run on the boardwalk along the edge of the lake. You should go there. Make lots of friends – all nice people take their dogs to the Beaches. You can swim there or sunbathe on the sand.'

'Not at this time of year, surely.'

He laughs, leaning his head back, showing his strong, even teeth. The laugh is musical, open, good-natured. 'I take my kids there in summer. Make them happy. Four kids. Big Italian family.'

Kate pictures them on the beach. Four diminutive children, rolling around in the sand, the soft grains dusting their dark skin as they squabble over buckets and spades, dogs tumbling into the fray, the taxi driver sitting on a blanket, sketching their round, healthy limbs, while his wife—

'Is your wife Italian?'

His face closes down and becomes solemn. 'My wife left me. She found someone more handsome and took kids with her.'

'Oh.' Kate doesn't know what to say. Perhaps taxi-driving is a hazardous occupation. Like being a policeman. Never there when you need them. 'I'm sorry.'

Felix isn't always there when she needs him. He travels a lot. But he comes home every time, laden with presents, bringing his enthusiasms with him, ready to tackle any problem, however trivial. She trusts him. She's convinced his loyalty is a genetic gift, a hand-me-down from the parents he doesn't remember. And he's proud of his self-made image, the capable, reliable family man. They haven't quite managed the four children he always wanted, but he's settled for the smaller quota with easy resignation.

She has a sudden mental picture of Rory playing in the sand in Barbados last summer. Her last child, her final achievement, conceived when she was forty. A complete surprise, three years after Millie, arriving with a flourish and a fanfare. He has an inexhaustible bounce. Every time he appears before her, he claims his right to exist, convinced that he is welcome. 'Here I am,' he seems to say. 'It's me. I've arrived.' And he knows she will be delighted to see him.

'I have wonderful life,' says the taxi driver. 'My wife always nagging before. "Why don't you make more money? Why don't you put shelves up, do breakfast, wash up? Why are you always under my feet? Shouldn't you be working?" I glad to see her go.'

Kate asks Felix to wash up, do the breakfast, put up shelves. Is she nagging? But he does them cheerfully enough when he's there. They have a gardener, Donovan, who comes in for a few hours every week and he'll often do odd jobs when Felix is away. Felix likes gardening – he wouldn't want Donovan to take over – but he needs help with it. Even with Rory as an assistant, it would be difficult to keep it all under control.

'Got nice little flat in centre of Toronto,' says the taxi driver. 'Nice girlfriend too, comes over three times a week and cooks me dinner. I see kids once a fortnight at the weekends and everyone happy. Me, ex-wife, kids, girlfriend. I love Canada. You can do what you want here.'

They drive up to the entrance of her hotel. A huge man with a Russian hat and a greatcoat with brass buttons down the front comes out to open the car door. He's always there – he must work long hours. He doesn't speak much English – 'Hello, thank you' – but he accepts her tips with a huge grin, revealing a mouthful of crooked and broken teeth.

At eleven o'clock the following morning, Kate sits on the edge of her king-size bed. She estimates that at least six people could lie comfortably side by side on it. Once or twice she's woken in the night, finding herself rolling across the wide empty spaces, searching for Felix.

Make the most of it, he whispers in her ear. *It'll be back to your two-foot-six slot when you get home.*

She misses the presence of his feet, often entwined with hers, the jutting angle of his heels, the softness of the skin underneath, the coolness of his toes.

She checks her documents. Tickets, passports, plane times. Her suitcase is packed, fastened and labelled. The Inuit art she has bought will be sent separately by the gallery, but she has three small sculptures of polar bears in her hand luggage for the children when she gets back. Rory and Millie will love them. She's not sure about Lawrence, because he's unpredictable, but he will appreciate the fact that she's supporting the Inuit community.

She picks up the phone and dials her home number. Nobody answers. She leaves a message. 'Felix, it's Kate. How was your trip? I'm just about to leave for the airport. There's been a lot of snow, but I don't think the flights are delayed. See you soon. Bye.'

She puts the receiver down, feeling lonely. There's an hour to go before the taxi comes to take her to the airport, so she puts on the television and flicks through the channels for a news programme, hoping for another passing reference to Felix Kendall. She would like some proof of his existence.

But there's nothing. She turns to the weather channel for a few last minutes, watching the forecast drift through each day of the week, while soothing music plays in the background. The local forecast, Toronto, Ontario, the whole of Canada, the United States, the world. She turns it off.

She takes one last look round the hotel room, standing by the window for a while, gazing over the rooftops of Toronto. Buses are going in and out of the depot, people are hurrying towards the Eaton Centre, struggling in the icy wind. Steam pours out of some of the big buildings. The sky is so blue it hurts her eyes. Toronto in the morning.

She wheels her case out of the door and shuts it for the last time. She takes the lift downstairs.

The man in Reception is unfamiliar. 'I'd like to pay my bill,' she says. 'I think you already have my debit-card details.'

He checks the computer and nods. 'OK,' he says. He presses keys and examines the screen.

Kate watches a couple set out for a walk. They're wrapped in fur-lined anoraks and heavy boots, with rucksacks on their backs. Indoors, they're surrounded by the luxury of marble floors, chandeliers, low tables and soft leather sofas. But everyone is disguised by outdoor clothing, unable to reflect the elegance of their surroundings. How do people manage business meetings, light lunches, drinks with friends after work? Do they carry a change of clothes in their bags – high heels and short skirts? A quick change in the toilets?

The man behind the desk coughs.

'Sorry?' she says.

'There seems to be a problem.'

'What sort of a problem?'

'It's not accepting your card.'

She's confused. 'What do you mean?'

'It won't go through.'

She stares at him. Has Felix forgotten to transfer money into the current account? Has she spent so much that she's overdrawn? But they have an overdraft arrangement for just that eventuality. 'I don't understand. Try again.'

He looks embarrassed. 'I have tried again.'

This has never happened to Kate before. She has never considered it to be the kind of emergency she should prepare for. 'It must be a mistake. There's plenty of money in the account.'

'Perhaps there's a fault on the system. Do you have a credit card? We could try that.'

She brightens. 'Oh, yes, what a good idea.'

He takes it and enters. After a few seconds, his face clears. 'That's fine,' he says.

'Well, thank goodness for that,' says Kate.

Chapter 3

Rory Kendall thinks it's time for the parents to come home. It's OK staying with Theo, but it's getting to be hard work now. You can't just live your own life. You have to be polite to Theo's parents, who expect to be called Sian and Edward, instead of Mr and Mrs Holliday, which Rory would much prefer. He can't see why he should call adults by their first names. It's not exactly as if they're his *friends*.

His father often goes away for his work. Rory doesn't mind too much because he comes back with models of Boeing 747s and stories about travelling business class – 'You get so much leg-room, Rory, that even Great-aunt Beatrice would be satisfied' – but this is the first time his mum has gone too.

She's in Canada. 'She wants to see the art,' his dad said, in a mock-serious voice. Rory wasn't quite sure if he should laugh or not. He thought his mum might not like it, so he shrugged his shoulders in a nonchalant sort of way and nodded seriously at the same time. For some reason, his mum laughed instead. She said she might go to Niagara Falls while she's in the area, which seemed unfair, because Rory wants to go there too. 'Next time,' his mother said. 'We'll probably go as a family.'

'I don't think you should go,' he said, at the airport, when they were saying goodbye. 'I'm only nine. It could damage me for life. I might end up being a bus driver because I didn't get into the right senior school and then never got any GCSEs.'

But she just laughed again. 'There's no chance of that,' she says. 'I'll soon be back. It's only a short break.'

Theo comes into the bedroom where Rory is curled up on his bed, reading *Stormbreaker* for the tenth time. 'Come on,' he says. 'We're going out.'

'Where to?'

Theo rolls his eyes. 'Shopping.'

Boring. Rory follows him downstairs. Halfway down, on the middle landing, he pauses and checks for anything unusual. Are the pictures still hanging straight? Is there a rush of breeze that shouldn't be there? An unusual coldness? These aliens are clever. They get in everywhere. It's the subtle details that tell you they're around. You can never be too careful.

Rory and Theo stop at the front door and put on their trainers, a rule that Rory finds deeply irritating. In his house they're allowed to wear shoes all the time.

'Come on, boys,' calls Sian, from the people-carrier. Theo shuts the front door and they run to the car.

'In you get,' she says, with the pretend enthusiasm that Rory finds so unnecessary. What else would they do, with the door open and the engine running?

'Seatbelts on,' she calls, as she slams the door behind them.

As if he'd trust her driving without the security of a seatbelt. She hesitates at T-junctions, revs up too much, then pulls out just at the wrong moment when a BMW is speeding towards them at 40 m.p.h. Still, at least the car is only six months old. It's got airbags for passengers.

'Can we go to Pizza Hut after the shopping?' says Theo.

'Maybe, darling,' she says. 'But I thought we ought to go for a run on the beach before lunch. Take advantage, now it's finally stopped raining.'

Hasn't she spotted it's freezing out there?

'Exmouth beach?' asks Theo.

'No, Budleigh. I haven't got time to go to Exmouth.'

Typical, thinks Rory. Just what I wanted to do. Stagger over giant pebbles, trying not to break an ankle, and pretend to get excited about throwing stones into the sea when the sea is perfectly capable of moving stones on its own. All because Sian thinks it's healthy.

'Did you see that?' calls Sian, from the front of the car. 'A snowflake!'

'I spy with my little eye,' says Theo, 'something beginning with S.'

'Snowflake,' says Rory. 'I spy with my little eye something beginning with AS.'

'Another Snowflake,' says Theo. 'I spy with my little eye something beginning with YABS.'

Rory picks his way through. 'Yet – Another—'

'Boring—'

'Snowflake.'

They chuckle quietly so that Sian won't be offended.

'Here we are,' she calls, five minutes later.

Really? thinks Rory. I'd never have guessed. The big letters that say 'TESCO' wouldn't have warned me.

They get out and weave their way through the parked cars to the trolleys.

'I'll do the trolley, Sian,' says Rory.

'You're welcome,' says Sian, giving him the pound coin.

He slips it into the slot and releases the connecting chain, which gets caught in the side of the trolley. He untangles it, his hands growing numb with cold, then pulls the trolley out. As he pushes it over to Sian and Theo, he leans on the handle and lifts his feet for a brief glide.

'I want to push it,' says Theo.

Rory lets him take over. You have to humour people if you want to keep the peace. And it means he can warm his hands in his pockets. He glances back over his shoulder. It's the best way to see if you're being followed. Turn when they're not expecting it. It catches them out, and they react by stopping suddenly.

But there's no one suspicious today. They're safe to get on with the shopping.

He follows Sian and Theo, avoiding the white tiles and hopping on to the black ones. You can't see discarded chewing-gum on white surfaces.

'Come on, Rory,' calls Sian. 'You're not keeping up.' She stops by the newspaper rack. 'Oh,' she says.

Theo raises his eyebrows at Rory. 'I expect Madonna's adopted another baby,' he mutters.

The newspapers rise above them. *The Times*, the *Sun*, the *Telegraph*, the *Mirror*. Big black boring headlines. Newspapers are so unnecessary.

'Look!' says Sian.

There's a photograph on the front of every paper. A man smiling, his red hair springing out of his head in corkscrews, a gleam in his eyes.

'Isn't that your father, Rory?'

Chapter 4

'Lovely day for flying,' says the taxi driver to Kate, as they head for Pearson airport. He's a tall, broadly built Asian man, with wiry eyebrows that stick out too far and intensely black hair gelled into curled ridges. Indian? Pakistani? Bangladeshi? How can you tell? 'Have you been to Niagara?'

'Yes,' says Kate. 'It was frozen.'

'In its entirety?'

His voice rises and falls with an Asian lilt, stressing unexpected syllables. She has to play the words over in her head again, to make sense of them. 'Well, not the water that was falling, the horseshoe bit, but the river at the bottom was solid and most of the American falls.'

That was what she had seen first, after walking down the hill past the takeaways, the joke shops, the Incredible Hulk on the side of a building, the sound of hollow laughter echoing from the ghost trains as they tried to entice her to take a ride. When she finally saw the American falls in the distance, they seemed vaguely disappointing. A frozen sculpture of swollen, distorted shapes, with only a thin trickle of water still falling.

'I have been told it's overcrowded,' says the taxi driver.

'Well, it wasn't two days ago. There was just me, one German lady and a group of Japanese men who were all trying to warm their ears with their hands. They weren't even wearing coats.'

'Don't they have snow in Japan?'

'That's what I thought. Perhaps it's a different kind of snow.'

It had been better further up, when she had walked to the edge of the horseshoe where the water surged over the precipice. She had stood there with the German lady, just able to see over the iced-up railings, and watched the power of the water. The sky was a brilliant blue. Outlines of small trees, their bare branches coated with layers of snow, dotted the hill behind her. It was bitterly cold. They took photographs of each other with the bridge to America in the background to prove they were really there. Then they went to warm up with coffee in the deserted café.

The taxi driver swerves unexpectedly and overtakes a truck, gliding round it with effortless acceleration. He opens his window, leaning out into the cold to gesture at the driver. 'He's in the wrong lane,' he says, winding the window up again. 'That's why he's not a brain surgeon.'

It's the kind of thing Kate's elder son, Lawrence, would have said. He's supposed to be studying for a degree, but spends most of his time in a state of blissful inactivity, drinking coffee and discussing philosophy, being cynical about everyone else. The height of his ambition is a trip on a tandem with a friend in the summer. They intend to go from Land's End to John o' Groats and want people to sponsor them in aid of the homeless. All very worthy, although Kate can't help thinking that he should do something more practical to earn the money. Actually help the homeless, for example, instead of having a bit of fun on a tandem. She's tempted to warn people that it would be unwise to sponsor him, that they should just donate money directly to the charity, since there's no way he'll complete the journey, but she realises this would be disloyal. She should give him the benefit of the doubt.

Lawrence lacks his father's drive. He famously handed in his geography A level coursework at the last possible moment with writing on the top sheet and all the pages underneath blank. There was a huge fuss and Kate had to stand over him every day for a week until he'd completed it.

'I trust you have enjoyed an excellent vacation in Toronto,' says the taxi driver. 'Have you admired my country?'

'Yes, very much. But I haven't met a single person who was born in Canada.' They're all proud to be Canadians, but underneath they're something else. Their histories separate them without appearing to divide them.

'Ah, this is the greatness of Canada. We like each other.'

How easy he makes it sound.

'You are eagerly anticipating your return to England?'

'Yes.' She's looking forward to seeing the children again. Rory will be fine – he has too much bounce to be downhearted for long – but she wonders how Millie's coped with boarding. She imagines her watching the other girls, taking her cue from them, desperate to be part of the world that she believes to be passing her by. Kate suspects she'll be secretly longing to go home but unable to acknowledge it, even to herself.

They arrive early at the airport so there'll be a long wait. Kate goes to the KLM check-in desk, where multiple lanes are marked out by ropes, prepared for huge crowds. There are three people in the queue.

At the desk, she puts her suitcase on the scales. 'It's a bit heavy,' she says, with embarrassment.

'Do you have your passport?' says the man.

She hands it to him.

He fiddles with the computer and she waits quietly, letting him concentrate. She's distracted by the woman at the next desk, who is engaged in a furious argument. The four-inch heels on her knee-length boots click with a hectic impatience as she paces on the spot.

'What do you mean I can't take this on as hand luggage? I always take this amount with me.'

'Times have changed, ma'am. Hand luggage has been restricted.'

Kate turns back to her desk, where the man is still studying the computer. 'Will I have to pay a surcharge?' she says.

He stares at her intently and she feels uncomfortable. 'Is anything the matter?' she asks. The croissants and coffee she had for breakfast lie uneasily in her stomach, heavy and unsettled. It can't be the card problem again. The ticket was paid for before she left home.

'Sorry,' he says. He must be Dutch. His blond hair is parted in the middle, the two divided waves of hair flowing down on either side with a bushy breeziness. 'Nearly there.'

He continues to type into the computer.

'Aren't I booked in?' she says. 'Have I got the wrong flight?'

'No, no, everything's fine.'

Except it can't be because she's still waiting. The woman next to her has given in. Two cases have been taken for the hold and she has been left with one small piece of hand luggage. She strides away, her irritation expressed by the set of her shoulders, the imperious sway of her hair.

'Mrs Kendall?'

Surprised, she turns round. There's a man at her elbow.

'You are Mrs Kendall?'

'Yes. Who are you?'

'My name is Detective Sergeant Wright – Interpol.' He flashes a card in her face and she pretends to read it even though it's impossible. It's all too quick. She can't think.

'I wonder if I could have a word.'

Chapter 5

Millie Kendall can't believe she's actually allowed to board for a whole week at Hillyard School. It's only her first year in seniors. Things move fast once you're twelve, like a high-speed train – only one more stop and she'll be a teenager. She's slightly worried that she might have to give up her ballet annuals and *Harry Potter*, but she has faith that something more sophisticated will turn up.

Millie loves school. She adores her uniform, with the pleated skirt and the beige blouse covered with pale brown spots. The way the crisp collar sticks out over the green V-neck jumper, which is edged with two thin lines of brown. And the bottle-green blazer with the emblem of her house sewn on the pocket. Millie, Karishma and Esther are in Margaret Atwood House. There's a perfect circle embroidered on their badges, with a textured centre in pale and dark blue. An older girl explained it to them. 'It's a marble – the middle is a cat's eye. It's from a book by Margaret Atwood about bullying.' It's all changed since her mother was at Hillyard's. The houses were named after female saints in her day.

Millie's other best friend, Helen, is in Virginia's and her badge is a lighthouse. Nobody in year seven quite gets that one, but they're not too bothered. Someone will tell them eventually. Millie and Helen started together in the lower school at seven, and expect to be here until they leave at eighteen.

'Come along, girls,' the voice of Mrs Watkins, the house mistress, calls up the stairs. 'We're going over for breakfast.'

Millie peers into the mirror and adjusts a slide over her left ear. It's so unfair. She'll never ever be beautiful, never be approached by a model scout, never get a part as an unknown newcomer in a film. She bounces downstairs in her trainers and jeans, two steps at a time. She would prefer to wear uniform at the weekend, like they do in *Malory Towers* – although of course she's far too old for Enid Blyton now – but it would be considered uncool at Hillyard's and unwritten rules are much more important than written ones. It can't be helped.

All twelve girls have congregated downstairs, ready to go to the dining room. There are about forty boarders altogether, divided into four houses, a small exclusive group with parents who work abroad or are too busy and too far away for the daily commute. Most of the school is made up of day pupils who can be dropped off at eight o'clock in the morning and stay until six o'clock at night. Millie has often been one of the last to leave and she's seen the boarders of Margaret's settle down to prep together. They sit round two large oak tables under the supervision of Mrs Watkins, the lights bright above them, the atmosphere calm and so much better for homework than at home. She used to *ache* with envy.

Just inside the front door, making sure that everyone is wearing a coat, is Samantha Thomas.

Samantha: upper sixth, head of house, incredibly clever, beautiful, destined for Oxford. Even as Millie joins the end of the line, she can feel her face flushing. She wants to be like Samantha when she's in the sixth form.

'Hello, Millie,' says Samantha. 'Is everything going well?'

Millie nods, unable to speak. Just the sight of Samantha's glossy dark hair, hanging loose down her back, makes her feel ugly and clumsy. If only her own hair had been straight her whole life would be different. But it's ginger, curly, wayward, springing out with an obstinate independence that makes her despair. On some mornings she just knows that one day it will send her into clinical depression.

They start to walk over to the dining room, meeting the girls from Virginia, Iris and Sylvia on the way. Helen sees Millie with Karishma and Esther and runs over to join them. 'Look!' she says. 'It's snowing.'

A few solitary flakes drift down in a half-hearted manner, as if they've fallen by mistake and lost their way. The girls eagerly scan the leaden sky between the trees, a delicious anticipation fluttering through them.

'I bet we'll be stranded by tomorrow.'

'Wicked!' says Helen.

'It's so not going to snow,' says Karishma. 'It never snows here.'

Millie wishes they could be snowed in, cut off, inaccessible to the outside world. For about two days. If the electricity went off too, they could do everything by candlelight, creeping around unseen, spying on the older girls, listening to other people's conversations. You can find out so much just from listening.

And if they were snowed in, Millie's family would miss her. They'd appreciate her so much more after the enforced absence that her mother might even rush out and buy her the Top Shop coat she's had her eye on for the last month – emerald green with three very large black buttons down the front. Her mother will probably want to talk to her every night on the phone while they're cut off, of course, and Millie will tolerate this good-naturedly. Although it's possible her flight will be delayed because of the weather and she'll have to stay in Canada longer, in which case Millie can talk to her father. That'll be fine. He does good phone calls.

Actually, she could talk to her mother in Canada. You can phone anywhere in the world.

All four girls have the same breakfast. Sausages, scrambled eggs, fried bread and baked beans. Brilliant. Much better than Frosties and toast, which she's forced to have at home. 'You need the milk,' her mother always says, if she complains about the Frosties.

'They're disgusting,' says Millie. 'All that sugar.'

'You can have cornflakes without the sugar if you'd prefer,' says her mother.

'Yuk,' says Millie, and forces down the Frosties. It's just not worth the hassle.

'How are you enjoying boarding, Millie?'

Samantha's voice floats down from behind them and they swing round in their seats. She's leaning over slightly and her silky hair brushes against Millie's hand on the back of her chair. Her eyes are grey, tinged with green, and her voice soft and thoughtful. Samantha fills the whole of her immediate surroundings with her presence, as if she's a flat-screen forty-two-inch plasma television and everyone just has to watch her.

'It's fantastic,' says Millie, her voice high and squeaky. She wants to say, 'I *love* your hair – I wish mine could be so soft and straight. Thank you so much for talking to me, I'm having a wonderful time.' But her voice isn't working properly.

'Do you think it'll snow?' says Helen.

Samantha straightens slightly and looks out of the long windows of the dining room. 'It's possible,' she says.

'No,' says Karishma. 'It won't.'

'Love the top, Samantha,' says Helen.

I wish I'd said that, thinks Millie.

'Thank you, Helen,' says Samantha, smiling. The top is a pale, shimmery pink, which flows into a silvery blue whenever she moves, every curve and fold fluctuating with the change of light. It clings to her. It's sexy. It's short-sleeved. How come she doesn't feel the cold?

After breakfast they wander back to the house. There's no sign of snow now, but the ground is hard and ungiving, the sky bleak.

'Let's not do hockey today,' says Karishma.

They'd spent most of Saturday outside, practising their tackling and dribbling, and didn't realise until they came in how cold they'd been. Millie's knees ached, and when she looked in a mirror she was appalled to discover that her face had become strawberry red, the colour of her nose even eclipsing that of the colossal spot that was building up on her chin.

Mrs Watkins is waiting for them by the entrance to Margaret. 'Come in out of the cold,' she says, holding the door open for them. She's pulling the edges of her cardigan together across her front, dithering slightly. The girls have noticed before that her hands often tremble.

'She drinks too much coffee,' Esther says. 'It's the caffeine.'

'No,' says Helen. 'She's probably going through the change. It does that to you.'

They clatter into the hall and Mrs Watkins lets the door shut behind them. 'Millie,' she says, 'can I have a word?'

Millie's stomach contracts as she tries to remember what she has done. Did she forget to make her bed, or leave her muddy shoes by the door yesterday where everyone could fall over them?

The other girls stare at her. 'Go on, then, Millie,' says Esther. 'Tell us what you've been up to.'

Mrs Watkins is ushering her into her private living room, the inner sanctum. Nobody ever gets invited in here. Millie follows her, conscious of the round, startled eyes of her friends behind her.

There are two policewomen in the living room, standing by the fireplace with mugs of coffee in their hands.

Something terrible has happened. Her mother's flight home, her father, Rory—

'Hello, Millie,' says one of them.

Millie tries to say hello back but her throat has dried up.

'We were wondering,' says the other policewoman, 'if you could tell us where your mother is staying in Toronto.'

Chapter 6

Kate can't work out what has happened. One minute she was standing with her luggage, checking in, perfectly normal, expecting to be issued with a boarding pass, and the next she is in a small room, sitting opposite two men, neither of whom she has seen before in her life. A cup of coffee has been placed on the table in front of her, but she could no more pick it up than she could leap out of her chair and run for the door. She knows her legs would not perform, however authoritative her command.

The scene feels artificial, as if she is observing it from outside, through an invisible window. She can see herself, bolt upright on the edge of a sofa. Such an ordinary person. White, blonde-highlighted hair cut into a neat bob, varifocals giving her a touch of earnestness, three-quarter-length corduroy skirt from Marks & Spencer with an elasticated waist for comfort, flat round shoes with thick soles.

Whichever angle you come from, she is an occupier of the middle ground. She has pitched her sensible, capable tent in the centre of a plateau, exposed on all sides, easy to read from a distance, nothing to hide. So why is she here? They can't seriously believe she's a drug-smuggler.

A thought jumps into her mind with excruciating clarity. 'Rory,' she says. 'It's Rory, isn't it?'

The men look at each other, confused. 'No,' says one. 'It's not Rory.'

'Who's Rory?' says the other.

'My son,' she says. 'Has he had an accident?'

'Rory's fine, Mrs Kendall.'

How can he be so sure? He doesn't even know who Rory is. She tries again, struggling to control her voice. 'Millie, then? Or Lawrence? Are they all right?'

The first man leans forward and smiles. 'As far as I know, Mrs Kendall, your family is fine.' He's elderly, with sagging patches under his eyes that are magnified by the thick lenses of his glasses, and a loose, insecure chin that trembles when he talks. He looks ready for retirement.

'So why am I here? You still haven't told me what's going on.' Will they search her? Embarrassment spreads through her at the thought.

They're trying to be inscrutable, but they're not very good at it. She sees their uncertainty. 'We're waiting for DS Wright,' says the younger man.

DS Wright was the man who led her away from the check-in desk. When did he disappear? Why? 'I demand to know what's going on.' That's good. Demand. Felix would approve. Be more assertive, he always says. So here she goes. 'I hope this isn't going to take too long. I have a plane to catch.'

'We're aware of that,' says the younger man. 'Rest assured, you will not miss your plane.'

So they don't suspect her of being a terrorist or a smuggler or a bank robber. What do they want from her?

The door opens and the sergeant enters. His legs are slightly bowed and he bounces as he walks. A rubbery man, but not Action Man. He's too heavy for that, the expanse of his stomach straining over his belt, his shirt stretched to its limits. He's carrying a pile of papers in one hand and a polystyrene cup in the other. He nods at the two men and they get up, making room for him. They walk over to the window and look out at the runway beyond. A KLM airliner has come to a halt outside and the hold is being opened, a gaping dark wound in the huge underbelly of the aircraft.

That might be my plane, thinks Kate.

The man smiles. 'Hello again,' he says. His accent is Canadian – or maybe American. She can't tell the difference. His knees creak as he sits down. 'I must apologise for all this, Mrs Kendall. I realise it must seem over-dramatic, but I'm hoping you may be able to help us.'

'I can't begin to imagine how,' she says. 'I have no idea what this is all about.'

The sergeant shuffles through the papers. 'It's to do with your husband.'

Everything in the room has sharp edges: the table, the window frame, the creases in the sergeant's forehead, just above his nose. Somewhere in Europe, as Felix travelled back from Hamburg, there's been a freak storm or a train crash or a bomb. Or his heart has stopped suddenly, a double betrayal because his body failed him and he wasn't safely at home with his family when it happened. 'Is he – dead?' she says.

The sergeant has very clear green eyes. 'No,' he said. 'We don't think he's dead.'

'He's injured, then? I have to speak to him.' She tries to stand, but finds it difficult to co-ordinate her movements.

'The truth is,' says the sergeant, 'we don't know where he is and we were rather hoping you might be able to tell us.'

The mildness of his tone confuses her and she sinks down again. 'What do you mean?'

'He seems to have disappeared off the face of the earth.'

There's a great heaviness in Kate's legs. 'Don't be ridiculous,' she says. 'He's been to Hamburg.'

'Apparently not, Mrs Kendall.'

What's that supposed to mean? 'Yes, he has. Have you looked for him there?'

'We've looked for him everywhere.'

'He's just travelling, that's why you can't find him. It's hard to find people when they're on the move.' What does he know about her husband's habits? Felix likes to sleep on the train – he can't keep his eyes open once he's in motion. He doesn't drive himself anywhere any more: he uses a driver. In the early days of their relationship, he had had two accidents after falling asleep at the wheel. The first time, he ended up in a ditch with bruised ribs, and the second, he went into the back of a BMW in slow-moving traffic. The driver was terrifyingly angry and threatened to break both his legs – he was more alarming than the ditch and Felix was forced to take action, so he stopped driving. Their GP told them that Felix suffers from narcolepsy, but Kate and Felix don't agree with this diagnosis because it only happens when he's travelling. It's something to do with the movement, the sound of the engine. Together they trigger an overwhelming desire to sleep.

Maybe his insomnia makes it happen. Four hours' sleep a night is normal for him. He spends the spare time working at the computer or cooking. Kate often wakes at six o'clock in the morning to the smell of freshly baked muffins. She goes down to the kitchen, and is welcomed by her cheerful husband. 'I'm not the least bit tired,' he says. She doesn't mind. She loves to sit with him at the kitchen table over coffee and muffins, warm and comfortable by the Aga, until one of the children wakes up, smells the baking and comes down to join in.

'I don't understand,' she says to the sergeant. 'Why do you want to know where he is? What's he got to do with you?'

'Well,' he says slowly, 'we believe he has valuable information that could help us with our enquiries.'

'What enquiries?'

'I can't tell you that, of course,' he says. 'But I'm sure you realise that Interpol deals with international crime.'

'And you want Felix? My husband? Are you sure?' She relaxes as everything becomes clear. 'No, you've made a mistake. Felix has never broken the law in his entire life. He wouldn't know how to.'

The sergeant doesn't reply. She can see why he's a policeman. He has an impressive lack of reaction.

'You're obviously looking for the wrong man.'

'When was the last time you saw him?'

The question chills her and she feels like a small child, standing in front of a committee. And when did you last see your father? As if she will never see him again. Her mouth dries and she has a wild desire to drink something. The coffee. There's a cup of coffee in front of her. She grasps it with both hands to counteract the shaking of her fingers and raises it to her mouth. What if it's too hot? She gulps it down, not caring. It's not too hot. It's lukewarm. How long has it been sitting there? How long has she been here?

'My flight,' she says. 'I mustn't miss my flight. The children will be expecting me back.' And Felix will be meeting me at the airport, she wants to say, but doesn't.

The sergeant nods. 'We're aware of the time of your flight,' he says. 'Don't worry, you'll be on it. If necessary we can delay it.'

Kate stares at him. That's the most frightening thing anyone has ever said to her. 'Please could you just explain?' she says. 'I don't understand.'

He leans back in his chair and smiles at her. It's a genuine smile – it reaches his eyes. 'I'm so sorry about all this, Mrs Kendall. I realise how distressing it must be. But we need to find your husband with some urgency. I would really appreciate it if you could tell us when you last saw him.' His voice is kind and courteous, but he expects an answer. He's like Rory. He believes in himself. He knows that if he keeps asking, she will respond.

'Well,' she says, 'when I set off for my flight to Canada, Felix came, with the children, to see me off.'

'What day are we talking about?'

'Last Saturday. I flew from Heathrow in the morning. Felix's driver took us to the airport.'

'The name of the driver?'

'Ken – I don't know his last name. Felix always just calls him Ken.'

'How can we contact him?'

'He works for Luxury Cars, Exeter.'

He nods and writes it down. 'And have you spoken to your husband on the phone since then?'

'Yes, when I reached my hotel – you know, to tell him I'd arrived safely. He likes me to do that. It reassures him.'

'So that was what time?'

'I don't know, about seven o'clock.'

'Canadian time or British time?'

'Canadian.'

'And you haven't spoken to him since?'

'No. I tried to phone, but once he'd left for Hamburg on Tuesday morning, I couldn't get through to his mobile. He'd told me he'd be really busy and the time difference made it difficult.'

'Did you email?'

'I think I emailed him about three times.'

'Did he reply?'

'Yes – well, the first two times. Not the third.'

'When was his last reply?'

'I'm not sure. About Thursday, I think.'

'And where was he then?'

'Hamburg, of course.'

'How do you know?'

She hesitates and experiences a jolt of panic. 'Because that's where he was.' But she doesn't know that for certain. She'd just assumed it.

'Could we see the emails?'

She's shocked. 'No, they're personal.'

He smiles at her again, gently. 'I'm afraid we have the power to read your emails anyway, Mrs Kendall. I just thought you might prefer to give your permission first.'

One of the policemen comes over from the window and places a laptop on the table in front of her. He turns it on.

Kate had thought her emails were cheerful chronicles of her time away, a kind of amateur travel writing. Now it all seems so banal – the weather, the food, an episode on the subway when they were invaded by a group of children with recorders.

And what did Felix say? In the first one, on Monday, he talks about the children, taking Millie into school on Sunday evening and leaving Rory at Sian's. 'Rory's designing a gadget to put in a hat so he can see out of the back of his head,' he writes. In the second, on Thursday, he must have been in Hamburg. The message is shorter. 'Good flight – busy.' He's not chatty any more. Kate hadn't noticed this before. 'I love you,' he says at the end. 'Always and for ever.'

The room has become too oppressive, absurdly hot. Kate starts to take off her cardigan. She can see that they would interpret this email as signing off, preparing to disappear. 'He always ends like that,' she says. 'That was just his way.'

'He didn't end the first email like that,' says the sergeant.

'Well, not every time, but he often does. He's very affectionate.'

There's a long silence. Little trucks have driven up to the stationary KLM aeroplane, each one pulling a line of containers. Men sort through the suitcases, checking labels and transferring a few to the hold. They're distracted, shouting to each other, laughing at a joke. It's a miracle they ever get the right luggage on the right aeroplane.

There had been no reply to her next email.

'And you haven't spoken to him since?'

'No.'

The sergeant writes a few notes on the paper in front of him. 'Do you have any idea where he might have gone if he didn't go to Hamburg?'

But he had gone to Hamburg. 'Why wouldn't he do what he'd said he would do? What makes you think he didn't go there?'

He doesn't reply.

'He travels all over the world. He has a responsible job, you know. He's an accountant.'

'Yes, we know.'

What does that mean? Why does he say it in that sinister way, as if he knows more about it than she does? Is he implying that there's something wrong with Felix's job, that he isn't an accountant at all? 'Why don't you ask his partners – at Maine and Selwick.'

The sergeant nods. 'I know the name of the firm he works for, Mrs Kendall.'

Kate experiences sudden irritation. 'If you know all about him, why are you asking me?'

'Because nobody knows where he is.'

This was where they had started. 'Have you tried our home?' she says. It's not that unreasonable. 'Maybe everyone's so tied up looking for him that they've missed the obvious.'

A flicker of amusement drifts across the sergeant's face. 'I think the British police will already have tried your home, but I'll pass on your suggestion.' He drinks some coffee. 'Might he have gone to Iceland?'

'Iceland? Why would he go there?'

'I thought you said he went all over the world.'

'Well – yes, he does.'

'Has he ever been to Iceland?'

Kate feels as if she's losing track of the conversation. 'Yes, he has in the past.'

'When exactly?'

'I'm not sure. I'd have to check. About three years ago, maybe.'

'Did you go with him?'

'To Iceland? No.'

'Why didn't you tell anyone where you were staying in Toronto?'

'I did. I told Felix.'

'Didn't you feel your children's carers should know where you were?'

He's suggesting she's been negligent. 'They had Felix's contact details. He was nearer than me. I phoned them from Canada, so I was in touch all the time.' She sounds too defensive. A sign of guilt. She's suddenly urgently cold and puts her cardigan back on.

'When did you expect your husband to return from Hamburg?'

'He wasn't sure how long he'd be. He just said he'd be home before me.'

'Who is George Rangarajan?'

It's like a jump backwards in time. Kate hasn't heard George's name in so long she'd almost forgotten about him. 'George? What's he got to do with this?'

Sergeant Wright is examining her face as if he's expecting a particular response.

'I don't understand,' she said. 'Why are you asking me about George?'

'Is he a friend of your husband's?'

'They were at school together, but they haven't seen each other for years.'

'And do you know Kristin Petursdottir?'

'No, I've never heard of her.'

The sergeant watches her for a bit longer, then jots down some notes. He stands up. 'Thank you for your help, Mrs Kendall. I'm sorry to have taken up so much of your time.'

'But you haven't told me anything,' says Kate, struggling to her feet. 'I want to know what's going on. Has Felix broken the law in some way? What's it got to do with George Rangarajan? Who's the woman with the strange name?'

Felix is one of the most honest people she has ever met. He puts money in the box on those stands where you can take your own newspaper; he refuses to take unused soap or shampoo from hotel rooms; he goes back to the till if they've given him too much change. He always tells the children the truth, even if it causes problems, because truth is what matters most. Once you start to lie, he says, you go on doing it. It's a never-ending game of pass-the-parcel. You can't stop it, so don't start. He always rewards honesty, even if it reveals bad behaviour.

The sergeant stands in front of her, apparently deep in thought. He doesn't reply.

I should have asked for a lawyer. That's what people do in these circumstances. She glares at him. 'Are you Canadian?'

He looks surprised. 'Yes,' he says. 'Fourth generation.'

'Congratulations,' she says. 'You're my first genuine Canadian.' Talk to him nicely. Be friendly. He owes her some information.

'It's money-laundering,' he says. 'George Rangarajan and Kristin Petursdottir have been arrested and we're still looking for your husband.'

She stares at him.

'I'm sorry, Mrs Kendall,' he says. 'There's no mistake.'

Part Two

Chapter 7

Kate has a window seat and spends the first hour looking out at the frozen land below. They're flying over the east of Canada. The country is divided into a raised map of snowbound jigsaw pieces. Frozen rivers and roads edge the open spaces, strands of thin cotton in a landscape of crumpled white sheets. Clusters of lights shine out in the gathering dusk, evidence of tiny isolated settlements that are perhaps not as insignificant as they look from the air. Electricity has reached even these remote places. How did they do it, take cables so far, over such vast distances? How much did it cost? The roads snake through miles of uninhabited land, proof of civilisation's ability to reach the furthest, bleakest parts of the world.

Kate would like to live in one of these settlements, far away from her present life. She feels the need to withdraw, shrink inside a tight blanket, let everyone carry on without her.

She understands a bit about money-laundering. She wishes she had paid more attention whenever Felix talked about his work. She tries to banish the image of piles of banknotes drifting past on a conveyor-belt towards monster washing-machines. She knows this is childish nonsense. But why would Felix have anything to do with the criminal world? It doesn't make sense. She tries to remember details about the Enron scandal – something to do with accountants ignoring warning signals and turning a blind eye. Maybe it's like that. Maybe Felix didn't realise that something was going on. Maybe he was just careless.

But Felix isn't careless.

Two elderly American women in front of Kate are discussing their grandchildren. 'He's very intellectual,' says one. 'He's reading *Lord of the Rings*.'

'He's the star of the team,' says the other. 'He runs so fast round the pitch he nearly catches up with himself.'

If something was going on, Felix would know. There's no way he wouldn't have seen it. He's too clever.

She tries to remember his trip to Iceland. Had there been anything significant about it? Was that the occasion, a few years ago, when he'd come home feeling unwell? He'd been unusually subdued and tense and gone straight to bed. Probably a virus, he'd said. Must have picked it up on the plane. All that recirculated air. But he had been fine the next day and had taken the family out on to Dartmoor for a picnic.

The picnic stands out in Kate's mind as a particularly good day, although it had initially threatened to be a disaster. Lawrence was being difficult, refusing to revise for his school exams. Felix had intended to go over some history with him for an hour after lunch, but Lawrence had just got up and walked away. He joined Rory and Millie, who were attempting to dam a stream. He hadn't been aggressive, or even unpleasant. He had simply refused to discuss it.

'Never mind,' said Felix. 'He'll learn.'

'But we don't want him to fail.'

'He won't. He's too bright for that. He's a survivor.'

Kate had lain on her stomach and examined the coarse, springy grass in front of her. It was as resilient as a mattress, teeming with hidden life. She picked up a stone and discovered a mass of wriggling, squirming creatures scurrying around, frantic to escape the light. It was ancient land, polished and beaten by the weather, where sounds were muffled by perpetual wind and the rocky tors were bleached by their proximity to the sun. 'He might end up a drop-out,' she said.

Felix had smiled and put his arm round her shoulders. 'I didn't go to university,' he said, 'and look at me now.'

She leant back against him, conscious of his heat, his breathing. His wide knuckles and capable fingers rested easily against her cardigan, relaxed and comfortable. She knew those hands so well. They had explored every inch of her body with a controlled, methodical strength, but their familiarity was still, after all these years, achingly desirable.

'You've got drive,' she said.

'I didn't when I was Lawrence's age.'

That wasn't true. He was more tenacious than Lawrence, with an urgent desire to succeed. It had always been apparent, right from the first time she had met him. You could sense that he was on a quest, ascending a ladder that would have no top rung. She had learnt to accept his ambition. It was part of him, part of his personality.

The children spent the rest of the afternoon in a rare state of co-operation, paddling in the clear cold Dartmoor water, hauling stones around, yelling with irrational excitement every time the stream breached their dam. Felix eventually went to join in and Kate lay on the blanket, blissfully not needed by anyone, the music of their voices blending in the background with a pleasing harmony. The sky above was a pale, precious blue, the air fresh with a crystal clarity. She had fallen asleep.

The flight attendants are moving along the aisles with their trolley, serving dinner. Kate pulls down the little table in front of her, feeling suddenly exhausted. The flight could have been delayed because of her. Everyone would have had to eat late.

There's an empty seat between her and a man in his thirties. He has a laptop in front of him and is concentrating on the screen, tension tightening his cheek muscles. Every now and again he makes a conscious effort to relax, his face softening briefly before he stops thinking about it and the skin pulls itself taut again. Making international deals, perhaps, or saving his firm from bankruptcy by negotiating last-minute contracts.

Kate wants to lean over and ask him to look up money-laundering, but she knows how obsessive people become about their computers. Rory and Felix will sit for hours at a screen, playing games, refusing to let anyone else near them. Has Felix been teaching Rory to cheat, showing him how to commit silent crimes, send out viruses, take on secret identities?

'Beef or vegetarian?' says the flight attendant, smiling at her.

'Beef,' says Kate.

The attendant places a tray in front of her. Kate takes the lid off the beef stew and examines the food.

They were having beef when Felix first came to have a meal with Kate's family. Yorkshire pudding, sprouts, roast potatoes, gravy. Fragrant fumes from the cooking had been drifting through the house all morning, a soft, restful aroma, the smell of Sunday.

'I've invited Adam Kent, Piers Watkins, George Rangarajan and Felix Kendall,' said Kate's father. 'I don't think we've had any of them before.'

'Surely Felix and George are only upper fifth?' said Kate's mother, in surprise. They entertained four boys a week, but usually only sixth-formers.

'I thought I'd make an exception. Felix is an interesting boy.'

'Wasn't it George you caught halfway up the chapel roof last month?'

Kate's father smiled. 'I'm afraid so. The "OUT OUT OUT SEMOLINA" banner. It was just high spirits. George likes to make a splash.'

'So you offer him the privilege of Sunday lunch? Does he deserve it?'

'Probably not, but he and Felix are very close friends. Always together. It would be churlish to invite one without the other.'

'And where was Felix during the semolina episode?'

'Holding the ladder.'

'Why are you interested in Felix?' asked Kate's mother as she prepared the gravy, her tight grey perm bent over the top of the stove. She poured the juice from the meat into the saucepan and started to stir. It sizzled and the smell of beef intensified.

'He's unusually clever, very controlled.'

'Except when he's foolish enough to hold the ladder for George.'

'And his parents died when he was about five, I believe.'

'Could you lay the table, Kate?' said her mother.

But Kate wanted to know about the dead parents. She was fourteen. A boy whose parents had died was romantic. 'How did they die?' she asked.

Her father frowned slightly. 'It was rather unpleasant,' he said.

'Well, it would be,' said Kate's mother. 'Nobody dies pleasantly.'

'There was a burglary and his parents put up a bit of a fight. They were both stabbed.'

'Goodness,' said Kate's mother. 'Poor boy. Did he witness it?'

'I don't know if he actually saw it happen, but they found him sitting in the blood by his mother's body.'

Kate's mother stopped stirring and looked up, her eyebrows raised and her small dark eyes wide with shock. 'How dreadful.' A glug from the gravy drew her attention back to the saucepan. 'Who pays his fees?'

'There's a trust fund for his education. Surely you've noticed his guardians – two aunts?' He chuckled. 'You must have seen them. They're an extraordinary pair.'

'Oh, yes,' said Kate's mother. 'I hadn't realised they belonged to him.'

'Did they catch them?' asked Kate. 'The burglars?'

55

Her father paused before leaving the kitchen. 'Do you know? I have no idea.'

Kate went into the dining room. The story seemed so remote, like an item on the news, a report from a distant land that didn't touch her. She had never met anyone whose parents had been murdered before. Could you forget about it when you talked to him?

The long windows of the dining room looked out on to the sports fields where the home team were playing a cricket match. Light slanted into the room, filtered through the oaks that marked the boundary between the school grounds and a neighbouring farm.

She laid the table precisely, lining up the knives and forks, folding paper napkins and placing them on the left of each place, checking the wine glasses were clean and sparkling. Kate's father was a fair headmaster and enjoyed offering hospitality to his pupils. The boys liked him and called him Big Man. They enjoyed the irony. He was five foot six.

She could hear the crack of the ball against a bat and the faint ripple of applause. Walking over to the french windows, she gazed out at the white figures dotted round the field, the handful of parents sitting in deck-chairs by the pavilion, or standing in small groups, chatting. A Sunday-morning match was unusual, but the visiting school had a concert in the afternoon and there was a conflict of interest for several of the pupils.

On an impulse, Kate stepped outside on to the patio and sniffed at the warm air, wondering if she could recognise any of the members of the team. She walked over to the Mexican Orange and broke off a leaf, crushing it in her hand and savouring its sweet smell. The heat was rising rapidly as the sun crept round the side of the building, burning away the refreshing coolness of early morning.

The doorbell announced the arrival of their visitors, and Kate went along the patio to the kitchen door, which was standing open to let out the steam from the cooking. Her mother, cheeks hot and flushed, was tipping the vegetables into dishes and transferring them to the lower compartment of the Aga to keep warm. 'Go and join your father,' she said. 'He's talking to them all.'

Kate went into the hall and hesitated outside the drawing room, nervous at the prospect of meeting yet more young men.

'Glorious weather,' said her father.

'Yes, sir.'

'Absolutely sweltering.'

There were too many of them, an exhausting stream of seventeen- and eighteen-year-olds who knew everything – science, politics, history, geography – inhabiting a different world from her own. It was hard to remember all their names. She was a weekly boarder at Hillyard's, and coming back to this masculine world at weekends wasn't easy. She knew that her school friends would willingly hand over all their pocket money to be in her position, but the reality didn't live up to their fantasies. These intense boys, anxious to please her father, competing with each other for the cleverest sentence, the most original thought, were never the dreamboats her friends imagined.

'Kate!' called her father, catching sight of her. 'Come and meet the boys.'

She went in, immediately awkward, aware that she was too tall for her age, every movement distorted into an exaggerated clumsiness. Two of the boys were nearly six foot, thank goodness, but she was on a level with the others. Her father introduced her to them all individually. Felix was the shortest, but the most striking. His ginger hair, bushy and long, challenged the limits permitted by school regulations with curls that clustered around his shoulders. His face had a pleasing symmetry. Hazel eyes, slightly hooded, gave him a tragic look, Kate decided, although they gleamed with intelligent curiosity as he studied his surroundings. He smiled a lot, and whenever his mouth stretched outwards, she could see a thin mist of downy hair on his top lip. He had presence. Everyone's eyes were drawn towards him.

George towered over his friend. He was thin and angular, as if his bones had grown faster than his skin, but he moved with an unexpected ease, without any self-consciousness about his surprising height. He had large, eager eyes, slightly bulging, which darted round the room, assessing the décor, the laid table, the drinks cabinet. He had an air of certainty, a willingness to take over the proceedings at any time if necessary. When Kate's father poured the sherry, George distributed the glasses, as if he alone had the authority.

Kate shook hands with them all, as her father expected of her. The two older boys simply rested their palms against hers awkwardly, unresisting and expressionless. Their hands were slimy with sweat and she had to force herself to make contact, hiding her natural distaste, pretending to be pleased to meet them. George winked at her in a strangely familiar way, squeezing her hand with an alarming energy as if he had known her all his life and they shared some significant secret. Kate found his frank gaze intrusive and embarrassing. Felix also put a firm pressure into his handshake, but his grip managed to be more reassuring. She liked the fact that he seemed different, more thoughtful than the others.

'Adam and Piers are applying for medicine,' said her father. 'And George wants to be an artist.' They're all clever boys, he was saying. As you would expect from boys in my school.

Kate kept her head low, and studied George out of the corner of her eye. It was difficult to imagine him as an artist. He was very comfortable with his place in the world, fitting in almost too well. She thought an artist should be freer, more different.

'What about you, Felix?' said her father. 'Have you had any more thoughts about your future?'

'Oh, I just want to make a lot of money,' said Felix, with an easy grin.

'Not ambitious, then,' said George, slapping Felix on the back and nearly spilling his sherry. Everyone laughed.

'I'm serious,' said Felix. 'I intend to be a millionaire before I'm thirty.'

'No chance,' said George. 'Once I've got my Ferrari, you'll be lost in the distance behind me.'

'I'd rather be behind you where I can keep an eye on you,' said Felix. 'Nobody could trust a man who wears blue socks with grey diamonds on them.'

'They're not grey,' said George. 'They're a subtle silver.'

'Job fulfilment is as important as money,' said Adam.

'Of course it is,' replied Felix. 'But there's no point in starving while you spend years creating a masterpiece. I'd rather enjoy my life when I'm still young. And you need money for that.'

'It's a good thing Michelangelo or Leonardo da Vinci didn't think like you,' said Piers.

'They did. But they expected to make the money while they created, which is a bit more difficult nowadays. Anyway, I'm not artistic, so it's hardly a matter for concern.'

'It can be done,' said George. 'Just watch me.'

'Lunch is ready!' called Kate's mother, from the kitchen.

'Ah,' said her father, ushering them out. 'Splendid.'

'You're going into medicine,' said Felix to Piers. 'You obviously expect to make a lot of money.'

'Eventually, perhaps,' said Piers, strolling along with his hands in his pockets. 'But I'm most interested in the humanitarian side of medicine.'

'Very worthy,' said George, with raised eyebrows.

'Would you consider medicine?' asked Adam.

'Oh, no,' said Felix. 'I'm not keen on all that blood.'

Kate held her breath, remembering Felix's background, but he didn't seem to make any connection.

'Yorkshire pudding!' exclaimed George, as they entered the dining room. 'Brilliant!'

Kate's mother glowed, a faint pink patch appearing in each cheek. 'Oh, good,' she said. 'I'm glad you're pleased.'

All that ambition, thinks Kate, as she attempts to watch the video on the back of the seat in front of her. It's difficult because the angle isn't right.

Felix had done what he'd always intended. He'd gone to London and entered the financial world straight from school, shocking everyone by not going to university, and started earning very quickly. He had a formidable intellect, a calm ability to work his way through problems, a natural skill at making people like him. Once he was qualified, he came back to Devon and married Kate. Now he was a partner in a reputable firm and had written a book. He had the family he'd always wanted, an impressive house. Why would he need to do anything dishonest when he already had everything?

George had ambitions too. She vaguely remembers that he went to London at the same time as Felix. He was like Felix's shadow – or had it been the other way round? – irritating, but charming. Even her mother seemed to have a soft spot for him, inviting him for lunch more often than the other boys, as if she could fatten him up, fill out that sparse, stretched skin.

It seems odd now that Felix and George didn't stay in touch. In the early days of her marriage, whenever she mentioned George, Felix became strangely silent, not wanting to talk about him. She'd assumed that they'd followed their own interests and lost touch. Had they recently met up again – in Iceland perhaps? But why hadn't Felix told her? Why would he try to hide his connection with George?

She closes her eyes and drifts into a half-sleep. The words

from the film wander in and out of her consciousness, but her mind is in another place: after Felix had passed his accountancy exams and come back to visit them.

He had asked her to go with him to the Northcote Theatre in Exeter, to see *As You Like It*. As they walked back down the hill, from the university to the station, Felix suddenly halted. 'Look!' he said.

She stopped with him, not certain where to look, expecting to see something extraordinary. But there was nothing obvious. She gazed around with bewilderment.

Felix was staring at the lit window of a small terraced house. Inside, a family sat together, a father and two sons, crammed on a sofa, concentrating on the television screen.

'I wonder why they don't draw the curtains,' said Kate. 'Don't they know how exposed they are?'

'I love it when you can see in,' said Felix.

Kate couldn't understand what the attraction was. 'Come on,' she said uncomfortably. 'We'll miss the train.'

But he wouldn't move. It was as if he were watching a programme on the television, unable to take his eyes off the screen. Kate tried touching his arm, but he didn't respond. 'It's a family,' he said at last, very softly.

'They really should draw the curtains,' she said. 'They're too close to the road. Anybody'd think they wanted us to watch them.'

One of the boys nudged the other and they laughed. Felix sighed and half smiled with them.

The mother entered the room with a tray of drinks and offered them round. The boys' trainers were resting on the edge of the coffee-table as they stretched out their long legs; the father's suit was baggy and shapeless, as if he lived in it every day of his life. The mother was wearing a red and orange striped jumper, loose and sloppy, to hide her bulky shape. They were all overweight. The mother handed over Mars bars, smiling. The boys tore off the wrapping and started eating, not taking their eyes from the screen.

'No wonder they're fat,' said Kate.

'I want that,' said Felix. 'I'm going to have a family.' He turned away from the window and they continued down the street. 'Only I'm going to have a bigger house.'

'Well, just make sure you draw the curtains, then,' said Kate.

Chapter 8

Once they've landed, Kate remains in her seat, still dancing through time with Felix. Foxtrots and waltzes from the past, and a jitterbug for the present, the beat cascading through her with the energy of a teenage party. They've flown through the night and lost five hours. Everyone else had drifted into sleep, but her thoughts had continued to jump and shake and leap into the air. It is now eight o'clock in the morning and the whole of Britain will be getting up, sitting down to breakfast, rushing off to work. In those hours of travelling, surrounded by snoring passengers and subdued half-light, she has gone over and over her life, Felix's life, their marriage, pulling at threads to see if they will unravel, worrying away at knots that she didn't know were there. But nothing gives, nothing reveals itself. There's a clarity inside her head, a feverish energy that sends her racing through decades, yet still manages to linger over minute details.

She's pulled out a conversation with Felix from years ago after he returned from a weekend course. 'You have to report any suspicions of money-laundering the moment you realise, wherever you are, otherwise you're criminally liable. If you're standing in the bathroom cleaning your teeth and you suddenly think, That's odd, you have to do something about it. Immediately.'

Kate had been impressed. 'So clean money takes precedence over clean teeth.'

'Absolutely.'

The other passengers get up, remove hand luggage from the overhead lockers and queue to leave the plane. Kate watches them. She would like to stay there indefinitely. A flight attendant leans over, her face pale and weary, but still polite. 'Are you all right?' she says. Her breath smells from lack of sleep.

'Yes, thank you,' says Kate. 'I'm fine.' Her own breath is stale and yeasty.

She stands up and reaches for her bag, thinking about her presents for the children, the three little polar bears. Back in her Canadian hotel, when the world was predictable, she had wrapped each one with maternal care, with innocent love, and placed them in her hand luggage. She didn't want to lose them.

At Passport Control, someone is waiting for her. 'Inspector Williams, from SOCA,' he says, offering his hand. 'Serious Organised Crime Agency.' He looks too young to be an inspector, with short, spiked hair and a nose that bends very slightly to the right.

He accompanies her to pick up her suitcase. They stand side by side at the carousel and watch the bags drifting past. He reminds Kate of Lawrence. He has that same careless interest in everything going on around him that delights and infuriates her. A mixture of endless curiosity and a refusal to focus. But Inspector Williams is older. He must have learnt to channel his interests, or he wouldn't be an inspector. Maybe there's hope for Lawrence after all.

'Tell me when you see your case,' he says, 'and I'll grab it for you.'

'I'd really like to go home,' she says.

His face folds into a well-worn pattern of sympathy and immediately looks older. More responsible. 'I can appreciate how you feel, but I'd like to have a talk first, if you don't mind too much. We can do it here, and then I'll make sure you get home as soon as possible.'

'There's my case.'

It's lurching towards them, blue and black, still new but bulging with her Canadian purchases. Inspector Williams steps forward and grabs it, swinging it on to the trolley with easy strength. 'What have you got in there?' he says. 'An iceberg?'

Kate knows she should smile but she doesn't want to. Her eyes skitter round the groups of waiting people, examining their faces, still half expecting to see Felix. Confirmation that the last twenty-four hours have been nothing more than a spectacular misunderstanding.

But there are no familiar faces.

'Come along, Mrs Kendall,' says Inspector Williams.

'I want to check,' she says. 'My children might have come to meet me.'

'They're not here,' he says.

'How can you be so sure?'

'Because I know where they are. Someone is with them.'

'What do you mean, "someone"? Who? I left them in safe hands. You can't go changing my arrangements. It will upset them.'

'I can assure you they're completely safe. They'll be setting off for school exactly as they should be.'

She refuses to move. 'Where are they? Who's looking after them?'

'Millie has joined Rory at your friends' house – the Hollidays.'

He's too familiar. He's using the children's names as if he knows them. They need their parents. That's what he doesn't seem to be getting. 'May I go to the toilet?' she says.

'Certainly.' He leads her to the Ladies. 'Leave your bags with me. I'll wait here.'

'Of course.' She's seen the films. She knows that the police wait and watch, that she couldn't possibly escape. She should climb out of a window, find a panel that leads into the heating ducts, but she doesn't think she's quite up to that.

She locks herself into a cubicle and takes her mobile phone out of an inside pocket. She dials hurriedly, her hands shaking, terrified that someone will burst in and snatch the phone from her hand.

It rings twice. 'Mummy?'

'Millie – are you all right?'

'Mummy, what's going on?' She can hear the tears in Millie's voice.

'I don't really know. I'm trying to find out now.'

'They keep talking about Daddy. I don't understand.'

Tears prickle Kate's eyes and wash down her cheeks but she brushes them aside, somehow believing that Millie can see her. 'Where are you?'

'Sian and Edward's. They came to fetch me from school.'

'Is Rory with you?'

'Yes. Do you want to speak to him? He's just here.'

'All right. Put him on.'

'Mummy?' It's Rory's voice, thin and sleepy.

'Hello, Rory. Are you all right?'

'Yes – Mummy, why do I have to share a bedroom with Millie? She keeps blubbing and I can't sleep. It's so unnecessary.'

Kate can imagine his earnest, indignant face. 'Don't fuss, Rory. It won't be for long.'

'Have you landed? Are you back?'

'Yes,' she says. 'I'll be home any time now.'

'Well, thank goodness for that. There's such a fuss going on here – it's horrible. They've all got the wrong stick about Daddy. I keep telling them they don't know what they're talking about, but nobody listens.'

'It's not the wrong stick. It's just the wrong end of it.'

'Whatever.'

He's picked up 'whatever' from Lawrence. Even now Kate can feel the usual irritation rising inside her.

'Rory . . .'

'I know, I know. Was it a 787?'

'What?'

'The aeroplane. Was it a Boeing 787?'

'It might have been. I'll see if I can find out. Can you put Millie back on?'

'OK. Bye, then.' He has such confidence. He believes Kate can sort everything out. She wishes he was right.

Millie is back. 'When are you coming home?'

'Today. I'm at Heathrow, but we should all be home tonight.'

'Including Daddy?'

Kate hesitates. 'I'm not quite sure – but everything will be fine, you'll see. I'm going to have to go now. Speak to you later.'

'Bye,' says Millie. 'Bye.'

Kate shuts the mobile phone and replaces it in her pocket. She wipes her face with a piece of tissue and decides at the last minute to flush the toilet in case someone is listening. Then she realises that, if they were, they'd have heard the phone conversation anyway. She stops outside to wash her hands, rubbing them under the dryer for some time, determined not to show any sign of urgency.

They're all wrong. They just don't know it yet. I'm not going to let these people destroy my family.

'Have you seen the newspapers?' asks Inspector Williams.

'How could I?' says Kate. 'I've been on a plane for the last ten hours and then I came straight here.'

He looks at her for a second, his eyes still and thoughtful. 'I'm afraid the press are having a field day.'

'What do you mean?'

'We've made several high-profile arrests all round the world.'

'You've arrested Felix?' But they don't know where he is.

'No, he got away.'

'This is all about money-laundering?' Kate's voice sounds as if it belongs to someone else.

'And the criminal activity that produces the money.'

'What sort of criminal activity?'

'The smuggling of illegal immigrants into the country, prostitution, extortion. But that's only for starters. I have a feeling it's going to get a whole lot more interesting.'

Outside, people are waiting for flights, boarding aeroplanes, eating meals, phoning wives and husbands, waiting to greet long-lost brothers from America, Australia, Singapore, Beijing. Kate can hear them talking, pushing trolleys. Children are running around, falling over, wailing. A calm female voice is making announcements about which gate to go to, which flights are delayed. An airport is a city, a place where so many things can happen, where lives touch, where departures and arrivals overlap, losses and gains, where heightened emotions cast an artificial light. Everything is intensified into a few hours of isolation, cut off by a wall of security that you only notice if you look. An airport is the most exciting place in the world, the gateway to freedom, travel and enlightenment, and yet it is the most secure, the most monitored, the most watched.

Inside the room with Inspector Williams and an unnamed policewoman, Kate is struggling to make sense of this fresh information. She wants to wake up, discover she's only dreaming. 'You're suggesting Felix is involved in exploiting vulnerable people?' Felix, who has always hated any form of bullying, who refused to buy apples from South Africa in the days of apartheid, who checked all the labels of new clothes in case they came from China at the time of Tiananmen Square?

The inspector sits back and pauses. 'No, it's unlikely he's been getting his hands dirty with illegal immigrants.'

'Then – I don't understand.'

'Money-laundering, Mrs Kendall, means getting the proceeds of crime into the banking system and making it legitimate. You need experts to hide the progress of the money, an accountant who's prepared to turn a blind eye. He may not be implicated in the original criminal activity, but he's equally culpable. He hides the evidence and makes everything happen.'

'Felix wouldn't do that,' says Kate. 'You're chasing the wrong man.'

'Then why has he run away?'

I don't know. I don't know. 'Why would he get involved? What would he gain from it?'

'That's what we would like to know. Money, perhaps?'

'He has a good income. We don't need any more.'

'Perhaps he can't maintain your lifestyle as well as you thought he could.'

'But he has a high-paying job. He's never given any indication that we were struggling.'

'Pride, then, perhaps. He made a mistake, recognised it, but couldn't bring himself to own up.'

Kate takes a slow breath. Felix's reputation is important to him and this theory makes some sense, but she doesn't want to discuss it with a stranger. She needs to think about it later, when she's on her own and her mind is clearer. 'My husband is an honourable man,' she says.

Inspector Williams's mouth twists to one side, the opposite side to his nose. It takes her a second to realise he's smiling. 'Then let's hope he doesn't do a Cassius and attempt to assassinate someone.'

She allows him a thin smile in return. She hadn't expected him to know *Julius Caesar*. 'I meant that he has a strong sense of morality.' He doesn't lie. He never lies.

'What do you know about George Rangarajan?'

George again. Always at Felix's side, undermining his chat-up lines, forever in the way when she and Felix were trying to get to know each other. And now here he is again, roaring back into their lives, refusing to allow them their ordinary uneventful existence. 'You've just arrested him, haven't you? Why don't you ask him?'

'Answer the question, please, Mrs Kendall.'

His formality shocks her and she has to pause to think. 'I haven't seen him for years. He was friends with Felix at school – I told this to the policeman in Canada.'

'Did they stay in contact when they left school?'

'They both studied in London for a while. But then Felix came back to Devon, and, as far as I know, they lost touch.'

'I want you think about this very carefully, Mrs Kendall. Did Felix ever mention him? Did he get letters, postcards, emails? Any form of communication?'

'No, nothing.'

The inspector pauses for a long time, as if he expects her to offer further information, but there's nothing more she can tell him. He looks down at his notes. 'I'd like to go over Felix's movements during the last few weeks in more detail. We're still faced with the fact that we don't know where he is.'

Two hours later, Kate is dull with exhaustion. Cups of tea have been brought in and she has consumed them greedily, but a tuna and cucumber baguette sits uneaten on the table. She's tried to take a bite, but the food stuck in her throat and a wild nausea engulfed her as her stomach refused to accept it. The atmosphere in the room is stuffy and oppressive, and she feels as if she's drifting further and further away from the situation, as if her real self has withdrawn, leaving only an image of herself sitting there. She's watching the conversation from a distance, and wants to tell the inspector that she's an impostor. The original Kate is elsewhere, returning to the family home, where everyone will be waiting for her, the same as always.

'Well, I think we've covered everything for now,' says Inspector Williams, 'although I'm sure we'll meet again several times before things get sorted.'

'Am I free to go?' says Kate.

'Of course.'

'You're not going to arrest me?'

'Whatever for?'

'Well, I could have helped Felix, couldn't I? Perhaps I put him up to it. Sent him to Iceland, made the contacts, kept the records—' She can't go on. She knows she sounds ridiculous.

Inspector Williams watches her, waiting politely for her to finish. She can see compassion in him again, a kindness that softens the edges of his professional manner. 'I'll arrange for a car to drive you home,' he says.

'All the way to Budleigh Salterton?'

'Do you have transport already arranged?'

She hasn't given it a thought. Felix was supposed to be meeting her. She'd have to find out about buses, trains, taxis. Her debit card doesn't even work. 'Thank you,' she says.

'There are a couple of things I should warn you about.'

'What things?'

'We've had to search your house.'

'Oh.' She has a vision of men pulling books off shelves, taking up the floorboards, lifting the lids off cisterns. 'How bad will it be?'

'Well, it's difficult to say. I haven't personally seen it. We do try and put things back when we've finished, but there will inevitably be some disruption.'

'When did this happen?'

'Only yesterday, I'm afraid, but it should be finished by now.'

Kate imagines Felix coming home from Hamburg, being dropped off at the end of the drive by Ken. She can see him standing by the front door, travelling bag in hand, as policemen in yellow jackets brush past him, two of them carrying his filing cabinet down the front steps, loading it into their van . . . 'Whatever will the neighbours think?'

'The neighbours will be very aware of what's going on. The

whole country should be keeping an eye out for Felix Kendall by now.'

Kate snorts. 'So why haven't they found him, then? He's not a man who just disappears into a crowd. He's got red hair, for goodness' sake.'

'There's such a thing as dye, I believe.'

In twenty-four hours the world has shifted and split apart at the seams. The coat that always fitted comfortably has inexplicably shrunk and looks as if it belongs to someone else. This is how it must feel if one of your children is murdered, if a mud slide buries your house, if your husband turns out to be a spy and you never knew . . .

'Another thing, Mrs Kendall, is that we've had to freeze all your husband's bank accounts. We have the power to do this, if we suspect connections with organised crime.'

'I see,' says Kate. The words echo inside her head. *Freeze, bank accounts, freeze*— 'You mean I've got no money?'

'Not from any accounts that you share with your husband.'

'But they're all joint accounts. We don't separate our finances.'

He looks worried. 'You don't have any money of your own?'

'No.' She can feel panic rising in her stomach. 'What am I supposed to do? How do I feed the children?'

'Do you work?'

'No, I'm a housewife, as I assume you know. I like it,' she adds, in case he should think that Felix has been exploiting her.

'Do you have any family? How about parents?'

'I can't ask them for money.'

'I think you might have to. At least for the time being. The courts can release money for you and the children to live on, but it will take time.'

Kate closes her eyes and takes several deep breaths. What about the men who have just finished decorating the hall? What about the gas bill, the electricity? How will she buy petrol so that she can get the children to school? She has never had to worry about money before.

There's been an earthquake on her home territory, at the heart of her existence. She's standing on a cracked floor, at the edge of a precipice, looking down at a cavernous unknown space. The husband she has always depended on is standing next to her, but he's not real. He's fading as she turns to him, vanishing into a world that no longer exists. And the lights are off.

They're all wrong. They don't know Felix – they don't know that he's incapable of doing something like this.

Chapter 9

Rory sits in the back of the people-carrier between Theo and Millie, trying to think. Millie keeps sniffing and blowing her snot into a paper hanky. She's disgusting. Why can't she make an effort? If he can do it, then so can she.

'You're allowed to cry,' his father had said to him last year on Budleigh beach, 'but it's not necessary to make a meal of it.' Rory had been wailing as he staggered out of the sea, his feet soft and sensitive on the stones. It was his own fault. He hated taking his shoes down to the water's edge because they made him look like a little kid. His father was standing on the shingle in his pale green swimming trunks with water foaming round his feet. Strands of hair were springing out from his muscly legs like wire and he was wearing white plastic shoes. He should have looked gross, but he didn't. You just knew he was a champion swimmer, captain of his old school swimming squad, and still better than everyone else on the beach. Rory stopped crying. 'Come on,' said his father, and gave him a piggy-back up the beach to their towels and rugs.

Rory wonders if he should tell Millie not to make a meal of it, but decides against it. 'We have to keep in touch,' he whispers to Theo.

Theo blinks at him. 'Yes,' he says, although it's obvious to Rory that he doesn't know what he's talking about.

'In case we get confined to the house. You know, security. There'll be policemen and MI6 and Special Branch and people like that involved.'

'Really?' Theo looks interested.

'The telephone will probably be bugged.' Rory feels important when he says this. 'We'll have to have a special code that nobody else understands.'

'Is your dad a spy?' asks Theo.

Rory takes a deep breath and tries to decide if he wants his dad to be a spy. There could be certain advantages. 'It's possible,' he says.

'Ethan says he's a terrorist.'

Rory is outraged. 'Well, he's not,' he says, a little too loudly. Millie stops sniffing and Sian's head turns sideways as if she's listening. He lowers his voice to a furious whisper: 'And if you ever say that again, I'll pull your hair out. One hair at a time, so it really hurts, until you're bald all over. It won't grow back again, you know. You'll be bald for ever.'

'Then I'll do the same to you.'

Rory stops being angry as he considers Theo's shocking lack of imagination. You'd think he could at least pretend to be clever and come up with a different form of torture. One thing's for sure. They won't be offering Theo a place on the course for gifted children that will be held at their school next August.

'Anyway,' says Theo, 'I'd like to be bald. I wouldn't have to go to the barber's any more. I hate barbers.'

Rory stares out of the window and pretends not to hear him. There's no sign of yesterday's snowflakes, but it's very windy. They descend the hill that runs parallel to the beach. Waves are pounding down on to the pebbles, exploding like bombs, shooting streaks of white foam into the air. He's glad he's in the car and not outside, but he wouldn't be amazed if Sian or his mother suggested a walk along the beach later today. 'Fresh air and exercise,' his mother will say. 'Clear the cobwebs away.'

'We've got to have codenames, so no one knows who we are,' he says to Theo. 'I'll be Alex Rider.'

'You can't be Alex Rider. That's not fair.'

'OK,' says Rory, shrugging. He hadn't really believed he'd get away with it, but it had been worth a try. 'I'll be . . .' He has to think for a minute. 'I'll be Scarface.'

'Why? You haven't got a scar.'

'They won't know who I am, then, will they?'

'Oh. Right.'

'So who do you want to be?'

'Harry Potter.'

'No way. You've got to think of something cleverer. Like Piranha Man, or Hookeye, or Mad Dog.'

Theo thinks for a moment. 'OK, I'll be Mad Dog. I like dogs.'

'And before you say anything important, you've got to tap the phone three times with your fingernail. That means I'll know it's you and not MI6 eavesdropping.'

'Why would MI6—'

'Oh, my goodness,' says Sian. 'Who are all these people? Where am I supposed to park?'

Rory stares at the cars and vans lining the road, some of them double-parked. 'It's the BBC,' he says, as they pass a large white van.

Millie stops snivelling. 'Where?' she says.

Sian pulls up in front of the gates and a crowd immediately surrounds the car. Faces appear at the windows and cameras flash through the glass, flickering and confusing. Rory shrinks back in his seat, convinced the windows will break.

'I don't know what to do,' says Sian.

'Hoot at them,' says Rory. 'They shouldn't be blocking our driveway. It's illegal.'

Surprisingly, she follows his advice, pressing her hand on the horn and holding it there. It's a wicked sound. So loud it hurts your ears.

'Stop it!' screams Millie. 'I can't stand it.'

'How else do you think we'll get them to move?' shouts Rory.

The gates open slowly and Sian drives in, surrounded by people. Then his mother is there, pulling open the car door. Sian takes her hand off the horn.

'Mummy!' cries Millie, into the sudden silence, jumping out and throwing her arms round her.

A short man in glasses shoves a microphone forward. '*News of the World*, Mrs Kendall. How do you and your children feel about your husband now?'

A woman in a Russian-style fur hat pushes in front of him. 'Amanda Flyte from the BBC. Could we have a few words, Mrs Kendall?'

Rory unclips his seatbelt, but his legs seem to have frozen and he can't move.

'Quickly, Rory,' says his mother, struggling to get away from Millie. She reaches out a hand for him.

'I'll park round the corner and walk back,' says Sian.

'Hurry up, Rory.'

He still can't move.

Theo has started to cry. He's as bad as Millie. Why does everyone have to keep crying?

'Let me help.' The voice is deep and hoarse. His mother steps back and a man takes her place, leaning into the car. Rory draws away from him. The man's eyes are green and red-rimmed. He's an alien. You can see the cunning lurking behind his pretend kindness. His face swells up as he leans over Rory, the skin puffy and artificial. 'Come on, Rory,' he says.

He knows my name, thinks Rory in a panic. He grabs the seatbelt and tries to clip it back in, but the man clamps a hand over his and removes it. 'Help!' shouts Rory. 'Theo! Help me!'

The man places his arms round Rory, lifts him and pulls him out of the car.

'No!' screams Rory. I'll never see my mother again. He kicks, but can't seem to reach the man properly, so he tries to twist his body round and wrench himself free.

He can just hear his mother in the background. 'Rory, it's all right. He's trying to help. Stop it!'

Then the man lowers him to the ground and they stand facing each other, panting heavily.

'Strong guy, huh?' says the man, and grins.

His face is twisted and evil, his eyes leering out of the huge cheeks. There's a mole on the side of his nose, evidence of a creeping disease that he's probably already passed on to Rory.

Then someone else grabs Rory from behind. He bends and squirms. They won't get him. A voice speaks in his ear: 'Rory, it's me. Mum.'

He stops fighting, but he stands stiff and awkward, slowly turning round to check it really is her, careful not to take his eyes off the alien.

'Thank you,' his mum says to the man.

'Any time,' he says. 'I'm used to boys. I've got four of my own.'

I'll bet he has, thinks Rory. He's probably abducted them and uses them as slaves.

His mother guides him and Millie through the crowd and Rory can hear Sian driving away. 'Shut the gate,' he says. 'Then they can't get in.'

'I know,' says his mother. 'I know.'

She has the remote control in her hand and aims it at the gate. 'You'd better leave,' she shouts. 'You won't be able to get out.'

Most people drop back, but two women stay inside the drive.

'You'll be trapped,' says his mother.

At the last moment, they dash out. One catches her scarf between the closing gates and has to pull it through.

'It's all right,' says his mother. 'We're safe now.'

It's funny how the house has changed. The three of them stand in the hall and Rory stares round. Something's not quite right, but he can't work out what it is.

The clock is still there, above the hall table, but it's not ticking. The pendulum hangs down without moving and the hands are stuck at ten to nine. There are scratches in the wooden floor, as if someone has dragged heavy things across it. The school photographs of Rory and Millie and Lawrence at the side of the staircase are crooked, not even tilting in the same direction. The green sofa is pushed up against the wall below the big mirror and Rory's football kit has gone from the corner. He remembers leaving it there before he went to Sian's because he expected to be back before the next match. But his mum could have tidied it away. She does things like that. He looks back at the sofa. He can see the dark patch on the top corner where his dad spilt his coffee that time when he was playing charades with them and got carried away with Millie's skateboard.

'Mum!' says Rory. 'Someone's been in here.' A cold sweat is creeping down his back. He was right all along. The aliens have arrived. It's the wrong sofa. 'It should be the red and white striped sofa. The green one goes in the conservatory.'

She doesn't react as he expects, even with the evidence in front of her eyes. She doesn't do anything except stare at him.

'Mum,' he says, more urgently. 'They've moved the furniture around.'

'Let's go in the kitchen,' she says. 'I need a cup of tea.'

Why doesn't she say anything? She can see the sofa. She can't have forgotten where her own furniture goes, can she? Rory follows her into the kitchen. 'Mum, what's happened? Who's been in here?'

She sits down and he sees that her eyes are watering. Everybody's the same. Things go a bit wrong and they just become hysterical. He tries to be calm. He should be taking charge. 'We'll have to ring the police,' he says.

'Rory, they are the police.'

'Who?'

'The people who've been in here. They've searched the whole house.'

'The whole house?' says Millie, with a squeaky voice. 'Including my room?'

'Well, I suppose they must have done.'

'My diaries!' shrieks Millie, and runs out. Rory can hear her pounding up the stairs. They won't have taken the diaries. He tried reading them once, when she went on holiday with a friend. They were deadly, brain-freezingly boring.

The phone rings, but his mother ignores it.

'Mum, the phone.'

She just looks at him. Hopeless. Feeling grown-up and responsible, Rory crosses the room and picks it up. 'Hello?'

'Is that Rory? Where's Mum?'

Rory hands the phone to her. 'It's Lawrence,' he says.

She takes it. 'Lawrence?'

Rory doesn't listen to much of the conversation. He wanders round the kitchen, picking things up, examining them, as if he's never seen any of them before. As if he's a stranger in his own kitchen. He finds he can't remember where things were in the first place, so he can't tell if they've been moved.

'I don't know any more than you do,' his mother is saying. 'Well, I've talked to the police – money-laundering.'

How can she be sure it's the police who've been in? Wouldn't they have put everything back where they'd found it? Why have they swapped the sofas? Is there something hidden inside one of them, a secret transmitter that the aliens use to contact the mothership? It might have to be placed in the hall so that they can get better reception.

'No, don't come home. It's bedlam here. Just get on with your work . . .'

Rory would like to search the sofa in the hall, but he thinks he shouldn't leave his mother. She needs his help and, anyway, the house is too cold. The heating isn't on. At least the Aga keeps the kitchen warm.

'Lawrence, you must get on with your assignment. It wouldn't help coming home. You can't do anything. Nobody can do anything.'

It might be the sofa in the conservatory that has the hidden receiver. It'll be even colder in there. Aliens prefer the cold.

His mother puts the phone down. 'Oh, Rory,' she says, and pulls him towards her. There are still tears in her eyes, but he doesn't want to see them. He turns his face away.

His mother rests her chin on his hair. Rory stands stiff and alert, moving his eyes slowly round the kitchen. Someone's got to be sensible.

Chapter 10

Opening a corner of her bedroom curtains the next morning, Kate peers out into the early-morning gloom, then lets it drop back again with dismay. For about three seconds, she'd fooled herself into believing that the events of yesterday were just an over-vivid dream. But it's no good. It's all still there.

A handful of people are huddled together outside her gate, cupping their hands round steam-clouded mugs. Where did they get hot drinks at this time of the morning? Did they bring flasks? Nowhere in Budleigh could have supplied them. There aren't any all-night cafés – it's not that kind of place. Has someone local brought cups of coffee? A disloyal neighbour, a traitor in their midst, someone who thrives on drama? Will he or she be bringing bacon sandwiches next?

The night has been everlasting. A jetstream of insomnia stretches out behind Kate, a zone of lost hours, days, aeons, where sleep has become an elusive art. As she was tossing round the bed, the invisible presence of Felix lay beside her. On several occasions, she put her hand out to touch him, certain that she had just emerged from a nightmare, only to feel her arm drifting down through empty space, unresisted, unconsoled.

Where are you, Felix? Are you still alive?

She occasionally drifted into sleep, but kept jumping awake with hands of panic round her throat, threatening to throttle her. She had to sit up each time, fighting for breath. Her mind won't slow down. A matrix of interconnecting worries builds inside her, the spaces between the grid offering only emptiness, uncertainty, disbelief. Maybe Felix will turn up today as if nothing's happened. Can I ask Mum and Dad for money? How? Do the aunts know what's going on? What if Felix comes home while I'm out and there's no one here except the journalists?

And a thin, piercing laser-beam pulses through her. How could Felix possibly be mixed up in a criminal underworld? How did George persuade him? It's as if he's somehow been transported from one end of the earth to the other. The man she is now examining from afar is a stranger, a man who no longer looks like Felix.

His first work trip abroad – so long ago. Zürich. His new luggage. An expensive suitcase, navy, rigid. They'd never bought anything so extravagant before.

'Look,' he says. 'Wheels on the bottom. All this spare room to pack presents for you.'

'I don't want you to go.'

'I'll be back before you can say Jack Richardson.'

Jack Richardson? Who's he? 'What if the plane crashes?'

Felix like a child before a party, over-excited, proud of his job and his place in the world. His laugh booming round the bedroom, echoing up through the ceiling and into the roof, filling the space of their first home, their modest two-bedroomed terraced house. How could she resent such happiness? The joy that he expressed so openly and wildly, as if he was drunk even when he wasn't.

Did he keep drinking that joy? More and more until it turned into madness? Had she been looking the wrong way at the crucial moment, the turning point, when it had all gone bad?

No, they're hunting the wrong man.

Leaping back into bed that morning. Frantic, desperate love with an illicit urgency, as if it might be the last time. Conscious that the taxi was about to turn up, muffling their giggles so that they wouldn't wake six-month-old Lawrence, who had slept through the earlier laughter.

Is that his hand on her back now? The tips of his fingers so sensual as they brush her skin that her nerve-ends rise to the surface, recognising the delicacy of his touch, hyper-sensitive, hungry for him.

Her stomach aches with tension. She has to get breakfast for the children. She has to pretend to be normal.

'Can't I stay at home today?' says Rory, as he climbs into the car. His face is pale and there are dark smudges under his eyes.

'No.' She needs to get them to school. Out of the way.

He turns away from her, his mouth tight and sulky.

'Come here,' she says, leaning through the gap between the front seats and grabbing his tie. She loosens the knot and eases it into a more acceptable shape, pulling it up to cover his top button. 'That's better. Now the shoes.'

He raises each foot in turn and she adjusts the Velcro straps, tugging them firmly.

'Ow!' he yells.

She ignores him.

'We'll be late,' says Millie.

'That's the least of my worries,' says Kate, conscious of an uncontrollable trembling in her arms. Her eyes are on the gates as she presses the remote control. They shudder a little and then swing open. Journalists swarm through, waving cameras and microphones. She edges forward, terrified she's going to hit someone. 'Don't touch the windows,' she says sharply, seeing Rory's hand reaching for the handle.

'But they want to speak to us,' he says.

'We don't want to speak to them.'

'Why not? We can't tell them anything important because we don't know where Daddy is, any more than they do.'

'That's not the point.' *Shut up!* she is screaming in her head. *Shut up! Shut up!*

But Rory won't stop. 'I could sell them my story.'

Opening her mouth to reply is too exhausting. The words seem so slow, so heavy in her mouth. 'You haven't got a story.'

'Mum!' says Millie, suddenly. 'I've left my maths book at home. We have to go back.'

'We're not going back.'

'We have to.'

Kate keeps moving in first gear, her eyes darting, trying to keep everyone in sight. 'If you can find a way to turn round and get back, you tell me. Would you like to drive? Show me how it's done?'

'I can't go to maths without my book,' wails Millie, her voice cracking. 'Mr Harrison'll kill me!'

'I bet they'd pay us just to take some photos,' says Rory.

'Be quiet!' shouts Kate.

There's a shocked, painful silence. They creep on to the road and the gates close behind them. Kate accelerates, her eyes forward, refusing to look back. She is throbbing with guilt.

They drive to Hillyard's without another word and pull up at the back of Margaret's, where Millie's friend Helen is talking to an older girl with very long hair.

'That's Samantha Thomas,' says Millie, her voice shrill with excitement. 'I have to go.' She tugs at the door handle. 'Bye.'

She jumps out, grabbing her school bag and her hockey stick.

'Tell Mr Harrison it was my fault about the maths homework,' calls Kate. 'I'll write a letter tomorrow.'

But Millie isn't listening. She's flying over to Helen and Samantha, a broad smile stretched across her face. She's all right. Kate sighs with relief.

They reach Rory's school. 'I think I'm getting a cold,' he says, not even undoing his seatbelt.

Kate turns to face him. *Please get out without a fuss. Just go. I can't deal with this.* She examines his tight, anxious face. He must still believe there are kidnappers out there, waiting for him. Or Martians about to invade. 'Come on, Rory,' she says gently. 'Please.'

His eyes are old man's eyes, framed by hooded lids, which are normally endearing but now give him a haggard appearance. 'It's all right for you,' he says. 'You can just go home.'

'I can't,' she says. 'You wouldn't believe how much I have to sort out.'

'At least you don't have to play rugby in a dirty shirt.' He unclicks his seatbelt and slides out of the car. 'Bye,' he says, and slams the door.

She watches him go. He's walking like someone who thinks he won't return.

Kate's parents live near the station in Topsham, just outside Exeter, in a house that overlooks the river Exe. It has Dutch gables, built by the merchants who sailed up the Exe in the seventeenth century to trade, met the local girls and never went home again. The garden is on the opposite side of the road, kept private by a four-foot wall, thriving despite the wind and salt from the estuary.

Kate leaves the car in the station car park and walks down to the house. She doesn't want to face her parents. She has no idea what to say. If she didn't need money, she probably wouldn't have come. The air is bitingly cold. She digs her hands into her pockets and lowers her head against the wind, wishing she'd remembered to bring a hat and scarf. The last time she came here, Felix was with her. He believed in visiting her parents more than she did.

Let's pop into the second-hand bookshop on our way back, he says now. They might have something to please Aunt Beatrice.

Where are you? I need to know where you are.

It's all a game, he says. Just you wait and see.

She trusts him. She's always trusted him. He knows what he's doing. They've all got it wrong.

There have always been strong threads of affection running between Felix and her parents, criss-crossing in both directions, wrapping themselves round Kate as she stands in the middle, growing thicker and more solid with the passing of time. When Felix proposed to Kate and she accepted, she discovered that he had already discussed it with her father.

'You asked him before you asked me?'

'It seemed the right thing to do,' said Felix, running his hand through his red hair, slightly sheepish in the face of her indignation. 'I know it's a bit old-fashioned. Anyway, you must have realised—'

It felt as if there was a conspiracy between him and her parents. About her, but without her. 'Most people come to an arrangement first.'

His hand stops on the side of his head. 'Do they? I didn't know that.'

Perhaps she was mistaken. All her knowledge had been gleaned from novels and television.

Her delighted parents organised a celebratory meal, cooked by Kate's mother, in the large dining room of the headmaster's house. They closed the long red and green striped curtains for the first time ever, turned off the lights and covered the table with candles.

Kate was embarrassed by the intimacy of the candlelight. 'We should have gone out to a restaurant,' she said.

'Nonsense,' said her father. 'Why would we eat something cooked by a stranger when your mother can do it so much better?' Even now, he refuses to eat out. He'll accept ready-made meals from Marks & Spencer, because they don't have additives, but apart from that, only home cooking is good enough for him.

'But Mum never gets a break.'

'Oh, she doesn't mind. She likes it.'

Kate's mother put a forkful of roast pork into her mouth and chewed thoughtfully. She looked as if she might say something, but remained silent.

'Nothing compares with your mum's cooking,' said Felix, helping himself to a large portion of vegetables. 'I have never, in my entire life, eaten such superb cauliflower cheese.'

This was not surprising. He'd spent years consuming canteen food at boarding-school or surviving on the nutritious but eccentric meals conjured up by his aunts.

Kate's mother's face glowed and she directed a beaming smile at Felix. 'Have as much as you like, Felix,' she said. 'Nothing is more pleasing to a cook than a healthy appetite.'

'How's George?' asked Kate's father. 'Has he finished his art course?'

'George is fine,' said Felix. 'Not doing much art, but he seems to be busy.'

Kate wasn't interested in George. She was glad that Felix was there without him, no longer dividing his attention between the two of them.

'What are his plans for the future?' asked Kate's father.

'I've no idea,' said Felix. 'He hasn't told me.'

'How extraordinary,' said Kate's mother. 'You two were always inseparable – you knew everything about each other.'

'We're older now,' said Felix. 'We have different interests.' He leant over and took another spoonful of roast potatoes. He seemed unwilling to discuss George any more. The old dark furniture along the walls of the dining room loomed out of the half-light. Tall sideboards with the best china and cut glass hidden away in cupboards. Bottles of French wines, cocktails, whisky, brandy. How many Sunday lunches had Kate endured in this room?

How many sixth-formers had passed through here, how many sweaty hands had she shaken? They'd all moved on, left the school, none of them satisfying her secret desire for some kind of passion, none of them seeing her as anything more than the old-fashioned furniture that was part of their headmaster's background.

Except Felix. He was the one who had noticed her.

'Are you missing any important activities at university this weekend, Kate?' asked her mother.

'No,' said Kate. She was in the final year of a history degree at York university. 'Just an essay that has to be in by Tuesday.'

'Your mother and I are so thrilled about the engagement,' said her father.

'You two were made for each other,' said her mother. 'It seems so – right.'

It felt right to Kate as well, but she didn't want to discuss it with her parents. It was unlike them to be so enthusiastic about anything, or to express themselves in such an emotional way.

'You're already like a son to me,' said her father to Felix. 'The son I never had.'

Was he implying that he would have preferred a son to a daughter? Felix and George had become regular visitors after their first invitation to Sunday lunch, often added on as extra guests. Did her parents have their eye on Felix as a prospective son-in-law, even at that early stage? Certainly, during his last two years at school, he was encouraged to pop in for extra coaching from the headmaster without George. He would sneak into the kitchen afterwards for a slice of cake and a chat with Kate's mum, or catch Kate on the stairs and stop for a long, earnest discussion.

Was it a carefully thought-out campaign? Did he always have in mind that marrying the headmaster's daughter would be a good career move? Was he just yearning for a family, for acceptance, for the cosy world of the full-time mother who baked and cleaned and had time to sit around for a gossip? Or had he come because he liked to talk to Kate?

'We're also pleased about the job in Exeter,' said her father. 'It means we'll still see a lot of you.'

'It's great to be back,' said Felix, who had spent the morning wandering round the school. 'Everything's exactly as it used to be.'

'Not really,' said Kate's father. 'We've had the new canteen built on the field at the side of the science labs, and the gym's been refurbished.'

'Oh, yes, yes,' said Felix. 'But it feels the same. All that shouting in the changing rooms, the smell of dirty socks and cooked cabbage, the same boys scribbling out their prep at the last minute.'

'Charming,' said Kate.

'I thought you were implying that we didn't move with the times,' said Kate's father.

'Of course not,' said Felix. 'I know you're a modern, free-thinking headmaster. Best in the country, if you ask me.'

Kate's father took the compliment modestly but easily, as if he knew this to be a sound observation.

'I have the ring with me,' said Felix, into the hush that followed.

'Oh,' said Kate's mother, with a gasp of excitement.

Kate and Felix had chosen it on Friday evening, but left it at the shop in Exeter to have the size altered. Felix must have picked it up without telling her. He produced the box and placed it on the table in front of him. Stylish blue, compact, the symbol of all that was going to change in Kate's life.

He passed it to her and she opened it very slowly.

The ring sat in the middle of white satin, two diamonds on either side of a central sapphire. The three stones caught the light from the candles and flashed with tiny pinpoints of colour.

It was more impressive than Kate remembered, more imbued with significance, and she felt suddenly frightened.

What was she supposed to say? She'd seen too many films – how did you avoid cliché?

'Perhaps we should leave them to it,' said Kate's mother. 'Let them put it on when they're on their own.'

'Nonsense,' said her father. 'Put it on her finger, Felix. Let's see how it looks.'

Kate rings the doorbell of her parents' house and waits. It takes ages for one of them to struggle out of an armchair, descend the stairs, unlock the inside door, reach the outside door. Felix has often asked for keys. 'To make it easier for you,' he always says.

But they prevaricate, promise to get some made, forget. As if they're afraid of being caught in compromising circumstances. As if they're capable of outrageous, shameful behaviour.

Her father appears. 'Ah,' he says. 'There you are.' He looks exhausted, as if he's been up all night.

Kate breathes out slowly. They've been expecting her. They'll be waiting for answers, but she doesn't have any to give.

They walk through the downstairs garage that used to be a stable, past the Fiesta that hasn't seen daylight for about five years and a small, upturned wooden dinghy. Her father still spends hours on the boat, removing the barnacles, varnishing, rubbing down, revarnishing, while he listens to Radio 4 and argues with everyone's opinions. The door into the house is on a side wall, insignificant behind peeling blue paint.

They climb the stairs to the living room on the first floor. A large plate-glass window dominates the room, offering a spectacular view of the river Exe. Her parents spend much of their time watching the local boating world from here, hanging on to every last possible ray of light, drawing it into themselves as their eyes grow dim. The walls are crowded with her mother's pictures. She paints the sun setting over the estuary, gnarled trees that overhang the incoming tide, the acres of mud that glisten and glow at low tide.

'Hello, dear,' says her mother, putting down her book in the same way that she always does. But her eyes are red and swollen, as if she's been crying. 'How was Canada?'

Canada? That all happened in another life, centuries ago. She searches her memory for a brief description. 'It was very – clean.' She's seeing the snow, blinding white in the sunshine, camouflaging the reality. It was impossible to know what was underneath.

'I'm just about to make some coffee. Would you like some?'

'Yes,' says Kate. 'Thank you.' Anything to postpone the inevitable conversation.

She sits down. All the chairs are set out in a semi-circle, side by side, facing the window. Her father sits opposite, grasping the arms of the chair and lowering himself carefully. His knees creak and he drops the last few inches in a rush, letting out a sigh as he plops down.

Radio 4 is on, the volume too high. 'Can I turn the radio down?' says Kate.

'What?' says her father.

'The radio. Can I turn it down?'

'I won't hear it if you turn it down.'

'But we can't talk against it.' She gets up to turn it off and stops abruptly.

'Felix Kendall . . .' says the newsreader '. . . still missing . . . unable to trace . . .'

She presses the off-button and looks across at her father, who is frowning into the distance. The sun pouring into the room is too bright. Pressure is building inside her head.

'So, where exactly is he?' he asks. Her pulse is hammering in her ears. 'I don't know,' she says. His eyes turn towards her, headmaster's eyes, intelligent and penetrating under abundant eyebrows. He makes her feel as if she's lying.

'Money-laundering? Illegal immigrants? Prostitution? Where's all this come from?'

She's compelled to look at him. She remembers a time when she was very young – four, perhaps, or five – when he'd caught her taking an extra custard cream from the biscuit barrel. 'I'm very disappointed in you,' he'd said. He doesn't say that now, but his expression is exactly the same. Confess, he seems to be saying. Tell the truth and we'll all feel much better.

'I had no idea,' she says. 'He's never told me anything. As far as I was aware, there wasn't anything to know.'

'The police were here yesterday.'

Of course. 'What did you tell them?'

'What can I tell them when I have no information?' He snorts. 'They were barely out of their teens. No manners, slurped their coffee, talked with biscuits in their mouths. If I'd been in charge of them, they'd have had to smarten up their act, I can tell you.'

'What did they ask you?'

'They were more interested in George Rangarajan than Felix, I thought.'

'What did you say?'

'Not a lot. Couldn't help them much. Told them I hadn't seen George since he left school.'

Her mother returns with three cups of coffee and a plate of home-made biscuits on a small tray. She places it on the low table in front of the chairs and sits between Kate and her father. 'There were people here earlier,' she says, leaning over and taking a raisin and cinnamon cookie. 'They turned up at eight o'clock. Such an uncivilised hour.'

'The police?' asks Kate.

'No,' says her father. 'I told you. The police came yesterday.'

'So who were they?'

'They said they were from the *Sun*.'

Kate is appalled. 'You didn't speak to them?'

'Of course not, dear. I told them I had nothing to say. I think that's the correct response, isn't it?'

'I might have considered talking to them if they'd been from *The Times*,' says her father.

'No,' says Kate. 'You can't talk to anyone.'

'Why ever not?' Her mother turns to her in surprise. 'It's only the tabloids you have to worry about.'

'They want to find things out, things they have no right to know. If you let them in, they take advantage of you, twist your words – you didn't let them in, did you?'

Her father chuckles. 'I did as a matter of fact. Showed them your mother's pictures, told them prices, gave them some leaflets about the museum. I thought we might as well take advantage.' He channels his remaining energy into research for the small local museum.

Kate tries to smile. Her parents are not as helpless as they like to pretend. It's an act. They've taken to asking advice on where to go on holiday, how to make a major purchase, when to go to the optician, the doctor, the dentist, but none of it's genuine. They just like Felix to come over. It's become such a habit that even now, when Felix isn't here, they're expecting him to turn up.

'So, has he been in touch?' says her father.

'No.'

'He will be, you'll see. He's got some great plan going on and he hasn't told us about it yet.' He nods to himself.

'I might have known that George Rangarajan would be mixed up in it somewhere,' said Kate's mother. 'I always thought that boy would get himself into trouble.'

'But he's not a boy any longer,' said Kate.

'I've heard about him every now and then,' says Kate's father. He keeps in touch with large numbers of ex-pupils, who keep him informed about each other. 'Successful businessman, entrepreneur, the kind of person everyone wants on their side. He sponsors good causes, sports, art

projects, that kind of thing. In fact, he's a Tory Party donor, I believe. And all this time he's been making a nice little place for himself in the world as a kind of Godfather figure.'

'I know he used to cause trouble,' says Kate's mother, 'but I always rather liked him.'

'Nonsense,' says Kate's father. 'You just liked the fact that he liked your cooking.' He sighs. 'He had the kind of dangerous charm that wins people over, persuades them to do things they wouldn't normally do.'

'So it seems,' says Kate.

'Are the children all right?' asks Kate's mother.

'Fine.'

'It must be hard for them with all this fuss. You must bring them over.' It sounds as if she wants them to stay, but Kate knows she doesn't mean it. The idea is good. The practicalities are a bit wearing.

'Nice biscuits,' says Kate's father.

'Thank you,' says her mother. 'I made them yesterday while you were out with Margaret Jefferson.' They both go quiet for a while.

Kate's mind begins to slow down and her eyelids feel heavy. The tide is coming in. Water is creeping over the mud flats, almost imperceptible at first, until the shine of the mud becomes the shine of water. Tiny waves appear, ripples of brown water that cover wider and wider areas. Boats separate themselves gently from the mud, bobbing against their moorings. Seagulls squabble, swooping over the rising water, flapping their wings with increasing excitement.

'The thing is,' she says, forcing herself awake, 'I was wondering if you could lend me some money.'

Nobody replies. She waits, her stomach fluttering, and can't decide if she should try again, go through the embarrassment of it a second time, but with different words. 'They've frozen our bank accounts. I can't withdraw any money.'

'Yes,' says her father. 'I was afraid they might.'

'Why would they do that?' asks her mother. She takes another biscuit and bites into it with enthusiasm. She's put on weight since they moved here. She likes baking and she's never adjusted to smaller quantities, so she eats most of the cakes and biscuits herself.

'Apparently, they have the power to do it if they suspect involvement in organised crime.'

'Do you really have no idea of what's going on?' asks her father.

His voice is like the abrasive scrape of a match inside Kate's head, igniting a resentful spark of anger. She tries to contain it, fearing that she will alienate them. 'No,' she says. 'I only know what the police have told me and what I've seen on the news. Same as you.'

Her mother swallows a mouthful of coffee. 'It'll be to do with his childhood. Losing his parents like that. I always thought it affected him more than he let on.'

'He's completely adjusted,' says Kate. 'It's nothing to do with that.'

'You should never underestimate the damage that is done to a child who loses his parents, especially in such traumatic circumstances. The brain no longer functions in the same way.'

'How much money do you need?' asks her father.

'I'm not sure,' says Kate. 'I have no cash at all and I need to buy food and petrol. In the long run, there are all sorts of things – I don't really know what I'll do.'

'There won't be a long run,' says her father. 'Once Felix is back, he'll sort things out, you'll see.' He heaves himself to his feet and goes over to his desk. He pulls the front open and roots around in various compartments until he finds a cheque book and fountain pen. Holding the pen carefully, he unscrews the top, places it on the end of the pen, and then bends over awkwardly to write. The nib scratches on the paper. The comforting smell of ink fills the room. He tears the cheque out of the book, waves it briefly in the air to dry and hands it over. 'Five hundred should keep you going for a bit,' he says, handing it to her. 'You'll have to let me know if you need more.'

'Thank you.' Kate takes it, thinking about the house. She can hardly ask her father to pay the mortgage. The terror of the school fees looms over her.

But Felix will be back. He'll have a perfectly reasonable explanation and everything will return to normal. There's nothing to worry about.

What if he's dead? There would be insurance. But she doesn't want him to die. She wants him home with the family, the old Felix, the only Felix she knows, paying the mortgage himself. 'I can't cash a cheque,' she says. 'I haven't got a bank account.'

Her father looks surprised. 'You don't have a separate account?'

'No – there never seemed to be any point. We managed the finances together.'

'That shouldn't pose any serious problems,' says her father. 'Open a new one in your name.'

'But I won't be able to take anything out until the cheque clears. I need money now.' I've never asked anyone for money before. I didn't know how it would feel. Asking because you have no choice. Demanding money without menaces. Falling into emotional blackmail to get money. I'm your daughter. Millie and Rory are your grandchildren. If not for me, give me money for them. Why can't they make it easier?

Her father goes out into the hall and comes back with his overcoat. 'We'd better go to the cash machine, then,' he says. He buttons up the coat, wraps a grey cashmere scarf round his neck and pulls on his leather gloves, pushing down between each finger to make them fit snugly.

'Good idea,' says Kate's mother. 'Can you get some Brie on your way back, and some of that nice French bread they sell at the greengrocer's? Are you staying for lunch, Kate?'

'No,' says Kate. 'I have to go and see various people.'

'Asking around for money?' says her father, and laughs, his voice echoing round the room and bouncing back off the window. 'That's the spirit.'

Kate opens her mouth to protest and closes it again. He doesn't want a comment from her. He wants her to laugh at his joke.

Chapter 11

'Kate, you're not at home. Where are you?' Beatrice's voice blasts down the mobile phone into Kate's ear.

The aunts never phone her on her mobile. 'I can't talk now.' She tries to sound calm and in control, but she's walking and her voice bounces up and down. Please go away. I don't want to talk to you.

'Can you come round? We need to talk.'

'As soon as I'm free. I have a lot to do.'

'Of course,' says Beatrice, and rings off.

They think it's her fault. It's inevitable. They would never blame Felix.

Kate has left her car in Topsham and taken the train to Exeter. She's heading for Felix's office in Walter Raleigh House, the largest, newest office block in the city. Sixteenth floor. It's half an hour's walk from the station, but she doesn't mind. She finds herself moving faster and faster, her feet slapping on the paving slabs in a persistent rhythm, somehow independent from the rest of her, tap-dancing towards the truth, or at least an explanation that would help her make sense of things.

Felix, Felix—

It's not possible to disappear. There are cameras everywhere – everyone complains about it. On a single day, each individual will be filmed at least ten times. Or is it twenty? Either way, someone knows where you are. It's just a question of time.

She imagines rows of policemen sitting at desks, watching hours and hours of film. The tedium of it all. How can you concentrate for long, observing things like that? Mothers shouting at their children; men in suits eating bagels, sushi, pots of fruit; lonely people walking along studying the pavement . . .

Felix, Felix—

I can be seen on all those cameras too. Someone is watching me now.

The thought wanders away, bounces and comes back. Her stomach lurches. They want to find Felix. Who is he most likely to contact? Me. They can't afford to let me wander off on my own. I'm being followed.

She stops abruptly. A man in a pale pink checked blazer nearly bumps into her, but manages to swerve at the last minute.

'Sorry,' they say together. He walks on, anxious and irritable, as if he's late for an appointment.

She studies the street. There are people everywhere. They're shopping, going somewhere, coming back. Shoes dance around each other nimbly, setting their own beat: high heels, flat heels, knee-high boots, ankle boots, strappy sandals – in this weather? – thick-soled pumps, trainers. Coats are buttoned to the neck and collars pulled high. Scarves are knotted fashionably, doubled up, the ends pulled through the loop: cashmere, wool, polyester, acrylic. Faces down, protecting themselves against the cold.

Someone must be watching her. Who? Nobody seems to be still enough to watch. Feet, faces blurring. They seem to be speeding up, rushing through the cold air like an old film, trying to get away from the winter chill as quickly as possible. Any one of them could be following her. Or a whole group. The man in the pink jacket, the woman in sandals, the girl with the Next carrier-bag. She knows how it works. She's watched the John le Carré series on television. *Tinker, Tailor, Soldier, Spy*; *Smiley's People*; *A Perfect Spy*.

She starts to run. Should she try to trick them, double back on herself, jump on a bus, dodge into Laura Ashley and out again? But she knows she's hopelessly outclassed. If they're out there, behind her, watching, they're probably good enough to be invisible. Perhaps it would be better to ignore them, pretend she doesn't know.

She's too old for this. Her knees ache, her feet hurt. She slows down to a walk. She jumps as a man clips her arm with his briefcase, which he's holding in the air as he negotiates his way through a gap. He dashes off, waving a hand in apology.

Maybe they're right. Surely Felix would let her know that he was all right if he could. The more she thinks about it, the more likely it seems. How would he get a message to her? Telephone? No, they can bug telephones. Everyone knows that. Email? But experts can read computers, even deleted information. Besides, he must know there's a good chance the computer will be sitting down at the police station right now, in the process of being examined. He wouldn't risk his email pinging through while they're working on it. 'Hi, Kate. I'm fine, working in Brighton. Love you, Felix.' Text? Possibly. But they can trace mobiles. None of those methods, then. He'll find a way. He's a clever man.

There's a group of people outside the Walter Raleigh building when Kate arrives. Journalists or police? She straightens her shoulders, walks round them with authority and strides in as if she has every right to be there. As she approaches the lift, a security man in a grey uniform with red stripes down the side of his trousers steps forward to stop her. He looks like a 1930s American bellhop.

'Can I help you?' he says.

'No, thank you. I know where I'm going.'

'I'm sorry,' he says. 'I can't let you go up on your own. If you give me your name, I'll phone through to see if they're expecting you.'

'They're not expecting me. But they know me.'

'Fine,' he says. 'Where are you heading?'

'Maine and Selwick.'

'Ah,' he says, and his face becomes more alert. 'And who do you work for?'

'No one. I want to speak to them.'

He goes over to the reception desk and picks up a phone. 'Who shall I say you are?'

Kate wants to make up a name, but can't produce anything except Jane Smith, which she knows would be unconvincing. Besides, they won't let her in if they don't know who she is. 'Tell them it's – Kate.'

'Kate who?'

She tries to make her voice icy. 'Kendall.'

He becomes even more interested. 'Ah,' he says again, and she knows that he knows who she is. 'Just a moment, Kate.'

'Mrs Kendall,' she says, but he doesn't hear her.

A man appears at her elbow, unshaven, with very short hair. 'Mrs Kendall?'

Where had he come from? There was no one there when she last looked. 'Who are you?'

'DC Pargiter. Why are you here, Mrs Kendall?'

'Why do you think? I'm looking for my husband. Same as you.' She glares at him and he looks calmly back.

'I'm afraid you won't be able to go up to the office right now.'

Suddenly she wants to sit down. It feels as if all the sleep she's missed has decided to impose itself at this precise moment, a pillow hovering over her head, waiting to smother her. But she remains standing, her feet sinking into the thick carpet, and wonders what to do next.

Her phone rings. She scrabbles in her bag. It's Felix. She can't talk to him now. They'll be overheard.

It's not Felix: it's Beatrice again. 'Kate, what time do you think you can make it? If you could give us some idea . . .'

'I'm sorry,' says Kate, her voice tight. 'I just don't know.'

'Very well,' says Beatrice, and rings off.

Robbie Maine steps out of the lift. His round stomach protrudes with reassuring normality and the dome of his bald head rises above the thin circle of wispy hair like a polished acorn, shiny with sweat. His usual ruddy, florid complexion now appears unnatural, giving the impression of a clumsy layer of face-paint. His eyes are dark and sunken. He looks like a man on the verge of a heart-attack. He stares at Kate from behind DC Pargiter, but doesn't speak. He gestures with his eyes towards a door at the side of the lift.

'I have to go,' she says to DC Pargiter, and heads towards the entrance. When he turns to talk to the security man, she steps aside and darts towards Robbie. He eases her through the door, pausing on the other side by the stairs.

'Robbie,' she says. She clings to his arm for a few seconds, overwhelmed by the rush of affection she has for him.

'Sorry about the drama,' says Robbie, leading her through a fire door and out of the back of the building. 'It's becoming impossible to speak to anyone without a policeman listening in.'

'They're everywhere,' says Kate. 'Nothing's been left untouched in our house.'

He turns to her. 'It must have been very distressing, having people go through all your personal things, invading your home.'

'It hardly feels like home any more.'

'We need to talk. I'll give Bill a quick ring.'

At first, Kate had not wanted to move to the house in Budleigh Salterton. She was happy in Exmouth. She could walk to the shops and take Lawrence to the beach every day in the summer, while Felix went to work in Exeter by train. She had friends nearby.

'There's a house for sale in Budleigh,' said Felix one day, over supper. 'I've just picked up some details.'

'Whatever for?' she said. She liked the small rooms of their terraced house, the cosiness, the way the doors didn't fit properly and the sea winds blew through the eaves on stormy nights, rattling the roof, making the old yew tree in the back garden creak and moan. 'We have plenty of space here.'

'Not if we have another baby.'

But Lawrence was three. They'd been trying seriously for two years and nothing had happened. 'What if I don't get pregnant again?'

'You will,' he said, with his usual certainty. Didn't he have any fear of failure? Would he still be expecting babies when she was fifty? He leant over and started to stroke her neck. Lawrence looked up from his train set at their feet, studying the situation, his eyebrows creased with interest. Kate felt uncomfortable, as if they were encouraging him to be a voyeur like his father. He might not settle for watching happy family meals through windows, but develop an appetite for the more intimate stuff, wanting to see into the bedroom or watch the activity on the sofa. She moved away from Felix.

'Shall we go and look round?' he said. 'I think you might like it.'

You can't possibly know that, she thought. You can't anticipate my personal likes and dislikes. But she was afraid that he could. He knew how to please her in ways that she couldn't have articulated if he had asked her in advance. She worried about this sometimes. How did he do it? Was it right that he could read her so well, that he understood her better than she understood herself? Why could she not do the same thing back? Why were her presents never quite right, even though he pretended they were?

'I suppose it can't do any harm,' she said, 'just to look.'

'I'll make an appointment.' Felix picked Lawrence up from the floor and swung him in the air.

Lawrence shrieked in protest. 'My train! I want my train!'

'We've got to play cricket before supper,' said Felix. He put Lawrence down and led the way out into the garden. 'I'll be Ian Botham. You can be Graham Gooch.'

Kate watched Lawrence through the window as he trotted after his father, his plump, sturdy legs stumbling to keep up, the perfectly formed ginger curls at the back of his neck bouncing up and down. He wasn't very co-ordinated, but Felix didn't seem to mind. He was showing Lawrence how to warm up by running on the spot, throwing his arms around theatrically, knowing Kate was watching. Lawrence tried hard to copy him, but kept losing his balance and falling over.

They were the happy family that Felix had wanted, but he wasn't satisfied. He was too conscious of his original ideal – lots of children. He always drew the curtains whenever they sat down together at the table. 'We need to keep the darkness away,' he said, 'and the warmth in.' As if it would leak out and charm an outside observer, another Felix who couldn't quite grasp it for himself.

He had an endless supply of good humour. When others became annoyed, he smiled at them, talked them round. There was something about him, the way he took everyone seriously, showing respect even when they were just plain irritating, that won people over. He was a good man.

Was it possible to be so unremittingly nice? Didn't everyone have a breaking point, a moment when the goodwill drained away and the nerves became weighed down with the dirty washing of family life, too many pairs of damp jeans or heavy, dripping sheets, and the line snapped? Sometimes Kate wondered if she was waiting for that moment, holding her breath, convinced he would suddenly collapse. But it never happened.

'Do they remind you of your own parents?' she asked him once, as they sat in the sand dunes at Exmouth and watched her parents picking their way through the seaweed and shells with Lawrence between them, stepping delicately into the sea.

This wasn't the first time she had asked. Every now and again when they were alone, when he was relaxed, she slipped a question in, wanting him to open something, let her into a deeper level. Or just encourage him to go in on his own, knowing she was behind him, offering support. But he never responded, and it puzzled her.

The edge of the water was busy with families. Children were running into the water and out again, shrieking at the cold, shaking themselves like dogs. Kate's parents recoiled from the random splashes, struggling to appear oblivious in case they frightened Lawrence.

'We should have gone to Budleigh Salterton,' he said. 'They're out of place here.'

'I know,' she said, 'but it's nice to let Lawrence play in the sand occasionally.' She leant back. 'And I must say, I prefer the comfort of the sand.'

'The air never feels as fresh here as it does at Budleigh,' he said. He was shielding his eyes with a hand, squinting into the bright mirror of the sea, his face set in a sun-stretched smile as he looked out across the bay past Dawlish, past the most distant headland and beyond to the open sea. A white cotton hat was rammed down on his head, pushed too far back, shading his neck but missing his face.

'Do you remember your parents?' asked Kate again.

He didn't reply for ages. Kate's father waded out to where the water was deeper, nearly up to his waist, then launched himself into a leisurely, easy crawl. Her mother was struggling with Lawrence, holding him round the waist while he thrashed about, grimly determined to prove he could swim.

'No,' said Felix, at last. 'Not at all.'

It didn't feel right. Surely he needed to talk about them, discover happy memories that would erase the horror of the robbery. Otherwise there would always be a hollow at the heart of his life, eroding the foundations of his existence. She thought he should tell her about them, what they were like, but there was nothing. It was as if his mind had been wiped clean of his first five years and only started once he had moved in with the aunts.

He was right about the house, of course. It was Edwardian, white and draped with wisteria, looking out to sea from its position at the top of a cliff. Felix and Kate drove up the gravel drive and stopped in front of it.

'What do you think?'

'Are you serious?' Kate couldn't believe he was even considering something so impressive.

'Business is good.' He'd been made a partner six months ago. 'Why not?'

The estate agent's car crunched up behind them.

'Let's go and have a look inside,' said Felix, opening the car door.

The house was warm and dry, suffused with light. The spacious rooms had high ceilings and long elegant windows. It was easy to imagine family photographs on the walls, thick draped curtains, period furniture scattered throughout. Displays of dried flowers in front of the fireplaces. Embroidered firescreens.

Upstairs, you could see right out to sea, waves rolling in the distance, merging with the sky into a distant grey-blue horizon. 'Are you sure this is realistic?' said Kate.

Felix stood next to her and put an arm round her waist. 'To be honest,' he said, 'it'll be a bit tight at first, but I think it's worth the risk. It's a terrific investment. Robbie and Bill would approve. And in a year or two, the mortgage will be a drop in the ocean.'

They went out into the garden and pushed their way down through the overgrown grass, leaving a crushed trail behind them. A series of descending terraces led to a clematis-covered wall at the bottom. 'It's enormous,' said Kate, gazing around in amazement. 'Could we manage it?'

'The previous owners had a gardener,' said the estate agent. 'I believe he's still available.'

'No,' said Felix. 'We can do it ourselves. We'll have the evenings and weekends. The children will help us when they get older.'

'We may not have any more children,' said Kate.

He grinned at her.

They went back through the house to the front drive. The estate agent locked up and drove away. Felix and Kate sat in the car for a while, studying the house from outside.

'Well?' said Felix.

She couldn't even bring herself to believe it was possible to live here. 'It's lovely,' she said.

And he didn't gloat, didn't look pleased with himself. He simply shared the excitement with her and made her feel they were going into this together. A slow shuffle on the dance-floor. The lights dim, the music smoochy, her head on his shoulder.

Kate sits in Costa, her legs jittering under the table, and waits while the waitress sets down the drinks on the table between her and Robbie and Bill Selwick. It's impossible to know where to start. Bill and Robbie say nothing to explain or comfort her.

The fluorescent lighting flickers on the surface of the coffee, harsh and over-bright. The coffee machine grinds and grates, thunderous in the small space.

Say something! Shout at me!

But they seem to be trapped under a blanket of hopelessness.

'Is it true?' she asks eventually, unable to bear the tension any longer. 'What the media are saying?'

'Put it this way,' says Robbie. 'There's no way he could have missed the implications of the Rangarajan account. It screams out at you. One of our trainees could have spotted it on his first day at work.'

Kate grips the edge of the table. 'So he was working with George?'

Robbie nods. 'He's been managing the Iceland account for three years.'

Robbie and Bill knew about George. Why didn't she? Was it such a big secret?

'We've seen the figures,' says Bill. 'They're pretty damning.'

'What do you mean?' says Kate. 'In what way?'

'We have clear guidelines about money-laundering. There's a process called layering, which means the money is divided up into small quantities and paid into different places to make it appear harmless – offshore accounts in dodgy countries, small businesses, charities, companies that don't exist, that kind of thing. We have to be alert for large cash payments, fake invoices, too many regular payments that are just below the reporting limit.'

'And you saw this in the Rangarajan account?'

Robbie nods. 'It was a classic case.'

'So all Felix did was not report it?'

'You're missing the point, Kate. It's not carelessness. It's a criminal offence. I'm the money-laundering officer he should have reported to. This case is absolutely clear. Felix had a legal obligation to report it, but for some reason he chose not to.'

Nausea is rising in Kate's stomach. She had been hoping that Bill and Robbie would offer a rational explanation, but they're confirming his guilt. It's not a mistake. He knew what he was doing. He has betrayed all of them.

A man sits down at the table next to them with a cup of coffee and opens up a copy of the *Independent*. He has a gold ring in his left ear. He seems to be outlined in black against the bright glow of the window, but he's insignificant, dwarfed by the enormous truth sitting in the middle of their table.

'Are you sure it can't be a mistake?' she asks, desperation making her voice uneven. 'Someone else making him appear guilty?'

'I'm sorry, Kate,' says Robbie. 'The evidence is over-whelming. The sooner we all accept that, the sooner we can move on.'

'He's ruined us,' says Bill, stirring three teaspoonfuls of sugar into his herbal tea. 'We've already lost three major clients.' He's the most imposing of the three partners, towering above Robbie and Felix, a worrier. His face normally droops, but it's sagging even more today, his cheeks as loose and shrivelled as empty carrier-bags.

'Four,' says Robbie. 'United Warehouses rang me this morning. Half an hour ago.'

They're going to lose everything. What about their twenty-three employees who will lose their jobs because of Felix?

'According to the press,' says Bill, 'Felix was the brains behind the whole illegal-immigration business. Difficult to believe.'

Impossible to believe.

'We don't know that's true,' says Robbie. 'Nobody's found any money.'

'Yet.'

'But why would he have done this?' says Kate.

Bill sighs. 'Why does anyone go rotten? It happens all the time.'

'I wouldn't have expected it of Felix,' says Robbie. 'He didn't seem the type.'

He wasn't the type. It's impossible to reconcile the two images. The husband who's shared your intimate spaces for most of your life and a man who's involved in international crime: how can he be the same person?

'You must have known something was going on,' says Bill, his voice rising with barely suppressed resentment. 'You lived with him. He must have said something.'

'Bill,' says Robbie, laying a restraining hand on his arm.

Bill turns away from them, his face submerging into his chin.

He's right, I should have known. I was the one who was married to him. 'I didn't know. Really I didn't.' Tears are forming in her eyes. She blinks rapidly, but can't avoid a few drops spilling on to her cheeks.

Robbie leans over and rubs her arm gently. He's always been a kind man. 'I think we've probably got so caught up in our own disaster that we've forgotten how difficult it must be for you.'

A car parks just outside the window on the double yellow lines. Pale blue. The driver doesn't get out. He gazes into space and taps his hand up and down on the dashboard as if he's listening to music.

'How did you find out?' asks Kate.

'We got a phone call from Hamburg, the day he was meant to be there – Tuesday – to tell us he hadn't arrived. Then the police just turned up. They've been investigating for weeks apparently. We tried contacting you, but you weren't at home and we didn't know how to get in touch with you.'

'It started when he went to Iceland,' says Bill.

'What happened in Iceland?' asks Kate.

'What indeed?' says Bill. 'All we know is that he went to visit George and his partner, Kristin Petursdottir. It was supposed to be more of a pleasure than business trip, but he was expecting to be shown their factory while he was there.'

'He didn't discuss it with you?' asks Robbie.

Kate shakes her head.

'He was different after he came back,' says Robbie. 'We both noticed.'

So they saw something I didn't. I wasn't observant enough. 'How was he different? I didn't notice anything.'

Bill and Robbie exchange glances. 'It's difficult to pinpoint exactly,' says Bill, 'but he was less open with us, not so talkative. It wasn't like him.'

'Are you sure you're not just imagining it?' says Kate. 'Now you know things weren't as they seemed?' What had she missed? Had she become so used to him that she was part of him, so if he changed, she changed with him? Had there been an imperceptible shift in their outlook, a mutual decline, without her even being aware of it? A gradual loosening of their connections? But she can't see it, not even now, sitting here with his two partners. Right up to the last minute, their farewell at Heathrow before she left for Toronto, everything seemed normal.

'No,' says Bill, slowly. 'I didn't imagine it. I actually thought . . .' His voice fades. There's an awkward silence. 'Well,' he says, 'I thought – I know it sounds crazy – that perhaps he was having an affair.'

'It was just his age,' says Robbie, hastily. 'You know, middle-aged men. We did wonder, but couldn't really decide.'

An affair? A wave of relieved horror rushes through Kate at the more rational explanation. That's it. Everyone's been jumping to the wrong conclusions. Except – 'Don't be ridiculous,' she says. 'He wouldn't have known how to.'

Which is worse? Infidelity or criminality? An affair or money-laundering? I don't know, I don't know . . .

'Now, of course, that's obvious,' says Bill.

The man next to them sips his coffee slowly and stares at his newspaper. He doesn't turn any pages.

Kate's phone rings. 'Sorry,' she says to Robbie and Bill, with an irritable sigh.

'Kate?' says Beatrice.

So many voices in my head, everyone talking at once, nobody making sense. Leave me alone. She takes a breath. 'I'll be there in about an hour.'

'An hour,' says Beatrice, to Agnes in the background.

'I told you,' says Agnes.

'You were only speculating,' says Beatrice. 'We'll be here,' she says to Kate.

'Please don't call me again. I'm very busy.' Kate turns off her mobile. 'He wouldn't talk about his trip to Iceland,' she says. 'Whenever I asked him, he changed the subject.'

'We found the same thing,' says Bill. 'It was as if he had never been there. He didn't want to tell us about anything – not the hot springs, the volcanoes.'

'Something happened there,' said Robbie, 'but we don't know what.'

Felix in his hotel room, cleaning his teeth, suddenly knowing that something was wrong.

'Of course, we do know now that there was no factory,' says Bill. 'It was just a front.'

'But – why didn't he do something about it?'

'That's what we've spent hours discussing with the police and with each other. Money is the obvious reason. Have you got direct access to any of his accounts?'

'I haven't got access to any accounts. They've all been frozen.' I don't have any money. I'm sitting here drinking coffee and I'm destitute. Her legs are on the move, joggling, jiggling. She blows into a tissue. The sound blasts out, unnaturally loud.

'My dear,' says Robbie, 'how dreadful. If you need money, we'll help you, of course.'

'Providing we can manage to hang on to the last vestiges of our business,' says Bill, his voice low and bitter. 'Otherwise we'll be penniless ourselves.'

'It's all right,' says Kate. 'I'm fine. My parents are helping.'

For how long? A week, two weeks? Even if she's eventually allowed to use some of her and Felix's money, she won't be able to maintain things for very long. Not without Felix's salary.

'Did he have any expensive hobbies?' says Bill. 'Boats, aeroplanes, villas in the sun?'

'Don't you think I'd know if he was spending a lot? I'm not stupid.' I am stupid, I must be. 'Do you think he couldn't afford the mortgage and didn't want to admit it?'

'No,' says Robbie. 'He should have been able to afford it easily.'

'Gambling,' says Bill. 'Did he gamble?'

'No,' says Kate. They're talking about a stranger, not the Felix she knows. He had no secrets from her. He didn't lead a double life – it wouldn't have been possible. She knew everything about him, how he thought, how he spent his money.

Except that she didn't. He had a secret, a terrifying jagged gash concealed below the surface, and she hadn't even suspected.

Have they turned off the heating? The room is getting colder.

'I can't see any reason for it at all,' she says.

'No,' says Robbie. 'Neither can we.'

What's his weakness? She goes back over his life, his behaviour, his relationships with others. Could Inspector Williams's suggestion be close to the truth? He was ashamed that he'd made a mistake and hadn't been able to admit it. People have always liked him. He needs people to respect him.

'They've taken our computers away,' says Robbie. 'I went up there again this morning, hoping to get some files to work on, but they wouldn't let me in. That's when I saw you.'

The man in the blue car is on his phone, gazing into the café as he talks.

They had been so proud of their new office when they moved in three years ago. The windows look out over Exeter and beyond. You can see the university in one direction, the physics tower standing like a sentinel at the top of the hill, and the river Exe snaking towards the coast at Exmouth in the other direction, past the docks and the bridges. They had a celebratory dinner with all their employees and their partners on the day they moved in and toasted each other long into the night.

'Felix has been a great asset to the firm,' said Bill at the time. 'He's inspired us all to greater things than we ever anticipated.'

Felix sitting next to her, glowing with the achievement. But every word, every movement he made exuded modesty, quiet deprecation, a shared pleasure.

'What are we going to do?' says Kate.

'I have absolutely no idea,' says Bill.

Chapter 12

Millie knows she's being watched. The bell has sounded for Assembly and the building echoes with doors opening and shutting, urgent, chattering feet as the girls file out of their classrooms and into the corridors. Queues form on the staircases that meet at the entrance to the school hall. She can see girls on the opposite side pointing her out. They're whispering without breaking the official silence, sliding their eyes in her direction, indicating her presence by discreet movements of their heads.

'I've left my maths book at home,' she says to Helen. 'My mum wouldn't go back for it.' She wants to look as if she doesn't care about being watched, as if it's normal to have your father's photograph plastered all over the newspapers, to see him on *News at Ten*, presented as a criminal, even if no one actually says so. *We need him to assist us with our enquiries.* But everyone knows that means they think he's guilty. 'Do you think I'll get slaughtered?'

Helen doesn't reply. Her eyes are narrowed and focused on someone behind Millie's shoulder.

'Amelia Kendall,' says a quiet voice.

Millie turns round. It's Nicole. The deputy head. Mrs Kidman.

'We do not talk in the corridors.'

'Sorry, Mrs Kidman,' whispers Millie, conscious of everyone's eyes on her. Even those who've been pretending not to stare are now openly watching. Typical, they're thinking. What can you expect from someone whose father is a crook?

But instead of threatening terrifying penalties like memorising a poem, or writing a detailed report on the life-cycle of a slug, Mrs Kidman's face relaxes and she almost smiles. 'Don't let it happen again, Amelia.'

'No, Mrs Kidman.'

Helen's face is really, really good. Her mouth has fallen open with disbelief and her eyes are wide and amazed. Millie grins at her. I have hidden powers, she wants to tell Helen. I can freeze Nicole with a look. She'll do whatever I tell her.

Putting her new-found skills to the test, she tries to will Mrs Kidman into going back up to her office so that she misses Assembly. Go up the stairs, she says, inside her head. Up the stairs, up, up—

'Do get a move on, girls,' says Mrs Kidman. 'You're causing congestion.'

Inside the hall, the sixth form are already on the platform, prefects at the back, facing the rest of the school as they file in. Samantha's on the top row, with her friends from Margaret's, gazing into space.

Dreaming about her boyfriend, thinks Millie.

But then Samantha looks down at the girls in front of her, moving her eyes along the rows until they come to rest on Millie.

Millie wonders if Samantha is staring at someone else and turns to check. But it's only the Hooper twins behind her and they're doing their usual thing, tangling their feet together in discreet fury, arguing silently with their faces, oblivious to everything around them.

It's me she's watching.

Samantha's lips move. She's smiling. I have to smile back. Nervously, keeping an eye on everyone round her, Millie smiles, making sure her mouth is stretched as wide as it will go, squeezing her eyelids together with sincerity, desperate to demonstrate warmth and friendship.

Samantha continues to smile, nodding very slightly, while the head, Miss Dobson, climbs the steps at the side of the platform and takes her place between the senior members of staff.

'Please be seated, girls.'

There's a rumble of feet, a rustle of skirts and everybody sits down. It seems to Millie that the day has altered, that the thundercloud above her head has shifted, elbowed aside by a brief but brilliant shaft of sun.

She's standing with Helen in the queue for milk and fruit at break when someone prods her in the back. It's Karishma and Esther.

'Hi,' she says. 'Did you see Samantha Thompson—'

'Your father was on television last night,' says Karishma. 'I saw him.'

'Cool,' says Millie.

'He's a crook,' says Esther. She has short dark hair cut into a bob. Millie has never noticed this before, but there's something cruel about the sharpness of the cut, the way the hair ends so abruptly, with no warning.

'No,' says Millie. 'They've got it wrong.'

'How can they be wrong?' says Esther. 'It's obviously him.'

'How does it feel to see your dad on the news all the time?' says Karishma. Her voice is soft and gentle and, for a moment, Millie is fooled into thinking her interest is genuine.

'Well,' she says, 'it's not actually—'

'My uncle was killed by a bomb in Mumbai,' says Karishma, and she doesn't sound gentle any more. 'My dad says it's people like your father who raise money for bombs and things like that. He says all accountants are just greedy people who make a fortune while everyone else suffers.' She stands in front of Millie, hands on hips, her eyes narrowed. This is not the Karishma who played hockey on Saturday, or the friend who sat around with Helen, Esther and Millie yesterday and analysed the situation in the light of their limited information.

'Don't worry,' she had said then. 'I'm sure it's a mistake. Your dad's really nice.' She even fetched her own box of paper hankies, each tissue decorated with miniature fluffy rabbits, smelling of aloe vera, and put her arm round Millie.

Millie stares at her, her face burning.

'Move along,' shout some girls further back.

The queue has shuffled forward, leaving a gap in front of Helen and Millie.

Helen grabs her arm. 'Ignore them,' she says. 'They don't know what they're talking about. I'll bet Karishma's never met her uncle. He's probably a great-uncle, three times removed, and she doesn't even know what he looks like.'

But Millie pulls away, abandoning the queue and running out of the canteen, down the steps, faster and faster, round the gym, away from the school buildings, wanting to put as much space between her and Karishma as she possibly can.

When she finally comes to a halt, she finds herself by the netball courts, next to the outside toilets. She leans against the wall, crippled by a stitch in her side, and bends over, gasping for breath. The place is deserted – it's nearly the end of break and most girls hover nearer the school's entrances at this time of year, anxious to get out of the cold as soon as possible. Millie enters a cubicle, sits down on the toilet seat and allows herself to cry, letting the tears flow and her nose run.

When the bell rings for the end of break, she stands up, blows her nose and tucks in her blouse. There's no one outside the cubicle, so she checks her face in the mirror. Red, blotchy, puffy. She splashes some water over her cheeks, pats them dry with a paper towel, then takes several deep breaths. She imagines her dad standing next to her. 'Breathe in, out, slowly, slowly, now in again . . .' She makes her way to history with her eyes on the floor, refusing to acknowledge anyone.

The last lesson of the day is maths. Millie has spent the day avoiding everyone, even Helen, who's clearly offended. I'll talk to her tomorrow, Millie promises herself. I'll tell her I was stressed. She'll understand.

Mr Harrison, the maths teacher, is solving equations on the blackboard. He's asking for the homework to be handed in, so he won't know yet that Millie hasn't brought her book. A section of chalk breaks off and falls to the floor every time he writes something, and white clouds of dust spring out into the atmosphere. There's something wrong with the chalk. It's too crumbly. Every time it happens he sighs, starts to say something and restrains himself. Millie knows that the rest of the class are holding their breath, longing for him to swear, even though he's never used bad language in front of them before, but she can't bring herself to be part of the excitement. It seems so childish.

'Other schools have whiteboards,' he says. 'We should be moving with the times.'

She gazes through the window. She can do equations. You don't need the illustration of balancing scales. It's obvious. There has to be an equal amount on each side. Why don't some people get it?

The radiators are belting out heat. It's always too hot or too cold. They normally don't get this level of heat until the height of summer. The engineers must have been in over the weekend and done something right for a change. But the unexpectedly high temperature is making them sleepy. Millie can't concentrate on the maths.

Where's my father? Where's my dad? Where's Daddy? She doesn't know what to call him any more. Is he even the same person? Is he still the daddy who knew how much she wanted pierced ears when her mum said she couldn't have them?

'You're too young,' said Mummy. 'You need to be at least sixteen.'

Millie could tell that she didn't want her to have it done at all. Her mother has always failed to see how much things have changed since she was young, thinking that twenty-first-century children should be like she was. It was easy for her, growing up in a boys' school, surrounded by hundreds of teenage boys. She'd had plenty of choice. Millie doesn't have that kind of opportunity. She goes to a girls' school, her older brother is too old, no use for introducing her to fit boys, and her younger brother is just a pest. How can she make an impact without using every weapon at her disposal?

But Daddy had understood. 'Sixteen might be a little unreasonable,' he said.

Mummy had stopped what she was doing – chopping leeks and garlic for a stew – and stared at him. 'You're not suggesting she should go around like some Hollywood starlet, are you?' she said. 'I wasn't allowed to wear makeup until I was eighteen.'

He smiled. 'The world has moved on a little since then,' he said. How Millie loves his smile. His teeth are white and even, except for two on the lower jaw, at the front, where the edge of one tooth is bent slightly over the next-door one. His face slips so easily into niceness – the creases aren't even wrinkles – and his eyes are warm and twinkling. He makes you feel special, as if you have an important place in his mind. 'Why don't we review it in a year's time?' he said.

Millie was disappointed. She'd hoped he would persuade her mother to give in straight away.

'Well,' said her mother, 'maybe . . .'

Daddy put his arms round her waist from behind and snuggled his chin into her shoulder. He was slightly shorter than Mummy, so it was easy to do. 'You're such a wise woman,' he said.

Mummy laughed and pushed him away.

'Amelia?'

Millie stares at Mr Harrison. He's looking directly at her from the front of the room. The whole class has turned to watch. They're waiting for something, but she has no idea what it is. Heat radiates from her cheeks and sweat forms so rapidly that it trickles down her back.

'Yes?' she says.

'Do you have the answer?'

Are they supposed to have worked something out? On the edge of her vision, she can see rough-books open on other desks, full of scribble. Lines of figures, juggled, crossed out, rewritten, muddled. She would normally have the answer long before everyone else. But her page is blank. She hasn't even picked up a pencil.

'I don't know,' she says.

Mr Harrison reacts with genuine disappointment. She's the one who follows his reasoning when nobody else can. She's let him down.

'Sorry,' she says, just above a whisper. She can see the knowing looks from the class, the raised eyebrows, the weary nods. What can you expect from the daughter of a terrorist?

'Right,' says Mr Harrison. 'Back to the drawing board.' His thin grey hair wafts slightly in the waves of heat from a nearby radiator. He's removed his jacket and pulled his shirt sleeves up to the elbows. You can see freckles between the thick, springy hair on his arms as he picks up the chalk again.

The clock ticks with agonising slowness. Ten minutes to go. Then ballet for an hour and a half, but after that she'll have to go back to her house to be picked up at six. With any luck, her mother will be waiting for her, so she'll only have to dash in, pick up her bag and sign out.

The bell rings. Millie packs her books and pencil case into her bag, avoiding everyone else. She looks out of the window. Samantha Thompson has just stepped out of Margaret's in her cool red woollen coat and cream scarf. She's heading for the main gate.

Where's she going, thinks Millie, at this time of day?

She's seized by a desperate urge to find out. She grabs her bag and dashes to the door.

'Are you all right, Amelia?'

She likes Mr Harrison. Must he choose this particular moment to talk to her? 'I'm fine,' she says, edging towards the door.

'If you'd like a sympathetic ear, I'm always available.'

'Thank you,' she says. 'Only I've got to dash.' She backs out of the door, pushing past the other girls, and runs down the corridor.

Millie catches up with Samantha just inside the school gates. She slows down and allows a bigger gap to open between them. Now that she's no longer in such a hurry, she fastens the buttons on her coat, her hands dithering in the cold. She rummages in the bottom of her bag and finds her gloves and scarf, but no hat. A plan is forming in her mind. There's a notebook sitting on her desk at home with tortoiseshell kittens on the cover, a present from Lawrence. It's ideal. Exactly the right size to carry around. She could have a page a day and put important times in the margin. She could keep records, map out Samantha's life. Then she would know how to live her own.

She follows Samantha up the road. Girls are pouring out of school now, so it's easy to be invisible. They walk along Pembridge Road, turn right at the corner and head up Harlech Street. Then left, a quick right, and they're in the shopping centre.

She's meeting someone, thinks Millie in excitement. It must be the boyfriend. She hadn't expected to see him so early in the investigation. This could be much better than she'd hoped.

She follows Samantha into WHSmith and hides round the side of the books section, watching her pick up magazines, a packet of automatic pencils, fiddle with files, examine a small globe. She goes to the counter to pay for her pencils and magazines and then leaves, heading for the jeweller's, where she stands outside the window, examining the contents.

Millie watches every movement, careful to stand a long distance away when Samantha is looking into shop windows, realising that she could be spotted in the reflection.

The cold is intense. Her toes are rapidly losing sensation, the numbness spreading along her feet. She wishes Samantha would go into Laura Ashley or Boots, where they could warm up.

She's going to be in big trouble for missing ballet. If only the boyfriend would appear. Then everything would be worth it.

Chapter 13

Kate stands on the opposite pavement and looks across at the house where Felix grew up. She doesn't want to go in. The ground floor used to be a shop, part of a four-storey building that's squeezed into a narrow gap between Suzy's Babes, a massage parlour and Kwik Klean, a dry-cleaning business. A grille protects the brown, dusty downstairs window, and through it you can just pick out the ghostly figures of old clocks. They're clocks with inner workings – levers, pendulums, weights that need pulling down every eight days – built with care and precision in an era before batteries existed. But they've all stopped. They were there long before Kate's first visit twenty-nine years ago, standing in silence, shoulder to shoulder, gold-plated carriage clocks, grandfather clocks, cuckoo clocks. A notice inside the door says 'CLOSED'. It's permanently closed. It hasn't been open since Felix's grandfather last lived there fifty-one years ago. Kate knows the story of how he died, his head bent over a sturdy English mechanism, his thick-lensed glasses pushed up on top of his bald head, a pair of delicate tweezers in his hand. His heart stopped – just like that – and he slumped forward. They found him later, his face squashed up against the hands of the mahogany clock, their shape imprinted in his cheek.

Kate crosses the road, squeezing between the parked cars on both sides. She ignores the sign that says 'PLEASE RING FOR ATTENTION' and uses the knocker, a large brass disc with a clock face engraved on the surface. She waits thirty seconds, then knocks again. Car doors are opening behind her.

A window on the first floor opens and a head of red ringlets leans out. 'Hello?'

'It's me,' Kate calls up. 'Kate.'

'Hold on.' The window shuts and Kate waits.

'Mrs Kendall?'

She half turns and sees a cluster of people approaching, cameras, microphones—

The bulky shape of Beatrice appears behind the window in the door. She's short but very wide, with a Pre-Raphaelite mane that draws attention away from her size. It hasn't faded in all the years since Kate has known her, and there isn't a grey strand in sight, even though Beatrice must be well over seventy. Kate suspects that it's dyed, although it's difficult to imagine her going to a hairdresser's, sitting in front of the mirror, telling a blonde girl in a skimpy black overall that her trips abroad are connected with work, so there's no point in asking about her holidays.

'Kate,' she says, as she opens the door. 'Come in. Quickly.'

A voice calls from behind: 'Have you heard from your husband?'

Beatrice grabs her arm and pulls her in, closing the door behind them with a sharp bang. 'Journalists!' she says, with contempt.

'Have they been bothering you?' asks Kate.

'They've been ringing the doorbell.' Beatrice's voice is low and husky. 'Of course we haven't answered it, but they keep coming back. I've been considering pouring my washing-up bowl on them from above. You know, medieval style. Not quite up to the raw sewage, though, I regret to say.'

Kate follows her upstairs. The wooden spiral staircase creaks with every step, echoing in the uncarpeted space. If Beatrice gets any wider, she'll no longer be able to squeeze up or down. She's wearing a loose dress that hangs from the shoulders, making no attempt to conform to the normal female shape. The material is an exotic blue-green, sewn with metallic gold thread that glints as she moves. She must have bought it from an Indian shop and put it together herself on her treadle Singer sewing-machine. It would be beautiful as a sari, tailored to a different person. The same grey cardigan as usual sits on top of the dress, transparent at the elbows, covered with bobbles and pulled threads. And she's wearing open sandals, immune to the cold.

On the first floor, they pass rows of shelves bursting with books and academic journals, which overflow into random piles on the floor. There's a bicycle in one corner, rusty from lack of use, the sewing-machine set up under the window, and heaps of vinyl records, their rims melted and distorted after years of abandonment in intense sunlight.

On the second floor, they step directly into the rooms where Beatrice and Agnes live: a tiny kitchen, a bathroom and a long living room that stretches from the front to the back of the house. There's no landing.

'Here we are,' says Beatrice. 'Same as always.'

Very little has changed since the first time that Felix brought Kate here. He had been full of apologies and clumsy explanations, but nothing had prepared her for the chaos. There were books everywhere and crumbs littering every available surface, along with half-eaten sandwiches, Jammie Dodgers – a particular favourite of Beatrice's – and apple cores. The light was on throughout the day, a single central bulb hanging from the ceiling without a shade, though both aunts had lamps on their desks. Since then, they have each acquired a computer, selected and regularly updated by Felix. Every now and again he would respond to an urgent phone call and drive over to unfreeze a program, check the anti-virus, show them how to access lost material. The apple cores are still there, passing the mouldy stage and solidifying, eventually disintegrating and making room for the next abandoned meal.

What will they do now? Who will they phone for assistance?

There's a musky, overripe smell, which comes from the pet rats. They occupy a cage in the corner of the room, nibbling, scrabbling, peering out with shiny, intelligent eyes.

'Sorry about the mess,' says Beatrice, gesturing at piles of paper on the floor. 'I'm proof-reading.' She's an expert in medieval secular literature, specialising in courtly love, and she still goes into the university to give guest lectures. She's written four books so far, part of an intended series of eight volumes. Felix and Kate have copies of them at home, thick, densely printed, with tasteful dust covers, breathtakingly expensive. Kate has tried to read them, but the language is too archaic, the sentences too full of subsidiary clauses, the thoughts too obscure. She wonders who does read them. She can't imagine undergraduates poring over them with any chance of enlightenment.

Agnes is sitting in a small chair with wooden arms. Tufts of foam peep out from the corners of the mottled green upholstery where the stitching has split. She's studying a picture leaning against the wall. It's a John Singer Sargent portrait of two sisters in ballgowns, tall, elegant, quintessentially American as they stare out at the viewer with easy, bold expressions.

'Agnes,' says Beatrice. 'It's Kate.'

Agnes turns round as if she has only just heard them. She's short, like Beatrice, but thin, her scrawny body creased into sharp, precise folds and angles, like a piece of origami. Her hair is so thin on top that you can see the skull gleaming through, pale and shiny. For a while, she wore a wig, an immaculate curled grey perm, but she has given up in recent years with the explanation that it makes her too hot and prevents her hearing properly.

'At last!' she says. 'The kettle's been on for hours.'

'Good,' says Kate. She would prefer not to eat or drink here, but she's never been able to refuse in case they recognise her revulsion.

Felix constantly reassures her. 'We don't get food poisoning,' he's said, on more than one occasion. 'It can't be that bad.'

He would have been immune to any germs, of course, since he grew up with them. But he was right about Kate and the children. They'd never had upset stomachs after visiting.

Beatrice cleans occasionally, vacuuming the parts of the carpet that are still visible and wiping the kitchen table with a dubious grey cloth, but it doesn't make much difference.

Agnes gets up from her chair. 'Magnificent painting,' she says, waving at the Singer Sargent. 'The way they look like sisters without being exactly alike.'

'It reminds her of us,' says Beatrice. 'In our heyday.'

But you aren't alike at all, thinks Kate. You don't look like sisters.

'Of course, we were more the same shape then,' says Beatrice, with a girlish giggle. 'We sort of met in the middle before we passed by, if you see what I mean.'

How can they laugh? How can they discuss art as if everything is the same as always?

One of the rats starts to crawl up the netting on the front of the cage, his back feet hanging in the air, his tail waving wildly.

'Bertie's hungry,' says Agnes. 'It's his way of telling us, bless him.'

'Didn't you feed him this morning?' asks Beatrice.

'It was your turn.'

'But you're the one who leaves half of your Shredded Wheat. You always give it to them.'

'I was busy today,' says Agnes. 'I had important emails to send.'

Beatrice sniffs and takes a handful of feed from a bag by the side. She throws it in. There's a mad scramble from the rats. 'Good boy, Bertie,' she says, in a soft, gentle voice. 'Good boy, Jeeves.'

'What *is* all this about Felix?' says Agnes, suddenly.

Kate takes a deep breath. 'You've heard what they're saying on the news?' she asks.

'I never listen,' says Beatrice. 'It's too depressing. Wars, starvation, bombs. It's better not to know these things. Don't think about anything outside a five-mile radius from where you live, that's my motto. Concentrate on getting on with your neighbours and let everyone else kill each other elsewhere.'

'Terrific item on *Woman's Hour* yesterday, though,' says Agnes. 'About Salvador Dalí. Exceptional. They nearly got it right.'

Agnes is an art historian. She used to have a punishing schedule, lecturing round the world, until her health let her down and she gave in to exhaustion. She will still do the occasional lecture if there's a direct train line and she's met at the station. She enjoys the limelight, standing on a stage, gazing down at respectful faces, knowing they're all more ignorant than she is. Everyone is more ignorant than she is.

'Have the police been?' says Kate.

'Man and a woman,' says Beatrice. 'Privileged treatment. They thought a policewoman ought to be present because we're old ladies and might faint or something. Absurd.'

'They were hardly an enlightening source of information,' says Agnes. 'They expected answers to their questions but wouldn't answer ours.'

'What did they want to know?' says Kate.

'When did we last see Felix,' says Beatrice. 'Had he been in touch.'

'What did you say?'

'Nothing, of course. Never trust the police. It's none of their business. This is a private matter.'

'Not true,' says Agnes. 'You know what Hassan said in the greengrocer's yesterday.'

'Oh, that,' says Beatrice. 'I thought he was making it up. Trying to frighten us.'

129

'Hassan doesn't make things up. He's a man of integrity.'
Like Felix.

'I realise there's a slight problem,' says Beatrice.

'Hassan comes from Afghanistan, you know,' says Agnes, 'from a city in the mountains where they have ten feet of snow in the winter.'

'It's not a slight problem,' says Kate. 'It's a big one. Felix is in serious trouble and I have no idea where he is.'

'The police eventually imparted this information to us,' says Beatrice. 'But what exactly do they mean when they say he's disappeared? Is he not in the place where everyone expects him to be, or has he literally faded away? In which case, you'd probably say he was dead, I suppose.'

Kate breathes in, breathes out. 'You must have read about it in *The Times*.'

Beatrice brushes some crumbs from a previous meal off her desk and on to the floor. 'You can't believe what you read in the newspapers. You must know that – a headmaster's daughter.'

'They're making just as much fuss over George Rangarajan,' says Agnes. 'Can't think why. I remember him when he was friends with Felix. Not an impressive mind. No intellectual rigour.'

'Felix and George seem to have been working together,' says Kate.

'Utter balderdash,' says Beatrice.

'He was meant to be going to Hamburg,' says Kate, 'while I was away in Toronto, but he didn't get on the plane. Nobody knows where he is.'

'See?' says Agnes to Beatrice. 'Hassan was right. It's something to do with money.'

'Of course it's to do with money. That's what Felix does.'

They have absolute faith in him, thinks Kate. It's not a pretence.

There are dozens of photographs of Felix on the mantelpiece, leaning up against each other, some in cardboard frames, mostly simple snapshots. He's there at all his stages: a child of five; a boy of ten; fourteen years old, oozing confidence but somehow vulnerable in his school uniform; a delighted, satisfied bridegroom at their wedding. There are pictures of Lawrence, Millie and Rory too, but only if Felix is with them. Even as a child, he is immediately recognisable, staring earnestly out with a boyish charm that has never left him. There's innocence in his face, integrity, a belief in himself that is strangely attractive.

'I wasn't here that much when I was a teenager,' he'd said on her first visit, seeing her interest in the early photographs. 'All those holidays abroad with George.' He'd been all over the world with George and his parents, and yet he rarely mentioned the travelling once they were married.

'Didn't the aunts mind you going away so much?'

'I'm not sure they noticed.'

'They must have done after all those years' looking after you.'

'Well, yes, I suppose that's true. But they were very busy people. They had careers. And they thought it would add to my education.'

'Did you mind that they didn't mind?'

He'd looked surprised. 'I don't know. I didn't think about it. I was having a nice life. They wanted the best for me.'

'They were very good to take you on.'

'They loved me. They told me that all the time.'

'But it could have been just words.'

'No,' he'd said. 'It was more than words. They did love me. Still do.'

She'd examined the bedroom where he had grown up. A tiny attic room on the third floor, stuffed with objects – books, fossils, star charts, a microscope, rows of test tubes, replicas of ancient coins. It was the room of a Victorian child, Kate thought, with its emphasis on intellectual pursuits

– astronomy, archaeology, biology. There were ancient children's encyclopedias, books about pioneers, mountaineers, Scott of the Antarctic, out-of-date knowledge from a long-ago world of heroes. She imagined him up there on his own, reading, making calculations, discovering trigonometry.

When he first used to bring her here, she'd hoped that his aunts would talk about his parents, that the shadowy figures he never mentioned would come to life and become real to her. It always seemed as if they no longer existed for him, that they were just names from a distant past he didn't remember, and she thought the aunts might have been able to describe them to her. But they never mentioned them.

She'd attempted to broach the subject once. 'He must have missed his parents when he first came here,' she said to Beatrice, as they prepared cucumber sandwiches in the kitchen.

'Who?' said Beatrice, with apparently genuine surprise.

'Felix,' said Kate. 'He never talks about his parents.'

'Oh,' said Beatrice, as she unwrapped a Sainsbury's fruit cake and placed it on a plate. 'We're his parents. Agnes and I.'

Now, as Kate sits opposite them and sips tea, struggling to tell them about what has happened, she wonders again if this refusal to discuss his parents has damaged him. Surely you can't just remove the first five years of a boy's life and pretend they'd never happened. It's as if 'before' is irrelevant and 'after' is the only thing that matters. But the 'before' must be somewhere, imprinted on his mind, a deep groove that might seem to be filled in and painted over but, nevertheless, is still there, waiting patiently, ready to assert itself at any moment.

And now the solid rock base that should be there beneath him, the strength and flexibility that ought to withstand lightning, tornadoes, floods, has let him down. His foundations have turned out to be porous, and everything he's built above ground, apparently firm and secure, has just seeped through, trickled away, leaving nothing more than a shadowy outline. He couldn't hold on to the man they'd all thought he was.

'Did he have many friends before he went to boarding-school?' she'd asked once. 'It must have been very hard for him at first, losing his home as well as his parents and having to come and live with you.'

'Friends?' said Agnes. 'He had us. We were his friends.'

And, to a certain extent, that was true. Felix told her how they had spent hours with him when he was young, organising their lecturing timetables to make sure there was always someone at home with him, taking it in turns to accompany him to and from school until he became a boarder. They took him to London regularly, exploring the National Gallery, the Tate, the British Museum, the Science Museum, allowing him time to examine everything, answering all his questions with meticulous care. They drove out to Lyme Regis to examine the fossils, Bath for the Roman architecture, Plymouth for HMS *Victory*. They visited every castle within driving distance many times, and arranged overnight stays to see places further away. As soon as it became clear that his interests lay in maths, they found a tutor to stretch his abilities, searched for courses, went with him when he was too young to go on his own.

They were good to him. They were academics and he became part of their academic existence. They were unmarried women, yet they were able to conduct an experiment in child-rearing that they would normally never have anticipated.

Why are the aunts pretending to know nothing? They must have discussed the situation after the visit from the police. 'So has Felix been in touch?' she asks.

'When?' says Beatrice. 'Recently?'

'He phoned us about a month ago,' says Agnes. 'He was checking to see if the gas people had been. They condemned the cooker, you know. We had to buy a new one.'

'The police wanted to know if he'd phoned,' says Beatrice. 'If he had, I wouldn't be telling them.'

So he hasn't contacted them, but they don't want to admit it.

'Money-laundering!' says Agnes. 'Felix is the most honest person I know. Why would he do that?'

They're choosing indignation rather than shock – it's a strategy to convince themselves of his innocence.

'He hardly needs the money,' says Beatrice.

'I know,' says Kate. 'I've thought all these things.'

'There'll be a reasonable explanation,' says Agnes. 'He's a clever man. Always was, right from the beginning. There's no possibility that he would break the law. He wouldn't know how to.'

Frustration and irritation are fluttering through Kate's mind. I'm worrying. Why aren't they? 'So where is he?' she says.

'He'll turn up,' says Beatrice. She settles back in her chair, resting her teacup on her enormous stomach. It tinkles on its saucer every time she breathes out.

He might be dead.

'If they find him,' says Kate, 'he could end up in prison.'

'They'll have to catch him first,' says Agnes.

Beatrice sits up, puts her cup and saucer on the table. 'Try not to be too melodramatic,' she says, putting out a hand and patting Kate's arm gently. 'Felix knows what he's doing. Don't underestimate him.'

Agnes is smiling thinly. 'I think you'll find they're mistaken,' she says.

They're right. Felix knows what he's doing. He's in control. He's never let her down before.

But there's evidence.

'Don't talk to the press,' says Kate. 'They twist everything you say.'

Beatrice looks at her fondly, like an indulgent teacher.

'My dear, we've been handling journalists as long as we can remember,' she says.

'They never tell the truth,' says Agnes. 'They get their facts wrong, they don't listen properly. Nobody takes any notice of them.'

But their journalists are arts specialists, people who move in the world of culture, not the world of international news. 'These will be different,' says Kate. 'They'll twist everything. They'll have opinions and they won't be interested in protecting people's reputations.'

She imagines an article describing the house where Felix grew up. 'You mustn't let them in. You mustn't talk to them.'

Beatrice's expression becomes more solemn. 'My dear,' she says, 'we've been ignoring them since they first turned up. There's nothing to say to them, anyway.'

Agnes smiles. 'It'll be all right,' she says. 'You'll see.'

Millie is waiting outside Margaret's when Kate arrives at school. She climbs into the back seat without a word and gazes out of the window.

'Did you get into trouble with the maths?' asks Kate.

'No,' says Millie.

'How was ballet?'

'Fine.'

They find Rory standing by his school gates. It's almost dark by now and Kate nearly doesn't see him. She stops sharply. He clambers in next to her and they drive further into the school grounds so that they can turn round. 'You shouldn't be down by the gates,' she says. 'It's against the rules.'

'Rules are meant to be broken,' he says.

This is not normal. Rory's interested in laws. He likes structure.

'How was your day?' says Kate.

'Rubbish,' he says.

'What happened?'

'Nothing.'

Kate imagines Felix in a new place, sitting in a café, perhaps, eating eggs and chips, coating them with tomato sauce in a way he has never done before. He doesn't approve of chips, only allowing them on rare occasions when they're on holiday.

Was he ever the man she'd thought he was? Was he a real person at all? It now seems as if he was little more than a model of Action Man, designed to bend and adapt to all circumstances. The loss of his parents and his adolescence in a boarding-school encouraged him to create a flexible personality that he could redesign whenever necessary. He had learnt how to please others, fit in with their ideas of how he should be. He was a blank space, inviting creativity, a man for all seasons. As she gazes through the unknown window of a dingy café, miles from anywhere, it seems as if she is watching a stranger.

They drive in silence for a while. The same car seems to be hovering behind them in the traffic. When Kate turns off the main road, she glances in her mirror and there it is again. It's rounding the corner, apparently innocent but becoming sinister by its constant presence. She hopes it's the police rather than journalists. Have they been watching her all day? Spies or protectors?

'Mummy,' says Rory, 'can I change my name?'

'What would you like to change it to? Fred? Caspar?'

'Not that bit. Rory's OK. It's the Kendall I don't like.'

Kate sighs. 'Don't be silly,' she says.

It'll be another ordeal getting past the press again when they arrive. Her hair must be standing on end, her face blotchy and crumpled. She should have thought about this before. If she put on some lipstick, brushed her hair, smoothed down her clothes, she would at least look in control. She glances across at Rory. She can hardly stop now and smarten herself up.

He and Millie would think she was mad. She runs the fingers of her left hand through her hair, pulling out a few tangles, patting it back into place, and forces herself to relax. She needs to appear calm and rational, a loyal wife with absolute faith in the integrity of her husband. If they think she's got doubts, they'll have a field day.

The same people are there, waiting, watching for her approach, cameras ready and pointing directly into the car. She remembers Rory's panic yesterday. 'Get down on the floor,' she says to him and Millie, 'where they can't see you.'

He stares at her, on the verge of tears, struggling to keep his face still.

'Hurry,' she says. 'If you crouch down, you won't see them and we can just go straight through the gate.'

He unclicks his seatbelt and slips down into the footwell.

'That's it,' says Kate. 'Pretend we're smuggling you in to steal the diamonds. You're our secret weapon. The one they don't know about.'

Millie refuses to move. 'I'm fine,' she says, her head turned towards the window. 'I don't mind if they photograph me.' She's sitting very upright, her curls resting on her shoulders, a deep rich auburn in the glare of the outside security light. She's beautiful, thinks Kate, in surprise.

The car behind them suddenly overtakes and skids to a halt. It looks like the blue car that was parked outside Costa when she was talking to Bill and Robbie. A man with a gold ring in his left ear leaps out of the passenger seat and starts to shout at the journalists, pushing them away. He waves Kate forward.

She points the remote control at the gates and watches them shudder slightly, then swing open with painful slowness. A man is standing just outside her window. She can see his mouth opening, moving up and down, but she refuses to work out what he's saying. The air is thick with flashes. She keeps her eyes fixed on the opening gate, inching in very carefully. The man with the earring clears the way for her. She's halfway there. A woman bangs on the bonnet. Kate ignores her. She drives as close to the front door as she can. A small sports car she doesn't recognise is parked outside the kitchen window.

'Wait there,' she says, and gets out with the key in her hand. She can hear shouting behind her and turns.

'It's OK, Mrs Kendall. I'll remove them.' It's the man with the earring. 'DC Atkins,' he says, and flashes her a grin. I'm on your side, he's saying. He's enjoying himself. 'You can close the gates now.'

'Did you know about the money-laundering?' shouts a voice.

She fumbles with the key, drops it, picks it up, tries again, and then the door opens in front of her.

'Mum, quick, get in!'

'Lawrence!' Her grown-up son, her lazy, clever son, who should be at university worrying about Sophocles and Kant, not standing in front of her.

She drops her bag in the hall and runs back for Millie and Rory. Millie is already getting out, turning to the crowd and smiling slightly, pushing a strand of hair away from her face in a nervous but carefully poised gesture.

'Get inside,' says Kate.

She opens the car door and finds Rory huddled on the floor, misery etched into his face. 'Come on,' she says. 'We're all right now.' She bundles him out, up the steps and into the house, closing the front door behind them.

Chapter 14

'What exactly are you doing here?' Kate stands in front of Lawrence, trembling with anger. She'd told him not to come home. Why can't he just do as he's told for once in his life? 'Did you get the essay done?'

Lawrence produces an apologetic lopsided grin. 'I just thought I'd come home to support you in your hour of need.'

Kate wants to grab him by the shoulders, shake him, scream at him. 'I assume that means you didn't write it,' she says, in an icy voice.

A girl appears in the doorway to the living room. 'He didn't have any choice, Mrs Kendall,' she says. 'There were journalists waiting outside the lecture rooms, camping in the grounds of our hall, getting in under false pretences, pretending to be students. It was impossible.'

Who is this girl? She's taller than Lawrence, elegant in an ankle-length skirt and flat shoes. She has a very long neck that rises, white and slender, from her open-necked shirt and her face exudes an air of calm authority. She walks towards Kate with her hand outstretched. 'I'm Zoë,' she says. 'Lawrence's friend.'

What does that mean? Friend or girlfriend? Kate takes her hand, intimidated by her poise.

'Zoë drove me here,' says Lawrence. 'My car's off the road at the moment. We'll have to go back tomorrow, but I said she could stay the night. I knew you wouldn't mind.' He puts his arm round her and they smile at each other. 'She's been wonderful.'

They think it's exciting, a great adventure.

'Well, I don't know what I'm going to feed you on,' she says, a weary sense of defeat settling over her. 'There's not enough food in the house and I can't face going out there again.'

'That's all right, Mrs Kendall,' says Zoë. 'We could go shopping for you. In fact, I could cook for us tonight if you wanted me to.'

Oh. She's a practical person, not at all like Lawrence.

'Thank you, that would be – nice.' Kate feels she needs to say more, but it's difficult to organise her thoughts. Her tiredness is confusing everything, lining up random words and knocking them over before she has the chance to put them into any logical order.

'Shall we see what you need?' says Zoë.

They go into the kitchen and search through the cupboards. Zoë produces a small notebook from her bag and starts to make a list. Bread, coffee, potatoes, oranges, bananas, yoghurt, washing powder – Kate counts out fifty pounds and gives the notes to Lawrence, knowing it may not be enough. 'Put something back if it comes to more,' she says.

'But how will I know what you don't want?'

'Use your common sense.'

He looks confused.

'Don't worry,' says Zoë. 'We'll manage.'

'OK,' he says. 'Put your coat on, Zoë. You look good in turquoise. Give the cameras a treat.'

Stop behaving like a child. It's not a game. 'Be careful when you drive out,' says Kate.

'No problem,' says Lawrence. He opens the front door. 'Ready?' he says to Zoë. She nods. They slip out and run to the car.

Kate watches them from the hall window. Zoë gets into the driving seat. She lines the car up before they open the gates, then crawls out, nudging her way through the crowd. Lawrence opens his window before they're clear and a huddle of men rushes round to his side of the car. What's he doing? Camera flashes rip through the night air. He puts out an arm and waves. Kate can see him laughing. Then he closes the window, the car accelerates with a squeal of tyres and they drive off, scattering the journalists behind them.

Kate almost smiles. Lawrence is always infuriating. Why would he be any different in a crisis? And why has he never mentioned Zoë?

She walks through to the back of the house and gazes out. The garden is illuminated by light from the house, but a heavy mist has rolled in and the trees and shrubs are shrouded in gloom. The sea beyond is a solid black mass, indistinguishable from the sky. She's dull with tiredness. How long can you go without sleep? Don't you start hallucinating? The house feels so different from that last normal day before she left for Toronto.

Felix had insisted they all went to Heathrow to see that she boarded her flight safely. At the airport, he delayed their parting until the last minute, making her wait and join the end of the queue. They stood behind Asian families with babies and toddlers, young adults with skiing equipment, elderly couples, a group of Americans organised by tour guides.

'Mum,' said Rory, 'I'm starving.' He'd spotted a café with a display of chocolate muffins behind the counter.

'Wait, Rory,' said Felix.

'I can't. I might die of starvation.'

'You've just had a croissant. You can't possibly be hungry,' said Millie.

'I didn't have one. I don't like them.'

'So whose fault's that, then?'

'Millie,' said Kate, absently, 'leave it to me. I can cope.'

Felix was looking through the window where an aeroplane was landing. 'I bet that's your flight.'

But no one was interested. They were a much-travelled family and flying no longer held any novelty value for the children. They were used to the world being there for their convenience. Independent schools, holidays abroad, an abundance of fruit and vegetables, a home with space, meals out, an army of tradesmen to look after the house. They could afford hobbies, sports, culture. All the things that made life good.

Kate watched a man sweeping up by the barriers. 'I wonder if he's actually been on an aeroplane,' she said to Felix. He was too old for manual work, his legs bowed at an alarming angle, his knees bent outwards in a rubbery, convex arch, as if they were too weak to hold him up. His grey hair had only a few strands of black left and his eyes were large and blank. 'What chances do his children have?'

'They must be grown-up,' said Felix. 'It's the grandchildren you'd have to worry about. Or the great-grandchildren.'

Was Felix too insular? He believed in happy families. That was his creed, his religion. But the happy family had to be his.

'You'll have to go in a minute,' he said, checking the clock.

'Are you trying to get rid of me?' she said, with a smile.

'What do you think?' he said.

Was there anything unusual in his manner? Had he known he wouldn't be there when she came home?

Millie gave her a hug. 'Have a lovely time,' she said. 'Bring me something nice.'

'Of course I will,' said Kate.

'Watch out for people with funny eyes,' said Rory. 'If they look at you out of the side of their eyes like this –' he slid his eyes sideways and lowered the lids '– they might be trying to abduct you. Don't talk to them under any circumstances.'

'I'll bear it in mind,' said Kate.

'Bye,' said Felix, giving her a last squeeze. 'Enjoy the art. Spare no expense.'

'Of course,' she said.

The queue had nearly gone. 'You'd better go now,' she said. 'There's no point in waiting.'

'OK,' said Felix. 'Ring me when you get there.' He kissed her lightly on the cheek.

'Have a good time in Hamburg,' she said.

They smiled at each other. Had his smile been different? Had there been something significant in the way his lips parted, a hidden message in his crinkled eyes? He turned away. Rory was pulling at his arm. 'Can I have a chocolate muffin?'

She could just pick out Felix's mild response, the voice of reason. He turned back for a final wave and a smile.

That was the last she had seen of him. Even now, playing it back in her mind, she can't see any clues that would have led her to believe things weren't normal. Her husband must be the greatest actor in human history. Playing out his life exactly as he thought it ought to be, even when it wasn't. It was three years since the trip to Iceland, and she'd never even suspected.

The telephone answering service is crowded with messages from people she doesn't know. The *Guardian* financial correspondent, an expert on immigration from the *Independent*, complete strangers with long, ranting, incomprehensible accusations. Kate listens to them with disbelief, then realises she'll have to delete them without listening to the rest. Just before she presses the button, she hears the voice of Donovan, the man who comes in three times a week to do gardening and odd jobs.

'Kate, I came today and sorted the stuff for the tip. It's in a pile by the side of the house. I'll pick it up tomorrow in the van. I thought the old table and chairs from the conservatory should go to a charity shop so I've left them in the shed. I didn't talk to the parasites outside the gate. I could turn the hose on them if you'd like me to.' She can hear his slow laugh before he rings off.

I can't pay him. I'll have to warn him. He's got a family to feed.

She picks up the phone, not knowing what to say. To her relief, nobody answers and she goes through to the answering service. 'Donovan, it's Kate. Look, don't come tomorrow. We're all a bit upside down here . . .' She pauses. Donovan has been coming for sixteen years. He's an old family friend. She knows his children, his grandchildren. She can't just dismiss him. 'I'll be in touch,' she says. She puts the phone down.

The intercom on the gate buzzes. She looks out of the front window, but it's too dark to see individuals. She picks up the phone. 'Yes?'

'It's Inspector Williams. Can you let me in?'

'Hold on.'

He drives through and parks next to her car. She opens the door for him and his companion. 'Hurry up,' she says, her voice tight with anxiety.

'Hello again,' he says. She shuts the door behind them. 'This is DS Will Nichols, my partner in crime.'

'Hi,' says Sergeant Nichols. He has fine blond hair that surrounds his head in a frizzy tangle. A man who doesn't appear to believe in combs.

'Have you found him?'

'That's why we've come,' says the inspector. 'I wanted to fill you in on the situation.'

'Have you found him?' she says again. Why isn't he telling her? A picture of Felix hanging from a tree flashes into her mind. Then he is lying in a ditch with his wrists cut.

'No,' he says. 'We haven't found him.'

She looks past him into the blackness of the hall window. 'So have you got any information at all?'

'Can we sit down?' he says.

'Oh – yes, of course.' She leads them into the living room.

They settle themselves on the sofa. 'I need to ask you about these bank accounts,' says Inspector Williams.

He produces a handful of statements and passes them to her. There are several accounts: one for the business, payments from clients, one for everyday expenses, another for tax and VAT. 'I assume this one is for your household accounts.' He holds it out for Kate to examine.

She looks down the list of direct debits – mortgage, electricity, gas, telephone, wages for Donovan. The figures roll round in front of her, dancing across the page, disintegrating. She can't possibly pay all these bills, even with her father's help. She feels sick.

'Could you just confirm for me that all these bills are legitimate?'

'They seem to be,' she says.

'And do you have any more bank accounts?'

'No, I don't think so.'

'Are you certain? Did Felix have any he used separately?'

'You'd have to ask the bank. I'm not aware of any.'

The sergeant leans forward. 'Did Felix ever tell you he had extra money he could use in emergencies?'

'We didn't have emergencies. There was always enough money. We didn't even need an overdraft – although we had an arrangement in case we went over by mistake.'

He nods. 'Have you had any more ideas about where he might have gone?'

'No. He told me he was going to Hamburg.'

'What about close friends? Could he be with anyone he knows?'

Kate realises something odd about Felix. He has never kept in contact with people. It wasn't only George he lost touch with, but all his past friends and associates. They seem to have vanished, as if he'd run away, leaving them all behind them. Why wasn't there anyone else, someone from school, from his accountancy training, his first job? Most people have a history that you can trace back, people they remember, even if they don't keep in close touch. What happened to them, all those people who knew him once? Apart from his family and his aunts, he only appears to exist in the present.

'No,' she says. 'I can't think of anyone.'

'Really? No nights out with the lads? No Friends Reunited? No Facebook?'

'He liked being at home. He didn't really have a social life.'

'Are you hiding anything from me, Mrs Kendall?' There's an almost imperceptible change in the inspector's tone, scepticism, an edge of suspicion.

Indignation makes Kate's voice sharp. 'No, there's nothing to hide.'

Inspector Williams sits back and his voice becomes gentler. 'I understand Felix's parents died when he was a child.'

'Yes.'

'And he was brought up by his aunts?'

She nods. 'They were like parents to him.' A nagging headache has lodged itself over her right eye. She wants to sit here alone in her house, Felix's house, where she can feel his presence. Felix is going to walk in, any minute now, throw his briefcase on the hall table, lean over and plant a kiss on her head. 'What's for dinner?' he'll say. 'Is there time for a quick game of billiards with Rory?'

'Did he have any favourite places? Somewhere he might go on his own?'

'He liked Dartmoor,' she says. 'He preferred places to people.'

That's not true. He was good with people. But he wasn't close to anyone except the family. 'The newspapers are saying Felix influenced George, that he was the one behind it all. Do you really believe that?'

Inspector Williams hesitates. 'Actually, that hasn't come from us.'

'So you don't see Felix as the mastermind?'

He won't commit himself. 'It's too early to say.' They get up to leave. 'I'll put a man by the gate,' says Inspector

Williams. 'It'll make it a bit easier for you to get in and out.'

The telephone rings a few times before Sian answers. 'Hello?'

Kate feels an immediate relief at the familiarity of Sian's voice. The first adult she has spoken to who might be on her side. 'Sian—'

'I've been phoning, but I've had to leave messages.'

'I'm sorry. There are so many and most of them are from people I don't know. I wiped them all in the end.'

'Of course – how silly of me. How are you coping?'

'I don't know. It's all very difficult.'

'You poor thing. It must be terrible.'

'It is.' Tears are threatening again at this display of sympathy, but Kate resists them. 'I just wanted to thank you for having Millie and Rory.'

'It's no trouble at all. They can stay here any time you need it. Just let me know. Theo is always delighted to have Rory. He's such a polite boy – very good for Theo. And Millie's a darling.'

Not at the moment, thinks Kate. Right now, she's hardly speaking.

'Can I do anything to help?' says Sian. 'Anything at all?'

Suddenly Kate can't reply. She'd thought it might be helpful to talk to a friend, but now she knows she can't do it. Anything she says would be disloyal to Felix. He's her best friend, the one she talks things over with. Her other friends are good for coffee, worries about the children, debates about school, but she can't share her real fears with them.

She hears the front door bang.

'Mum!' shouts Lawrence. 'We're back. Get everyone into the kitchen. We've bought KFC.'

'Thanks,' says Kate to Sian. 'I really appreciate your offer. I'll let you know.' She knows she mustn't rush and risk alienating Sian. 'Is Theo all right?'

'He's fine. Listen, I'll come over tomorrow, after I've taken him to school. Or shall I pick up your two and take them as well? Then I can come back and we can talk.'

'Yes,' says Kate. 'Thanks, that's a good idea.'

'OK, see you tomorrow.'

Kate puts the phone down. She doesn't want to see Sian. She doesn't want to see anyone. She can't explain the unexplainable.

'Come on, Mum,' shouts Lawrence. 'It's getting cold.'

'Kentucky Fried Chicken is expensive,' she says, going into the kitchen. 'Did you get the other things on the list?'

'Yes, yes,' he says vaguely. 'Like you said, there wasn't enough to get everything.'

Chapter 15

The dream used to come occasionally, once a year, perhaps, creeping stealthily through Felix's body, immobilising the muscles, slowly filling his head with poison while he slept. Now it comes every night, and he wakes up sweating, frozen into an enforced rigidity, only his mind working. He has to lie and wait until the sweat dries, until his heart stops racing and his limbs begin to function again.

It's the inability to move that is most distressing. He wants to scream, feeling his head framed on both sides by the varnished grain of wood, his hands glued to the ridges and bulbous spirals of the banisters, but his vocal cords have seized up. He can hear things that he can't make sense of. The animal wail of a voice he should know but can't identify, sounds that don't mean anything, hammering against his eardrums.

'Get out! Get out!' He understands these words are coming from downstairs, but he can't get out. He can't move.

The bang of the front door. Running footsteps.

And silence. Deep, endless silence.

The wood digs into his cheeks, while his mind searches out something more familiar – what time does *The Woodentops* start? Where's his Dinky red bus? A smell crawls up the stairs. A bitter, metallic smell coming towards him, filling the bottomless silence, the wrong smell for his house. Now he's an adult, he knows it's the smell of blood.

And George is there with him, crouching beside him. There's a knife in Felix's hand and he tries to throw it away but it's attached to his hand with invisible glue. He can't let go.

He can't move.

Why hadn't he taken that final step in the hotel room and ended all this agony? His hand had simply refused to act, couldn't produce enough strength to plunge the knife into his heart. He'd made a startling discovery. Without Kate beside him, he was weak, unable to carry out his intentions. Alone, he was powerless.

When dawn broke on his pathetic little tableau in the hotel room, he'd risen, stiff with shame, and made himself a breakfast of cheese and biscuits. He couldn't even kill himself. Felix Kendall, the great accountant, the head of his family, the crook, couldn't perform a final, honourable act.

He went out early the next day and bought himself some hair dye and a newspaper, returning to his bathroom to go through the messy business of changing his appearance. He read the newspaper. People-smuggling, exploitation, human misery. George and Kristin had been arrested in Manchester, followed by other arrests around the world. Felix was portrayed as the mastermind who operated behind the scenes from the safety of his profession, deeply involved in the whole corrupt network.

George at fourteen, standing on the edge of a fountain in Rome, clutching an ice cream, swaying precariously, losing his balance and falling backwards. Howling with laughter. 'Come on in, the water's lovely.'

No guns, no drugs, no terrorism, George had said. A wave of shame and disgust swept through Felix. He could have stopped it – but he hadn't.

He left the hotel early the next morning, settling the bill with the last of his cash. Nobody recognised him.

He stands outside the newsagent's and studies the advert. It's roughly written on green paper with a thick black felt-tipped pen, and it's between the poster about the animal sanctuary and the postcard plea for a council-house exchange.

WANTED
WO/MAN TO COME AT 5AM EVERY MORNING
TO HELP SORT NEWSPAPERS
GOOD RATES MUST BE RELIABLE!

The word 'WANTED' upsets Felix at first. They're on to me, he thinks. They know where I am. But the face underneath is only a reflection in the window, a man with dark brown hair, a fierce beard and weary lines round his eyes. The ginger-haired Felix had disappeared four weeks ago.

He reads the notice again. The spelling is all correct and he likes the final exclamation mark in the absence of any other punctuation. The word 'RELIABLE' attracts him. That's me, he thinks. Most of the time. I could easily do this job. I'm always awake at five o'clock.

If he got this job, he could go out long before the students on the floor below surface from their night-club hangovers and rush off for nine o'clock lectures, or before the lady with the blue perm and yellow hair-band comes out of her bedsit on the ground floor with her mop. She asks too many questions and stares at him. It's as if she's waiting by her front door with a bucket of water ready beside her, peering through her spy-hole, listening for his tread on the stairs.

He's lucky to have the room, which belongs to a guy called Jinhai Su. It's a welcome improvement on the shop doors, skips and unlocked outhouses where he slept for the first two weeks. Felix and Jinhai worked together unloading mysterious boxes from the back of lorries in the middle of the night, the only two English-speaking adults among illegal immigrants from Ethiopia and thin, twitchy sixteen-year-olds from Romania. Jinhai was looking for someone to pay the rent for him while he went up to Scotland for a few months for a temporary legitimate job in construction, and Felix needed somewhere to stay that didn't require references. They came to an agreement. Felix goes to the renting agency once a week, pays in cash and receives a receipt made out to Jinhai. The girls in the office either haven't registered, or choose not to notice, that he doesn't look much like Jinhai Su. Nobody asks why he talks with a native English accent.

The bed is creaky and uncomfortable, but sleep is a luxury that he knows he doesn't deserve. In the early hours of every morning, jerked awake from the recurring dream, he lies on his back, waiting for dawn, examining the network of cracks in the ceiling, which are just visible in the glow from the streetlights. Landmarks flash past him as he clings to an out-of-control merry-go-round. Rory leaping into the air to catch a ball, his skinny, uncontoured legs kicking out into imperfect right angles. The pale softness of Kate's stomach, spreading and swelling gently over the years. Lawrence arguing with Millie about the last sliver of lemon meringue pie. 'I should have it. Your first slice was bigger than mine.'

'That's such a lie.'

'No, it isn't.'

'Yes, it is.'

Felix's first term at school, sharing George's tuck, marvelling at the crumbly texture of home-made cakes. The loneliness and fear that they recognised in each other.

Will Kate remember to pay the telephone bill? It's underneath some papers on my desk – she might not find it. Is Lawrence getting his essays done? What about Millie's concert? Will she get back safely from all those extra rehearsals? Did Rory's team win the match against Blackwell's last Saturday? Did he play all right without me there to cheer him on?

They can manage without me, of course they can, of *course* they can – they'll adjust.

The pain inside his chest is crushing. He must be the only person in the world who would welcome a heart-attack. But it never happens. He just goes on living.

Rage sweeps through him every now and again. Rage at himself, rage at circumstances, rage at George.

Felix and George in London, old school friends, walking back from the pub in the small hours of the morning, a little unsteady on their feet.

'Are you going to let the Big Man know you've passed your accountancy exams?' asked George.

'Eventually,' said Felix.

'I thought the intention was to claim the hand of the gorgeous Kate.'

'I want to build up some savings first, present myself to her parents as a good prospect.'

George poked him in the side with his elbow. 'Lighten up, man. Get in there while you can, seize the day.'

A figure emerged out of the shadows, dark and solid, running towards them. Felix and George moved to one side to let him past, but he didn't pass. He stopped in front of them, silently staring, his face coated with a sheen of sweat, his breath warm and rancid.

Felix and George looked at each other, half amused by the ridiculous drama of his appearance.

'Give me your wallets,' said the man, in a harsh whisper, only just discernible above the rumble of a bus in the next street.

They stopped smiling. 'You've got to be kidding,' said George.

'Shut up!' hissed the same voice and, with a sudden swift movement, he engulfed George's neck with his arm and thrust the point of a knife against his throat. The whites of his eyes glittered in the light from the streetlamps.

It took Felix a second to grasp that it wasn't a joke, that the danger was real. A wave of uncontrollable shaking swept through him and a desperate shriek was reverberating in his head: Do something! Run! Do something!

'Give me your money,' said the man, in a low voice. He was groping through George's pockets with his free hand, but George never had any spare cash. His pockets were always empty. Felix could hear the man's frustration, his breath rattling in his throat, a gargle of fury.

'Look,' he said quickly – calm him down, defuse the situation. 'I can help. I've got money.' His voice came out in a dry, high-pitched croak. He reached for his wallet in the inside pocket of his jacket.

His movements must have been too fast, too threatening. The man swung round to him with a snarl. 'Don't even think it,' he growled. He removed the knife from George's throat, pushed him aside and swung round, the blade slicing towards Felix.

But George recovered quickly. He launched himself through the air and brought the man down in a classic rugby tackle. Felix grabbed the knife as it clattered to the pavement, then fell heavily as the man seized his legs. All three of them struggled in the darkness. The man was unbelievably strong, a source of terrifying energy, unassailable—

Felix has never been able to recall what happened next, but when he was finally able to stagger to his feet, George was next to him, his chest heaving as he fought to regain his breath, and the man was on the ground at their feet. Felix was holding the knife.

He stared down. There was a dark liquid, black in the artificial light, oozing slowly away from the man's inert body, flowing into a thick, viscous puddle. Blood.

Felix stopped breathing.

He had been here before.

He knew the smell. From a long, long time ago. Sharp, metallic.

He was five years old again. The blood was on the kitchen floor, pouring out in a stream, a river, a torrent.

George was speaking to him, jostling his arm, but the words were empty noise, garbled, meaningless.

Slowly, slowly, he allowed George to lead him away. Every movement took more energy than he'd thought he possessed. His five-year-old legs wanted to escape, his twenty-two-year-old legs wanted to run, but the message was not coming through from the brain. He moved achingly, weighed down by confusion.

George was pulling him, talking in his ear. 'Come on, Felix, come on!'

Gradually, his legs warmed up, and he started to run, keeping up with George, his hand still clamped round the handle of the knife.

He ran and ran and ran.

When they finally stopped, they found themselves on the towpath of a canal. There were trees on one side and an industrial estate on the other. It was a dark, silent, deserted place.

'OK?' asked George.

'Yes,' said Felix, bending over and gasping for breath, his voice cracked and unreal.

'Here we go, then,' said George, and pushing Felix in front of him, he leapt over the grass and into the canal.

The water hit Felix like a wall of ice. He could feel himself sinking, dropping the knife, astonished by the cold. Then he instinctively started to flap his hands and rose to the surface. George was bobbing in front of him, his hair flattened by the water, laughing.

Laughing?

'What did you do that for?' yelled Felix, furious.

'We've just got rid of the evidence,' said George. 'Come on.' Felix followed him as he swam to the opposite side and they pulled themselves out, water streaming from their clothes. Felix crouched on the hard concrete surface, shivering violently, his head between his knees.

'Are you all right?' asked George.

'I don't know,' said Felix. He might have been seriously injured, but he was too numb with cold to tell. 'What about you?'

'Just frozen. I thought you were never going to move back there. You scared me to death.' George was too loud, too full of adrenalin.

Felix sat up. 'Hadn't we better phone the police?'

George turned towards him, his eyes wide and startled. 'You've got to be joking. We've probably killed him. Do you want to be the defendant in a murder trial?'

Felix's teeth were chattering. 'But we didn't do anything.'

'We killed him.'

'It was self-defence.'

George snorted. 'Come on,' he said. 'Two half-drunk lads out on their own, no witnesses, a dead man? We can't even prove it was his knife and not ours.'

Felix needed more time to think about it. 'How come you've worked all this out?' he said. 'Have you done this sort of thing before?'

And then George was rolling around, hooting with laughter, taking great gasps of air, spitting out water. Felix watched him, realising that this must be shock, but unsure how to deal with it. He rose to his feet and started to pull George upright. 'Stop this,' he said. 'We have to start moving or we'll freeze to death.'

Half shoving, half punching, he managed to manoeuvre them both along the road between rows of tall, closed factories, not knowing where they were, but away from the canal.

George eventually stopped laughing and they stumbled along in silence. 'Look,' said George, after a while, 'there's nothing to link us with the stabbing. No blood on us, no knife. We were simply a bit drunk and fell in the canal. The stabbing was miles away. Let's just go home, forget it ever happened.'

'What if he's not dead?' said Felix. 'What if he needs medical attention?'

'Then someone else will find him and send for an ambulance. It's not our problem. He was the aggressor – he was going to rob us, remember?'

Day after day, Felix pored over the local papers, desperate to know if the man had survived, but he couldn't find any information. He kept asking George if he'd heard anything, but George refused to discuss it. 'The guy was a drug addict,' he said. 'A no-hoper. Forget the whole thing, it's history.'

Had Felix killed the mugger, somehow managing to stab him in the confusion of the fight? Or had George done it and dropped the knife, which Felix had then picked up? Or did the man just fall against the knife?

Sometimes the mugger appeared in his dreams, huge and dark in front of him, breathing into his space, his eyes growing dull as his life dripped away. Felix lay awake in the middle of the night, wrestling with remorse, trying to decide if he was any better than the intruders who had stabbed his parents all those years ago.

But he and George had been the victims. They had been mugged and anything they had done had been in self-defence. George was right. What was to be gained by reporting it to the police? The man was dead and nothing they did now would make any difference.

Felix and George met up again once or twice, but it became increasingly difficult for them to talk to each other. Their guilty secret hung between them and, in the end, Felix found he couldn't even look directly into George's eyes. His words dried up. Putting a physical distance between them seemed to offer the only solution.

He applied for a position in Exeter, went for the interview, got the job and stayed there. He liked the remoteness of Devon, away from London, comforted by the proximity of his childhood, his old school, Kate. He allowed the incident and all its associated worries to slide down a long chute into the same lost place as his early childhood. He locked it into a remote, inaccessible part of his mind.

By the time he proposed to Kate, George had become a memory, a friend from the past, someone he had once known.

Then Felix went to Amsterdam.

Felix takes a breath and walks into the newsagent's. A bell rings as he opens the door and a tall, big-boned Asian woman behind the counter glances across at him. She's sitting on a stool, leafing through the pages of *Hello!* and chattering into her mobile, her voice high-pitched and rapid, squeezing out breathless words as fast as possible. There's no chance that anyone at the other end could be contributing to the conversation. She smiles at Felix and carries on talking.

Will they want a National Insurance number? Everybody wants so much information. Name, address, phone number, mobile number, email address, referees.

He walks up and down the aisles. It's much more than a newsagent's. They stock everything here, crowded shelves reaching to the ceiling, stacks of unpacked boxes clogging the space between the shelves. There's a hum of fridges, the glug of a fruit slush-maker, the smell of onions, lemon disinfectant, curry. The newspapers have been thrown on to the floor in piles and the racks behind are full of magazines. Car magazines, children's comics, teenagers' magazines with free nail varnish, free flip-flops, free mobile-phone covers. If you're an antiques collector, a garden enthusiast, a classical musician or a man in a raincoat, it's all there, waiting for you.

Felix approaches the counter and waits. The woman says a few last words into her phone, rings off and closes it with a snap. She places it below the counter and turns to Felix, beaming broadly. One of her front teeth is missing, and the two on either side of it have grown towards the hole, twisting slightly in an effort to meet each other. She's wearing a yellow and green sari of light, floaty cotton, topped with a voluminous navy fleece. 'You want cigarettes?' Her voice is strongly accented.

'No,' he says, uncomfortable under her intense gaze. 'I was interested in the job.'

'Job?'

'In the window. Sorting newspapers in the morning.'

She studies him, her eyes dark and curious.

She can see into my mind – she's recognised me. She reads newspapers all day, she probably watches television all evening.

She turns suddenly and shouts. 'Salik!'

For a few seconds nothing happens. Then a door opens at the back of the store and a man comes out, presumably her husband. Felix catches a glimpse of young children – black hair, bare feet, and a red plastic tractor being manoeuvred round a hall table. The door bangs shut and the woman at the till starts to talk in her furious fast language. Salik asks a few questions, which she answers with too many words.

'You have come about the job?' he says to Felix. His English is clearer than his wife's.

'Yes, the one advertised in the window.'

Salik looks at him. He's wearing jeans and a red and navy check shirt. A tangle of wiry black hair emerges from the open neck of his shirt. 'You mean sorting newspapers?'

'Yes.'

'You are prepared to come in at five o'clock every morning? Including Sunday?'

'If that's what you want.'

He walks round Felix, examining him with embarrassing thoroughness. Felix can feel his eyes behind him, reading his secrets from the shape of his head, the set of his shoulders. Prickles of sweat break out down his back, but he resists the urge to turn round.

'Why do you want to work for me?'

I didn't know I'd have to produce a reason. I just want to take the job, do the work, get paid, go back to my bedsit. 'I need the money.'

Salik emerges in front of him again and stops. His moustache twitches with amused interest. He has the longest eyelashes Felix has ever seen. 'No,' he says. 'This is an error. You are a prosperous man. Look at your clothes.' He puts out a hand and touches the collar of Felix's shirt, rubbing it softly between his fingers. 'This . . . this is expensive. You are respectable man, a man with a wife and children. You own your house, yes?'

'No,' says Felix. 'I don't own a house. I have a room, nearby, that's all.' I'm no good at this. Why did I put on my suit to get the job? I should have gone to a market stall and bought some cheap clothes, walked through puddles, got splashed by passing cars, spilled food down my shirt. He takes a deep breath and resigns himself to giving up. The only difficulty is how to leave with dignity. 'It's OK,' he says. 'I—'

'So,' says Salik, 'you have fallen on hard times.'

Fallen? Jumped would be closer to the truth. 'Yes,' he says. 'That's it.'

Salik chuckles, his face creasing with an unexpected sympathy. 'Your wife, she has thrown you out?'

'Well . . .'

'And she won't let you near the children?'

Felix allows himself a rueful grin.

'She has taken you to court and kept the house, the children, the money and you have nowhere to go?'

'Sort of,' says Felix.

Salik claps him on the shoulder. 'Then, my friend, you will work for me and you will keep the money for yourself and forget your ungrateful wife. My brother – this happens to my brother and he lives with us now.' He goes to the back door and opens it. 'Tahir!' he yells, making Felix jump.

A second man emerges, smaller than Salik, more overweight, but neat and compact.

'My brother,' says Salik, to Felix. 'This man has the same wife as you, Tahir, the fire-breathing dragon, the money-grabber. He wants to come and work with me.'

Tahir presumably understands English but doesn't speak it. A torrent of passionate words bursts out of his mouth, then both men stand close to Felix, patting his shoulder, beaming at him, feeling the quality of the material in his shirt, his jacket, his trousers. Salik's wife looks on, smiling through her crooked teeth, apparently taking no offence at their abuse of intolerant wives.

'So,' says Salik, 'you are a man of my own heart. You will work for me. Four pounds an hour.'

Well below the minimum wage. Salik watches Felix with steady, intelligent eyes. There's a suggestion of a deal here. No questions asked. 'How many hours?' asks Felix.

'Twenty-one. Three hours a day, sorting, doing a paper round if one of the boys doesn't turn up, sweeping up. Yes?'

'I would prefer more hours.'

'In time, my friend. Let's see what you can do first. Yes?'

'Yes,' says Felix.

'Done,' says Salik, and they shake hands vigorously. 'What is your name?'

'Tom,' says Felix. 'Tom Sawyer.'

'Tomorrow morning, then, Tom. Five o'clock. Let us see how well you English work.'

As he leaves the shop, Felix looks up at the windows of the flat above. He meets the gaze of a young girl, huge eyes, pale skin, a black plait hanging over one shoulder. She draws back as soon as she sees she has been spotted.

He relives his flight every night. Waking from the nightmare of his childhood, he drifts back into sleep and finds himself sitting on the train, speeding away from the appalling humiliation of discovery and the inevitable disgrace. He stares through the window at the landscape of his life as it drops away behind him, separating him for ever from his family. He can see George and Kristin reflected in the glass, watching him.

He changed trains four times, checking for CCTV, taking his coat off, putting it on again, trying to walk differently, hiding his head in a newspaper. He doesn't know which bit worked, but something did, because nobody was on a platform waiting for him, nobody stepped out of the crowd to arrest him.

And now, in his nightly reconstruction, he is being chased by a small, insignificant man who runs faster than seems possible, gaining on him, catching up with him until he comes to a halt among the frost-bound nettles and thistles along the side of the train. He comes face to face with a sightless, drug-addicted mugger. He can't move. The terror races through him, wild and eager, while his arms and legs stiffen into paralysis.

Eventually his limbs unfreeze and he climbs out of bed, walks in the darkness to the kitchen and pours himself a glass of water, letting the water splash out over the side of the sink, soaking his pyjamas. He drinks the whole glass greedily and puts it down on the draining-board. Then he goes to the window and stares out. The night road has become familiar in the week he has been here. Orange streetlights; an old Fiesta with the side mirror on the passenger side drooping sadly, held together with masking tape; bin-bags piled up on the opposite pavement, broken into by foxes, cats, magpies, spilling out their contents of margarine boxes and mouldy bread for public inspection; a pushchair without wheels, tossed on its side against a wall, teddies marching along the edges of a cushion that once held a child, a potential adult, a hope for the future.

There's a hint of rain in the wind. It slants across the window frame, then runs down the glass in a shining, distorted orange, a trickle of water that's swept away before it has time to make a real impression. A steady stream of air seeps through the badly fitting frames, cold with the night, bringing a musty damp into the bedsit.

The smell is still there in his nostrils . . .

And his mind is completely blank.

Felix sits on his lumpy mattress, eating fish and chips straight out of the paper. He's halfway through *War and Peace*, but the Asian family from the shop keep chattering in his ears and populating the pages. Where are they from? India, Pakistan, Bengal? He has no way of telling without asking them. They're a large family – at least four children, if not more, a brother living with them, perhaps parents as well, all squeezed together in a few upstairs rooms. He sees the little boy on the tricycle, curls over his ears, round cheeks, a look of determination as he races towards the door, desperate to get out before it closes in his face. They're a family and they run a shop. They came together from wherever they used to live, learnt a new language, a new culture. It's the togetherness that Felix thinks about.

There's no one to play football with Rory, no one to sit on Millie's bed and discuss her day, no one to hire a van for transporting Lawrence's stuff when he moves out of hall.

How will Kate cope?

My fatherless children – I need to be there, to help. But I'd only make everything worse for them—

There's a knock on the door.

Felix stops eating, prickles of fear shooting up his arms.

They've come for him.

'Are you there?' calls a voice from outside. The voice of a young man, soft and hesitant.

The knock comes again. Felix gets off the bed, his knees creaking, goes to the door. He puts his hand on the catch. He sees himself from a distance, poised, about to commit himself to someone else by the innocuous act of opening the door.

He turns the handle. The young man outside has pale hair and a gaunt, bony face, his eyes framed by deep sockets. His hands hang loose at his sides and there's an expression of imminent panic on his face. He attempts a smile. It's not confident and wavers slightly, as if a single unkind word would knock it off.

'Yes?' says Felix. He wants to say 'Who are you?' but he can't bring himself to be rude.

'I've moved in next door,' says the young man, 'and my cooker won't work.'

Felix sighs to himself. What else can he do? 'Hold on,' he says, and reaches behind the door for his keys. 'I'll come and have a look.'

Another tentative smile lights up the boy's face. 'Thanks,' he says. 'I don't know nothing about cookers, see.' He hesitates. 'My name's Brandon.' He offers a hand, but doesn't seem to know what to do with it when Felix takes it, letting it lie pale and limp in Felix's experienced grasp.

'I'm—' Felix stops for a second, aware that he has nearly given his real name. 'Tom.' He wants to ask about Brandon's age. He doesn't look old enough to be living on his own. 'Let's see what we can do with this cooker.'

There are two other rooms on the same floor, but Felix has never met anyone up here before. He doesn't even know if the rooms are occupied, although someone is using the bathroom, leaving shaved hairs round the wash-basin. But the culprit could be from the floor below, trying to avoid a queue for his own bathroom.

Brandon's room is more cramped than his, with a cold, unlived-in atmosphere. It smells of gas. On a small table a chopping-board has been laid out with an onion, two cloves of garlic, a red pepper and a small pile of diced chicken. It's all neat, the knife ready, the oil on the side for the frying-pan. There isn't a shelf by the cooker, so he'll have to carry all the ingredients over and bring them back when they're cooked.

Brandon smiles apologetically. 'I'm, like, just, you know, a learner.' He picks up a grubby, food-stained book from the sofa and shows it to Felix. Delia Smith, *Complete Illustrated Cookery Course*. It falls open to 'Stir-Fried Cooking'. 'I never done it before.'

'Good for you,' says Felix, trying not to smile. 'Let's have a look at this cooker.'

'It's my first home, see. It's, like, all right, i'n't it?' His mouth twists into an eager, childish smile. Felix can picture him swapping Pokémon cards in the playground, hiding at the back of a classroom so that he won't have to answer any questions.

A large chipped plate is resting on the cooker, next to the frying-pan. It has a pink edge decorated with little bunches of roses.

'It was only, like, ten pence,' says Brandon, putting the recipe book on the sofa 'I got it down the market.'

Felix fiddles with the cooker. Nothing happens when he presses the ignition. 'Must be the battery,' he says.

'Oh, no,' says Brandon, with dismay. 'My week's money's all spent.'

'Not to worry,' says Felix, deciding to buy a battery for the boy. He should be able to light his cooker. 'How about matches?'

'Here,' says Brandon. 'Mrs Baker said to get them, see, for the fire, so I did. But it's not, like, cold enough yet.' He picks them up from the coffee-table and hands them to Felix. The box is icy to touch.

'It should work with matches,' says Felix. 'You can hear the gas coming through.' He pauses so that they can hear the thin whistle and Brandon nods solemnly. Then Felix lights a match and puts it over the ring. It bursts into flame with a satisfying whoosh.

'Ace!' says Brandon. 'Why didn't I think of that?'

Why indeed? 'Where did you live before?' Felix asks.

Brandon's face closes up. He has such instant reactions. As if no one has ever taught him how to disguise things, how to be something other than the vulnerable person he knows he is. 'My mum and dad's place,' he mutters, turning away.

'Didn't you get on with them?'

'They was – they, you know, didn't like me.'

Felix wonders if he's exaggerating. 'Was one a step-parent?' he asks. 'Your dad, perhaps?'

Brandon looks confused. 'No. They never wanted me, see. So, soon's I was old enough, I, you know, left home and found myself this place.' His face opens into a sudden, shining smile. 'It's cracking here, isn't it?'

'It is,' says Felix. And perhaps it's true if you've never had anything else. 'How old are you?'

'Sixteen.'

'Do you have a job?'

'Just started. It's a factory. They make, like, taps – on sinks and things.'

'Great,' says Felix. 'I hope it goes well.'

They stand side by side for a few seconds, contemplating the cooker.

'Well,' says Felix, 'I'd better be getting back.'

'Thanks, Tom,' says Brandon, and sticks out his hand again.

Felix takes it, feels the soft skin, the evidence of a sad, untaught life that may be about to begin. 'I hope the meal goes well.'

'You're a good mate,' says Brandon.

No, thinks Felix, as he goes back to his room. I'm nobody's mate and I don't belong here or anywhere else. I need to be on my own, not touching anyone. There's blackness in me, around me, behind me, a dark shadow, hovering, accusing, thick with blood.

Part Three

Chapter 16

Six months later, Kate lingers in the empty sunlit living room and feels the weight of change heavy on her shoulders. With the removal of the furniture, the space around her no longer feels familiar. Everything she loved about this house has gone sour and she wouldn't want to stay here even if it were possible. It's nothing to do with finances, but the betrayal in every room, every object, every memory. Even the sunshine, as it gathers through the long window-panes, slanting across the floorboards, fails to move her. Once it was comforting. Now it seems tainted.

Yellow roses are scrambling along the wall at the end of the garden, overwhelming the long-established clematis. Kate planted the roses three years ago – about the time when Felix went to Iceland. 'Golden Showers', scented and extravagant, a vigorous, disease-resistant climber. Brilliant blue globes of agapanthus rise from the lower lawn, while branches of mixed fuchsias droop gracefully between them: 'Tom Thumb', 'Lindisfarne', 'Mrs Popple'.

She imagines other people, another family, taking over the house. They'll rip out the inside and redesign everything, wiping away all traces of their occupation. It will be as if the Kendalls have never existed.

Kate has considered digging up some of the plants and taking them with her, but she can't quite believe in the tiny rectangular garden outside the flat that will be their temporary new home. It's a tangle of wild fertility, populated by dandelions, brambles, nettles, untouched and unloved for many years.

We have been happy here. I'm not imagining it. It was true once.

Kate's parents have been helping her financially for the last few months. 'Once you've finished your MA,' said her father, 'you'll be in a much stronger position.'

They were sitting in her parents' room watching the sun go down. Long, thin bands of cloud stretched across the sky, shining streaks of gold against the orange of the setting sun. On the opposite side of the river, a patchwork of fields rose up, each one a different shade of green, punctuated with the occasional yellow flash of rape. It's gentle, benign, so unlike the vast frozen world of Canada that Kate flew over on her way back to her altered life.

Her parents were comfortable, but not rich. They had made the mistake of not investing in a house until her father retired, so a considerable amount of their savings went into the purchase of their present home in Topsham. Her father had been able to indulge his passion for sailing until a few years ago when he had become less mobile, but they were not in a position to pour money into Kate's house.

'I can't let you use up all your money on us,' said Kate. 'It should be put aside for your old age, when you might need nursing care—' She stopped. Her mother didn't like talking about their uncertain future. 'The house is too big. The maintenance, the bills, they're too much of a worry.'

'Why don't you just sell it and buy somewhere smaller?' said her mother. 'You probably wouldn't need a mortgage at all.'

'Can't be done at the moment,' said her father. 'The house is in both their names, so Kate can't sell it without a signature from Felix.'

'How ridiculous. What if Felix died?'

'That's different. The insurance would cover that.'

'I think it would be better to let it be repossessed,' said Kate. The house reminded her too much of Felix. He was there in every room, strong and stifling. She kept hearing his voice in the distance. 'Kate! Come and look at this!' 'Kate, where are you?' 'Kate, guess what's happened?' She would never be able to think clearly while she was still there.

'But where would you live?' said her mother, offering her a plate of banana muffins. 'Do have one. They've just come out of the oven.'

'You could rent a place,' said her father. 'We'd help you until you're on your feet.'

'What about the aunts?' said her mother. 'Couldn't they help you financially?'

'They've offered,' said Kate, 'but I'd really rather not take anything from them.' They were too committed to Felix. It would be like accepting money from him – not illegal exactly, but unsuitable in some way. She needed to act independently now, make her own way towards the future.

'Quite right,' said her father. 'You shouldn't accept money from anyone except your immediate family.'

'I've been looking,' said Kate. 'There aren't many houses around for a long-term let – they make more money from tourists.' She bit into the cake. A burst of comforting sweetness filled her with brief pleasure. 'But I have found something – it's an ex-council flat.'

Her mother looked appalled. 'On a council estate?'

'It's not that terrible,' said Kate. 'All sorts of people live on council estates, these days.'

'But it'll be so hard on the children.'

That was the big worry. Millie, especially, would struggle with the changed lifestyle. 'I know they'll find it difficult, but we don't have much choice. They'll just have to adapt.'

'But what about gangs and drugs and things?'

'Mum, this is Budleigh, not some inner-city estate. It won't be that bad. They only show the worst places on the news.'

Kate's mother took another muffin and nibbled at the edge, as if convincing herself that eating slowly would cancel out the effect of too much fattening food. 'What if Felix comes back?' she said. 'He'll be so upset to find his house sold.'

Kate exchanged glances with her father. Her mother simply refused to accept the situation. She still believed there was a rational explanation and that Felix would just turn up again one day and explain. 'It really isn't very likely,' she said.

'Even so,' said her mother.

There was a long silence. Her father was also struggling to make sense of Felix's betrayal, but at least he was realistic. 'I'm not normally such a bad judge of character,' he muttered every now and again. 'There was always something uncertain about George, an unpredictability, the sense that he could go either way. But Felix – how did I get it so wrong?'

He had aged in the last few months. He was doing all the things he used to do, but now they seemed to drain his energy more, wearing him out, slowing his mind.

'He fooled everyone,' said Kate. 'For a very long time.'

'Well, if you ask me,' said her mother, 'nobody could live a lie for all those years. Something has happened that he has no control over.'

Kate's father eased himself to his feet. 'It's up to you, Kate. When you're ready to buy a new home, I'll help as much as I can.'

Kate rose with him. 'Thank you,' she said. She didn't know how to express her appreciation of their support. She knew the shock had damaged them nearly as much as it had damaged her, but they had never tried to blame her for not seeing what had been going on. They were aware that they had shared her blindness.

'Did you get the extension on the MA?' asked her father.

For some time she hadn't been able to think about anything, let alone the thesis, but she wanted to continue. It seemed important that she should achieve something on her own.

'Yes, they were very understanding. I'm hoping to get on with it as soon as we've moved. Once I've passed, I can look for a proper job.'

'You know we'll have the children any time,' said her mother. 'They needn't be neglected.'

'I have no intention of neglecting them,' said Kate.

'I have to be off now,' said her father, moving awkwardly towards the hall and taking his linen jacket off the peg.

'You didn't tell me you were going out,' said Kate's mother.

'Yes, I did. It's a meeting in the village hall.'

'Margaret again, I suppose,' said Kate's mother. She let a silence fall for a few seconds. 'Well, lunch will be ready at one o'clock exactly. Make sure you're back.'

He winked at Kate and his face collapsed into a thousand amiable creases. 'You mean you want me to bring the proceedings to an early close and leave the den of iniquity that is otherwise known as the village hall for the sake of chicken and mushroom pie? Be reasonable, woman.'

At first the flat was a bit of a shock. Kate and the children went to view it as soon as she was given the keys. It was on the first floor of a two-storey block, but it had its own entrance from the garden path, with the staircase directly inside the front door.

'It'll be nice living upstairs,' she said to Millie. 'We should have a good view.' Rory thundered up ahead of them. There was a faint smell of rotting cabbage, damp, something else that she didn't want to think about. Millie pulled her coat closely round her, avoiding the walls and the banisters, her face set in a rigid expression of disgust.

'What's the black stuff on the bathroom walls?' asked Rory, coming back along the hallway.

Kate studied the mould under the window. 'It's nothing,' she said. 'It just needs a good scrub with disinfectant.'

They made their way to the living room. Their feet stuck to the carpet. Previous tenants had left rubbish behind. A chair with a broken seat, piles of screwed up newspaper, off-cuts of splintered wood, an open container of what looked like motor oil.

'Well,' said Kate, gazing round with dismay, 'it's not as small as I'd thought . . .'

'I'm having this bedroom,' said Rory, coming out of a room that led off the living room.

Kate peered through the door. 'No, Rory,' she said. 'That's the main bedroom. You'll have to have the one next door.'

He looked incredulous. 'That's not a bedroom, it's a cupboard. There's no room to play on the Wii.'

Millie refused to move from the middle of the room. 'It's gross,' she said. 'I cannot believe you're even contemplating living here.'

'We don't have much choice,' said Kate. 'There's nowhere else available at this time of year. We're not in a position to be fussy.'

'Fussy? You think I'm being fussy? Why should we live in this pigsty?'

Kate was fighting her own prejudices, struggling to believe they could make it into an acceptable place to live. Please, Millie, we can't be too precious. This is what happens to families when the father walks out on them. We're not the first and we won't be the last. 'It's not so bad,' she said. 'It's a roof over our heads.'

'I'd rather sleep in a tent,' said Millie.

'You wouldn't say that if it was snowing.'

'You can see Sandy Bay from the bedroom,' said Rory.

'No, you can't,' said Millie. 'It's just more revolting flats.'

'Come with me.' He led them into the largest bedroom and pointed through the top corner of the left window. It was just possible to pick out the cliffs, the rows of caravans stretched over distant fields.

'Big deal,' said Millie.

'It'll only be for a short while,' said Kate. 'We can decorate, paint the walls – get the carpets cleaned. You won't recognise it when we've finished.'

'What's the point if we're not staying? Anyway, it'll still be disgusting.'

Bleakness settled over Kate. She had a strong desire to run out of the flat, jump in the car and drive as far away as possible – on and on without stopping.

'Perhaps I could use the Wii in the living room,' said Rory.

'The smell will get into our clothes,' said Millie.

'No, it won't,' said Kate. 'It'll be clean and nice-smelling in no time, once we get going. This is nothing compared to the hardship people in other countries have to put up with. Shanty towns or mud huts or houses without any walls.'

'Lucky them,' said Millie. 'At least they don't have to live here. And, anyway, they always have hot weather.'

'Except when it rains,' said Kate.

'How do they get the roof to stay on,' said Rory, 'if there aren't any walls?'

Kate put an arm round Millie's shoulders. 'It'll be all right,' she said gently. 'You'll see.'

But Millie remained stiff and hostile, refusing to allow herself any comfort from her mother's touch.

Standing in the deserted living room and looking down into the garden, Kate can see the Wendy house that Felix built for Millie. It would make a far more desirable home than the council flat. Felix had embarked upon its construction almost immediately after she was born, spending hours out there with the eight-year-old Lawrence, discussing details with him, designing little alcoves, windows, a tiny staircase to an upstairs room.

'She's only just been born,' said Kate, when he showed her his early plans.

Energy radiated from him, fuelled by impatience. As if he needed to construct something external to make up for the fact that he couldn't nourish the newborn baby himself. 'No time like the present,' he said.

'Can't it wait a bit?'

'Oh.' His face dropped with disappointment. 'I thought it would be a good time.'

Kate felt a twinge of guilt. 'It's a nice idea,' she said.

'I know it's premature, but I might as well get on with it while I'm off work. Little girls love Wendy houses.'

How could he possibly have known that? He'd never had any contact with little girls. Any memories of childhood that his aunts might have conjured up would have been hopelessly untypical. Perhaps he was remembering Enid Blyton or Arthur Ransome. Did he see girls as little housekeepers or female pirates? Who knows? The mind that Kate believed to be transparent and believable had turned out to be nothing more than an elaborate fiction.

He leant over the cot and put his finger on Millie's baby cheek, his face soft with tenderness. 'I always knew we'd have a girl. It was just a question of time.'

'Rubbish,' said Kate. 'You can't pretend you knew the future after it's already happened.'

He became obsessed with the Wendy house. Deliveries of wood turned up almost every day, window units, roof tiles. He wouldn't consider a pre-designed kit. He wanted to do it from scratch. He acquired a mysterious expertise, as if he had built hundreds of play houses in the past. And, of course, he turned out to be good at it.

'Is it necessary to make it so complicated?' asked Kate.

'Oh, yes. If you're going to do something, you should do it properly.'

Naturally, she thinks now, watching him in her memory

as he dances up and down the garden, never still. The whole building experience acted like a stimulant, jerking his body into ever-growing feats of ingenuity and endurance. You should always do things properly. When you decide to break the law and abandon your family, there must be no half-measures. No point in being semi-criminal.

He had taken time off work. 'They can manage without me for a few weeks,' he said.

Kate wasn't sure if he was a help or not. It was useful to have someone to fetch Lawrence from school and test him on his spellings, but he wasn't willing to change nappies and it was tiring watching all his energy.

'You have to relax,' he said to Kate, who was finding the breast-feeding more difficult with Millie than she had with Lawrence.

'Don't be naïve,' she said. 'It's impossible to relax with a baby.'

'I know,' he said, coming to sit next to her on the sofa where she was nursing Millie. 'You're quite right.'

Kate looked down at his hair as he bent over Millie. Curled into neat ginger spirals that compelled you to reach out and touch. She had seen this impulse in many people, children and adults: the involuntary movement of a hand creeping stealthily towards his head, then falling away with embarrassment as the owner of the hand became aware of what was happening.

She ran a finger through one of the curls, pulling it out to its fullest length and letting it spring back to its original shape. The hair of a small boy. He was an adult, a partner in a reputable firm, earning enough money for a comfortable and pleasant lifestyle yet there was something childlike about him. Something unfinished that she couldn't define.

'Back to the Wendy house,' he said, leaping up as if an alarm had just gone off in his head.

He wanted the baby, he wanted the family, but he was too itchy to just sit and appreciate things. He had to be doing something. All the time. A powerful motor was chugging away inside him, compelling him to clear out the loft, move shrubs around, build a Wendy house.

'Mum!' Lawrence's voice breaks into her thoughts. 'Where are you?'

It's time to go. Time to forget all this.

The sea is choppy today, despite the sun. White-tipped waves appear occasionally in the expanse of blueness that stretches out to the distant horizon. From here, you can believe it's calm if you don't interpret the glimpses of white correctly. It's only when you get up close that you discover how rough it is, how deceptive, how willing to pull you in and submerge you.

She can feel anger inside her all the time now, bubbling away, brewing up into a hurricane as it pulls in every drop of low pressure, building up its strength, preparing itself for landfall and an explosion of epic proportions.

Sometimes she wakes in the night, believing Felix to be lying next to her, and leaps up, ready to attack him, pummel him with her fists, immobilise him before he can do them any more damage. Her hands fly through the air and find an empty space, a nothingness, when she wants a warm, breathing body that she can fight. She finds herself sobbing helplessly, weak with bitterness and fury that she can't share with anyone.

'I hate him,' says a voice behind her.

She turns. Lawrence has come into the room and is standing with his hands in his pockets, watching her. His face is set in an unnatural resentment, so unlike the easy-going softness that has accompanied him all through his life.

'No, you don't,' she says, putting an arm round his waist. I hate him much more than you do. 'You don't know why he's done it, so you're resentful. But he's been a good father most of the time.' Why shouldn't he hate him? It's perfectly reasonable.

'It doesn't make any difference what he was before,' he says. 'It's what he's done now. He's destroyed everything.'

She rubs his back, feeling his youthful strength under her fingers, the powerful muscles, the skin's ability to spring back into shape. 'It needn't destroy your life,' she says. 'You can do whatever you want to do.' It's harder for me. What can I do?

She can hear Rory running around upstairs, his feet thumping through the empty rooms. He's yelling, roaring at the top of his voice, producing a wordless sound, almost joyful. 'Whatever is he doing?' she says.

'He likes the echo. He says it means the aliens have gone.'

'Thank goodness for that.'

'He'll get a sore throat if he carries on,' says Lawrence.

How sad that he sounds sensible at last. 'At least he's happy,' she says.

And this is true. Moving schools seems to have changed Rory. At first, after Felix left, he sank into himself, hiding in his room, panicking about aliens, not speaking unless she asked him a question. Now that he has a new school, a new life, he comes and discusses things with her again. Time passes in a different way when you're nine. The earth takes longer to complete a circuit, days stretch out less predictably, cuts and bruises heal quicker.

She had fought furiously to let him stay at his school, but encountered an unexpected resistance. She had to deal with the deputy head, Simon Harries. He was an oddly detached man who could only operate according to correct procedures.

'You must understand, Mrs Kendall, that Rory can't stay indefinitely unless his fees are paid.'

He used to call her Kate. They often met at the edge of the

rugby pitch, vocal supporters of the school team. They would huddle into their fleeced anoraks, feet growing numb despite the army socks inside their wellies, while drizzle engulfed them in a sheet of fine mist. She had thought she liked him. 'Rory's a credit to the school,' he said at every match, never aware of how much he repeated himself. He just wanted the goals, she knew, even then, and he lived for the trophies, the heady roar of victory. Rory was a goal scorer, a furnace of energy and skilled footwork, a fast mover. But she had always believed there was more to Simon Harries than the desire for success. He was loyal, hard-working, nice to her. And he reminded her a little of her father.

'So what about foundation places?' she said. 'Why can't he have one of those?' Some people would rather starve to death than ask for charity. I don't care. I'll do whatever's necessary for Rory.

'Unfortunately they've all been taken.'

'Oh, come on,' she exploded. 'How much can it possibly cost to allow one more child into a classroom?'

'I'm afraid we can't reason like that. Once you make an exception, the floodgates open—'

'Oh, yes, of course,' she said. 'I've seen them all, queuing up at the gates every day, holding demonstrations, demanding places.'

He turned away from her. They didn't really care about Rory at all. He might be clever, a great rugby player, but without the money he no longer counted.

The secretary wouldn't put her calls through to the headmaster. 'I'm sorry, Mrs Kendall, Mr Blakelock is on the other line. Could you call back later?'

She came into the school, sat in the waiting room. 'Mr Blakelock isn't available today. He's out visiting other prep schools. They like to keep in touch.' 'He's teaching science all day. Mr Huntingdon is off sick.' 'The board of governors is here – their meetings go on for the whole day.'

Finally, she ignored the procedures and walked straight into his office. She was the daughter of a headmaster. She would not be intimidated. Piers Blakelock was sitting at his desk making lists, but as soon as he recognised her, he rose and came towards her, stretching out his hand. 'Kate, do come in.'

'You have to let Rory stay here,' she said, hearing a slight tremble in her voice and struggling to control it. She mustn't show weakness.

He smiled at her as if they were old friends – which they were. 'Shall we sit down?' he said.

'No,' she said. 'I want to stand.' If she sat down, she might feel less strong, more likely to burst into tears.

He took her gently by the elbow and led her to a small group of armchairs at the other end of the room. 'We need to be comfortable if we're to discuss the serious matter of a child's education.'

He was too nice. She wasn't equipped with the necessary ruthlessness for this. She sat down.

'It's cruel,' she said. 'You can't ask Rory to leave at this stage, when he's doing so well. How would he survive in a state school? His whole future can't just hang on money. Surely you have to show some integrity, some loyalty to your pupils and their families. It can't be right that at the first hint of difficulties you chuck them out, wave goodbye, wash your hands of them. Children have feelings, you know. They've got friends and patterns of life. You can't uproot them like this. Where's your compassion?'

Piers Blakelock was nodding, as if he agreed with every word she said. 'I'd like to believe that we do have compassion, Kate,' he said, 'and that we have the best interests of all our children at heart—'

There was a knock on the door and the secretary put her head round. 'Oh,' she said, when she saw Kate. 'Miss Millard is here, Headmaster.'

He nodded. 'I'm going to be a bit late, I'm afraid. Unforeseeable circumstances. Could you apologise and offer her a cup of coffee if she's willing to wait? Otherwise I think you'll have to ask her to make another appointment.'

The secretary left and Kate took a deep breath. 'So how can you just throw him out?'

'I must assure you that we'll do our best for him. The school will take on the responsibility of finding Rory a place at some other suitable school—'

'You mean another private school?'

He hesitated. 'Well, there aren't that many independent schools in the area, as you already know, but we would certainly make enquiries to see if any of them have funding available. Meanwhile we'll talk to the local state schools and see if we can find the best place for him.'

'But it would be so difficult for him to adjust.'

He smiled again. 'I think that reports of the condition of state schools have been greatly exaggerated. Most of them are perfectly capable of educating the children in their care – some of them as well as we do, but don't tell anyone I said so. The local primary school uses our facilities, the swimming-pool and the cricket pitches, so I know what I'm talking about. A boy with Rory's abilities and intelligence will survive in any school and rise easily to the top.'

Kate could feel her resolve ebbing away in the face of his reasonableness. She reached out desperately for her original anger. 'But this is what he knows. He fits in here.'

Piers Blakelock turned and looked out of the window. Kate followed his gaze. Children were emerging from the classrooms for break. Some raced on to the playing-field, springing into life after sitting down for so long, while others sauntered in groups, hands in their pockets, talking earnestly.

'I'm really very fond of Rory,' he said, as if he meant it. 'But I'm afraid there are too many administrative problems.

We're at capacity with foundation pupils at the moment, and although we'd love to keep him, we can't afford to do so. It's not possible to simply wave a benevolent hand and change the situation, however much we might wish to.'

'But you're the headmaster. You can intervene.'

He sighed. 'I'm afraid my powers are strictly limited.'

Kate was struggling to hold on to her desire to fight. He was too pleasant, too sympathetic. 'I'm just thinking of Rory,' she said.

'Of course,' he said. 'We all want the best for him.'

On her way out, she met Simon Harries in the corridor. 'You'll be pleased to know you were right,' she said. 'Rory can't stay.'

'I'm sure it's for the best,' he said.

'What's that supposed to mean?'

He half smiled. 'It's very difficult to keep everyone happy. I'm sure you must have appreciated that some of the parents have been talking—'

Kate found that she was clenching her fists. 'You mean you listen to gossip and innuendo? You care more about the reputation of the school than the welfare of a child who cannot be held responsible for his parent's actions?'

He put up his hands and stepped backwards. 'I'm sorry, Mrs Kendall.'

She couldn't speak. She turned her back on him and walked away, slamming the door behind her. But it was weighted and glided shut without making a sound.

She'd find a school for Rory today. She wouldn't let him stay with these bigoted, over-privileged, patronising—

'Mrs Kendall.' Rory's form teacher, Mr Wickenham, had come up behind her. 'I'll be so sorry to lose Rory,' he said. He appeared to be genuinely upset. 'We're really going to miss him.'

'Thank you,' said Kate. 'It's very kind of you to say so.' She felt exhausted. She could no longer tell if people cared or not and, in the end, it didn't make any difference. They weren't going to let him stay.

Kate listens to Rory racing around upstairs. She shouldn't have worried about him. He has an extraordinary resilience, going off to school more eagerly than in the past, bringing children home to play, already part of a local football team, bouncing back to life in a way she hadn't expected.

She goes into the hall and calls up the stairs. 'Come on, Rory! Time to go.'

'Coming!'

'Where's Millie?' she asks Lawrence.

'Outside in the car. She says goodbyes are futile and we shouldn't try to live in the past.'

'Hmm.' Kate takes one last look round. She won't ever see this room again. She's lived here all these years and has only now understood that it was all a lie. Felix, the impostor, the fake, the confidence-trickster. He'd fooled her completely, but she isn't having any more of it. 'Let's go,' she said.

Chapter 17

'Right,' says Rory, gazing round at the circle of his new mates. 'What are we going to call ourselves?' There were six of them, seven with Rory, crouched together in the corner of the playground, between the big bush with stinky white flowers and the wall of year four's classroom.

'The Budleigh Boys,' suggests Matt, a short fat child who wears the same clothes every day for a whole week. It's Friday. Monday's rice pudding and Wednesday's beef stew mingle on his shirt with grass stains and dust from the playground.

Rory looks at him with contempt. 'I bet that's been used before.'

'Yeah,' says Darren, who lives next door to the school and knows all the local history. 'Them as used to get into fights with the Exmouth Evvies, until they was both banned by the police.'

Banned by the police. It's like an electric current buzzing through the group. This could happen to them. They could get a reputation, get known by the police, have car chases—

'You're missing the point,' says Rory. He knows exactly what they're thinking. He thought it himself – only for three seconds, until his brain took over. 'We're forming this group to hunt for aliens who are infiltrating the world, not get into stupid fights.' He likes using good words like 'infiltrating' with these boys. It impresses them.

'That's right,' says Jack.

Rory contemplates him in silence for a moment. Jack seems too keen to agree with whatever he says. Is he planning to be deputy leader, or does he have ideas about taking over? He'll need to be watched. It might be worth testing him some time with a junky theory and see if he agrees with him then.

'How about Space Warriors?' he says. He's wanted this name all the time, but he's been waiting for the right moment to introduce it. He holds his breath and watches them think. It's like watching the tide coming in.

'OK,' says Jack.

'Yeah,' says Darren.

They're all nodding. Rory relaxes. Now comes the exciting bit. 'We have to prove our loyalty. There can't be any chickening out.'

He produces a small package from his pocket and carefully unwraps the folds of Andrex toilet tissue, revealing a needle that he's lifted from his sister's sewing box. She won't know it's missing. She never sews anything, ever. He's not at all sure why she's got it. He holds up the needle, moving it slowly so that it glints in the sunlight, but makes sure it can't be seen by anyone else in the playground. He's got this idea from a book that Great-aunt Beatrice gave him recently from his father's old collection. *An Encyclopedia of Extraordinary Things*. He might sell the book some time, on eBay. It's really ancient and must be worth a fortune.

He waits as long as possible before speaking. 'In Sierra Leone,' he says at last, 'they make the child soldiers kill someone . . .' He pauses. Six pairs of eyes stare at him.

'It's all right.' He produces the short, terse laugh he's been practising at home. 'I'm not going to ask you to kill anyone. But we have to share our blood.'

'Blood?' says Jason. 'Blood makes me pass out.'

'Then you're never going to be a Space Warrior,' says Rory.

'That's not fair.'

'What about AIDS?' says Reese.

For a horrible moment, Rory's brain stops working. The authors of *An Encyclopedia of Extraordinary Things* hadn't known about AIDS. They'd thought you had to worry about snakes and deadly injections and Martians.

'It's OK,' he says, recovering himself. 'I've sterilised it. In steam from the kettle.' This isn't strictly true. He held it under hot water from the tap. But it's good enough. It was nearly boiling.

They still look doubtful.

'Anyway,' he says, 'has anyone here got AIDS?'

They all shake their heads.

'HIV?'

They shake again.

'There you are, then. No problem.' He hesitates for another second. If anyone does have AIDS, would they say so? He dismisses the thought. 'I'll go first.' He holds his finger up in the air and stabs it quickly with the needle, holding himself upright and blinking fast to hide the watering of his eyes. He wipes the needle on the tissue and passes it to Darren. 'Your turn.'

The needle goes round the circle, but nobody refuses until it reaches Jason. 'I can't do it,' he says.

'Yes, you can,' says Rory. He locks eyes with Jason. This is his first great test as leader.

Jason holds the needle out. 'You do it for me.' He turns his head away.

Rory leans over and jabs Jason's finger before he has time to realise what's happening.

'Ah!' Jason lets out a strangled howl.

They watch with interest to see if he's going to faint. His face goes very white and he sways briefly, but remains upright. It's disappointing.

'OK,' says Rory. 'Now we've got to mingle our blood.' They lean forward and rub their fingers together. Some of the blood has already clotted and it's difficult to be sure if each one has made contact with everyone else, but they do their best.

Rory examines the scene with considerable pleasure. 'We're a real gang now,' he says.

The bell rings for the end of break and they scramble to their feet. 'Race you,' says a voice just behind Rory. It's Jack.

'You've got no chance,' he yells, and puts all his energy into running. He's fast, he can beat anyone, he's Superman. But when he staggers to a halt beside the school entrance, Jack's there beside him. They gasp for air together, bending over as they fight for breath, watching each other.

'Pretty good,' says Rory, his chest heaving.

'Not so bad yourself,' says Jack.

They stare at each other and grin. Rory knows that it's going to be all right.

For the first time in his life, Rory is allowed to cycle home on his own. Now they've moved and everything is much closer, his mum has finally agreed. It wasn't easy to persuade her.

'I bet you went out on your own when you were nine.' He was only guessing – he couldn't actually imagine his mother being nine years old – but it seemed a good line of argument to pursue.

'That was then. It's all different now.'

'I don't see why. No one's going to grab me and shove me in the back of a car if I'm on my bike. I'll just pedal away. And if you give me a good supply of sweets I can say no when they offer me some.'

He was fairly sure he could wear her down. She wasn't as certain as she used to be. He won in the end, although she insisted on walking to school with him, making him wait for her at every junction. It was so unnecessary. He just hoped Jack was nowhere around to see.

He's got plenty of time to get home. His mum will be on the crossing for another half-hour, so he goes the long way round, getting off to walk up the steep roads to the top of the cliffs. Once there, he glides down the other side, faster and faster, the wind singing in his ears.

He's about halfway down when there's a sudden pop and the back wheel starts to judder. He presses the brakes gently, knowing that if he stops too abruptly, he'll go head-first over the handlebars, but it's difficult to control the bike and he's afraid he'll fall off anyway. He skids to a halt, brakes squealing, weaving a zig-zag path across the pavement – he's seen Lewis Hamilton do this in a Grand Prix. He dismounts, pushes the bike to a lamp-post where he can prop it up and bends down to examine the back wheel.

The tyre is completely flat, bulging outwards, loose and empty. Rory sighs with frustration. He's going to be late home now. He runs his hand along the surface of the tyre and finds the culprit: a large nail embedded up to its head. He pulls it out and throws it into the gutter. With a jolt of guilt he sees his mobile sitting on his bedside table instead of in his schoolbag, beside the list of rules he has drawn up for the Space Warriors. She'll kill me, he thinks, as he sets off down the hill.

At the bottom, his attention is diverted by a cluster of people on the beach. They're watching a small boat being dragged out of the water by two divers in wetsuits. Rory props his bike against some railings and heads down to the water's edge to see what's going on, picking his way through the moored boats, avoiding patches of seaweed and tar. The round flat pebbles creak under his feet.

Something is lying in the boat, long and stiff, wrapped in a tarpaulin.

An ambulance pulls up by his bike. Two men in yellow fluorescent jackets get out, open the doors at the back and remove a stretcher. They stumble over the pebbles with it, past Rory, to the boat that is still half in and half out of the water.

'What's going on?' says a voice behind Rory.

He turns and sees a middle-aged woman in an anorak and walking boots, her hair all tangled in the wind.

He shrugs. 'Don't know,' he says. 'I've only just got here.'

They join the small group of onlookers. Wind tugs at the rucksack on Rory's back, ruffles his jacket and whips up the edges of the tarpaulin with sharp cracks.

The two ambulance men lift the object from the boat onto the stretcher. Then they bend over it.

'It's a body,' says a man, who's walked up behind them. He must know the woman. His anorak is the same colour as hers – bright blue and yellow, almost certainly brand new. 'They've just pulled it out of the water.'

Rory leans forward to see more clearly. He's never seen a dead body before. As they pull the tarpaulin back, he catches a brief glimpse of a white face, swollen and puffy, with staring eyes.

'It looks like he's been in the water for some time.'

A body in the water for a long time. Someone who's been missing for ages. Someone who's had an accident and no one knew. They all thought he'd run away. It could be – it could be—

The woman next to him puts a hand on his arm. 'You don't want to look,' she says. 'It's not very nice.'

He does want to look. He wants to see it more than anything else he's ever seen before. He pulls away from the woman, darts out from the edge of the small crowd, and runs towards the ambulance men.

They turn round in surprise.

'Who are you?' says one of them.

'I want to see who it is,' he says. The face is covered again and now it's just the long, still shape of a person.

'I don't think so,' says the ambulance man. 'Drowned bodies aren't pretty.'

Rory struggles to appear calm and sensible. He can feel his legs shaking, his body straining forward against the wind. 'It might be my dad,' he says. He wants to sound sensible, but he can hear his voice trailing away, shrill and whining.

The man bends over him. He's enormous in his yellow uniform, towering above Rory, wide and fluorescent. 'Is your dad missing then?'

Rory nods.

'What's your name?'

Rory freezes. He can't reveal himself here. It wouldn't be a good idea in front of all these people. 'I just want to see if it's my dad.'

'How long's he been missing?' The man's voice is deep, calm, reassuring.

'I don't know – a long time. I want to see him. Can I just see him? I need to check.' He leans forward, determined to pull the tarpaulin back and get another view of the face, but the ambulance man grabs his arm.

'Sorry, son. Can't let you do that. You wouldn't like it.'

Rory stares at him. He can't understand why they won't let him just look. It would make it all so much easier.

One of the divers comes over to them. 'What's going on?'

'I want to see him,' says Rory. 'I want to check.'

'He thinks it's his dad,' says the ambulance man. 'Apparently his dad's gone missing.'

They both study him for a moment in silence. He knows what they're thinking. They reckon his dad's just left, gone off with someone, and he's just a stupid kid believing his dad's had an accident. It's not like that, he wants to say, but he can't start that sort of conversation. They might guess who he is.

'Look, son,' says the diver, bending down towards him. 'It's not your dad.'

'You don't know that.'

'It's a woman.'

'Are you sure?' says the ambulance man.

The diver nods. 'No question. Long hair, waist-length, I'd say. She's only been in the water twelve hours.'

Rory steps back, his eyes wet and blurred. They're wrong, completely wrong. While they're talking, he darts round them, grabs the tarpaulin and pulls it back.

He's appalled by what he sees. A face so swollen that you can hardly recognise it. What he'd thought were eyes were just sockets, dark, empty holes. And the diver is right about the hair. It's long, blonde, tangled with seaweed, not his father's hair at all.

Someone puts a hand on his shoulder. 'Come on,' says a voice, firm but gentle, in his ear. 'You shouldn't be here.'

Rory jumps away from the hand. Then he's running, across the stones, along the seashore, away from all those people.

How could he have been so stupid? Why would his dad end up in the sea?

He runs until he's exhausted and finally stops, looking back to see if he's been followed. The people are a long way behind him, small in the distance, not as many as he'd thought, just a few dark shapes gathered round a small boat. They don't look important at all, standing there at the edge of the sea.

He sits down, shifting the stones underneath him until he's comfortable, and hugs his knees to his chest. A wave pounds down, sending a long unstoppable trail of white foam up the beach, then pulls back with a squeal, turning the stones with it. He watches the water flow into the Otter river, a deep current, guarded by a group of rocks at the entrance. Seagulls whirl and scream, swoop for fish, ride the waves.

The dead woman's face floats in front of him. Huge and swollen, hardly a face at all, a fat, ugly, cartoon woman.

He picks up a stone. Smooth, round, pleasing to hold. It feels so right in his hand, exactly the right shape, comfortable against his skin.

'Hi, Kendall.'

Rory jumps at the voice just behind him, drops the pebble and turns round slowly. He can't believe he's been caught out here alone.

It's them. James Peterson, William Holt, Richard Wong, Rohit Sammerji.

They walk round and stand in front of him. Now would be a good moment for the aliens to invade. 'So this is where you've been hiding, Kendall. Making plans for your future criminal career?'

Rory pulls himself up, and turns to run, but Richard Wong moves behind him and blocks his way, grabbing his arms and holding them firmly.

'We don't like crooks round here,' says William Holt.

'I'm not a crook,' says Rory. He's said it a thousand times, over and over again from the moment his father disappeared until the glorious day when he left his old school.

Why are they here on their own? They're only year six – eleven-year-olds. Their parents should be with them.

Everything slows down, like an action replay, while Rohit takes a cigarette and some matches out of his pocket. It seems to take hours for him to shake out a match and scrape it against the side of the box. Everyone's eyes are fixed on it as a small flame flares up, flickers in the sea air, blows to the side – and goes out.

'Scum like your dad shouldn't be allowed to exist,' says Rohit, and takes out another match.

Rory tries to release himself from Richard, but the grip on his arms is too strong.

'That dead body over there should be your dad,' says James. 'I'd have helped drown him myself, given the chance. It would have been a pleasure to hold him down. A service to our country.'

The cigarette is lit now, and Rohit takes a small puff, pulling in his cheeks and drawing on the cigarette so that the end glows red. He takes it out of his mouth, lets the smoke drift easily away, and steps towards Rory.

William pulls up Rory's sleeve. On the inside of his arm, there's a row of small scars from the past, dark and round, starting to fade. Rohit waves the cigarette in the air. 'I don't know why I lit this,' he says. 'I've given up smoking. Where shall I stub it out?'

The four of them smile at each other, as if they really don't know what to do with it.

'I know,' says Rohit. 'Here's a good place.' He holds the cigarette two centimetres away from Rory's arm. Rory feels his powerlessness like a suffocating weight on his chest. He clamps his teeth together, determined not to cry, not prepared to beg for mercy, and watches the cigarette quivering over his skin, getting closer and closer—

'James! William! Where are you?'

Heads appear over the banks of pebbles. Mothers are advancing in waterproof coats, scarves, hair streaming behind them, curls swept over faces by the wind.

One of them – Rory recognises her as Richard's mother – rushes down the slope towards them, struggling to keep her balance. 'Why did you scuttle off like that?' she's calling. 'We're just going home for tea.'

Rory can feel William's grasp on his arm relaxing. He pulls himself away and doesn't encounter any resistance. Rohit drops the cigarette on the beach and kicks stones over it. The box of matches has disappeared into his pocket.

Rory runs.

As he passes Richard's mother, he hears her calling, 'Hello, Rory! How's your mother?'

But he doesn't intend to answer. He's clambering up the stones to the path at the top, pushing himself forwards even as his feet slip backwards, then flying into the wind, back home, away from his broken bicycle.

Chapter 18

The wallpaper is yellow, embossed with huge swirls of flowers in purple flock, surely designed for function rooms in hotels or pubs. Kate can't understand why her predecessors would consider it suitable for a living room in a small council flat, but she's decided to leave it in place since it's in reasonably good condition. The clock is ticking louder than usual, a harsh, insistent rhythm, the boom of a magnified pulse, the tapping of high heels as a woman walks past the house. Not the footsteps of a small boy who is late, who wouldn't make walking sounds anyway because he should be on his bike.

Is this her destiny? To be perpetually waiting for someone who will never come home again? One by one, her family could disappear, simply not turn up one day, and she'll be left sitting here for ever, wondering where they all went.

She stares at the print of Lawren Harris's *Above Lake Superior* in front of her. The branches of the bare birches rise up through the snow, round and polished as they catch the light. She needs words to describe his technique but all she can see is the bleak dark mountain in the background.

A key scrapes in the front-door lock.

She leaps to her feet, runs down the stairs and meets Rory as he steps in. His pinched face stares up at her, his eyes pink and puffy, as if he's holding back tears.

'Where have you been?' She expects him to offer an explanation, to cry, or at least look pleased to see her, but he shrugs and pushes past her.

'I'm starving,' he says. He runs up the stairs, his feet clattering on the uncarpeted steps.

'Rory, your shoes,' she says. 'Take them off.'

He ignores her.

She steps outside and peers around nervously, hoping that Irene from downstairs can't see her. She walks down the garden path in her bare feet, assuming Rory's left his bike on the road, but there's no sign of it.

She goes back in and shuts the door. 'Rory!' she calls.

There's no reply.

'Rory!' She runs up the stairs. He usually heads for the kitchen straight after school, desperate for biscuits or crisps, but he's not there today. She finds him sitting on the bed in his room, leaning against the wall and concentrating on his Nintendo. He doesn't acknowledge her.

She bends down to pick up his shoes and a pair of discarded trousers. There's barely room to turn round, and every inch of space needs to be used wisely. She folds the trousers and squeezes them into an already overflowing drawer, but there's nowhere for the shoes except under the bed, so she eases them there with her foot. 'What's happened, Rory?'

He continues to press buttons, absorbed in his game, behaving as if she's not there.

'The bike, Rory. Where's your bike?'

He still doesn't answer.

She leans over and takes the Nintendo away from him with one quick movement, before he has time to resist. She puts her face close to his and speaks slowly and clearly. 'Where is your bike?'

He tries to turn away, but she's too close and won't let him. He mumbles something.

'What? I can't hear you.'

'I was mugged,' he says.

'Mugged?' she repeats, trying to grasp the word and make sense of it. She sits down abruptly on the bed next to him, afraid to touch him in case he's injured. 'Did they hurt you?'

'No, of course not,' he says.

He seems so unconcerned. It must be shock. 'So what happened?'

'Nothing.'

'What do you mean, nothing? Mugging isn't nothing. Tell me exactly what happened.' She wants to shake him, squeeze the information out of him, but it's clear that she needs to tread more cautiously.

She can see people in the flats opposite, a window propped open with a box of cat food, curtains billowing out through the gap, tellies flickering. A powerful beat blasts out from a downstairs flat, the bass turned up so high it's impossible to hear a tune.

'It was just some kids,' he says. 'They said they'd break my arm if I didn't give them the bike, so I gave it to them.'

'What kids? Who were they?'

He shrugs again. 'I don't know. I've never met them before.'

Why is he so calm, so accepting? 'We'll have to go to the police.'

His face crumples. 'I couldn't help it,' he says. 'There were too many of them.'

She puts an arm round him, hoping he'll give in and cry. 'I'm sorry, Rory. I wish I could have prevented it.' But although he tolerates her, he remains rigid and unresponsive.

'We could go and look for it,' he says, pulling away. 'They might have just used it for a bit and then left it.'

'I don't think that's very likely, Rory.'

'Why not? It could just be lying around.'

'Where were you when they took it?'

'By the beach.'

She's about to ask why he went that way when she remembers the day when she'd driven past his old school by mistake and forgotten that everyone would be coming out. She recalls her burning embarrassment, her fear of examining faces in car windows in case she recognised someone looking back.

Why should she have felt ashamed? It wasn't her fault or her children's fault. It was all down to Felix. But she'd married him, they would say, she'd allowed him to do this thing, even if she hadn't known anything about it. She was condemned by association.

Rory knows why she goes the long way round. He has that same fear of being seen. It's not right. He's only a child. I haven't protected him enough.

Kate's hands tingle with the desire to hit out at Felix's absent body. How could he have done this – made his own son frightened of being seen by former friends? She wants to save Rory from the fear, pass over some of her own strength, assure him that everything is all right, but he's refusing to allow her to express any sympathy.

'OK,' she says. 'There's plenty of time before we pick up Millie. Let's drive down to the sea front.' She needs to prepare him for disappointment. 'But we probably won't find it.'

They manage to locate a parking space on the hill overlooking the beach and Kate starts to reverse into it.

'You're too far over,' says Rory.

'I'm fine,' she says. Her back wheel touches the kerb and she has to come out again.

'You turned the steering-wheel too soon,' says Rory.

'Thanks for the advice, Mr Lewis Hamilton.'

But once they've parked, he shrivels into his seat, not wanting to move. 'Can't I stay here?'

'Don't be ridiculous. You need to show me where it happened.' His eyelids flicker and his mouth sets in a taut, unnatural line. 'Look,' she says, 'it'll be fine. You're with me.'

He gets out reluctantly, his eyes swivelling as he examines every small movement with a heightened alertness. They walk down the hill together. Rory keeps in step with her, unnaturally close.

'If we can't find it,' she says, 'we'll go to the police station. Could you describe the boys?'

A flash of fear jumps across his face, but it's replaced almost immediately by a closed, dull expression. 'No,' he mutters. 'I didn't see them properly.'

They're reaching the point where the road levels out and diverts to the right, away from the sea front, heading for the shops. Kate stops and looks across the beach. Two women are walking together with their dogs, trudging over the pebbles with grim perseverance, not talking. A family close to the edge of the water is having a stone-throwing competition. The air is heavy with salt. She turns in the direction of the shops.

And there it is, leaning against a lamp-post.

'Look, Rory!' she says. 'Isn't that your bike?'

He's already seen it. He's standing with his back to the beach, his face softened with relief. They walk over to examine it.

She has a moment of doubt. All bikes look the same to her. 'It is yours, isn't it, Rory?'

He nods. 'It's got a puncture,' he says.

'That must be why they left it here. Lucky for us.'

He's still watching, tense and uneasy, examining passing faces, distracted by each passing car. Kate wants to reassure him, so she rotates through a slow 360 degrees, searching for groups of youths, anyone who looks threatening. But they're all old people, solitary schoolchildren walking home, families.

'No aliens,' she says. 'Or if there are, you can't see them.'

He's not amused. 'Ha ha,' he says.

They walk back up the hill with the bike, the damaged tyre flapping on the pavement. 'I hope we can get it into the car,' she says.

She's driving her father's old, neglected Fiesta, which they rescued from his garage. He paid to have it serviced. The boot isn't big enough, so they have to leave it open with one bicycle wheel dangling out. 'It'll be all right,' says Kate. 'It's not far.'

'Let's hope a police car doesn't spot us,' says Rory.

She looks at her watch. It's later than she'd thought. 'We have to get this home before picking up Millie,' she says.

'Of course Millie can stay,' said Mrs Harper, the headmistress of Millie's school, when Kate went to speak to her armed with a list of convincing arguments. 'We're all very fond of her.'

'But what about the money?'

'You mustn't worry about that. We have plenty of schemes and I'm sure we can sort things out. Just leave it to us.' She's a big woman with wild hair that refuses to lie down, and she talks very fast, using her hands to emphasise her thoughts. Visual aids in case you're having trouble keeping up.

'But aren't your foundation places already taken?'

Mrs Harper dismissed Kate's concerns with airy confidence. 'Then she can stay here for free. I'll authorise it.'

Kate was appalled to find that her eyes were watering. She mustn't cry. She gave up crying a long time ago. 'Thank you,' she said. 'Thank you so much.' She wanted to go on saying thank you, but realised there had to be a limit or she would become irritating. Mrs Harper didn't make her feel like the wife of a criminal – in fact, she didn't even mention Felix.

But did she understand all the implications? 'Won't there be complaints?'

'From whom?'

'Other parents. They might not be very pleased.'

Mrs Harper looked at her with a genuine astonishment. 'What does it have to do with them? They won't know that Millie's getting assistance.'

'It's not that. It's just that my husband—'

Mrs Harper laid a hand on her arm. 'My dear, it's not your fault and it's certainly not Millie's fault. We wouldn't dream of penalising a child for the actions of a parent.'

Kate didn't know how to respond. She hadn't expected such kindness after the trauma of going to Rory's school. 'Thank you,' she said. 'Thank you.'

'Actually,' said Mrs Harper, leaning forward slightly, 'we once had the daughter of a murderer here. Nobody knew, of course. Not even most of the staff. He went to prison for twenty years and the grandparents paid the fees.'

Millie has apparently never considered that her school would react like Rory's school. She's carried on in her normal way, as far as Kate can tell, often preoccupied but following her routines without fuss. She doesn't invite friends round any more, but that's hardly surprising, since the flat is so small. She stays late at school instead, even when there aren't any activities.

She doesn't talk as much as she used to. She used to chatter to Kate all the time, but she's become vague and rarely volunteers any information about her life. Kate misses the warmth of their old relationship and wonders if she should contact the school to ask if she's coping with her work. But it's a fine balance between showing an interest and interfering. She's waiting for something, although she's not sure what. Changing traffic-lights, a road sign, a flashing indicator that will tell her which way to turn so that she can follow Millie into her private world.

Sometimes the three of them squeeze round their tiny table for supper in complete silence, each strolling through a private landscape. They only seem to be shaken out of their separateness by conflict.

'Mum – Millie kicked me.'

'No, I didn't.'

'Yes, you did.'

'Try to keep your feet still,' says Kate. 'There isn't much room.'

'Duh!' says Millie. 'I would never have noticed.'

Kate sighs. The kitchen is too small for a table and chairs, but they have to sit down together somewhere and moving the table into the living room would make it unbearably overcrowded. 'Just try to show some consideration for each other,' she says. 'We won't be here for ever.'

Millie snorts. 'I don't think Rory knows what consideration is.'

Kate looks up at the framed prints of the Group of Seven that she's put on the wall above the fridge. MacDonald's *Stormy Weather, Georgian Bay* and Harris's *Above Lake Superior*. There's such strength in the landscapes, their ability to capture something enormous and powerful. Squabbles round the kitchen table seem so insignificant.

'What's for pudding?' says Rory.

'An apple.'

He groans. 'Why can't we have proper puddings any more?'

'It's not good for you. You have to eat more fruit.' And because she can't afford any extras. She's determined to be self-sufficient.

'Pigs eat apples,' said Rory. 'We're not pigs.'

'Don't be ridiculous,' says Kate. 'Everyone eats apples. They're designed for human consumption.'

'How do you know that?' says Millie. 'About pigs.'

'Everyone knows it. They take all the rotting apples and feed them to the pigs.'

'Not any more,' says Millie. 'Any food that goes past its sell-by date has to be destroyed. It's food hygiene.'

'You don't know everything,' says Rory. 'You just think you do.' He stands up and pushes his chair back. It catches the edge of the fridge and threatens to fall over. Kate saves it just in time.

'Anyway, pigs eat anything,' says Millie. 'What does that prove?'

Most of their furniture was too big for the flat. Everything they took with them had been dictated by size and the rest was sold. A second-hand dealer – specialising in house clearances, it said in the *Yellow Pages* – had arrived in a rusty truck, rung the doorbell for longer than necessary, shaken hands with her and gazed round the hall with bright, eager eyes. 'You want everything to go?' he asked.

'No,' said Kate, 'but most of it.' Did he know? Had he seen the house on the news, viewed through the lens of a camera, framed by the locked gates?

They went round each room while he made a list on a small pad. He was shorter than Kate, with greasy hair that was slicked back with no parting and gathered at the base of his neck into a bunch of curls. She glanced over his shoulder as he wrote. He couldn't spell. He mixed capitals with lower-case and pressed too hard with his biro, so the indentation went through to the next page.

'Hmm,' he remarked occasionally. 'Nice sofa.'

It cost me two thousand pounds, says Felix's voice behind her. *It jolly well ought to be nice.*

White leather, three-seater, perfect in front of the bay window in the study. Cool, stylish and deliciously comfortable. Kate used to sink into it after a tiring day in the garden. Sometimes Felix would have to work during the weekend and she liked to watch him at his desk, the late-afternoon sun slanting in behind her, warming the back of her head. The light washed through the room, softening the oak of the desk, drawing a polished glow out of the wooden floor, bleaching the red dahlias in the curtains. Felix would continue working but look up and smile at her every now and again, not minding that she was interrupting his work.

Turning a blind eye, presumably.

'How much is the sofa worth?' she asked the second-hand dealer.

Don't let him give you less than a grand. It's worth more, even second-hand.

'I'll send you an overall assessment,' he says. 'I never quote for individual items.'

The offer, when it arrived in the post, seemed far too low, but there wasn't much time and Kate couldn't summon the energy to negotiate. She accepted it anyway and didn't tell her father, who would have been outraged.

There was so much furniture. She tried to decide if anything had sentimental value, but she found she wanted to cling to all of it, everything too precious to lose. Her memory echoed with moments of acquisition, the discovery of rustic second-hand kitchen chairs, tables, swathes of glorious curtains, ornate beds. They're congregated in a huge mental warehouse, stuffed with significance. She could remember buying every item with Felix. They'd travelled round in the early days, with Lawrence strapped into the back of the car, searching for antiques shops, going to auctions, visiting all the local showrooms. They didn't worry about consistency of style.

'Eclectic is fine,' Felix reassured her. 'Everyone does it now. You have what you like, what's comfortable, and let them blend in together.'

She had loved the deliveries, the men who arrived in lorries and carried everything into the house with such ease. Some even took their shoes off or covered their boots with little plastic bags. They were nearly always cheerful, lifting with a strength and technique that she admired.

'Would it be possible to take it upstairs?' she would say, and be amazed at their willingness. She made them cups of tea, which they drank quickly, never apparently burning their tongues, before offering her their forms to sign.

The artwork and antiques went to auction and Kate has saved the money in a separate account. It's for a rainy day, she thinks, remembering her parents' lessons in thrift, their desire to anticipate emergencies. It's becoming apparent that there will be quite a few emergencies. Bicycles stolen, windscreen wipers disappearing off the car overnight, a school trip to the Eden Project.

She decided to keep a few things – a small eighteenth-century walnut table, a mahogany cabinet, Millie's art-deco dressing-table and a few pictures. She thought that familiar pictures on the walls of the flat might make them feel more comfortable. Give them a sense of continuity.

She worked so hard at the beginning, getting the carpets up, hauling them downstairs to the hired skip, with advice from Millie and hindrance from Rory as he found the prospect of rolled-up carpets irresistible and spent much of his time leaping over them and getting in the way. Most of the help came from Sian and Edward, who came kitted out in their oldest and shabbiest jeans and T-shirts to help with the lifting. Kate has polished the dark vinyl floor tiles and bought cheerful mats from Ikea. She's scraped off wallpaper, sanded woodwork, painted, emulsioned. She consulted with Millie and Rory about the colours for their rooms and helped them decide what they would like to keep from the old house.

She's pleased with all her work. The flat is now clean and cosy. It's hers and everything in it belongs to her.

It's the space she misses, the ability to walk in a straight line without having to be careful about bumping into something. Wealth means that you can pay for emptiness and the understanding that no one will encroach upon your privacy. The yardstick for measuring a person's affluence is how many square feet of empty space he possesses. The ultimate goal is nothingness.

Their neighbour downstairs is a small blonde woman with a high-pitched voice. She knocked on Kate's door the day after they moved in.

'Hello,' she said. 'My name's Irene.'

'Hello,' said Kate, wondering if she was supposed to invite her in, but worried about the state of the flat. 'I'm Kate.'

'Where are you from?'

'Oh – Budleigh,' said Kate, vaguely. 'But further over.'

'Towards Sandy Bay?'

'Mmm.'

'My sister lives over there – Jasmine Avenue. Do you know it?'

'Yes,' said Kate, although she didn't. She needed to change the subject. 'Have you lived here long?'

Irene rolled her eyes. They were pale blue and surrounded by thick black mascara. 'No way. It's just a dumping ground for the council. They only use the estate for urgent cases. You know, asylum seekers, homeless people, things like that.' She studied Kate with an uncomfortable intensity. 'Your flat's privately rented, isn't it? Can't think why you'd want to come here.'

Kate felt she ought to be evasive, but couldn't think of a plausible explanation. 'My house was repossessed.'

Irene put a hand on her arm. 'You poor thing,' she said. Her voice dropped a few tones, softened by a compassion she couldn't possibly feel since they'd only just met.

Kate was embarrassed. 'Oh, it's all right – we'll be moving again soon, once the money's sorted out.'

'That's what they all say. Where's your husband?'

'We're separated.' It sounded like a lie.

'I'm here because my boyfriend got into trouble. Drugs. They did a dawn raid. Four o'clock in the morning, there I am all tucked up and cosy in my bed, and I wake up to find three dirty great policemen in riot gear standing there looking down at me. They ripped up all the floorboards and made it uninhabitable so we had to move out.'

'Goodness,' said Kate. These were events you watched on the news or documentaries, not what you expected from people who lived below you.

'Serves him right. I kept telling him, but you know what men are like. They always know best.'

'It seems a bit hard on you.'

'Oh, we'll be gone in no time. We're lucky – my daughter's got asthma, so we've got lots of points. The flats are damp, you know.'

Kate had a vision of walls running with water. More black mould, ceilings falling in.

'Only,' said Irene, 'you haven't got any carpet on the stairs.'

'No,' said Kate. There hadn't seemed much point in replacing the existing carpets, so she'd varnished the steps instead. Hopefully, they wouldn't be here for long . . .

'It's the baby, you see, he's only three months, wakes up all the time. Slightest noise and he's off, bawling the place down.'

It took Kate a few seconds to understand that Irene was complaining about the noise. 'Oh,' she said. 'I see. I'll ask the children to take their shoes off when they come in.'

'Great,' said Irene. She didn't show much interest in leaving.

'Well,' said Kate, 'I'll have to get on.' She closed the door slowly, wanting to be firm, but unwilling to appear unfriendly.

'You were so patronising,' said Millie, from the top of the stairs.

'Was I? I didn't mean to be.'

'You don't have to mean it. It just comes over that way.'

Irene has proved to be a problem. She wants to stand around and talk about babies and errant husbands and irritating neighbours. It's very difficult to get away from her. The best strategy is to avoid her in the first place.

Kate, Millie and Rory walk in single file along the river Otter. When they're at home, it's too easy to disappear into their separate rooms and think isolated thoughts. It's a sunny day. Walks are free. It should be an opportunity to relax and start to talk again. It's not working.

'Do we have to go?' said Millie, when Kate told them her plan at breakfast.

'Yes,' said Kate.

'But I've got things to do.'

'Do them when we get back.'

Millie scowled at her bowl of Frosties. 'I have too much homework for this sort of thing.'

'It's called relaxation. Nobody works all day non-stop.'

'Can I take my bike?' said Rory.

'No, of course not. We're going for a walk.'

A tight, sullen atmosphere descended.

They often used to come on this walk in the past. She can remember a particularly good day when Lawrence was about seven, just before she became pregnant with Millie.

The sky had been an intense, unbroken blue, stretching from horizon to horizon without a blemish. On the opposite side of the river, trees projected their image onto the water so perfectly that, if the world was turned upside down, no one would ever know the reflection wasn't the reality. They walked along a narrow path, Felix and Kate squeezed together, holding hands, Lawrence leaping ahead with inexhaustible energy. Long grassheads, heavy with seeds, swished around them, interspersed with bright cornflowers and pungent white clusters of hedge-parsley. Bees droned in the background, while lacy strands from dandelion clocks drifted in the still air around them.

Lawrence was fascinated by a stile. He climbed backwards and forwards over it several times until an elderly couple approached and he had to get out of the way. The woman smiled at him and he ran shyly back to Felix and Kate. At the edge of a field, they flopped down into the long grass and watched the river. The water moved slowly, the surface smooth and heavy as it dragged itself along in the heat.

'Can I have a drink?' said Lawrence.

Felix took off his backpack and handed him a bottle of orange squash. Lawrence gulped a few mouthfuls and gave it back. He wandered over to the side of the river.

'Careful,' called Kate.

'All right, Mummy,' he said.

'He'll be fine,' said Felix. 'We have to trust him a little,' but he propped his head on an arm and watched him.

Kate lay back and looked up at the sky. The way it went on and on and on. She leaned her head against the side of Felix's chest, feeling his ribs through the shirt, the slight dampness of sweat in the cotton under her cheek. He reached over and put his hand very gently on her chest, placing his thumb in the hollow at the base of her neck. He rubbed his fingers gently over the soft skin where the first swell of her breast was exposed above her T-shirt. A warm thrill swept through her, but somehow the fact that they couldn't do any more than this in public didn't matter. There was a sense of perfection, of being held in his hand and savoured. The rays of the sun enclosed them, bathing them in liquid heat. They both knew that they would have to wait until later, much later, when they had returned home and Lawrence had gone to bed. The delay simply heightened the sense of pleasure.

They lay there together, and Kate was conscious of a deep contentment. It was an exquisite moment that she would never lose, whatever might happen in the future. She turned her head and saw that Felix was still watching Lawrence, perpetually alert for danger, but willing to allow a perception of freedom.

She has always believed that Millie was conceived later that night. An intended consequence of love.

Millie and Rory are striding ahead of Kate, presumably with the hope that if they go far enough as quickly as possible they can turn round and come back sooner. There is no attempt at communication. Every comment from Kate is met with stubborn silence.

'Look, you can see the fish.' A silvery flash below the surface of the water.

'Can we go home yet?' says Rory.

'No, we've come for a walk and we've only just got here.'

'Only old people go for walks.'

It's true. Everyone they meet is over fifty, brown and weathered by years of exposure to the sun. They're experienced walkers in boots and parkas.

Rory picks up a stick and starts swishing it around.

Millie shrieks. 'Mum – he's trying to kill me.'

'Don't be ridiculous,' says Kate. 'Of course he's not.'

Rory swipes at Millie, his stick dangerously close to her face.

Millie tries to grab it and they fall to the ground, wrestling with furious energy. They shriek with genuine or imagined pain.

A man walks past with his dog. He looks at them with distaste.

'Be quiet,' says Kate. 'You're disturbing the peace.'

'Who cares about stupid peace?' says Rory, and runs towards the river, still brandishing his stick.

'Be careful, Rory,' shouts Kate.

She thinks again of that idyllic time with Felix. It was all so perfect. It had seemed real.

Then she realises what she's doing. She's watching the family through a lit window. Felix was fixated by images of a world that had become idealised in his mind, envying something he didn't have. Now she's viewing her life with him as a single moment, a picture of happiness that couldn't have been real. The whole scene was an elaborate tableau, constructed by Felix. He never was what she'd thought he was.

'Mum!' screams Millie. 'Rory's fallen in.'

'No, I haven't,' says Rory. 'Anyway, it's only up to my knees.'

Chapter 19

Millie likes Latin. The rhythm of the words, the way you can chant them out loud or in your head. *Amo, amas, amat, amamus, amatis, amant.* I love, you love, he loves, we love, you love, they love. Everybody loves, apparently. They did *amare* months ago, of course – it's prepositions today, the accusative case – but *amare* remains Millie's favourite.

Does Samantha love her boyfriend? Does he love her? He waits for her every Thursday by the swimming-pool, lounging against the wall, holding his jacket nonchalantly over his shoulder. Millie has watched him waiting and admired the shape he makes, the long lean legs crossed with such casual elegance. His hair is unusually black – from behind you might think he's Indian or Chinese – and he always looks as if he's forgotten to shave.

His name is Crispin. Exactly the right name. A real man. He's in the sixth form at Merchant Venturers' School for Boys, just up the road from Hillyard's.

Her father's face used to develop a similar shadow by the end of the day. He would sometimes shave for a second time if he was going out for the evening. She can remember the prickles against her cheek when he kissed her, the abrasive sting— Her stomach twists and she feels briefly sick. Samantha's boyfriend is not like her father.

'They don't do Latin at my brother's school,' says a voice behind her, as they come out of the classroom. 'I don't see why we have to.'

'Nor me,' says another voice. 'It's a dead language. What's the point if nobody speaks it?'

'We should be doing Mandarin. That's what my dad says.'

It's Helen and Esther. For a moment, Millie forgets she isn't friends with them any more and turns round. 'Latin's all right,' she says. 'It's only like learning to recite poetry.'

They stop, surprise interrupting their conversation. Then a beaming smile transforms Helen's face. 'You're right,' she says. 'I hadn't thought of it like that.'

Esther pushes past them, her shoulder brushing against Millie's arm, her head tilted upwards slightly so that she has to look down her nose to see where she's going. All she needs to do now is toss her hair.

There's an awkward silence while they stare at each other. It's not clear if Helen is smiling because she agrees with the comparison of Latin with poetry, or because Millie has spoken to her. Then, aware that she has broken her self-imposed rule of non-communication, Millie turns away and runs off down the corridor. Why did she speak to them? It must have been because she was thinking about her father.

They wouldn't understand. If she starts to talk to them again, Helen will ask her questions, penetrate the private rooms inside her head that she's carefully organised and doesn't want to share with anyone. And, anyway, they believe things about her father that aren't true.

Although perhaps they are true . . .

She doesn't want to think about it. Instead, she pictures Crispin walking to his rendezvous with Samantha in the soft light of late afternoon, the sun behind him. Black curls spiral over his head, tight and wiry. He walks with a comfortable confidence, dropping an arm over Samantha's shoulders. There's something so easy about him, the way he moves, as if he's been walking through the world for ever.

Millie rearranges herself on the grass and stretches her legs out in front of her, wiggling her toes to relieve the pins and needles. Her blazer is stuffed into the bag at her side and she's wearing a navy jumper over her school blouse so that she won't be easily recognised. Her aim is invisibility, to blend into the background. She's holding a 3B pencil and every now and again she makes little strokes on the pad resting on her knees. She's pretending to sketch the cathedral, but she's actually waiting to see Samantha and Crispin. Occasionally, she becomes interested in her drawing – she's good at art – and bends her head to shade in a shadow, or outline the curve of a window.

Samantha and Crispin meet here on Mondays. Millie knows their patterns. Dates, times, movements, all listed in her notebook. They follow the same routines every week and she's started to wonder why they don't get bored. But she doesn't mind too much. She's learning.

She can see them now, strolling along hand in hand. Samantha's hair is tied back in a loose pony-tail, but she's arranged it so that wisps hang down the side of her face, all gentle and ethereal.

'Ethereal'. A good word. Millie jots it down in her notebook. She's conscious of her own red hair, all spikes and corkscrews, spitting and fizzing. She should have brought a hat.

Samantha's wearing a low-cut T-shirt, white and close-fitting, which says 'PRESS HERE TO TURN ON' across the front. Millie is a bit dubious about that T-shirt and she's fighting the suspicion that it's not in very good taste. Her dad – her mum wouldn't approve. But this is Samantha. She must know what she's doing.

They seem to be talking all the time. What do they talk about? They're coming closer. Millie usually watches them for a short while before getting up, checking her watch in an obvious manner, as if it's time to catch her bus, then walks behind them at a discreet distance. She likes to follow them round the shops, making a note of what they buy.

They stop abruptly, right in the middle of the path, and he takes her chin in his hand, turning her face towards his. They're kissing! Millie feels as if she should be looking the other way, but she can't take her eyes off them. Then something happens. Samantha rises on the tips of her toes, and raises her arms into the air, holding them up like a bird soaring into the wind.

Millie's seen that gesture before. Her mother used to kiss her father like that. Often. In the garden, in the kitchen when they thought they were on their own, occasionally when they were out, once on the beach at Exmouth as they stood in the shallows in their swimming costumes, pretending to watch Rory swim.

A hammer slams into Millie's heart. She doesn't want to see this. There's a hard, persistent thumping in her ears, a red film in front of her eyes. She gathers her things together, her hands shaking, and stuffs them into her bag. *Amo, amas, amat . . .* Wrong verb. She needs another. Something more suitable. What's the Latin for 'I walk, you walk, he walks'? *Promenado? Strollo?*

'Millie!'

Aghast, she looks up and Samantha and Crispin are above her, only three metres away. She scrambles to her feet, dropping her sketchpad, bending down to pick it up, staring at their legs.

'What are you doing here, Millie?'

'I – I was sketching.' She gestures towards her pad, unable to meet their eyes.

'Every week?' says Crispin. His voice is dark, like his hair, and much lower than she expected. 'How long does it take to draw a cathedral? Let me see.'

'No,' she says. 'It's not good enough, I have to keep trying, that's why I keep coming.' She knows she doesn't sound convincing, but she hasn't prepared a proper cover story. It's never crossed her mind that she's been spotted.

'Are you following us?' Samantha's voice is quiet, but warmer than Crispin's, faintly amused.

'No, of course not.' She can feel herself going hot all over, and still can't face them, certain that the heat is radiating out towards them, proof of her guilt.

Crispin bends down towards her and she finally raises her eyes. There are spots on his chin, tiny red dots among the black hairs, which she's not been close enough to observe before. 'I don't want to see you, ever again. Do you understand me?'

Millie nods.

'Scram!' he says, loudly and suddenly, making her jump.

She runs as fast as she can, conscious of their eyes following her, choking on the tears that pour down her cheeks in thick, salty torrents.

She can hear them laughing behind her.

'Where in the world have you been?'

Her mother is standing at the top of the stairs, gazing down at Millie as she comes through the front door.

'Karishma invited me back to her house,' she says, struggling to make her voice casual. 'I didn't have anything to eat, though. We just did a bit of homework. It's a project . . .' Her voice tails off.

'Did you forget?'

Millie runs through all the possibilities in her mind and can't work out what she is supposed to have forgotten. 'What?'

'We're going to Grandad and Grandma's for tea.'

'Oh, yes.' Millie can't remember being told this, but she doesn't take much notice of anything her mother says these days – it's all moaning and fussing – so it's quite possible she wasn't listening at the crucial moment. 'Sorry.'

Rory and her mother are coming down the stairs. 'Leave

your bag there at the bottom. We'll have to go straight off. You know they worry if we're late.'

They step out of the front door and her mother glances nervously around. 'Quick,' she mutters. 'She's coming.'

Irene's front door is opening. They walk very fast down the pathway.

'Can I sit in the front?' says Rory.

'No,' says Millie. 'It's my turn.' In her opinion, she should always sit in the front. She's older and she's the girl, and it's undignified climbing into the back.

'Please don't argue,' says their mother. 'We'll get caught.'

They can hear footsteps. Millie decides it would be advisable to climb quickly into the back for once. At least if Irene reaches them before they leave, she won't have to join in the conversation. But Rory must have reached the same conclusion. He clicks the seat forward and jumps in while their mother dashes round to the driving seat. She starts the engine immediately and turns the steering-wheel.

'Wave,' says their mother. 'Look friendly, not as if you're escaping.'

Irene is standing on the edge of the path, holding her baby in one arm and gesturing with the other as if she has something important to say. Her mouth is moving up and down.

'I reckon she talks all the time,' says Millie, 'even when she's on her own.'

'Drive,' says Rory. 'Drive.'

'Our flat is like yours,' says Rory. 'You have to go up the stairs to get in.'

'So I've heard,' says Grandad.

'It's not exactly the same,' says Millie. 'Ours is disgusting.'

She's standing by the big window in the living room, watching the muddy water lapping against the sides of the moored boats. There are people on one boat, a man and a woman, standing together but not looking at each other. They seem annoyed. She rather hopes that he'll tip her over the edge and she'll be the only witness of a murder.

It'll be all right, she decides. I'll just have to be more discreet in future and not let Crispin see me. I can do it. I'm an expert at invisibility.

'Supper will be ready in a moment,' says Grandma. There's a big table in the living room behind the semi-circle of chairs. 'Can you lay the table for me, Millie?'

'I don't see why Rory can't help,' she says.

'Millie,' says her mother. 'Please . . .'

Millie takes the knives and forks from her grandmother and starts to place them on the table. Her mother is sitting back in a chair, her legs stretched out and her eyes half closed. She doesn't look much like a woman who used to kiss her husband. Millie tries to imagine her lifting her arms softly into the air now, and it seems impossible. Her mother is solid, old, grumpy, a different mother from the one she used to know. She doesn't bother to put on makeup any more. Not that she ever did very often, but occasionally she would dress up, become glamorous for a particular event. Now she wears the same clothes every day for a week. She doesn't show any interest in anything important.

'So, how's school, Amelia?' says her grandad.

'Great,' says Millie. 'Great.'

'Good,' he says, as if she's told him something new or unusual. He was a headmaster once: he should know how to talk to schoolchildren. But he seems to have forgotten how to do it.

'I'm in the football team,' says Rory.

'They have a football team in your school?'

'Why shouldn't they?'

'Well, I just thought . . .'

'Rory's school is very good,' says Millie's mother, her voice hard and edgy. 'You'd be surprised by how much sport they do.'

'Don't suppose they play rugby, though.'

'There's more to life than rugby.'

'Supper's ready,' called her grandma, bringing in two plates, already dished out, her hands protected from the heat with tea towels. 'Come and sit down.' She goes back for the rest.

Millie's grandma buys ready-meals from Marks & Spencer and heats them up in the microwave. Millie is interested in this. It seems so much easier than peeling potatoes, steaming up the kitchen with cauliflower, cutting up disgusting pieces of raw dead creatures. 'We should have meals like this,' she says.

'I don't think so,' says her mother.

'They're very healthy,' says her grandmother. 'No hydrogenated fats or anything like that.'

'Maybe,' says her mother. 'But they're extremely expensive.'

It's the same old story. They can't afford it. Of course. She watches her grandfather ease himself out of his chair and limp over to the dinner table, his slippers shuffling over the carpet to his seat. He lowers himself as if it's really painful. He's probably exaggerating. It can't hurt that much just to sit down. He wants their sympathy. He's like Rory when he falls over and you'd think it was the end of the world.

Millie is seized by the desire to do something terrible, like pushing her grandfather over, pulling off the tablecloth, screaming at the top of her voice. Everyone starts eating, not talking any more, concentrating on chewing and swallowing. She can hear teeth clicking, the slurp of saliva mixing with the food in their mouths. The whole process of eating is so degenerate.

She looks down at her plate and very slowly lifts the fork, placing it in her mouth with the utmost care.

Chapter 20

When Kate's alarm goes off at half past five, she's already awake, lying there waiting for the measured tones of Radio 4 to signal the time. Sleep has become an elusive stranger. Sometimes she sinks down into that preliminary world of semi-sleep, where her limbs go heavy and she can feel the weight of imminent unconsciousness pushing her down. Her thoughts lose their intensity and begin to drift. But then there's a sudden drop, as if she's stepped down further than she expected, and her mind leaps back to attention. Chattering voices in her head, endless debates with herself.

Rory has nightmares every few nights, usually at the moment when she has just managed to doze off, and she has to grope her way through the darkness to soothe him.

'Bodies – ' he whispers. 'Long hair – on the beach – '

It makes a diversion, sitting with him until he settles back to sleep.

She's planning the next chapter of her thesis. *Georgian Bay, Source of Inspiration*. There are so many paintings of the bay that she can easily fill a chapter with comparisons. Working out the order of her points, thinking logically, calms her.

The dawn is a relief. It gives her a point of reference, an indication that it's all right to be awake. Getting up is easy.

She slips out of bed, pulls on the candy-pink polyester overalls and clips back the strands of hair that overhang her face. She avoids looking into the mirror. Then she pads down the stairs in slippers, changes into her shoes at the bottom, and goes out of the front door.

She likes being on her own at this hour. Everything is still, the sky washed and empty. It's chilly, even in July, but it's a refreshing sharpness, a zip in the air.

She gets into her car as quickly as possible, shutting the door in one clean, firm movement, hoping that no one is awake to hear. Sometimes, glancing back, she can see Irene through an opened curtain in her living room, holding the baby, standing at the window watching, her mouth miraculously closed. Kate is ashamed that she can never remember if the child is a boy or a girl. It seems to be perpetually awake, crying, grizzling, whining, in training for a lifetime of talking like its mother. They're both wired for communication that is not communication, the capacity to extract pleasure from the sound of their own voices.

It takes her ten minutes to reach the factory, a large Victorian building situated between a nursery and a council-run home for children. She unlocks the front door and punches in the code for the burglar alarm. The cleaning equipment is stored in a cupboard under the stairs and she has to carry it up to the offices on the third floor, where maids would once have lived. Each room is individually shaped with sloping ceilings, eccentric alcoves and blocked-off fireplaces, reminders of the building's respectable past. The heavy aroma of chocolate rises up through the building, even after a night of non-production, permeating every corner, every carpet, every speck of dust.

Mr Addenbrooke – 'Call me Trevor' – had given her the history of Horton's Chocolates during her interview. 'Founded in 1932. We export all over the world, even to Belgium,' he said. 'If you want quality hand-made chocolates, this is the place to come.' He's not part of the original family who founded the firm. He took over as managing director three years ago, after the last surviving member of the Horton family had died in a tragic accident involving a bus and a wedding limousine, but he's very hands-on and clearly loves his job.

'So, what experience do you have?' he asked her.

She had never been for a job interview in her life. She'd married Felix as soon as she'd finished university and had cheerfully become a housewife. She didn't know about CVs, references, previous experience. 'Well,' she said, realising she had no chance of getting this job, 'I clean my own house, of course – is it very different?'

Mr Addenbrooke leant back in his chair and roared with laughter. He was wearing an electric blue bow-tie, which jiggled up and down as he laughed. 'No, Kate, that's not the way to do interviews. You're supposed to impress me.'

His desk was cluttered with piles of papers and files, overflowing in-boxes and out-boxes, leftover crusts of pasties, cakes, sandwiches. There was an array of half-finished mugs of coffee with slogans on the side. *Trevor's Mug*, *Mummy's Little Helper*, *Who's a Clever Boy, Then?*.

It was a parallel world, existing alongside Kate's old life, which she hadn't known about until now. 'I'm a quick learner,' she said, hearing the desperation in her voice. 'I can pick things up – I'm doing an MA in art history.'

He stopped laughing and studied her with more interest. 'I'd have done art if my father had let me. What's the subject of your thesis?'

Kate was not at all sure that this was the way the interview should be developing. 'You may not know them – the Group of Seven. They were Canadian.'

'Hey!' he said. 'Lawren Harris, Arthur Lismer . . . '

She couldn't quite believe this. 'No one else has ever heard of them.'

'I've got an uncle and aunt in Canada. We did all the art galleries and museums when I was a child.' He swivelled from side to side in his chair for a while, his eyes turning inwards towards distant memories. 'Happy days, happy days.'

But what about the job? She needs to earn some money. 'Do I need experience to clean?' she said.

He hesitates. 'You're not really the sort of person I had in mind. You're over-qualified.'

She'd messed it up. She shouldn't have mentioned the MA. 'Does it matter?' she said. 'I can do the same work as anyone else.'

'But once you have your MA, you'll be off looking for something better.'

'That won't be for ages,' she said. 'I need the money now.'

He hesitated, thought for a few moments, then came to a decision. 'Why not?' he said. 'There's something about an educated cleaning lady that appeals to me. Why don't we give you a trial period? I'll get Ivy to show you what to do. She's been with us for thirty years, but it's all getting a bit much for her. Arthritis. She can hardly climb the stairs nowadays.'

Kate wanted to jump up and shake his hand. 'Thank you,' she said.

He eyed her. 'Fallen on hard times, then?'

Kate avoided his gaze. 'You could say that.' She wasn't going to tell him anything. He was the kind of man who would watch the news and listen to discussions on the economy. He might have recognised the name. How many Kendalls were there in the area?

'I'll need a reference,' he said. 'You know, to prove you're who you say you are, that you're of fine, upstanding character, that kind of thing.'

Sian would do it. She was a part-time solicitor. 'No problem,' she said.

'Come on,' he said. 'I'll show you round the factory.'

Ivy, the cleaner, was tiny, with wispy grey hair and widely spaced flat feet. Her body was hunched painfully in on itself, shrivelled and distorted like the branches of an old tree. She lurched into the factory car park at five forty-five two days later and peered through her large round glasses into the open window of Kate's car. 'You the new cleaner?' she asked.

'Hello,' said Kate. 'You must be Ivy.'

Ivy laughed, a deep cackle that ended in a wheezing sound that made her cough. 'Eee – you're a bit posh, ain't you?' she said.

'I don't think so,' said Kate.

'It's your voice, dearie. If I was you, I'd keep your mouth shut if you meet the workers. Don't want to give the wrong impression.'

What's the right impression?

Ivy's fingers curled towards her palms and she found it difficult to negotiate the keys. She punched the numbers on the burglar alarm with a crooked thumb. 'It's dead easy,' she said, 'but you got to do it right or Trevor gets all in a tiswas.' She chuckled with obvious affection. 'But he's OK, our Trevor. He's been good to me.'

The cleaning was straightforward, with or without experience. Kate thought she could whiz through it all in an hour.

'Do you smoke?' asked Ivy, who smelt strongly of stale cigarettes.

'No,' said Kate.

'Trevor reckons I've been smoking in here. I says if he doesn't trust me it's time for us to part company. He says he does trust me, but he doesn't want no smoking inside. I says he can't trust me if he says that, and isn't he satisfied with my work? He says he's more than satisfied, but maybe it's getting a bit difficult for me now I'm older. I says how dare he tell me what I can or can't do. He says he's sorry if he's offended me. I says I ain't offended. He says in that case perhaps I could refrain from smoking indoors. I says in that case I'm resigning and that's what I did. I'm getting a bit old for all this kind of thing anyway. Time to put me feet up, I say.'

They went into Trevor Addenbrooke's office.

'Don't you touch that desk, now,' said Ivy. 'He's touchy about this stuff. Dust round the edges, but don't move his papers. He gets in a right paddy about things like that.' She portrayed Trevor as an arrogant, demanding employer, yet at the same time she couldn't hide her affection for him. As if he was a wayward grandchild who needed constant correction.

'You'll do,' said Ivy, as they made their way downstairs together.

Kate was proud of herself. Praise from Ivy was clearly to be valued.

On her way home, she forgot where she was going and found herself pulling up outside their old home, the white house on the hill.

A young woman stepped out of the front door and closed it behind her. She was wearing pink jeans and a tight-fitting T-shirt. Her hair was tied back into a pony-tail that swung behind her as she walked confidently towards her car in the drive. She looked so young.

That was me once.

I hope her husband's reliable.

Trevor Addenbrooke's presence is everywhere, his smell – a vibrant, masculine, clean smell – welcoming her as soon as she opens the door. Five pairs of shoes are always thrown into the corner in an untidy heap. Why does he need five pairs – six if you count the ones he goes home in? Does he change them regularly during the day as his feet expand? Does he have business-like shoes for board meetings, smart shoes that pinch for entertaining clients, wider, baggy shoes for everyday? And then there are all the jackets hanging on the back of the door, draped over spare chairs, dropped on the floor behind the desk; the multi-coloured scarves that jostle for position with the jackets, even though it's the middle of summer; the assortment of overalls for his sorties down into the manufacturing rooms; spare balls of socks, presumably a substitute for golfballs, congregating among a pile of clubs in an alcove.

His secretary's office, by contrast, is immaculate, the desk open and bare, a pleasure to polish. Kate had met Glenda briefly when she came for her interview, waiting in her office for a while before Mr Addenbrooke called her in. Glenda was a middle-aged woman with short hair and no makeup, who answered the phone in a gentle, precise voice. 'Hello, Delia. How are you today? I'm afraid Trevor's not going to be able to talk to you this morning. He's tied up until lunch – meetings, I'm afraid. Can I ask him to call you back? This afternoon?' An unexpected, musical chuckle. 'I'm sure you have. Take care now.'

There are three other permanent members of staff: Mrs Stevenson, who has pictures of her family on the desk – her husband and three children, with herself mysteriously absent – lists of people to ring that never seem to get any shorter, pot plants in every available space; Mr Lucas, who posts memos to himself on his desk, pinned to his noticeboard, Blu-tacked to the wall. Kate imagines him sitting at his desk with his feet up, on the phone all the time, doodling as he talks, airy and good-natured, producing nothing; and Mr Plunkett, who manages to achieve near-anonymity, leaving no traces of his personality. His office is easy to clean – up and down with the vacuum, no clutter. She dusts the shelves, neatens the files, lines up the computer and the keyboard and tucks the chair under the desk.

Sometimes they leave notes for Kate:

To the Cleaner, please could you put more toilet rolls in the Ladies?

Kate, would you be a darling and polish the leaves on my cheeseplant?

Kate, have you seen my pen, black enamel with red poppies down the side? I seem to have mislaid it.

How do they remember her name when they only saw her for two minutes? It's easier for her. Their names are on their doors. Mr S. Lucas, Mr J. Plunkett. She imagines them as Stephen/Sean/Scott, and Jonathan/Julian/Jeremy. Young men, breezing through their days with equanimity, killing time until they can go home and start their lives, spending all day planning the evening's entertainment, the girlfriends, the pubs and clubs.

Kate cleans methodically, satisfied by the gradual drawing of things into place, the imposition of order, surprised to discover that she is more demanding than she's ever been at home. She once had her own cleaning lady. Did she talk to her enough? Did she show her enough respect?

She likes the silence, the way she occupies the building alone, the absolute control she has over everything. The ever-present smell of chocolate is warm and familiar, a comforting escape from the realities of her small flat.

She returns home to noise. Millie is in the bathroom, the radio on in her bedroom and blasting out through the entire flat. The first thing Kate does is go into her room and turn it down.

'Hey!' says Millie, coming out of the bathroom with her hair in a turban. 'I didn't give you permission to go into my room.'

'Are you going to get that hair dry in time?' says Kate. 'Sian will be here in fifteen minutes.'

'Have I ever been late?' says Millie. 'The coffee's made, the cereal's on the table. Where's the problem?' She's a morning person. She wakes with a sunny disposition, amiable, willing to help, softening their chaos with surprising good nature.

Kate changes out of her overalls and goes into the kitchen. 'Rory!' she calls. 'Breakfast's ready.'

He appears, still in his pyjamas, rubbing his eyes. 'Hurry up,' says Kate. 'You've only got half an hour.' She fetches the milk from the fridge. 'Come on, Millie!'

'Coming!' She joins them in the kitchen, her wet hair clinging to her head, combed and flat.

They sit down together. Rory is silent, unable to engage his mind so early, focused entirely on his Frosties.

'Don't pick me up until six,' says Millie.

'Why?'

'There's an extra orchestra practice – for the concert next week.'

Is there a concert? Kate can't remember anything about it. 'What day did you say it was?'

'Oh, it's not a public concert. You can't come. It's just for the house.'

There's a hoot outside. 'It's Sian. She's early,' says Kate, in a panic.

'It's OK,' says Millie. 'I've finished. I'll just get my bag.'

Kate runs down the stairs and approaches Sian in the car. 'Hi,' she says. 'Millie's on her way.'

Sian leans her elbow on the edge of the window and smiles at her. 'How are you doing?' she says. She's pushed up her sunglasses to the top of her head and looks elegant and poised in a smart dress. It's not one of her working days so she must be going out somewhere, but she hasn't mentioned it to Kate. They don't share much any more.

'I'm OK,' says Kate. And, actually, she is. She's working, earning money, becoming a different person.

Sian stares with distaste at an abandoned car parked in front of her. All four tyres are completely flat, squashed on to the road, and someone has smashed the back window. 'Sorry, I'm a bit early,' she says. 'We seemed especially well organised today. It won't happen again.'

'Organised? What's that?' says Kate, with a smile. She feels guilty about her lack of communication, but doesn't know how to interrupt it and resume their old relationship. Barriers seem to have been constructed between the two of them, erected during a night when no one was looking, and now they're too tall, too solid, to scale. Sian is always willing to help and Kate uses her because she feels that Sian would be offended if she didn't, but it's difficult to know what to talk about.

'Rory must come over some time,' says Sian. 'Theo has missed him.'

'Yes,' says Kate. 'That would be lovely.'

Millie runs out, swinging her bag on to her shoulder as she tears down the path. 'Bye,' she calls to Kate, and jumps in beside Theo. Her hair has started to dry and random red curls are springing up and out.

'Thanks for taking her,' says Kate. As they drive off, she wonders why Millie didn't have her flute with her. How will she manage a rehearsal without it?

Rory refuses to walk with Kate if she wears her fluorescent yellow coat, so she carries it in an Asda bag and puts it on when she arrives.

'I'm off,' says Rory, as they approach the school crossing.

'Have a good day,' she says. She longs for him to reach up and kiss her as he used to, but he doesn't. It's his age, not the circumstances, she tells herself.

He's assured her that he's allowed to arrive at school early and play football in the playground with his friends. Neglected children, she thinks. Children whose parents have to leave them to fend for themselves. Once she would never have done this. She always used to be there for them, dropping them off, picking them up, going to all their matches and concerts.

She fetches the lollipop stick from the garden of a nearby house.

'Morning, Mrs Kendall,' calls the owner of the house from an upstairs window.

'Morning,' calls Kate. She has never actually seen this woman in her entirety. Just a head of grey hair, red lipstick, good-natured scrunched cheeks.

She positions herself on the edge of the kerb and waits for the first child to arrive. A car hoots as it drives past. She waves, not sure if it's someone she knows or just a friendly passer-by. She's discovering a whole new support network. Lorry drivers honk their horns at her, policemen wave, cyclists shout hello and sometimes dismount to have a conversation.

The difficult ones are the people in a perpetual hurry. They accelerate as they approach, hoping to get past before she stops the traffic. She usually lets them go because it's safer, but she dreams of stepping out suddenly and bringing them to a seething, quivering halt. There's power in a lollipop. She smiles at them as they roar past. I've let you go this time, she thinks, but there's always another day.

Her first encounter with a bus was easier than she'd expected. She hovered on the edge of the pavement, her lollipop ready, waiting for the bus to pass before she stepped out. But, unexpectedly, it stopped and the driver sat back, watching her. She went out with trembling legs, not sure if she'd read the signs properly, while he leant on his steering-wheel, grinning as if he had known her for years. Thank you, she mouthed at him and he put his thumb up.

She worries about meeting people from her previous life and often thinks she's seen the back of some old school acquaintances who have either not recognised her or not acknowledged her. But others have surprised her.

One father from Rory's school who had always been very remote – an accountant she'd suspected of leading the disapproval of Rory's presence in the school – had stopped one day, just past the crossing, wound down his window and called to her. She felt obliged to walk over to him.

'Mrs Kendall?'

'Yes?' As she recognised him, panic caused her voice to falter.

'You're the new lollipop lady?'

'They prefer to call us crossing patrols.' She laughed nervously.

He hesitated for a second. 'I just wanted to say how much I admire you,' he said.

'Oh,' she said, not sure that she had heard correctly. She checked over her shoulder but the pavement was clear, so she peered through his window, wondering if he was mocking her. But he appeared calm and sincere. 'Thank you,' she said.

Sian's predictions had all been negative. 'The children are mainly from the council estate,' she said. 'They won't treat you with respect.'

I'm from the council estate now, thought Kate.

The mothers, large, cheerful women with pushchairs laden down by carrier bags on the handles, are mostly friendly. And the children seem like children everywhere – brushed hair and clean shirts in the morning, tangled heads and the debris of the day plastered all over their clothes by the afternoon.

The headmaster has been out to meet her. 'We're delighted to have you, Mrs Kendall,' he said. 'We've been missing our lollipop lady.'

'What happened to her?'

'Too old. She wanted to carry on, but I'm afraid we were starting to help her across in the end. She loved the children, though.'

He sounded vaguely patronising, as if her uniform placed Kate in a different social category from himself. I haven't always done this, she wanted to say. I have a degree. I'm doing a master's. But her desire to impress him seemed to be a surrender to his inbuilt prejudices, so she said nothing.

Some of the children are cheeky, mostly boys and only if they're in groups of three or more. Only one boy has caused her any serious anxiety. He walks to school on his own, small and stocky, with an air of tough independence, always late. From her very first morning, he refused to acknowledge her existence, his whole attitude resentful and challenging. I'm not a kid, he seemed to be saying. I don't need you.

'Hello,' she said to him.

He ignored her.

As soon as the traffic slowed, she prepared to step out, but he was ahead of her, running across without waiting. She followed him, too late, and he'd gone. She was left alone in the middle of the road, feeling foolish. He did it again the next day. After a few days, she decided to stand in front of him so that he couldn't go. When he tried to push past her, she moved as he moved, trying to block his way.

'You have to wait for me,' she said.

'Don't you touch me!' he shouted. 'I'll set my dad on you!'

For the next few days, she didn't attempt to help, standing back and watching him weave his way expertly through the traffic. She worried about it. What if he made a mistake? It was her responsibility to protect him.

Then one day, as he leapt out into the road, he stumbled slightly and nearly lost his balance. Instead of carrying on, he froze, watching a car approach, its brakes shrieking. Barely pausing for breath, Kate jumped out, grabbed him and pulled him back to the pavement.

The car skidded towards the kerb before managing to stop. The driver threw open his door and leapt out. 'Why aren't you doing your job?' he yelled. 'I nearly killed him!' His voice was shrill with hysteria.

Kate was shaking too much to reply.

'I could report you!'

They glared at each other. Kate couldn't think of anything to say. After a few seconds of tense silence the man climbed back into his car and drove away.

Kate's uncertainty was replaced by an overwhelming fury and she grabbed the boy by the shoulders. 'You could be dead!' she shouted. 'You stupid boy!' She put all her energy into the word 'stupid'.

He kept his eyes on the ground and said nothing.

'What's the matter with you? Don't you have any intelligence?' She wanted to hit him, knock some sense into him. She had never been so angry in her entire life.

He didn't move and it suddenly occurred to her that he was scared. She loosened her grip on his shoulders and took several very large gulps of air. Calm down, she said to herself. Calm down. He's only a child.

'It's all right,' she said. She put her hand under his chin, making him look up at her. 'But don't ever do that again.' She attempted a laugh. 'Otherwise if the traffic doesn't kill you, I will. Is that clear?'

He nodded, his eyes sliding away from her gaze.

'Right,' she said. 'We'll have another go. You wait here until I tell you it's safe to go.'

She tilted her lollipop stick towards the road. The traffic slowed. She stepped out and the cars stopped. She reached the middle of the road, stood her lollipop on its end and turned to the boy. 'OK,' she called. 'You can go now.'

He put his head down and ran across.

He hasn't caused any trouble since.

The phone is ringing as she returns home from the crossing.

'Hi, Mum.'

'Lawrence, is everything all right?'

'Yes, great. Look, you know I said I'd come home for some of the holiday?'

'Yes?' He's not coming back. Relief floods through her. There's so little room. He would have to sleep on the sofa and he gets such pleasure out of winding up Millie about everything. There's no room for him round the table. There's nothing for him to do. His old school friends are all abroad, scuba-diving in Australia or climbing the Alps or backpacking in Thailand.

'Well, Zoë and I thought we'd still do our cycle ride to John o' Groats, if you don't mind.'

'I thought you were going with Josh.'

'Mum, stop quibbling. I'm doing it with Zoë. Have you any serious objections?'

'No, of course not. I think it's a splendid idea. Can you afford it?'

'Well, I've been saving some money from the job in the bar. We can always sleep in a field.'

'I don't think you can any more. It's not as easy as it used to be. There are laws about trespassing.'

'And the bank's offered me a good overdraft.'

'Don't forget you'll have to pay it back.'

'Mum, you don't need to lecture me about money.'

'I'm not so sure about that.'

There's a silence.

'I was exaggerating,' he says. 'Zoë's dad's helping out – we'll manage between us. Is that all right?'

'Of course it is.' Nothing she says will make any difference anyway.

'We're leaving tomorrow.'

So he wasn't exactly waiting for her approval before going ahead.

'Have a wonderful time. Make sure you stay warm and dry and have enough to eat.'

'Yes, Mum.'

'Send me a postcard.'

'Yes, Mum. Will you manage all right without me?'

'I think so, Lawrence.'

Kate puts on her coat and walks down to the beach. There's a soft breeze, but the sun is shining and the water is sparkling.

She walks briskly along the pathway above the pebbles. The sea stretches out to the horizon, wide and open.

She doesn't want Lawrence to feel responsible for her. It's upsetting that her older son is slipping away, transforming himself into an adult before he needs to. She knows it's perverse and that she and Felix would have been delighted once to see him showing signs of concern for others. But that would have been a shared pleasure. Now that she's on her own she doesn't want it. She wants her carefree son back, the young man who would take his friends out for a meal with thoughtless generosity, who would forget to let her know he was going to be late home when he offered to drive someone all the way back to Barnstaple. He shouldn't have to worry about his family or grow mean because he can't afford to help people.

She reaches the end of the beach and gazes across the river at the cluster of pines opposite. They stand tall and spindly against the yellow corn in the fields behind them. The tide is low and the thin remains of the river flow sluggishly between the banks of mud. The colours are strong and powerful.

The Group of Seven would have painted this scene. They created something original and individual, an acceptance of their new land, an acknowledgement that they could ignore other great artistic movements and make their own heritage.

She turns back to the sea and gazes out to the horizon. There's a tanker out there, almost motionless with distance, travelling across the world, passing Budleigh Salterton without acknowledgement.

Felix is dead, she thinks. He must be. The police have enough evidence to arrest him, charge him, take him to court, but they still haven't been able to find him. He has sunk below the horizon and will never appear again. I don't know what motivated him, I'll probably never know, but I think he must have loved us.

Chapter 21

Felix misses the sea. He misses many things, but it's the sound of the sea, that ferocious, unpredictable monster at the bottom of his garden, that he feels most keenly. It was a constant presence in his life for seventeen years, a Greek chorus, murmuring and commenting in the background, but he's only now come to understand its importance. He goes to bed at nine o'clock in the evening, dreading the nightmares but too exhausted to do anything else. And as he drags himself towards consciousness at four, he finds he's listening, expecting to hear the muffled growl of moving water in the distance, the wind as it whooshes over the top of the cliff, the boom of the waves as they crash against the rocks below the end of his garden.

But there's only the sound of a hyperactive city: passing cars – where are they all going in the middle of the night? – drunken teenagers throwing up at the side of the pavement, the chatter of magpies as they scavenge in the litter-strewn gutters. Every now and again he hears the forlorn cry of a seagull, but he knows it's just veered off course, driven inland by storms, lured by the promise of easy pickings from torn bin-bags. There's no salt in the air, no lawn leading to the wall at the end of the garden, no sea.

No family.

He's living a kind of half-life, sneaking along on the edges, in the shadows, too numb to think clearly or work out how to do anything else.

He arrives home from work at about six o'clock. The building is active and humming at this hour. Students are conducting shouted conversations through their open doors, heating Indian takeaways in their microwaves; someone practises the oboe every evening; the blue-rinsed lady on the ground floor watches the television at full volume. He can hear the news as he climbs the stairs to the top floor.

Wearily, he puts the key in the lock and Brandon's door opens. It never fails. He's tried varying the time of his arrival, tiptoeing, putting the key in so slowly that you can't hear it grate against the side of the lock, but Brandon still knows. He must be standing by his door, waiting, longing for Felix to come home.

'I've done a stew. It's been cooking all day.'

'That's wonderful, Brandon.' It's a struggle to talk through the fog that's wrapped round his exhausted mind.

'D'you want me to bring it round?'

'No, no. I'll come to you. Give me a minute.'

In his own room, Felix takes off his jacket and hangs it on the back of the door. He places the contents of his carrier-bag in the fridge, puts the bag into a box for re-use as a rubbish bin, then comes back out on to the landing again. He sighs. He knows Brandon has been deprived of attention all his life, and inevitably lacks balance in his adult relationships. But he's been up since four. He doesn't want to do anything.

Brandon has bought an extra plate from the market for twenty-five pence – fat jolly cows strolling round the edges and a large chip out of one side like an open wound. He's started to experiment with casseroles, lamb stew, spaghetti Bolognese. Felix sits next to him on the sofa and they balance their plates on their knees.

'This is very good,' says Felix. 'You've got a real talent for cooking.'

A shy smile of pleasure creeps across Brandon's angular face. ''S all right, i'n't it?' he says.

'How's work?' asks Felix.

The hint of a smile fades and his face settles back into its normal bony structure, cheekbones protruding like crude ledges carved by wind out of a rugged cliff. 'OK, I suppose.'

Felix fishes out a strip of black vegetable. 'Is this aubergine?'

Brandon nods. 'Got it cheap down the market, left over when they was closing.'

'What do you think of it?'

'Well . . .' He can't find the words, but he's clearly disappointed.

'So what's wrong with work?'

'It's, like . . .' He's stacking shelves at Tesco. The factory job hadn't lasted more than three days. He was too nervous and they didn't give him a proper chance. He nearly caused a major incident by dropping some hot metal. Fortunately no one was hurt, but it spattered over his overall and riddled it with tiny burnt holes. His foreman had bawled at him so convincingly that Brandon had walked out in tears. 'They laugh at me.'

'Who?'

'Like – all of them.'

'The customers, or the people you work with?'

'Both.'

Felix chews a chunk of beef. He can see why they laugh at Brandon. His limbs seem too big for his size and he's too anxious, his movements quick and jittery, so he bumps into sharp corners and drops things. He would make other people nervous. 'Give it time,' he says. 'They'll get used to you.'

Brandon examines his empty plate with surprise, as if he's wondering where the food has gone. He eats much faster than Felix, taking huge mouthfuls and swallowing them without enough chewing. 'I suppose,' he says.

Felix has a sudden image of Lawrence, tall and thin, with a voracious appetite that's never satisfied. He can eat Mars bars all morning, a full roast meal at lunchtime, crisps in the afternoon, and still have room for Kate's home-baked tea. Scones, fruit cake, Victoria sponge, flapjacks.

'Nobody would laugh at you if they tried your cooking,' he says.

Brandon's face softens again with an uncertain glow of pleasure. 'D'you reckon?'

'I should know. You feed me almost every night now.'

Brandon nods. 'Thanks, Tom.'

For a minute, Felix wonders who Tom is. Then he remembers he has two names. 'I think you've got that the wrong way round. I'm the one who should be thanking you.' A dull weight is settling in his stomach and it's not the beef stew. It's the discovery that he's been drawn into Brandon's life, formed a bond with him. This shouldn't have happened. He needs to remain anonymous. He's not in a position to be friends with anyone. He feels sorry for Brandon, but that's all. It shouldn't be necessary to get involved with him.

He struggles to clear his thoughts. 'Couldn't you look for a job as a cook?'

Brandon frowns. 'Didn't get no qualifications, did I?'

Felix watches him contemplating his empty plate, a mass of sharp angles and nervy twitches. It's hardly surprising that he doesn't have any GCSEs. It's difficult, if not impossible, to imagine him tackling quadratic equations, the periodic table, or *Romeo and Juliet*. 'Not even woodwork?' This is patronising, he realises, and wishes he could take it back.

But Brandon isn't tuned in to sarcasm. 'Di'n't do woodwork at my school.'

'So did you actually sit the exams?'

Brandon shrugs. 'Didn't go into school.'

'What – at all?'

'You don't know how it was,' he mumbles. 'They all said I was thick. Well, I am thick, i'n't I? So I stopped going.'

'That's rubbish,' says Felix. 'You can follow recipes, budget your money, go out to work. That all shows intelligence.'

'You reckon?' Brandon half smiles, unconvinced, but flattered.

'Where did you go when you should have been in school?'

'Dunno – anywhere. Home if there wasn't nobody there. Shops, like, arcades – '

'Did your parents know?'

'They sent some letters from school and my dad was mad at me, but they wasn't bothered.'

Felix remembers his aunts and their mission to fill him with knowledge and make him think, how they encouraged a thirst for information. Education was their lifeblood. The concept of anyone wanting to miss school was so far from their agenda that they wouldn't have believed it. They took for granted his desire to learn. That was probably their greatest gift.

'It must be possible to find you a course, or an apprenticeship, or something like that, where you can train to be a chef.'

Brandon looks down, his sparse blond eyelashes fluttering with uncertainty. 'Dunno,' he says. 'I wouldn't be no good. I'd just drop everything.'

'No, you wouldn't. Not once you'd settled down. You don't drop things when you're cooking at home.'

'It's a dream, see,' says Brandon, softly. 'I keep thinking, if there was a nice little café somewhere, where people was nice, I could go and cook for them and learn how to do really clever things and then people will like me.'

'People will like you anyway, Brandon. You just haven't met the right people yet.'

'I've met you.'

'Yes.' Felix can feel the burden of friendship pulsing through him. 'Look,' he says, 'I'll see what I can find out about apprenticeships and things like that.'

Brandon's large head drops down, a poppy head blown over by a blast of unfamiliar emotion. 'You're like a father to me, Tom,' he says, his voice thick and muffled.

An arrow shoots into Felix's heart, quivering and exquisitely painful.

He jumps to his feet and puts his half-finished meal down on the coffee-table. 'No, I'm not. You already have a father.'

His voice is hard and cold. I've got three children already. I don't need any more.

Brandon stares at him, bewildered, his mouth trembling, a flush spreading across his dry, flaky cheeks. Rory appears behind him, his childish face round and earnest, his brain fizzing with intelligence, his eyes creased with concentration. That's my son, thinks Felix. Not this poor, underdeveloped misfit.

He pulls out a fiver from his pocket and throws it on the table. 'Here, that's for the last two meals. Thanks for the food.' He walks quickly to the door and opens it.

Brandon struggles to his feet, confused, his eyes watering. 'I di'n't mean it, Tom, I di'n't mean no harm—'

'Then don't say things you don't mean.'

Felix slams the door behind him. He crosses the landing to his own door, puts the key in the lock and stops.

He examines himself standing there with a key in his hand. He's like a cartoon, a hard man, drawn with strong, straight lines, with the cruel strokes of an uncaring pencil. Is this really him? Felix Kendall? A man who used to like his image of himself, a good man who loved his family? Suppose that boy back there was Lawrence?

He takes several deep breaths and returns to Brandon's door. He knocks softly.

The door flies open and Brandon's gaunt white face peers out. His eyes are swollen and pink.

'What's the recipe for tomorrow, Brandon?'

He can see Brandon forcing himself to think, pretending he's not upset. 'Sweet and sour chicken,' he says at last.

'Great. I'll look forward to it all day.'

Relief smoothes out the anxiety that is creasing Brandon's tight-skinned forehead. He tries to smile but tears come gushing out instead.

There are several large crates outside the store when Felix arrives for work the next morning, piled neatly near the edge of the kerb. The labels are hand-written in a flamboyant, flowery style, all addressed to the same person in Bangladesh. Salik's father.

'Another pick-up?' asks Felix, as he goes in and finds Salik throwing bundles of newspapers into a corner, ready for sorting.

Salik grunts. 'Relief work never stops.' His parents are still there, and many uncles and aunts. He tries to keep them well supplied, but the floods continue to come every year.

Felix takes a penknife out of his pocket and slits through the string tying the newspapers and magazines together. 'Wouldn't it be easier to send money?'

'They can't always get to banks, and no point in having money if nothing to buy. Better to send things they can have straight away. No fuss.'

Felix places a large pile of the *Sun* on a shelf next to the *Mirror*. They sell far more copies of these newspapers than they do of *The Times* or the *Guardian*. He can now imagine the headlines when he disappeared: BETRAYAL!! MONEY MAN SHOCK! THE FLIGHT OF FRAUDULENT FELIX!

He checks the papers every day for news of George and Kristin, but now they've been charged and let out on bail, everything has gone silent. The hunt for Felix has faded from the news. Have George and Kristin implicated him further, or have they told the truth about his lack of involvement in George's complicated affairs? He's waiting, watching, ready for the trial.

'Where's that delivery of orange juice? Came yesterday,' asks Salik.

Felix straightens up. 'At the back, under the box of milkshakes.'

The aisles are clearer than they used to be. Felix has given a lot of thought to the layout of the store. 'You're not making the best use of space,' he had said to Salik after a few weeks. 'You don't need all these piles of stuff here. You want people to browse. They'll always buy more if they can see more.'

They've made a space at the back, next to the fridges, where they stack new deliveries. They sort them out together at the beginning of the day, before the early-morning rush. 'Why don't you put the chocolate at the front?' suggested Felix, recently. 'The big supermarkets have stopped doing this because parents complain that their children want whatever they see. You don't have to worry about that. Your customers aren't middle class.'

Salik is not always convinced. 'You come here, ask for small job and then take over. You want to run the shop, Tom? How much? Make me offer.' He waves his hands through the air, fighting off invisible competitors. Then he slaps Felix on the back, hard. 'You're a good employee, Tom. My wife thinks God sent you to me.'

'That's because she doesn't have to get up so early in the morning any more,' says Felix.

Sales have started to improve.

Felix fetches the list for the delivery boys. He starts to sort out the papers and put them into the bags. Turning around after a while, he sees that Salik is watching him. 'What?' he says.

'I don't understand you, Tom,' he says.

Felix straightens, nervous under Salik's frank stare. 'There's nothing to understand,' he says.

'You are clever man. I knew that from first day we met. You could be doing anything. You know everything. You work everything out. You improve my business. Why?'

Felix shrugs. 'Why not? You pay my wages.'

'But they not good wages. We don't pay tax, National Insurance—' He stops.

Felix can feel sweat between his shoulder-blades, at the

back of his knees. 'It doesn't matter. I don't need much. Why bother with details?'

'You are hiding, Tom. Even I can see that. It's not a wife at all, is it?'

The sweat cools on Felix's skin and a damp chill creeps down his back. 'I don't know what you're talking about.'

A little smile hovers on Salik's lips. 'Your secret is safe with me, my friend. Would I betray you?'

Does he know, or is he just guessing? 'Look,' says Felix, 'you're making something out of nothing. There are no secrets. Let's just get on with the work, shall we?'

'I come to this country because I want to be safe,' says Salik. 'I do not like the English – they are the ones who dictated to us where we should live when they left India, who gave us a country that spends much of its time under water. I do not want to like them, I just want to keep my family dry. And then I meet you, a polite, clever Englishman, and I find that I like you. I do not want to intrude, but why will you not trust me? Perhaps I can help you.'

'You already help me,' says Felix. 'By giving me a job.'

At eight fifteen, Salik's family come down from their flat above the shop, dressed in uniform, ready for school. There are four older children and two younger ones. The babies stay at home with their mother now that Felix can take over in the shop. Salik's brother, Tahir, used to help out, but he's gone now, moved to Manchester to open his own shop. Felix often hears the toddlers above him during the day, fractious wailing, the sound of quick, frantic steps across the floor, occasional bursts of boisterous giggles.

Runa, the oldest girl, is fourteen, confident in her uniform – navy jumper over trousers – with a thick plait falling to her waist, and her rich brown face consciously calm. I am the oldest, she seems to be saying, I am beautiful. People will always give me whatever I want from them. She's clever, her father says, preparing for ten GCSEs. She will be a doctor, a lawyer. Perhaps. Perhaps she will do what she wants to do and not what her father wants. Felix wonders if Salik intends to marry her off in the Bangladeshi way and she doesn't know this yet. He would like to ask, certain it couldn't happen, but holds back, worried that Salik might give the wrong answer. Runa watches Felix with an amused glint in her eye, a blossoming sexuality that she's aware of, without appreciating its power. Her provocative stare seems to be inviting him to do something, but she might not know what the invitation is.

Abbas, twelve years old, is in his first year at senior school. He's tall for his age, just beginning to develop a casual ease, the manner of a boy training to be a man. His teeth stick out. He will have to wear a brace soon, and Salik can't understand why the dentist is delaying. Abbas likes to play mathematical games with Felix.

'If a man buys three cows for thirty-seven pounds thirty-four each, slaughters them and cuts them into twenty different parts, how much must he charge for each bit if he wants to make a fifty per cent profit?'

'This boy,' says Salik, his hand perpetually hovering over Abbas's head, itching to ruffle his hair, but holding back because Abbas gets annoyed if anyone interferes with his image, 'he will be a great businessman, yes?'

'Governor of the Bank of England,' says Felix, making calculations in his head. 'Two pounds eighty each.'

'The answer is,' says Abbas, 'you can't possibly work it out because the kidneys are always going to be worth more than the feet. Only a butcher would have the expertise to know.'

Felix rolls his eyes. 'So why ask?'

'It's the business side of things, you see. It's to do with understanding your market and showing faith in the true experts.'

'Right,' says Felix.

Nazrul, seven years old, the second son, hides behind his father, peering out occasionally through slanted black eyes, but never speaking. His face has retained its babyish chubbiness, and a strand of hair flops permanently over his eyes, allowing him a natural refuge from anyone who looks directly at him. His sturdy, slightly overweight body, moves with slow awkwardness, lacking the grace of his siblings.

And Amina, the five-year-old girl who spends most of her time singing and dancing, always happy, always giggling: whenever Felix looks at her, she dashes behind a shelf in the shop and pops her head round, her cheeks dimpling like a baby's, her eyes creased with laughter, a silver ring glinting in each ear.

'I won't be back until about eleven,' says Salik to Felix. 'Abbas has appointment with orthodontist.'

'No problem,' says Felix.

He stands in the doorway of the shop and watches them climb into the Subaru, the four-wheel drive that is parked on double yellow lines outside the shop. It's a busy road and a large queue builds up on one side behind the parked car. A howl of protest comes from Amina as she's strapped into her seat by Runa. A laugh from Abbas. Nazrul's head droops, but he glances to the side to see if he's being watched. He drops his eyelids immediately when he sees Felix looking back. Salik runs round the car, slamming all the doors.

That was me, once. A long time ago.

Runa smiles slightly from the front seat, her face still and alert, as if she's reading his thoughts.

Millie—

Salik starts the engine. For a moment, they are all framed in the windows of the car, the morning sun lighting them from behind. A photograph of a large family. All individuals, but working together.

The cars behind hoot as Salik pulls out with complete disregard for anyone else, edging his way into the traffic.

Nazrul raises a hand and waves. Felix stares after them with disbelief. Nazrul has never waved before.

The traffic starts to flow normally again.

Pain hits him like a tornado, tearing at his eyes, his ears, the pressure rippling the skin on his face. He can barely remain standing. His family crowds round him, elbowing their way into his vision, pushing aside the Bangladeshi family. I miss them, I miss them, I miss them.

Where are you, Dad?

Did you have to leave us like that?

Why don't you come back?

The boy comes into the shop in the middle of the morning. He's small and wiry, in faded jeans dotted with torn and frayed holes. His denim jacket is covered with badges. I WOZ AT GLASTONBURY; CHIPS FOR CONSUMPTION, NOT COMPUTERS. He looks about thirteen.

Felix is perched on the stool at the counter, leafing through a copy of the *Guardian* as he attempts to distract his jittering thoughts. 'Shouldn't you be in school?' he says.

The boy sneers at him and mutters something under his breath. He dodges round the corner of an aisle.

Felix waits and listens. He can hear the soft rustle of sweet wrappings, the boy's footsteps as he walks, his trainers squeaking slightly on the newly washed floor. After a few minutes, he swaggers up to the counter and puts down a packet of chewing-gum. His jacket is bulging, much wider than when he came in. He stares at Felix, his eyes wide and unblinking.

'And the rest,' says Felix.

'Don't know what you mean.'

'Yes, you do,' says Felix, softly. 'Let's have a look inside your jacket.'

'No way,' says the boy.

Felix comes round to the front of the counter. The boy makes a dash for the door, but he's not quick enough and Felix grabs his arm.

'Get off!' screams the boy, wriggling with unexpected strength. He lashes out with his other arm and punches Felix on the mouth. Felix staggers back and the boy breaks away. Felix throws himself forwards, reaches for the boy's waist and they tumble on to the floor together, rolling on top of each other. Felix manages to scramble to his feet and pulls the boy up.

'Now,' he says. 'Let's see what you've really got, shall we?'

Holding the boy's arms behind his back with one hand, he reaches round, unzipping the jacket and searching inside the pockets. He finds handfuls of Mars bars, Snickers, Rolos, Milky Ways. He drops them on to the counter one by one, then turns the boy round, keeping a tight grip on his arms. 'Going to pay for them, were we?'

The boy scowls at him and goes limp.

Salik comes through the door. 'Tom, my friend,' he shouts. 'They're finally going to give Abbas a brace—' He sees the boy in Felix's grasp. 'What's going on?'

'Shoplifting,' says Felix, through tight lips.

The boy's face crumples. 'I didn't mean it,' he says. 'I was hungry. Didn't have no breakfast.'

Felix takes a deep breath and relaxes his grip, but remains alert. 'Don't get any ideas,' he says.

'Must call police,' says Salik, taking his mobile out of his pocket. 'Make an example.'

'No,' says Felix. He doesn't want to talk to the police. Give statements, his name, his address.

'Please,' says the boy. 'They'll lock me up.' He's transformed into a clinging, frightened child. 'Me dad'll kill me.'

But Salik is unmoved. He dials, speaks to someone and shuts the phone. 'Ten minutes,' he says.

Felix wants to take him aside, whisper that it seems a bit harsh. Couldn't they cancel the police? He contemplates letting the boy go, letting him run, but Salik is beside him, pushing the boy on to the floor, running his hands through his pockets.

'Sit there,' he says. 'Don't move an inch.'

The boy starts to sob loudly, his face dripping with tears.

Rory at Budleigh, crying because he's left his shoes further up the beach and his feet hurt.

Felix picks up a bar of Cadbury's Dairy Milk. 'Here,' he says, handing it to the boy. 'Eat that.'

The boy unwraps it, tearing the paper, and stuffs two chunks into his mouth. He stops sobbing.

Salik hands Felix a tissue. 'The mouth,' he says.

Felix puts a finger up to his lip and discovers it's bleeding.

At six o'clock, Felix leaves the store and walks home. He's given his name, Thomas Sawyer, to the police. They have his address. They wrote it down, not particularly interested. But he's uncomfortable. Coincidences change things. They could prosecute the boy. He might have to go to court, swear he's telling the truth, when he isn't even the person he says he is. Someone will wonder why an educated man is working for Salik.

Brandon opens the door almost as soon as Felix knocks. 'Tom,' he says. 'What's happened to your mouth?'

'Nothing,' says Felix. 'A shoplifter. It's all sorted. That sweet and sour smells good.'

Brandon dishes up. They sit side by side on the sofa and start eating.

'You'll be on the television one day,' says Felix. '*Brandon's Kitchen*.'

Brandon grins shyly. 'Go on,' he says. 'Not me.'

'Just wait and see,' says Felix.

Neither of them mentions the day before. Brandon is more careful before he speaks, as if he's checking the words in his mind before committing himself, so their conversation becomes laborious, and every subject seems heavy and significant.

Felix's mind slips in and out of the present, unable to hold on to anything solid.

Anyone can be an entrepreneur, says Abbas, his eyes shining. *You just need to want to.*

It's Lawrence really, taller than Abbas, but not much more mature. *Cool it, Dad. Nobody cares about reputation any more. It's so old news.* An untroubled young man who believes in all sorts of things but doesn't do any of them.

Dad! calls Rory, along the A30, across the M25, up the stairs. *Where are you?*

Felix, says Kate. The voice of reason. *We need you here. Now.*

Felix returns to his room, weak with the frustration of slow discussion. He washes some empty mugs in the sink and leaves them on the draining-board. He changes and folds his working clothes neatly into a drawer. He opens the wardrobe, rummages in the back and pulls out the briefcase he brought with him. The one he was carrying when he received George's phone call.

He's needed here, he's needed there. You think you can keep moving, brushing past people, making no impression. But it doesn't work. Suddenly you're not a stranger any more. You're someone people know. Anonymity is unattainable. And you take everyone with you, carry them round in your mind so that they start to inhabit the faces of people you meet.

He puts some library books into the empty briefcase and stands in the middle of the room, looking round. There's no trace of him as an individual. The chest of drawers and the wardrobe contain evidence of his existence if anyone opens them, but they're unclaimed possessions, things that hold no significance for him. They could belong to anyone. Jinhai will be back in a couple of weeks' time and he might find a use for them. The rent is up to date, the room is ready for him.

He goes out and locks the door behind him.

He walks to the library and takes the books to the returns desk. Eileen, the librarian, recognises him. Her tanned cheeks – sunbed, Felix suspects – crease into a smile that fades when she sees the cut on his lip. 'What happened to you, Mr Sawyer?'

'Nothing,' he says. 'I caught a shoplifter.' He goes over to the computers. It's not busy this evening, only one other person, a Chinese man, peering earnestly into a screen. Felix settles himself into a corner and starts work.

After an hour, he has accumulated several pages about training courses for chefs. He prints out the most relevant. Then he types two letters and prints them. When he's finished, he slips everything into the envelopes he brought with him and addresses them to Brandon and Salik. He can't get them weighed, so he attaches several stamps, knowing he is overpaying, but wanting to be certain they will reach their destination.

I can't abandon Brandon. He has no friends.

I'll write again. I'll send him a forwarding address when I have one.

Will Salik find someone reliable so his wife doesn't have to start getting up early again?

He can taste the guilt at the back of his throat.

He walks back through the library.

'No more books?' says Eileen.

'No, not today.'

Outside, the sun is sinking and the street is bathed in an uncharacteristic rosy glow. A man shoots past him on a bicycle, singing. A dog, tied by his lead to a lamp-post, looks up at him with patient, trusting eyes.

There's no one in the police station when he walks in. He waits at the desk, examining the posters about burglary, speeding, fraud, counterfeiting.

He wonders if the station is closed and the door has been left unlocked by mistake. He considers leaving and coming back later, but knows he couldn't do that. He stands still and waits.

Finally, a door opens behind the desk and a policeman comes out in shirt sleeves. He sees Felix and brief surprise flashes across his face. It's replaced by a calm, controlled expression, as if he'd always known Felix was there, but wanted to do things in his own good time. 'Hello, sir. Looks like you've been in a fight.'

'No,' says Felix. 'It was nothing.'

'Can I help you?'

'Yes,' says Felix.

The policeman studies him tolerantly. 'And?'

'I'm Felix Kendall.'

There's no immediate reaction. 'Pleased to meet you. I'm Constable Peters.'

Felix doesn't know what to do. 'I think you might want to arrest me,' he says.

'And why would that be, Mr Kendall?'

'Well, a few months ago—'

'Yes?' Constable Peters manages a mild interest, as if he's hoping that Felix is going to confess to half a dozen murders but doesn't really believe that to be likely and, anyway, he's not going to encourage any confession.

'Look,' says Felix, 'go and check my name on your computer. Felix Kendall.'

Constable Peters doesn't react.

'Please,' says Felix. 'I think you'll find it becomes clear.'

'How do you spell your name, then?'

Felix takes a leaflet about burglar alarms and writes his name on the top.

'OK,' says Constable Peters. 'You wait here.'

He's gone for about a quarter of an hour. When he returns, he's more alert, more motivated. 'Can you prove you are who you say you are?'

Felix sighs. He hadn't expected it to be so difficult. 'I don't have any documents, if that's what you mean. I got rid of them. But I'm sure you could find people who can identify me.'

Constable Peters lifts a section of the desk and holds it open. 'I think you'd better come with me, Mr Kendall. There's quite a few important people who want a word with you.'

'Yes,' says Felix. 'I thought there might be.'

'They'll be here shortly.'

'Before they arrive, I need to tell you about something else, something that happened thirty years ago.'

Constable Peters raises an eyebrow. 'You mean we can produce an extra little surprise for the big boys?' he says. 'It'll be a pleasure.'

Part Four

Chapter 22

Kate is in the kitchen when the phone rings. She's working on her thesis – eight thousand words completed, another twelve to go. She's surrounded by images of rocky islands growing cube-like out of remote lakes and dense forests. Pieces of paper keep dropping to the floor whenever she searches for a particular picture.

The lazy sound of the signature tune from *Coronation Street* wafts out of the living room where Millie is sprawled on the sofa. It offers a temporary respite from the background sound of heavy rock that thuds insistently and monotonously from a neighbouring flat. Rory is in his room with the door shut. He's drawing up guidelines for the Space Warriors, he says. They have to be prepared for invasion. He wants to know how to contact the prime minister when the time is right, and he's been disappointed by Kate's lack of expertise in this area.

The heat is oppressive, soaking through the thin walls of the flat, hanging motionless in the claustrophobic rooms. It presses up against the skin, an overbearing presence that doesn't respect personal space. Kate can hear Irene downstairs, sitting on a sun-lounger outside her back door with her sister and her mother, their voices rising indignantly as they discuss and complain and laugh with high-pitched voices, passing the baby from person to person, talking to it with exaggerated baby-voices.

'Ooh, those cheeks. I could just munch you to death.'

A petulant wail.

'What is it, my precious? Isn't Mummy looking after you properly?'

255

The voices blend into each other and settle into a familiar, almost comfortable background music, no longer irritating to Kate. The noise is present but distant because her mind is engaged in an intellectual process that refreshes and invigorates her. Now that she's working on her thesis more consistently, she's finding it soothing and satisfying. The family is managing – they've gone past the mere survival stage – and they're making a way for themselves that is their own, not Felix's.

The ringing of the phone penetrates the background noise with a demanding shrillness. Hardly anyone phones now, except Lawrence – and that's not very often. Millie's friends never contact her on the landline, so she's presumably conducting her social life by text. Occasionally someone calls for Rory – some members of the vast network of acquaintances that he's recently built up who don't possess a mobile – or a tele-salesman from India rings to ask baffling questions about personal security, but that's all.

Kate goes into the hall and picks up the phone. 'Hello?'

'Mrs Kendall?'

'Yes?'

'Inspector Williams.'

How quickly everything restarts. It's so easy: just press a button and it's back to the beginning. Kate has convinced herself that she's rewritten her history and moved past Felix. The shock has started to fade and she's now constructing a new life. She doesn't want to go back through it all over again.

She can't answer for a few seconds.

'Are you all right, Mrs Kendall?'

'Yes – yes. He's dead, isn't he?'

'Well,' he says, 'not exactly.'

A rolling of the stomach, a shuffling of the cards, which are thrown on to the table into an unexpected pattern that bears no relation to the previous configuration. A new game has started and she isn't prepared.

'What's that supposed to mean?' she says.

'He walked into a police station in London yesterday. Deptford. I thought you ought to know before anyone else gets hold of it.'

There's shouting on *Coronation Street*, Irene's family are having an argument over the screaming baby, someone has turned up the volume across the gardens. Everything is magnified, a crescendo of strident discords. But none of them can compete with the violent pulse that is thundering in her head.

She puts the phone down.

Rory puts his head round his bedroom door. 'Is it for me?' he says.

'No,' she says.

Rory returns to his bedroom and shuts the door. The hall is dark and narrow, a long corridor with doors leading off it. They have no shape cut into them, no mouldings, they're just plywood constructions, smooth and characterless.

There's no air. It's difficult to breathe.

Just as Kate decides she should move, experimentally putting out one foot, letting the leg take her weight, shifting forward in the direction of the kitchen, the phone rings again.

She picks it up.

'Are you all right, Mrs Kendall?'

'I'm fine,' she says.

'The thing is, we need someone to identify him.'

Now she finds she wants to talk too much, to drown all the other noises. 'I thought that only happens with dead people. Because they can't tell you who they are and you need someone else to prove you've guessed right.'

He pauses. He's too serious, she thinks. He was meant to laugh. 'That's true,' he says, 'but he claims he's destroyed all his identification. He could be someone pretending to be your husband.'

'You mean like that man who came back from the war and claimed to be someone else and his wife went along with it because he was much nicer than her original husband? Martin Guerre, or something.'

'That's it, more or less.'

'But I might lie too, mightn't I? Because I don't want Felix back.'

'I would trust you, Mrs Kendall.'

'Find someone else. I don't want to see him.'

'It would be helpful—'

'No,' she says. 'I won't do it.' She puts the telephone down again.

'Mum!' calls Millie. 'There are loads of cars outside.'

I can't do this, thinks Kate.

'The good news is,' says Inspector Williams, during his third attempt to talk to Kate on the phone, 'the press won't bother you for long. They can't report anything once he's charged.'

'How long will that take?'

'No more than a couple of days. There'll be a preliminary hearing, and the judge will almost certainly give him bail.'

'Does someone have to put up money for that?'

'No, that rarely happens these days. They might ask for his passport, so he can't disappear abroad. Then he's free to go until the trial.'

'Free to go?' Kate is horrified. 'Where to?'

Inspector Williams hesitates. 'That depends on who wants to put him up.'

'Not me,' says Kate. 'He's not coming here.'

After a moment's silence, the inspector says, 'By the way, you should know that we now believe your husband was not as heavily involved in illegal activities as we originally thought.'

'How do you know?'

'Rangarajan has made it clear that Felix had no knowledge of where the money came from. And there is no evidence to link him to anything other than the money-laundering.'

'Does that mean he's not guilty after all?'

'I'm afraid not. Failure to disclose suspicions of money-laundering, tipping off, prejudicing an investigation – they're all criminal offences with heavy penalties.'

'Will he go to prison?'

'I'd be amazed if he didn't.'

Why does she experience a pang of shock when he says this?

Felix's arrest arouses almost as much interest and speculation as his disappearance. On the regional news that evening, Kate, Millie and Rory watch him being bundled out of a van and into a local police station with a blanket over his head. Kate doesn't want to look, but her curiosity is too great and when she does, she can't recognise him anyway. Just a hunched figure, staggering up the steps, surrounded by a huddle of policemen. Does she know those trainers? They're not new, but they're as clean and white as if they were, maintained with the precise care that she would expect from Felix.

The reporter analyses the consequences of money-laundering, gives a profile of Felix's life and a reconstruction of the circumstances of his disappearance. Maine and Selwick have now ceased to exist, taken over by another, bigger accountancy firm. George's business affairs are listed but not commented on because of the impending trial. Apparently, large numbers of witnesses have come forward. Someone has filmed Kate's flat, the street, the block, her front door, the closed windows.

'Look!' says Millie. 'You can see the picture of Sydney Harbour in my bedroom.'

'We'll have to draw the curtains,' says Kate, terrified that they can be seen, but unable to move away from the television.

Suddenly, Irene appears on the screen, standing outside her front door, holding the baby. She's wearing a tight-fitting T-shirt with a low front. Her plump arms wobble slightly as she rocks the baby up and down. 'They've only recently moved in,' she says, 'but they're not the sort you'd expect round here.'

'The traitor,' breathes Millie.

'They seemed OK, but I always thought there was something odd about them. You just can't tell about people, can you?'

'We should have talked to her more,' says Kate. 'She must have known we were avoiding her.'

Irene has made a big effort. Black eyeliner, long, luxuriant lashes, shimmering lipstick that glints in the lights from the cameras. Close-up filming doesn't flatter her. Her face seems large and loose, and her mouth drops open too easily into a distorted, gaping smile, as if the facial muscles have never developed properly.

'She's ugly,' says Rory.

Kate doesn't want to think of Felix doing normal things again. She can no longer be certain that she won't meet him somewhere. Is he suffering from amnesia? But he knows who he is: he didn't lose his identification, he destroyed it. How does he explain himself to himself?

When she looks back on their life together, she sees him as controlling everything, taking her on to the dance-floor, guiding her in the directions he wanted to go, aggressively leading her through a waltz in an old-fashioned protocol. It seems to her now that his steps were too slick, his technique too polished, as if he'd practised for so long that he'd lost all spontaneity. She remembers a discussion about wallpaper for the small television room they called the snug.

'What about this one?' said Kate, picking out a gentle duck-egg blue with tiny rosebuds scattered over the surface as if they had been blown by a random gust of wind.

An expression passed over his face that she couldn't understand at the time. Now she decides, as she gazes at the darkened ceiling at ten past two in the morning, that he was sneering. She didn't know about sneering then. She'd always thought well of him. Why? Why didn't she challenge him? Why had she always believed that he was right? It doesn't seem to make any sense now.

'Possibly,' he says, after a while. 'I don't think it's what we need. A bit dated, perhaps.'

'I thought you said we were looking for a classic style. Surely that's going to be out of date, by definition.'

He smiled. A superior, knowing smile. She should have recognised it as such at the time. She should have argued more, pushed for her own preferences. 'That's a good point.' Patronising. 'Although I suspect the experts wouldn't agree with you. We need something tasteful – timeless, I suppose – that never looks dated, whatever period you're in.'

What was he talking about? Who decides what is tasteful? Why should they listen to them anyway? If she likes something, why shouldn't she have it, even if other people don't like it? If the previous occupants of this flat adored yellow and purple flock wallpaper and it made them happy, then who is she to pass judgement on them? Why should Felix have decided that his taste was better than hers?

He picked out a striped paper, pale yellow and cream, uncluttered. 'What do you think of this one?' he asked.

She hesitated and tried to imagine it in the room. He was probably right. She could see it reflecting the brightness of morning sunshine or cosy in the light of an evening lamp. But she still had duck-egg blue in her mind. 'It's all right,' she said. She felt guilty. 'Actually, it's rather nice.'

But then he discovered that it was cheaper than he'd expected. 'I'm not sure,' he said.

'You said you liked it.'

'It's too cheap,' he said. 'We must consider the quality.'

She couldn't understand why the price mattered, but clearly it did. He told her that expensive paper goes up more easily; it doesn't stretch or tear and decorators always prefer it. She wonders now if it was more than that. That he needed the personal satisfaction of knowing he had the best. It wasn't necessary for anyone else to know, but it was essential that he knew. She'd always believed he despised materialism, not wanting their financial position to be readable to people who came to the house. He would refuse to reveal his income or discuss how much he had spent on anything. But now she can see a more subtle type of ostentation that she hadn't recognised at the time. He wanted everything to be quietly wealthy, the kind of richness that spoke of class, of taste, of secure luxury.

At the time, this disagreement in the wallpaper shop seemed normal, to be expected, a moment of conflict that could be experienced by any couple. She'd thought she agreed with his final choice.

'I think we've got it,' he said eventually, finding a very expensive designer wallpaper. Clean straight lines, so pale it was almost white. 'What do you think?'

'It's lovely,' she said.

They furnished the snug with soft sofas, an antique walnut coffee-table and a small television placed discreetly in the corner. The room felt warm and comfortable, beautifully designed.

But now Kate finds herself getting more and more annoyed as she turns in her bed, rolling over, sweeping her legs from side to side, plumping up the pillows endlessly. It's too hot, too sweaty for sleep.

Why didn't she argue with him more? Why did he always get his own way? What would have happened if she had really challenged him? That's what she finds impossible to know. She was too compliant, too willing to be guided by his hand on her back. *Forward, one, two, three; sideways, one, two, three* . . . So the luxury crept up on her, unnoticed, and she started to cultivate the same love of expensive things, the same taste for discreet colours and textures, cleanness and simplicity.

But is that what she really likes? She doesn't know. She can't even begin to make herself follow her own instincts because she doesn't have any left. All her taste has been moulded by Felix, as if he'd sat her down in a classroom, a solitary, impressionable schoolchild, and lectured her from the blackboard. Rules, formulae learnt by rote, chanted every day, recorded in a mental notebook. There was never any opportunity to experiment. She wakes from a hazy doze with a jolt. She's never been allowed to make mistakes. She has no sense of her own personality, only that of Felix. How impossible it would have been to challenge such wisdom.

Haphazard patterns of light seep through the curtains and play hopscotch on her walls. She listens to the silence of the night. Did she hear something? There it is again, a soft snuffling sound, coming from one of the children's bedrooms.

She switches on her lamp and swings her legs over the side of the bed, keeping her eyes shut until she has become accustomed to the light. After a few seconds she hears the sound again, so she tiptoes out into the hall, the vinyl tiles cool and soothing under her feet.

She stands still and listens. It's Millie.

Very gently, she pushes open the door, letting the light from her bedroom filter in. Millie is lying on top of her sheet, uncovered, with her back to the door. Her breathing is uneven and ragged, as if she's crying and trying to keep it quiet. 'Are you all right, Millie?' whispers Kate, anxious to let her know she's there.

Millie freezes and the noise stops immediately. She seems to be holding her breath.

Kate approaches the bed. 'I heard you moving around so I thought perhaps you couldn't sleep, like me.'

There's a long pause, then Millie turns over. She's pretending she has just woken up. 'What? What did you say?' Her voice is slurred and confused, louder than a whisper.

'Sssh,' says Kate. 'We mustn't wake Rory. I don't want to interrupt his beauty sleep.'

Millie manages a scornful grin, her lips trembling slightly. 'Sleep wouldn't make any difference. Nothing improves his appearance.'

Kate smiles and sits on the side of the bed. 'Would you like me to make some hot chocolate to help you sleep?'

'No, it's all right.' Millie pulls herself into a sitting position and hugs her knees, wrapping herself in the spare sheet that Kate has given her to use in the hot weather instead of the duvet. 'Why did he have to come back?' she says after a while.

Kate sighs. 'I don't know. I don't understand any of it.'

'It's so unfair. Just when everyone was starting to forget about it all.'

'I know,' says Kate.

'How can you live with someone all your life and never know them?'

'Well . . .' Kate pauses. 'I suppose nobody ever knows anyone else properly. You just think you do. I'm not sure we even know ourselves.'

'But that means you can't trust anyone.'

'I don't think it's usually that bad. Most people only hide small things that don't really matter. Everyone just gets excited by the exceptions – you know, the men who turn out to have two families on the go at the same time – but it's very rare.'

'What about men who only pretend to love people?'

'Do you really think Dad didn't mean it when he said he loved you?'

Millie rests her face against her knees. 'No,' she says, in a muffled voice. 'I don't know. How can you tell?'

Kate doesn't know what to say. The same dark thoughts have been racing through her mind. How can she answer a question that has no answer?

'If Dad had been lying to us all this time, I'm sure we'd have found out sooner.'

'We didn't know he was a money-launderer.'

No, they didn't know anything. It's so easy to read exactly what is put before you. Why would you be suspicious? 'That was only one side of him. You shouldn't forget the good bits, the parts you saw when he was with us.' She is advising Millie to do something she can't do herself.

'*The Times* says that white-collar criminals should be dealt with as severely as gangs of drug-dealers and racketeers.'

'Since when have you been reading *The Times?*'

'Ages. They have all the papers in the school library. I go there and read them in the lunch hour.'

'Then stop reading them,' says Kate. 'It's only opinions you're reading, nothing else. They don't have any more facts than we do.'

'But you can't say opinions don't count. That's how you get new ideas, people thinking different things, not agreeing.'

Kate sighs. 'You're right, Millie. That's a very good thought.'

Millie sits back and looks pleased with herself. 'What's a racketeer?' she says.

'Someone who uses illegal methods to make money.'

'Like George Ranga – Raja . . .'

'Yes.'

'I wish we could just go back to where we used to be. I'm tired of everything being different. We were all right before.'

Kate leans over and puts her arms round her daughter. Millie relaxes, accepting the embrace, and Kate rests her head on Millie's, feeling the warmth of her thick hair. They stay together for a while. 'The trouble is,' says Kate, 'you can't go backwards. But things will get better. We won't be here for ever.'

'It's not that bad, really,' says Millie. 'You get used to it.' I didn't mean to complain, she's saying. I don't want to be difficult.

I don't want you to get used to it. I want to give you a nicer home. Kate strokes Millie's back gently. It's so hard to know that you can't just make things better for your children. 'Come on,' she says eventually. 'Let's go back to bed. We need to get some sleep.'

Millie lies down and Kate pulls the sheet up over her. She smoothes it with her hands, then leans over and kisses Millie's forehead. Millie smiles up at her. For a few seconds, Kate drifts back to a more innocent time when they lived without having to calculate every step, when it was easy to be a mother because there was an accepted structure within the family.

Kate pops her head round Rory's door on her way back to her bedroom, hoping they haven't woken him. There's a sudden scuffle, followed by an unnatural silence. She goes in and leans over him. He's curled up tightly under his sheet, his eyes squeezed shut. Suspecting that something's going on, Kate pulls back the sheet. He rolls away from her and she catches sight of his Nintendo clutched between his hands as he tries to hide it.

'Give me that,' she says, wondering why she's whispering when all three of them are awake.

Rory starts to snore loudly and unconvincingly.

Kate reaches for the Nintendo, but he resists her. 'If you were really asleep,' she says, 'you wouldn't be able to keep on holding it.'

An eyelid flickers and opens halfway, one eye staring at her blankly. 'I'm having an out-of-world experience,' he says, in a flat, mechanical voice. 'Aliens are communicating with me telepathetically.'

'No problem. Give me the Nintendo or I'll be signalling to them out of the window to take them with you.'

'They won't recognise your signals. You're an ignorant earthling.'

'And you're not? Give it to me.'

She goes to the bottom of the bed and tickles his feet.

He yelps. 'Stop it,' he begs, giggling and trying to get away from her. As he draws up his legs, she makes a grab for the Nintendo. They struggle for a few seconds until she manages to loosen his grip and prise it out of his hands.

'No!' he wails.

'Sssh,' says Kate. 'We'll disturb Millie.'

But she's too late. There's the click of a switch and they're flooded with blinding light. Millie is standing by the open door, glaring at them. 'Whatever's going on?' she demands, managing the role of an outraged parent very well. 'How am I supposed to get any sleep?'

They stare blearily at each other as their eyes adjust to the brightness. Then Millie rushes to the bed and leaps on top of Rory. Kate tries to pull them apart, not sure why they're fighting, whether they mean it or if it's just over-excitement. She's reassured by their gurgles of laughter as they kick and grab anything that moves.

Rory lets out a triumphant cry.

'Stop!' says Kate. 'You'll wake Irene.'

In the guilty silence that follows, they hear a sudden flurry of movement beneath them and the baby starts to cry.

'Serves her right,' says Millie. 'Using television cameras to please herself.'

'That's very uncharitable,' says Kate. 'A crying baby in the middle of the night is no laughing matter.'

At seven o'clock the following evening, Kate settles down again at her laptop, ready to type up the latest notes on her thesis.

I mustn't forget to dead-head the roses at the bottom of the garden. I left it too late last year.

There are no roses. There isn't a garden any more.

'Look at this, Mum,' calls Rory, from his bedroom.

She joins him at his window and sees a Mercedes pull up alongside the kerb. *Luxury Cars,* it says. *Exeter.* Felix used to use Luxury Cars. Kate holds her breath for a second, but then lets it out again as she recognises the two people emerging from the vehicle.

'It's the great-aunts,' says Rory.

'Mum!' calls Millie, from her bedroom.

'It's all right,' calls Kate. 'I've seen.'

They run down the stairs and out on to the path. Agnes is stepping delicately out of the taxi, balancing herself against the door. Beatrice has gone round to pay the driver.

'Nonsense, the journey only took forty minutes,' she is saying. Her clear, articulate voice rings out in the evening air, and every other sound shrinks back into obscurity. Two teenage boys shuffling past with their hands in their pockets stop and stare at her. Kate runs forward to help Agnes, who is swaying alarmingly.

'Ah, there you are, dear,' she says.

'So you'll be back in an hour's time,' says Beatrice.

'What a surprise,' says Kate.

The taxi driver is nodding up and down. 'Yes. No trouble. I be here.' He has a strong foreign accent and Beatrice is having difficulty understanding him.

'One hour,' she repeats. 'One hour.'

'I think he's got it, Aunt Beatrice,' says Rory.

Beatrice slams the door and the taxi drives away. Everyone stands together on the pavement while Beatrice and Agnes look around.

'Hmm,' says Beatrice, examining the block of flats. 'Nineteen fifties, I'd say. Replacing the slums.'

'But did they have slums in Budleigh Salterton?' asks Agnes.

'Good point,' says Beatrice. 'Are you upstairs?'

'Yes,' says Rory. 'Everyone in our family lives upstairs – even Grandad and Grandma.'

He's right, thinks Kate. How odd. Why has it turned out like that? An inability to keep our feet firmly on the ground, perhaps? Or are our ambitions too grand? Are we reaching for the sky, our heads in the clouds?

'At least we'll never have to worry about floods,' says Millie.

As they walk slowly up the path in a procession to their front door, Irene comes out of her flat with the baby on her shoulder like a fur stole.

'Good evening,' says Beatrice, who is in the lead.

'No,' whispers Millie. 'You mustn't talk to her.'

Beatrice stops on the path, causing everyone else to come to a halt behind her. 'Why ever not?'

'You'll never get away,' murmurs Kate, into her ear. 'She never stops talking.'

'I think I can manage to conclude a conversation whenever I want to,' says Beatrice.

'She betrayed us,' says Millie. 'She talked to the television cameras.'

'Ah,' says Beatrice. 'I see.'

She sweeps past Irene, who is compelled to retreat to the edge of the path. Irene jiggles the baby up and down and tries to meet someone's eye. 'How are you all coping with the heat?' she says. She says it again. 'How are you all coping with the heat?'

Everyone ignores her.

'Yes!' says Millie, with delight, as they reach their front door. 'We've cracked it. That's the way to deal with her.'

'Millie!' says Kate. 'You mustn't be so rude.' She turns back, anxious to soften their rejection. She will have to meet Irene again tomorrow and the next day. Their front doors are only a foot apart. She smiles vaguely, but doesn't let her eyes rest on Irene's face long enough to see the response. Then she follows everyone inside and shuts the door.

She has a moment of panic. Is the flat clean? Is it tidy?

Progress up the stairs is slow. Once on the landing, Beatrice opens each of the doors in turn and peers in, inspecting every room. Kate can hear her muttering: 'Hmm, bit small for Rory. Bathroom's adequate. You could do with more space in the kitchen.'

When they reach the living room, Agnes sinks thankfully into an armchair. 'Goodness,' she says. 'Such hard work, all those stairs.'

'That's what happens when you live upstairs,' says Rory. 'You must be used to it.'

She smiles at him fondly. 'I think we've had this conversation already, Rory,' she says.

Beatrice settles herself in the centre of the sofa, making it impossible for anyone to sit beside her.

'Rory,' says Kate, 'bring in some kitchen chairs.'

Agnes looks out of the back window. 'The grass needs cutting,' she says.

'Nobody does gardening,' says Kate. 'I'd like to hang the washing out there, but everyone says it would get stolen.'

'The flat's very small,' says Beatrice. 'You have to be tidy in such a confined space.'

Well, you're the expert, thinks Kate.

'Ah,' says Agnes. 'You've kept the Picasso sketch.' She's looking at the small picture next to the window. 'Felix will be so pleased.'

There's an embarrassed silence.

'Would you like some tea?' says Kate.

'That would be wonderful,' says Beatrice.

Kate goes out into the kitchen, but she can still hear the conversation.

'Have you spoken to Dad?' asks Millie.

'Yes, of course. He's staying with us.'

'I didn't know that.'

'Silly arrangement, the law. They make all this fuss, must find him, must catch him, must lock him up in prison, but when they do, they send him home again, telling him to be a good boy for six months until the trial. If he was a real villain, he could be off murdering people every night while he waits for the trial.'

'I think,' says Agnes, 'they would keep him locked up if he was a danger to the public.'

'Don't forget all the hoo-hah was about finding him because he'd disappeared. He could just go and get lost again.'

But where's home? Kate thinks. Rory and Millie are silent, and she wonders if they're thinking the same thing. She comes out of the kitchen. 'It's lovely to see you,' she says, wondering why they're here. They never used to visit, even in the old house, which wasn't upstairs. They always said it was too difficult to get out and they didn't drive and it was easier to receive guests than to visit.

'What do you mean, home?' says Millie, suddenly. 'There isn't a home any more. We live here now.'

Agnes looks up and beams. 'His old home, my dear. Where he grew up.'

The kettle boils and Kate returns to the kitchen to pour the water into the teapot. She brings a tray into the living room and sets it down on the coffee-table. 'Millie, Rory,' she says, 'I think it might be best if you go to your rooms now, so that I can talk to Aunt Beatrice and Aunt Agnes in private.' What she wants to do is be angry with the aunts, coming here with no notice, announcing to the children that their father is in the area, that he hasn't returned to his real family. She needs more time to explain it to Millie and Rory, to give them her reasons for refusing to have him come and live with them.

'No,' says Millie. 'I want to know what's going on.'

'Me too,' says Rory.

'Quite right,' says Beatrice. 'Children should not be denied important information.'

Not that you can talk, thinks Kate, living there on your own in your academic, unreal life, imagining you know all about families. Not that you ever shared any information about Felix's parents with him.

'We have come,' says Agnes, leaning forward to take her cup of tea from Kate, 'to ask if you—'

'He wants to talk to you,' says Beatrice. 'He's asked us to fix up a meeting.'

'No!' says Kate. She is handing a cup of tea to Beatrice, but her wrist turns, quite spontaneously, as if she no longer has any control of her movements and the cup and saucer tumble to the floor, the contents spilling on to the Ikea rug.

Chapter 23

Rory reaches the crossing before his mum and prepares to take off as soon as she gives the word, his left foot on the ground, the right poised on a raised pedal. His head is down, watching behind him. He's seen cyclists in this position in the Tour de France, waiting for the signal. She's so slow. Why can't she have a sense of urgency? He wants to be the first one there when the school caretaker unlocks the gates to the playground. Doesn't she understand about timetables? She ought to. She grew up in a school where the bell went every forty minutes. Maybe that's it. Maybe she can't cope without bells.

He wants to leave before she arrives, but he knows she won't like it. She likes saying goodbye and checking he has his packed lunch and all that sort of stuff. If he goes now, she'll go on and on about manners when he gets home from school.

'OK,' she says, when she finally reaches the crossing. She starts taking her yellow jacket out of the Tesco bag and putting her arms through the sleeves. She looks like someone pretending to be a policewoman in the wrong hat. 'You must come straight home today. Remember we're going to Grandma and Grandad's for supper.'

He nods. His foot is itching on the pedal, a millisecond away from launch time. Nought to thirty in sixty seconds. He'd like to make it fifty, but that's probably expecting a bit much.

There's a voice behind them.

'Kate.'

They turn round. A man is standing a few yards away. He's wearing a black anorak – an *anorak* in a week when it's been touching twenty-eight degrees by ten o'clock every morning? – jeans and trainers, and his hair is so short he's nearly bald. He has a yukky beard like a Russian spy. There's something about him . . . He almost looks like—

His mother gasps. 'Felix,' she says.

What's she talking about? Rory looks more carefully and the man starts to change. A bit like the Incredible Hulk, only not so many muscles and his clothes don't all come apart. His shape – his lips pressing together even though they're now surrounded by hair – the way his left ear sticks out more than the right—

Dad?

Rory doesn't know what to do. His foot loosens on the pedal and the handlebars become heavy in his hands. The bike feels as if it will topple over and he's not sure he can stop it.

His mum's no use either. Hours seem to pass before she jerks into life. 'Go away,' she says. 'I'm working.' She walks towards the house where the lollipop stick is kept.

'Morning, Mrs Kendall,' calls the face from the upstairs window.

Rory's mum waves, but doesn't speak. She picks up her stick and comes back to the crossing, watched silently by Rory and his dad.

'Go away,' she says again.

'I just wanted to . . .' His voice is odd, weaker than Rory remembers, as if he's nervous. It's not right. His dad always knew exactly what he was going to say.

'No!' she says. 'I *don't* want to. Go away.'

There's another pause and then, amazingly, his father just turns round, walks down the road and disappears into a side-street. Rory can't believe it. Is that it? She says no, so he just gives in? He doesn't do that sort of thing. He's always been – in charge.

'Off you go, Rory,' says his mum, in a funny voice. 'You'll be late for school.'

No, he won't. She knows he's always half an hour early. Is she expecting his dad to come back?

'Go on,' says his mum.

He wants to say something to her. About his dad. Ask if she knows why he's there. But he can't work out how to say it. 'Bye then,' he says.

She tries to smile, but he can tell she's only pretending. He turns away, gets on his bike and starts pedalling in the direction of his school.

After riding for a couple of minutes, he brakes, glides to a halt and turns back. He wants to know if she's talking to his father right now. He pushes the bike up a narrow pathway and comes out at the top of a hill, which overlooks the road and the crossing. He can see his mum as she takes a child across. There's someone else on the side of the road, waiting for her. Another mother with a group of children. Rory's mother takes them across and returns to the kerb. She's alone. No one is standing nearby, waiting to speak to her. His father hasn't gone back.

'Rory!'

Rory swings round and his father is standing a few metres away.

Rory doesn't know what to do. One half of him wants to turn away and pretend his father isn't there. This seems the logical thing to do, bearing in mind what his mother did. He knows he should be loyal to her because she was the one who didn't go off and leave him. But the other half of him wants to cheer because his father has come back.

He feels as if he's been caught by the pause button on the DVD, interrupted in the middle of a scene. He could go forwards or backwards. Which way? What should he do? He could run to his father and throw his arms round him. But that wouldn't be fair. His father made them poor, changed his mum, caused the boys at his old school to try and get him. Everything has been his fault.

But he's my dad.

Two teenage girls approach them, their school blouses untucked and tight over their hips, their skirts rolled over at the waist and ending about six inches above the knee. They're applying lipstick as they walk and talk.

'Anyway,' says one, 'it was Billy Goat Gruff.'

'What did he say?' says the other.

'He said, "I thought we had a date." It was, like, awesome . . . '

They drift past slowly. One is wearing flip-flops and they have to keep stopping as she struggles to keep them on. Rory can still hear their voices as they move out of sight.

'Thank you, Rory,' says his dad.

'What for?'

'For not running away.'

Rory shrugs. 'Doesn't mean anything.' He wants to give the impression that he's not really interested in the conversation, but the words come out as a thin squeak.

His father's voice is flat and funny. 'No, of course not.'

Stop it! Rory wants to shout. You don't really talk like that. You're just pretending. Go back to being normal.

He finds that he can't meet his father's eyes, so he stares past him, over the parked cars, into gardens where flowers are drooping and the grass is going brown, through small gaps between houses at the sea beyond. A seagull circles above them, occasionally opening its beak to give a creaky moan.

'You off to school?'

Rory nods.

'Mum lets you cycle, then? Aren't you going in the wrong direction?'

'No,' says Rory. 'I go to a different school now.' He looks directly at his father's face for a moment, to see what he thinks of this. He wants him to be shocked or something, but he just stays the same.

'What time do you have to be at school?'

'Nine fifteen.'

His father checks the watch on his arm. It's like the ones you can buy in the market for five pounds. What's happened to the stainless-steel chronograph watch that would withstand pressure up to fifty metres, five bar, under water? 'You've got ages yet. Do you fancy a walk along the sea front first?'

Rory hesitates. He's fairly sure his mum wouldn't like it. On the other hand, she'll be on the crossing for at least three-quarters of an hour and will never know. 'OK,' he says.

They walk side by side down the hill in the opposite direction from his mother. Rory wheels his bike between them. It's funny, he thinks. It's like walking next to someone he doesn't know. It doesn't even feel like his father. He has no idea what to say to him.

'So, where are you living now?' his father says.

'In a flat.'

'Do you like it there?'

'It's all right. It's nearer the beach than we used to be.' He wants to tell his dad about his new friends, about the game he's playing on his Nintendo, about football before school, but he finds that none of the words will come out. He opens his mouth to try a couple of times, but nothing seems right and he closes it again.

'How are the aliens?'

Stupid question. What's he supposed to say to that? 'Oh – around,' he says, in the end. Not too bad an answer. He's not really giving anything away. He can't tell him about the Space Warriors. That's private.

At the edge of the beach, Rory lays his bike on its side so that they can walk on the pebbles. His father picks it up, wheels it a few metres and props it against a bin. 'Don't you have any security for it?' he asks.

Rory pulls a chain and combination lock out of his pocket. He's only recently bought it from Halfords. He loves it – he's spent hours spinning the dials round, trying to work out how easy it would be to break the code. He thinks it gets very slightly looser at the moment when each correct number comes up, although he can't be absolutely certain. It's not possible to test it properly because he can't forget the right numbers. He hands it over.

'Do you know the code?' says his dad.

Rory rolls his eyes. 'What do you think?'

They walk down to the sea. The water is lapping in and out against the pebbles, revealing some of the orange sand that appears at low tide along this part of the beach. This is where most people come if they want to swim.

'How's your mum?' says his dad, as they stand side by side, gazing out to sea.

Rory thinks about this. He doesn't really know how she is. She just is. 'All right,' he says.

'Do you think she'd speak to me?'

'No. She said she wouldn't.'

'You mean just now? When she was in her yellow jacket?'

Rory nods.

'I meant later, another time, once she'd got used to the idea.'

How is Rory supposed to know what his mother wants? If she says no, doesn't that mean no? He's not a mind-reader. 'I don't know,' he says. 'Maybe.'

His father bends over and picks up a stone. He tries to skim it along the surface of the water, but it's not thin enough so it bounces slightly, then drops with a feeble plop into the water. 'I was hoping she might. D'you reckon you could persuade her?'

'Me?' says Rory, in amazement. How come his father is asking such a dumb question? 'She won't take any notice of me.'

His father picks up another pebble. Two seagulls hover over their heads, circling like helicopters, hoping for food. 'She might.'

Rory watches him. In one way, the man at his side is exactly his father. The way he turns over lots of stones, trying to find one that satisfies him, changing his mind at the last minute, then straightens up, thinking he's found the perfect shape. The way he leans backwards, his arm bent behind him, and the circular movement as he throws it, his body zooming forward just the right amount, as if he's bowling for England.

But in another way he's a stranger, a man he's never seen before, someone who makes Rory shy. He can't talk to him about his mother. This is not the man who used to live with them, who taught Rory how to listen to the Test match on the radio, who made all those jokes about blueberries.

'How did you know Mum was a lollipop lady?' he asks suddenly.

His father seems surprised at the question. He thinks for a while, as if he doesn't know the answer. 'It was just luck,' he says at last. 'I happened to catch sight of her one morning and followed her to the crossing. My lucky day.'

He's lying. Nobody goes for walks in Budleigh at eight o'clock in the morning if they haven't got a dog. Anyway, Rory would have been with her and he'd definitely have noticed if someone was following. There's no such thing as coincidence, everyone knows that. It must have been the great-aunts. He's protecting them.

Except the great-aunts might not know about the lollipop job, and if they do, they certainly won't know where it is and they couldn't have come across her by mistake because they don't drive.

So his dad has another source of information. Someone who's betrayed them, given away their whereabouts. He might even know where they live.

To hide his suspicions, Rory picks up a stone and throws it at a group of seagulls bobbing up and down on a wave. They see it coming, drift apart and let it fall into the gap between them.

'I've got to go,' says Rory, turning away. 'I'll be late for school.'

'Of course,' says his father. He makes no attempt to follow.

Rory stops halfway up the beach and looks back. His father raises his hand in a sort of salute. He's smiling. From this distance, he appears normal. It could be a whole year ago, and his dad is the dad he used to know. On holiday, beachcombing together, collecting all the peculiar things you can find washed up on the high-tide mark. Shells, coloured glass, plastic dolls' legs, feathers, bits of rope. They could have just eaten ice-creams, biting off the point at the bottom and sucking from there, seeing who could make it last longest without dripping.

His father seems so small on his own with the wide sea behind him, as if he's just going to fade into the background.

A great pain is growing inside Rory. It starts in his stomach and spreads outwards, through his arms and legs, choking him as it reaches his throat, expanding into his head, a sick-making roar that travels so fast he can't keep track of it.

His father is shrinking in front of him, squeezing into a tiny dot against the light, disappearing.

Rory charges back down the beach, his head lowered, stumbling over the stones, his mouth open and making sounds he can't control, and he throws himself into his father's waiting arms. Boys don't cry, he thinks briefly. My dad doesn't like it. But he can't stop the bone-shaking sobs that force their way out of him.

Chapter 24

By the time Kate returns to the flat, she is shaking with disbelief. She'd recognised Felix immediately. The beard, the strange clothes, the shaved head, none of these could disguise the essential reality of him. Her initial reaction took her by surprise – a leap of joy that jolted through her like electricity. He'd come to find her! It was followed by choking anger. How dare he just turn up, after all this time, not dead at all? His appearance confirms his disloyalty and dishonesty. Did he really expect her to speak to him, as if they knew each other? As if they could just pick up where they'd left off, husband and wife, after a little tiff?

The phone rings and she picks it up. 'Hello?'

'Mum, is that you? You sound funny.'

Lawrence. She swallows and forces herself to concentrate. 'Yes, it's me. How's it going? How far have you cycled?'

'Oh, miles. We're making great progress.'

There's something about the way he says this. 'How far?'

'Well, we're still in Cornwall.'

'What part of Cornwall? You're approaching the Tamar bridge, right, about to cross over into Devon?'

'Well . . .'

'Lawrence? Where are you?'

'We've got to Penzance.'

But Penzance was where the train terminated. They were supposed to cycle down to Land's End and start from there. That was two weeks ago. 'Lawrence, have you actually been to Land's End?'

'Zoë's got some friends here – they've hired a cottage by the beach for the whole summer. We've been camping on their floor.'

'And do you intend to stay there?'

'No, no. We're setting off in a few days' time. We just thought we ought to have a bit of a holiday before we started. You know, after all the exams.'

Kate gives up. If he's happy and not starving, perhaps he's better kicking around on Cornish beaches with his friends than cycling along busy roads to the north. 'Do you have enough money to live on?'

'Are you offering?'

'No, I was thinking it might be worth looking for a job in Penzance since you're there.'

'Yeah, yeah.' He pauses. 'Mum . . .'

'Yes?'

'Zoë bought the *Guardian* yesterday.'

Ah. He knows. Kate had intended to tell him, then decided not to. Why spoil his holiday? Why force him to confront the future before he needs to? He won't be able to change anything. 'And?'

'Dad's come back.'

'Yes.'

'And you didn't think you ought to tell me?'

'I was going to ring you, but it's been so hectic here. And I wanted to confirm it. You can't always trust newspapers, you know.'

'Have you been to see him?' asks Lawrence.

'He's not in custody any more. He's out on bail.'

'Mum! You haven't let him come home?'

'No, of course not. He's staying with the aunts.'

'The traitors!'

Kate agrees with Lawrence on this. She thinks Felix should be made to stay in a hostel for homeless people, endure some hardship. She doesn't see why he should live in comfort, have his meals cooked for him, his shirts ironed. 'Well,' she says, 'I suppose they feel some loyalty to him.'

'Make sure he doesn't try and move in with you, Mum.'

'Don't give me orders, Lawrence. I can make my own decisions.'

'I just don't like the idea of him wheedling his way back into our life. He doesn't deserve anything from us. Let him sort himself out.'

Lawrence is saying all the things that Kate has been thinking, but at the same time . . . Remember the way he used to be, she wants to say. We loved him once. You can't just wipe away all that love as if it never was. Some of it must have been real.

'Mum? Are you still there?'

'Yes.'

'Did you hear me?'

'Of course I heard you. What about looking for work in a bar or a restaurant? They must be quite busy at this time of year, especially with all the good weather. You and Zoë could do it together.'

'Mum, stop it. We were talking about Dad.'

'No, you were talking about Dad. I wasn't.'

'So what are you going to do?'

'I've got a thesis to write. I'm going to get on with it.'

'OK.' He sounds relieved. 'So you're not going to have Dad back?'

'I've already told you, Lawrence. I'm not accountable to you. But, as it happens, I have no intention of speaking to your father.'

'OK, Mum.' His voice changes and she can hear murmuring in the background. 'I'm off now. Zoë wants to go swimming. Bye.'

It was inevitable that the aunts would support Felix, that they would act as a go-between, just to please him. He's always been the joy of their life. The model son they never expected to have, the only person they have ever cared about except themselves. They've invested all their energies and resources and intelligence in his upbringing. They wouldn't be able to disown him.

Beatrice was shocked when Kate refused to see him. 'He's made some mistakes,' she said, 'but he never expected things to come to this.'

'He should have thought about that before he abandoned us,' said Kate.

'He was caught up in difficult circumstances,' said Agnes. 'He wanted to be loyal to George. The burden of friendship can be overwhelming.'

'Never mind George,' said Kate. 'What about his responsibilities to his family? You can't go on making excuses for him.'

'We've never done that,' said Beatrice. 'He wasn't spoilt. He always had to accept the consequences if he behaved badly.'

But she meant things like reading in bed with a torch, taking the last slice of cake without asking, watching the *Flintstones* when his aunts were out.

'Anyway, nothing's been proved,' said Agnes, her face stiff and prim.

'Yet,' said Kate.

'Why don't you ask Felix for his explanation?' said Beatrice.

'No,' said Kate.

After talking to Lawrence on the phone, she goes into Rory's bedroom to change the sheets. It's not easy. He's decided to reorganise everything, but hasn't got past the stage of emptying all the cupboards and shelves and piling his possessions on the floor in random groups. Why is his *Dangerous Book for Boys* sitting in a box of dried seaweed? Or his CD collection divided up and placed between heaps of T-shirts and jeans? Kate steps delicately over the clutter to the bed and pulls the sheet off the mattress.

A movement outside the window attracts her attention and she looks up.

Felix is standing on the pavement.

He has his back to the road and his head slightly raised. He's examining their flat.

Kate steps away, her heart pounding. What is she supposed to do now? She doesn't want him to know that she's here, that she can see him.

After a while, she leans forward very slowly to see if he's still there. He is. She takes a deep breath, turns her back on the window and decides to finish changing Rory's sheets.

She pulls off the Power Rangers cover and throws it through the door to the landing, then wrestles the Transformers cover over the duvet. She shakes it out more violently than usual, pounding it down on the bed several times before letting it settle.

He can't do this to me. I shall carry on as normal. He doesn't exist.

She goes into the kitchen where she can't see the road and starts working on her thesis. She's still comparing Lismer's *A September Gale, Georgian Bay* with Varley's *Stormy Weather, Georgian Bay*. The similarities are striking. There's a single isolated tree in each painting. It appears frail and bent, but it's deep-rooted enough to survive the force of the wind, resilient enough to keep standing. In the background, threatening waves rip through the lake and dark, tormented clouds tear across the sky, but the eye is drawn to the tree, the survivor.

What does Felix want? Does he intend to knock at the door? Halfway through the morning, she edges to Rory's room and peers through the window.

He's gone. Relief floods through her and she takes several deep breaths. She goes back to the kitchen and studies the sky in both pictures. Lismer's is fierce and angry; Varley's is calmer in the background.

Ten minutes later, the doorbell rings. What if it's him? She hesitates, not sure what to do, then creeps down, peering through the opaque glass from the safety of the stairs, hoping to see who it is. Someone oddly shaped is standing there, too slight, too short for Felix. She opens the door.

It's Irene, with the baby draped over her shoulder.

'Oh,' says Kate. 'It's you.'

'Can I come in?' says Irene.

Normally Kate would never have considered it, but today is not normal and she's almost pleased to see Irene. She stands back to let her step in. 'Go ahead,' she says, closing the door behind her.

Irene climbs the stairs and heads straight for the living room. She knows the layout of the flat, of course. It's identical to hers.

'Do sit down,' says Kate.

Irene sinks to the sofa, jiggling the baby up and down. It's asleep. If she doesn't stop all this moving around, it'll wake up and start crying. 'What a lovely sofa,' says Irene. She sounds nervous.

'Would you like a cup of coffee?' says Kate, wondering if she should tell her that the soft cream leather sofa was bought in the days of Felix, when money was no object.

'No, it's OK.'

'Is anything wrong?'

'It was him, wasn't it?' says Irene.

'Who?' Has her boyfriend turned up? Has she escaped, leaving him downstairs on his own as he hides the drugs?

'Outside. The man on the pavement. It was your husband, wasn't it?'

It hasn't occurred to Kate that other people in the flats might have noticed him. He shouldn't be a presence in anyone else's life. He's a shadow in her mind, not theirs. 'Yes,' she says. 'Did he alarm you?'

Irene takes the baby off her shoulder and lays it on the sofa next to her. It gurgles, wriggles a little, continues to sleep. Kate has never seen it behave so charmingly. It sucks a thumb, its breath whistling softly in its nostrils. For the first time, it looks like a proper baby, an individual, not an extension of Irene. The wailing that Kate hears in the evenings must be a sideshow, not the main act.

'He came yesterday as well,' says Irene. 'When you were out. He walked up the pathway as if he was going to ring the bell, but then he didn't.'

He must be mad. Didn't she make herself clear at the crossing? 'I'm sorry if he worried you.'

'Oh, he doesn't bother me. But he's a bit scary, isn't he?'

Kate doesn't think that 'scary' is the right word, but she can't decide what is. 'Persistent'? 'Annoying'? 'I don't think he's going to do anything nasty, if that's what you're worried about.'

'I wasn't worrying,' says Irene, 'but I thought you might be.'

'That's very kind of you,' says Kate. 'But—'

'I know about men, see. Had to put up with difficult men all my life. My father was one, then my brothers, and then Kevin – I was stupid to go with him, I always knew that, really. But you think they'll be different with you, don't you? Until they get angry and put one on you.'

'What do you mean?' says Kate.

'You know, knock you around, hit you.'

'Oh,' says Kate. 'I don't think my husband's like that.'

'Those telly people, them that came here with cameras, they said he was a crook.'

'Well, maybe ... He's not exactly. It's all to do with money.' Is she defending Felix or herself for being taken in by him?

Irene leans over and pats her arm. 'Doesn't make any difference. Money or not, it's what they do to you that matters. I should know. My dad went to prison for fraud.'

'Really?' says Kate.

'Fiddled the state, didn't he? Claimed thousands on benefits by pretending he was three different men, all with a wife and four children. Social Security didn't find out for ten years.'

'Goodness,' says Kate. 'Don't they make checks?'

'Course not. Not unless someone reports you. You fill in a form and they give you the money. He had it sent to mates' houses.'

But that's real dishonesty, thinks Kate. Felix isn't like that. He didn't make things up. He just didn't tell anyone. 'It's not quite the same,' she says.

'Comes to the same thing,' says Irene. 'If they're not honest, they're not honest and you can't trust them.'

Kate can feel herself becoming resentful. She doesn't want to establish a link with Irene. 'Would you like a cup of tea?' she says, wanting a change of subject.

Tea is obviously more appealing than coffee. Irene's face lights up. 'I thought you'd never ask,' she says, and produces a packet of Chocolate Digestives from her bag. 'I brought these.'

'How kind,' says Kate.

Irene's face relaxes into a cheeky smile. 'Nothing like a treat every now and again. These are the best – more chocolate than biscuit.'

She's not that bad, thinks Kate, as she goes into the kitchen to make the tea.

'You could ring the police – ask them to move him on next time he comes,' says Irene, when Kate returns.

'Ask the police to move on my own husband? I couldn't do that.'

'Why not? They're used to it. They have a special way of dealing with domestics nowadays. Much better than they used to be.'

So it's a domestic now. Kate is shocked. Up until this year, she hasn't lived the kind of life that involves the police. She's always been respectable.

But what makes someone respectable? Is it the way you live now, the way you used to live, or the way you think? What's the difference between her and Irene? They've both ended up in the same position. Partners of men who've broken the law, men who've deceived them. Given the opportunity, wouldn't Irene have taken up Kate's old way of life with pleasure, fitted in, expanded into a big house and sent her children to private schools?

'No,' says Kate. 'I don't want to involve the police – it would just get him into more trouble.'

Instead of laughing, as Kate expects, Irene puts out a hand and touches her arm. She's getting sentimental, thinks Kate, in a panic.

'We're hopeless, aren't we?' says Irene. 'We always feel sorry for them, whatever they've done. I know when Kevin gets out of prison, I'll take him back in, feed him, forgive him, pretend he's mended his ways. You can't help it, can you?'

'Oh, I don't think I'll do that,' says Kate. 'I didn't mean I'd have him back. In fact, I know I won't. I just don't like the idea of calling the police. It seems too dramatic.'

Irene opens her wide, loose mouth and laughs. 'Dramatic!' she gasps. 'You get all these reporters outside your home, he gets his mug into the papers, even the telly, he turns into a stalker, and you think calling the police is a bit dramatic!' She leans back and her peals of laughter echo through the room.

The baby, thinks Kate. You'll wake the baby. She's not at all sure what Irene finds so funny, but somehow the spectacle of her laughing becomes entertaining in itself. Kate smiles and allows herself to join in, still wary, still cynical. Then something whooshes through her like water through an unblocked drain and she gives way to helpless giggles. Tears stream down her face. She can't remember what the joke was, but it doesn't seem to matter very much. All she knows is that she's laughing about something very funny. She laughs and laughs and laughs.

Eventually she feels a firm hand on her arm. She takes deep breaths and struggles to assert some control. 'Come on,' says Irene, with unexpected gentleness. 'Drink your tea.'

Kate takes the cup and sips slowly, letting the heat seep down with reassuring familiarity. Waves of giggles are still hovering below the surface, threatening to engulf her again, but she manages to resist them this time. They subside into trembling and finally calmness. 'Sorry,' she says. 'I got a bit carried away.'

'Have a biscuit,' says Irene, offering her the opened packet.

Kate takes one. 'It's a good thing Rory isn't here. He'd have devoured the packet by now.'

The baby on the sofa is squirming, screwing up its face, curling its hands into fists. Irene looks down at it. 'Typical boy,' she says. 'Nothing's going to stop him getting just what he wants whenever he wants it. Thinks the world revolves round him. Same as every other man I ever met.'

Kate sits among the other parents in Millie's school hall and tries not to meet anyone's eyes. It's the summer concert. They've heard the orchestra twice, the string quartet, the wind band, and the gifted thirteen-year-old Winifred Ho, the next potential concert pianist – although she's more likely to study medicine if she follows the same path as all the other brilliant musicians who've passed through the school.

Kate watches the choir file on to the platform. They're organised by height. Millie is in the second row and Kate can just see her red curls as she peers out between two of her classmates.

The junior girls think they're so grown-up before they go into the senior school. But as soon as they arrive they revert to being children, back at the bottom of the heap. All of the nearly-teenagers in the front two rows are yearning to be the girls behind them, longing for sophistication, counting down the milestones to adulthood. Nail varnish, heels, boyfriends. But to their parents in the audience they're just little girls with hair-bands and bunches, balancing evenly on sturdy legs as they prepare to sing. The older girls are allowed to wear tights and their uniform is more sophisticated, but years seven and eight are still in black ankle socks, although block heels and platforms are creeping in, surreptitiously replacing the regulation flat shoes. Their low-waisted cotton summer dresses rise in the middle, pulled up by developing busts or padded bras, and form an unintentional arch over their knees.

> *Early one morning, just as the sun was rising,*
> *I heard a maiden sing in the valley below . . .*

The sopranos are sweet against the mellow tones of the altos. Kate lets her eyes wander round the hall. Fathers and mothers are here together, younger brothers and sisters, babies, aunties, grannies. Late-comers are standing against the walls at the back, craning their necks to see properly.

> *Oh, don't deceive me,*
> *Oh, never leave me . . .*

There seems to be some disturbance at the back, the hint of a whisper, heads moving slightly to the side to enable a discreet search.

Felix is standing at the back of the hall. Just inside the doorway.

Kate's eyes dart away in shock. She stops listening and prickles of sweat break out down her back. How could he possibly have known when Millie was performing?

He's been recognised. People will be embarrassed. Kate won't be able to speak to anyone.

> *How could you use*
> *A poor maiden so?*

Everyone is applauding. The girls file off the stage, grinning at each other and their parents in the audience. Kate glances over her shoulder at the back of the hall again.

He's gone.

She cranes her neck, trying to check if he's hidden behind someone else, but she can't see him. She breathes more easily and the sweat starts to dry. Was he really there at all?

He seems to be everywhere, waiting outside the house during the day, hovering near the crossing after Rory has left, a shadow that somehow fades when she can't bear it any longer. Just as she summons the courage to confront him and tell him to go away, he's disappeared, slipping into the background and frustrating her.

She knows she should say something to Rory, explain why she couldn't talk to his father that day when he approached them. But she can't find the words. So she says nothing and hopes that it will somehow fade from Rory's memory. He doesn't seem concerned. His mind is on his gang, on football, his Nintendo. Millie seems to be distracted by end-of-term events. She's hardly talking at all at the moment.

Three days after the concert, at five fifty-five in the morning, Kate arrives at Horton's Chocolates, gets out of the car, unlocks the door to the factory and turns off the alarm.

'Kate . . .'

The soft voice doesn't surprise her as much as it ought to. Somehow she has always known that she will have to speak to him in the end. She turns and stares at him. He's uncharacteristically scruffy, his jacket open and dishevelled, his face creased and puffy. 'It's a bit early, isn't it?' she says. 'Are the buses running already?'

He grins, familiarity and strangeness mingling in the framework of his beard. 'I slept the night in one of the boats – under the tarpaulin.'

'Which boat?'

'The red and white one. It's called *Patience*. From Teignmouth, it says.'

'By the beach huts?' Why are they talking about a boat? He comes back from the dead and they need to discuss the details of his night's sleep?

He nods. 'That's the one.'

She steps into the building. 'I'm working,' she says, over her shoulder. 'If you want to say anything, you'll have to talk while I work.'

He follows her in and shuts the front door behind them.

Chapter 25

Felix stands just inside the office marked 'Mr T. Addenbrooke' and watches Kate as she collects mugs from around the room. He takes a breath, opens his mouth – and nothing comes out.

He's prepared a speech. He's gone over it a hundred times – in his head, into the empty air in the tiny bedroom at the top of his aunts' house, into the round shaving mirror in the bathroom, his lips magnified and distorted. The words are queuing up in his mind, falling over each other in their anxiety to push themselves forward, but he can't organise them into a practical order. Nazrul, Runa, Brandon are watching him—

'I don't know why you're here,' says Kate. She dumps the mugs in an untidy group at the edge of the desk and sweeps a half-eaten pork pie, a container of left-over coleslaw, cake crumbs and broken chocolates into a black bin-bag. There's a frantic energy in her, hard and brittle, a barely suppressed anger that is waiting for an opportunity to ignite. 'I have nothing to say to you.'

She knocks over one of the mugs. Felix leans forward and grabs it just before it topples off the side of the desk. She glares at him as if he was the one who had knocked it over. 'I can't see why we've had to go through all this performance if you haven't got anything to say. Why don't you just clear off?'

He has got things to say. 'I thought I should—'

Kate doesn't stop working. 'Whatever it is, you'd better get on with it. I'll be vacuuming in a minute.' The air around her shimmers, radioactive and dangerous. She picks up stray papers and throws them savagely into the in-tray, where they tremble with cringing obedience.

'You've changed, Kate.'

She freezes halfway through the action of bending down to pick up some scrunched papers that had missed the wastepaper bin and an expression of disbelief passes across her face. 'You think I've changed?' she says. 'Well, now, I wonder how that could have happened. There I was, getting on with my nice, slightly boring, ordinary life, looking after my family in the best way I knew, and what happened? My husband disappeared off the face of the earth. There one day, gone the next. It turns out he's a money-launderer, a crook. What on earth makes you think I'd remain the same?'

Amsterdam, four years ago. Felix and Robbie had completed a two-week audit and Robbie had left a day early, leaving Felix to tidy up the details. On his last evening, after a meal, Felix wandered into the hotel bar. He could feel restlessness pulsing inside him, a release of tension after finishing an assignment that had left a vacuum, and he knew he wouldn't sleep if he just went to bed.

The bar was active and noisy. Several large groups were engaged in passionate debate, their voices raised in disagreement. Felix ordered a glass of wine and sat down in a corner, listening for an English voice, an argument he could follow.

A couple came in and sat at the bar, close to Felix. They murmured with the comfortable, intimate sound of people who knew each other well. Felix was struck by the clarity of the woman's profile, the long line of her nose, the flatness of her forehead above her delicately arched eyebrows. Her straight hair ebbed and flowed, panther-black, against her white cheek.

Her companion, a man in a pale herringbone jacket, had his back to Felix and was leaning towards her, talking intently.

The language seemed to be English, but their voices were too low for Felix to catch more than the occasional word. When they broke off their conversation to sip from their glasses, the woman noticed Felix watching them and smiled vaguely.

He looked away, conscious that he had been observing them too closely. He felt as if he was a child again, creeping down the darkened stairs to the toilet, hearing his aunts' murmured conversations in the living room, a burst of suppressed laughter. He couldn't distinguish the words. He just knew that he was apart from them, a child with no autonomy.

It was a mistake to come here on his own. The warm atmosphere, the groups of friends, their raucous laughter, isolated him. As he considered returning to his room and reading a book, his eyes were drawn back to the couple. They were picking up their debate again, softly but intently, when the man unexpectedly turned round, as if he knew he was being watched.

They recognised each other at the same moment.

George leapt from his stool, almost overturning it, and stepped over to Felix, who had also risen to his feet. 'Felix, my man!'

'George!'

They grasped each other's hands, smiling broadly, speechless in a way they had never been when they were younger. George was bigger than Felix remembered, the skin on his face loose and fleshy. He had become the mirror image of his father.

'Ah, so you have met before,' said the woman, standing up to join them.

'We're old school friends,' said Felix.

'But we kind of lost touch. We haven't seen each other in—'

'Thirty years,' said Felix.

George laughed. 'Figures were always his thing.'

The woman offered her hand. 'I am Kristin Petursdottir.'

Her hand was tiny and Felix could feel the delicate structure of bones underneath her skin. 'Icelandic?' he said.

'Very good,' she said, nodding.

They sat down and ordered more drinks. Felix knew he had had enough already, but the night was slipping sideways, and none of his normal reactions seemed appropriate.

George and Kristin had just set up a business in Iceland – Olafsson's School Supplies – and they were in Amsterdam to negotiate a contract with a new customer.

'You're a businessman?' said Felix, with amazement. 'The great George Rangarajan has joined the rest of the world and taken up a conventional career?'

George grinned. 'Actually, I have several businesses. An antiques shop in Paris, a casino in Hong Kong and I'm a landlord – I've got property in Manchester, London and Leeds. Oh, and a charity for displaced Tamils.'

'Goodness,' said Felix. 'You're running a global empire.'

'Felix is an accountant,' said George to Kristin.

'Really?' She turned towards him, studying him with more care. 'How interesting.'

'Not that interesting,' said Felix. 'It can sometimes be a little boring.'

'Come on,' said George, getting up. 'We can't just sit here on such a glorious night. We should go out and explore. Eat, drink and be merry, that sort of thing.'

'Well,' said Felix, 'I'm afraid I've already eaten, but I'm willing to be merry.'

Kristin smiled at him, her face pale and luminous in the half-light. 'At least we can walk,' she said. 'And talk about George's past.'

'So, did you marry Kate?' asked George, as they strolled along beside a canal.

'I did.'

'Children?'

'Three. How about you?'

George sighed and looked briefly at Kristin. 'Divorced,' he said. 'Twice.'

This was no surprise. 'And now?' asked Felix, looking from George to Kristin.

'Ha!' said Kristin. 'He thinks we are lovers.' She and George laughed loudly.

'My fault,' said George. 'Must have given the wrong impression. We're just business partners. Kristin has her own husband back home, a doctor.'

'But no children,' said Kristin.

'I'm sorry,' said Felix.

'There is no sorry,' she said. 'I do not want children. I enjoy my job, my beautiful house, my trips to the theatre, my holidays abroad.'

Their footsteps were light on the pavement, the night air warm and companionable. Felix started to see everything with an unnatural clarity. The mass of still water in the canals, black as oil but overlaid with glittering reflected lights, the metal whorls and curls on the side of the footbridges, the ornate carvings under the roofs of the tall terraced houses.

'Do you remember when we came to Amsterdam before?' said George. 'We stayed in a house just like this.' He started to climb the front steps of an imposing double-fronted house with a wide mahogany door.

'George!' said Kristin. 'Behave yourself. Someone lives in this house.'

'You're quite right,' said George, jumping down. He collided with Felix and they clung to each other in an effort to keep their balance. Felix experienced a delicious slide backwards to his teenage years, the only time in his life when he had been able to surrender himself to enjoyment without consequences, swept along in the wake of George's irresponsible impulses. He allowed himself to enjoy the pleasure of uninhibited laughter.

'You are like children,' said Kristin. 'Come, we must leave this area before we are arrested.'

They stumbled away from the house, led by Kristin, and their hilarity gradually subsided, settling into the more comfortable glow of long-term friendship.

'I've just remembered,' said George. 'Felix's ambition was to be a millionaire. Do you remember telling all of us in front of the Big Man and the comely Kate?'

'I was very young at the time,' said Felix.

'And did you make the million once you came face to face with real life?'

'What do you think?' said Felix. 'Money slips through your fingers when you have a family.'

Kristin and George stopped and looked at each other with unexpected seriousness. George raised an eyebrow in query and Kristin gave a slight nod.

'We've been looking for an accountant to manage our Iceland account,' said George. 'Have we mentioned that yet?'

'Oh, I see,' said Felix. 'You want to hire my professional expertise.'

'We do indeed,' said George.

He went over the whole episode again the next day on the flight home. He had a dull headache and his eyes ached from lack of sleep. He had never expected to meet George again. He hadn't been prepared. He felt that he had climbed some steps and was standing before a wide, locked door, which, given certain circumstances, might just swing open. A sense of unease scratched the back of his mind, like the tickle of a threatening sore throat.

But when he closed his eyes, he saw himself at sixteen with George, on the deck of the boat his parents had hired for the summer to sail round the Greek islands. George was crouched in the bows, watching the water flow past, his shoulder-length hair streaming out behind him in the breeze. Their O-level results had arrived at the hotel in the morning post. Felix's were outstanding, as everyone had expected. George's were less good, with passes in only five subjects, although he had an A in art.

'Well done, both of you,' said George's mother, as she buttered her toast. 'They've forgotten the jam again. Why is everyone so incompetent?'

'And are you proud of your results, George?' said his father.

'I am, actually,' said George, his voice brittle and defensive.

'And what exactly will an A in art do for you? If you'd worked harder, you might have had a more impressive set of results.'

'I did work hard.'

'Clearly not hard enough.'

At the prow George was uncharacteristically still and distant. Felix watched the back of his head, uncertain if he should approach him. He thought of how his aunts would respond when he arrived home. There would be a celebratory meal, champagne. He was shocked by George's father's attitude, acutely embarrassed by his own success, and overwhelmed by a desire to make everything all right for George.

Kate plugs in the vacuum-cleaner.

'I'm sorry,' says Felix. 'I never intended to hurt you.'

She ignores him and presses the switch. The dusty roar fills the space between them and cancels out his words. She flings the vacuum around, banging into skirting-boards, ploughing through a pile of shoes, sweeping a ball of socks in front of her towards some golf clubs in the corner. She heads for Felix's feet until he jumps out of the way. When she's covered every section several times, she switches off the vacuum and pulls the plug out of the socket. She wheels it into the corridor.

'Oh, you're sorry. Is that supposed to make me feel better?'

she says, over her shoulder. She goes back for the empty mugs and nearly bumps into him. He steps aside just in time.

'Are the children all right?' asks Felix, following Kate into the corridor. He knows the answer already. When he sees Rory, he sees himself as a child, bewildered, struggling to find reasons for events that have no explanation. And he's followed Millie while she wanders through Exeter as if she's lost her way. He wants to approach her, offer to help her, but he knows how much she must hate him. He's written to Lawrence, but there hasn't been any reply. Felix lies in bed at night and the air pulses with their sense of betrayal and rage. If he turns away now, he might never be able to approach her again. He has to try, he has to.

Kate stops and turns back, her face thunderous. 'What do you think? Rory's been chucked out by his school, Millie doesn't have her friends round any more – too ashamed of our flat, I assume – and Lawrence is cycling from Penzance to John o' Groats, except that he can't be bothered to get on his bicycle.'

So Lawrence wouldn't even have received his letters. 'No change there, then,' he says, and smiles. He has forgotten for a moment how careful he has to be.

Her mouth compresses and her eyes narrow. She's as outraged as if he had hit her. 'If you find that funny,' she says, 'I can't begin to imagine what you think you're doing here.' She turns away and walks into the next office.

Felix follows her. He examines a family photograph on the desk.

'You won't find anything in common with Mrs Stevenson,' she says. 'She's got a nice family. Her husband's an engineer. He comes home every night.'

'I was placed in an impossible position,' says Felix.

She stops abruptly and stares at him. 'I see. So George was more important to you than me and the children?'

'No, no – it wasn't like that.'

'That's exactly how it looks to me.'

He can't find the right words. 'I made a wrong decision.'

'Yes,' she said. 'You did.'

At first, there were no problems with the accounts of Olafsson's School Supplies. Felix had expected to go out to Iceland for his quarterly audits, but George sent everything to him by courier and it all seemed straightforward.

But as time went on, a niggling uncertainty crept over him. The profits seemed excessive for such a new company. Why were there so many cash payments? Why were so many bills being paid into offshore accounts in Nigeria, the Cayman Islands, the Bahamas, countries well known for their stringent privacy laws that prevented investigators from knowing who controlled a company or bank account?

He emailed George. 'Can I come and see the factory?' If George responded and invited him to Iceland, all would be well. If not, he would have to extricate himself.

A card arrived. *Greetings from Iceland*, it said. It was elaborate and beautifully designed, a work of art. An invitation to visit. Pleased and relieved, Felix placed it on his office mantelpiece.

'Lucky you,' said Bill. 'I hear Iceland's a great place to go.'

Felix experienced an unexpected moment of panic, suddenly doubting his logic. Was he standing in front of the door that had been closed for decades? Had he been handed a key he shouldn't use?

'Let them spoil you,' said Robbie. 'Take you round, show off their facilities.'

This was nothing to do with anything that had happened in the past. He and George were thirty years away from the streets of London. They were no longer the same people.

'OK,' said Felix. 'I'll make arrangements.'

George and Kristin greeted Felix with delight, hugging him, kissing his cheeks, escorting him from the airport to the hotel with plenty of jokes and bursts of laughter. Felix felt himself being drawn in again, gathered up into the warmth of their friendship.

'Did you bring photos of your family?' asked George.

'I've brought several,' said Felix.

During dinner, they pored over them. 'Such a beautiful family, Felix,' said Kristin. 'Have you told them about us, how much you have helped in our success?'

'We need to talk about that,' said Felix.

But they were in no hurry. 'First,' said Kristin, 'you must see my country.'

'Tomorrow we're going to take a trip,' said George. 'They have the most spectacular waterfalls in the world here. I want to show you one of the largest at Gullfoss.'

'Will I be able to go and see the factory?' said Felix.

'Of course,' said Kristin. 'We'll all go the day after.'

But the next day there was a drive to the Blue Lagoon. 'I thought we were going to see the factory,' said Felix.

'Later,' said George.

'When?' said Felix.

George hesitated for a few seconds. 'There is a small problem,' he said.

'A problem?'

'There has been an unfortunate incident.'

'It is nothing,' said Kristin. 'We will soon fix it.'

'So can we go there anyway?'

'Of course,' she said. 'Tomorrow.'

On the fourth day, Felix went back to the hotel room in Reykjavik and looked out of his window at the sea in the distance. The landscape was frozen, still and beautiful. He was warm behind the double glazing, relaxed in the heat from the radiator. He'd just had an excellent meal at the Pearl, a restaurant under a dome on top of the city's heating system – hot-water tanks heated from geothermal sources.

There isn't a factory, he thought.

His stomach was suddenly uncomfortable, overfull, cramping up – he dashed into the bathroom and was sick.

He was regularly briefed on money-laundering. There was a procedure to follow. He had ignored it.

He phoned George.

'I'll come round,' said George.

Felix wanted to be calm and rational, politely withdrawing from the situation. It wasn't too late. He hadn't done anything wrong yet, at least not knowingly, so he should still be able to walk away from it.

George came on his own. The moment he had entered the room and closed the door, Felix was aware of electricity in the air between them, shimmering, vibrating.

'Don't you think you owe me an explanation?' Felix heard his voice rising and tried to moderate it.

George held up his hands in a gesture of surrender and chuckled as if he couldn't feel the tension. 'That's the Felix I remember. Straight to the point.'

A picture sprang into Felix's head. George bobbing up and down in the canal, laughing. 'You think this is funny?'

George kept smiling as he went over to the sofa. 'Sit down, Felix. Let's talk.'

Reluctantly, Felix sat in the chair opposite and glared at him. He couldn't shake off the sensation that they were fourteen again and George was organising a homework scam. The idea was to pair up each thick boy with an Einstein, who would be paid to do his homework for him. George had a little book in which he had compiled a list of rates and strict rules, which involved commission for each transaction. 'It's a charity,' he had said. 'Everyone gains. I can't imagine why nobody's ever thought of it before.' It went on for three glorious weeks until Bradley Junior stole the book, attempted blackmail and handed it in to the Big Man when George refused to pay up. Felix and George were put on a fortnight's litter patrol for that offence.

'OK,' said George. 'What's the problem?'

'You know perfectly well what the problem is. You're using me to legitimise your money – dirty money.'

'Have you got anything to drink?' said George, getting up. He located the mini-bar and went over to help himself. 'How about you?'

'No!' said Felix, more violently than he intended. George was just creating a diversion, avoiding the issue. 'Well?' he said. 'You haven't answered the question.'

George came and sat down again. 'I don't remember you asking me a question.'

'So you don't deny it?'

'I wasn't aware that there was anything to deny.'

'You're money-laundering. And you've involved me. Did you seriously believe I wouldn't notice? When you can't even produce a factory?'

George sipped his drink slowly and looked out of the window. 'Are you suggesting there's no factory?'

'Of course there's no factory. It doesn't exist. It's just a way of getting your money into the system legitimately. Fake invoices, receipts, shipping documents. You know that, I know that. Why pretend?'

George turned his gaze towards Felix. He studied him thoughtfully for some time. 'Do you really think I would involve you in anything dishonest?'

Felix couldn't understand his lack of agitation. Wasn't he worried that Felix would report him? 'Stop pretending, George. I know about these things. It's my job.'

George leant forward, suddenly serious. 'And my job is to run a business. If I have to sail close to the wind to do that, then so be it. I take the risks, everyone benefits. I support local charities. I donate to the Tory Party – did you know that?

Everyone loves me. I'm an entrepreneur, a man who makes things happen. Do you seriously believe you can undermine my ability to make something of myself, to be someone?'

'Where's the money coming from?'

George smiled. 'You really don't want to know that. I can promise you it's minor stuff. No guns, no drugs, no terrorism. Does that reassure you?' He stared straight at Felix, his eyes wide and open with the confidence Felix remembered from their schooldays. The boy who believed in himself, even if his parents didn't.

'Nevertheless, it's illegal. A crime.'

George sat back and spread his arm along the back of the sofa. 'Come on, Felix, lighten up. Look on it as a favour to me. We've been friends for years.'

Felix stood up. He had to make his position absolutely clear before he was drawn in too far. 'No,' he said. 'Find someone else. I'm not your man.'

'But, Felix, old friend,' said George softly. 'You're already my man.'

Felix stared at him. With a lurch of the stomach, he realised that George was right. He'd known something was wrong and he should have reported it immediately. Talking to George now, like this, was tipping off. A criminal offence.

He sat down. He wondered if he could appeal to the George he'd once known, his great friend and ally. They would have lied to protect each other once. 'Come on, George, people trust me. I couldn't betray that trust, even for you.'

George watched him, not responding for a few seconds. He placed the ankle of one leg over the knee of the other. 'Felix . . .' he began. He sighed heavily, as if he was reluctant to continue. 'But do these people know about the other Felix? London, just qualified, walking home from the pub – do they know you've killed a man, Felix?'

This was it. The tension in the room burst into a thousand points of light, pulsing outwards in waves. The body of their attacker was between them, his blood on the ground, black and deadly, the knife glued to Felix's hand – Felix's hand, not George's.

They had arrived at the point that had been mapped out thirty years ago. It had been smouldering away all this time, pretending to be buried, waiting for precisely this moment. The conversation had been inevitable.

'We don't know what really happened. It was difficult to tell – it was dark . . .' Felix was stammering.

'You were holding the knife, remember? I saved you that night. I made you run, made you jump into the canal to destroy the evidence. Without me, you'd have been standing there when the police arrived and you'd almost certainly have ended up in prison. There would have been no wedding, no kids, no career. You owe me.' He stood up and went back to the mini-bar. He poured out two whiskies and handed one to Felix. 'Here, get that down you. You'll feel better for it.'

Felix drank without tasting anything. 'And is Kristin part of all this?'

'I don't think you need to be concerned about Kristin.'

He should never have come. It would have been better to carry on, pretend he hadn't noticed anything, let it all rush by him without comment.

'Felix . . .'

He was startled to hear a softer tone in George's voice.

'I'm asking you as a friend. You were always much cleverer than me. You could do anything you wanted to, while I couldn't even stick out an art course because I knew I wasn't good enough to succeed. I know what I'm good at. I can make money, spread it around for good causes, help other people. This has been my chance to be someone, not the son of my father, but me, George Rangarajan. People treat me with respect. OK, some of my methods may be a little off the beaten track, but I'm not bad. I'm just doing what I do best. All I need from you is a little understanding, a little help.'

Felix felt himself being sucked back to that time of powerlessness, when he was only five years old, unable to act . . .

'It's your turn to save me,' said George.

It was more complicated than he'd expected. Much more complicated.

'Why don't you think about it?' said George, brisk now. 'Mull it over tonight and give me a ring tomorrow before you go.' He made it sound as if he thought there was a real choice. He went to the door. As he put his hand on the lock he turned back. 'It's not as if you won't benefit from it,' he said. 'There's money in it for all of us.'

'You can't be serious,' said Felix. 'If I took money from you, I'd be committing a much more serious crime.'

'We go back a long way,' said George, opening the door. 'Don't forget that.' And he left the room.

On the flight home, Felix thought of Kate and the children. He studied the clouds below him – white, fluffy, rosy in the setting sun.

I am an honourable man. I put my family before everything.

Honesty is the quality I most need to instil in my children.

They can solve old crimes now – they can prove things with DNA evidence. They would send me to prison.

How could I explain it to Kate and the children? How could I face them once they know I'm not the person they thought I was?

George at twelve, coming into the toilets, finding Felix surrounded by a group of upper-fourths demanding his watch. Felix huddled up against a wall, water gushing in the background. 'Come on,' a boy was saying. 'Let's put his head down the toilet.' It sounded like fun, an interesting game.

'What's going on?' George, silhouetted against the light of the outside corridor, standing with his legs apart, towering above some of the older boys, arms hanging loosely against his sides. A gunfighter on the side of right.

Relief flooding through Felix, his legs shaking with the release of tension.

'If you lay another finger on Kendall, I'm up there, talking to the Big Man. The only way you're going to stop me is to kill me. Is anyone ready for that?'

Felix and George walking stiffly through the door, careful not to rush, leaving behind an uncertain silence. Running down the corridor once they were out of sight, not quite certain how they'd got away with it, sharing the exhilaration of triumph.

As the plane flew through the darkening skies, calm settled over Felix. He was starting to lock up, moving through his mind and sealing the doors, one by one, until he was walking through clean, uncontaminated corridors. All the clutter, the debris he didn't need, was scattered behind him in the frozen spaces of Iceland.

When they landed, he walked off the plane, showed his passport, passed through the green channel and went home.

Kate's cleaning is too diligent. She's determined to scrub and polish everything until it gleams. 'I didn't know you liked cleaning,' says Felix. 'You're very good.'

He's underestimated her fury. 'What do you know of what I like or dislike?' she shouts. 'Do you think I have a choice? Someone has to go out and earn a living for the family.' She pushes him aside as she heads for another office.

Felix stands still in the now empty room. She's become powerful. It feels as if he's standing at the foot of a wall that reaches so far into the sky he can't even see the top. He doesn't know if he can ever scale it.

He has to try. Without his family, he will cease to exist.

After a few seconds, he follows her into the next office. 'I'm sorry,' he says again. 'I'm sorry.' But however hard he tries to inject meaning into what he says, he can't seem to make it convincing. How can he? It's all too big for words.

'Don't you think you're a bit late for that?' she says. She pushes the vacuum-cleaner plug into the socket. 'So where exactly does the money-laundering fit in?' This is the first time she's asked a question. 'It's not exactly as if you needed the money.'

Felix hesitates. 'It wasn't about money. I wasn't paid a penny.'

He can see her hands shaking as she reaches for the switch on the vacuum. 'Oh, yes, I can believe that. I'll be a crook for absolutely no reason. I'll just pretend I'm an honest man, I'll teach my children to be as upright as me.' She turns on the vacuum and shouts over the sound. 'You're a hypocrite! A confidence-trickster – a counterfeit!'

Felix waits until she's finished vacuuming. 'I accept all your blame,' he says. 'I just wanted to say that I know how hard it's been for you and that I deeply regret my mistakes.'

There's nothing else to say. He can hear her breathing into the silence. Ragged gasps as if she's trying not to cry.

'All I've ever cared about is you and the children.'

'Get out of here!' she screams. 'Get out!'

Her voice penetrates deep inside him. The force of her hate is so strong that it pushes him physically backwards, towards the stairs and down. His feet clatter on the bare wood.

'And stop spying on me!'

A book flies through the air after him, followed by a large ring-binder, heavy with filed documents.

He opens the front door and leaves.

Chapter 26

Millie has seen her father several times, outside the school gates, in shop entrances as she walks past, sitting on a bench along the sea front. He has never attempted to speak to her, but it's as if he wants her to know he's there.

Should she tell her mother?

At night, she dreams of him watching her while she's watching Samantha and her boyfriend. They walk through the streets of Exeter in a straight line. Samantha and Crispin are in front, holding hands, gazing into each other's eyes every few seconds. Millie follows ten metres behind, her face cleverly disguised by a school scarf. And her father is ten metres behind her. He has a beard and doesn't look like her father at all, but she knows it's him. The ten metres between them never varies. If one person moves faster or slower and the gap alters, everyone else adjusts to put it back to where it should be.

Millie feels that she's being suffocated in the middle. There's no way out, forwards or backwards. She wants to escape, but can't. She's tied there, held in place, even while she's walking, compelled to follow and be followed. She wakes up aching all over, her mouth dry and sore, as if she's been shouting for hours.

She and Helen are talking to each other again. The first time was their short conversation about Latin, but things got going properly during one lunchtime about a fortnight before the end of term. Millie was sitting on her own, swallowing pasta and chicken as fast as possible, not taking any notice of anyone else, when a plate appeared next to hers on the table and she heard a chair being pulled out. She looked up.

'Hi,' said Helen.

'Hi,' said Millie, in surprise. Then she put her head down and continued eating, not sure if this was intentional or if Helen had made a mistake. Nobody had wanted to sit next to her for ages.

'Could you pass the water, please?' said Helen.

It was within reach of both of them, but Millie leant over and handed the jug to her.

'Thank you,' said Helen, and smiled.

Millie smiled back, wondering if Helen had forgotten that they weren't friends any more.

'Who do you think is going to win the rounders match this afternoon?' said Helen. 'I reckon it'll be Virginia's. They've got Hilary Martin. She's an ace runner.'

'More likely to be Sylvia's. Their fielders are so good. It doesn't make any difference how fast Hilary can run if they bowl her out.'

They continued eating for a while, not talking, but Millie could feel a change taking place. A comfortable companionship. There'd been a blockage inside her chest for so long that she'd forgotten what it felt like to breathe easily. She'd grown so used to the pain of it that she was startled to feel something like a thin trickle of liquid managing to work its way through her lungs. Like ice melting. Helen hadn't said much. Just a few words. But she had chosen to sit next to Millie. She was saying something without actually saying it.

They have fallen into a regular pattern of sitting together every lunchtime. Now if she's late, Millie finds Helen waiting for her at the entrance to the canteen. Gradually, their conversation is easing its way back to an ordinary level, although they're more cautious than they used to be. There's still a barrier between them, but now it's more like a sheet of glass.

After a few days, she decides to tell Helen about her father. 'I keep seeing him,' she says. 'He's watching me.'

Helen looks alarmed. 'Is he safe? He wouldn't kidnap you or anything?'

Millie finds this funny, but she doesn't laugh because she doesn't want Helen to think she isn't taking her seriously. 'No, I don't think so,' she says. 'I just don't know what to do. Suppose he speaks to me?'

'Well, you don't have to reply if you don't want to. He can't force you.'

'That's true.'

'Do you reckon he's dangerous?'

Millie thinks of bank robbers, men with guns, James Bond villains. 'Not really,' she says, although she doesn't want to deny herself the exciting image of being in danger. 'I just don't know what he wants.'

'He probably wants to talk to you.'

But he doesn't. Millie goes over and over what she would say to him, working out the exact words. 'I would prefer not to speak to you.' 'Leave me alone. You're no longer my father. You gave up that right when you left us.' 'Who are you? I don't recognise you.'

But he never gives her the chance. When she looks again, he's gone.

It's the end of Millie's first year in senior school. She's heard about end-of-term celebrations. Some of them have gone down in history – the day the sixth form came in early and moved the entire contents of the staff room on to the front lawn, or the day they covered everything, including the headmistress, with glitter that stuck and wouldn't come off. But this will be Samantha's last day of school. She's going to uni next term and Millie might never see her or Crispin again.

In the last Assembly, teachers who are leaving have to walk through the massed rows of shrieking, clapping, stamping girls to the platform to receive their leaving gifts from the head girl. The girls even cheer for Miss Jennings, the geography teacher, who can strike terror into their hearts simply by writing 'See Me' at the bottom of a piece of work. Suddenly it's desperately sad that she's leaving. Several girls are crying.

'She wasn't that bad, really,' shouts Helen, into Millie's ear.

But Millie can't answer. She's screaming with everyone else, her hands burning from the clapping. She unexpectedly loves Miss Jennings. She loves the school, the girls, the teachers . . .

The sound dies down as Miss Jennings turns to address them. 'Well, girls, all good things must come to an end.'

Samantha is on the platform among the rest of the sixth form, her flushed face split by an enormous grin. Maybe she actually liked Miss Jennings, who treated the older girls with more respect than the younger ones and shared jokes with them. It's easy to love her now, here, in the middle of a great big crowd like this, but to *like* her?

'I shall miss you all.' Miss Jennings wipes her eyes.

She's crying, thinks Millie, with astonishment. She doesn't want to go. There are tears in Millie's eyes too, but she's thinking of Samantha – and Crispin. There's a kind of dangerous charm about Crispin that forces her to keep watching him. He makes her nervous, but she likes the gleaming dark coils of his hair, the way the muscles of his back move under his shirt. He seems to have forgotten his earlier threat. Now when he encloses Samantha in his arms, it's as if he organises his position so that he can look directly over her shoulder at Millie with a confusing expression. Once he winked at her and she was so shocked she turned away in a panic and ran, dropping her Parker pen on the way, not going back for it. She doesn't know how to react to him. He hasn't told her to scram again, but he knows she's there and he doesn't seem to mind any more. Sometimes it seems as if he's putting on a play just for her, keeping his eyes open when he kisses Samantha, to make sure Millie is watching.

'I will follow your careers with interest,' says Miss Jennings, stepping down from the platform with a huge bouquet of lilies and the Royal Worcester vase that has been presented to her.

Millie is watching Samantha, her stomach fluttering. She might never see her again. How will she know how to be a sixth-former herself if she can't keep learning from Samantha?

Most of the upper sixth are crying, letting the tears flow down their cheeks, almost as if they're proud of them, but a few are standing apart, stiff with disapproval. It's all so childish, they seem to be saying, so juvenile. Millie studies both reactions and wonders what she will do when she's that old.

Cars crowd chaotically into the front car park at twelve o'clock as parents arrive to pick up their daughters. Millie's mum won't be coming – she doesn't pick her up so often these days – and Millie is going to take the train to Exmouth, then a bus to Budleigh.

She walks down the drive with Helen, who's carrying a bag crammed with end-of-term presents. Millie has only one present in hers – from Helen. It's a bracelet, sterling silver, studded with diamanté and pretend rubies. She adores it. They stop at the gates. 'You can come back to my place if you want,' says Helen. 'My mum wouldn't mind. She'd give you lunch.'

'Thanks,' said Millie, 'but I'd better get home.'

Glancing sideways, she sees her father on a corner by the school. Girls are streaming past him, but he remains motionless, his eyes fixed on Millie. She looks away.

'I'll ring you,' says Helen.

'Great,' says Millie.

They hug. A long, drawn-out hug, the first in ages. Millie tries to enjoy the warmth of Helen's body against her own, the offer of friendship. But she's waiting for Samantha. She wants to say goodbye.

And her father is still there, watching.

They set off in opposite directions, pausing to wave to each other every now and again. Once Helen is out of sight, Millie stops and looks across to where her father was standing. He's not there any more.

She pauses for a second, makes a decision and runs back to the school. If she stands by the gates long enough, she's bound to catch Samantha. She would just like to end properly and she's been rehearsing the words. 'Thank you for being nice to me,' she will say. 'I'm glad I've known you. I hope all goes well in the future.' That would do it. A signing off, a recognition of her debt to Samantha.

As she approaches the school gates, she catches sight of her father walking away, up the road that borders the side walls of the school grounds. She hesitates. It's the first time she's seen him without him seeing her.

She doesn't know what to do.

She wants to speak to Samantha. She wants to follow her father.

Which is most important? Samantha will soon be gone for ever. How much does it matter? Samantha has been inside Millie's head for such a long time, and given her something to think about when everyone else was so nasty. Millie can't just let her disappear without a word.

But this is her father.

She wants to know why he keeps watching but never speaks. He must think about her and, let's face it, he's the only one who does. Nobody else cares about what she's going through. Her mother hardly ever talks about anything serious any more, just how expensive oranges are, or 'How many times have I told you to hang your coat up? There's no room for untidiness here. We don't live in a mansion.' All Rory talks about is football, aliens and food, and Lawrence is miles away.

She leaves the school gates and follows her father.

At first, she has to run to get herself into a reasonable position behind him. She's been following Samantha for so long, she knows how to do it. Move fast, stop every now and again and blend into a group of nearby people, look natural. Stay near the inside of the pavement where you're less visible. Notice any suitable hiding-places – entrances to drives, alleyways leading to garages or the backs of gardens – in case he turns round. Be aware of parked cars, which you could crouch behind in an emergency.

She wants to know where he's going, although she's not at all sure what she'll do when she finds out. But it's reassuring to keep him in sight, as if she's talking to him without talking to him.

They turn left past the leisure centre, up the hill past the bus garage and down the road that leads to the back of the station. This is where she should be heading anyway. He goes straight past, and she follows, beginning to feel tired, but determined not to lose him. He heads towards the university.

He must be going to the great-aunts'. She makes all this effort and the only thing that's going to happen is that she'll find out where he's living. Which she already knows.

He disappears round a corner at the top of the road, and she hurries to catch up, breathing heavily, wondering how much longer she can keep going.

She turns the corner and he's standing in the middle of the pavement, waiting for her.

She stops and doesn't know what to do.

He tries to smile, but it's a rubbish sort of smile. He's just pretending, stretching his lips inside that stupid beard. Who does he think he's kidding? 'Millie,' he says.

She stares at him. She can't remember any of her prepared speeches.

Nothing happens. He seems to be waiting, but she doesn't know what for. A bus drives past, the engine rattling as it accelerates up the next hill. Two boys who've been walking behind her jostle her arm, deliberately maybe, but she doesn't take any notice of them. They fade into the distance.

What should she do? What should she say?

She opens her mouth, wondering if words will come out on their own anyway, even though she's forgotten them. But there's only silence.

He takes a step towards her. 'Millie,' he says again.

'How could you do it?' she says, in a low voice. 'You've ruined our lives.'

He doesn't come any closer. 'I know,' he says. 'I did a terrible thing.'

She stares at him and a wave of anger crashes over her. 'Is that all you've got to say?' Doesn't he even have an explanation? 'Why did you do it? Why? Why? Why?' She can hear her voice rising into a shriek. She can't stop it. 'I hate you!'

He stands in front of her, swaying slightly as if he's being hit by a violent wind, but not giving way. 'I don't blame you for hating me,' he says. 'I'd do the same if I were you.'

'Well, you're not me,' she shouts, and turns away from him.

She finds herself running down the hill, her feet tumbling over themselves, her breath jagged and uneven, tears dripping down her cheeks. Her schoolbag bangs against her side, threatening to fall off her shoulder. She grabs it and holds it in one hand.

She runs and runs and runs until she can't run any further. When she finally stops, she leans against a wall and bends over, panting.

After a while, she manages to straighten up, but keeps her head lowered, afraid to look round in case he's standing close by. But there's no one there. She's in an unfamiliar street, completely alone. The large, elegant Victorian houses are set back from the road, surrounded by trees and bushes and gravel drives, partially hidden behind brick walls. There's no sound of traffic, no sound at all, except her own pathetic whimpering.

She shuts her mouth and checks her bag. Everything seems to be inside, including her purse. She sighs with relief.

That'll teach him, she thinks.

She smoothes her dress down, making sure it's hanging properly, and bends over to neaten her socks. She runs her fingers through her hair and refastens the clasp that pins the curls off her face.

OK. She's fine now.

She walks down to the end of the road and finds herself in the area where Samantha lives. She's been here before – just walking past, pretending she was on her way to somewhere else, checking what kind of house Samantha lives in, so she'd recognise it again if she needed to.

Thank goodness she did. Now she can get her bearings and work out how to get back to the station. She might even manage to see Samantha and say goodbye to her after all. Or catch a glimpse of Crispin for a last time.

A group of young people turns the corner and walks up the road towards her. They're talking loudly, passing a can of Diet Coke between them and drinking deeply. Bursts of indignant voices leap out into the quiet road.

'You can earn seven quid an hour—'

'He's so uncool—'

'I'm sure it was her that borrowed my hockey stick—'

If Millie crosses the road to avoid them, they'll definitely see her, so she decides to squeeze herself against a wall and let them walk past as if she's not there. As they draw closer, she keeps her eyes down, convincing herself that she's invisible. Rosebushes lean out over the top of the garden wall behind her back, the brown-tinged petals spilling on to the pavement. She can feel the tip of a branch just touching her head.

'Well, hello,' says a man's voice, sounding as if he's just found a ten-pound note. 'What have we here?'

Slowly, she raises her eyes and finds herself looking up into the dark eyes of Crispin. 'Hello,' she whispers, unable to make her voice work properly.

He's with Samantha and her three friends, Cassie, Frances and Anthea. They gather round Millie with a kind of pretend curiosity, as if they're all taking part in a complicated joke.

'Millie!' says Crispin, sounding artificial, like an actor. 'What in the world are you doing round here?'

She tries to shrug. 'Nothing. Going home.' She manages to produce more sound this time.

'This is hardly on the way home for you, though, is it?'

'It might be. Depends where I've been.' She's pleased with that answer. It shows she's not scared of him.

But, alarmingly, he takes her arm. 'Look, Sam,' he says, turning to speak over his shoulder. 'We've caught your stalker.'

She can feel the heat of his skin against her bare arm.

'I tell you what, Millie, we're going back to my parents' house for a few beers. Why don't you join us, since you seem so keen to be in our company?'

Millie stares at him. The invitation doesn't make sense. They don't want her with them. They're nearly grown-up. 'I – I can't drink beer,' she says. 'I'm not old enough.'

Two of the girls giggle loudly. 'Join the club,' says Cassie.

'How old do you reckon you have to be?' asks Frances.

'Eighteen,' says Millie. 'That's the law.'

'Only in public, sweetheart,' says Crispin. 'Not in private.'

'Duh!' says Cassie.

'Sweetheart'? What's going on here?

'Come on,' says Samantha. 'Leave her. We're wasting time.'

'Yeah,' says Cassie. 'She's just a kid.'

'I don't think we should leave her,' says Crispin.

He's very close to Millie. She can feel heat coming off his body, smell his sweat, strong and sour. What had once seemed fascinating has become menacing. An overwhelming sense of revulsion is welling up inside her. She pulls her arm back. 'I've got to go,' she says.

'No,' says Crispin. He puts out his hand and strokes her cheek gently. 'You're a stalker. We should take you to the police station.'

Millie goes rigid. A tremble starts up deep inside her stomach. She can't move. Crispin is so much taller than her, so alien and masculine. He's an enormous, powerful man and she feels like a little girl, tiny, with no strength—

He bends over and murmurs softly into her ear so that no one else can hear. 'You fancy me, don't you? I've seen you looking at me. I know.'

He's angry because I've been watching him with Samantha. He wants to punish me.

'Stop it,' says Samantha, somewhere in the distance. 'You're frightening her.'

He laughs. 'That is my intention.' His voice is unnaturally loud, so close to Millie's ear. She can feel the damp warmth of his breath on her cheek.

An appalling thought pops into her mind. He's going to kiss me.

This cannot be happening.

She clamps her teeth together. She can smell alcohol, aftershave, the sweetness of the roses.

She can hear a passing car going up the hill, a dog barking in the distance.

'That's enough,' says Samantha's voice, much louder, as she pulls at Crispin's free arm.

Millie feels his muscles tense for a second, then he relaxes and steps away from her.

'Come on,' says Frances, sounding bored. 'It's getting late. I want to put a DVD on.'

'It wouldn't suit you,' says Anthea.

Crispin separates himself from Millie, and laughs with the others, a cheerful, easy-going laugh. 'I just thought Millie and I should have a little chat. She's been spying on us for far too long.'

Millie stares straight ahead, unable to move or look directly at any of them. Her face is burning.

'Are you all right, Millie?' says Samantha.

Millie nods.

'She's fine,' says Crispin. 'Aren't you, Millie?'

Millie nods again. She shrinks into herself, desperate to disappear, and edges past them all.

Don't do anything suspicious, she thinks. Act normal.

She starts walking away from them, towards the station, resisting the temptation to run.

'Millie!'

She stops. She can hear steps approaching her from behind.

Samantha comes round in front of her. 'Are you sure you're all right?' she says, peering at Millie's face. 'You look a bit strange.'

'I'm fine,' says Millie.

'Crispin was only teasing you.' Her voice is soft but insistent. 'He didn't really mean it.'

'It's OK,' says Millie. 'Really.'

'You'll have to stop following us, you know.'

Millie nods. 'I'm sorry,' she says. 'I'm sorry.'

Samantha studies her for a bit longer and apparently decides to accept this. 'OK,' she says. 'Have a good holiday.'

And that seems to be it.

'See you around.'

Millie nods. Samantha walks back up the road. 'Crispin!' she calls. 'Wait for me!'

Millie hears them meet up again, their low, confidential voices.

A great surge of laughter bursts out from behind her. Loud and hysterical.

She feels completely humiliated.

She reaches the end of the road, turns the corner and leans against a wall, shaking uncontrollably. Fat tears ooze out. Huge, thick and hot, pouring down, merging and becoming a waterfall. Her nose is running, her mouth open, catching some of the water as it cascades past, and the tears keep coming, on and on, enough water to feed a lake, the sea, all the oceans on the planet.

Slowly, slowly, after a long time, the shaking becomes less violent, subsiding into slight tremors, and the tears fade to a thin trickle. It's nearly all gone. Millie becomes aware of a strange lightness, as if she's managed to get rid of more than she'd known was there. As if she'd been building up to this for months, her body filling with a toxic gas that needed to be let out. She takes a few deep breaths, feeling the air reaching down into her lungs, clearing pathways, penetrating further than she's used to.

She lifts her head and examines her surroundings. A man is standing two metres away from her, watching.

For one startled second, she thinks it's Crispin. Then she recognises her father. 'Oh,' she says, 'it's you.'

'Are you all right?' His voice is familiar, but somehow old. A sound that comes from a distant past.

She nods.

'I'm sorry,' he says. 'I didn't mean to frighten you like that.'

He doesn't know. He didn't see what happened with Crispin and Samantha. He thinks Millie's upset because he tried to talk to her. Relief sweeps through her. She doesn't have to tell anyone about it. There's no need to explain. She can just forget it, walk past, let it fade away.

'Why do you keep following me?' she says. They're not the right words. Not what she had intended.

'I'd like to talk to you,' he says.

'So talk.'

'Well,' he says, 'it'll take a bit longer than that. Do you have time for some lunch somewhere?'

Millie hesitates. It sounds so formal.

'It doesn't have to be lunch,' he says. 'Perhaps a coffee.'

'I don't like coffee.'

He's watching her, a familiar half-smile just touching his lips. 'OK, then. A Diet Coke? Going down, going down . . .'

He's right, she thinks. I'm in a lift. I've been too high, wandering around, expecting the wrong things on the top floor when all I really need to do is get back to the ground. Suddenly she's exhausted. It's too difficult pretending she knows what she's doing. She just wants things to be normal.

She can feel herself starting to cry again, but it's different this time. Easy, gentle tears. 'All right,' she whispers.

Chapter 27

At four thirty, after finishing her lollipop duty, Kate walks to the beach for a swim. She heads for the far end where there won't be so many people and undresses quickly, leaving her clothes in a small pile near the edge of the water. She wades in. The beach descends in ridges, like a giant stairway, and you lose contact with the bottom within a few yards. But once you're there, lifted by the natural buoyancy of the water, it's glorious. Fresh, open and clean, with the arc of the sky soaring above you.

Eventually, she swims back to the shore, stopping at the water's edge to put on her plastic sandals. Looking up, she sees a figure at the top of the beach, a silhouette. A compartment deep in the centre of her heart opens and shuts abruptly at the sight of him, but not before a tiny drop of unexpected pleasure has squeezed out. It's Felix. The droop of his shoulders, the position of his head, the angle of his feet.

She ignores him as she stumbles back up the beach to her belongings, unable to decide how she should react. On the one hand, he really should have got the point from their last encounter. On the other, she acknowledges and almost admires his persistence, his refusal to give up. She doesn't regret throwing the ring-binder at him when he ran down the stairs at Horton's Chocolates, but she is ashamed of her anger, her obvious loss of control.

The prickle of goose pimples breaks out along her arms and she starts to rub herself vigorously with a towel. She knows Felix is approaching slowly, sliding down the stones. 'Do you want a hand?' he says, as he reaches her.

Once he would have helped to dry her back, her arms, her legs. She shivers at the thought of his touch. 'Go away,' she says.

But he sits down and stretches out his legs, watching her. Kate looks round the beach. Will people recognise him? What will they say? She huddles into her towel, not wanting to draw unnecessary attention to herself. A warm breeze blows off the sea towards them.

'You've lied to me,' she says. 'Right from the beginning.'

'No,' he says. 'That's not true.'

'You were never who you said you were.'

'I was. I was Felix Kendall. It was only at the end that things went wrong.'

'You mean they didn't quite fit into your plan.'

'There was no plan. It just happened.'

She's shivering.

'You'd better get dressed,' he says. 'Do you want me to help?'

She moves away from him. 'No.' He used to hold the towel round her while she manoeuvred into her underwear. He was good at it. Now she does it on her own, as she has learnt to do this summer, wriggling awkwardly. She keeps an eye on him as she does it, but he's looking out to sea, his eyes narrowed against the glare of the sun.

She pulls on her skirt and T-shirt and feels more in control. Felix hasn't moved from his position. 'What do you want?' she says.

'Just to talk to you.'

She's trying to be angry again, but it's harder out here in the wide fresh air, with the soft ripple of the waves a few yards away. The sea rocks in and out, massaging the pebbles with a soothing, rhythmic roll. 'But you don't seem to have anything to say.'

'I think I have, but it's not easy.'

'Well, it wouldn't be, would it?'

A mother walks across the beach towards the sea, holding the hand of her toddler. The child is licking an ice-cream, but just as they decide to sit down, she stumbles. The ice-cream leaps out of the cone, arches through the air and falls on to the stones. 'Mum!' she shouts.

The mother examines the situation with a weary bleakness on her face. 'It's no good,' she says. 'We can't do anything about it.'

The little girl starts to shriek. They turn round and head back up the beach, the screams echoing in their wake, strangely remote in the still air.

The heat of the sun penetrates, and a comfortable relaxation spreads across Kate's back. 'Why?' she says.

'Why what?'

'Why everything? Why did you do it, go off and leave us like that instead of sorting it out? Why didn't you tell me what was going on?'

'I don't know,' he says.

'That's not good enough. You must know.'

'I'm still trying to make sense of it myself.'

'I thought you were dead.'

They're dancing an old-fashioned dance. The Virginia reel. Coming together as part of a big circle and holding hands while they twirl round, *dos-à-dos*, back to back, avoiding each other's eyes. They form an arch, watch other people pass underneath, and skip between the rows of couples. They divide and march in opposite directions, not meeting again for some time. Then they line up again, watching, but too far away to touch.

'I've been living in Deptford,' he says.

'Really?'

'And I've been working in a grocery store.'

'Thus are the mighty fallen.'

He chuckles softly. She knows the sound. The intonation, the way he starts, the way he trails off.

'It was run by a family of Bengalis,' he says. 'I grew quite fond of them. They had five children.'

'Well, well. A family. I wonder what drew you to a family.'

He moves restlessly on the stones. 'It all started when I went to Amsterdam – about four years ago,' he says. 'I met George again – and Kristin.'

'I thought it was Iceland.'

'That was later.'

'I suppose she seduced you – that's how they do these things, isn't it?'

'No!' he says. He seems genuinely shocked. 'I've never been unfaithful to you, Kate. You have to believe me.'

She doesn't want to hear this. 'Did you know about the illegal immigrants and all the rest of it?'

'No, of course not. They wanted an accountant, that was all. But the business wasn't exactly as he portrayed it. They didn't tell me the truth—'

'Oh, come on, Felix. You're not stupid. You must have seen through them.'

'It wasn't obvious. Not at first – not until I went to Iceland.'

She's wrong. He is stupid. 'That was three years ago. Why didn't you just report it?'

'There were other considerations – something that happened when we were much younger.'

'Oh, I see. A secret schoolboy pact that meant more to you than your family.'

He shakes his head slowly. 'No, of course not. But it was very complicated. Do you remember when we bought the wallpaper for the snug?'

She's startled. Has he been having the same thoughts and memories as her? Do their minds still run along parallel lines? 'You overruled me,' she says. 'I never had a real choice.'

'That's not how I recall it. You were the one who made the final decision.'

'Was I?' He's remembered it wrong. If it was true, he'd manoeuvred her into that position.

'I'm not complaining,' he says. 'I liked the way you had confidence in your own taste.'

Confidence? She can't remember it. She can only remember Felix taking the lead, making the decisions, moulding her.

'You were so good for me,' he says. 'Without your involvement, I couldn't make a decision – but I thought I could.'

Is he saying he can't decide anything unless he can convince her first? That he needs her to help him think? She picks up a stone and examines it. It's smooth and grey, flecked with an uneven brown line that goes right through the middle. Like all the stones, it is perfect, smoothed by years of battering by the sea, made for holding, placed there for her pleasure. It would have had a rough surface once but the elements have transformed it, polished it so completely that you can rub your fingers along it endlessly and never feel a flaw.

'I think you were bored,' she says. 'That's what it was all about.'

'Bored with what?'

'Family life, work, everything. Your existence was so normal, so conventional. You wanted more excitement.'

'You're quite wrong,' he says quietly. 'I was happy.'

'Happiness is subjective,' says Kate. 'You can talk yourself into it.' Doesn't he see the irony? He has spent his whole life wanting a family, doing everything to achieve an ideal, and when he gets there, he blows it. 'You could at least have found a way to let me know you were all right – once you came to your senses. I assume you did eventually come to your senses?'

'Yes.' He doesn't look at her. 'I wanted to contact you, but it was difficult.' He hesitates. 'In the end, I decided it would be best if you never saw me again.'

'Well, you were right there.' Kate is finding it hard to equate the man next to her with the Felix she lived with for twenty-seven years. He used to be so sure of himself. Now it's as if someone else has dressed up in his skin, studied the intonation of his speech and learnt all his mannerisms, but somehow missed the essence of him. She ought to know him, she does know him – but she doesn't. 'So what changed?' she asks.

'It was several things. We had a shoplifter and I might have had to go to court to testify. And earlier – Nazrul waved at me. He's seven years old, the son of the man who owned the shop where I worked. He never looked me in the eye, but suddenly he did, for no reason. Finally, I thought, he trusts me.' He stops for a second, his eyes gazing into the distance. 'They were all in the car together, going off to school. How many times have we done that in our lives? It was as if I was watching my own family. Everyone waiting, ready to go – with no one to look after them. I was in the wrong place. I was there and I should have been here. I thought I'd done you all a favour by removing myself, when what I had actually done was rip a wall away from the side of the house.'

'You flatter yourself,' says Kate. 'We can manage without that wall. We've moved. We've got a new home.'

'I know,' he says.

'You seem to think I can't look after the children myself. We haven't exactly been sitting around waiting for someone to rescue us.'

'I know that too,' he says.

The sun is fierce, wrapping itself around her, as tangible and protective as a coat. It penetrates her clothes and passes through to her skin. What makes someone become a different person? Felix must have had an inborn talent for creating a counterfeit life. Most people wouldn't have been able to carry on as if everything was fine. Was it the death of his parents, the interruption to his early life that gave him the ability to remodel himself whenever he wanted to, that made him into someone who could put on whatever covering he required? Had he ever been the man she'd thought he was? 'Why didn't you ever talk about your parents?' she says.

He thinks for a long time before answering. 'I'm not sure. I never thought about them.'

'But you must have.'

'No, I didn't.'

Kate doesn't believe him. 'They're part of your earliest memories. You can't just forget them. The first five years are the most formative period of your life. Everybody knows that.'

'Nobody thought it was important then.'

That may be true. She thinks back to her parents. She can't recall any demonstration of fierce love from them when she was little, of the kind she has experienced with Lawrence, Millie and Rory, but she does remember lying in bed listening to her mother reading *Noddy*, clinging to her father's hand as they walked along a country path, sitting on the kitchen table while her mother dabbed at torn, bloody knees with cotton wool and a plaster. Normal life, things everyone must remember.

'Did you go to the funeral?'

'I don't think so. I don't have any memories of it.'

'Do you remember when you first went to live with your aunts?'

'I remember being frightened of the clocks. I found out later that they hadn't been working for years, but at the time, I could have sworn they were ticking away – all together, really loudly, as if they were watching me and disapproving. And I remember sitting on my bed, wondering what I was supposed to do next.'

Kate can so easily picture the earnest little boy she has seen in photographs, listening to the silence of his new home, completely alone, inside his head as well as in his surroundings. Lost. Has he changed at all since then? Or is he still that lost boy, wandering around in the body of a man, never fully grown up? 'You remember the way you felt abandoned as a child, yet you end up doing the same thing to your own children. How could you do it?'

He lowers his head and seems to shrink into himself. 'It wasn't meant to be like that. All I ever wanted was to give the children a better life than I . . .' His voice falters and fades into silence.

This won't do. She doesn't want to feel sorry for him. 'Did the aunts give you hugs, sit you on their laps, kiss you goodnight?'

He answers her seriously, as if it's important that he gets things right. 'No, I don't think they hugged me, and I probably wouldn't have wanted to sit on their laps. Would you? They were a bit too grand for that, really. I think they may have kissed me goodnight. They did everything they thought would be expected of them. They were very thorough.'

'But nothing interrupted their work, their lecture tours, their writing. They just fitted you into their schedules.'

'And why not? Lots of working parents do that sort of thing today.'

Like me, thinks Kate. It's nearly six o'clock. Millie has had the afternoon off, so she'll have been on her own for ages before Rory got home from school. I should be there, preparing supper, not here. 'They packed you off to boarding-school.'

'Yes, but I had long holidays and the aunts came to all the parents' nights, the concerts, the Speech Days. They came to cricket matches with their folding chairs and bottles of Piat d'Or. They weren't monsters. They didn't neglect me, they loved me, and that's all that matters.'

Kate knows this is true. She's seen the evidence over the years. Their total commitment to Felix, their devotion, their absolute certainty of his innocence. She doesn't know why she's arguing about it. 'But they didn't talk to you about your parents.'

'They might have been waiting for me to say something.'

'Children don't always do that. They wait for signals from the adults.'

'Maybe there were signals and I didn't pick them up.'

'Or maybe there weren't any signals.'

'I can't see that it makes any difference. You can't blame the aunts for anything I've done. They were good to me, they did their best. My mistakes are my responsibility.'

'I don't want to blame them. I'm just trying to work it out. And you're right. It is your responsibility.' Kate bends down and picks up a razor shell. The white mother-of-pearl centre gleams, bordered by long blue-black streaks. She runs her finger along the edge and it slices into her skin, sharp as a knife, drawing a thin line of blood. How deceptive it is, lying innocently on a crowded beach, waiting for someone, anyone, a child, to pick it up or step on it and experience pain.

She sucks the finger to ease the sting. 'I was a bit of a fool to believe in you, wasn't I, refusing to accept what everyone was saying? Considering you actually did it.'

He looks confused for a second, and then his face twists into a half-smile. 'Oh, I see. We've abandoned the childhood trauma. Back to the present day.' He laughs quietly.

Even now, after all that's happened, he can do cynicism, react with quick wit. Is he ever genuine? Does he even know what the word means? She pulls herself to her feet, picks up her things and walks away from him, awkwardly, across the stones. She hates him again. She wants to shake him, scream at him, dig her fingernails into his complacent cheeks. How dare he come back here like this, imagining he can simply apologise and worm his way back into her life?

'Kate!' he calls. He's behind her, jogging to catch up. 'What did I do?'

She stops and turns round. 'You laughed,' she says.

'Kate – I'm sorry, I'm sorry.'

'I don't want to hear that you're sorry. It's not good enough. I don't want your explanations. Why should I care?' She's raising her voice, aware that people are watching but not caring.

He faces her, his hands up with the palms towards her. He's an expert in appeasement. She feels as if she's being made into the aggressor, the knife-wielding hooligan, the madwoman with a grievance. 'It's all right,' he says, his voice gentle.

But it makes her angrier. He can't do this. He can't just turn up, offer explanations, or non-explanations if he doesn't have the answers, and expect her to listen. Why should she? He's abandoned her. Why can't she abandon him?

'I've told you to go away so many times,' she says. 'Why can't you just do it?'

She wants him to shout or even cry. Anything but this calm, rational approach, this desire to talk things through, this persistent, patient reasoning, as if eventually they'll arrive at a truth that satisfies both of them. She hates him for his even temper.

'Please, Kate,' he says. 'Give me another chance. I know I'm not doing it right. I need you to believe in me, even if no one else does.'

'A chance for what?' Surely he's not suggesting that she'd have him back.

'A chance to make it up to you.'

'Meaning what exactly?'

He's trying to find the right words. She can see him running through the possibilities. It's all so familiar. Felix the arbitrator, the man who understands human nature, the finder of resolutions.

'Forget it,' she says abruptly. 'I don't want reasons. I don't want apologies. I don't want you. Go away.'

She looks directly into his face and sees with a shock that he has taken her seriously. Bleakness is settling over him and he stiffens in front of her eyes. She has finally managed to wound him. 'Please, Kate,' he says. 'Please . . .'

But is he as desperate as he sounds? How does she know that the hurt in his eyes isn't something he's worked on, something he can produce whenever he wants to make people feel sorry for him? She remembers the time when she first met him in her father's dining room, when he boasted about how much money he was going to make. She'd thought she understood him then. The over-confidence, the need to impress. She'd recognised that it was all a cover. A need to make a mark, to imprint himself on other people so that he could then exist.

But maybe what she'd read in him was what he'd intended. Maybe she'd believed she'd gone down a layer and understood the real Felix, when all the time it was just his next act. Maybe he'd known exactly what she would think. She'd always assumed he married her because he could see beyond her shyness to the qualities that were hidden to everyone else, but it occurs to her now that he might have been looking for something more subtle. A quiet and amenable woman who could be moulded, who would fit in with his vision of happy family life. He'd wanted malleability and transparency more than anything else. He's certainly been good at knowing what she was thinking for all their years of married life. Could this be the first time that he's not quite sure he can lead her in the way he wants?

'Please leave me alone,' she says, lowering her voice, but determined not to be swayed by his apparent surrender. 'I've had enough. Go and sort out your problems elsewhere. Find someone else to manipulate. I don't want to know.'

She turns away quickly because she knows she'll waver if he appears too distressed. But if he does, it will be manufactured. She has never in her entire life seen him lose control. He doesn't know how to. Even in the past, in rows with Lawrence during his difficult teenage stage, Felix's anger wasn't real. She can see that now. Everything was carefully contrived. Measured. Exactly the right degree of anger to frighten Lawrence, but not too much.

'Kate!' He's begging.

She doubts herself. How can she be so sure he's insincere? Something must be genuine otherwise he wouldn't be here. Would he even know how to portray the difference between real and pretend emotion? What means does he have at his disposal to convince her, apart from the same arsenal that he always uses? If you have a supply of fake weapons that you've used all your life, how can anyone tell if the final weapon is loaded? It would be impossible to know until it goes off.

She hovers, still uncertain.

Her mobile rings. For a moment, she doesn't recognise her own ring-tone. A Mozart symphony blasts into the sea air, background music, swallowed up by the surrounding space, nothing to do with her.

She gropes in her pocket and takes out the phone. 'Hello?'

'Mum? Where are you?'

'Sorry, Millie. I got delayed.'

'It's nearly six o'clock. You finished work ages ago.'

'I know. I lost track of time. I didn't mean to be so late.' She turns her back on Felix, who is still standing beside her.

'I've been home for hours.' Millie's voice is flat and weary.

'Are you all right? You sound fed up.'

'No, I'm fine.' But she doesn't sound fine. She sounds as if she's been crying. 'I'm just hungry.'

'Look, I'll be about a quarter of an hour. Do you want to peel some potatoes? That'll speed things up a bit. Ask Rory to lay the table.'

'He isn't here.'

'What do you mean?'

'I mean he isn't here.'

'Where's he gone?'

'How would I know?'

'Didn't he tell you when he went out?'

'He hasn't been home.'

Kate's stomach flutters. 'But he must have been. He promised me he was going to cycle straight back from school. Perhaps he's popped out for something. You know what he's like – he doesn't always think.'

'Mum,' says Millie, and her voice is slow and patient, as if she's talking to a child, 'I've been here most of the afternoon. Rory has not been home.'

'Is his bike in the hall?'

'No. Obviously.'

'Has he left it outside? Can you go and check?'

Millie sighs.

'Just do it, Millie,' says Kate, forcing herself to be calm. She hears Millie's footsteps running down the stairs, the door banging, the pounding of her feet as she comes back up.

'What's the matter?' says Felix. She shakes her head, not wanting to divert her attention.

'No,' says Millie, from outside. 'It's not there.'

'OK,' she says, keeping her voice level. 'I'm coming back now. I'll be as quick as possible. Ring me if he turns up.'

She snaps the phone shut.

'What is it?' says Felix.

She stares at him without seeing his face. 'Rory hasn't come home,' she says. She starts to climb back up the beach towards the road, her feet stumbling over the stones. Each sliding step is a laborious, exhausting process. Her breath comes out in ragged gasps.

'I could drive you back,' he says. 'I have a hired car.'

'Why are you driving? You're dangerous. You go to sleep.'

'Not any more,' he says. 'I've changed.'

'I can walk in fifteen minutes.'

'I can drive in five.'

Rory is missing. What does it matter who gives her a lift? 'OK,' she says.

They reach the top of the beach and run down the steps to the car park. Felix leads the way to his car.

Rory, where are you? She examines the pavements as they drive past the shops, looking into cars going in the opposite direction. Could he have been kidnapped? She's overreacting. He'll be heading for home now, whizzing up the side-streets on his bike, skidding down the hills at an alarming speed, scaring the old ladies. She watches for police cars, ambulances, signs of an accident. But the street is normal. Lined with parked cars, congested. Oblivious.

Chapter 28

Rory's life is becoming too complicated. There are so many different parts of it and he's worried he's going to make a mistake soon and have the right conversation with the wrong person. There's school, Mum, Millie and the flat, the Space Warriors – and then there's his father. He keeps turning up, somewhere between the crossing and school, as if he just happened to be walking past. He's like the figure that steps out of the mist in those old horror films. There isn't any mist, but he's definitely got the knack of appearing out of nowhere.

It happened again yesterday afternoon. Rory was whizzing down a hill, enjoying the breeze in his face, when his father was suddenly standing in the middle of the road a few metres in front of him. He squeezed his brakes hard and skidded to a halt.

'Hi,' said his father, as if he'd thought Rory would be expecting him.

Rory still can't decide if it's all right to be pleased to see him. 'I can't stop,' he said. 'I'm meeting Mum.'

'No problem. I'll just walk with you for a while.'

So Rory climbed off his bike and they continued side by side. They didn't talk about why his dad had gone away, or why he'd come back, or whether he had broken the law. They discussed trains and black holes and Rory's gang.

'Space Warriors,' said his dad, rolling the words round in his mouth, as if he was trying to get a feel for them. It made Rory think of the old father, the old house, the old life. 'OK. Why are you warriors? Who are you going to fight?'

'Extra-terrestrial beings. When they invade.' This was the first time Rory had said it to an adult and he had to admit it sounded a bit childish. But he wasn't going to let his dad know this.

'When's it going to happen?'

'If we knew that, everybody would be ready for them and they're not. That's where we come in. They'll need us then.' None of it seemed very important right now. He'd had a quick game of football before leaving school and Jack had come over to speak to him as he unlocked his bike.

'Great goal, pal,' he'd said, and stuck out his hand.

Rory shook it and resisted the grin that wanted to break out all over his face. It wouldn't be cool to smile. 'Thanks, mate,' he said. As he pedalled away, his handlebars gleamed and every time he glanced down, he could see the wheel spokes glinting in the sun.

'What about weapons?' said his dad.

'What do you mean?'

'Well, if you're going to be warriors, you need weapons.'

Trust his dad to expose the main flaw in their plan. 'Don't worry,' he said. 'We'll be getting round to it soon.'

His father didn't question him further, but Rory was aware that the situation was unsatisfactory. You can't fight anyone without weapons. 'Cunning,' he said, after a pause. 'We'll defeat them because we'll be cleverer than them.'

'That goes without saying,' said his dad.

But the thing that's nagging away at Rory as he trails home today is that his mum doesn't know he's talking to his dad. How bad is this on the scale of dishonesty? It's not right up there with important people who turn out to have been spying for Russia all their lives, or rock stars who say they don't take drugs when everyone knows they do. It's not as if he's been helping criminals, so if he's comparing himself with his dad, he wins every time. But lying isn't quite his sort of thing. He tries to tell himself it's not lying, just not saying the truth. It's like seeing someone steal something in the supermarket and not telling. But even that works in degrees. A single Curly

Wurly doesn't seem too bad – although he wouldn't do it – but what about a frozen chicken or a DVD player? On the other hand, that's a rubbish question, because you couldn't exactly smuggle a DVD player out under your coat. Even a frozen chicken would be difficult, come to think of it. It might melt a bit and drip, it would be cold, and you might get infected with salmonella . . .

He's going home on his own today. His mum is going to the library after the crossing and Millie will be back early because her school has just broken up. Strictly speaking, he should have been home hours ago, but he got carried away, playing football. Mr Joliffe, the caretaker, joined them for the first time today and he was brilliant. They'd asked him to be their coach and he'd agreed. He'd had them doing things like keeping the ball in the air with their heads, press-ups (they were all rubbish at it) and running in a circle lifting their knees up high. It was wicked, like on the telly when they're interviewing the England coach and you can see the players in the background doing funny actions.

And afterwards he and Jack had gone down to Budleigh beach, near the shops where there were plenty of people around, and they'd thrown stones into the sea for ages, pretending they were Olympic shot-putters. After that, they'd started to dodge the waves, following the water as it sucked backwards and built up its strength, then running for their lives when it whooshed forward. Rory got caught a few times, so his feet were a bit wet, but he didn't mind. He couldn't remember having such a great time ever before. He and Jack had laughed so much that they'd fallen over and rolled painfully through the wet stones, and Rory thought he was going to be sick. Jack never said, 'I'll have to get back. My mum'll be worrying where I am.' Rory really liked this lack of concern, the grown-upness of it all.

He knew he ought to say it himself, but since it was only Millie, it didn't seem very important. He thought about texting her, but there never seemed to be enough time. And if Jack could stay out until he wanted, so could he.

Then, long after Rory had decided he could be as cool as Jack, Jack suddenly said, 'Got to go now. Me and my mum are off to see my gran. We're getting the bus to Exmouth, then the train.'

Now that Rory's heading for home on his own, he has an uncomfortable ache inside. His mum was probably back ages ago. He can't help thinking that perhaps he's overdone it and he's fairly sure he's going to be in big trouble. He wonders if his mum will send him to bed without any supper. That would be unfair considering how hungry he is. She's never done it before, but she might be really angry. She probably won't shout at him – although you can never tell nowadays – but she'll certainly talk to him in the serious way he hates about how she's trusted him and how he's let her down. She might even ban him from using his bike, which would be a total disaster.

There's a taste of guilt at the back of his throat, trickling down like a really nasty medicine. He knows he's been irresponsible. He should jump on his bike and pedal home as fast as possible, but he can't bring himself to do it. He's walking slower than normal and his feet feel too heavy. He's trying to put off the moment when he arrives home.

Should he run away? If she thinks she's lost him, she might be so glad to have him back that she won't bother to be angry. It's a good idea, but he can't be sure she'll react like that. And he's starving. Anyway, he can't think of anywhere to go. He can't exactly turn up at his grandparents' or the great-aunts' house. That wouldn't count as real running away.

No, he'll have to go home, even though he's doomed.

'Well, well, well.'

Rory stops. He knows the voice.

Richard Wong is standing a few yards in front of Rory, shoulder to shoulder with William Holt.

In an instant, Rory's tiredness zaps away and he's making calculations. It would take too long to get on his bike, they'd pull him off. In any case, it would be impossible to get going fast enough up the hill. And to go down, he'd have to head straight for them. He decides to run. It's his best bet. The narrow lane is deserted, but once he gets to the top, he can double back down a parallel road and get to the main street. There'll be plenty of people around there and he'll be safe.

He can hear their pounding footsteps, their panting as they gain on him. He can't run and push the bike at the same time. He has a stroke of genius and flings it behind him, directly into their path. Then he runs, the backs of his legs pulling and stretching as he drives himself up the steep hill. The bike has the right effect. He can hear their footsteps falling behind.

He ploughs straight into James Peterson and Rohit Mehta at the top of the lane. The collision results in them all losing their balance and they collapse in a chaotic heap. By the time Rory has struggled to his feet, Richard and William have caught up.

'Well, well, well,' says Richard again, although his voice is less smug after the effort of the uphill chase.

Rory finds himself surrounded. There are two older kids with them.

'So,' says one. 'This is Kendall. The son of an extortioner.'

'No,' says Rory. 'That's not right.'

'Oh, I think it is. I know all about your pathetic family.' He's almost grown-up, but not grown-up enough to be like a dad or a teacher. More a stretched version of James.

'Meet my brother, Charles,' says James.

Rory swallows. The surrounding street seems to flicker slightly. If they have older brothers with them, it means they've been allowed out on their own. There won't be any mothers hovering round the corner ready to rescue him.

'And my brother, Samay,' says Rohit. A brother for Rohit is even worse news. Rohit is the hard man. He doesn't do the talking, he does the doing. He's the one who lights the cigarettes, who applies them to the skin, who watches with cold, interested eyes to see what happens. He'd have made a brilliant Nazi. There's no chance that his brother would be any nicer. He probably taught Rohit.

Samay has a thin face and a long nose with a bump in the middle that looks like it's going to push out further and break through.

Rory has seen Charles and Samay around on the beach, but he's never taken much notice of them before and he certainly hasn't connected them with James or Rohit. He decides to go for the charm approach. Be nice. Smile. Let them think he's not worried. 'Hi,' he says, in his politest voice. 'It's nice to meet you.'

He might as well have said nothing.

'Where's your dad?' says Samay.

'I don't know,' says Rory.

'That's not what I've heard.'

'Well,' says Rory, 'I don't know what you've heard, but I'm fairly sure it's wrong. My dad may be back, but he doesn't live with us.' He wants to say, We don't have anything to do with him any more, but there's something inside him that prevents this. He's still my dad. I can't pretend I don't speak to him. It would be a kind of betrayal.

'People like your dad don't deserve to live,' says Charles.

Rory stares at him. 'So what are you going to do about it?' he demands. 'Kill him off?'

'We believe in justice,' says Samay.

They do want to kill off his dad. 'Well,' says Rory, trying very hard to keep his voice steady, 'a man can't be guilty until it's proved.' Or something like that. He tries again. 'A man is innocent until proved guilty.' That's it. He can do this. He can be on their side and they'll leave him alone long enough for him to escape. Without moving his head, he checks for escape routes. How far is it to the end of the road? How long

343

would it take him to run down the hill? Could he outrun them? He wonders if he could stop a passing car, although there's no sign of any traffic in either direction.

'Your dad's continuing existence is an insult to decent people,' says Samay.

'It won't worry you, then,' says Rory, thinking a joke might help. Someone behind him chuckles.

A hand comes out of nowhere and slaps his face. 'Don't be cheeky,' says Samay.

The force of it jerks Rory's head to one side, but it feels as if his brain has been left behind. He shakes his head, anxious to collect his thoughts, pick them up from where they're scattered and put them back together again. 'What was that for?'

Samay is rubbing his hands and looking pleased with himself. 'I asked you a question,' he says. 'Where's your father?'

'What's it to you?' says Rory, forgetting his clever strategy of being nice. 'It's none of your business.'

The hand comes again and this time he loses his balance with the momentum of the slap. 'Is that the best you can do?' he shouts, as he falls backwards into a hedge. 'Only losers resort to violence!' His father used to say that. It seems appropriate right now. He can hear Samay laughing. Yes! he thinks. I've made him laugh. It'll be OK.

'Hey!' calls a woman's voice.

Charles and Samay haul Rory back up between them and dust him down. 'I'm really sorry,' says Samay. 'He fell over.'

The woman is elderly, dressed in baggy tracksuit bottoms and a long beige cardigan. 'What are you doing to my hedge?'

'Hello, Mrs Butterfield,' says Charles, in a clear, friendly way.

Help! shouts Rory, in his head. They're beating me up! He opens his mouth to say something, but a heavy hand clamps down on his shoulder.

'Oh, it's you, Charles. Is your mother with you?' says Mrs Butterfield.

'We're just going for an evening swim,' says James.

'How nice,' says Mrs Butterfield, looking at them all. 'I'd invite you in for a cold drink, but there are rather a lot of you.'

'Thank you anyway,' says Charles. 'It was kind of you to think of it.'

'All right,' she says. 'Have a nice swim.'

'Thanks,' says James.

She smiles and goes back through her front door.

'Bye!' calls Rory.

The boys carry on up the hill. Charles's hand stays on Rory's shoulder. 'Well done,' he says. 'I like guys who stay cool in a crisis.'

'That's me,' says Rory. 'A cool guy.'

Suddenly he seems to have become part of their gang. Even Rohit looks friendly. He's done it! He's passed some secret test and they're not seeing him as the kid to pick on any more.

Charles takes his hand away from Rory's shoulder. Rory watches him put it into his pocket and slip something in and out, a long shiny metallic object. 'Is that a knife?' he asks, trying to sound nonchalant.

'Not for you, my son,' says Charles. 'Unless you want to come crabbing with us.'

'We have a fire on the beach,' says Rohit. 'And cook them.'

Rory has a sudden picture of them round a bonfire, roasting crabs, scraping the white flesh out of the shells, drinking Coke, laughing. His stomach rumbles. He wants to be part of it.

'That's where we're going,' says James. 'Lympstone. They have massive crabs there. Big as your baby face.'

'Can I come?' says Rory.

'Depends if there's room in the car,' says Charles.

A car! They've got a car! Suddenly the Space Warriors

seem tame. 'You took it well back there,' says Rohit to Rory. 'Some kids would have cried.'

'Not me,' says Rory, narrowing his eyes and standing up straight.

'I can't go crabbing,' says William. 'Got to get back.'

'And me,' says Richard. 'My parents are taking us out for a meal tonight.'

'Wimps,' says Rohit.

'OK,' says Charles to Rory. 'You're in.'

A surge of joy races through Rory at this easy acceptance, but he knows he has to be casual. 'If you want,' he says, with a shrug. He can see that William and Richard are annoyed, but he works hard at hiding his satisfaction. Rohit is right. They are wimps. He's in. They're out.

'Let's get the car,' says Samay.

Richard and William leave them and go back down the hill. Rory tries to walk like Samay, taking longer strides, rocking his shoulders, but he keeps stumbling because his legs won't reach as far.

At the top of the road, they stop by a black Astra. New, very shiny, very expensive. Samay flicks the car keys out of his pocket and presses the button. The doors click open. 'OK,' he says. 'James and Charles in the back, with young Mr Kendall. Me and Rohit in the front.' He gets in, turns on the ignition and revs the engine. 'Let's burn some rubber,' he says, and pulls away, the tyres screaming.

'Give that man a house point,' shouts Charles, from the back seat.

They're playing a game, thinks Rory. They think they're in a film. For a brief moment, he remembers Millie at home waiting for him, and then his mum, who will probably be back by now, but they're a long way in the distance, fading fast. He's part of a real gang now. This is what it's all about.

They drive across Woodbury Common, along narrow roads between dense trees, which arch over and hide the sun. Samay drives too fast, only slowing down if the wheels threaten to leave the road as they lurch round tight double bends. When they meet a car coming the other way, Samay slams his brakes on and skids into the ditch at the side of the road, but refuses to give way, forcing the other car to back up to a wider part of the road. They race up behind a red Volvo driving at thirty miles an hour and Samay pulls out to overtake it without hesitating.

'Sunday drivers!' shouts Charles, gesturing at the Volvo through an open side window.

There's a tense silence in the car. Rory holds his breath. If they meet a car coming the other way now, heading straight for them in the opposite lane, they'll all be dead. Faster, thinks Rory. Faster. As they pull back in again, he finds that his hands are slippery with sweat. Rohit and Charles whoop with pleasure. 'Way to go!' shouts James. Rory feels as if he's surrounded by a brilliant light that's lifting him up, teaching him to fly. He can do anything. Nobody will ever harm him again.

'That was brilliant!' he says.

They cross the main road and head down an even narrower lane, before turning a sharp corner and pulling up on the edge of a muddy, pebbled beach. There's a row of benches going up the hill along the side of the road, overlooking the estuary, but they're unoccupied. The place is deserted.

'Everyone out,' says Samay.

The tide is coming in, creeping quietly over the mud and pebbles. The air is very still. A few solitary birds are bobbing up and down and moored boats are being picked up and set free by the rising water. They swing round with the tide towards the river, away from the sea, straining at their ropes. In the distance, a train hoots as it approaches Exmouth.

'Come on,' says Charles, and they crunch over the shingle along the beach beside the railway line.

'The tide's coming in,' says Rory.

'So?' says James.

'Who asked you?' says Rohit.

Rory realises that they're not pleased to have him with them. He has interfered with their place in the group. It might be better not to talk for a bit, in case he annoys them too much.

'OK,' says Samay, 'you lot start looking under the rocks, in the pools. That's where the beasties hide out. We'll get some driftwood for the fire.'

'But the tide'll be up before you get the fire going,' says Rory.

Samay looks at him coldly. 'Give it a rest, criminal boy,' he says.

'I'm not a—'

'Just shut up,' says James, pushing Rory's shoulder violently.

'Hey!' shouts Rory. 'Leave me alone.' He kicks out at James and manages to make contact with his legs.

'Aargh!' screams James. 'Charles, he kicked me!'

Charles has been wandering around picking up dry pieces of driftwood. He looks over to where Rory and James are standing. 'Just shut up and get on with it!' he yells.

Rory stands back from James, breathing heavily, waiting to see what he'll do. James approaches him again, his face furious. 'Don't think you can get away with that,' he says.

Suddenly Rory's arms are grabbed from behind. It's Samay. A deep voice rumbles in his ear: 'Like father like son, eh?' he says. 'You enjoy a bit of violence, don't you?'

'I don't know what you mean,' says Rory. 'He started it.'

Charles looks up and sees what's going on. He runs back towards them, but his foot gets caught in a dip between two rocks. He stumbles awkwardly for a few paces, trying to recover his balance, then topples over, face first, into the wet shingle. When he gets up again, his clothes are black with mud and his face is dark with anger. He walks towards them slowly. 'OK,' he says to Rory. 'You want trouble, you're going to get it.'

'No,' says Rory. 'I don't want any trouble. I want to catch crabs and cook them.'

But the atmosphere has changed and he can see that he's in a bad position. He shouldn't have come. He'd thought they'd accepted him, when really they were just putting up with him because he amused them. He's not making them laugh any more.

Charles comes up to him and stares into his face. 'So why not get your dad to catch crabs, then?'

Rory tries to lighten the situation by sighing tolerantly. It doesn't quite come out like that because his breathing isn't as normal as he would like it to be. 'We've been through all that.'

'And we're going through it again. Have you got cloth ears? We want to know where your dad is.'

'I don't know!' says Rory. 'I don't know! I don't know!'

'Well, it's time you started to remember.'

Charles hits him across the face, hard enough to knock him over, but Samay is holding his arms, keeping him upright.

A car swoops past the entrance to the beach and hoots loudly as it approaches the corner. Startled, everyone turns round.

Rory can feel Samay's arms loosen and he pulls himself free. With the advantage of surprise, he starts to run. Putting his head down, he races towards Exmouth, alongside the railway track, knowing he has to keep moving. Their yells ring out behind him, but they've taken time to react. He's smaller than them, he plays football every day, he's a fast runner. They're probably rugby players, very fit, but that makes them more bulky. They can't dodge over the uneven surfaces as easily as he can.

He wades through a shallow stream. A train is approaching, gathering speed as it leaves Exmouth and heads for Lympstone. If he can get past the bushes someone might see him and raise the alarm. He runs faster. The train hoots twice.

He can't see the train yet, so no one can see him either. He pushes himself along the beach, stumbling over rocks and pebbles and driftwood until the railway track comes into view. He looks up, just in time, and waves his arms wildly.

'Help!' he screams. 'Help!'

But he'd forgotten that they wouldn't be able to hear him. He can see the passengers inside, white moons of faces looking out, watching him play on the beach, running away from his friends in a game of tag.

'No!' he cries. 'They're chasing me! I'm in danger!'

And then the train is gone. He can see the end of it trailing away towards Lympstone, the little blue and yellow back door rocking uncertainly, rolling on its tracks as if it's finding it difficult to remain upright. He turns round and Charles and Samay are gaining on him, with Rohit and James close behind.

He takes a deep breath and starts to run again.

Chapter 29

The car is crawling in slow traffic along the main street of Budleigh when Kate's phone rings. She gropes in her bag with her left hand, finds the phone and flips it open. 'Hello?'

'Mum? It's Millie.'

'Is he back?'

'No – I've just had this weird phone call.'

It's the police. He's had an accident. 'What's happened?'

'It was this boy called Jack—'

'Rory's friend?' Relief washes through her. It's all right. Rory's been playing with Jack and he's forgotten the time. She's been overreacting, seeing disaster when it's just typical Rory-style carelessness.

But why has Jack phoned and not Rory?

Felix stops at the traffic-lights and turns to face Kate, raising his eyebrows in enquiry.

'He was phoning from the train to Exeter,' says Millie.

Kate ignores Felix. 'What on earth are they doing on the train?' She's listening to Millie, knowing there's more, that it's not as straightforward as she'd hoped.

'He says he's just seen Rory on the beach at Lympstone – heading for Exmouth.'

This doesn't make sense. Rory wouldn't be all the way over there. It's miles away. 'So he's not on the train with Jack?'

'No, Jack just happened to look out and saw him. There were some older boys running behind Rory, and he was waving and shouting at the train, as if he wanted it to stop.' Panic edges into Millie's voice. 'Mum, something's going on. Jack seemed scared.'

'Who were the other boys? Did he know them?'

'No, he didn't have a clue. What are you going to do?'

Kate forces herself to remain calm. 'Look, it'll be all right. I'm sure it's nothing – just Jack getting carried away. If he's anything like Rory he'll be seeing a drama round every corner.' She doesn't believe this, but it helps to say it. 'Ring me if anything else happens, anything at all.'

She rings off. 'Rory's being chased by some older boys, along the beach from Lympstone to Exmouth,' she says to Felix. 'He was spotted from the train by one of his friends.'

'OK,' says Felix, instantly calm. 'Let's drive to Exmouth. If we get down to the beach near the station and walk along the river from there, we should be able to meet him coming the other way.'

Kate can see Rory in her mind, running, running, terrified, shouting for help and no one hearing him. 'Hurry,' she says.

'It's probably nothing,' he says.

'You don't know that. Boys can be dangerous when they get carried away.'

He turns into a side-street, does a screeching three-point turn, narrowly missing an elderly couple, and heads back up the high street.

'Should I phone the police?' asks Kate.

'Yes,' he says. 'Tell them he's in serious danger.'

The interior of the car closes round Kate, hot and stuffy, preventing her from breathing properly. 'Do you think he is?' she says.

'He'll be fine,' he says. 'They're just boys. But the police won't come unless they believe it's serious.'

She opens the window and lets the wind rush into her face. Her hair lifts from her damp neck and swirls away, flapping wildly. There are too many pictures in her mind. She's seen it all on the news. Gangs of teenagers kicking grown men to death, young lads with knives who've killed other boys, children drowned by bullies. Every picture that flashes into

352

her mind has the face of Rory superimposed on the body. She can sense his fear, experience the urgency in her own legs as he runs along the beach.

She dials 999 and explains the situation. 'He's in serious danger,' she says.

The man at the end of the phone takes all the details and assures Kate that they'll send a car to Lympstone beach. When she rings off, her hands are trembling. It'll be all right, she says to herself. They know what they're doing.

What if they're too late?

Felix pulls up outside the station and gets out of the car. 'Come on,' he says, heading for the station.

The barriers are open and groups of people are moving on to the platform so a train must be due in. Felix approaches the ticket office. 'Two singles to Lympstone,' he says.

'What are you doing?' asks Kate, confused. 'Why are we going on the train? I thought you said . . .'

He ignores her and produces a ten-pound note from his pocket. The man patiently prints the tickets, sorting the change with slow, ponderous precision. Kate has to force herself not to scream at him.

Felix leads her towards the barrier, hands the tickets over to be clipped and walks swiftly on to the platform.

'But we have to get to the beach,' she says. She tries to imagine jumping off a moving train when they catch sight of Rory. The train doesn't go very fast, they might be able to do it. Do they have communication cords on trains any more? That's another possibility.

But Felix is dodging past the waiting passengers. 'Think about it,' he says, over his shoulder. 'The most direct route to the beach is along the railway track.'

As they reach the end of the platform, he glances back and she follows his gaze. People are talking, reading newspapers or looking past them at the bend where the train will appear. Nobody is interested in Felix or Kate.

'Quickly,' he says. 'I don't think anyone's seen us.' He hurries down the slope at the end of the platform and on to the narrow pathway, which runs between a high wall and the railway track.

She follows him. 'But there's a train due.'

'So let's get a move on,' he says. 'We just need to get past this narrow bit.'

'What if someone's spotted us?'

'I doubt they've got enough staff to chase us – they're more likely to contact the police. That would be useful.'

He's enjoying this, she realises. It's the next great adventure. The old Felix has come back to life, found something he knows he can do. He's in control again.

She runs behind him, peering ahead every now and again, searching for the oncoming train.

They hear the hoot just before it appears round the bend, rattling lazily towards them, shimmering in the haze of its own generated heat, toy-like and self-important.

By this time, they've passed the wall and reached a boat-building yard situated between the railway line and the beach, so they scramble into the wild buddleia and rosebay willowherb. Once they're far enough back from the line, they stop, panting, and watch the train rumble past. They're close enough to smell the diesel, feel the hot blast of the engine. It hoots again – maybe the driver has seen them and sounded a warning, or maybe he's announcing his arrival. It's a sound that Kate used to hear dozens of times a day when they lived in Exmouth. A pull of nostalgia momentarily distracts her. She was happy in that old, cramped house. Everything was so uncomplicated then.

Once the train has passed, they climb back down on to the track and start to run along the sleepers. They're now well past the boatyard and heading towards the beach. 'It can't be far,' says Felix. 'They could be anywhere along here.'

Kate wants to look up and search, but she's finding it

difficult to keep her balance and has to watch her feet to avoid tripping. It must be twenty minutes since Jack phoned – he was on the previous train. Anything could have happened to Rory in that time.

'This'll do,' says Felix, stopping abruptly. 'We can get down here.' Kate joins him, gasping for breath. He hovers for a few seconds, gauging the distance, then jumps off the side of the bank on to the beach. Kate bends down, grasps a bush and lowers herself more carefully. Her feet skid on the stone embankment, scrabbling for a foothold and then she lets go, rushing down the last section. Felix grabs her to prevent her from falling over.

They examine their surroundings. The tide is coming up the estuary rapidly, racing up the river, and there's only a narrow strip of beach left uncovered. All sounds are delayed and muted. The lapping of the water, the distant banging of doors as the train arrives at Exmouth and the occasional gurgle as a bird lands on the river and dips its beak in search of food. It doesn't feel like a scene of violence or cruelty. It's remote and peaceful.

We're in the wrong place, she thinks. We should never have taken any notice of Jack. The phone call was a practical joke. Rory is somewhere else entirely and Jack was just trying to put us off the scent—

'There,' says Felix.

She follows the line of his pointing finger and sees five figures in the distance, at the edge of the water. It's difficult to tell what they're doing. Fishermen digging for cockles, wading out towards their boats?

But Felix doesn't hesitate. He sets out towards them, no longer checking to see if she's behind him, his feet pounding across the shingle, splashing in and out of the muddy water as he increases his speed. She runs after him, determined to keep up, her breathing shallow and uneven.

As they draw nearer, it becomes clear that they are in the

355

right place. A struggle is taking place between two of the people in the rising water. It's a slow-motion dance. They come together with difficulty in a frenetic embrace. The smaller of the two falls over and pulls himself up, staggering away in the ever-deepening water. The other, a much older boy, goes after him, clumsily reaches out and loses his balance, tumbling over and briefly submerging. He pulls himself up, spluttering and screaming with rage. The other three are standing on the beach and watching, apparently incapable of action, mesmerised by the spectacle before them. Both of the two in the water are shouting. It's impossible to hear any words, but the raw anger in their voices travels across the empty, open beach. They stop and face each other, water draining out of their clothes as they fight for breath and continue to shout, neither pausing to listen to the other. The words are becoming more distinct.

' – mad – ' It's Rory. 'My dad – get you!'

'Scum!' shouts the other boy. 'Filth!'

None of the watchers sees Kate and Felix approach. They're too involved in the struggle taking place in front of them, watching with the same intense absorption as they might have had in a cinema.

The taller boy suddenly throws himself on top of Rory and grabs him, pushing him down, forcing his head under the water and holding him there. Rory's arms flap frantically, churning up the water as they break the surface. The older boy almost falls over again with the strength of Rory's reaction, but he manages to maintain his hold on him. The splashing weakens, becomes less aggressive.

'Rory!' screams Kate.

Felix explodes into the middle of the watchers with a terrifying, animal roar. They're caught by surprise and scatter, their cries of fear echoing across the river. He storms through them as if they're not there and wades into the water, lifting his legs high to make quicker progress. The older boy looks up, sees him and straightens, his face transfixed with shock. He lets go of Rory. Felix throws him to one side and gropes under the water, pulling Rory up and out. He shakes the water from him and slaps his face, but gets no reaction. He turns and struggles back to the shore with him in his arms.

Kate is up to her knees in water, unable to move as quickly as Felix, paralysed by the sight of Rory. His arms are hanging down, his head flopping lifelessly on Felix's chest.

Just as Felix reaches the beach, Rory moves. He squirms in Felix's arms, rolling his head from side to side, and coughs, weakly at first, then more violently. He vomits a stream of muddy water.

'Rory!' cries Kate, and bursts into tears.

'He's OK,' says Felix. He sits Rory down and leans him over, patting his back rhythmically. Rory coughs and coughs, then sags back against his father. 'It's all right,' says Felix, rubbing him more gently. 'Everything's going to be fine.'

He takes his eyes away from his son and looks round for the boy who was responsible for all this. 'Can you take Rory?' he says to Kate. They transfer Rory's weight from Felix to Kate. Felix heads back into the river.

The older boy is heading towards Lympstone, still in the water, but Felix cuts him off by running along the beach. Once he has caught up with him, he plunges back into the water. The boy wades further out, panicking as he sees Felix getting closer. He loses his footing and starts to swim, a clumsy crawl, slowed down by his waterlogged clothes. But Felix has been swimming all his life. He easily outpaces him.

The current, thinks Kate, watching them from the shore. They mustn't get caught in the central channel – they'll be dragged down.

Felix reaches the boy and grabs him. There's a short struggle, then Felix starts to swim back to the shore, his arm under the boy's chin, a model performance of his life-saving technique. Once they reach the shallow water, he hauls the boy to his feet. They stumble through the shallows, breathing heavily, streaming with brown water and strands of seaweed, until they're not far from Kate and Rory.

Felix stops. 'What's your name?' he demands.

The boy tries to look away.

'Answer the question,' says Felix, his face two centimetres from the boy's. 'What's your name?'

The boy mumbles something.

'Again?' says Felix.

'Charles.'

'Charles who?'

'Peterson.'

Felix drops him back into the water. 'OK, Charles, what will your parents have to say about this?'

'We were just having a bit of fun,' says Charles, struggling to his feet. 'We didn't mean anything by it.'

'Fun? *Fun?*' Felix spits the word. 'Perhaps you'd care to explain to me what is funny about drowning a young boy. I call that attempted murder.'

Charles puts a hand into one of his pockets.

'Mum,' whispers Rory, struggling to sit up.

'It's all right, Rory,' says Kate. 'You don't need to do anything. Your father is capable of managing the situation.'

'Knife—' says Rory, his voice thin and hoarse.

'Felix!' calls Kate. 'He's got a knife.'

Felix grabs Charles's arm and lifts the hand slowly out of the pocket. 'Is this true?'

'No,' says Charles. 'Of course not.'

'Empty your pockets.'

Charles pulls out his phone, a packet of Polos, some cigarettes, a few coins. He holds them, watching the water drain off them.

'And the rest.'

'That's it.'

Felix reaches down and pats the pockets of Charles's leather jacket. Kate experiences a moment of panic. If Charles has a knife, what if he stabs Felix?

But it's a clever move. Charles can't prevent Felix from checking without dropping his possessions into the water.

Felix pulls out a kitchen chopping knife, about six inches long, and grips it between his finger and thumb as if it's almost too hot to hold. It hangs in the air, the blade catching the sun, dazzling and menacing. There's a strained silence.

Charles drops everything and reaches for the knife.

He almost succeeds, but Felix responds in time and grasps it more firmly. Their hands clamp together over the handle and they freeze into a battle of strength with the blade between them, quivering with the tension.

There's a moment of unnatural calm. The air glitters with bright specks of sharp sunlight. The water laps against their legs, cold and deadening. The sky above them is immense.

The tip inches towards Charles. 'How does it feel?' shouts Felix. 'Scared?'

Charles pushes it back.

'Felix!' yells Kate. She leaves Rory and plunges into the water, running towards them. 'Let him go!' she shouts as she reaches them. 'Let him have the knife.'

Momentarily distracted, Felix loses his concentration and Charles lurches forward, overreacting to the loss of pressure. The knife jerks towards Felix.

'No!' screams Kate, throwing herself at Charles at the same time, pushing him to one side.

The knife drops into the water.

Charles pulls himself up and stumbles away, staggering through the rising tide, his arms flapping to keep his balance.

Felix and Kate cling to each other and manage to stay upright.

Felix summons one last burst of energy. 'I'll come looking for you, Charles Peterson!' he yells.

Charles pauses at a safe distance and turns round. 'No, you won't. You'll be in prison.'

'Maybe! But you'd better hope it's not the same one that you're going to.'

Something flickers in the edge of Kate's vision and she turns. 'Look!' she says.

Several yellow-jacketed figures are picking their way along the edge of the beach from the direction of Lympstone. They've already caught the other three boys and two men are escorting them back towards the road.

'Come on,' says Felix and he leads Kate back to Rory, who has been watching with increasing interest. The water is creeping up to the corner of beach in front of the railway embankment, isolating them on a small, rapidly diminishing section of seaweed-covered rocks.

A boat is chugging towards them, cutting a quiet pathway through the water. Two more men in yellow jackets peer out at them, shading their eyes with their hands against the glare of the lowering sun.

'Were you going to kill him?' Rory asks Felix.

'No,' says Felix. 'I just didn't want him to kill me.'

Kate turns to Rory. 'Jack saw you on the train,' she says.

Rory tries to smile. 'Good old Jack,' he whispers.

'How did you manage to hold them off for so long?' says Felix.

'I ran,' he says. 'I ran and ran and ran.'

'That's my boy,' says Felix, and he's perfectly calm, in control. He and Rory are still familiar with each other, even now. This can't be the first time they've made contact since Felix's disappearance. Kate feels foolish, weak, left out. She thought they were managing well without Felix. They didn't need him. And all the time he was there in the background, part of their lives without her knowledge.

But if he hadn't been, what would have happened to Rory?

The train from Exmouth judders past them with its cheerful hoot. It rattles and buzzes on its way to Lympstone.

Part Five

Chapter 30

'Felix will be coming out of prison in two days' time,' says Beatrice, almost before Kate has time to put the receiver to her ear.

'Oh,' says Kate, jolted out of her contemplation of curtain material in the Laura Ashley catalogue. 'I hadn't realised.' But she's done the calculations. She'd known it would be soon.

'It'll be early. About eight o'clock in the morning. They like to confuse the press if it's a high-profile case.'

In fact, it's no longer a high-profile case. George was sentenced to eighteen years and Kristin, who was not directly involved in all his criminal activities, seven. It was clear from the trial that George liked to be in control – he didn't share responsibility unless he had to – and the media no longer portray Felix as a master criminal. But Kate doesn't want to minimise Felix's importance in his aunts' eyes, so she doesn't comment.

Beatrice's voice is brisk and matter-of-fact. 'I thought you should know.'

Kate can't decide how to respond. Her thoughts are not flowing coherently.

'We'll be meeting him in a taxi,' says Beatrice. 'Unless you'd prefer to pick him up.'

'No,' says Kate. 'I don't think so.' Please don't try to persuade me. 'But thank you for letting me know.'

'I've got to go,' says Beatrice. 'Agnes has let Bertie out and he's eating the paint on her little Francis Bacon – you know, the sketch she picked out of a skip that time we went to Stratford . . .' Her voice fades.

And Agnes's voice in the distance: 'Naughty Bertie. Naughty, naughty . . .'

'Goodbye,' says Beatrice, and puts the phone down.

Three days after the call, Kate sees Felix.

She's parked in a space on the hill overlooking the beach, intending to take a brisk walk, but it's raining and she's reluctant to get out. So she sits and watches the rhythmical coming and going of the waves.

The rain descends in intense bursts, drumming on the car roof with angry fists. In the periods between downpours, moisture hangs in the air in a static mist, washing across the windscreen lightly, separating into feather-like rivulets.

During one of the milder interludes, Felix appears on the path below, his hands stuffed into his pockets. At first, Kate doesn't recognise him. So small from this distance, insignificant. Clean-shaven. In a black jacket, zipped up tightly to the neck, which makes him appear young and vulnerable. He is very wet. He pauses once or twice and takes several deep breaths. He doesn't lower his head under the rain, but looks straight ahead and Kate knows it's him. His refusal to be defeated by the weather is achingly familiar.

They only talked about the events on the beach once, while they sat in the waiting room at the hospital, waiting for Rory to be discharged.

'Would you have stabbed Charles?' she asked.

'No,' he said. 'I don't think so.' He hesitated, started to say something, stopped, started again. 'Something like this has happened to me before – possibly – a long time ago . . .'

She stared at him.

'In London, when I was qualifying—'

364

'What are you talking about?'

'I was with George and a man with a knife tried to mug us.'

'Really? I didn't know anything about this.'

'No, well – he ended up dead, but I can't remember how it happened.'

'What do you mean you can't remember?'

'Exactly that. Neither of us knew what happened. We fought back and we were all rolling around on the ground and then he was just lying there.'

'So it could have been George, or even an accident?'

'I was the one left holding the knife.'

Kate rubbed her hands backwards and forwards, listening to the comforting, rhythmical sound of skin sliding over skin. 'You don't think you should have told me this?'

He nodded. 'It was a mistake not to tell you.'

Perhaps a child who witnesses violence becomes damaged in a way that can never be healed and gains an immunity to the shock of further violence. Everyone assumed that Felix had managed to recover from his parents' death and live a normal life, when all the time the trauma was incubating, growing shoots, seeking out its own nourishment. A sleeper waiting to be activated. Waiting, waiting . . .

'This time, there was a moment – just a second . . . It was like . . .' He paused for a long time. 'It was like confronting the burglar downstairs, making up for what I hadn't been able to do then.'

He had finally arrived at his own truth. The event that he had always refused to talk about or acknowledge.

'You're an adult now. You have more power over the situation. You can choose how to act.'

He paused, then turned to look at her. 'I wouldn't have killed him unless he gave me no choice.'

On the day of the trial, Kate arrived early at Exeter Crown Court and passed through a small group of local reporters to reach the entrance.

Beatrice and Agnes turned up with Felix a few minutes later in a taxi. The journalists gathered round, but Beatrice organised them in grand style. Her clear voice rang out for everyone to hear. 'Kindly stand aside, gentlemen,' she said, ignoring the women.

Felix climbed out of the taxi and leant in to help Agnes out, taking her weight as she cautiously emerged. They then headed towards the entrance.

'Gangway!' called Beatrice, and everyone obediently stepped back.

'Felix, do you have any comments?'

'Mr Kendall—'

Felix, walking very slowly with Agnes on his arm, acted as if the journalists didn't exist.

'Kate!' boomed Beatrice, as they came through the door and spotted her inside. 'Where are the children? Haven't you brought them?'

'I've discussed it with them,' said Kate, speaking softly, conscious that their conversation was threatening the hushed, respectful murmuring going on around them. 'We agreed that it would be better for them not to come.' She hadn't felt it was appropriate for them to see their father humiliated. 'They're too young.'

'You can never be too young to learn from experience,' said Agnes. 'It's wrong to shield them.'

'Maybe,' said Kate. 'But it's too late now. They've gone to school.'

'They do know about the trial?' asks Agnes.

'Of course,' said Kate.

'Do they do refreshments?' said Beatrice, looking round. 'I simply must have a decent cup of coffee before we start.'

'I've brought a flask and some Jammie Dodgers,' said Agnes. 'Just in case.'

There was no sign of Bill or Robbie, Felix's old business partners – they probably had other things on their minds. Kate's father had offered to come with her, but she'd talked him out of it. He wouldn't be able to sit for long with his arthritis and she didn't want him there, seeing Felix exposed and guilty, stripped of everything except his clothes.

The Crown Prosecution Service had decided not to charge Felix and George with the stabbing of the mugger. It transpired that the man had survived after all, though he went on to die of an overdose eight months later. So neither Felix nor George had killed him, and it couldn't be proved that the knifing hadn't been an accident or self-defence.

The trial for the money-laundering only took a day. Kate sat in the court room with the aunts and listened to the presentation of technical details about the money-laundering, struggling to follow it all. At the end, Felix was sentenced to eighteen months, but might be released on parole after nine. It helped that he had regretted his actions, turned himself in and pleaded guilty. The judge accepted that Felix had not known where the money had come from or where it was going to, and that he had had no knowledge of George's criminal activities. But money-laundering was a serious crime, so a custodial sentence was inevitable.

Agnes gasped when the sentence was read out. 'Prison,' she said, and went very white. She slumped back in her seat, but didn't manage to faint.

'The barrister warned us,' said Beatrice.

'I know, dear, but one does hope, of course.'

'You can't hope for reasonableness from a judge,' said Beatrice. 'He probably had kippers for breakfast and arrived in a chauffeur-driven Mercedes. He wouldn't understand ordinary people like us.'

Agnes sighed. 'I thought he had a sound mind,' she said. 'I didn't expect him to be so harsh.'

Kate was simply relieved it was all over. She thought that Felix would cope with prison. He was a chameleon, an expert with image. He could change to any colour that was needed, be the right individual for every circumstance. He knew how to eliminate anything painful, press the delete button and act as if it had never happened. He'd been doing it since he was five years old – he'd been in training all his life.

'What about his career?' said Agnes, sniffing into a lace handkerchief that looked as if it had survived from the nineteenth century. 'He won't be able to work in the financial world when he gets out.'

'Felix can do anything,' said Beatrice. She sat up straight – to show that she had no sympathy with Agnes's weak response – expanded to an even larger version of herself and filled the air with confidence. 'He'll be successful, whatever he decides to do.'

She was right. Kate watched him walk out of the court, calm, composed, in absolute control, as if he was being directed to a hotel room. He looked satisfied now that he had a way of paying for his mistakes. He thought he could take the punishment and come out cleansed, ready to start all over again.

The road is grey and bleak. A thin layer of water covers the surface, streaming down the hill in fluctuating shades of grey, glinting occasionally in the struggling daylight. A woman walks past on the opposite side, huddling against the wall and shielding herself with her umbrella every time a car swishes past.

Why has Felix come back to Budleigh Salterton? He could have gone anywhere in the country, or at least stayed in Exeter with the aunts. The man Kate can see walking along the sea front reminds her of a younger version of Felix, the one she had first known: apparently confident, determined to impress, feeling he had to run faster than everyone else just to keep up, but not quite managing to hide his anxiety. He was not as he seemed. She had realised that even then, and it was this very quality that had attracted her to him.

She turns on the ignition. There's so much to do. Her parents have lent her a deposit and she's just bought a small semi-detached house in a quiet cul-de-sac. Cardboard boxes that she's picked up from Tesco fill the boot and the back seat of the car. She needs to get on with the packing. They're itching to go, to leave the flat behind them.

Felix's shadow has faded, become insignificant as they've all found alternative ways of existing. Kate has finished her thesis, been awarded her MA and started a job as an administrator with a lottery-funded organisation that backs local arts projects.

Everyone went to her graduation, six months after Felix's trial. At the end of the ceremony, they came out of the Great Hall, surrounded by young people in mortar boards and flapping gowns. Leaving the aunts sitting down inside, they climbed up through the university gardens until they found a secluded spot by some stone steps. It was windy, as always, but the sun had broken out between the clouds, granting a few dazzling minutes of welcome colour.

Her father had brought his new digital camera and organised them into a group. Kate stood between Millie and Lawrence, with Rory in front of her. Zoë, who had come with Lawrence, stood politely to the side, resisting the temptation to interfere.

'Smile!' called her father, holding out the camera.

'No,' said her mother, watching over his shoulder. 'You're cutting their heads off.'

Her father squinted at the screen and frowned. He took his glasses off and peered again. 'It's difficult to see at this distance,' he said.

'Let me do it,' said her mother. She took the camera. 'Smile!' she called, and they held their smiles until they were frozen.

The grandparents examined the camera together. 'It's blurred,' said Kate's father.

'No, it's not,' said her mother. 'It's crystal clear.'

'Can we move now?' asked Lawrence.

'No,' said her father. 'We're going to give it another go.'

'It's a bit cold,' said Millie. She was wearing a short-sleeved sequined top and very tight black trousers. She had refused to keep her coat on for the photographs.

Kate watched her parents. They were looking better – not so tired. Her father was moving well, despite the arthritis, and her mother was uncharacteristically splendid in a voluminous hot-pink suit.

The wind ruffled their hair and Kate saw Millie shiver. Carefully, she put an arm round her shoulders and drew her closer. Millie didn't resist.

She had been subdued for some time after the events on the beach, more affected by them than Kate would have expected. But once she had begun the new autumn term and settled into school work, she began to regain some of her confidence. She's joined a local orchestra that puts on musicals, taken up judo with Helen, started to chatter about a boy called Brett whom she's met on the train.

'Come on!' shouted Rory. 'It's boring.' He has his eyes on some students jogging along a nearby path. He's not good at standing still.

Occasionally, he still has nightmares, his cries echoing through the flat in the dark hollow time of early morning, waking Kate. She goes to comfort him, listens to his rambling descriptions of dead aliens, and allows him half an hour on his Nintendo to calm his mind. Otherwise, he seems to be thriving from the publicity after his struggle on the beach. Kate has heard him relating the story to friends on the phone and the knife becomes bigger with every telling.

Kate finds her new job exciting but tiring. She enjoyed the solitude of the cleaning and her association with other people's children every morning and afternoon at the crossing. The mothers used to stand and talk, sharing their problems with her. She has learnt from them. Nobody saunters through life on a clear straight road with no red lights, roundabouts or traffic jams.

'One more photo,' called her father, 'then we'll go for our meal.'

'Hurry up,' said Lawrence. 'I'm starving.'

'Done!' said Kate's father, unexpectedly. 'Perfect.'

'I can't see how,' said Lawrence. 'It's too windy.'

They pored over the camera to examine the photos. The last one was best. Everyone's hair and clothes were blowing to the right of the frame, but this produced a relaxed, natural charm. Lawrence was caught in an unguarded moment, creased and comfortable, grinning at Zoë behind his grandparents. Millie was still leaning against her mother, but peering round at Lawrence and laughing. Rory appeared to be dancing a jig, one leg in the air at a very odd angle, with his arms flapping wildly. And Kate was standing upright in her gown and the floppy hat with tassels that had presumably been designed in the middle ages for male academics, staring out at the camera with a strong, direct gaze. She looked like a woman who knew where she was going.

Coming out of Marks & Spencer in Exeter, she sees Felix again. He's carrying a briefcase and wearing a suit, looking more like he used to. He's either found himself a job, or he's going to an interview.

She follows him along the pavement, down Queen Street towards the station. She watches the way he walks, the way the briefcase swings in his hand. The aunts must have financed the suit, which has an expensive sheen. He'd have needed several months' job-seeker's allowance to buy it himself. She hurries to keep up with him as he strides purposefully along the pavement, stepping aside when too many people come the other way, stopping to allow a woman with a pushchair enough space.

She comes to an abrupt halt. Why is she following this man, this stranger she no longer knows?

Felix's great skill, his lifetime achievement, has been to build an image for himself, an image that fits the surroundings. He has learnt, with huge success until now, how to make people like him. He's filled in any cracks, plastered over them, reconstructed himself each time he has needed to. Now he needs to strip away the surface repairs and start again.

But there would be danger in stripping away everything. He might be left with nothing. There's something to be said for pretending. The disguise is the protective cashmere coat, the bit everyone sees, the reality that walks down the road every morning. The coat reflects the man as much as the clothes underneath. Maybe the pretending simply becomes the reality in the end.

He looks so normal as he passes the station and heads for the university. It's almost as if nothing has happened. As if she can run after his departing back, call him, force him to stop. She imagines him turning round. 'Kate,' he will say. 'I didn't know you were in Exeter today. Let's take the train back together.'

He was helpful with the children in the last few months while he was still on bail. He took Rory on several day trips during the holidays, re-creating the expeditions he had been on with his aunts when he was a child, when education masqueraded as fun. Rory came home full of interesting facts and stories, talking endlessly, bursting with vitality.

Felix went down to Penzance twice to meet Lawrence, who

never actually set off for John o' Groats. Once Lawrence discovered that he didn't have the energy for long, drawn-out hatred, he was pleased to see his father. He seemed contented – 'Zoë sends her love. We might go travelling next year . . .'

Felix even took Millie shopping in Exeter on a few occasions. Entering the claustrophobic world of girls' shops is a stressful activity – fighting through packs of teenagers and their boyfriends against a background of mind-battering music, hanging around outside changing rooms, admiring every outfit, while negotiating the tricky matter of decency. Watching the necklines and hemlines come closer together, wondering if any area of flesh is still sacred. Not Kate's favourite activity.

He was always scrupulously polite with Kate, only meeting her occasionally to pick the children up and bring them home, without setting foot inside the front door.

She'd thought he would be angry when the police decided not to take action over Charles Peterson and the other boys. They'd only been given a caution.

But he'd shrugged. 'They're young. They'll regret it one day.'

A week later, she sees him in Budleigh again. This time she is walking along the path above the beach, breathing in the cool autumn air, invigorated by the sharpness of the wind. The ocean is grey in anticipation of winter storms, but there's still a hint of warmth in the sun's rays.

He's at the water's edge, throwing stones into the sea. The wind is tugging at his jacket, puffing it out and pulling it to one side. Red curls are emerging from his once-shaved head, and they're ruffling in the wind.

His appearance is so familiar, so *known*, to Kate that for a brief, mad moment, she forgets everything. Without thought, she jumps over the low wall and runs across the beach, skating over the rain-soaked surface of stones, her feet dizzy with an old rhythm.

But this is a new dance, a wild, dangerous dance where no one leads and no one follows. The tea-dances, the ballroom dances of the past have faded into antiques. Even rock-and-roll seems quaint. This is a dance from the jungle, raw and powerful, driven by the relentless beat of a drum, a dance so primitive, so exhausting that it might not be possible to keep standing.

She stops.

What is she doing? This is not the way to behave. She is living her own life now. She has power. She is not dependent on anyone or anything. She is watching a man who is capable of killing someone.

But he is the same Felix she married, the father to her children, the man who led her to the elegant white house in Budleigh and made her happy. The difference is within her. She's the one who's changed.

She can see beyond the image he presents to the world. She can see the child who lost his parents, who was frightened of stopped clocks, who has always pursued with determination the security of a home and a family around him. She realises that she is the one who holds the thin thread of their connection in her hands.

Maybe this was always true and she just didn't know it.

She can snap it apart or she can use a sharp, painful needle to sew something back together again. It couldn't be the same shape, but it might work.

She can feel the children behind her.

'You're good at sewing,' says Millie. 'You've already made curtains for the new house.'

'Get the sewing-machine out,' says Lawrence.

'*Please*,' says Rory.

The wind catches her hair and pulls it out to the side like a flag, buffeting against her ears so that she can hardly hear her own thoughts. She can taste salt on her lips. It's wild out here, uncertain: you never know how big the waves will be, how far up the beach they'll penetrate after they've crashed down. You come down here in all weathers to test yourself, see how well you can stand up to the elements, see if you're as strong as you think you are.

A man walks past with a Doberman. The dog is pushing forwards, pulling so hard that its collar digs deep into its neck. But the man is determined to control it. He holds the end of the lead with both hands, wraps it round his arm, leans backwards to take the strain. It's not easy, but he's determined to win.

Felix stops throwing stones and turns to head back up the beach. He sees Kate and stops.

She faces him, strangely calm.

'Hello,' he shouts, into the wind.

'Hello,' she yells.

He walks over to her and she doesn't back away.

He's much thinner than he used to be. Now he's closer, she can see the lack of colour in his skin. Some of the new hair that has begun to sprout so vigorously is white, as if the physical part of him has given up fighting and he's resigned to growing old.

He stands next to her and, side by side with half a metre between them, they look out at the sea. On a calm day the horizon curves, as if you can see the shape of the earth, but on a day like this it's just thick brown waves tinged with green, weaving round and over each other, fighting their way to land.

'It's good to see you,' he says.

She nods, but doesn't reply.

He moves closer and she can sense his desperation. 'Kate – I know you must hate me—' Some of the words are being lost on the wind, captured and whisked away before she can hear them, their insignificance made clear. '—want to put things right – forgive me.'

Forgive? Such a strong word. Forgiveness implies that

375

she owes him something. If she forgives him, she gives him credibility, treats him as if he is legitimate when what he did was unforgivable.

'Forgive is the wrong word,' she shouts. 'The word you're looking for is "accept".'

She can see him straining to catch what she says. She doesn't want to repeat it. It would take away her conviction.

He carries on. He seems to be taking her unheard words as a rejection. '—won't have me back, but – for the children – help you when you need it – friends.'

She reacts without thinking. 'I don't know!' she says.

'—don't want a divorce – love you – let me be around for you – please.'

He knows now. He needs her to help him make decisions. She has more power than she ever realised. He can only be strong if she is behind him.

Side by side. Turning to face each other. One step forwards, one step back. The chord at the beginning of the dance when he bows and she curtsies. Will you dance? he is saying. She consults her card, the list of people she intends to dance with. There is only one name on it. She can accept or she can spend the rest of the time alone.

She leans over and shouts in his ear, 'I'm thinking about it!'

The wind catches her words and throws them into the air so that they mingle with the salt and the spray.

Acknowledgements

I would like to thank the following:

My writing group, who have been as patiently critical as always.

The Gateley family, who let me get on with things in peace.

James Gordon for his helpful information on the subject of financial crime.

Everyone at Sceptre. In particular: Carole Welch for her thoughtful and meticulous approach; Ruth Tross for her prompt and cheerful emails; Hazel Orme for her impressive attention to detail; Henry Jeffreys for his calm support.

My agent, Laura Longrigg, who is always so encouraging.

Not
The End

Go to channel4.com/tvbookclub for more great reads,
brought to you by Specsavers.

Enjoy a good read with